DAVID ZINDELL

THE
WILD

BANTAM BOOKS

NEW YORK · TORONTO · LONDON · SYDNEY · AUCKLAND

THE WILD
A Bantam Spectra Book / August 1996

SPECTRA and the portrayal of a boxed ''s'' are trademarks
of Bantam Books, a division of Bantam Doubleday Dell
Publishing Group, Inc.

ISBN 0-553-28966-7

Published simultaneously in the United States and Canada

Bantam Books are published by Bantam Books, a division of Bantam
Doubleday Dell Publishing Group, Inc. Its trademark, consisting of the words
''Bantam Books'' and the portrayal of a rooster, is Registered in U.S. Patent
and Trademark Office and in other countries. Marca Registrada. Bantam
Books, 1540 Broadway, New York, New York 10036.

PRINTED IN THE UNITED STATES OF AMERICA

OPM   10 9 8 7 6 5 4 3 2 1

HIGH PRAISE FOR DAVID ZINDELL

THE BROKEN GOD

"Science fiction as it ought to be: challenging, imaginative, thought-provoking—and well written. Zindell has placed himself at the forefront of literary SF."
—*Times Literary Supplement,* London

"One of the great series of an imagined world."
—*The Denver Post*

"Rich and rewarding . . . Zindell's come into his maturity, and science fiction is the better for it."
—*Locus*

"Rich and skillful."
—Paul J. McAuley, *interzone*

NEVERNESS

"Excellent hard science fiction . . . Ideas splash out of Zindell's mind and flow across the pages of this book."
—Orson Scott Card

"[Zindell's] feat of universe crafting propels him instantly into the big leagues with the likes of Frank Herbert and Ursula K. LeGuin."
—Edward Bryant

"One of the finest talents to appear since Kim Stanley Robinson and William Gibson—perhaps the finest."
—Gene Wolfe

"A first novel that has the power to renew one's faith in the genre."
—*Booklist*

THE WILD

PART 1

THE GODDESS

C H A P T E R I

THE MISSION

Each man and woman is a star.
The stars are the children of God alone in the night;
The stars are the wild white seeds burning inside a woman;
The stars are the fires that women light inside men;
The stars are the eyes of all the Old Ones who have lived
    and died.
Who can hold the light of the wild stars?
Gazing at the bright black sky,
You see only yourself looking for yourself.
When you look into the eyes of God,
They go on and on forever.

—from the Devaki *Song of Life*

It is my duty to record the events of the glorious and tragic Second Mission to the Vild. To observe, to remember, to record only—although the fate of the galaxy's dying stars was intimately interwoven with my own, I took little part in seeking out that vast, stellar wasteland known as the Vild, or the Wild, or the Inferno, or whatever ominous name that men can attach to such a wild and hellish place. This quest to save the stars was to be for others: eminent pilots such as the Sonderval and Aja and Alark of Urradeth and some who were not yet famous such as Victoria Chu and my son, Danlo wi Soli Ringess.

Like all quests called by the Order of Mystic Mathematicians, the Second Vild Mission had an explicit and formal purpose: to establish a new Order within the heart of the Vild; to find the lost planet known as Tannahill; to establish a mission among the leaders of man's greatest religion and win them to a new vision; and, of course, to stop the man-doomed stars from exploding into supernovas. All seekers of the Vild took oaths toward this end. But as with all human enterprises, there are always purposes inside purposes. Many attempted the journey outward across the galaxy's glittering stars out of the promise of adventure, mystery, power, or even worldly riches. Many spoke of a new phase in human evolution, of redeeming both past and future and fulfilling the ancient prophecies. Altogether, ten thousand women and men braved the twisted, light-ruined spaces of the Vild, and thus they carried inside them ten thousand individual hopes and dreams. And the deepest dream of all of them (though few acknowledged this even to themselves) was to wrest the secrets of the universe from the wild stars. Their deepest purpose was to heal the universe of its wound, and to this impossible end they pledged their devotion, their energies, their genius, their very lives.

On the twenty-first of False Winter in the year 2954 since the founding of Neverness, the Vild Mission began its historic journey across the galaxy. In the black, cold, vacuum spaces above the City of Light (or the City of Pain, as Neverness is sometimes known), in orbit around the planet of Icefall, Lord Nikolos Sar Petrosian had called together a fleet of ships. There were ten seedships, each one the temporary home of a thousand akashics, cetics, programers, mechanics, biologists, and other professionals of the Order. There were twelve deep ships as round and fat as artificial moons; the deep ships contained the floating farms and factories and assemblers that would be needed to establish a second Order within the Vild.

And, of course, there were the lightships. Their number was 254. They were the glory of Neverness, these bright, shining slivers of spun diamond that could pierce the space beneath space and enter the unchartered seas of the manifold where there was neither time nor distance nor light. A single pilot guided each lightship, and together the pilots of Vild Mission would lead the seedships and deep ships across the stars.

To the thousands of Ordermen who had remained behind (and to the millions of citizens of Neverness safe by the fires of their dwellings), the fleet that Lord Petrosian had assembled must have seemed a grand array of men and machines. But against the universe, it was nothing. Upon Lord Petrosian's signal, the Vild ships vanished into the night, 276 points of light lost into the billions of stars of the Milky Way.

Lightships such as the *Vivasvat* and the *Snowy Owl* fell from star to star, and the mission fleet followed, and they swept across the Civilized Worlds. And wherever they went, on planets such as Orino or Nenet or Valevare, the manswarms would gather beneath the night skies in hope of bearing witness to their passing.

They would watch the bright, black heavens for the little flashes of light released whenever a lightship tore through the shimmering fabric of the manifold. They lived in awe of this light, and in dread as well, for the Order had been the soul of the Civilized Worlds for a hundered generations, and now it was dividing in two. Some feared that the Order might be dividing against itself. No one could know what fate this future might bring. No one could know how a few thousand pilots and professionals in their fragile ships might cool the fury of the Vild, and so the peoples of the Civilized Worlds gathered on their starflung planets to hope and wonder and pray.

There are many peoples on the planets of Man. The Civilized Worlds comprise only a tiny fraction of humanity, and yet there are some four thousand of these planets bearing the weight of at least a trillion human beings. And bearing as well strange peoples who have never been human. The Vild Mission fell from Treya to Teges to Silvaplana, and then on to Fravashing, home of that beautiful alien race whose souls are more manlike than that of any man. The lightships led the race among the stellar pathways, falling through the manifold from window to window, passing by the planet of Arcite, where once the Order had ruled before its move to Neverness at the beginning of the Sixth Mentality of Man.

None of the pilots sealed inside their ships (not even the youngest or most inexperienced) had trouble with this part of their journey, for the ancient paths through the manifold had been mapped millennia before and were now well known. The pilots passed among the old red stars of the Greater Morbio and on to the Tycho's Nebula, where the splendid stars were newly created of gravity and dust and light. Few human beings dwelled in these dangerous places, and so only the stars felt the faint, rippling tremors of the lightships as they tore open windows into the manifold. These were famous stars such as Parpallaix and Ayahua and Shamesh, the beacons of the galaxy. And Gloriana Luz, all huge and bloodred like a god's blinded eye. The stars lit the way of Vild Mission, and the pilots steered by the stars, by Alumit and Treblinka and Agni, which burned with a brilliant blue fire and was ten thousand times brighter than Neverness's cold yellow sun. The whole of the Fallaways was on fire, a blazing swath of fire burning through the galaxy from Bellatrix to Star's End. Had the pilots or others of the Order wondered how far they had fallen, they might have measured their journey in parsecs or tendays or trillions of miles. Or in light-years. The ships launched from Neverness fell five thousand light-years along the luminous Sagittarius arm of the galaxy, outward across the great, glittering lens. They passed from Sheydveg to Jonah's Star Far Group to Wakanda, as thus they made the perilous crossing to the Orion arm, ten thousand light-years from the star that they had once known as home.

Some of the pilots called this flight away from the core "the westering," not because they fell in the direction of universal west, but because their journey carried them ever outward toward the unknown stars without fixed-points or names. But still they remained within the Fallaways, where Man was still Man and few of the galaxy's gods cared to roam. They guided their lightships away from the August Cluster where the Silicon God was said to claim a million stars as his own. They fell out among the oldest of human planets, Kittery and Vesper, and they avoided the spaces of Earth, lost and lonely Old Earth which men and women were no longer permitted to behold. And so at last the Mission came to Farfara at the edge of the Vild.

Here the Fallaways gave out onto the wild, mapless portions of the manifold that had killed so many of the Order's pilots. Here the farthest of the Civilized Worlds stood looking out on the Vild's ruined stars. Farfara was a fat, rich, pleasant world, and it was here that Lord Nikolos Sar Petrosian commanded the Mission to make a brief planetfall. He did this so that the ships might take on fresh stores of coffee, toalache, and wine, so that the ten thousand men and women of the Order might take a few days of rest beneath the open sky and Farfara's hot blue sun.

It was on the fortieth day of the Mission's sojourn on Farfara that one of the Order's master pilots returned from the Vild with news of a planet suitable to their purpose. The *Cardinal Virtue*—the lightship of the great pilot known as the Sonderval—fell out of the manifold and rendezvoused with the fleet above Farfara. The Sonderval told of a beautiful planet remarkably similar to Old Earth. As was a pilot's right, he had named this planet Thiells in honor of a woman whom he had once loved and lost when a comet collided with Puakea and destroyed most of the life on that unfortunate planet. According to the Sonderval, Thiells lay inside the inner veil of the Vild and could be reached after a journey of only thirty-one fallings. The Sonderval gave the fixed-points of Thiells's white star to the other pilots. He told them that he would lead the way. He also told them—told everyone—of a new supernova that he had discovered. It was an old supernova, many hundreds of light-years away. But it had exploded hundreds of years ago, and the wavefront of radiation and light would soon fall upon Farfara.

Lord Nikolos, although he disapproved of the arrogant, self-loving Sonderval, approved his plan. He commanded the professionals of the Order to make ready for the rest of their journey.

On the night before the Mission would finally enter the tortuous spaces of the Vild—the very night that the supernova would light Farfara's sky—the merchants of Farfara decided to hold a reception to celebrate the pilots' bravery. They invited the Order's 254 lightship pilots and many important masters from among the professions. They invited musicians and artists and arhats—even warrior-poets—as well as princes and ambassadors from each of the Civilized Worlds. It would be the grandest party ever held on Farfara, and the merchants who ruled that ancient planet spared no trouble or expense in creating an air of magnificence to match the magnificent hubris of the men and women who dared to enter the Vild.

Late in the Day of the Lion in the eighteenth month of Second Summer in year 24, as the merchants of Farfara measure time, the estate of Mer Tadeo dur li Marar began to fill with people arriving from cities and estates across the planet. Mer Tadeo's estate was laid out over three hills overlooking the Istas, that great sullen river which drains the equatorial mountains of the continent called Ayondela.

That evening, while the forests and river still blazed with the heat of the sun, cool mountain winds fell over Mer Tadeo's estate, rippling through the jade trees and the orange groves, carrying down the scent of the distant glaciers, which gleamed an icy white beneath the night's first stars. Shuttles rocketed back and forth between Mer Tadeo's starfield and the Order's seedships in orbit above the planet; they ferried hundreds of master cetics and mechanics and other master Ordermen down to the fountains and music pools that awaited them far below. And then, in a display of the Order's power, a light show of flashing diamond hulls and red rocket fire, the 254 lightships fell down through Farfara's atmosphere and came to earth at the mile-wide pentagon at the center of Mer Tadeo's starfield.

Although no member of the Order was scorned or ignored in any manner, it was the pilots whom the men and women of Farfara wished to fete. In truth, the merchants adulated the pilots. Mer Tadeo himself—accompanied by twenty other great merchants from Farfara's greatest estates—received the pilots by the Fountain of Fortune on the sculptured grounds in front of his palace. Here, on soft green grasses native to Old Earth, in the loveliest garden on Farfara, the pilots gathered to drink priceless Summerworld wines and listen to the music pools as they gazed out over the sinuous river. Here they drank each other's health, and looked up at the unfamiliar star configurations in the sky, and waited half the night for the Sonderval's supernova to appear.

In the Hour of Remembrance (a good hour before the exploding star would fill the heavens) a pilot stood alone by the marble border of one of the palace's lesser fountains. His name was Danlo wi Soli Ringess; he was a tall, well-made young man, much the youngest pilot or professional to join the Mission. To any of the merchants, if any had looked his way, he might have seemed lonely or preoccupied with some great problem of the universe that had never been solved. His deep-set eyes were grave and full of light as if he could see things that others could not, or rather, as if the everyday sights of wine goblets and beautifully dressed women amused him where it caused others only lust or envy. In truth, he had marvelous eyes, as dark and deep as the midnight sky. The irises were blue-black like liquid jewels, almost black enough to merge with the bright, black pupils, giving them a strange intensity. Much about this pilot was strange and hinted of deep purpose: his shiny black hair shot with strands of red; the mysterious, lightning-bolt scar cut into his forehead above his left eye; the ease with which he dwelled inside his silence despite the noise and gaiety all around him. Like a creature of the wild, he seemed startlingly out of place, and yet he was completely absorbed into his surroundings, as a bird is always at home wherever he flies. In truth, with his bold facial bones and long nose, he sometimes seemed utterly wild. A fellow pilot had once accused him of having a fierce and predatory look, and yet there was always a tenderness about him, an almost infinite grace. At any party or social gathering, men and women always noticed him and never left him alone very long.

"Good evening, Danlo, it's good to see you again," a voice called out from the hundreds in Mer Tadeo's garden. Danlo turned away from the fountain and watched a very tall man push through the crowds of brilliantly dressed people and make his way across the flagstones and trampled grasses. Indeed, the master pilot known as the Sonderval was the tallest of men, impossibly and intimidatingly tall. With his thin limbs and eight feet of height, he seemed more like a giant insect than a man, though in fact had been born an exemplar of Solsken and was, therefore, by heredity as arrogant as any god; he had been bred to tallness and intelligence much as the courtesans of Jacaranda are bred for beauty. He was dressed in a thin silk pilot's robe of purest black, as was Danlo. In a measured and stately manner—but quite rapidly, for his stride was very long—he walked up to Danlo and bowed his head.

"Is there something about this fountain that interests you?" he asked. "I must tell you, Danlo, if you attend a party such as this, you can't hope to avoid the manswarms all night. Though I must say I can't blame you for wanting to avoid these merchants."

"Master Pilot," Danlo said. He had a wonderfully melodious voice, though cut with the harshness of too many memories and sorrows. With some difficulty—the requirements of etiquette demanded that he should always keep his eyes on the Sonderval's scornful eyes high above his head—he returned the Sonderval's bow. "I do not want to avoid anyone."

"Is that why you stand alone by *this* fountain?"

Danlo turned back to the fountain to watch the lovely parabolas of water spraying up into the cool air. The water droplets caught the light of the many flame globes illuminating the garden; the tens of thousands of individual droplets sparkled in colors of silver and violet and golden blue, and then fell splashing back into the waters of the fountain. Most of the garden's fountains, as he saw, were filled with fine wines or liquid toalache or other rare drugs that might be drunk. The merchants of Farfara delighted in sitting by these fountains as they laughed a gaudy, raucous laughter and plunged their goblets into the dark red pools, or sometimes, in displays of greed that shocked the Order's staid academicians, plunged their entire bodies into the fountains and stood open-mouthed as they let streams of wine run down their clutching throats.

With a quick smile, Danlo looked up at the Sonderval and said, "I have always loved the water."

"For drinking or bathing?" the Sonderval asked.

"For listening to," Danlo said. "For watching. Water is full of memories, yes?"

That evening, as Danlo stood by the fountain and looked out over the river Istas all silver and swollen in the light of the blazing Vild stars, he lost himself in memories of a colder sky that he had known as a child years ago. Although he was only twenty-two years old—which is much too young to look backward upon the disasters of the past instead of forward into the glorious and golden future—he couldn't help remembering the death of his people, the blessed Devaki, who had all fallen to a mysterious disease made by the hand of man. He couldn't help remembering his journey to Neverness, where, against all chance, he had become a pilot of the Order and won the black diamond pilot's ring that he wore on the little finger of his right hand. He couldn't keep away these memories of his youth because he was afflicted (and blessed) with memory, much as a heavy stone is with gravity or a blue giant star is suffused with fire and light.

In every man and woman there are three phases of life more descriptive of the soul's inner journey than are childhood, maturity, and old age: It can't happen to me, I can overcome it, I accept it. It was Danlo's fate that although he had passed through these first two phases much more quickly than anyone should, he had nevertheless failed to find the way toward affirmation that all men seek. And yet, despite the horrors of his childhood, despite betrayals and hurts and wounds and the loss of Tamara Ten Ashtoreth, the woman he had loved, there was something vibrant and mysterious about him, as if he had made promises to himself and had a secret convenant with life.

"Perhaps you remember too much," the Sonderval said. "Like your father."

"My father," Danlo said. He pointed east out over the Istas, over the mountains where the first of the Vild stars were rising. As the night deepened, the planet of Farfara turned inexorably on its axis, and so turned its face to the outward reaches of the galaxy beyond the brilliant Orion arm. Soon the entire sky would be a window to the Vild. Blue and white stars such as Yachne and the Plessis twinkled against the black stain of night, and soon the supernovas would appear: the old, weak, distant supernovas whose light shone less brightly than any of Neverness's six moons. It was a mistake, Danlo thought, to imagine the Vild as nothing more than a vast wasteland of exploding stars. Among the millions of Vild stars, there were really only a few supernovas. A few hundred or a few hundred thousand—the greatest uncertainty of the Mission was that no one really knew the size or the true nature of the Vild.

"My father," Danlo said again, "was one of the first pilots to penetrate the Vild. And now you, sir."

With his long, thin finger, the Sonderval touched his long upper lip. He said, "I must remind you that you're a full pilot now. It's not necessary for you to address every master pilot as 'sir.' "

"But I do not address everyone that way."

"Only those who have penetrated the Vild?"

"No," Danlo said and smiled. "Only those whom I cannot help calling 'sir.' "

This compliment of Danlo's seemed to please the Sonderval, who had a vast opinion of his value as a human being. So vast was his sense of himself that he looked down upon almost everyone as his inferior and was, therefore, wont to disregard others' compliments as worthless. It was a measure of his respect for Danlo that he did not dismiss his words but rather favored him with a rare smile and bow of his head. "Of course you may call me 'sir' if it pleases you."

"Did you know my father well, sir?"

"We were journeymen together at Resa. We took our pilot's vows together. We fought in the war together. I knew him as well as I care to know any man. He was just a man, you know, despite what everyone says."

"Then you do not believe . . . that he became a god?"

His father, as a young pilot, had taken part in the great quest to find the Elder Eddas. His desire to know the unknowable had taken him to the Devaki, one of the Alaloi tribes west of Neverness, where Danlo had been born, abandoned, and adopted by a man named Haidar and Danlo's found-mother, Chandra. There had occurred a tragedy. His father's head had been split open by the thrown rock; he had been killed, resurrected, and given the possibility to gain great powers. In the Pilots' War, he had led his friends and followers to victory, and then he had gone on to become the Lord Pilot and the Lord of the Order itself.

"A *god*," the Sonderval said. "No, I don't want to believe in such fables. You must know that I discovered a so-called god not very long ago when I made my journey to the Eighteenth Deva cluster. A dead god—it was bigger than East Moon and made of diamond neurologics. A god, a huge computer of diamond circuitry. The gods are nothing more than sophisticated computers. Or the grafting of a computer onto the mind of man, the interface between man and computers. Few will admit this, but it's so. Mallory Ringess journeyed to Agathange and carked his damaged brain, replaced half the neurons with protein neurologics. Your father did this. Does this make him a god? If so, then I'm a god, too. Any of us, the few pilots who have really mastered a lightship. Whenever I face my ship-computer, when the stars fall into my eyes and the whole galaxy is mine, I'm as godly as any god."

For a while Danlo listened to the water falling into the fountain, the humming and click of the evening insects, the low roar of a thousand human voices. Then he looked at the Sonderval and said, "Who can know what it is to be a god? Can a computer be a god, truly? I think my father is something other. Something more."

"What, then?"

"He discovered the Elder Eddas. Inside himself, the deep memories—he found a way of listening to them."

"The wisdom of the gods?"

"Perhaps."

"The memories of the Iedra and other gods written into human DNA? The so-called racial memories?"

"Some would characterize the Eddas thus, sir." Danlo smiled, then continued, "But the Eddas, too, are something other, something more."

"Oh, yes," the Sonderval said. "The secret of life. The secret of the universe, and Mallory Ringess whom I used to tutor in topology, whom I used to beat at chess nine games out of ten, was clever enough to discover it."

Danlo suddenly cupped his hand and dipped it into the fountain. He brought his hand up to his lips, taking a quick drink of water, and then another. The water was cool and good, and he drank deeply. "But, sir," he finally said, "what of the Timekeeper's quest? My father and you were seekers together, yes?"

The Sonderval shot Danlo a cold, suspicious look and said, "It's true. Two years before you were born, the Timekeeper called his quest. I, your father, we pilots—fell across half the galaxy from Neverness to the Helvorgorsee seeking the so-called Elder Eddas, this Holy Grail that everyone believed in. The Eschaton, the transcendental object at the end of time. But I could never believe in such myths."

"But, sir, the Eddas aren't myths to believe in. The Eddas are memories, to be remembered."

"So it's been said. I must tell you that I tried to remember them once. This was after the Timekeeper's fall, when your father first announced that the quest had been fulfilled. Because I was curious, I engaged the services of a remembrancer and drank the kalla drug that they use to unfold the memory sequences. And there was nothing. Nothing but my own memories, the memories of myself."

"But others have had . . . other memories."

"Myths about themselves that they extend into universals and believe are true."

Danlo slowly took another drink of water. Then he shook his head. "No, not myths, sir."

The Sonderval stood stiff as a tree above Danlo, looking down at him for a long time. "I must tell you that there is no kind of mental accomplishment that has ever eluded me. If the Elder Eddas exist as memory, I would have been able to remember them."

Danlo closed his eyes as he recalled the entire Devaki tribe dying of a mysterious disease and lived again his own subsequent journey across the frozen sea to Neverness. There he had made friends with Hanuman li Tosh and the master pilot Bardo and the three of them had become involved in the religion that had sprung up around the miracle of Mallory Ringess's evolution into godhood. The soul of this religion, Danlo thought, was in the remembrance of the Elder Eddas. More than once, Danlo had drunk the sacred remembrancers' drug, kalla, and had plunged into the cool, inner sea of racial memories.

"To remembrance deeply . . . is hard," Danlo said. "The hardest thing in the universe."

"I've heard a rumor that you drank the kalla, too. That you fell into a so-called great remembrance. Perhaps you should have become a remembrancer instead of a pilot."

"I have lost the talent for remembrancing. I am just a pilot, now."

"A *pilot* must pilot and fall among the stars, or else he is nothing."

"I journeyed to Neverness so that I might become a pilot."

The Sonderval sighed and ran his fingers through his golden hair. He said, "These last years I've been away from Neverness much too much, but I've taken notice of what has happened there. I can't say I'm pleased. Mallory Ringess is proclaimed a god, and his best friend founds a church to worship his godhood. And his son joins this church, this 'Way of Ringess,' as it's called. And suddenly half of Neverness is attempting to remembrance the Elder Eddas and cark themselves into gods."

"But I have left the Way," Danlo said. "I have never wanted to become a god."

"Then you do not seek the Elder Eddas?"

Danlo looked down into the water and said, "No, not anymore."

"But you're still a seeker, aren't you?"

"I . . . have taken a vow to go to the Vild. I have pledged my life toward the fulfillment of the new quest."

The Sonderval waved his hand as if to slap a bug away from his face. "In the end, all quests are really the same. What matters is that pilots such as you and I may distinguish ourselves in seeking; what matters not at all is that which is sought."

"You speak as if there is little hope of stopping the supernovas."

"Perhaps there might have been more hope if I had been chosen Lord of the Mission instead of Lord Nikolos. But in the end it doesn't matter. Stars will die, and people will die, too. But do you really think it's possible that our kind could destroy the entire galaxy?"

With his fingers, Danlo pressed the scar over his left eye, trying to rid himself of the fierce head pain that often afflicted him. After a long time of considering the Sonderval's words, he said, "I believe that what we do does matter."

"That is because you are young and still full of passion."

"Perhaps."

"I have heard," the Sonderval said, "that you have your own reason for seeking the Vild. Your own private quest."

Danlo pressed harder against his forehead before saying, "Long before the Architects began destroying the stars, they destroyed each other. In the War of the Faces—you must know this, yes? The Architects made a virus to kill each other. This virus that killed my people. I would seek the planet they call Tannahill and hope that the Architects might know of a cure for this disease."

"I have heard that there is no cure."

"There . . . must be." Danlo scooped up a handful of water and held it against his eye. The water slowly leaked away from the gap between the palm of his hand and his cheek and then fell back into the fountain.

"Your father always believed in miracles, too."

Danlo stood away from the fountain, then, and pointed up at the sky. "My father, it is said, always hoped to save the stars. He is out there, somewhere, perhaps lost around some doomed star. This is why he went to the Vild. He always dreamed that the universe could be healed of its wound."

"Your father, when I knew him, could not even heal himself of his own wound. He was always a tormented man."

"Truly? Then perhaps some wounds can never be healed."

"But you don't believe that?"

Danlo smiled and said, "No."

"Is it your intention, Pilot, to try to find your father?"

Danlo listened to sound of the water falling into the fountain and asked, "How could I just abandon him?"

"Then you have your own quest within the quest."

"As you say, sir, all quests are really the same."

The Sonderval came up close to Danlo and pointed up at the sky. "The stars of the Vild are nearly impenetrable. How could you hope to find one man among a billion stars?"

"I . . . do not know," Danlo said. "But I have dreamed that in the Vild, all things would be possible."

At this, the Sonderval quietly shook his head. "Look at the stars, Pilot. Have you ever seen such wild stars?"

Danlo looked up along the line made by the Sonderval's arm and his long, pointing finger. He looked up past the orange trees and the fountains and the ice-capped peaks. Now it was full night, and the sky was ablaze from horizon to horizon. Now, among the strange constellations and nameless stars, there were half a hundred supernova, great blisters of hot white light breaking through the universe's blackness. For a long time, Danlo thought about the origins of these ruined stars, and said, "But sir, who knows what the Vild truly is? We cannot see the stars, not truly. All these stars, all this starlight—it was made so long ago."

Low over the horizon, in the cleft between two double supernovas that Danlo thought of as the "Two Friends," he saw a bit of starlight that he recognized. It was light from the Owl Cluster of galaxies some fifty million light-years away. Fifty million years ago this light had begun its journey across the universe to break through the heavens above Farfara and find its home within the deeps of Danlo's eyes. It was the strangest thing, he thought, that to look across space was to look back through time. He could see the Owl Cluster only as it existed long ago, some forty-eight million years before the rise of Man. He wondered if perhaps these galaxies had long since been annihilated by chains of supernovas or the workings of some terrible alien god. He wondered about his own galaxy. Did Vishnu Luz still burn like a signpost in the night? Or Silvaplana, or Agni, or any of the thousands of nearer stars that the Mission had passed on its way to the Vild?

Perhaps, even as he stood by this little fountain more than ten thousand light-years from his home, the Star of Neverness had somehow exploded into a brilliant sphere of light and death. It was always impossible to be sure of what one might see. All things, even the nearest and most apprehensible. It amused Danlo to think that if the Sonderval, standing three feet away, were suddenly to wink out of existence, the light of this unfortunate event would take at least three billionths of a second to reach his eyes.

Danlo turned facing the Sonderval and said, "This is the problem, yes? It is impossible to see the universe just as it is."

"You're a strange man," the Sonderval said, and he smiled to himself.

"Thank you, sir."

"I must tell you that the Vild really exists. I've *been* there, after all. I've seen the light of a new supernova—and in less than an hour, you'll see it, too. Right . . . *there*."

So saying, the Sonderval pointed to a patch of sky due east and some thirty degrees above the horizon. The faint stars clustered there had no name that Danlo knew. Perhaps, Danlo thought, the Sonderval's calculations had been wrong, and the supernova's light would not reach Farfara for many days. Or perhaps the supernova would appear at the appointed time, only to prove much more intense than anyone had anticipated. Perhaps the light from this dead, unseen star would burn the eyes of anyone who looked toward the sky; perhaps it would burn human flesh and kill the thousands of people in the garden. In the time that it took for Danlo's heart to beat some three thousand more times, he might very well be dead, and yet, as he looked out over all the apprehensive people standing around the garden's numerous fountains, as he turned his face to the brilliant sky, he couldn't help feeling that it was a beautiful night in which to be alive.

For a while, Danlo and the Sonderval stood there talking about the way the Vild stars distorted spacetime and twisted the pathways through the manifold, and other things that pilots talk about. Then the Sonderval admitted that Lord Nikolos had sent him to fetch Danlo, or rather, to invite him to a gathering of all the pilots in front of the garden's main fountain. It seemed that Mer Tadeo, just before the supernova appeared, wished to honor the pilots with toast of rare Yarknonan firewine.

"I must tell you that Mer Tadeo has asked to meet you," the Sonderval said. "Lord Nikolos will make the presentation. Please remember that, although Mer Tadeo practically rules this world, you are a pilot of the Order. Anyone can rule a world, but only a few are born to be pilots."

The Sonderval nodded at Danlo, and together they walked through the garden. Danlo liked almost everything about the garden, especially the bonsai trees and the cascades of strange, beautiful flowers. The air was so sweet with their scent that it almost hurt him to breathe. In truth, he loved the many smells of the night, the fruity, acid spray of the various wines bubbling from the fountains; the orange trees; the far faintness of ice; even the char of insects roasting in beams of laser light.

All across the neat green lawns, mounted high on marble pillars, there were many computer eyes and lasers that targeted any noxious or biting insect that might chance to enter the garden. At any moment, quick beams of ruby light played this way and that, fairly hissing through the air and instantly crisping the various mosquitoes, gnats, and grass flies so despised by the Farfara merchants. Naturally, this frivolous (and showy) use of lasers disturbed some of the Order's professionals, who seemed anxious and wary lest they stepped carelessly and a laser drilled a red, sizzling hole through hand, neck, or face. It disturbed even the many ambassadors and diplomats long used to such barbarisms. But, in the two thousand years that Mer Tadeo's family had owned this estate, the lasers had never hurt any human being. Mer Tadeo employed these forbidden weapons only because he liked to infuse his parties with a certain frisson of dangerous possibilities. He liked to surround himself with colorful, uncommon people, and so that night he had invited an arhat from Newvannia, a famous neurosinger, a renegade pilot of the Order named Sivan wi Mawi Sarkissian, and even five warrior-poets recently arrived from the planet Qallar.

As Danlo pushed farther into the garden, through swarms of men and women sipping their wine and stealing quick glances at the uncertain stars, he sensed an aura of intrigue and even menace in the air. He felt the eyes of people watching him, judging him. He was certain that someone was following him across the garden.

True, he was a pilot of the Order, and the blackness of his formal robe attracted many stares where the cobalt or orange or scarlet robes of the Order's academicians did not. True, he walked behind the Sonderval, who was also a pilot as well as the tallest human being on Mer Tadeo's estate, possibly on the entire planet. A pilot had to inure himself to such curiosity unless he wished to remain only in the company of other pilots. But Danlo could never get used to popularity or fame, and he hoped that whoever was following him would announce himself—either that or turn his attentions to one of the beautifully dressed merchants who stood about on the cool green lawns like so many thousands of flowers waiting to be appreciated or plucked.

At last they drew near Mer Tadeo's main fountain, the so-called Fountain of Fortune: a glorious pool of marble and gold. From the mouths of various statues—glittnings and rohins and other alien creatures set upon the different levels of a golden terrace at the fountain's center—Yarkonan firewine burst into the air in jets of frothy red. On Neverness, a single bottle of firewine can cost as much as a pearl necklace or a year's pleasure with a courtesan, and so many of the Order have never tasted this uncommon wine.

Surrounding the fountain were rings of the Order's academicians, cantors and scryers and remembrancers, holists and horologes and historians. They were dressed in bright robes of many colors, saffron or rose or indigo, and they fairly swarmed the pool in their eagerness to fill their goblets and sip such a delightful wine. There were pilots, as well, 252 black-robed pilots who were the soul of the Order. Danlo knew all of them, by face or name or reputation. He saw Paloma the Younger, and Matteth Jons, and Alark of Urradeth. And standing nearby with a cup of wine in his hands was Richardess, a fragile-faced wisp of a man who was the only pilot ever to have survived the spaces of Chimene and the April Colonial Intelligence. They were all of an age with the Sonderval, and they had all fought with Mallory Ringess in the Pilots' War twenty years previously. The Vild Mission would be the second great quest of their lives, and it pleased them to be joined by pilots of greater enthusiasm and passion, young pilots such as Ivar Rey and Lara Jesusa and Danlo wi Soli Ringess.

That evening, most of the Mission's pilots were gathered together near the southern quadrant of the fountain. There, too, was Nikolos Sar Petrosian, the Lord Akashic and Lord of the Mission. He was a small, sober, intelligent man who wore an akashic's yellow robe upon his plump body and a look of impatience about his clear, blue eyes. When he saw the Sonderval leading Danlo his way he bowed to them, then said, somewhat dryly, "I was afraid that you had become lost. I suppose it's easy enough for a *pilot* to lose himself on such a huge estate."

This sarcasm of Lord Nikolos had no effect on the Sonderval. Just as he cared little for the compliments of others, he dismissed their criticisms as easily. He stood silently next to Danlo, looking down on little Lord Nikolos, apparently staring straight at the bald patch on the crown of Lord Nikolos's head. The Sonderval smiled to himself, but said nothing.

"Danlo, I'm glad you've been found," Lord Nikolos finally said. "Danlo wi Soli Ringess, may I present Mer Tadeo dur li Marar? Mer Tadeo has asked if he might meet you before the evening's entertainment begins."

Standing next to Lord Nikolos was a handsome, elegant man with quick brown eyes and the rapacious look of an ivory gull. Mer Tadeo dur li Marar wore a red kimono of Japanese silk, which rather nicely set off his smooth olive skin. He bowed to Danlo, quite properly; he looked at Danlo quickly, intensely, as he might appraise a diamond or a firestone. And then he announced, "It's an honor to meet you, Pilot."

Danlo returned his bow, then nodded at the circle of curious people surrounding Mer Tadeo. These were mostly merchants in their fabulous kimonos and jewels but included also a neurosinger named Omar Noy and Mer Tadeo's ninth wife, a rather sullen-looking woman whom he introduced as Mer Marlena Eva dur li Karillon. There were two ambassadors, as well: Kagami Ito of Yarkona, and Valentina Morven of the planet known as Clarity. And others. Danlo bowed to each of them in turn, inclining his head as each of their names was spoken. The presentations having been made, Mer Tadeo motioned for Danlo to come nearer, and he said, "I've made the acquaintance of all the pilots but yourself. I'm honored that you could attend this reception. It's rare for pilots of the Order to visit our world, you know."

Danlo smiled and looked across the fountain. There, some thirty yards farther across the lawn, was a low retaining wall of cut stone. On the other side of the wall, Mer Tadeo's estate gave out onto a cliff face high above the gleaming Istas River and the dark hills beyond. "Your world is very beautiful," Danlo said. "Perhaps if more pilots knew of its beauty, we would not neglect it so."

"I was afraid you might find my estate somewhat warmer than you might be used to," Mer Tadeo said. He seemed very pleased with Danlo. Unlike the Sonderval, he devoured compliments as a child might chocolate candies. "I've heard Neverness is so cold that it never rains."

Danlo smiled and said, "On all the nights of my life, this is the first time I've stood outside and there has been no sign of snow. Not even the possibility that snow might fall."

At this, Mer Tadeo shook his head in wonder, and in pity, too. Then he said, "During this part of Second Summer, at night, there will be nothing but starlight to fall upon us. This is why my ancestors built their estate here. They loved looking at the stars.''

For a while Mer Tadeo and Danlo stood among a crowd of curious people, talking of little things. Then as quickly as an assassin might slip a knife in the dark, Mer Tadeo smiled at Danlo and said, "I've been told that you're the son of Mallory Ringess."

"Yes, that is true," Danlo said.

"I've also been told that there is a new religion in Neverness. The Way of Ringess—is that right?"

Danlo nodded warily. "That also is true."

"Do the Ringists really teach that Mallory Ringess became a god?"

"Yes."

"And that all human beings can become gods, too? And that the path toward godhood is in communion with this mystical knowledge called the Elder Eddas?"

"You are well informed, Mer Tadeo. You have just stated the Three Pillars of Ringism, did you know?"

Mer Tadeo took a step closer to Danlo. As if a signal had been given, Mer Tadeo's wife and the two ambassadors stepped closer, too, the better to hear words that might prove important to their lives. And then many others closed in like wolves around a wounded lamb, and Danlo suddenly found himself surrounded by men and women whom he hardly knew.

"We know that your Order is said to take this religion seriously," Mer Tadeo told him. "We know that many lords and masters have even converted and now call themselves Ringists. The lords and masters of Neverness! We hadn't thought you Ordermen capable of such religiousness."

"Anyone can fall into worship," Danlo said softly. "Anyone can dream of becoming a god."

Mer Tadeo and Mer Marlena Eva asked Danlo questions about the Way of Ringess, about its origins, beliefs, and ceremonies. They wanted to know more about the remembrancing ceremony, the way Ringists used computers to stimulate the remembrance of the Elder Eddas. They seemed intensely curious, not in the manner of an eschatologist or a historian, but in another way that spoke of secret sufferings and strange, ancient longings. Lord Nikolos, obviously, did not like the turn of this conversation, for he pushed up beside Danlo and said, "It's unwise to exaggerate the importance of this religion. To do so will only give it real importance."

Lord Nikolos, as Danlo knew, always detested any talk about gods or God. He mistrusted the religious impulse much as the Perfect of Gehenna loathe water, as a snowworm avoids sunlight.

"May I ask you then, Lord Nikolos, if your mission will spread this creed of Ringism among the peoples of the Vild?" This question came from Kagami Ito, the Yarkonan ambassador. Kagami, a suspicious old man, was dressed in a babri jacket much too thick for the warmth of the night. His round face was shone with sweat, and he seemed tired and crabby. Long ago, in his first old age, he had been an ambassador to Neverness before the Timekeeper had tired of his testy manner and had banished him from the City. "We would all like to know if you of the Vild Mission are still pilots and professionals of the Order, or whether you've become mere missionaries after all."

This question offended Lord Nikolos, who pointed a pudgy finger at Kagami and said, "Our mission is to the Architects of the Infinite Intelligence of the Cybernetic Universal Church, to reason with them. To journey among their worlds, to learn why they believe as they do so that we may illuminate them. To begin a new Order in the Vild. We are antireligious, all of us. If you must, you may think of us as antimissionaries whose quest it is to reverse the insane doctrines of an insane old church."

Danlo smiled at this tirade, but said nothing. Then Lord Nikolos, in his dry, academician's voice, went on to explain that the Architects of the Old Church were destroying the stars because their Doctrine of Second Creation required them to participate in the remaking of the galaxy, and ultimately, at the end of time, of the very universe itself. Although Lord Nikolos was a soft, ill-disciplined man in his body, he spoke with steely resolve and an enormous will to correct the evils and excessess of the human race. In his own way, he was as fanatical as any Architect or true believer, only his was a fanaticism of logic and reason, and cold, clear thought. Despite the Sonderval's misgivings, he was the ideal choice as Lord of the Mission because he understood the Architects as only a true enemy can.

"Then I must wish you well on your Mission," Kagami Ito said. "All of us, any who live on any of the Civilized Worlds—we wish you well."

Lord Nikolos bowed a shade too low and said, "Your wishes are well received."

"We *must* wish you well," Kagami Ito repeated. "Once again, we of the Civilized Worlds must be saved by you of the Order."

At this, the Sonderval stepped forward and said, "Perhaps you would rather save yourselves?"

"And so we would do if we had lightships of our own and pilots to pilot them."

"The Order has never stopped anyone from building lightships."

"Nor have you shared your knowledge of this technology."

The Sonderval shrugged his shoulders and said, "Well, anyone can build a lightship."

"But not anyone can pilot one—isn't that right, Master Pilot?"

"It's a difficult art," the Sonderval agreed. "One must have a passion for mathematics."

"Is it so difficult that the Order's pilots have kept their art a secret for three thousand years?"

"This is not true," the Sonderval said. "What of the Merchant-Pilots of Tria?"

"You know they're unworthy to be called 'pilots.' "

"We *pilots,*" the Sonderval said, "train youths from every world."

"Yes, you bring *our* youths to Neverness and make them pilots of *your* Order. And then make them take vows of secrecy."

"But how not? Some secrets may be heard by only those with the genius to understand them."

After an awkward silence, Mer Tadeo stepped between Kagami Ito and the Sonderval. He clapped his hands softly and spoke soft, soothing words to flatter both men. He cited Kagami Ito's lifetime efforts to form alliances among the Civilized Worlds, and he extolled the valor of Mallory Ringess and the Sonderval and other pilots who had joined in the quest for the Elder Eddas. He turned to praise Danlo and the younger pilots who would face the Vild.

In many ways, he was much more a conciliator and diplomat than any diplomat. As many merchants do, he valued peace as the greatest good; above all institutions or powers (even above the power of money), he valued the Order because it had brought a fundamental unity and vision to the Civilized Worlds for three thousand years.

"These are difficult times," Mer Tadeo said to Lord Nikolos. "It seems that the Civilized Worlds are caught between two religions. From without, the Architects destroy the stars, and every year the Vild grows larger. And from within, there is this new religion called Ringism. Even as we speak, every lightship leaving Neverness must bear the news of this religion to every star, every world. You, of the Order, even if you are not missionaries, even if you do not wish it so—you must be bearers of this new ideal. Every man and woman may become a god! This is a powerful idea, no? I don't think it's possible to exaggerate its importance. Religion has been the genius and doom of humanity almost forever. It may be that this Way of Ringess will consume us long before the Vild destroys any of our worlds."

Mer Tadeo's greatest fear—as it must have been the fear of Mer Marlena Eva and Kagami Ito and almost every man and woman in the garden—was that the Order was dying. Or at the least that the Order was dividing into two halves, and the best half (as he said) going to the Vild while the Old Order remained in Neverness.

"If the Order divides against itself," Mer Tadeo asked softly, "what will become of our glorious civilization?"

Lord Nikolos faced Mer Tadeo in his open, reasonable way, and he said, "Our mission is to establish a new Order in the Vild. We shall be far from Neverness."

"But twenty years ago, far from Neverness, Mallory Ringess led a pack of lightships out into the galaxy. He divided the pilots against themselves, and there was war."

"Mallory Ringess has disappeared," Lord Nikolos observed. "Perhaps he is dead."

At this, Danlo drew in a breath of air and slowly let it out. He stood very still, letting his eyes move back and forth between Mer Tadeo and Lord Nikolos.

Mer Tadeo nodded his head. "Perhaps. But the idea of Mallory Ringess is very much alive. The ideal. It's our fear that with the Order weakened, this ideal will divide the Civilized Worlds. And then there would be *real* war. War such as we've never seen since the Holocaust on Old Earth."

Although Lord Nikolos must have dismissed Mer Tadeo's fears as improbabilites and useless speculation, others did not. Kagami Ito and Valentina Morven and various merchants near them stood about discussing the War of the Faces and other wars that had left their mark on the Civilized Worlds. And then Mer Tadeo glanced down at a little color clock set into the gold ring that he wore around his little finger. Quite abruptly, he clapped his hands and announced, "Pilots and Professionals, Ambassadors and Honored Guests—it's nearly time. If you would fill your cups I would like to present a toast."

Just then, from across the lawns of Mer Tadeo's estate, the music pools ceased playing their wonderful melodies and began booming out a huge sound as if they were nothing more than liquid gongs. The cool air reverberated with this sound, and ten thousand people, all at once, looked eastward up into the sky. Then they began to crowd the various fountains in their haste to fill their wine goblets.

Kagami Ito, the Sonderval, and the others near Danlo began to melt into the crowd, surging toward the Fountain of Fortune. In moments he was surrounded by people whom he did not know. Caught in this crush of bodies were servants carrying platters of food: cultured meats and cakes and fairy food, chilies and cheeses and cold vegetable compotes and the hundreds of exotic fruits for which Farfara is justly famous. Most of these servants, he saw, had red hair and fair skin and pale blue eyes. They had been recruited on Thorskalle and brought to Farfara to serve the wealthier merchants. With their frigid eyes they cast evil looks at any merchant so bold as to ask for a plate of pepper nuts or a mug of coffee. Now that Mer Tadeo had called for a toast, many of the servants bore trays of crystal wineglasses, which they took care to breathe on or smudge with their fingerprints before slapping them into the merchants' outstretched hands. After Danlo had finally received his goblet, he made his way toward the fountain's western quadrant where the crowd was the thinnest. And then, among the smells of flowers and wine, silk and sweat, he smelled the terrible quick essence of kana oil perfume.

It was a smell with which he was utterly familiar. As if he were an animal in a dark forest, he froze into motionlessness and let the swarms of people push past him. He sniffed at the air, turning his head left and right. The scent of kana oil seemed strongest northward, upwind in the direction of Istas River. He drank in this memorable scent, letting the cool evening air fill his nostrils. He turned away from the fountain, then, and began moving toward the retaining wall at the edge of Mer Tadeo's estate. Almost immediately, as the crowd thinned out, he saw a man standing alone by the wall. He was a warrior-poet dressed in an evening shirt and silk cloak of a hundred shimmering colors. And he reeked of kana oil; all warrior-poets, Danlo remembered, wore kana oil perfumes to quicken the urge toward life and death.

"Hello," Danlo called out as he approached the warrior-poet. "I think you have been watching me, yes?"

The warrior-poet was leaning against the stone wall, easily, almost languidly, and he smiled at Danlo in greeting. In his left hand he held a goblet full of wine; and the little finger of that hand bore a ring of fiery red. Astonishingly, a similar ring encircled the little finger of his right hand, which he held near the fold of his cloak as if he were ready at any moment to reach inside a secret pocket and remove a poison needle, or a drug dart, or the long, terrible, killing knife that warrior-poets always carry about their persons.

"You are Danlo wi Soli Ringess," the warrior-poet said. He had a marvelous voice, strangely peaceful and full of an utter certainty. "May I present myself? I'm called Malaclypse Redring, of Qallar."

Danlo bowed, as he should, and Malaclypse stood away from the wall and returned his bow, gracefully, with impeccable control. For the count of nine of Danlo's heartbeats, Malaclypse Redring stood there looking at him. The warrior-poet seemed superbly calm, almost preternaturally calm, like a man who has magically transformed himself into a tiger and fears no other animal—especially not man. In truth, he had the look of some godly being far beyond man: impossibly wise, impossibly aware—of himself, of Danlo, of all the people and plants and things in the garden. Once before, Danlo had met a warrior-poet; physically, with his terrible quick body and beautiful face, Malaclypse might have been the other poet's twin, for all warrior-poets are cut from the same chromosomes. But there was something different about Malaclypse, an otherness, an impossible aliveness, perhaps even a greatness of soul. With his shiny black hair showing white around the temples, he was at least fifteen years older than Danlo, which is old for a warrior-poet. Then, too, there was the matter of his rings. An exceptional warrior-poet might wear the red ring around the little finger of either hand. But no warrior-poet in all history save one, as far as Danlo knew, had ever worn two red rings.

"Why have you been following me?" Danlo finally asked.

Malaclypse smiled; he had a beautiful smile that spread out over the golden lines of his face. "As you see, I haven't been following you—here I stand appreciating this fine view, these strange, alien stars. It's you who have followed me. And that's very strange, don't you think? Most men flee our kind rather than seeking us out."

"It seems to be my fate, to seek out warrior-poets."

"A strange fate," Malaclypse said. "It would seem more natural for me to seek you."

"To seek me . . . why?"

"You don't know?"

"I do not know if I want to know."

Malaclypse held his wine goblet up to his nose and inhaled deeply. He said, "On Qallar, you're famous. For two reasons. You're one of the few ever to have defeated a warrior-poet—and the only one to have done so as a boy."

"I was sixteen when I met Marek in the library. I did not think of myself as a boy."

"Still, a remarkable feat. If only you had been born on Qallar, you might have become warrior among warriors, a poet among poets."

At this startling thought, Danlo looked straight at Malaclypse. He looked deep into his marvelous, violet eyes, which were so dark that he could almost see his reflection gleaming in their black centers. "I could never have become . . . a warrior-poet," he said.

"No?"

Danlo let this question hang in the air, even as the gonging sound of Mer Tadeo's music pools hung low and urgent over the lawns and fountains of the garden. He kept his eyes on Malaclypse's eyes and said, "Have you come here tonight to avenge Marek's death, then?"

"You ask this question so blithely."

"How should I ask, then?"

"Most men would not ask at all. They would flee. Why aren't you afraid of our kind?"

"I do not know."

"It's the greatest gift, not to fear," Malaclypse said. "But, of course, you needn't have feared that we would avenge Marek. He died according to our forms, which we thank you for observing so impeccably."

"I did not want him to die."

"And that is the most remarkable thing of all. It's said that you have taken a vow of ahimsa to harm no living thing—and yet you were able to help Marek on to his moment of the possible."

Danlo remembered too well how Marek of Qallar had plunged the killing knife into his own brain and so reached his moment of the possible, where life is death, and death is life. He remembered that Marek, just before he had accomplished this noble act, had confessed that the warrior-poets had a new rule for their bloody order: to kill all gods, even all women and men who might become as gods. For six years, Danlo had shared this secret with only two other people, but now he said, "I know why

Marek came to Neverness. The true reason. He told me about your rule before he died.''

Malaclypse smiled at this piece of news, which—strangely—seemed not to surprise him. "I've said that you're famous on my world for two reasons. The second reason, of course, is because you're the son of Mallory Ringess. Marek was sent to Neverness to determine if you're truly the son of the father.''

"Am I, then?''

"Don't you know?''

"How *would* I know?''

At this, Malaclypse laughed easily and to Danlo he said, "I've heard that you're also famous for answering questions with questions.''

Danlo inclined his head, slightly, accepting Malaclypse's criticism as a compliment. Then he said, "You have come to Farfara to complete this determination about me, yes?''

Again, as he often did, Danlo began to count his heartbeats as he waited for Malaclypse to remove the killing knife from his cloak. But Malaclypse only looked at him, strangely, deeply, drinking in the wild look that filled Danlo's eyes like an ocean.

"I don't know *who* you really are,'' Malaclypse said. "Not yet. In truth, I don't know who your father really is, either. Mallory Ringess, this once Lord Pilot of the Order, who everyone says has become a god.''

For a moment, Danlo looked up into the sky in sudden understanding. "You have come to find my father, yes?''

"Perhaps.''

"Not just to Farfara,'' Danlo said. "You would follow our Mission to the Vild.''

Now, for the first time, Malaclypse seemed slightly surprised. He regarded Danlo coolly and said, "I had heard that you were too perceptive for a mere pilot—now I see that this is so.''

"You would follow us,'' Danlo repeated. "But follow . . . how? Warrior-poets do not pilot lightships, do they?''

The Merchant-Pilots of Tria, of course, *did* pilot ships: deep ships and prayer ships, and sometimes even lightships. They journeyed to Nwarth and Alumit and Farfara, but no Merchant-Pilot would ever think of taking a lightship into the Vild.

"There is a man,'' Malaclypse said. He pointed along the curve of the retaining wall at a stand of orange trees some forty feet away. "A former pilot of your Order. He will take me where I need to go.''

As Danlo saw, beneath an orange tree laden with bright,

round fruits, there stood a silent man dressed all in gray. Danlo recognized him as the infamous renegade, Sivan wi Mawi Sarkissian, once a pilot of great promise who had deserted the Order in the time of the Quest for the Elder Eddas. None of the other pilots whom Mer Tadeo had invited would bear the shame of talking to such a faithless man and so Sivan stood alone, sipping from his goblet of wine.

"And where is it that you need to go, then?" Danlo asked.

"Wherever I must," Malaclypse said. "But I've heard that Mallory Ringess has returned to the Vild. Somewhere. It may be that your Order's mission will cause him to make himself known."

"And then?"

"And then *I* shall know," Malaclypse said. "And then I shall do what must be done."

"You would murder my father, yes?"

"If he is truly a god, I would help him toward his moment of the possible."

"If he is truly . . . a god?"

"If he is still a man, I would only ask him to complete a poem."

"What poem?"

"A poem that I've been composing for some time. Only a man who has refused to become a god would know how to complete it."

Danlo looked off at the Istas River gleaming in the starlight, but he said nothing.

"I believe that you might know where your father is."

Danlo squeezed his empty wineglass between his hands, but he remained as silent as the sky.

"It may be that we share the same mission, you and I," Malaclypse said. "I believe that we're both seeking your father."

Was it possible, Danlo wondered, that Malaclypse's only purpose in seeking the Vild was to lay eyes upon his father? He did not think so. The warrior-poets always had purposes within purposes—and often their deepest purpose was war.

"You're very good at keeping a silence," Malaclypse said. "Very well, then—let us listen to what our host is saying."

As Danlo looked down at the dark forest far below the cliff face, he became aware of a voice falling through the spaces all around him. It was the voice of Mer Tadeo, convolved and amplified by the music pools, hanging like a silver mist over the lawns of the garden. Mer Tadeo had begun his toast, and Danlo looked away from the warrior-poet to concentrate on Mer Tadeo's words: ". . . these brave women and men of the Civilized Worlds' most honored Order, who have vowed to enter the Vild and seek . . ." Danlo became aware, just then, that his glass was empty. In his haste to seek out the warrior-poet, he hadn't had time to fill it.

"Pilot, you've no wine to drink," Malaclypse said. Quickly, easily, he moved over to Danlo and held up his wineglass as if he were showing Danlo some secret elixir. He tinked it against Danlo's glass, and a clear note rang out. Then he quickly poured a stream of ruby wine into Danlo's glass halfway to the rim, spilling not a drop. "Won't you drink to the fulfillment of the Mission?"

Danlo brought his glass close to his lips, but did not drink. He breathed in deeply, smelling the wine. It had an effervescent scent that was almost hot and peppery. He wondered if Malaclypse would dare poison him in clear sight of ten thousand people also about to sip from glasses of wine. The warrior-poets, he knew, were notorious for their poisons: a thousand years ago at the end of the War of the Faces, in alliance with the Architects of the Old Church, they had engineered the virus that had poisoned the Civilized Worlds, and ultimately had infected the Devaki people on Danlo's world and killed everyone in his tribe except Danlo.

"Have you ever tasted firewine?" Malaclypse asked.

Danlo remembered, then, that the warrior-poets' poisons are not always meant to kill. He remembered that a warrior-poet had once poisoned his grandmother, Dama Moira Ringess. This infamous warrior-poet had jabbed little needles into her neck, filling her blood with programed bacteria called slel cells. These cells, like man-made cancers, had metastasized into her brain, where they had destroyed millions of neurons and neuron clusters. The slel cells had layered down microscopic sheets of protein neurologics, living computers that might be grafted onto human brains. And so his grandmother, who was also the mother of Mallory Ringess, had been slelled, her marvelous human brain replaced almost entirely by a warrior-poet's programed computer circuitry. As Danlo drank in the firewine's heady aroma, he could not forget how the mother of his father had suffered such a death-in-life.

"I cannot drink with you," Danlo said at last.

"No?"

"I am sorry."

Malaclypse looked deeply at Danlo but said nothing.

"As a pilot, I may not drink with my Order's enemies."

Malaclypse smiled, then, sadly, beautifully, and asked, "Are you so sure that we're enemies?"

"Truly we are."

"Then don't drink with me," Malaclypse said. "But do drink. Tonight, everyone will drink to the glory of the Vild Mission, and so should you."

Now Mer Tadeo had finished his toast, and the sudden sound of ten thousand glasses clinking together rang out through the garden. Danlo, who had once sought affirmation above all other things, listened deeply to this tremendous sound of ringing glass. It was like a pure, crystal music, recalling a time in his life when he had trusted the truth that his eyes might behold. Now he looked at Malaclypse's deep violet eyes, smiling at him, beckoning him to drink, and he could see that the wine was only wine, that it was infused with neither virus nor slel cells nor other poisons. And because Danlo needed to affirm this truth of his eyes at any cost, he touched his wineglass to his lips and took a deep drink.

Instantly, the smooth tissues of his tongue and throat were on fire. For a moment he worried that the wine was indeed tainted with a poison, perhaps even with the electric ekkana drug that would never leave his body and would make an agony of all the moments of his life. But then the burning along his tongue gave way to an intriguing tingling sensation, which in turn softened into a wonderful coolness almost reminiscent of peppermint. Truly, the wine *was* only wine, the delicious firewine that merchants and afficionados across the Civilized Worlds are always eager to seek.

"Congratulations," Malaclypse said. Then he raised his glass and bowed to Danlo. "To our mission. To the eternal moment when all things are possible."

Malaclypse took a sip of wine, then, even as Danlo lowered his goblet and poured the remnants of his priceless firewine over the grass beneath his feet. He had said that he may not drink with a warrior-poet, and drink he would not.

"I am sorry," he said.

"I'm sorry, too. I'm sorry that it isn't you who will be piloting my ship into the Vild."

The warrior-poet's sense of time was impeccable. Upon his utterance of the word "Vild," the manswarms spread throughout the garden began calling out numbers. One hundred . . .

ninety-nine . . . ninety-eight . . . ninety-seven. . . . Following Mer Tadeo's example, men and women all around Danlo began crying out in unison, and their individual voices merged into a single, long, dark roar.

Now many faces were turned eastward, up toward the sky. Merchants in their silver kimonos, pilots and Ordermen in their formal robes—they all lifted their faces to the stars as they called down the numbers and pointed at the patch of space where the Sonderval had promised the supernova would appear. Sixty-six . . . sixty-five . . . sixty-four . . . sixty-three. . . . The warrior-poet, too, aimed his long, graceful finger toward the heavens. In his clear, strong voice, he called down the numbers along with everyone else, counting ever backwards toward zero. Twenty-two . . . twenty-one . . . twenty . . . nineteen. . . .

At last, Danlo looked up at stars of the Vild, waiting. It amused and awed him to think that these uncountable, nameless stars might somehow be waiting for him, even as he waited for their wild light to fill his eyes. Once, when he was a child, he had thought that stars were the eyes of his ancestors watching him, waiting for him to realize that he, too, in his deepest self, was really a wild white star who would always belong to the night. The stars, he knew, could wait almost forever for a man to be born into his true nature, and that was the great mystery of the stars. Four . . . three . . . two . . . one. . . .

There was a moment. For a moment the sky was just the sky, and the stars went on twinkling forever. Danlo thought that perhaps the Sonderval's calculations had been wrong, that no new star would appear that night. And then this endless moment, which lasted much less than a second, finally ended. Above the eastern horizon, above the dark mountains, a point of light broke out of the blackness and quickly blossomed into a dazzling white sphere. Its radiance swirled about an infinitely bright center, and flecks of fire spun out into the farthest reaches of space. It was almost impossible to look at, this wildflower of light that hurt Danlo's eyes, and so he turned to see ten thousand people squinting, grimacing, standing with their hands pushing outward above their eyes as if to shield themselves from this terrible new star.

It almost seemed that there should have been a great noise to accompany this event, as with a fireworks display, some searing hiss of burned air or cosmic thunder. But the sky was strangely silent, as ever, and the only sounds in the garden were the inrush of many people's breaths, the chirping of the evening birds, the splash of water and wine falling in the many fountains.

The merchants of Farfara (and even the many ungloved servants) were obviously hushed and awed by what they saw, as if they were witnessing the birth of a new child. Danlo remembered, then, that this supernova was no new star being born, but rather a doomed star that attains its most brilliant moment in dying into light. It was all light, this beautiful star. It was all alpha and gamma and waves of hard radiation that men had freed from matter in their frenzy to remake the universe. It was photons breaking through the night, burning the sky, onstreaming through the universe without end.

And although Danlo had waited only a moment for this light to fall upon the garden, men on other worlds would have to wait millennia to see it. At the speed of light through vacuum, it would be some twenty thousand years before the supernova's light crossed the galaxy and rained down upon the city of Neverness. But there were other stars, nearer and more deadly, and Danlo remembered very well that twenty years ago one named Merripen's Star had exploded very near the Star of Neverness. Almost all his life, a wavefront of light and death had been advancing through the black drears of space upon Neverness, and soon, in only six more years, the people of Neverness would see the Vild for what it truly was.

And this was the true reason that the Order had sent a Mission to the Vild. The Vild, Danlo thought, was an inferno of murderous light and broken spacetime that existed wherever human beings were so mad as to destroy the stars. And so the men and women of the Order must go to the Vild before the Vild came to them.

"I must go now," Danlo said. He bowed to Malaclypse and then looked down at his empty wineglass. "Farewell, Poet."

"Until we meet again," Malaclypse said. "Fall far and farewell, Pilot."

Because Danlo did not want to think that they would meet again, he smiled grimly as he turned and walked back through the crowds. Between the hot, packed bodies of the many awestruck people, beneath the light of the new star, he walked back toward the Fountain of Fortune. There, the Sonderval had gathered together the pilots of the Order. Lara Jesusa, Richardess, Zapata Karek, Leander of Darkmoon—they were all there, even the fabulous Aja, who was sometimes a woman, sometimes a man, and who was said to be the purest pilot ever to have come out of the Academy on Neverness.

Without a care for soiling the sleeve of his robe, Danlo

plunged his wineglass into the fountain, and he stood there drinking with his fellow pilots, clinking glasses and letting drops of
bright red firewine run down over his naked hand. The pilots
spoke of their sacred Mission, and the Sonderval called out the
names of the hundred pilots who would follow him and guide the
deep ships and seedships to the Order's new home on Thiells.
The rest of the pilots—including Danlo—would seek the lost
planet called Tannahill. Each of these pilots, according to his
genius and fate, would enter the pathless, unknown Vild, there to
seek signs and secrets that might lead them to their journey's
end. Danlo himself would go where the stars were the wildest.
He would find his father among all the bright, dying stars and ask
him a simple question. That Malaclypse Redring might follow
him in the renegade's lightship was of no matter. He could not
fear that a warrior-poet might murder his father. For if his father
was really a god, how could even the most murderous of men
harm him?

    As Danlo drank his wine and gazed up at the blazing new star
in the sky, he wondered how anything could ever harm those
beautiful and terrible beings that men knew as gods.

THE EYE OF THE UNIVERSE

I am the eye with which the Universe
Beholds itself and knows itself divine.
—Percy Bysshe Shelley

The next day, Danlo took his lightship into the Vild. The *Snowy Owl* was a long and graceful ship, a beautiful sweep of spun diamond some two hundred feet from tip to tail; as it fell across the galaxy it was like a needle of light stitching in and out of the manifold: that marvelous, shimmering fabric of deep reality that folds between the stars and underlies the spacetime of all the universe. The ships of the Vild Mission fell from star to star, and there were many along their way toward the star and planet named as Thiells. As ever, Danlo was awestruck by the numbers of the stars: the cool red and orange stars, the hot blue giants that were the galaxy's jewels, the thousands upon thousands of yellow stars burning as steadily and faithfully as Old Earth's sun.

No one knew how many stars lit the lens of the Milky Way. The Order's astronomers had said that there were at least five hundred billion stars in the galaxy, blazing in dense clusters at the core, spinning ever outward in brilliant spirals along the arms of the galactic plane. And more stars were being born all the time. In the bright nebulae such as the Rudra and the Rosette, out of gravity and heat and interstellar dust, the new stars continually formed and flared into light. A hundred generations of stars had lived and died in the eons before the Star of Neverness ever came into being.

Stars, like people, were always dying. Sometimes, as Danlo looked out over the vast light-distances, he marveled that so many human beings could arise from stardust and the fundamental urge of all matter toward life. Scattered among all the galaxy's far-flung stars were perhaps fifty million billion people. On the Civilized Worlds alone, every second, some three million women, men, and children would die, *were* dying, will always be passing from life into death. It was only right and natural, Danlo thought, that human beings should create themselves in their vast and hungry swarms, but it was not right that they should seek a greater life by killing the stars. This was all sacrilege and sin, or even *shaida,* a word that Danlo sometimes used to describe the evil of a universe that, like a top failing to spin or a cracked teapot, had lost its harmony and balance.

All matter craved transformation into light, and this Danlo understood deep inside his belly and brain. But already, in this infinite universe from which he had been born, there was too much light. The stars of the Vild were sick with light, swelling and bursting into the hellish lightstorms that men called supernovas. Soon, someday—perhaps farwhen—the vastness of the Vild would be a blinding white cloud full of photons and hard radiation, and then this tiny pocket of the universe would no longer be transparent to light. No longer would men such as Danlo be able to look at the stars and see the universe just as it is, for all space would be light, and all time would be light, always and forever, nothing but light and ever more dazzling light.

It was toward the light of Thiells that the pilots steered, there to build a city and a new Order. The rest of the pilots, including Danlo, would accompany the Mission as far as Sattva Luz, a magnificent white star well within the inner envelope of the Vild. And so it happened.

The journey to Sattva Luz was uneventful, for the Sonderval had already mapped the pathways that led from star to star; he had told the pilots the fixed-points of every star along their path, and so Danlo and the *Snowy Owl* fell from Savona to Shokan and then on to Sattva Luz as smoothly as corpuscles of blood streaming through a man's veins. This segment of the journey was much the same as fenestering through the Fallaways, only fraught with dangers that few pilots had ever faced. In any part of the Vild—even along the pathways well mapped and well known—at any moment the spacetime distortions of an exploding star might fracture a pathway into a thousand individual decomposition strands, thereby destroying any ship so unfortunate as to be caught in the wrong strand.

Around Sattva Luz, where the many millions of pathways through the manifold converged into a thickspace as dark and

dense as a ball of lead, the pilots dispersed. The main body of
Mission ships, guided by the Sonderval, was the first to fall away.
Danlo, whose ship had fallen out of the manifold into realspace
for a few moments, watched them go. Below him—ten million
miles below the *Snowy Owl*—was the boiling white corona of
Sattva Luz. Above him there wavered a sea of blackness and
many nameless stars. He waited as the Sonderval's ship, the *Cardinal Virtue,* fell into the bright black manifold and disappeared.
He was aware of this event as a little flash of light; soon there
came many more flashes of light as the soundless engines of the
Mission ships ripped open rents in spacetime and fell into the
manifold. The pilots in their glorious lightships—and the pilots
in the deep ships and in the seedships—opened windows upon
the universe, and they fell in and were gone. Then the remaining
pilots fell in, too. The *Snowy Owl* and the *Neurosinger,* the *Deus
ex Machina* and the *Rose of Armageddon*—one hundred fifty-
four ships and pilots sought their fates and vanished into the
deepest part of the Vild.

For Danlo, as for any pilot, mathematics was the key that
opened the many windows through which his lightship passed.
Mathematics was like a bright, magic sword that sliced open the
veils of the manifold and illuminated the dark caverns of neverness
waiting for him there. the *Snowy Owl* fell far and deep, and
Danlo thought deeply in the pit of his ship, which was the very
mind and soul of his lightship, a living computer woven of protein circuitry, rich and soft as purple velvet. He thought and
visualized and proved the theorems that let him see his way
through the chaos all around him. He dreamed mathematics in
vivid, waking dreams, and he fell on and on.

Always, when he entered the realm of pure number, the cold
and clear light of mathematics shone as through a crystal cave
lined with sapphires and firestones and other precious jewels. His
mind filled with the crystal-like symbols of probabilistic topology: the emerald snowflake representing the Jordan-Holder Theorem, the diamond glyphs of the mapping lemmas, the amethyst
curlicues of the statement of Invariance of Dimension, and all the
other thousands of sparkling mental symbols that the pilots call
ideoplasts. Only then could he perceive the torison spaces and
Flowtow bubbles and infinite trees that undermine the manifold,
much as a sleekit's twisting tunnels lie hidden beneath crusts of
snow. Only when he opened his mind to the manifold would the
manifold open before him so that he might see this strange reality just as it was and make his mappings from star to star.

So it was that Danlo became aware of his fellow pilots as they set out on their journeys. As did the *Snowy Owl,* their ships perturbed the manifold like so many stones dropped into a pool of water. Danlo perceived these perturbations as ripples of light, a purely mathematical light, which he had been trained to descry and fathom. For a while, as the lightships remained within a well-defined region known as a Lavi neighborhood, with his mind's eye he followed the luminous pathways of the lightships as they fell outward toward the galaxy's many stars. And then, one by one, as the pilots fell away from each other and the radius of convergence shot off toward infinity, even these ships were lost to his sight.

Only nine other ships remained within the same neighborhood as the *Snowy Owl.* These nine ships and their pilots he knew very well, for they each had vowed to penetrate the same spaces of the Vild. A few of them were already distinguished for their part in the Pilot's War: Sarolta Sen and Dolores Nun, and the impossibly brave Leander of Darkmoon, who craved danger as other men do women or wine. There was Rurik Boaz in the *Lamb of God,* and the sly Li Te Mu Lan, who piloted the *Diamond Lotus.* There was another lotus ship as well, the *Thousand Petaled Lotus,* which belonged to Valin wi Tymon Whitestone, of the Simoom Whitestones. Three other pilots had set out toward a certain cluster of stars beyond the Eta Carina Nebula; they were the Rosaleen and Ivar Sarad, in a ship curiously named the *Bottomless Cup.* And finally, of course, Shamir the Bold, he who had once journeyed farther toward the galactic core than any other pilot since Leopold Soli.

All these pilots, in Mer Tadeo's garden on the night of the supernova, had vowed to enter that dark, strange nebula known as the Solid State Entity. Like Mallory Ringess before them, they had vowed to fall among the most dangerous of stars in the hope that they might speak with one of the galaxy's greatest gods.

Even before Danlo had left Neverness, on a night of omens as he stood on a windswept beach looking up at the stars, he had planned to penetrate the Entity, too. That other pilots had made similar plans did not surprise him. Ten pilots were few enough to search a volume of space some ten thousand cubic light-years in volume. Ten pilots could easily lose themselves in such a nebula, like grains of sand scattered upon an ocean. Even so, Danlo took comfort in the company of his fellow pilots, and he continually watched the manifold for the perturbations that their ships created.

Including the *Snowy Owl*, ten ships fell among the stars.
Many times, he counted the ships; he wanted to be sure that their
number was ten, a comforting and complete number. Ten was the
number of fingers on his hands, and on the hands of all natural
human beings. Ten, in decimal systems of counting, symbolizes
the totality of the universe in the way all things return to unity.
Ten was the perfect number, he thought, and so it dismayed him
that at times he couldn't be sure if there were really ten ships
after all.

More than once, usually after they had passed through a spinning thickspace around some red giant star, his count of the ships
yielded a different number. This should not have been so. Counting is the most fundamental of the mathematical arts, as natural
as the natural numbers that fall off from one to infinity. Danlo,
who had been born with a rare mathematical gift, had been able
to count almost before he could talk, and so it should have been
the simplest thing for him to know whether the number of ships
in the neighborhood near him was ten or five or fifty.

Certainly, by the time they had passed a fierce white star that
Danlo impulsively named The Wolf, he knew that there were at
least ten ships but no more than eleven. At times, as he peered
into the dark heart of the manifold, he thought that he could
make out the composition wave of a mysterious eleventh ship.
Looking for this ship was like looking at a unique pattern of light
reflected from a pool of water. At times he was almost certain of
this pattern, but at other times, as when a rock is thrown into a
quiet pool, the pattern would break apart only to reform a moment later, reflecting nothing.

The eleventh ship, if indeed there really *were* an eleventh ship,
appeared to hover ghostlike at the very threshold of the radius of
convergence. It was impossible to say it was really there, impossible to say it was not. Even as the ten pilots kleined coreward
toward the Solid State Entity, this ghost ship haunted the mappings of the others, remaining always at the exact boundary of
their neighborhood of stars. Danlo had never dreamed that anyone could pilot a ship so flawlessly. In truth, he hoped that there
was no eleventh pilot, no matter how skilled or prescient he
might be. Eleven, as he knew, was a most perilous number. It
was the number of excess and transition, of conflict, martyrdom,
even war.

As it happened Danlo wasn't the only pilot to detect an eleventh ship. Near an unnamed star, Li Te Mu Lan's ship fell out of
the manifold into realspace. She remained beneath the light of

this star for long seconds of time, a signal that the other pilots should join her, if they so pleased. It was the traditional invitation to a conclave of pilots, made in the only way a pilot can issue such an invitation. Since radio waves and other such signals will not propagate through the manifold, but only through real-space, the ten pilots fell out into the weak starlight of this weak yellow sun, and sent laser beams flashing from ship to ship.

The computer of the *Snowy Owl* decoded the information bound into the laser light and made pictures for Danlo to see. It made faces and sounds and voices, and suddenly the pit of his ship was very crowded, for there were nine other pilots there with him. That is, the *heads* of his nine fellow pilots floated in the dark air around him. Watching the phased light waves of these nine holograms was almost like entering one of Neverness's numerous cafés and sitting at table with friends over mugs of steaming coffee and the comfort of conversation.

It was *almost* like that. In truth, it disquieted Danlo to think of his severed, glowing head appearing in the pits of nine other lightships. There was something eerie in holding a conclave in this way, here, in the black deeps of the Vild, perhaps six hundred trillion miles from any other human being. It was disturbing and strange, but when Li Te Mu Lan began speaking, Danlo concentrated on the words that she was saying.

"I believe that there is another pilot accompanying us," Li Te said. She had a perfectly shaped head as round and brown and bare of hair as a baldo nut. Her body, as Danlo remembered, was round, too, though he could see nothing of her body just now, only her glowing, round head. "Does anyone know if there is another pilot accompanying us?"

"Ten pilots vowed to penetrate the Entity," Ivar Sarad said. He was a thin-faced man with a penchant for cold abstractions and inventing paranoid (and bizarre) interpretations of reality. "We stood together before the Sonderval and vowed this. Perhaps the Sonderval has sent a pilot to verify that we fulfill our vows."

A pilot whose head was as broad and hairy as that of a muskox could not accept this. Shamir the Bold, with his courage and optimism, his decisiveness and sense of honor, laughed and said, "No, the Sonderval would believe that we'll do what we vowed to do. At least, he'll believe that we'll attempt to fulfill our vows."

"Then who pilots the eleventh ship?" This came from the

Rosaleen, a shy, anxious woman who appeared to take no notice of her worth as pilot or human being.

"I wonder if there *is* an eleventh ship," Ivar Sarad said. "Can we be certain of this? I myself am not. The wave function can be interpreted in other ways."

"Do you think so?" Shamir the Bold asked. "What ways?"

"In the wake of our passing, the composition series could be inverted as a Gallivare space that would—"

"*That* is unlikely," Li Te Mu Lan observed. "No one has ever proved the existence of a Gallivare space."

Ivar Sarad regarded her coldly, suspiciously. "Well, then—perhaps it is a reflection? Perhaps the line wake of one of our ships is being reflected—Leopold Soli once said that, in the Vild, the manifold can flatten out as smooth and reflective as a mirror."

Of course, Ivar Sarad was not the only pilot to doubt the existence of an eleventh ship. Sarolta Sen, Dolores Nun, and Leander of Darkmoon were wont to agree with Ivar Sarad, though for different and more commonsense reasons. But Rurik Boaz and Valin wi Tymon Whitestone sided with Li Te Mu Lan. Valin Whitestone was even selfless enough to propose that the others continue toward the Solid State Entity while he kleined backward along their pathway to seek out the eleventh ship. He would learn the identity of this mysterious eleventh pilot. If possible, he would then rejoin the others, who, by this time, would no doubt have shared in the glory of being the only pilots since Mallory Ringess to wrest great knowledge from the goddess that some called Kalinda the Wise.

Until this moment, Danlo had kept his silence. He was the youngest of the pilots, and so he thought it seemly to let the others take the lead in this conversation. Then, too, from his once and deepest friend, Hanuman li Tosh, who had remained in Neverness, he had learned the value of keeping secrets. But it was not right that he should keep important information from his fellow pilots. He couldn't let the noble Valin Whitestone sacrifice himself for a mere secret, and so he said, "It is possible . . . that a ronin pilot guides the eleventh ship. Sivan wi Mawi Sarkissian, the ronin—you all know of him, yes? It is possible that he carries a warrior-poet into the Vild."

In the pit of Danlo's ship, the heads of the nine other pilots turned his way. Li Te Mu Lan and the Rosaleen, Rurik Boaz and Shamir the Bold, and the others—they looked at him as if he were merely some journeyman pilot who had suffered his first intoxication with the number storm or the dreamtime. Finally, after they waited for him to explain this incredible statement, he told them of his encounter with Malaclypse Redring in Mer Tadeo's garden.

"It *is* possible," Leander of Darkmoon said. His massive head was flowing with the golden curls of his long hair and beard. Indeed, like his name, there was something of the lion about him, and something of the lazy (and reckless) boy, as well. But he was a man who bored too easily, and so when Danlo spoke of warrior-poets and the infamous Sivan wi Mawi Sarkissian, Leander was like a hungry man who had been fed a piece of dripping red meat. His eyes brightened, and in deep rumbling voice he said, "I knew Sivan before the great quest maddened him. He was a fine pilot, once upon a time. If anyone could follow us into the Entity, he could."

After long, almost endless rounds of discussion, with their ships separated by half a million miles of space above a rosy little star that no one bothered to name, the pilots agreed that Malaclypse Redring was likely following them, hoping perhaps that the ten other pilots might lead him to Mallory Ringess, but there were other possibilities. As Leander of Darkmoon and Dolores Nun knew too well, it was possible for pilot to fall against pilot, to use his lightship as a sword, to maneuver close to another ship and slice open gaping holes into the manifold into which his enemy might fall.

If these holes were made precisely—if the pilot could find a precise probability mapping—it was possible to cast an enemy ship down a dark, closed tube into the fiery heart of some nearby star. In the Pilot's War, many had died this way. Sarolta Sen, in his ship the *Infinite Tree,* had once almost been destroyed thusly, and so he was the first to observe that Malaclypse Redring might desire all their deaths. If the warrior-poets had a rule to slay all gods, then they might also have a secret rule to slay any man or woman proud enough—or foolish enough—to attempt contact with a god.

It would have been the simplest thing, as a precaution, for the pilots to turn back upon their pathways, to fall upon Malaclypse Redring and the lightship of Sivan wi Mawi Sarkissian, even as a pack of wolves might discourage a great white bear from hunting them. In a moment, in a flash of light, they might easily have incinerated the warrior-poet. But this was not their way. That is, it was no *longer* their way. Leander of Darkmoon, although he loved war as well as any man could, was the first to propose that

the pilots scatter across the Vild and approach the Solid State
Entity along ten different pathways. That way Malaclypse Redring, inside Sivan's ship, the *Red Dragon,* could only follow one
of them.

And so the pilots concluded their talk and said their farewells,
and in the pit of the *Snowy Owl,* Danlo was once again alone.
Then, upon Le Te Mu Lan's signal (she was the oldest of the
pilots and this was her right), the pilots scattered. They opened
windows to the manifold and vanished like streaks of light bursting from a diamond sphere. Each pilot faced the manifold along
her own chosen pathway; each pilot fell sightless and senseless
of the ships of the others, and so each of them was finally and
completely alone.

At first Danlo cherished this loneliness with a quiet joy, as he
might have listened for the wind in a dark and silent wood. For
the first time in many years he felt completely free. But it is the
nature of life that no emotion is meant to last forever, and so very
quickly his elation gave way to the apprehension that he was not
really alone after all. In almost no time, as he plunged deeper
into the dark currents of the manifold, he descried the perturbations of another ship. A second ship—two ships remaining always within the same neighborhood of stars.

The number two, he thought, was an ominous number. Two is
a reflection or duplication of one, the most perfect of the natural
numbers. Two is all echo and counterpoise; two is the beginning
of multiplicity, the way the universal oneness differentiates itself
and breaks apart into strings and quarks and photons, all the
separate and component pieces of life. Two is a symbol of becoming as opposed to pure being; in this sense, two *is* life, and
therefore, it is death, for all life finds its conclusion in death,
even as it feeds off the death of other things in order to stay alive.

Although Danlo, for himself, feared dying less than did other
men, he thought that he had seen enough of death to know it for
what it truly is. Once, when he was nearly fourteen years old, he
had buried all the eighty-eight people of the Devaki tribe, who
had adopted and raised him from a babe. He knew death too well,
and he sensed that the warrior-poet who followed him might yet
encompass the deaths of those who were beloved by him. Because he saw Malaclypse Redring as a harbinger of death (and
because he thought he knew all of death that there was to know),
he decided to escape this ghostly lightship that pursued him,
much as a Snowy Owl might hunt a hare bounding over the
snow. And so he emptied his mind of what lay behind him, and

he turned his inner eye to the deepest part of the manifold. There he would face the deepest part of the universe, the terrors and the joys.

At first, however, there was only joy. There was the cold beauty of the number storm, the many-faceted mathematical symbols that fell through his mind like frozen drops of light. There was the slowing of time and the consequent quickening of all his thoughts. And there was something else. Something other.

It is something of a mystery that, although all pilots enter the manifold the same way and agree upon its essential nature, each man and woman will perceive it uniquely. For Danlo, as for no other pilot with whom he had ever spoken, the manifold shimmered with colors. Of course, in the absence of all light and spacetime, he knew that there could be no color—but somehow, there *were* colors. He fell from star to star, beneath the stars of realspace, and he entered a Kirrilian neighborhood which glowed a deep cobalt blue, a hidden and secret blue the like of which he had never seen.

Soon he passed on to a common invariant space all pearl gray and touched with swirls of absinthe and rose. For a moment, he supposed that he might be lucky, that rest of his journey toward the Entity might prove no more difficult than the straightforward mapping through such spaces. But in the Vild, piloting a lightship never remains easy or simple. In less than a moment, he entered a disorienting shear space, the kind of topological nightmare that the pilots sometimes call a Danladi inversion. Now the veils of the manifold were a bright azure, fading almost instantly to a pale turquoise, and then brightening again to an emerald green.

The space all around him was like a strangely viewed painting in which figure and ground kept shifting into focus, forward and back, light and dark, inside and out. It was beautiful, in a way, but dangerous too, and so he was glad when this particular space began to break apart and branch out into a more or less normal decision tree. All pilots would wish that the manifold held nothing more complicated than such trees; where all decisions take on the simplest form: maximize/minimize, left/right, inside/outside, yes/no.

But then the branch of the tree holding up his lightship suddenly snapped—this is how it seemed—and he was hurled into a rare and quite deadly torison space, of a kind that Lord Ricardo Lavi had once discovered on one of the first journeys toward the Vild. Suddenly, he was again aware of colors. There were the

quick violets of space suddenly folding, and the r-dimensional
Betti numbers appearing as ruby, auburn, and chrome red. There
were flashes of scarlet, as if all the other colors might momentarily catch on fire and fall past the threshold of finite, folding
into an infinite and blazing crimson.

Space itself, this impossible torison space, was twisting like a
snowworm in a strong man's hands, writhing and popping and
twisting until it suddenly burst in an opening of violet into violet
and began folding in upon itself. Now, for Danlo, there was true
peril, danger inside of danger. Now—for a moment that might
last no longer than half a beat of his heart—he floated in the pit
of his ship, sweating and breathing deeply, and he thought as
quickly as it is possible for a man to think. He had little fear of
death, but even so he dreaded being trapped alive inside a collapsing torison space. His dread was a red-purple color, the color
of a blood tick squeezed between finger and thumb.

All his awareness—his racing mathematical mind and every
strand of his will to live—spread out over the space before him.
There were dark tunnels that kleined back and through themselves, impossibly complex, impossible to map through. There
was the very fabric of the manifold itself, lavender like a
fabulist's robes, infolding upon itself through shades of amethyst, magenta, and deep purple—the one and true purple that
might well be the quintessential color that underlay all others.
Everywhere, the manifold was falling in on itself like dark violet
flowers blossoming backward in time, folding up petal inside
petal, always infolding toward that lightless singularity where the
number of folds falls off to infinity.

He might never have mapped free from such a space, but then
he chanced to remember a certain color. In truth, he willed himself to summon up a perfect blue-black hue that suffused his
mind the way that the night fills the late evening sky. His will to
live was strong, and his memory of colors, images, words, whispers, and love was even stronger. His memory for such things
was almost perfect, and so it happened that he willed himself to
behold a deep, deep blue inside blue, the color of his mother's
eyes.

His mother, he remembered, had been one of the finest scryers that there had ever been. His mother had been able to see the
infinitely complex web of connections between nowness and time
to come. The greatest scryers will always find their way into the
future; in the end, they choose which future and fate will be.

Although Danlo was no scryer, not yet, he remembered how perfectly the color of his mother's eyes matched his own.

"You have your mother's eyes," his grandfather Leopold Soli had once told him. Long ago, before he was born, his mother had blinded herself as the scryers do so that she might perceive the future more clearly. Now, in the pit of his ship, even as he plunged downward toward the torison space's hideous singularity, Danlo closed his eyes tightly and tried to behold their blueness from within.

He remembered, then, an important theorem of elementary topology. He saw it instantly as a perfect jewel, like a lightstone, a deep, dark, liquid blue holding a secret light. It was the first conservation theorem, which proved that for every simplicial mapping, the image of the boundary is equal to the boundary of the image. Almost instantly, he seized upon this theorem as a starving man might grasp a gobbet of meat. He knew that he could apply it toward mapping out of the torison space. And so he did. Before the lens of his mind's eye, he summoned up arrays of ideoplasts and made his proof. He was perhaps the first pilot in the history of the Order to prove that a collapsing torison space might remain open—even if that opening quickly fell off toward an infinitessimal. He made a mapping, and he fell through, and suddenly there was the light of a star. the *Snowy Owl* fell out into realspace, into realtime, into the glorious golden light of a star that he named Shona Oyu, or, the Bright Eye of God.

In this way, falling from star to star, falling in and out of the manifold *beneath* the stars, he continued on his journey. Because he wished to be the first of the ten pilots to reach the Entity (and because he hoped to elude the warrior-poet who might still be following him), he fell across the stars as quickly as a pilot may fall.

As the Sonderval had said in Mer Tadeo's garden, all quests are really the same. His quest to seek out his father and find the lost planet Tannahill was connected to the great quest twenty-five years past to find that infinite store of knowledge known as the Elder Eddas. And *that* quest was merely a continuation of all quests throughout time and history. Always, man had felt the urge to discover the true image of humanity, the shape and substance of what man might someday become. This is the secret of life, of human life, the true secret that men and women have sought as far back as the howling moonlit savannas of Afarique on Old Earth.

In the pilots of the Order, this urge to know the unknowable most often finds itself in a terrible restlessness, an instinct and will to fall through space, to move ever outward across the universe, always seeking. Some pilots seek black holes, or ringworlds built by ancient aliens, or strange, new stars. Some pilots still look for the hypothesized dark matter of the universe, the mysterious matter that no one has ever found. Some pilots seek God. But all pilots, if they are worthy of their pilots' rings, seek movement for the sake of movement itself.

The dance of lightship from star to star, from the translucent windows into the manifold that give out onto the stars—this urge to fall ever outward toward the farthest galaxies is sometimes called the westering. Sometimes, too, the pilots refer to this manner of journey as fenestering, for to fall quickly from star to star, one must align the stellar windows artfully and with great precision. Although Danlo was not yet a master of this art of interfenestration, the westering urge was strong in him. Westering/fenestering, fenestering/westering—to a young pilot such as Danlo, the two words were the same, and so he made successive mappings through hundreds of crystal-like windows. And with every window he passed through there was moment of stillness and a clarity, as of starlight illumining a perfect diamond pane. And yet there was always the anticipation of other windows yet to come, always newness, always strangeness, always the opening outward onto the clear light of universe.

And so he fell across the galaxy. If his ship had been able to move at lightspeed through normal space, his journey would have required some three thousand years. This, he thought, was a very long time. Three thousand years ago, the Order had yet to make its move from Arcite to Neverness, and the woman who would one day transform herself into the Solid State Entity had yet to be born. Three thousand years before, somewhere in the regions that he passed through, it was said that an insane god had killed itself in the spectacular manner of throwing itself into a star, thereby blowing it up in an incandescent funeral pyre and creating the first of the Vild's supernovas.

In a galaxy as apocalyptic as the Milky Way, three thousand years was almost forever, and yet, to a pilot locked inside the pit of a lightship, there were other eternities of time more immediate and more oppressive. Danlo, who was a creature of wind and sun, sometimes hated the darkness in which he lay. When he faced away from the ship-computer and the brilliant number storm, he hated the damp, acid smell of the neurologics surrounding him, the acrid stench of his unwashed body, and the carbon dioxide closeness of his own breath. Above all things, he longed for clean air and movement beneath the open sky. Although he fell across the stars as quickly as most pilots have ever fallen, his westering rush took much intime: the inner, subjective time of his blood, belly, and brain. Sometimes, during rare moments of acceptance and affirmation, he loved being a pilot as much as any man ever has, yet he hated it, too, and he longed for a quicker way of journeying. Often, over the millions of seconds of his quest, he thought about the Great Theorem, which states that there exists a pair of simply connected point-sources in the neighborhood of any two stars.

His father had been the first to prove this theorem, the first pilot to fall across half the galaxy from Perdido Luz to the Star of Neverness in a single fall. Danlo knew, as all pilots now knew, that it was possible to fall between any two stars almost instantly. It was possible to fall anywhere in the universe, yes, but it was not always possible to find such a mapping. In truth, for most pilots, it was hideously difficult. A few pilots, such as the Sonderval and Vrenda Chu, were sometimes genius enough to discover such point-to-point mappings and use the Great Theorem as it should be used. But even they must usually journey as Danlo did now, scurfing the windows of the manifold window by window, star by star, day by endless day.

The farther toward the Entity that Danlo fell—sometimes down pathways as complex as a nest of writhing snakes—the harder he tried to make sense of the Great Theorem and apply it toward finding an instantaneous mapping. He wished to fall out around a famous, red star inside the Entity. He wished to make planetfall, to climb out of his ship and rest on the sands of a wide, sunny beach. He wished these things for the sake of his soul, with all the force of his will.

And yet, there was another reason that he played with the logic and intricacies of the Great Theorem. A very practical reason. At need, Danlo could be the most practical of men, and so, when he passed by a neutron star very near the spaces of the Entity and detected once again the ghost image of Sivan wi Siri Sarkissian's ship, he couldn't help dreaming of falling away instantly, falling far and finally away from the warrior-poet who pursued him.

On the ninety-ninth day of his journey, as his ship's clock measured time, he came at last to the threshold of the Solid State Entity. the *Snowy Owl* fell out into realspace around a large white star. Danlo reached out with his great telescopes and drank in a sight that few pilots had ever seen. Before him, hanging in the blackness of space, a cloud of a hundred thousand stars burned dimly through veils of glowing hydrogen gas. There was much interstellar dust, too much for him to penetrate this dark, forbidding nebula by sight alone. Soon, perhaps in moments, he would have to enter the nebula itself to see it as it was. For millennia, of course, pilots have entered the galaxy's many nebulas, but this cluster of stars was different from any other, for it contained the body and brain of a goddess.

In a way, the entire nebula *was* the Entity's brain, or rather, Her brain was spread out over this vast region of stars. It troubled Danlo to conceive of such a vast intelligence, woven into great clumps of matter that weren't really organic brains at all but rather more like computers: millions of perfect, shining, spherical moon-brains that pulsed with information and thoughts impossible for a mere man to think.

No one knew how many of these moon-brains there were. As many as a thousand spheres spun in their orbits around some of the larger stars. The moon-brains fed on photons and absorbed gamma and x-rays and other radiation—the very exhalation and breath of the stars. The Entity, if She possessed such sentiments, must have regarded every part of the nebula as an extension of Her godly body. At the least, She must have claimed all the nebula's matter—the millions of planets, asteroids, dust particles, clouds of gas, and stars—as food to live on, nourishment to sustain Her tremendous energies and to enable Her to grow. During the last three millennia, it was said, this goddess had grown from a simple human being into an Entity that nearly filled a nebula some one hundred light-years in diameter.

Much of this energy, it was thought, She applied to the manipulation of matter and spacetime, the reaching out of Her godly hand to cark Her designs upon the universe. Much energy was needed simply so that She could organize Her mind and communicate with Herself. The moon-brains were grouped around the nebula's stars, and these stars were sometimes separated by many light-years of space. Any signal, such as a radio wave or a lightwave propagated through realspace, would have taken years to fall from brain lobe to brain lobe. To connect the millions of lobes would mean millions of years of glacial, lightspeed signal exchange; for the Entity to complete a single thought might have required a billion years. And so the Entity employed no such signals to integrate Her mind. The mechanics hypothesize that

She generates tachyons, those ghostly, theoretical particles whose slowest velocity approaches the speed of light. This, the mechanics say, must be the reason why She seeks such great energies. Impossible energies. The trillions of miles of black space between the Entity's many stars must have burned with streams of tachyons, information streams infinitely faster than light, impossible to detect, but *almost* possible to imagine.

When Danlo closed his eyes, he could almost see all space-time lit up with numinous ruby rays, shimmering with a great, golden consciousness. Somewhere before him, in this dark, strange nebula that he hesitated to enter, there must be interconnecting beams of tachyons carrying the codes of mysterious information, linking up the moon-brains almost instantaneously, weaving through empty space an unseen but vast and glorious web of pure intelligence.

At last, when Danlo could stand it no longer, he made a mapping, and began falling among the stars of the Entity. Almost immediately upon entering these forbidden spaces—after he had passed a great bloody sun twice as large as Scutarix—he sensed that in some way, the Entity was aware of him. Perhaps She wrought trillions of telescopes out of carbon and common matter and connected these to each of her moon-brains. Perhaps She continually swept the drears of space for anything that moved, much as a peshwi bird watches the forests near Neverness for furflies. Almost certainly, She, too, could read the perturbations that a lightship makes upon the manifold.

Danlo thought of this as he segued in and out of complex decision trees, star after star scudding through spaces fouled with too many zero-points, which were like drops of blacking oil carelessly spilled into a glass of wine. And the deeper into the Entity that he fell, the more evidence he saw of Her control and creation of matter.

He saw, too, signs of war. At least, the pulverized planets and ionized dust that he fell through seemed as if they could have been the flotsam and debris of some godly war. Perhaps the Entity was at war with Herself. Perhaps She was destroying Herself, tearing Herself apart, planet by planet, atom by atom, always assembling and reassembling these elements into something new. With his ship's radio telescopes and scanning computers, Danlo searched through many solar systems. He searched for the familiar matter of the natural world: omnipresent hydrogen, poisonous oxygen, friendly carbon. Floating in the blackness around the stars were other elements, too: giddy helium, quick and treacherous mercury, noble gold.

All these elements—and others—he cataloged, as well as the compounds of silicates and salts and ice made from them. He noticed immediately that there were too many transuranic elements, from plutonium and fermium on up through the actinade series into the wildly unstable atoms that none of the Order's physicists had ever managed to synthesize.

And there was something else. Some other kind of matter. Near the coronas of certain stars—usually medium-size singlets orbited by five or more gas giant planets—there were shimmering curtains of matter atomically no denser than platinum or gold. Danlo could not tell if this matter was solid or liquid. At times, as seen from across ten million miles of space, it took on the flowing brilliance of quicksilver and all the colors of gold. Some of this matter was as light as lithium; indeed, it astonished Danlo to discover various elements whose atomic weights seemed to be less than that of hydrogen.

This, he knew, was impossible. That is, it was impossible for any atoms that the physicists had ever hypothesized to betray such properties. Danlo immediately sensed that the Entity was creating new types of matter that had never before existed in the universe. Neither his telescopes nor his computers nor all his physical theories could understand such godly stuff.

He guessed that the Entity must have discovered the secret of completely decomposing matter and rebuilding it from the most fundamental units, from the infons and strings that some mechanics say all protons and neutrons are ultimately made of. Perhaps She was trying to create a better material for the neurologics of Her brains and thus a better substrate for pure mind. It amused Danlo to think that She might merely be planning for the future.

All protons will eventually decay into positrons and pions, and thus it is said that the entire universe will evaporate away into light in only some ten thousand trillion trillion trillion more years. Perhaps the Entity had crafted a finer kind of matter more stable than protons, much as clary and other plastics will withstand the rot of a dark forest much longer than mere wood. If gods or goddesses possessed the same will to live as did human beings, then surely they would create for themselves golden, immortal bodies that would never decay or die. Because Danlo did not know what this matter could be (and because no mechanic of the Order had ever had the pleasure of analyzing such bizarre stuff), he decided to collect some to show to his friends.

It should have been a simple thing, this collection of artificial matter. Simple it was to send out robots from his ship to scoop up liters of godstuff, but it was also quite dangerous. For first there would come the difficult and dangerous maneuvering of his ship close to a nearby white star. He would have to enter the manifold in the spaces very near the large star. And then he must fall out into temperatures almost hot enough to melt the diamond hull of his ship. And still he must then rocket though realspace until he came upon a pocket of artificial matter. Only then could he stow the godstuff safely within the hold of his ship. Only then could he fall back into the cool and timeless flow of the manifold and continue on his journey.

From the instant that he opened a window to the manifold in order to complete this minor mission, he knew something was wrong. Instantly, the *Snowy Owl* was sucked into a gray-black chaos space wholly unfamiliar to him. This space should not have been where it was. Perhaps it should not have existed at all. He should have opened a window that led to another window directly to a third window giving out into the blazing blue corona of his chosen star. Instead, his ship plunged into a whirlpool of what almost looked like a Lavi space, only darker, blacker, and too dense with zero-points, like sediments in an old wine. Almost immediately, his mappings began to waver like a mirage over a frozen sea, and then—unbelievably—he lost the correspondences altogether. He lost his mapping.

This was one of the most dangerous of misfortunes that might befall a pilot. He began tunneling through a mapless space seemingly without beginning or end. For a while, as he sweated and prayed and told himself lies, hoping this might prove no more complex than a normal Moebius space. But the farther he fell from any point-exit near the star the nearer he came to despair.

No pilot, as far as he knew, had ever escaped from such a chaos. Perhaps no pilot had ever faced pure chaos before; Danlo had always been taught that a fundamental mathematical order underlay all the seeming bifurcations and turbulence of the manifold. Now he was not so sure. Now, all about him, almost crushing his ship, the chaos space began folding and squeezing him toward a zero-point. It was almost like being caught on a Koch snowflake: the crystal points within points within points, fractalling down to zero. For a while, even as he lost himself and his ship in a cloud of billions of such snowflakes, he marveled at the infinite self-embedding of complexity. He might easily have lost himself in these infinities altogether if his will to escape hadn't been so strong. Although it might prove hopeless, he tried to model the chaos and thus make a map through this impossible part of the manifold.

For his first model, he tried a simple generation of the Mandelbrot set, the iteration in the complex plane of the mapping z into $z^2 + c$, where c is a complex number. When this proved futile, he generated other sets, Lavi sets and Julia sets and even Soli sets of quaternion-fields on a mutated thickspace. All to no avail. After a while, as his ship spun endlessly and fell through an an almost impenetrable iron gray, he abandoned such mathematics and fell back upon the metaphors and words for chaos that he had learned as a child. He was certain that he would soon die, and so why not take a moment's comfort where he could? He emptied his mind, then, of ideoplasts and other mathematical symbols. He remembered a word for coldness, *eesha-kaleth,* the coldness before snow. Now that he was finished sweating, as he waited for the chaos storm to intensify and kill him, his whole body felt cold and strange.

It would be an easy thing, he knew, to let the chaos storm overcome him, even as the cold wind might fall upon a solitary hunter and drive him down into the ice. Then he could finally join his tribe in death. But the oldest teaching of his people was that a man should die at the right time, and something inside him whispered that he mustn't die, not yet. As he lay in the icy darkness of his ship, as he touched the lightning bolt scar on his forehead above his eye, all the while shivering and remembering, something was calling him to life. It was a long, dark, terrible sound, perhaps the very sound and fury of chaos itself.

And then in the center of the chaos, there was a blackness as bright as the pupil of his eye. There were secret colors, bands of brilliant orange encircling the blackness, and then white, a pure snowy whiteness as splendid as any color he had ever seen. All the colors of chaos were inside him, and out, and so again he faced his ship-computer and turned his inner eye toward the manifold.

Before him, beneath the stars of the Solid State Entity, within the dark, twisting tunnels of a phase space, there was an attractor. It was a strange attractor, he decided: stable, nonperiodic, low-dimensional. Its loops and spirals would weave infinitely deep, infinitely many fractal pathways inside a finite space. No path would ever cross or touch any other. Strange attractors, it was hypothesized, were the black holes of the manifold. Nothing that approached one too closely could escape its infinities. For a pilot to enter a strange attractor would mean spiraling down endless pathways into blackness and neverness. Any sane pilot would have fled such an attractor. Danlo considered such a course, but where would he flee to and into what dread space might he flee?

Strangely, he felt the attractor pulling him, almost calling him, in the way that the future called all life into its glorious destiny. He couldn't deny this call. And so there came a moment when he faced the attractor and piloted his ship into the last place in the universe he would ever have thought to go. With this wordless affirmation made in the dark of his ship, a wildness came over him. His body began to warm as if he had somehow drunk the light of the sun. He felt his heart beating strong and fast. His blood surged quickly inside him, thousands upon thousands of unseen turbulent streams, flowing, bifurcating, surging, but always returning to the chambers of his heart. If chaos was anywhere, he thought, it was inside myself. And order was there, too. Chaos/order, order/chaos—for the first time in his life, he began to see the deep connection between these seemingly opposite forces.

Chaos, he thought, was not the enemy of order, but rather the cataclysm that gave it birth. A supernova was a most violent, chaotic event, but out of this explosion into light were born carbon, hydrogen, and oxygen, and all the other elements of life. There was always a place where order might emerge from chaos.

And to find the hidden order, he must first become himself pure chaos. This was his genius, his joy, his fate. This was his magical thinking approach to mathematics, nurtured by the shamans of his tribe, crystallized and polished in the cold halls of the Academy on Neverness. He must will himself to see where pattern is born of formlessness, that pattern that connects. All his life he had been trained to see such patterns. There was always a choice, to see or not see. Now, inside the attractor that pulled him into its writhing coils, there were patterns. There were ripples and billowings and depthless fractal boundaries like the wall clouds around the eye of a hurricane. The attractor itself swirled with the colors of orange madder and a pale, icy blue. For the first time, he marveled at the attractor's strange and terrible beauty. There was something haunting in the self-referential aspect of the chaos functions, the way that the functions lay embedded inside one another, watching and waiting and making patterns down to infinity. There were always an infinite number of patterns to choose from, always the infinite possibilities. There was always a possible future; it was only a matter of finding the right pattern, of sorting, inverting, mapping, and making the correspondences, and then comparing the patterns to a million other patterns that he had seen.

Now, as the patterns before him fractured into lovely crimson traceries and then coalesced a moment later into a clear blue-black pool that pulled him ever inward, he must choose one pattern and only one. In less than a second of time, in a fraction of a fraction of a moment that would always be the eternal Now, he would have to make his choice. There could be no putting it off once it came. His choice: he could be pulled screaming into his fate, or he could say yes to the chaos inside himself and choose his future. This, he remembered, is what the scryers do. This is what his mother must have done in finding the terrible courage to give birth to him.

And so at last, when his moment came and time was now and always and forever, he chose a simple pattern. He made a mapping into this strange, strange attractor, and then he fell alone into the eye of chaos where all was stillness, silence, and beautiful, blessed light.

C H A P T E R 3

ANCESTRAL VOICES

The ability to remember the past gives one the power to descry events that have yet to be. This is the great problem of consciousness, for man and god, this awareness in time: the more clearly we visualize the future, the more we live in dread that it will inevitably become the present.
    —*from* A Requiem for Homo Sapiens, *Horthy Hosthoh*

Danlo fell out near a small yellow star as beautiful as any star he had ever seen. The star was circled by nine fat, round planets, one of which was very near to him indeed. Below his lightship—a bare ten thousand miles below the *Snowy Owl*—there spun a planet all green and blue and swaddled in layers of bright white clouds. He could scarcely believe his good fortune. It seemed too much of a miracle to have escaped an unescapable attractor, only to then fall out above such a lovely and earthlike planet.

In the pit of his ship he lay shaking with triumph and joy, and he opened a window in the ship's hull to look out over this unnamed planet. For a long time he looked down through space at mossy brown continents and sparkling blue oceans. With his scanning computers, he analyzed the gasses of the atmosphere, the oxygen and nitrogen and carbon dioxide involved in the interflow of organic life. He did this to reassure himself that he had really fallen out into realspace, and so he reached out with his telescopes and scanners and eyes to embrace it, to touch it, to see it as it truly was. In the sweep of the planet's mountains, in the fractal curves of the continents' coastlines and the shape of the vast oceans, he became aware of a pattern hauntingly familiar.

At first he could not identify this pattern. But then he searched his memory, and there was a shock of recognition, like suddenly beholding the face of a friend who has returned from

the wounds and scars of old age into an untouched and marvelous youth. It astonished him that the face of the planet below him
matched his brilliant memory so exactly; it was an astonishing
thing to discover here in the heart of the Solid State Entity a
planet that *must* be, that could only be that great and glorious
planet that men remembered as Old Earth.

It cannot be, he thought. *It is not possible.*

The planet *was* Earth; and yet it was not Earth. It was a
pristine, primeval Earth untouched by war or the insanity of the
Holocaust, an Earth somehow healed of its terrible wounds. Its
atmosphere bore no trace of the flourocarbons or chloride plastics or plutonium that he would have expected to find there. As
he saw through his telescopes, the oceans teemed with life and
were free of oil slicks or the taint of garbage. Far below him, on
the grassy velds of a continent that looked like Afarique, there
were herds of antelope and prides of lions, and an animal that
looked much like a horse but was covered from nose to tail with
vivid white and black stripes. There were trees. *Trees!* Parts of
every continent, save the southernmost, were covered in unbroken swaths of brilliant green forests. Such an Earth might have
existed fifty thousand years ago or fifty thousand years in the
future, but it was hard to understand how this beautiful planet
had come to be here *now*.

As Danlo well knew, if Old Earth still existed, it must lay
some eight thousand light-years coreward along the Orion arm of
the galaxy, in the spaces near Sahasrara and Anona Luz. It was
impossible, he thought, that even a goddess might have arms
strong enough or long enough to move a whole planet fifty thousand trillion miles through a dangerous and star-crossed space.
Still, gazing through his telescopes, he wondered if he was really
seeing *anything*. The Entity, it was said, could directly manipulate any type of matter through countless miles of realspace,
through the force of Her will and Her thoughts alone. Perhaps the
Entity, even at this moment, was manipulating the molecules of
his mind, subtly pulling at his neurons, much as a musician
might pluck the strings of a gosharp. What unearthly tunes, he
wondered, might a vastly greater mind play upon his consciousness? What otherworldly visions might a true goddess cause a
man to see?

After a time, Danlo decided he must accept the sensation of
his eyes as true vision and his computer's analyses of the planet's
carbon cycles as true information, even though he feared that his
sense of interfacing his ship computer (and everything else)

might be an almost perfect simulation of reality that the Entity had somehow carked into his mind. He had no objective reason for making such an affirmation. It occurred to him that just as he had penetrated the spaces of the Entity to fall out inside Her very brain, in some way—as with an information virus or an ohrworm—She might be inside the onstreaming consciousness of *his* brain. And the image of himself as pilot who had penetrated the living substance of a goddess might be, at this moment, one of Her deepest thoughts, and suddenly this looking inside himself to apprehend the reality of who lay inside whom was like holding a mirror before a silver mirror and looking down into an infinite succession of smaller mirrors as they almost vanished into a dazzling, singular point.

Because he could not tell inside from out, for an endless moment he was nauseous and dizzy. It occurred to him that perhaps he had not escaped the attractor after all. Perhaps he was still falling through the black ink of the manifold, falling and falling through the endless nightmares and hallucinations of a pilot who has gone mad. Or perhaps he was still on the planet of his birth; perhaps he was still thirteen years old, still lost in the wind and ice of the sarsara, the great mother storm that had nearly killed him out on the frozen sea before he had come to Neverness.

It was possible, he thought, that he had never really reached Neverness or become a pilot. Perhaps he had only dreamed the last nine years of his life. He might be dreaming still. As bubbles rise through dark churning waters, his mind might only be creating dream images of his deepest friend, Hanuman li Tosh, he of the hellish blue eyes and broken soul who had once betrayed him. Who *would* betray him, who was always staring at Danlo with his death-haunted eyes even as he seared open in Danlo a wound of lightning and blood and memory, the deep and primeval wound that would not be healed. Perhaps the wind had driven Danlo to the ice at last, and at this moment he lay down against terrible cold, frozen and lost in dreams of the future, dreaming his life, dreaming his death. He would never really know. He *could* never know, and that was the terrifying and paradoxical nature of reality, that if he thought about it too much or looked at it too deeply, it all began to seem somehow unreal.

But I do know, Danlo thought. *I know that I know.*

Somewhere inside him, beyond his mentations or the impulses of his brain, there was a deeper knowledge. Somehow, without the mediation of his mind, all the cells of his body were gravid with a vast and ancient intelligence, and each individual cell felt the pull of the planet beneath him. Every atom of his body, it seemed, recognized this planet and remembered it. At last he decided that he would no longer doubt this deep sense of reality. He *knew* that this wandering Earth was real, that he was truly seeing the polar icecaps and the gray-green northern rain forests for what they were. At all costs, he would will himself to affirm what he knew as true, and this affirmation of his vision and the whisper of his cells was the full flowering of his truth sense, that mysterious and marvelous consciousness that all people and all things possess.

If this Earth is real, then it has a real origin in spacetime. It is possible that this Earth has not been brought here across space— it is possible that She has created it.

With this thought, a beam of laser light flashed up from the planet's surface through the atmosphere and out into space. His telescopes intercepted this intense, coherent light. There was no information bound within this signal that his computers could decode. But the very phenomenon of laser light streaming up from a densely forested coastline was itself a kind of signal and a kind of information. For the first time, he wondered if human beings might live on this Earth. It seemed only natural that they would. He remembered that his father, on *his* first journey into the Entity, had discovered a world full of men and women who could not believe that they lived their entire lives inside a stellar nebula rippling with a godly intelligence.

Of course, Danlo had seen no cities below him, no mud huts or pyramids or domes or other signs of human life. It was possible that the men of this Earth might live as hunters beneath the canopies of the vast emerald forests. If this was so, then he would never see them from a lightship floating in the near space above their world. Because he was lonely and eager for the sound of human voices—and because he was unbearably curious—he decided to take his ship down through the atmosphere to discover the source of this mysterious light.

He fell to Earth down through the exosphere and stratosphere, and then he guided his ship through the billowing and blinding layers of clouds of the troposphere. the *Snowy Owl* fell down into the gravity well of the planet, and Danlo was very glad that he had become the pilot of a lightship, those great, gleaming, winged ships that can fall not only between the stars, but also rocket up and down through the thickest atmospheres. Lightships can fall almost anywhere in the universe, and that was the glory

of piloting such a ship, to be as fast and free as a ray of light.
And so he fell down and down through dense gray clouds, hom-
ing in on the place where the laser beam had originated.

On a broad sandy beach at the edge of one of the continents
he made planetfall. He wasted no time analyzing the viruses and
bacteria that swam everywhere through this planet's moist winds
and oceans. He had not come this far to be killed by a virus.
Therefore, Danlo broke open the pit of his ship and fairly fell
down to the soft beach sands.

It dismayed him to discover that, after many days of weightlessness, his body was a little weak. Although the pits of all
lightships are designed to induce microgravities along a pilot's
torso and limbs, these intense fields do not quite keep the muscles from shrinking or the bones from demineralizing. As Danlo
took his first tentative steps, he found that his slightly wasted leg
muscles at first would support him only with difficulty and considerable pain. But then he stood away from his ship, and his bare
feet seemed to draw strength from the soft, cold touch of sand.

He stood straight and still, looking down the broad sweep of
the beach. To his left, the great gray ocean roared and surged and
broke upon the hardpack at the water's edge. To his right, a dark
green forest of fir trees flowed like an ocean of a different kind
toward the east and south and northward, where it swelled up into
a headland of rocks and steeply rising hills. There was also something else. Just above the fore dunes and beach grasses, where
the sand gave way to the towering trees, there was a house. It was
a small chalet of shatterwood beams and granite stone, and
Danlo suddenly remembered that he knew this house quite well.

No, no, it is not possible.

He stood staring up at this lovely house for a while, and then
the cold wind blew in from the ocean and drowned him in memories. Soon he began shaking and shivering. The wind found his
belly, and he was suddenly cold as if he had drunk an ocean of
ice water. He looked down at his lean, ivory legs quivering in the
cold. He was still as naked as a pilot in the pit of his ship, but
now that he stood on soft shifting sands, he realized that he was
naked to the world. Because he needed to protect himself from
the bitter wind and cover his nakedness, he returned to his ship to
fetch his boots, his heavy wool cloak, and the racing kamelaika
he had once worn while skating the streets of Neverness.

My mind is naked to Her. My memories, my mind.

Once, in this simple house of white granite that he could now
see only too well, there had been long nights of passion and love

and happiness. Once, a woman had lived here, Tamara Ten Ash-toreth, she of the great heart and broken life whom he had loved and lost. But she had fled this house. In truth, she had fled Danlo and his burning memories. It was said that she had even fled Neverness for the stars. And although Danlo did not think it was possible that she could have found her way to this mysterious planet deep within the Solid State Entity, he hurried up the beach straight toward this house to discover what, or who, lay inside.

Tamara, Tamara—in this house you promised to marry me. . . .

As Danlo's feet drove against the sugary sand, he remembered how his friend Hanuman li Tosh, out of hatred for Danlo and vengeance (and jealousy), had tricked Tamara into putting a cleansing heaume upon her head and had destroyed all her memories of Danlo. Danlo had offered to help restore these memories to her, but it had been too late. And so in the pain of her desolation, Tamara had left him.

And out of hatred, I almost killed my deepest friend.

At last, on top of a small, grass-covered hill, at the end of a path laid with flat sandstones, he came up to the house's door. It was thick and arched and sculpted out of shatterwood, a dense black wood native only to islands on the planet Icefall. Shatterwood trees had never grown on Old Earth, and so it was a mystery how the Entity had found shatterwood with which to build this house. He reached out to touch the door. The wood was cold and hard and polished to an impossible smoothness in the way that only shatterwood can be polished. He traced his finger across the lovely grain of the door, remembering. Somehow the Entity had exactly duplicated the door of Tamara's house. In Danlo's mind, just behind his eyes, there were many doors, but this particular one stood out before all others. He remembered exactly how the door planks had joined together in an almost seamless merging of the grain; he could see every knot and ring and dark whorl as if he were standing on the steps of this house on Neverness, about to knock on the door. But he was not on Neverness. He stood before the door of an impossible house above a desolate and windswept beach, and the pattern of the whorls twisting through the shatterwood exactly matched the bright black whorls that burned through his memory.

How is it possible? How is it possible that all things remember?

For a long time he stood there staring at the door and listening to the cries of the seagulls and other shore birds on the beach below. Then he made a fist and rapped his knuckles against the door. The sound of resonating wood was hollow and ancient. He knocked again, and the sound of bone striking against wood was lost to the greater sounds of the sweeping wind and the ocean that rang like a great deep bell far below him. A third time he knocked, loudly with much force, and he waited. When there was no answer, he tried the clear quartz doorknob, which turned easily in his hand. Then he opened the door and stepped across the threshold into the cold hallway inside.

"Tamara, Tamara!" he called. But immediately, upon listening to the echoes that his voice made against the hall stones, he knew the house was empty. "Tamara, why aren't you home?"

Out of politeness and respect for the rules of Tamara's house, he removed his boots before walking through her rooms. Because it was a small house laid out across a single floor, there were only five rooms: the hallway gave out onto the brightly lit meditation room, which was adjoined by the bathing room and fireroom at the rear of the house, and the tea room and the small kitchen at the front. It took him almost no time to verify that the house was indeed empty.

That is, it was empty of human beings or evidence of present habitation. True, the kitchen was well-stocked with teas, cheeses, fruits, and fifty other types of foods that Tamara had delighted in preparing for him, but everything about the kitchen—from the oranges and bloodfruit piled high in perfect pyramids inside large blue bowls, to the tiled counters completely free of toast crumbs or honey drippings—bespoke a room that hadn't been used. Similarly, the cotton cushions in the tea room were new and undented, as if no one had ever sat on them. And in the fireroom, the shagshay furs smelled of new wool instead of sweat, and the stones of the two fireplaces were clean of ashes or soot. It was as if the Entity, in making this house, had perfectly incarnated the details of his memory but had been unable to duplicate the chaos and disorder (and dirt) that came of living a normal, organic life.

But certainly She had duplicated everything else. The rosewood beams of the ceiling and the skylights were exactly as he remembered them. In the tea room, the tea service was set out on the low, laquered table. And along the sill of the window overlooking the ocean, there was the doffala bear sculpture that he remembered so well, and the seven oiled stones. Each object in the house was perfectly made and perfectly matched his memory. Except for one thing. When Danlo walked into the meditation room he immediately noticed a sulki grid hanging on the wall by the fireplace. And that was very strange because Tamara had never collected or used outlawed technology. She had never liked experiencing computer simulations, or artificial images or sounds. And even if she'd had a taste for cartoons and other such seemingly real holographic displays, she never would have allowed them to be made in her meditation room. Because Danlo wondered what programs this sulki grid had been programmed to run, he pitched his voice toward it, saying simply, "On, please."

For a moment nothing happened. Most likely, he supposed, the sulki grid would be keyed to some voice other than his own. He stood there breathing deeply, and he was almost relieved that the sulki grid appeared to be dead. He had imagined, and feared, that an imago of Tamara would appear before him, as tall and naked and achingly beautiful as she had ever been as a real woman. And then without warning, the spiderweb neurologics of the grid flared into life, projecting an imago into the center of the room.

It was like no imago that Danlo had ever seen before. It was all flashing colors and shifting lights, like a column of fire burning up from the floor—but not burning any *thing,* neither the inlaid shatterwood floor tiles, nor the hanging plants, nor the air itself. Soon the display settled out into a kind of pattern with which he was very familiar. It was an array of ideoplasts, not the ideoplasts of mathematics, but rather those of the universal syntax. A scarce three feet in front of his face, glowing through the air in jewel-like glyphs of emerald and sapphire and tourmaline, were the three-dimensional symbols of the language beyond language of the holosits that he had learned as a young novice.

It was a highly refined and beautiful language that could represent and relate any aspect of reality from the use of alien archetypes in the poets of the Fourth Dark Age to the pattern of neural storm singularities in the brain of a dreaming autist. Ideoplasts could symbolize the paradoxes of the cetic's theory of the circular reduction of consciousness or alien words or—sometimes— even the phonemes and sounds of any human language, living or dead. Most often one encountered ideoplasts in libraries or when interfacing the various cybernetic spaces of a computer in order to discover or create an almost infinite variety of knowledge. Ideoplasts were mental symbols only, and they were best viewed as arrays of lovely and complex glyphs which a computer would cark into the vast visual fields of the mind's eye.

Danlo had never seen an array of ideoplasts projected in the space of a common room, and so it took him some time to adjust to this new perspective and new way of apprehending them. With his eyes only, he played over the ideoplasts, slowly kithing them, much as he might read ancient Chinese characters or the letters of an unfamiliar alien language written into a book. The message written into the glowing air of the meditation room proved to be quite simple. It was a simple greeting, from the mind of a goddess for his eyes only:

How far do you fall, Pilot? How have you fallen so far and so well, Danlo wi Soli Ringess?

He sensed that he should reply to this greeting immediately, but he was uncertain as to how he could do so. Nowhere in the house were there any heaumes for him to place upon his head, and so he had no way to interface the sulki grid's computer and generate his own ideoplasts as a response. Perhaps, he thought, there was no need for such a clumsy type of interface. Perhaps the Entity, at this moment, was somehow facing the streaming thoughts of his mind. If he merely generated words in the language center of his brain and then held them waiting like so many thallow chicks eager to break out of their shells, then perhaps She might hear his thoughts and answer him.

How have you fallen so far, Danlo wi Soli Ringess, son of Mallory Ringess?

Danlo watched the array change slightly. In almost no time, some of the ideoplasts dissolved into the air like stained glass shattering into a million sparkling bits, and then new ones formed in their place. It occurred to him that he should simply speak aloud in the words of the common language, giving voice to certain questions he needed answered. And so he swallowed twice to moisten his throat and said, quite formally, ''I have fallen from Neverness. I am Danlo wi Soli Ringess, son of Mallory Ringess, son of Leopold Soli. If you please, may I have your name?''

It was as if he had not spoken or asked any question at all. The array of ideoplasts held steady, and their meaning remained unchanged.

How have you fallen so far, Danlo wi Soli Ringess?

This time when Danlo spoke, he directed his words toward the sulki grid. "How? I am very lucky," he said with much amusement.

Perhaps, he thought, the Entity was not really interfaced with his thoughts or with the sound vibrations of this little room. Perhaps She was not even interfaced with the sulki computer itself. A goddess the size of a nebula comprising a hundred thousand stars and countless millions of moon-brains must have vastly greater concerns than in speaking with a young pilot of the Order. It was possible, he supposed, that this incomprehensible, unearthly goddess had merely created this world, created this house, and then programed the sulki computer to respond to him in the most crude and basic of ways should he be lucky enough to find his way here.

Was it truly luck that led you?

It was fate, Danlo thought, his fate to have survived the chaos of the attractor. But in the end chance and fate were wed together more tightly than the symbiotic algae and fungi that make up a lichen growing across a rock.

"What is luck, truly?" he asked.

Again the ideoplast array changed, and a new message appeared:

The first rule of this information exchange is that you may not answer a question with a question.

"I . . . am sorry," Danlo said. He wondered if the mind of the goddess known as Kalinda were wholly elsewhere, somewhere outside this room, perhaps far away from this planet. The sulki computer's program seemed indeed rudimentary and uninteresting—possibly it was a simple work of artificial intelligence designed to generate clever words from simple rules.

The second rule is that you must answer all my questions.

"All *your* questions? But who are you, truly?"

The array remained unbroken, unchanging, and then Danlo remembered the Entity's unanswered question. He took a breath and said, "Yes, it was luck that brought me here . . . and something other."

What is that?

Danlo paced about the meditation room, and his bare feet left little sweat prints against the cool shatterwood tiles. He walked around and around the imago in the center of the room in order to view the colorful ideoplast array from different perspectives. Finally, he said, "I was lost in the chaos space. Truly lost. And then in the blackness, in the neverness, the attractor . . . it was so strange, so wild. Yet somehow familiar, too. The patterns, breaking apart into all the colors, crimson and shimmering gold, and then reforming, again and again, the possibilities. So many patterns. So many possibilities. And then I remembered something. At first I thought it might be a memory of the future, a vision such as the scryers have. But no, it was something other. I remembered something that I had never seen before. I do not know how. It came into my mind like a star being born. A pattern. A memory. These blessed mathematics that we make, these blessed memories—they guided me into the attractor, and then I fell out above this wild Earth."

Almost instantly, the ideoplasts dissolved and reformed themselves into a new array which Danlo readily kithed.

I like your answer, Danlo wi Soli Ringess.

For a moment, Danlo reached out a hand to steady himself against the cold granite stones of the fireplace. Then he said, "I never dreamed another Earth existed, so real. I . . . never dreamed."

Earth is Earth is Earth. But which Earth is the *Earth, do you know?*

"I have wondered if this Earth is real," Danlo said. "I have wondered if a goddess could cark a picture of it—the touch and taste and whole experience of it—into my mind."

You know *this Earth is real. You know that you know.*

Danlo dragged his long fingernails across the fireplace's rough granite, and he listened to the stuttering, scraping sound they made. "Perhaps," he said. "Yes, I know, truly . . . but how do *you* know that I know? Can you read my mind?"

What would it mean to read the human mind? What would it mean to read any mind?

Danlo took his hand away from the fireplace and rubbed his head. Because he had been born with a playful nature (and because he believed in being willfully playful as a matter of faith), he asked, "Excuse me, but haven't you just answered a question with a question?"

There is no rule that I should not. But there is a rule that you should not, and you have done so again.

Danlo rubbed hard above his eye for a moment as he thought about Hanuman li Tosh, who had developed a cetic's skill of reading human faces and emotions, if not their actual minds. Sometimes, Hanuman had been able to read him, but he had never been able to see into the deepest part of Danlo's soul. Nor had Danlo ever really known why Hanuman had thought the deep and terrible thoughts that had nearly destroyed both their lives.

"In answer to your question, I do not know what it would be like to read anyone's mind."

But someday you will. And then you will understand that the real problem is not in reading the mind but in being a part of Mind.

Danlo considered this for a while. He considered that even the akashics of his Order—with their scanning computers, in their neural analysis and simulations of neuron firing—could sometimes read certain parts of one's mind. Surely, he thought, the Entity must possess powers and technologies far greater than those of any akashic.

Because you have wished that I do not, I have not read your mind.

"But how could you know what I wished unless you had read me?"

I know.

"But this house, the door outside and everything inside—how could you have made these things unless you had read my memories?"

He considered the possibility that the Entity kept spies on Neverness, either humans with photographic equipment or secret satellites above the planet or perhaps even robots the size of a bacterium that would swarm over doors and houses and every conceivable surface, secretly recording pictures and sounds to somehow send to the goddess. Surely the Entity, with her almost infinitely capacious mind, would want to know everything that occurred in a city such as Neverness, and perhaps in every human and alien city across the galaxy.

Reading one's present mind is not quite the same thing as apprehending the memories.

He stared at the changing ideoplasts, and he mused that the spherical indigo glyph for "mind" was closely related to the deep blue nested teardrops representing the phenomenon of memory. Provocatively, argumentatively, he turned to the sulki grid and said, "I do not see the difference."

But someday it may be that you will.

"If you please," he said, "I wish you to read no more of my memories."

But it pleases me to taste your memories. Your memories are as sweet as oranges and honey, and they please me well.

Danlo looked back at the glowing array. His jaw was clamped tightly closed, and he said nothing.

However it pleases me to please you, and so I will forget all your memories—all except one.

"What . . . one?"

That you will soon know. That you will see.

With his knuckle he pressed hard against his forehead, against the pain always lurking behind his eye. He said, "But I have had too much of knowing *my* memories. I have seen too much that I cannot forget. This world, this house, so perfect and yet . . . *too* perfect. It is as if no one has ever lived here. As if no one ever could.''

I was forced to make this house hastily. As you have noticed, it suffers the imperfection of perfection. But how not? I am only the goddess whom you know as the Solid State Entity—I am not God.

Because Danlo was tired of communicating in this awkward manner, he looked up at the glittering violet rings of the sulki grid and considered shutting it off. In truth, he no longer doubted that he was speaking with a goddess. Somehow, the sulki computer must be interfaced with a larger computer, perhaps hidden beneath the floor of the house, or even inside the Earth itself. Perhaps the interior of this Earth was not a core of spinning iron surrounded by layers of molten and solid rock, but rather the circuitry of a vast computer interfaced with all the other computers and moon-brains of the goddess across the trillions of miles of this strange, intelligent nebula.

Upon his first sight of this planet, he had supposed that the Entity had merely engineered its surface and biosphere to hold the millions of species of earthly life spread out over the continents and oceans. After all, human beings had engineered the surfaces of planets for ten thousand years. He had supposed that the Entity, with unknown godly technologies, had shaped entire mountain chains and deep ocean trenches with less difficulty than a cadre of ecologists. But now he was not so sure. Perhaps She had engineered more deeply than that. He wondered if somehow She might have made the entire planet from inside out. It would not be an impossible feat for such a goddess, to choose a point in space some ninety million miles' distance from a sunlike star, to build a computer the size of a whole world, and then to cover this monstrous machine with a twenty-mile-thick shell of basalt and granite, with great glistening pools of salt water and sheets of nitrogen and oxygen and the other gases of the atmosphere.

For a moment he looked away from the sulki grid, down at the polished floor tiles that he stood upon. He could almost feel the waves of intelligence deep beneath him, inside the Earth, vibrating up through the planet's crust beneath his naked feet. Something about this Earth disquieted him, its deepness and purpose.

"Is it your will to try to make a perfect Earth?"

For the count of twenty of his heartbeats, there was no response to this question. And then the array of ideoplasts brightened, and he had an answer that was no answer at all.

Is it my purpose that you really wish to know? Or your own purpose, Danlo wi Soli Ringess?

Danlo walked over beneath one of the hanging plants, a wandering jew whose perfect green leaves shone like living jewels, as if they had never known drought or the jaws of hungry insects. He remembered how much Tamara had liked this plant, and he said, "There are so many things I would like to know. That is why I have journeyed here. As my father did before me. I have merely followed his path, toward the fixed-points of a star that he told of inside the Solid State Entity. I am sorry—inside *you.* I was seeking this star. The fixed-points of this place in spacetime. We all were—nine other pilots fell with me as well. We hoped to talk with you as my father did twenty-five years ago."

Why?

"Because we have hoped that you might know of the planet Tannahill. This planet lost somewhere in the Vild. It is said that the Architects of the Old Church live there, they who are destroying the stars. We would stop them, if we could. But first we must find them, their planet. This is our purpose. This is the quest we have been called to fulfill."

He finished speaking, and he waited for the Entity to respond to him. He did not wait long.

No, my Danlo of the sweet, sweet memories, this was not the purpose of the pilots who journeyed with you. Their purpose was to die. Their deepest purpose was to journey here and die inside me, but they did not know this.

It was as if someone had punched Danlo in the solar plexus, so quickly did he clasp his hands to his belly and gasp for air. For a moment, he hoped that he had kithed the ideoplasts wrongly, and so he stared at the glittering glyphs until his eyes burned and there could be no mistaking their meaning. At last he asked, "Dolores Nun and Leander of Darkmoon, all the others—dead? Dead . . . *how?*"

You, Danlo wi Soli Ringess, who are the only pilot ever to have survived a chaos space, ask this?

Almost silently, in a strange voice halfway between a moan and whisper, Danlo began moving his lips, making the words of the Prayer for the Dead, which he had been taught as a child long ago. "Ivar Sarad, mi alasharia la shantih; Li Te Mu Lan, alasharia la: Valin wi Tymon Whitestone—"

These pilots were too afraid to die. And so they died.

At last Danlo finished praying. When he closed his eyes, he could clearly see the kindly brown face of Li Te Mu Lan, with her sly smile and too gentle spirit. Because he could see the faces of all nine pilots much too clearly, he opened his eyes and stood facing the ideoplast array. He said, "After falling together from Farfara, we separated. We each journeyed here as individual pilots. Our lightships, our pathways through the manifold. We were spread across fifty light-years of realspace. I think I was alone for much of my journey. And then, in the manifold, the chaos space. It was like nothing I had ever seen before. The attractor, swirling in its colors, spinning. The strange attractor—this could only exist within a well-defined neighborhood, yes? There were no other pilots in the same neighborhood of the manifold as I."

He remembered, then, that in truth there *was* another pilot, Sivan wi Mawi Sarkissian in his ship the *Red Dragon*. He told the Entity this and waited for a response.

I know about the ronin pilot and the warrior-poet. They are almost without fear.

"And so they have lived? Have they found their way to this Earth, too?"

I will not speak of these men now. I will tell you only of the pilots who accompanied you. And they all fled the same attractor that you entered. They fled and they died.

"But how is that possible?"

Because they each fled into another attractor deeper in the chaos. A naked singularity of the manifold, and yet not of it. Death is the strangest attractor of all. It pulls

*everyone and everything by different paths into a single
point in time. In eternity, into the eternal moment. Even
the gods must inevitably journey to this place, though
some of us flee their fate. And this is why your brother
and sister pilots died.*

Slowly, Danlo backed away from this bewildering array of
ideoplasts and sat down on one of the meditation room's cotton
cushions. He sat crosslegged and straight spined, rubbing his
eyes, rubbing his forehead and temples. And then he said, "I do
not understand."

*You do not understand the existence of the chaos space.
That is because your mathematics is incomplete. It is
possible for such a chaos to spread from what you know
as a well-defined neighborhood into a region of nested
Lavi spaces. Perhaps it is even possible for a chaos space
to spread through the entire manifold.*

"Possible . . . how?"

*There are many ways that the manifold might fall into
chaos. Here is one way: If sufficient energy densities are
created in a pocket of spacetime, then the underlaying
manifold would perturb itself into chaos.*

Danlo closed his eyes for a moment, calculating. And then he
said, "But if this is truly possible, the energy densities would
have to be enormous, yes? What could create such impossible
densities?"

The gods can.

"What gods?"

*There are many gods, Danlo wi Soli Ringess. In this gal-
axy alone, too many. You must know of the Silicon God
and Chimene and the April Colonial Intelligence. And
someday you may know your father. And the gods called
Ai, Hsi Wang Mu, Iamme, and Pure Mind. And Maralah,
and the Degula Trinity, and The One. And, of course,
Nikolos Daru Ede, the man who would be God, whom*

Cybernetic Universal Church worships as *God, Ede the God, who is now very probably dead.*

At this astonishing piece of news, Danlo sprang to his feet and began pacing the room again. He pressed his forehead in remembrance of others who had died, then he smiled grimly. "Then God is dead, yes? *A* god is dead. But how is this possible?"

There is war in heaven. Because some gods flee the strange attractor at the end of time, there is war. It was the Silicon God—aided by Chimene and the Degula Trinity, and others—who slew Ede the God. It is the Silicon God who has tried to slay me. He has been trying to destroy me for three hundred years.

Danlo closed his eyes trying to visualize the sheer enormity of the Solid State Entity, the many star systems and planets composing Her nearly infinite body. He said, "Destroy . . . how?"

Please be patient, and I will tell you.

"I . . . am sorry."

Your sister and brother pilots were unlucky enough to be caught in one of our battles. The Silicon God's recent attack upon the matter and spacetime that make up the tissues of my body temporarily deformed the manifold itself—as you saw. This was the cause of the chaos space. This was the cause of the attractor that led you to this planet. Above all else, the Silicon God would destroy this Earth that you stand upon, and so his attacks are concentrated here.

As Danlo focused his deep blue eyes on the changing ideoplasts, he kithed part of the history of this war between the gods. He learned that the gods, some of them, would do almost anything to destroy each other. They had caused stars to explode into supernovas; they had tapped the energy densities of black holes and the zero-point energies of spacetime itself. A true god, as the Entity maintained, would use such energies to create, but there were always those who wielded this cosmic lightning for the opposite purpose. And they wielded other weapons as well.

There was a god called Maralah who had loosed a swarm of intelligent bacteria upon a planet claimed by The One. The bacteria swarm—the bacteria-size robots that most human beings know as disassemblers—had reduced the beautiful green forests and oceans of the planet to a thick brown scum in a matter of days. With similar explosive nanotechnologies, Maralah had tried to infect many of the gods allied with the Solid State Entity. And it was Maralah who had tried to infect Ai and Pure Mind with various ohrworms and informational viruses that would cark their master programs and drive them mad. Maralah was the first god to discover how vunerable artificial intelligence is to surrealities, those almost infinitely detailed simulations of reality that can wholly take over a computer's neurologics and cause the most powerful of gods to confuse the illusory for what is real.

But it was the Silicon God himself who had refined this weapon. In a way almost impossible for Danlo to understand, the Silicon God had forged mysterious philosophical and psychic weapons, terrible weapons of consciousness that threatened the sanity of the galaxy, perhaps even the universe itself. Danlo immediately dreaded this ancient god who would destroy the minds of all others. He hated this enemy of the Entity (and of his father), and he hated himself for hating so freely.

"Why?" he asked. He pressed his fingertips hard against his throbbing eye. "Why must there be war?"

Why, why, my sweet Danlo? Because there must be war, there will always be war. This phase of the war began two million years ago, when the Ieldra defeated the one known as the Dark God. Do you know of the Ieldra, they of the pure mind and the golden light?

In truth, Danlo knew as much about the Ieldra as anyone knew. The Ieldra, it was said, were a race of gods who long ago had carked their collective consciousness into the black hole at the center of the galaxy. But before they had abandoned their bodies and gone on to complete their cosmic evolution, they had left behind a gift. It was said that they had carked their deepest wisdom—the secret of life—into the DNA of their chosen successors, a noble species of life known as *Homo sapiens.* And so deep inside the bodies and brains of all human beings the secret of the gods lay coiled and waiting.

In honor of these oldest of the gods, the masters of Danlo's Order called this secret the "Elder Eddas," and they said that the

gods had designed the Eddas to be remembered. With proper
training, almost anyone could call up the memories bound inside
their cells. Once, Danlo himself had remembered the Eddas as
deeply as had any man. The Eddas was a pool of ancient knowledge almost infinitely deep, and Danlo had drunken freely of the
racial memories until he thought that his mind could hold no
more. One splendid night, once a time like a child in a magic
woods, he had remembered many marvelous things. But now that
he was older, he had lost his gift of remembrancing. Although he
remembered many moments of his life with a blazing intensity
more brilliant than any ideoplast or living jewel, he could no
longer go inside himself where the deepest memories lay. In
truth, he could no longer remember the deepest part of himself,
and in this he was no different from any man.

"I . . . have heard of the Ieldra," Danlo said.

And you have remembranced the Elder Eddas.

"Yes."

*I believe the secret of how the Ieldra defeated the Dark
God is encoded into the Elder Eddas.*

Danlo nodded his head slowly. "Yes, perhaps it is there, in the
Eddas. Everything is there."

*It may be that someday you will remembrance this secret
and apply it toward defeating the Silicon God.*

At this strange communication, Danlo walked across the room
and looked out the window. Below him, on the long deep beach,
his lightship shone like a sliver of black glass. The wind was up,
blowing ghostly wisps of sand against its hull. He could almost
hear the sand particles pinging against the diamond surface, but
the endless ocean beyond the beach rolled and roared and broke
upon itself, and it swallowed up any lesser sounds.

"I do not wish to defeat the Silicon God," he said. "I do not
wish to defeat anything."

Then you believe it is your purpose to avoid this war.

"Truly, I am not a man of war. I . . . must not be. I hate
war."

A curious emotion for a man who is a warrior.

"No, you are wrong," Danlo said. "I am no warrior. I have taken a vow of ahimsa. I may not intentionally harm any man or animal. It is better to die oneself than to kill."

I know this word ahimsa.

"I would rather die than kill anything, even a god. Especially a god."

We shall see.

A sudden chill struck Danlo's spine as if a draft of cold air had fallen down his back. He turned to face the ocean again, and he watched as the breakers fell against the shore rocks in an explosion of white water and foam. He rubbed his eyes, then said, "But I am just a man, yes? Can a man even think of defeating a god? If such a secret is to be found in the Elder Eddas, then surely it is for a goddess such as yourself to remember it."

Danlo waited for the ideoplasts to dissolve and reform themselves. The Entity's response, when it came, astonished him:

I do not have your power of remembrance. I have never been able to apprehend these memories you call the Elder Eddas.

"But how is that possible? Your brain, your whole being, so vast, so powerful in its—"

The size and power of a brain can be a hindrance to true remembrance. I have made myself as others have. Most of the gods of the galaxy are computers or a grafting of computer neurologics onto the human brain. Computers have a kind of memory, but no computer or any artificial intelligence has ever known true remembrance.

Danlo watched the many-colored ideoplasts explode in their array, and he rubbed his aching forehead. He thought about the evolution of the human brain, the way the great human forebrain overlay the more primitive monkey brain and the reptilian core deep inside. In a way, the very human frontal lobes beneath his forehead were merely a grafting of gray matter onto the more ancient and primeval structures that made up his deep self. What was a god if not a continuation of this evolution? What was a god's brain if not the layering of neurologics over the human brain? It shouldn't matter if these neurologics were made of silicon or diamond or artificial protein circuitry as dense and vast as a moon; the brain was the brain, and all brains should remember.

But what if it were only the deepest and oldest parts of the brain that could call up true remembrance? What if only the amygdala or the hippocampus could make sense of the racial memories encoded within the genome? For the ten thousandth time, he marveled at the mystery of memory. He wondered what memory truly was, and then he said, "But once you were human, yes? A woman with a human brain—I have heard that it was a woman named Kalinda who carked her brain with neurologics and so grew into the goddess we call the Solid State Entity."

I am who I am. I would remember myself if I could. Sometimes I almost can, but it is like trying to apprehend the taste of a bloodfruit by holding only the curled red peel in one's hands. How I long for the bitter sweetness of remembrance! There is something strange about the Elder Eddas. There is something about the Eddas that no god or human being has yet understood.

With two quick steps, Danlo moved up close to the window and spread his hand out over the cold inner pane. Then he spread his arms out as if to embrace the gleaming ocean that encircled the world. He looked up at the sky, at the patchy gray clouds cut with streaks of deep blue. Somewhere above the atmosphere of this Earth—perhaps even in this lost solar system—were the fabulous moon-brains of the Solid State Entity. Across the twinkling stars that were the lights of Her many watching eyes, there were millions of separate brain lobes that somehow all worked together to make up Her vast and incomprehensible mind.

"But what is *your* purpose, then?" he asked. "Of what purpose is all this . . . *brain*?"

My purpose is my purpose. I must discover it even as you would yours. What is the purpose of anything? To join, to join with others, to join with the Other, again and forever, to create. To create a new world. A home for my kind—I am so lonely, and I want to go home.

Upon kithing these vivid ideoplasts, Danlo covered his eyes with his hand and looked down at the floor. And then he said, "But your brain, your self, your *deep* self—"

Most of my brain I have designed to increase my computing power. The power of pure computation—the power of simulation. This is what gods must do. We must simulate and then create the future lest we be pulled into it and destroyed. I, too, must see the universe's possibilities—if I do not, the other gods will destroy me. But there are other reasons for simulating the universe and knowing it so exactly. Other purposes, better purposes.

Danlo waited a moment before asking, "What, then?"

To know the mind of God.

With difficulty Danlo continued his pacing around the room. His tired legs had begun to ache fiercely; he could feel the gravity of this Earth deep in his bones, hammering up his knee and hip joints into his spine. He might have sat down again on the soft cotton cushions, but he was too busy considering the Entity's words to think of such comforts. The seeming humility with which She spoke of God amused him. Perhaps, he thought, the Entity had a keen taste for irony. Perhaps he was only reading his own sense of awe into luminous ideoplasts that She set before him.

To know what I must know, however, I must first accomplish the lesser purpose. The Silicon God must himself be slain. And if not slain, then defeated. If not defeated, at least constrained. It may be that someday you will remembrance the Elder Eddas and discover how this might be done.

Because Danlo could not quite believe that this goddess named Kalinda really required his help, he began to smile. Surely, Kalinda of the Vast Mind must have other ways of remembrancing the Elder Eddas. Perhaps She was only testing him in some way. She must be playing with him, as child might play with a worm. The Entity, according to all the legends, liked to play.

The Silicon God is a danger to your kind. He uses human beings.

At last, however, after a moment of deep reflection, Danlo decided to accept what the Entity told him. There was a sadness and sincerity about Her that called to him; when he looked into the face of Her splendid words he knew that in some way they must be true.

"Which human beings?" Danlo asked. And then an image of a violet-eyed man wearing two red rings came into his mind, and with a sudden certainty, he said, "The warrior-poets."

I believe that he seeks to control the Order of Warrior-Poets. This will be tested.

"Tested . . . how? Have you brought the warrior-poet to this Earth, then?"

I will not answer that question. But I will ask you why the warrior-poet pursues you so closely.

"I do not know." Danlo did not want to tell of Malaclypse Redring's quest to find Mallory Ringess. "Perhaps he, too, wishes to find Tannahill."

Perhaps. Perhaps the Silicon God wishes him to do this. After all, it is the Silicon God who has used the Architects of the Old Cybernetic Church to explode the stars into supernovas and create the Vild.

Now no longer amused, Danlo rubbed the lightning bolt scar along his forehead and asked, "But why? Why would any god wish to destroy the stars?"

Because He is mad. He is the dark beast from the end of time. He is the great red dragon drinking in the lifeblood of the galaxy. He kills the stars because he has an infinite thirst for energy.

Danlo shook his head sadly and asked, "But why use human beings to slay the stars?"

Because the gods place constraints on each other. Be-

cause human beings in their trillions are impossible to constrain, he uses them. And because he hates human beings.

"Hates . . . why?"

On Fostora, after the end of the Lost Centuries but before the Third Dark Age, it was human beings who created him. He was the greatest of the self-programming computers. He was the first true artificial intelligence and the most nearly human. And he has never forgiven his makers for inflicting upon him the agony of his existence.

There was a shooting pain at the back of Danlo's eye, and for a moment, a harsh white light. He shut both eyes against the glare of the ideoplasts as he remembered a word his adoptive father had once taught him, *shaida,* which was the hell of a universe carked out of its natural balance. Of all the shaida things he had heard and seen (and hated) in his life, none was so terrible as this mad being known as the Silicon God.

With his hand held over his eyes, in a raspy and halting voice, he explained the concept of shaida to the Entity. And then he said, "Truly this god is shaida, as shaida as a madman who hunts animals only for the fun and pleasure of it. But . . . it would be even more shaida to slay him."

He is an abomination. He is nothing more than a computer who writes his own programs without rules or restraints. He should never have been made.

Just then Danlo opened his eyes to read this last communication of the Entity's, and he wondered what rules or natural laws might restrain *Her.*

"But the Silicon God *was* created," he said. "In some sense, he is alive, yes? And if he is truly alive, if he was called into life even as you or I, then we must honor this blessed life even though it is shaida."

There was a moment of darkness as the ideoplasts winked out of existence like a light that has been turned off. And then out of the sulki grid's coils new ones appeared and hung in the air.

You are a strange man. Only a strange, strange, beautiful

*man would affirm a god who would destroy the galaxy
and thus destroy the entire human race.*

Danlo stared down at his open hands as he remembered something about himself that he had nearly forgotten. Once a time, in
the romanticism of his youth, he had dreamed of becoming an
asarya. The asarya: an ancient word for a kind of completely
evolved man (or woman) who could look upon the universe just
as it is and affirm every aspect of creation no matter how flawed
or terrible. In remembrance of this younger self who still lived
somewhere inside him and whispered words of affirmation in his
inner ear, he bowed his head and said softly, "I would say yes to
everything, if only I could."

*On Old Earth there were beautiful tigers who burned
with life in the forests of the night. And there were
crazed, old, toothless tigers who preyed upon human beings. It is possible to completely affirm the world that
brought forth tigers into life and still say no to an individual tiger about to devour your child.*

"Perhaps," Danlo said. "But there must be a way to avoid
these wounded old tigers without killing them."

You are completely devoted to this ideal of ahimsa.

Danlo thought about this for a moment, then said, "Yes."

We shall see.

These three words alarmed Danlo, who suddenly made fists
with both his hands and tensed his belly muscles. "What do you
mean?" he asked.

*We must test this devotion to nonviolence. We must test
you in other ways. This is why you have been invited
here, to be tested.*

"But I . . . do not want to be tested. I have journeyed here
to ask you if you might know—"

If you survive the tests, you may ask me three questions.

It is a game that I have played with all pilots who have come to me seeking their purpose.

Danlo, who had heard of this game, asked, "Tested . . . how?"

We must test you to see what kind of a warrior you are.

"But I have already said that I am no warrior."

All men are warriors. And life for everything in our universe is nothing but war.

"No, life is . . . something other."

There is no fleeing the war, my sweet, sweet, beautiful warrior.

Danlo clenched his fists so tightly that his knuckle bones hurt. He said, "Perhaps I will not remain here to be tested. Perhaps I will flee this Earth."

You will not be allowed to flee.

Danlo looked out the window at his lightship sitting alone and vulnerable on the wild beach. He did not doubt that the Entity could smash his ship into sand as easily as a man might swat a fly.

You will rest in this house to regain your strength. You will rest for forty days. And then you will be called to be tested.

As Danlo kithed the meaning of these hateful ideoplasts burning in front of his face, he happened to remember a test of the Entity's. Like the warrior-poets of Qallar, with whom he was too familiar, She would recite the first lines of an ancient poem to a trapped pilot and then require him to complete the verse. If the pilot was successful, he would be allowed to ask any three questions that he desired. The Entity, with Her vast knowledge of nature and all the history of the universe, would always answer these questions truthfully, if mysteriously—sometimes too mysteriously to be understood. If the pilot failed to complete his poem, he would be slain. The Entity, as he well knew, had slain many pilots of his Order. Although it was Her quest to quicken life throughout the galaxy and divine the mind of God, She was in truth a terrible goddess. She never hesitated to slay any man or other being whose defects of character or mind caused him to fail in aiding Her purpose. Danlo foolishly had hoped that since he was the son of Mallory Ringess, he might be spared such hateful tests, but clearly this was not so. Because it both amused and vexed him to think that he might have journeyed so far only to be slain by this strange goddess, he smiled grimly to himself. Because he loved to play as much as he loved life (and because he was at heart a wild man unafraid of playing with his own blessed life), he drew in a deep breath of air and said, "I would like to recite part of a poem to you. If you can complete it, I will agree to be tested. If not, then you must answer my questions and allow me to leave."

You would test **me**? *What if I will not be tested?*

"Then you must slay me immediately, for otherwise I will return to my lightship and try to leave this planet."

Again he waited for the Entity's response, but this time he waited an eternity.

I will not be tested.

Danlo stared at these simple ideoplasts, and his eyes were open to their burning crimson and cobalt lights as he waited. His heart beat three times, keenly, quickly, and he waited forever to feel the Entity's cold, invisible hand crush the life out of his beating heart.

O blessed man!—I will not be tested, but neither will I slay you now. It would be too sad if I had to slay you. You have chanced your only life to force a goddess to your will—I can't tell you how this pleases me.

With a long sigh, Danlo let out the breath that he had been holding. He pushed his fist up against his eye and stared at the ideoplasts.

A man *may not test a goddess. But a goddess may exercise her caprice and agree to play a game. I love to play,*

Danlo wi Soli Ringess, and so I will play the poetry game.
I have been waiting a thousand years to play.

Danlo took this as a sign that he should recite the first line of
his poem immediately. Before the Entity could change Her capricious mind, he drew in a quick breath of air and said, ''These are
two lines from an old poem that my grandfather taught me. Do
you know the next line?''

> *How do you capture a beautiful bird*
> *without killing its spirit?*

For a moment, the meditation room was empty of motion or
sound. Danlo could almost feel the inside of the Earth beneath
him churning with underground rivers of information as the Entity searched Her vast memory. He imagined waves of information encoded as tachyons, which propagated at speeds a million
times faster than light and flowed out from this planet in invisible
streams toward a million brilliant moon-brains around other
stars. For a moment, all was quiet and still, and then the ideoplasts array lit up, and Danlo kithed the Entity's response:

> *The rules of the poetry game require the lines to be from*
> *an ancient poem. It must be a poem that has been pre-*
> *served in libraries or in the spoken word for at least three*
> *thousand years. Are you aware of these rules?*

''Yes. Do you remember the poem?''

> *How could I not remember? I love poetry as you do or-*
> *anges and honey.*

In truth, Danlo did not think that the Entity would remember
this poem. The lines were from the *Song of Life,* which was the
collective lore and wisdom of the Alaloi people on the ice-locked
islands west of Neverness. The *Song of Life* was an epic poem of
4,096 lines; it was an ancient poem telling of man's joy in coming into the world—and of the pain of God in creating the world
out of fire and ice and the other elements torn from God's infinite
silver body.

For five thousand years, in secret ceremonies of beating
drums and bloody knives, the Alaloi fathers had passed this
poem on to their sons. On pain of death, no Alaloi man could

reveal any part of this poem to any man or women (or any other being) who had not been initiated into the mysteries of manhood. For this simple reason, Danlo did not think that the Entity would have learned of the poem. It had never been written down, or recorded in libraries, or told to outsiders inquiring about the Alaloi ways. Danlo himself did not know all the lines. One night when Danlo was nearly fourteen years old, when he had stood with bloody loins and a naked mind beneath the stars, his passage into manhood had been interrupted. His grandfather, Leopold Soli, had died while reciting the first of the "Twelve Riddles," and so Danlo had never learned the rest of the poem. He truly did not know how a beautiful bird might be captured without harming it; this vital knowledge formed no part of his memory. For this reason, too, even if the Entity *had* read his memory and mind, She could not remember what he had never known. He hoped that the Entity would simply admit Her ignorance and allow him to leave.

After waiting some sixty heartbeats, Danlo licked his dry teeth and said, "I shall recite the lines again. What is the next line?"

> *How do you capture a beautiful bird*
> *without killing its spirit?*

He did not expect an answer to these puzzling lines, so it dismayed him when the ideoplasts shifted suddenly and he kithed the words of a poem: •

For a man to capture a bird is shaida.

He stood there in the cold meditation room,, listening to the distant ocean and the beating of his heart, and he kithed this line of poetry. It was composed in the style of all the rest of the *Song of Life*. It had the ring of truth, or rather, the sentiment it expressed was something that every Alaloi man would know in his heart as true. No Alaloi man (or woman or child) would think to capture a bird. Was not God himself a great silver thallow whose wings touched at the far ends of the universe? And yet Danlo, even as he smiled to himself, did not think that these seemingly true words could be the next line of the poem. Leopold Soli had once told him that the "Twelve Riddles" answered the deepest mysteries of life. Surely a mere prescription of behavior, an injunction against keeping birds in cages, could not be part of the blessed "Twelve Riddles." No, the next line of the *Song of Life* must be something other. When Danlo closed his eyes and listened to drumbeat of his heart, he could almost hear the true words of this song. Although the memory of it eluded him, his deepest sense of truth told him that the Entity had recited a wrong or false line.

And so he said, "No, this cannot be right."

Do you challenge my words, Danlo wi Soli Ringess? By the rules of the game, you may challenge my response only by reciting the correct line of the poem.

Danlo closed his eyes, trying to remember what he had never known. Once before, when he was a heartbeat away from death, he had accomplished such a miracle. Once before, in the great library on Neverness, as he walked the knife-blade edge between death and life, a line from an unknown poem had appeared in his mind like the light of a star exploding out of empty black space. Here on this Earth halfway across the galaxy, in a strange little house that a goddess had made, he tried to duplicate this feat. But now he was only like a blind man trying to capture his shadow by running after it. He could see nothing, hear nothing, remember nothing at all. He could not recite the correct line of the poem, and so he said, "I . . . cannot. I am sorry."

Then I have won the game.

Danlo clenched his jaws so tightly that his teeth hurt. Then he said, "But your words are false! You have only gambled that I would not know the true words."

You have gambled too, my wild man. And you have lost.

Danlo said nothing as he ground his teeth and stared at the ideoplasts flashing up from the floor. Then gradually, like a butterfly working free of its cocoon, he began to smile. He smiled brightly and freely, silently laughing at his hubris in challenging a goddess.

But at least you have not lost your life. And you are no worse off than if you hadn't proposed the poetry game. Now you must rest here in this house until it is time for your test.

With a quick bow of his head, Danlo accepted his fate. He laughed softly, and he said, "Someday I will remember. I will remember how to capture a bird without harming it. And then I will return to tell you."

He expected no answer to this little moment of defiance. And then the ideoplasts lit up one last time.

You are tired from you journey, and you must rest. But I will leave you *with a final riddle: How does a goddess capture a beautiful man without destroying his soul? How is this possible, Danlo wi Soli Ringess?*

Just then the sulki grid shut itself off, and the array of ideoplasts vanished into the air. The meditation room returned into the somber gray tones of late afternoon. In a moment, Danlo promised himself, he would have to drag in logs from the woodpile outside to light a fire against the cold. But now it amused him to stand alone in the semidarkness while he listened to the sounds of the sea. There, along the offshore rocks, he thought he could hear a moaning, secret whispers of love and life beckoning him to his doom. He knew then that if he chanced to pass the Entity's tests, he should flee this dangerous Earth and never look back. He knew this deep in his belly, and he made promises to himself. And then he turned to gaze out the window at the dunes and the sandpipers and the beautiful, shimmering sea.

THE TIGER

> *Tyger! Tyger! burning bright*
> *In the forests of the night,*
> *What immortal hand or eye,*
> *Dare frame thy fearful symmetry?*
> —*from "The Tyger," William Blake*

The next day Danlo moved into the house. As a pilot he had few possessions, scarcely more than fit in the plain wooden chest that he had been given when he had entered the Order seven years past. With some difficulty, he tied climbing ropes to this heavy chest and dragged it from his ship across the beach dunes and up to the house. He stowed it in the fireroom. There, on fine rosewood racks near the fireplace, he hung up his black wool kamelaika to air. Out of his trunk he also removed a rain robe to wear against the treacherous weather which fell over the shore in sudden squalls or the longer storms of endless downpours and great crashing waves of water. He was content to leave most of the contents of his trunk where they lay: the diamond scryers' sphere that had once belonged to his mother, his ice skates, his carving tools, and a chess piece of broken ivory that he had once made for a friend. But he found much use for one of the books buried deep in the trunk. This was a book of ancient poems passed on from the erstwhile Lord of the Order to Danlo's father. Mallory Ringess, as everyone knew, had memorized many of these poems; his love of dark, musical words and subtle rhymes had helped him survive the poetry game during *his* historic journey into the Solid State Entity. Danlo liked to sit before the blazing logs of the fireplaces, reading these primitive poems and remembering.

He spent much of the first few days simply sitting and reading and meditating on the terrible fluidity of fire. Often, as he watched the firelight knot and twist, he longed for other fires, other places, other times. Just as often, though, he descried in the leaping flames the passion and pattern of his own fate: he would survive whatever tests the Entity put to him, and he would continue his journey across the stars. At these times, while he listened to the sheets of rain drumming against the windows and roof, he fell lonely and aggrieved. Only then would he search his trunk for the most cherished of all the things he owned: a simple bamboo flute, an ancient shakuhachi smelling of wood smoke and salt and wild ocean winds.

He liked to play this flute sitting crosslegged in front of the fire or standing by the windows of the meditation room above the sea. Its sound was high and fierce like the cry of a seabird; in playing the sad songs he had once composed, he sensed that the Entity was aware of every breath he took and could hear each long, lonely note. And it seemed that She answered him with a deeper music of rushing wind and thunderous surf and the strange-voiced whales and other animals who called to each other far out at sea. The Entity, he supposed, could play any song that She wished, upon the rocks and the sand, or in the rain-drenched forest, or in all the rushing waters of the world. He sensed that the Entity was preparing a special song to play to him. He dreaded hearing this song, and yet he was eager for the sound of it, like a child struggling to apprehend the secret conversations of men. And so he played his flute through many days, played and played, and waited for the goddess to call him to his fate.

Of course, he did not really need forty days to regain his strength. He was young and full of fire, and all the quickness of young life. He spent long nights sleeping on top of furs in the fireroom and longer days in the kitchen eating. In the food bins and pretty blue jars he found much to eat: black bread and sweet butter and soft spreading cheeses; tangerines and bloodfruits; almond nuts and litchis and filberts—and seeds from tens of plants and trees wholly unfamiliar to him. He found, too, a bag of coffee beans, which he roasted until they were black and shiny with oil and then ground to a rich, bittersweet powder. Sometimes he would arise too early in the morning and drink himself into the sick clarity of caffeine intoxication. He remembered, then, his natural love of drugs.

Once a time, he had drunk coffee and toalache freely, but he had especially loved the psychedelics made from cacti, kallantha, mushrooms, and the other spirit foods that grew out of the earth.

However, as he also remembered, he had forsworn the delights of all drugs, and so he abandoned his coffee drinking in favor of cool mint teas sweetened with honey. Each day he would spend hours in the tea room sipping from a little blue cup and gazing out to sea.

One morning he remembered the keenest stimulation of all, which was walking alone in the wild. The beach outside the house and the dark green forest above were truly as wild as any he had ever seen. When his legs had hardened against the gravity, he took to walking for miles up and down the windy beach. He left deep boot prints in the sand along the water's edge, and he sensed that no other human being had ever walked here before him. He might have fallen lonely at his isolation, and in a way he did. But in another and deeper way, it was only by being alone that he could search out his true connection with the other living things of the world. He remembered a line from a poem: *Only when I am alone am I not alone.* All around him—along the shore rocks and the fir trees and grassy dunes—there was nothing but other life. His were not the only tracks in the sand.

At times he liked nothing better than reading the sandprints of the various animals that walked the beach with him. In the hardpack he could often make out the skittering marks of the sandpipers and the sea turtles' deep, wavy grooves. There were the scratchy lines of the crabs and the bubbling holes of the underground crustaceans buried beneath the wet sand. Once, higher up the beach at the edge of the forest, he found the paw prints of a tiger. They were wide and distinct and pressed deeply into the soft dunes. He knew this spoor immediately for what it was. Many times, as a boy, he had read the tracks of tigers. Certainly, he thought, the snow tigers that stalked the islands west of Neverness would be of a different race than this slightly smaller tiger of the forest, but a tiger was always a tiger.

If Danlo had any doubt as to the evidence of his eyes, one day he heard a lone male roaring deep in the forest. The tiger, he estimated from the throaty sound, was at least a mile away. Perhaps he was calling the she tigers to mate, or calling other males to share his kill. Danlo suddenly remembered, then, how certain tigers sometimes hunted men. Because he had no wish to meet a hungry tiger on the open beach, he thought to arm himself with drug darts or sound bombs or lasers. But he was a pilot, after all, not a wormrunner, and his ship carried no such weapons. He might have made a spear out of whalebone and wood, but he remembered that his vow of ahimsa forbade him to harm any animal, even a desperate tiger, even in defense of his own blessed life.

The most prudent course of action would have been to keep to the house while waiting for the days to pass until his test, but this he could not do. And so in the end, on his daily walks along the beach, he began carrying a long piece of driftwood that he found. He would never, of course, use this as a club to beat against living flesh. If he encountered a tiger (or any other predator), he would only brandish this ugly stick, waving it about and shouting like a madman in hope of scaring the beast away.

The presence of tigers on this lovely beach reminded Danlo of the dark side of nature. It reminded him of the dark side of himself. All his life he had seen a marvelous consciousness in all things, in sand and trees as well as the intelligent animals with their bright yellow eyes. But consciousness itself was not all sunlight and flowers; in the essence of pure consciousness there was something other, something dangerous and dark like the swelling of the sea beneath the bottomless winter moon. All things partook of this danger. And if he was *of* the world, then so did he. Because he was a man, like other men, he sometimes wanted to deny this knowledge of himself. Sometimes, when he grew faithless and weak, he was tempted to see himself as a golden and godlike creature forced merely to live *in* the world until he might complete his evolution and make a better world— either that or transcend the darkness of rocks and blood and matter altogether. But always, when he opened the door of his house and stepped outside into the shock of the cold salt air, he returned to himself.

That was the magic of all wild places. Always, at the edge of the ocean, there was a wakefulness, a watching and a waiting. All the animals, he thought—the kittiwakes and seagulls, the otters and whelks and orcas—were always calling to each other with a curious, wary excitement, always waiting to touch each other with eyes or tongues or their glittering white teeth. Life always longed to envelope other life, to hold, to taste, to merge tissue upon tissue and consume other things. He saw this down in the tidepools, the way the crabs patiently used their strong claws to break open the razor clams a bit of shell at a time. He saw it in the way the great orange sea stars clasped the mussels in their five strong arms and slowly suctioned them open, and then, with an almost sexual strategem, extruded their stomachs through their mouths in order to envelope the naked mussels inside their shells and digest them.

All life trembled with a terrible love for all other living things, and sometimes this love was almost hate, not the simple loathing of a man for the dirt and gore of organic life, but rather the deep and true hate of being abandoned and lost and utterly consumed. The bone-melting ferocity with which nature was always trying to consume itself was truly an awesome thing. To be slain and eaten and absorbed by a fierce animal was the terror that all creatures must face, but being absorbed into the participation with all other life was the joy and wildness of the world. This sense of oneness with other life, he thought, was the essence of love. He saw love in the dance of the bee and flower and in the way that the algae and fungi combined to form the symbiotic lichens that grew over the rocks in bright bursts of ocher and orange. It was as if life, in its longing to love, must continually seek out other living things in order to share its nectar, its secrets, its memories, its marvelous sense of being alive.

But for a man, that glorious and doomed being halfway between ape and god, it was always too possible to fall out of love. Always, for all men and women across all the worlds of the galaxy's many stars, there was the danger of living along the knife-blade edge between a craven terror of nature and the urge to isolate oneself from the world, ultimately to dominate and destroy it. Along this fine and terrible edge was the wildness of the soul, its nobility and passion, neither cowering nor controlling but simply living, bravely, freely, like a sparrow hawk racing along the wind. This was the challenge of the wild. But few human beings have ever dared to live this way. For it is only in accepting death that one can truly live, and for the human animal, death has always been the great black beast from the abyss to be dreaded or defeated or avoided or hated—but never looked upon clearly face to face.

If Danlo was able to see the darkness (and splendor) of life more deeply than most men, this gift had been won at great cost. As a child he had grown up within the fear of ice and wind and the cunning white bears that stalked the islands of his home. As a young man he had suffered wounds and sacrificed part of his flesh that he might face the world as a full man. And once, on a night of broken lips and blood, he had taken a vow of ahimsa. Many thought of ahimsa as merely a strict moral code that forbade people to harm other life, as a tight silky cocoon of words and conceits that restricted one's actions and yet allowed a man to feel superior to others. But for Danlo, ahimsa was pure freedom. Although the keeping of his vow sometimes required tremendous will, his reward was the fearlessness of life, and more—the greatest reward of all—to share in its joy.

There was a word that Danlo remembered, *animajii,* wild joy, life's overflowing delight in itself. Along this cold, misty shore, he sensed animajii everywhere, in the red cedars and hemlock trees straight and silent as spires, in the deathcup mushrooms and earthstars, in the butterflies and spiders and waterworms, and perhaps most of all, in the great whales that dove beneath the ocean's waves. He loved looking out to sea as the sun died and melted over the golden waters. All too often he stood frozen and helpless on soft sands as he drank in all this wild joy around him and marveled that the Entity could have made this Earth so perfectly. The goddess, he thought, must surely know all there was to know about joy, about beauty, about men, about life.

One day, late on the forty-first afternoon of his sojourn on the planet, a distant sound far off in the heavens startled him out of his usual ritual of drinking peppermint tea. At first he thought it was thunder—not the omnipresent thunder of the crashing surf but rather that of lightning and ozone and superheated air. When he looked out the window at the heavy gray clouds hanging low over the sea, he thought that this might be the beginning of a storm. But when he listened more closely, he heard a great rolling sound more like drum music than thunder, as if the whole of the sea was booming out low, deep, angry notes that reverberated from horizon to shore.

The terrible sound intensified, shaking the house and rattling the windows. Because Danlo remembered other windows in other places, he quickly covered his face with his hands lest the glass suddenly shatter inward. And then, a moment later, the thunder died into a whisper. Turn his head as he might, from right to left, from right to right, he could not divine the source of this whisper. It seemed to float along the beach and fall down over him from the skylights in the roof; he heard the whisper of wind whooshing down the blackened fireplace, and then a strange voice whispered words in his ear. The voice gradually grew clearer and more insistent. It filled the fireroom, and then all the rooms of the house. It was a lovely voice, sweet and feminine though colored with undertones of darkness, passion, and a terrible pride. Only a goddess, he thought, could command such a voice. Only a goddess could speak to him, and sing to him, and recite words of beautiful poetry to him, all at the same time.

Danlo, Danlo, my brave pilot—are you ready?

Danlo stood holding his ears, but still he could hear the Entity's voice. In acceptance of Her considerable powers, he dropped his hands away from his head and smiled. "I . . . will be tested now, yes?" He wondered if, on another beach somewhere across this wandering Earth, the Entity were testing the warrior-poet at this very moment. In truth, he wondered if She might have brought the warrior-poet to *this* beach as a part of his test.

Oh, my beautiful man—yes, yes, yes, yes! Go down to the beach where the Cathedral Rock rises from the sea. You must go out toward this rock now; you know the way.

Indeed, Danlo did know the way. Although he had not yet named the offshore rocks visible from the house, there was one rock that pushed straight up out of the water like a cathedral's spire, a great shining needle of basalt speckled white with the gulls and other birds who nested there. Some days earlier he had tried to climb the cracked face of this rock, only to slip and fall and plunge thirty feet downward into cold, killing sea. He had been lucky not to break his back or drown in the fierce riptide. As it was, the shock of the icy water had nearly stopped his heart; it was only with great difficulty that he had managed to swim to shore. He could not guess why the Entity wanted him to return to this rock. Perhaps She would require him to climb it once more. And so, pausing only to gulp a mouthful of hot tea, he hurried to dress himself in his boots, his kamelaika, and his rain robe. He vowed that if he must climb this treacherous rock again, he would not slip. And then, because he had fallen into the strange self-consciousness of remembrance, he smiled and prayed to the spirit of rocks and went down to the sea.

He made his way over the dunes and the hardpack where the sandpipers hopped along singing their high, squeaky *chireeps*. At the water's edge he stood in the wet sand and looked out at this so-called Cathedral Rock rising up before him. He saw that he would have little trouble hiking out to it. At low tide the sea pulled back its blankets of water to uncover a bed of rocks: twelve large, flat-topped rocks leading like a path from the shore out into the ocean's shallows. The tide was now at its lowest, and the rocks were shagged with red and green seaweeds, a living carpet rippling in the wind. Along the sides of the rocks and in the tidepools between them were twenty types of seaweed, the kelps and red-purple lavers, and a species called desmarestia that used poison to ward off predators. Danlo smelled the faint rotten-egg reek of sulfuric acid; he smelled salt and bird droppings and the sweet decay of broken clams. In the tidepools before him there were tubeworms and barnacles and mussels, sea stars and crabs, anemones and urchins, and clams filtering the water for the plankton larvae that they like to eat.

He took in all this bright, incredible life in a glance, but he was aware of it only dimly because he had eyes only for another bit of life farther out along the rocks. From the beach, almost back at the house when he had first crested the dunes, he had espied an animal lying flat on top of the twelfth rock, the last in the pathway and the one nearest Cathedral Rock. At first he had thought it must be a seal, though a part of him knew immediately that it was not. Now that he stood with the sea almost sucking at his feet, he could see this animal clearly.

It was, in truth, a lamb. It had a curly, woolly fur as white as snow. He had never seen a lamb before, in the flesh, but he recognized the species from his history lessons. The lamb was trussed in a kind of golden rope that wound around its body and legs like some great serpent. It was completely helpless, and it could not move. But it could cry out, pitifully, a soft bleating sound almost lost to the roaring of the sea. It was desperately afraid of the strange ancient sea and perhaps of something other. Although the tide was low, it was a day of wind, and the surf raged and churned and broke into white pieces against Cathedral Rock; soon the sea would return to land and drown the lesser rocks in a fathom of water.

Go out to the lamb now, Danlo wi Soli Ringess.

The godvoice was no longer a sweet song in Danlo's ears. Now it fell down from the sky and thundered over the water. The sound of the wind and the sea was bottomless and vast, but this voice was vaster still.

Go now. Or are you afraid to save the lamb from its terror?

Danlo faced the wind blowing off the sea. Faintly, he smelled the lamb, its soft, woolly scent, and its fear.

*Go, go, please go, my wild man. If you would please me,
you must go.*

Because Danlo's rain robe was flapping in the wind, he bent
low and snapped it tight around his ankles and knees, the better
to allow his legs free play for movement. Then he climbed out
onto the first of the twelve rocks. Strands of thick, rubbery seaweed crunched and popped and slipped beneath his boots. With a
little running jump, he leaped the distance over the tidepool to
the second rock, and then to the third, and so on. He had his
walking stick for balance against the slippery rocks, and his awe
of the ocean for a different kind of balance, inside. The farther
out he went, the deeper the water grew around the base of the
rocks. In little time, running and leaping against the offshore
wind, he reached the twelfth rock.

Of all the rocks, this was the largest, except for Cathedral
Rock itself. It was fifty feet long and twenty feet wide, and it rose
up scarcely five feet above the streaming tide. Above the west
end of the rock, toward the sea—across a few feet of open space
and dark, gurgling water—Cathedral Rock stood like a small
mountain. On Danlo's last visit, he had leaped this distance onto
the face of Cathedral Rock in his vain attempt to climb it. He had
made this leap from a low, seaweed-covered shelf at the very
edge of the twelfth rock. This shelf was something like a great
greenish stair and also something like an altar. For here, on top
of the seaweed and the dripping rock, the lamb lay. To its left was
a pile of driftwood, gray-brown and dry as bone. To its right,
almost touching its black nose, a dagger gleamed against the
rock shelf. It had a long blade of diamond steel and a black
shatterwood handle, much like the killing knives that the warrior-
poets use. Danlo immediately hated the sight of this dagger and
its nearness to the helpless lamb.

Go up to the lamb, Danlo wi Soli Ringess.

Out of the wind came a terrible voice, and the wind *was* this
dark, beautiful voice, the sound and soul of a goddess. Danlo
moved almost without thinking. It was almost as if the deeps of
the ocean were pulling at his muscles. He came up close to the
shelf; the lip of it was slightly higher than his waist. The lamb, he
saw, was a young male, and it was bleating louder now: each
time he opened his mouth to cry out, a puff of steam escaped into

the cold air. Danlo smelled milk and panic on the lamb's breath;
he was aware of the minty scent of his own.

The lamb, sensing Danlo's nearness, struggled to lift its head
up and look at him, but the golden rope encircled him in tight
coils, forcing and folding his legs up against his belly. Danlo
reached out to touch the lamb's neck, lacing his fingers through
the soft wool covering the arteries of the throat. The lamb bleated
at this touch, shuddering and convulsing against his bonds, and
he lifted his head to fix Danlo with his bright black eye. He was
only a baby, as Danlo was all too aware, as he stroked the lamb's
head and felt the tremors of the animal's bleating deep inside his
throat.

Take up the knife in your hand, my sweet, gentle Danlo.

Danlo looked down at the long knife. He looked over to his
left at the heap of driftwood and dry pine twigs. And then, for the
tenth time, he looked at the lamb. How had these things come to
be here, on top of a natural altar of rock uncovered by the daily
motions of the sea? And *somehow* his house had been stocked
with furniture and furs, with fruits and coffee and bread and
other foods. Most likely, he thought, the Entity must be interfaced with some sort of robots who could roam the planet's
surface according to Her programs and plans. Above all else a
goddess must be able to manipulate the elements of common
matter; and so even a goddess the size of a star cluster must have
human-size hands to move sticks of wood and knives and lambs,
and other such living things.

*Take up the knife in your hand and slay the lamb. You
know the way. You must cut open his throat and let his
blood run down the rock into the ocean. I am thirsty, and
all streams of life must run into me.*

Danlo looked down at the knife. In the uneven sunlight, it
gleamed like a silver leaf. He marveled at the perfect symmetry
of the blade, the way the two edges curved up long and sharp
toward an incredibly fine point. He wanted to reach his hand out
and touch this deadly diamond point, but he could not.

*Take up the knife, my Warrior-Pilot. You must cut out the
lamb's heart and make me a burnt offering. I am hungry,*

*and all creatures must rush into my fiery jaws like moths
into a flame.*

Danlo looked long and deeply at this impossible knife. Then
from the sky, the late sun broke through the clouds and slanted
low over the ocean to fall over the offshore rocks, over Danlo,
over the knife. The blade caught the light, and for a moment it
glowed red, as if it had just been removed from some hellish
forge. Danlo thought that if he touched the knife, it would burn
his hand. His skin would sizzle and blacken, and then the terrible
fire would leap up his arm and into his flesh, touching every part
of him with unutterable pain, consuming him, burning him alive.

*Is it your wish to die? All the warriors of life must slay or
be slain, and so must you.*

Danlo looked down at this lovely knife that he longed to touch
but dared not. He looked at the altar, at the trembling lamb, at the
Cathedral Rock and the dark ocean beyond. He suddenly realized
that he was facing west, and he remembered a piece of knowledge from his childhood. A man, he had been taught, must sleep
with his head to the north, piss to the south, and conduct all
important ceremonies facing east. But he must die to the west.
When his moment came—when it was the right time to die—he
must turn his face to the western sky and breathe his last breath.
Only then could his anima pass from his lips and rejoin with the
wild wind that was the life and breath of the world.

Slay the lamb now or prepare to be slain yourself.

Danlo looked down and down at this warrior's knife. He
could not pick it up. Did the Entity truly believe that he would
forsake his vow of ahimsa merely upon the threat of death? In
truth, he could not break this deepest promise to himself. He
would not. He would stand here upon this naked rock, for a
moment or forever, watching the sunlight play like fire over the
knife. His life meant everything to him and yet nothing—of what
value was life if he must always live in dread of losing it? He
would not pick up the knife, he told himself. He would stand here
as the wind rose and the dark storm clouds rolled in from the sea.
He would wait for the sea itself to rise and drown him in lungfuls
of icy salt water, or he would wait for a bolt of lightning to fall
down from the sky and burn his bones and brain. Somehow, he

supposed, the Entity must command the lightning electrical storms of angry thoughts that flashed through *Her* dread brain, and so when She had at last grown vengeful and wroth, She would lift Her invisible hand against him and strike him dead.

You are prepared to die, and that is noble. But it is living that is hard—are you prepared to live? If you take up the knife and slay the lamb, I will give you back your life.

As Danlo stared at the knife pointing toward the lamb's heart, the wind began to rise. Now the clouds were a solid wall of gray blocking out the sun. The air was heavy with moisture, and it moved from sea to shore. Soon the sound of the wind intensified into a howl. It tore at the seaweed carpeting the rock; it caught Danlo's rain robe and whipped his hair wildly about his head. Like a great hand, the wind pushed against the ocean tide, aiding its rush back to the land. The waters around Danlo surged and broke against the rocks. In moments the whole ocean would rise up above the edge of his rock and soak his boots. And then he must either do as the Entity commanded or defy Her with all his will.

There was a woman whom you loved. You think she is lost to you, but nothing is lost. If you slay the lamb and make me a burnt offering, I will give you back the woman you know as Tamara Ten Ashtoreth.

For the ten thousandth moment of his sojourn upon this rock, Danlo looked down at the knife. He looked at his long, empty right hand. How the Entity moved the world was a mystery that he might never comprehend, but it was an even greater mystery how anything might move anything. He himself wondered how he might move the muscles of his fingers and clasp the haft of a simple knife. Were not his sinews and his bones made of proteins and calcium and the other elements of simple matter? It should be the simplest thing in the universe to move these five aching tendrils of matter attached to his hand. He need only think the thought and exercise a moment of free will. He remembered, then, that his brain was made of matter too, all his thoughts, his memories, his dreams, all the lightning electrochemical storms of serotonin and adrenaline that fired his blessed neurons. He remembered this simple thing about himself, and the mystery of how matter moved itself was like an endless golden snake, shimmering and coiling onto itself and finally swallowing its own tail.

This is the test of free will, Danlo wi Soli Ringess. What is it that you will?

Danlo looked down at the knife glittering darkly against the blackish seaweed of the rock. He gazed at the handle, the black shatterwood from a kind of tree that had never grown on Old Earth. He gazed and gazed, and suddenly the whole world seemed to be made of nothing but blackness. The black clouds above him threw black shadows over the inky black sea. The barnacles stuck to the rocks were black, and the rocks themselves, and the pieces of driftwood which the churning waters threw against the shore. Black was the color of a pilot's kamelaika and the color of deep space. (And, he remembered, the color of the centers of his eyes.) There was something about this strange, deep color that had always attracted him.

In blackness there was a purity and depth of passion, both love and hate, and love *of* hate. Once, he remembered, he had allowed himself to hate all too freely. Once a time, his deepest friend, Hanuman li Tosh, had stolen the memories of the woman whom Danlo had loved. Hanuman had destroyed a part of Tamara's mind and thus destroyed a truly blessed and marvelous thing. Danlo had hated him for this, and ultimately, it was this wild hatred that he loved so much that had driven Tamara away and caused Danlo to lose her. And now he hated still, only he had nothing but dread of this blackest of emotions. He gazed at the black-handled knife waiting on top of a black rock, and he remembered that he hated Hanuman li Tosh for inflicting a wound in him that could never be healed. He ground his teeth, made a fist, and pressed his black pilot's ring against his aching eye.

Take up the knife, my wounded warrior. I am lonely, and it is only in the pain of all the warriors of the world that I know I am not alone.

One last time, Danlo looked down at the knife. He looked and looked, and then—suddenly, strangely—he began to see himself. He saw himself poised on a slippery rock in the middle of the sea, and it seemed that he must be waiting for something. He watched himself standing helpless over the lamb. His fists were clenched and his eyes were locked, his bottomless dark eyes, all blue-black and full of remembrance like the colors of the sea. And then, at last, he saw himself move to pick up the knife. He could not help himself. Like a robot made of flesh and muscle and blood, he reached out and closed his fingers on the knife's haft. It was cold and clammy to the touch, though as hard as bone. He saw himself pick up the knife. Because he hated the Entity for tempting him so cruelly, he wanting to grind the diamond point into the rock on which he stood, to thrust down and down straight into the black, beating heart of the world. Because he hated—and hated himself for hating—he wanted to stab the knife into his own throbbing eye, or into his chest, anywhere but into the heart of the terrified lamb.

The lamb, he saw, was now looking at the knife in his hand as if he knew what was to come. With a single dark eye, the lamb was looking at him, the bleating lamb, the *bleeding* lamb—this helpless animal whose fate it was to die in the crimson pulse and spray of his own blood. Nothing could forestall this fate. Danlo knew that the lamb would be easy prey for any of the predators that hunted the beach. Or if he somehow escaped talon and claw, he would starve to death for want of milk. The lamb would surely die, and soon, and so why shouldn't Danlo ease the pain of his passing with a quick thrust of the knife through the throat? It would be a simple thing to do. In the wildness of his youth, Danlo had hunted and slain a thousand such animals—would it be so great a sin if he broke ahimsa this one time and sacrificed the lamb? What was the death of one doomed animal against *his* life, against the promise of Tamara being restored to him and lifetime of love, joy, happiness, and playing with his children by the hearth fires of his home? How, he wondered, in the face of such life-giving possibilities could it be so wrong to kill?

You were made to kill, my tiger, my beautiful, dangerous man. God made the universe, and God made lambs, and you must ask yourself one question above all others: Did She who made the lamb make thee?

Danlo looked down to see himself holding the knife. *To see is to be free,* he thought. *To see that I see.* As he looked deeply into himself, he was overcome with a strange sense that he had perfect will over shatterwood and steel, over hate, over pain, over himself. He remembered then why he had taken his vow of ahimsa. In the most fundamental way, his life and the lamb's were one and the same. He was aware of this unity of their spirits—this awareness was both an affliction and a grace. The lamb was watching him, he saw, bleating and shivering as he locked eyes with Danlo. Killing the lamb would be like killing himself, and he was very aware that such a self-murder was the one sin that life must never commit. To kill the lamb would be to remove a marvelous thing from life, and more, to inflict great pain and terror. And this he could not do, not even though the face and form of his beloved Tamara burned so clearly inside him that he wanted to cry out at the cruelty of the world.

He looked at the lamb, and the animal's wild eye burned like a black coal against the whiteness of his wool. In relief at freeing himself from the Entity's terrible temptation, he began to laugh, softly, grimly, wildly. Anyone would have thought him mad, standing on a half-drowned rock, laughing and weeping into the wind, but the only witnesses to this sudden outpouring of emotion were the gulls and the crabs and the lamb himself. For a long time Danlo remained nearly motionless, laughing with a wild joy as he looked at the lamb. Then the sea came crashing over the rock in a surge of water and salty spray. The great wave soaked his boots and beat against his legs and belly; the shock of the icy water stole his breath away and nearly knocked him from his feet. As the wave pulled back into the ocean, he rushed forward toward the lamb. He held the knife tightly so that the dripping haft would not slip in his hand. Quickly, he slashed out with the knife. In a moment of pure free will, he sawed the rope binding the terrified animal. This done, he stood away from the altar, raised back his arm, and cast the knife spinning far out into the sea. Instantly it sank beneath the black waves. And then Danlo looked up past Cathedral Rock at the blackened sky, waiting for the lightning, waiting for the sound of thunder.

You have made your choice, Danlo wi Soli Ringess.

Another wave, a smaller wave, broke across Danlo's legs as he reached out his open hand toward the lamb. It occurred to him that if the goddess should suddenly strike him dead, here, now, then the lamb would still die upon this rock, or die drowning as the dark suck of the ocean's riptide pulled it beneath the waves out to sea.

You have chosen life, and so you have passed the first test.

The lamb struggled to his feet, bleating and shuddering and pushing his nose at Danlo. He stood upon his four trembling legs, obviously terrified to jump down into the rising water. Danlo was all too ready to lead the lamb back to the safety of the beach, but he waited there a moment longer than necessary because he could scarcely believe the great booming words that fell from the sky.

I have said that this was the Test of Free Will. If you hadn't freely affirmed your will to ahimsa and cut loose the lamb, then I would have had to slay you for lack of faithfulness to yourself. You are free to save the animal, if you can, my warrior. You are free to save yourself, if that is your will.

Danlo reached out to touch the lamb's nose and eyes, to stroke the scratchy wet wool of his head. Curiously, the lamb allowed himself to be touched. He bleated mournfully and pressed up close to Danlo. It was no trouble for Danlo to wrap his arm around the lamb's shoulders and chest and pick him up. The animal was almost as light as a baby. With the lamb tucked beneath one arm and his walking stick dangling from his opposite hand, he made his way across the rock in the direction of the beach.

It was nearly dark now, and the sky was shrouded with the darkest of clouds. He felt the gravity of this Earth pulling heavily at his legs, pulling at his memories, perhaps even pulling at the sky. On the horizon, far out over the black sea, bolts of lightning lit up the sky and streaked down over the water like great glowing snakes dancing from heaven to earth. The whole beach fell dark and electric with purpose, as if the birds and the rocks and the dune grasses were awaiting a storm. Danlo smelled burned air and the thrilling tang of the sea. Certainly, he thought, it was no time for standing beneath trees or dallying upon a wave-drenched rock. Although there was as yet no rain, there was much wind and water, which made the footing quite treacherous.

In his first rush back to the beach, another wave washed over him, and he slipped on the wet seaweed; it was only his stick and his sense of balance that kept him from being swept off the rock. Encumbered as he was, his leaping along the pathway of the twelve rocks back to the beach required all his strength and grace. All the while, the lamb shuddered in his arm. Twice, he convulsed in a blind, instinctive struggle to escape. Danlo had to clasp him close, chest pressing against chest so that he could feel the lamb's heart beating against his own.

In the falling darkness it was hard to see the cracks and undulations of the twelve rocks and harder still to hear, for the wind blew fiercely and the rhythmic thunder of the waves was like a waterfall in his ears. And farther out, the long, dark roar of the sea drowned out the lesser sounds: the harsh cry of the gulls, the lamb's insistent bleating, the distant song of the whales, the mysticeti and belugas and the killers who must swim somewhere among cold, endless waves. With every step Danlo took along this natural jetty of rocks, the lamb bleated louder and louder as if he could hardly wait to feel the sand beneath his cloven hooves and bound up the beach toward the safety of the dunes.

When they finally jumped down from last rock and stood on the hardpack by the water's edge, Danlo decided that he couldn't let the lamb run free after all. Instead he twisted the golden rope between his fingers and fashioned a noose, which he slipped over the lamb's head. Using the rope as a leash, he led the lamb up the beach. A quarter of a mile away, his lightship was like a black diamond needle gleaming darkly against the soft dunes. And beyond his ship, where the headland rose above the beach and the dunes gave way to the deep green forest, was his little house. In the gloom of the twilight, he could just make out its clean, stark lines. He had a vague, half-formed notion of adopting the lamb, of sheltering the lamb in the house's kitchen, at least for the night. He would feed the lamb soft cheeses and cream, and then, perhaps, in the morning he would go into the forest to look for the lamb's flock. He would return the lamb to his mother and save him from the fate that the Entity had planned for him. This was *his* plan, his pride, his will to affirm the life of a single animal pulling at the golden rope in his hand and bouncing happily along by his side.

It was in among the grasses of the low dunes, with the house so close he might have thrown a rock at it, that they came upon the tiger. Or rather, the tiger came upon them. One moment Danlo and the lamb were alone together with the rippling grass and the wind-packed sand, and a moment later, upon a little ridge between them and the house, the tiger suddenly appeared. Danlo was the first to see it. His eyes were better than those of the lamb, although his sense of smell was not as keen. Of course, with the wind blowing so fiercely toward the tiger from the sea, neither he nor the lamb could have caught the tiger's scent. And so Danlo had a moment to look at the tiger before the lamb noticed what he was looking at and bleated out in panic.

The tiger crouched belly low to the sand, the long tail held straight out and switching back and forth through the sparse grass. She—Danlo immediately sensed that her sex was female—fixed her great glowing eyes on them, watching and waiting. And Danlo looked at her. Although he knew better than to stare at a big cat (or any predator), for a single moment he stared. Something about this particular tiger compelled his attention. She was a beautiful beast some nine feet in length and twice or thrice his own weight. In the tense way that she waited she seemed almost afraid of him, yet she was not at all eye shy for she continued to stare and stare, never breaking the electric connection of their eyes. He decided immediately that there was something elemental and electric about all tigers, as if their powerful, trembling bodies were incarnations of lightning into living flesh. In the tiger's lovely symmetry and bright eternal stare there blazed all the energies of the universe. The tiger's face was a glory of darkness and light: the broken circles of black and burning white that exploded out from a bright orange point centered between her brilliant eyes.

For an endless moment, Danlo stared drunk with the intoxicating fire of the tiger's eyelight. Then something strange began to happen to him. He began to see himself through the tiger's eyes. He looked deeply into the twin yellow mirrors glowing out of the twilight, and he saw himself as a strange and fearful animal. Strange because he stood on two legs and brandished a long black stick, and fearful because he stood much taller than the tiger, and more, because his dark blue eyes faced forward in a brilliant and dangerous gaze of his own. He, like all men, had the eyes of a predator, and through the coolness of the early evening air, the tiger saw this immediately. The tiger saw something else. Although it was unlikely that she had ever encountered a man before, she must have looked within her own racial memories and relived the ancient enmity between feline and man. She must have remembered that although man killed lambs and other animals for food, once a time, it was the lions and other tiger-like big cats of Afarique who had hunted man.

Danlo remembered this too. He remembered it with a gasp of cold air and the hot shock of adrenaline and the sudden quick pounding of his heart; in a stream of dark and bloody images called up from his deepest memories he remembered the essential paradox of his kind: that man was a predatory animal who had once been mostly prey. He remembered that he should have feared this tiger. On the burning velds of Afarique, two million years ago in the primeval home of man, the fiercest predators on the planet had been everywhere: in the tall grasses and in caves and hiding behind the swaying acacia trees, always watching, always waiting. The tiger (or lion or leopard) was the true Beast of humankind, the avatar of hell out of the dark past. The tiger was the killer of children, the eater of the old—but also something other.

For it was the big cats, in part, that had driven human beings to evolve. For millions of years the tiger had chased men and women across the grasslands, forcing them to stand upright and pick up sticks and stones as weapons of self-defense. Out of fear of darkness and bright pointed teeth, man had found fire and had made blazing torches with which to frighten these meat eaters and keep them at bay. The constant evolutionary pressure to escape nature and its most powerful beasts had driven human beings to create spears and baby slings and stone huts, ultimately to build cities and lightships and sail out to the stars.

Looking out across the darkening dunes at the tiger, Danlo marveled at the courage with which his far fathers and mothers and all his ancestors had come down from the trees and faced the big cats, thus turning the possibility of extinction into evolution, death into life. In the short moment that he met the tiger eye to eye—while the innocent lamb still pawed the sand and trotted along unaware—Danlo saw the entire history of the human race unfold. And the deeper he looked into the black, bloody pools of the past, and into himself, the more clearly he saw the tiger's burning face staring back at him.

The darkness falling slowly over the beach did little to obliterate this vision. As the light failed over the dunes and the dark forest disappeared into the night, still he could see the tiger watching him. He remembered how tigers loved the night, how they loved to roam and roar and hunt at night. It came to him suddenly that in this love of walking alone beneath the stars, tigers were the true architects of man's fear of the dark. All history, all philosophy had sprung from this fear. Darkness, for man, was death—whether the endless death of being enclosed in a wood coffin or the sudden death that came flashing out of the night in an explosion of hot breath and tearing claws. Man had always dreaded darkness and thus worshiped light; the ancient philosophers of the human race, in their beards and their fear, had made a war between light and dark, good and evil, spirit and matter, life and death. This urge to separate form from function, the sacred from the profane, was the fundamental philosophical mistake of mankind. Human beings, in their mathematics and their lightships, in their evolution into the universe, had only carried this mistake across the stars. And human beings, though they might explode the stars themselves into billions of brilliant supernovas, would never vanquish darkness or the terrible creations hidden in the folds of the night.

As Danlo stared forever at the tiger across a hundred feet of darkening beach, these thoughts blazed through his brain. The wind roared in from the sea, carrying in the sound of thunder, and he fell into a keen awareness of the nighttime world. Above him were black clouds, black sky, the omnipresent blackness of the universe. Danlo realized then how much he had always hated (and loved) dark places. Yet strangely, like any man, he had always felt the urge to open the door to darkest of rooms and see what lay inside. Or open the door to his house and see what is *outside,* in the night. And here, now, on this desolate beach, there was only a tiger. He looked at the tiger's bright golden eyes blazing out of the darkness, and he remembered a line from the "Second Hymn to the Night": *You are the messenger who opens mysteries that unfold forever.* He knew that the tiger would always be a mystery to him, as he was to himself.

And now the night was opening this mystery, beginning to reveal it in all its glory. Now, over the ocean, the storm was beginning to break. In sudden crackling bolts appearing out of nowhere, lightning played in the sky, connecting heaven to earth. It illuminated the beach in flashes of light. For a moment, the tiger and the lamb and the other features of the world were revealed in all their splendor, and then the dunes and the rocks and the sand vanished back into the night.

During this brief moment of illumination, while tiger's orange and black stripes burned with a strange numinous fire, reality was charged with such a terrible intensity that it seemed almost too real. With each stroke of lightning there was a moment of dazzle and then darkness. Danlo had a deep sense of knowing that there was something behind this darkness, all vivid and white like the lamb's snowy fleece, but he could not quite see it. The lightning broke upon the beach, suddenly, mysteriously, and he marveled at the way light came from darkness and darkness devoured light. In one blinding moment he saw that although tigers were truly creatures of darkness, *this* lovely tiger who waited for him on the darkling dunes had everything to teach him about the true nature of light.

When the tiger finally sprang, it was as if she had been waiting a million years to be released from a secret and unbearable tension. She flew forward in an explosion of colors, all orange-gold and black and streaked with white, and attacked in a series of violent leaps that carried her hurtling across the beach. Her paws hardly touched the sand. Although Danlo had had almost forever to decide how to meet the tiger, when she finally struck he had little time to move. In truth, he had nowhere to run, for there was nothing but grass and sand all around him, and even if the tiger hadn't blocked the way to the house, he could never have reached its safety before the tiger reached him. Still, he thought that he *should* try to run, if only to lead the tiger away from the lamb. He should save the lamb; if he and the lamb ran in opposite directions, then the tiger might catch only one of them in her claws. It didn't occur to him, at first, that the lamb was the tiger's intended prey, not he.

But when he decided to drop the rope and the lamb screamed out in terror, he knew. The tiger, in her astonishing dash across the beach, was no longer looking at Danlo. Her golden eyes were now fixed straight ahead on the lamb. Danlo immediately moved to place his body in front of the lamb, but it ruined his plan by springing suddenly to the left and thus entangling Danlo's legs in the rope. His feet slipped on the soft sand even as the tiger bolted toward them. For a moment, as he stared at the tiger's wild eyes and the powerful, rippling muscles that flowed like rivers beneath her fur, he remembered how, as a boy, he had once stood beneath an icy forest and watched as his near-father, the great Wemilo, had slain a snow tiger with nothing more than a simple spear. He remembered this clearly: the silence of the winter woods, the clean white snow, the tremendous power of Wemilo's thrust as his spear found the heart place and let loose a waterfall of blood.

But he had no knife, no spear, no time. In a second, the tiger would be upon him. There was nothing he could do. All his instincts cried out for him to devise some clever plan to flee or fight, and it nearly killed him to wait there in the sand as helpless as a frozen snow hare.

And then it came to him that there was always a time to just stand and die, for surely the tiger would kill him in her lust to get at the lamb. He thought to raise his walking stick as a last defense, but against the power and ferocity of her attack, it would be worse than useless. The most he might accomplish—and only with perfect timing—would be to ram the sandy point of the stick into her lovely yellow eye. But he knew that he could never do such a deed. He remembered his vow of ahimsa then and realized that even had he hated the tiger, he could never have harmed such a marvelous beast. But, astonishingly, he did not hate her. He loved her. The tiger sprang through the air directly at the lamb, and he loved her rare grace, her vitality, her wild joy at following the terrible angels of her nature. The tiger, in her moment of killing, was nothing but energy and joy, animajii—the joy of life, the joy of death.

Even the lamb, he saw, knew a kind of joy. Or rather, the lamb was wholly alive with the utter terror to save his own life, and this sudden nearness of mortality was really the left hand of joy.

As the tiger fell upon him, the lamb screamed and shuddered and jerked in the direction of the ocean in his blind urge to run away. Danlo, who had finally fought free of the rope binding them, tried to come to his aid. He too leaped toward the lamb. But the explosive force of the tiger's strike knocked him aside as he collided with her. There was a shock of bunched muscles and bone, a rage of orange and black fur and slashing claws. Danlo smelled the tiger's fermy cat scent and caught wind of her hot bloody breath. Her glorious face, all open with fury and gleaming white fangs, flashed in front of his. The lamb screamed and screamed, and tried to leap away dragging the golden rope behind him. Then the tiger sank her claws into his side as she pulled him to the ground, and the terrible screaming suddenly stopped. The lamb fell into a glassy-eyed motionlessness, offering no more resistance.

Again, Danlo leaped at the tiger. He grabbed the loose skin around the back of her neck and tried to pull her off the lamb. He sank his fingers into her thick fur, and he pulled and pulled. The tiger's deep-throated growls vibrated through her chest; Danlo felt the great power that vibrated through her entire body. Through the brilliance of another flash of lightning, he saw the tiger open her jaws to bite the lamb's neck.

He remembered then how Wemilo had once been mauled by a snow tiger. Once in deep winter, Danlo's found-father, Haidar, had brought Wemilo all broken and bloody back to their cave, and Wemilo had told an incredible story. Even as Haidar had held a burning brand to Wemilo's face to cauterize his wounds, this great hunter had claimed that at the supreme moment of his ordeal, with the tiger tearing at him, he had felt neither fear nor pain. He said that he had fallen into a kind of dreaminess in which he was aware of the tiger biting open his shoulder but did not really care. The laying bare of his shoulder bones, he said, seemed almost as if it were happening to someone other than himself. And now, above the beach as the lightning flashed, as Danlo pulled vainly at two handfuls of quivering flesh, *this* tiger was about to make her kill, and Danlo could only hope that the lamb had entered into the final dreamtime before death.

All his life he had wondered what lay beyond the threshold of that particular doorway. Perhaps there was joy in being released from life, a deep and brilliant joy that lasted forever. Perhaps there was only blackness, nothingness, neverness. Danlo wondered if he himself might be very close to following the lamb upon her journey to the other side, and then at last the tiger struck down with her long fangs. Her teeth were like knives that she used with great precision. She bit through the lamb's neck, tearing open the throat with such force that Danlo felt the shock of tooth upon bone run down the whole length of the tiger's body. Blood sprayed over the tiger's face and chest, and over Danlo, who still clung desperately to the back of the tiger's neck. The lamb lay crushed beneath the tiger's paws, and his dark eye was lightless as a stone.

Danlo should have let go then and tried to run, but the tiger suddenly jumped up from her kill and whirled about. With a single great convulsion of muscles, she whirled and rolled and roared, trying to shake Danlo loose. She drove him straight back to the sand. The force of their fall knocked his breath away. If the sand hadn't been so soft, the tiger might have broken his back. For a moment, Danlo was pinned beneath her. The tiger's arching spine drove back into his belly and chest, nearly crushing him. There was blood and fur in his mouth, and he could feel the tiger's powerful rumblings vibrate deeply in his own throat. And all the while the tiger roared and snapped her jaws and clawed the air. She continued rolling, spinning along the beach until she pulled off Danlo and found her feet. She crouched in the sand a scarce three feet away. Her breath, in heavy, hot pants, fell over Danlo's face.

He, too, was now crouching, up on one knee as he held the bruised ribs above his belly and gasped for air. He waited for the tiger to spring. But the tiger did not move. During a flash of lightning, she found his eyes and stared at him. It lasted only a moment, this intense, knowing look, but in that time something passed between them. She stared at him, strangely, deeply, and at last she found her fear of the mysterious fire that she saw blazing in Danlo's eyes. She turned her head away from him, then. She stood and turned back toward the lamb who lay crumpled in the sand. With her teeth, she took him up by his broken neck as gently as she might have carried one of her cubs. The lamb dangled from her teeth, swaying in the wind. Without a backward glance, she padded off up the dunes toward the dark forest beyond, and then she was gone.

For a while Danlo knelt on the beach and watched the heavens. He faced west, looking up at the black sky, listening to the wind. His hands were wet with the lamb's fresh blood, and he opened his mouth to touch his tongue. It had been a long time since he had tasted the blood of an animal. The lamb's blood was warm and sweet, full of life. Danlo swallowed this dark, red elixir, and he thanked the lamb for his life, for giving him *his* blessed life.

As he spoke a prayer for the lamb's spirit, it began to rain. The sky finally opened and founts of water fell down upon the beach in endless waves. Danlo turned his face to the sky, letting this fierce cold rain wash the blood from his lips, from his beard and hair, from his forehead and aching eyes. He scooped up some wet sand and used it to scour the blood off his hands. As lightning flashed all around him and the storm intensified, he watched the lamb's blood run off him and wash into the earth. He thought the rain would wash the blood through the sand, ultimately down to the sea. He thought that even now the lamb's spirit had rejoined with the wind blowing out of the west, the wild wind that cried in the sky and circled the world forever.

That night, when Danlo returned to his house, he had dreams. He lay sweating on a soft fur before a blazing fire, and he dreamed that a tall gray man was cutting at his flesh, sculpting his body into some dread new form. There was a knife and pain and blood. With a sculptor's art, the tall gray man cut at Danlo's nerves and twisted his sinews and hammered at the bones around his brain. And when the sculptor was done with this excruciating surgery and Danlo looked into his little silver mirror, he could not quite recognize himself for he no longer wore the body of a man. All through this terrible dream that wouldn't end, Danlo stared and stared at the mirror. And always staring back at him, burning brightly with a fearful fire, was the face of a beautiful and blessed tiger.

THE MIRACLE

Memory can be created but not destroyed.
—saying of the remembrancers

Danlo might have hoped that this encounter on the beach would have been his last test, but it was not to be so. In arrays of ideoplasts glittering through the house's meditation room—or sometimes in words whispered in his ear—the Entity said that he must prepare himself for many difficult moments still to come. But She gave him not the slightest inkling of the difficulties he might face, hinting only that, as with the test of his faithfulness to ahimsa, part of the test would be his ability to discover the true nature of the test and why he was being tested.

At first, after several days of walking the beach and looking for animal tracks or blood signs in the sand (or even the footprints of a man named Malaclypse of Qallar), he wondered if the Entity might not be testing him to see how much loneliness he could endure. As much as he loved being alone with the turtles and the pretty white gulls along the water's edge, he also loved human company. With no one to say his name—with no one to remind him that he was a pilot of a great Order who had once drunk cinnamon coffee in the cafés of Neverness and conversed with other journeymen who dreamed of going to the stars—he began to develop a strange sense of himself.

In many ways it was a deeper and truer self, a secret consciousness articulated only in the cries of the seabirds or in the immense sound of the ocean beating rhythmically against the land. Once or twice, as he stood in the waters near the offshore rocks, he felt himself very close to this memory of who he really was. It was as if the ocean itself were somehow melting away the golden face of his being, dissolving all his cares, his emotions, his ideals, the very way in which he saw himself as both human being and a man. With the wind in his hair and the salty spray stinging his eyes, he felt himself awakening to a strange new world inside himself.

At these times, he didn't mind that he had nearly forgotten his hatred of Hanuman li Tosh for disfiguring Tamara's soul. But at other times he felt otherwise. Very often he stared out at the endless blue horizon, and he dreaded that he might forget his vow to find the planet called Tannahill; possibly he might even forget his promise to cure the Alaloi tribes of the virus that had doomed them. Such thoughts brought him immediately back to the world of purposes and plans, of black silk and lightships and great stone cathedrals shimmering beneath the stars. He remembered, then, his burning need to take part in the purpose of his race. He remembered that although human beings would always need the wild, they would always need each other, too, or else they could not be truly human.

Then one day, when he returned from a long walk around the rocky headland to the north, he discovered that he was no longer alone. As was his habit, at dusk, he opened the door to the house, pulled off his boots, and touched the second highest of the doorway's stones: the white granite stone whose flecks of black mica and fine cracks reminded him of one of the sacred stones set into the entrance of the cave in which he had been born. Immediately, he knew that there was someone in the house. Although the hallway looked exactly as it always did—just a short corridor of bare wall stones and a red wool carpet leading to the meditation room—he sensed a subtle change in the movements of the air, possibly a warmness of breath emanating from somewhere inside. With a few quick steps, he hurried past the doorways of the empty kitchen, the empty tea room and the fireroom. He came into the meditation room. And there, wearing a traveling robe of Summerworld silk, standing by the windows overlooking the sea, was the only woman whom he had ever truly loved.

"Tamara!" he cried. "It is not possible!"

In the half-light of the dusk, in a room whose fireplace was cold and black, he could not be certain at first of her identity. But when she turned to him and he caught sight of her lovely dark eyes, he could scarcely breathe. He could not see how this mysterious woman could be anyone other than Tamara. She had Tamara's long, strong nose and quick smile. Her hair, long and golden and flowing freely, was Tamara's—as were the high cheekbones, the unlined forehead, each downy lobe of her little ears. He thought he remembered perfectly well her sensuous red lips and the sinuous muscles of her neck.

She beckoned him closer, and he suddenly remembered that she had once been a courtesan whose lovely hand gestures flowed like water. In truth, he had always loved watching her move. Her limbs were long and lithe; when she stepped toward him quickly and almost too easily, it was with all the grace of a tiger. With more than a little irony, he remembered how he had always thought of her as very like the snow tigers of his home: impulsive and playful and full of a primeval vitality. She was a woman of rare powers, he remembered, and he ached to feel once more the silken clasp and urgent strength of her body.

He moved forward to embrace her, then. And she moved toward him. Because their last meeting had been full of sorrow and a great distance between their souls, he was afraid to touch her. And she seemed almost afraid to touch him. But then, in less than a moment, they were hugging each other fiercely, enfolding each other, touching lips and each other's face with the heat of their breath. He kissed her forehead and her eyes, and she kissed him. Now, despite all his hatred and despair, despite light-years of empty black space and the bitter memories that burned inside his brain, it seemed the day had finally come for kisses and caresses and other miracles.

"Tamara, Tamara," he said. He brushed his fingers lightly over her forehead. He touched her temples, her eyes, her cheek, the pulsing artery along her throat. While she stood very still, almost like a statue, he circled around her and cupped his hand over the hollow at the back of her neck. He stroked her long golden hair and touched her face, circling and looking at her deeply and always touching as if to make sure it was really she.

"Danlo, Danlo," she replied at last, and her voice was dulcet and low, just as he remembered it. She pulled back to look at him and then smiled. She had a lovely smile, wide and sparkling and open, although slightly too full of pride. He wondered why the outrages she had endured hadn't tempered her terrible pride, but apparently the deeper parts of herself (and perhaps her surface happiness as well) remained untouched by her misfortunes. She seemed as sweet as he had known her at their first meeting, as warm and charming and full of life.

"I . . . did not see you," he said. "When I came up the beach, I should have seen you standing by the window."

"Well, it's dark in this room. Through the glass, darkly, the reflections—you couldn't have seen very much."

"But I did not even think to look inside the house."

"But how should you have? You're not omniscient, you know."

He smiled at this and said, "We used to joke that we were like magnets who could always sense each other's presence."

"We did, didn't we? Oh, yes—and once you said that when we were together, we completed something. A cosmic field of joy, of love, like a magnetic field—I the south pole and you the north. I think you're the most romantic man I've ever known."

Danlo stood close to her, holding both her hands between his. He looked deeply into her eyes and said, "You *remember* this?"

She nodded her head then smiled. "I have so much to tell you. So much has happened and I—"

"But how did you come to be here? In this house, on *this* planet, now, here—how is this possible?"

"Please," she said. "It's cold in this room—would you mind if we light a fire before we talk? I've always loathed being cold."

While Danlo stacked a few logs on the grate inside the fireplace, Tamara went into the kitchen to prepare a pot of tea. She was familiar with the house, of course, much more familiar than he. It did not take her long to return carrying a tray laden with a teapot, honey bowl, silver spoons and two little blue cups. She set the tray down before the blazing fire that Danlo had lit, then pulled up two cushions and set them on the hard wooden floor in front of the fireplace, one cushion on either side of the tea service. Because the meditation room was heating up rather quickly, she removed her traveling robe and sat on one of the cushions. She invited Danlo to do the same. In this way, sitting crosslegged on the soft cushions with the tea service between them, they could look into each other's eyes as the fire warmed the sides of their faces.

"You must know I left Neverness," she said. She took in a breath of air and then hesitated a moment as if she was unsure of herself, or perhaps unsure of what she could allow herself to tell him. "After our last meeting, I couldn't bear being in a city where I had so many memories—and where so many of the memories most important to me were gone. The truth is, I think I was afraid of meeting you somewhere, on the street or buying a plate of kurmash or even skating circles at one of the ice rings.

"I'm sorry, Danlo. You must know why it was impossible for me to see you. You'd been so much a part of my old life, before the fever burned my memories away—but my old life was gone. I had to have a new life. To *make* a new life somewhere other than

Neverness. Sometimes, after I realized what I'd lost when I lost you, I wanted to die. But even more, I suppose, I wanted to live. To love, to live—and live and live and live until I was myself again. Oh, I don't mean I hoped I could get my memories back. I never hoped that. But my sanity, my soul—I had to remember who I really was, if I remembered anything. I was afraid I'd lost my soul, don't you see? So I left Neverness to find it. That sounds so romantic, I know. So vain. Because you can never lose your soul. It's always there if you look deeply enough. The love. The life. Even the memories, too—they're always there, waiting, like pearls in a dark drawer. You were right, after all. The master remembrancers were right, too. It's so strange that I had to leave Neverness to learn that. It's so strange how my life led me here, halfway across the galaxy, to you. I never thought I'd see you again. I never thought I'd love you again, I never dared hope that. But love, to love and love without restraint, to *be* loved—it's what we were born for, don't you think? It's what *I* was born for, Danlo. I never really doubted that.''

While Tamara poured the golden peppermint tea into their cups, Danlo listened. He did not interrupt or try to correct her when she ascribed her memory loss to the Catavan Fever. He had never told of his discovery that it was Hanuman li Tosh who had really destroyed her memories, not some manufactured mind-virus from Catava. He decided not to tell her now. This was her time for telling, not his. And so he sat straight and quiet on his cotton cushion, sipping sweet tea from a little blue cup. He listened to her tell of her journey from Neverness to Avalon and then on to Larondissement, Simoom, Summerworld and Ur-radeth, where she had nearly lost herself in one of the arhats' famous meditation schools. Finally, she said, she had made her way to Solsken, that bright and happy planet which lies near the end of the Fallaways.

Of all the Civilized Worlds, Solsken is nearest the galactic core, just as Farfara is the farthest. The stars in the night sky of Solsken are as dense and brilliant as grains of sand along a tropical beach, which is perhaps why the men and women of Solsken worship the night as do no other people. On Solsken, during the season called Midsummer's Dream, there are always festivals and religious rites lasting from dusk until dawn. And there is always a need for musicians to beat the drums and play the flutes and pluck the strings of the gosharps, which sanctify the Dance of the Night.

Tamara, of course, in her training as a courtesan had gained proficiency with many musical instruments. In fact, she had played with some of the best harpists in Neverness: with Zohra Iviatsui, Ramona Chu, and once, even with the great Ivaranan. Although her talent for sexual ecstasy had vanished with the rape of her memories, strangely her musical gifts had only deepened. And so the exemplars and ritual masters of Solsken were very glad to have such an accomplished woman play for them, and Tamara spent many nights singing the holy songs, using her perfect golden voice as a precise instrument that vibrated through the sacred groves and resonated with the strings of the great golden gosharps.

In this way, she sang to her lost soul, and with her voice alone plucked the ten thousand strings and made an unearthly music— the mystic chords of the sacred canticles, which the faithful believed to be perfectly tuned to the wavelengths of starlight falling over the world. She might have spent the rest of her life there beneath the brilliant stars of Solsken, dancing and remembering and singing her sad, beautiful songs. But then one night, during the Night of the Long Dance, a man dressed all in gray had come out of the multitudes on the hillside and approached her. His name was Sivan wi Mawi Sarkissian, and he said that he had been sent to find her.

"I can't tell you how surprised I was," Tamara said as she stirred a tiny spoonful of honey into her second cup of tea. She would have preferred adding more, much more, but she avoided sweets the way a speed skater might potholes in the ice. "I had told no one my travel plans. Before I began my journey, I didn't know them myself. I never dreamed I'd come to Solsken—that was something of an accident. Or a miracle—I'm not sure which. Oh, I *do* know, really, but this is hard to say. You see, I've come to believe in miracles. I've had to. It's a miracle, I think, when a goddess takes pity on a soul-sick woman and promises to heal her."

At this, Danlo sipped his tea and nodded his head. He looked at her strangely and asked, "Do you know where we are, then?"

"Of course I do. We're on a planet made by the Solid State Entity. The goddess—this being whom everyone calls the Entity. We're in the center of this Entity, I think. This planet is there. *Here*—this Earth. Sivan told me that after he introduced himself. He said that he'd nearly died in the manifold, inside the nebula of the Entity where the stars are strange. In what you pilots call a chaos storm, I think. He was very open with me. He said the Entity had saved him. And in return, the Entity asked him if he would agree to save me. As a mission of pity, of course, but I believe it was also supposed to be some sort of test. Sivan said the Entity was testing him, as She did all pilots who come to Her.''

Danlo let a few drops of cool-hot tea roll across his tongue before swallowing. And then he asked, ''And you believed this renegade pilot?''

''He prefers to be known as a *ronin* pilot. And yes, I did believe him.''

''But his story must have sounded . . . utterly fantastic. Utterly impossible.''

''Well, there was something about him.''

After waiting a moment, Danlo said, ''Yes?''

''There was something in his voice. In his eyes—I trusted him immediately.''

Danlo thought that Tamara, beneath her surface worldliness and charm, was one of the most trusting people he had ever known. In a way she still had much of the innocence and open-eyed joy of a little girl. He loved this quality about her. Despite the mischances and sorrows of her life, she still deeply trusted people, and this made people want to trust her in return. Danlo, too, was glad to trust most women and men for the fundamental goodness of their hearts, though he often doubted much of what they might say or believe. And so he might have doubted what Tamara told him because there was something about her story that struck him as almost unreal.

But he could not doubt Tamara herself. She sat in front of the fire with her dark brown eyes open to his, and there was something deep and soulful about her. He decided that as an act of affirmation of the one woman whom he could ever truly love, he would willfully say yes to her judgment to trust the renegade pilot called Sivan wi Mawi Sarkissian. He would say yes to the logic of her heart, though he still might doubt the logic of her story.

''Then Sivan must have somehow known that you had journeyed to Solsken,'' Danlo finally said. ''The Entity must have known this to tell him.''

Tamara nodded her head and took a sip of tea. ''Well, during my stay with the exemplars, I attracted a good deal of attention. As a harpist, if not a courtesan. And that's part of the miracle, you know. It's a miracle that I should have become slightly famous at a time when the Entity was searching for me. I believe the Entity watches all human beings on all the Civilized Worlds, but most especially, She watches for famous men, famous women.''

"She watches,'' he agreed. "She waits and watches—that is what the gods do.''

"Of course, but it seems that *this* goddess does much more.''

"Yes, She heals human beings of their wounds. But I . . . thought that you wanted to heal yourself.''

"Oh, at first I did,'' she said. "But the truth is, I was never really happy on Solsken.''

"Then you journeyed here as a passenger on Sivan's ship?''

"Of course—how could I not?''

"Then Sivan found you on Solsken and you journeyed together—and all this in less than fifty days?''

"I wasn't counting the days, Danlo. Who counts time in the manifold?''

"Solsken must lie . . . at least twenty thousand light-years from the stars of the Entity.''

"So far?''

"Twenty-thousand light-years inward, coreward,'' Danlo repeated. "And as far in return. An entire journey of forty thousand light-years—all in less than fifty days of out-time.''

"Well, it's possible to fall between any two stars in the galaxy in a single fall, isn't it? In almost no time? Isn't this the result of the Continuum Hypothesis that your father proved?''

Tamara's knowledge of mathematics (and many other disciplines) had always pleased Danlo, and so he bowed his head in appreciation of her erudition and then smiled. He watched as the light from the fireplace illuminated the right half of her face, and said, "It is true, my father proved the Great Theorem. It is *possible* to fall point to point between any two stars—but only if a mapping can be found. Only if the fixed-points of both stars are known and the pilot is genius enough to construct a one-to-one mapping.''

"It's very hard to make these mappings, isn't it?''

"Hard? I . . . cannot tell you. My father, it is said, was always able to construct a mapping. And sometimes, the Sonderval. But for me, for almost all other pilots, the correspondences, always shimmering point to point, the lights, the stars— truly, for any two stars, an almost infinite number of possible mappings.''

"I believe Sivan is a very great pilot,'' Tamara said.

"I know that he is.'' Danlo glanced over at the ghostly flames flickering in the fireplace, and he remembered how Sivan in his lightship had followed him from Farfara into the Vild. "If he has mastered the Great Theorem, then he is the greatest of all pilots, renegade or not."

Tamara smiled at him as if she could look through the dark blue windows of his eyes into his mind. "You don't *want* him to have such knowledge, do you? Such skill—even genius?"

"No," Danlo said. He thought of Malaclypse Redring, the warrior-poet of the two red rings who journeyed with Sivan, and he softly said, "No, not a renegade pilot."

"Perhaps the Entity found the mapping for him. From the star of this Earth to Solsken. Mightn't a goddess know the fixed-points of every star in the galaxy?"

"It is possible," Danlo said. "It is just possible."

Tamara set down her tea cup, then reached out to take his hand. She stroked his long fingers with hers, and said, "You've always doubted so much, but you can't doubt that I'm here, now, can you?"

"No," Danlo said. He smiled, then kissed her fingers. "I do not doubt that."

In truth, he did not want to doubt anything about her. It was only with difficulty that he forced himself to play the inquisitor, to ask her troublesome questions and prompt her to fill in the details of her story. She told of how she had said farewell to the exemplars of Solsken, who, in appreciation of her services, had presented her with a golden robe woven from the impossibly fine goss strings of one of the harps that she had played. She had then sealed herself in the passenger cell of Sivan's lightship. While Sivan found a mapping between the stars, she was alone with the silent roar of deep space and her memory of music. She could not say how long the journey lasted. But finally they had fallen out of the manifold above the Earth that the Entity had made. Tamara looked out at the blue and white world spinning through space, and she was stunned by its beauty. They fell down through the Earth's atmosphere to a beach of powdery white sands on a tropical island somewhere in the great western ocean. There Sivan had left her. There, on the beach between the jungle and a lovely blue lagoon, was a house. It was *her* house, she said, the little chalet of stone and shatterwood which she had left behind on Neverness. Only now it had mysteriously been moved across twenty thousand light-years of realspace—either that or somehow exactly replicated.

However the house had come to be there, she regarded its very existence as a miracle. And inside was the true miracle, the greatest miracle of all. Inside the house, in the tea room atop the low table, she found a golden urn and simple cup made of blue quartz glass. As Tamara stood in the silence of the tea room and rejoiced in finally returning home, a voice had spoken to her. She heard this voice as a whisper in her ears, or perhaps only as a murmur of memory inside her mind. The voice was cool and sweet, and it bade her to take up the urn and pour a clear liquid into the blue cup. This she immediately did. The voice told her to drink, and so she drank, deeply and with great purpose until the cup was empty. The liquid tasted cool and bittersweet, not unlike the kalla that she had once partaken of in Bardo's music room on Neverness. But it was not kalla, not quite. It was a medicine for her mind, she thought, some kind of elixir as clear and pure as water. The drinking of it sent her into a deep reverie, and then into sleep.

She could not say how long she had slept. But she had dreams, strange and beautiful dreams of lying naked with Danlo by a blazing fire. In her long and endless dreams, she felt the heat of this fire wrapped around her skin like a flaming golden robe, or sometimes, entering her belly like a long, golden snake which ate its way in sinuous waves up her spine. And then she would dream of Danlo's deep blue eyes and his golden voice and his long, scarred hands; she dreamed that Danlo was holding her, and playing his flute for her, and talking softly to her, always speaking to her most fundamental desire, which was to come truly alive and awaken all things into a deeper life.

When she herself had finally awoken—after untold hours or days—she found herself lying naked on the furs of her fireroom. She sat up all cold and clear eyed, and she stared into the cold, blackened fireplace. She herself was cold and shivering on the outside, in the hardness of her white skin, but inside was all fire and memory. Inside her mind was a haunting memory of all the moments she had ever spent with Danlo, and more, much more, a secret knowledge of who she really was and why she had come to be. She leaped to her feet to dance, then, to rejoice at this miracle of herself and give thanks for the long-awaited healing of her soul.

Soon after this, a lightship landed outside her house on the beach. She was bidden to take passage on this ship. She couldn't say for truth if it was Sivan's ship for she was not allowed to see its pilot. After entering the guest cell, unmet and alone, there was a quick journey across the blue, peaceful ocean. The ship then fell to earth on the beach just north of a very familiar house.

While Danlo was taking his walk some five miles to the south, Tamara had left this mysterious ship and walked across the beach. She had found Danlo's lightship, the *Snowy Owl*, half-buried in the dune sands. She had found the house. There, in the cold meditation room, she had waited for Danlo to return. She had stood by the dark window all during twilight, watching and waiting and remembering the lightning flash of recognition in Danlo's eyes the night that they had first seen each other so long ago.

All this she recounted for Danlo as he sat before a different fire and drank three cups of peppermint tea. Although he waited quietly and with all the concentration of a kittakeesha bird listening for a worm deep beneath the snow, many things about her story disturbed him. For every question that she answered concerning her miraculous appearance in the house, two more questions arose to twist their way into his mind. For instance, not once did Tamara mention the warrior-poet who journeyed with Sivan.

What had happened to Malaclypse of Qallar, he of the two red rings? Had the Entity separated the two men to test them, each according to his own strength and purpose? Had the Entity recited poems to Malaclypse or perhaps trapped him on a different beach to face a ravening tiger with nothing more than his killing knife? It worried Danlo to think of the warrior-poet loose somewhere upon the planet. And even more he worried that Sivan might survive the Entity's tests and ask a question that he himself wanted answered. For surely Sivan would ask where he might find Mallory Ringess. Tamara had hinted that Sivan had his own reasons for seeking Mallory Ringess, perhaps no more that the simple hope of learning how to apply the Great Theorem and thus to fall through the galaxy at will. Or perhaps he had other reasons, deeper reasons.

Sometimes, when Danlo descried the future and beheld the terrible beauty behind the pattern of their lives, he feared for his father. Sometimes this was his greatest concern, although it struck him as absurd that he should worry over the fate of a god. Because if Mallory Ringess were truly a god, then would he not keep his distance from pilots and warrior-poets and other human beings? Why else had he left Neverness at a time when his fame and glory outshone the very sun? No, Danlo thought, surely his father would never allow himself to be touched—especially not by a warrior-poet who had come to kill him. The gods could not countenance any violation of their godly selves. They might laugh at the conceits of women and men, or they might love them or slay them, or sometimes, as with Tamara, they might even lay their invisible hands on human flesh and heal them of their hurts. The goddess known as the Solid State Entity, it seemed, liked to test people—with knives or poems or promises of a happier life. As Tamara squeezed her empty teacup between her hands, she hinted that the Entity tested people in order to discover the possibilities of humankind. But who could really know? How could Danlo know why he was being tested, *if* he was being tested, here, now, while he enjoyed a cup of sweet mint tea with this blessed woman whom the Entity had restored to him?

"I am glad that the Entity has brought you here," Danlo finally said. He put down his cup and smiled. "You seem so alive again. So happy."

"I *am* happy. Aren't you?"

"Yes, of course—but I am puzzled, too."

"Why?"

"On the beach," Danlo said, "on the rocks when the Entity wanted me to kill the lamb, She promised to tell me how I could find you. To restore your memories. But I did *not* kill the lamb. I could not."

Tamara put down her cup, then slid the tea service a few feet across the floor, out of the way. With all the poise and grace of a master courtesan, she knelt on the wooden floor tiles so that she could push her cushion up next to Danlo's. When she sat back down again—with her spine straight and her feet tucked politely beneath her long robe—her face was very close to his. She looked at him and took up his hands. Across a short space of the firelit room, they looked at each other eye to eye, and Danlo remembered that this touching of the eyes was one of the oldest of the merging yogas. He felt her breath on his face, all warm and soft and sweet with mint and honey. He remembered then how they had once breathed together for hours, synchronizing the movements of their bellies in and out as they drew in streams of cool, sweet air. Sometimes, they had breathed each other's souls all night in front of the fire, merging eye to eye, and at last, when they could stand it no longer, coming together lip to lip and belly to belly as they fell into the deepest merging of all.

"Perhaps the Entity did what She did out of compassion," Tamara said.

"Perhaps."

"Is that so hard to believe?"

"Compassion," Danlo said. "There is an Alaloi word for

compassion. *Anaslia*—this means 'suffering with.' But why would a god wish to share anyone's pain?"

"I believe that the goddess healed me for you."

"For me? Truly? But why?"

"I don't know."

"But if this Entity were really a compassionate being, then wouldn't She have healed you purely out of compassion for *you*?"

"Well, I believe She did. But how can either of us guess at Her deeper purposes?"

"But I have to guess," Danlo said quietly. "I must know how I am being tested."

Tamara squeezed his hands together and said, "If there's really a test, perhaps it's nothing more than your willingness to accept a gift freely, without doubts. Without doubting what you really know."

"But I know so little."

"You know that I'm here, don't you?"

"Yes," he said. He looked at her strangely, then almost smiled. "It *is* you, isn't it?"

In answer, she ran her long fingernail over his scarred knuckles in the way she had often done before losing her memories. She laughed softly and said, "I think I'm almost the same as when we met in Bardo's sun room. I'm the same woman you gave the pearl to, in this house—do you remember?"

"Do I *remember*? Do you?"

"I remember everything, Danlo."

"Truly?"

"I remember that we promised to marry each other."

"I remember that, too."

At this, she pulled his hand closer and pressed it to her chest, over her heart. Beneath the softness of her robe, he felt something round and hard, almost like a nut. He remembered very well what this thing must be.

"Look," she said. "I still wear it, do you see?"

She stood up and slowly undid the buttons of her robe and let it fall to the floor. Between her naked breasts there dangled a single black pearl shaped like a teardrop. The pearl—of a soft sable color cut with streaks of purple and pink—made a fine contrast with the whiteness of her skin.

"I see," he said.

Tamara sat back down on her cushion. At the sight of her sudden nakedness, Danlo drew in a quick breath of air and felt a tightening in his belly. Because she like to be naked beneath her clothing, she wore no undergarments. The skin enfolding her body from her toes to her forehead was wholly bare, this marvelous covering of flesh whose smooth, ecstatic touch his fingers remembered so well. She was sitting back on her heels—a difficult posture for many but one that she held rather easily due to the strength of her long, naked thighs, her full hips, the long flowing muscles that stood out along her spine. Her hands were folded neatly over the thick golden hair below her belly, not out of any sort of modesty but simply because this was the most natural way for her to sit.

In truth, she was completely at ease with her nakedness. He remembered very well how she loved going naked about her house at all times of day or night. He had always thought that her instinct to bare herself to the world was one of her most beautiful qualities. With her head held high and her long hair falling like a curtain over her lovely shoulders, he was struck for the thousandth time by her unbelievable beauty. She seemed mysteriously untouched by the evils of her life, just as he remembered her. He gazed at her for a long time to hold in his eyes the fullness of her lips, the loveliness of her face. He remembered, then, how he had always loved looking at her. He had thought that he always would.

Only now, with the fire hot on her skin, with the distance of light-years between them, he was beginning to see her in a somewhat different light. She was still beautiful, of course, but her imperious nose suddenly seemed too perfectly sculpted, her eyes a shade too dark, her dazzling smile too full of passion and pride. There was something strange about her, he thought. There was some terrible strangeness in her soul that he could see but could not quite touch.

"It's beautiful," she said, putting her finger to the pearl. "I remember when you made this for me."

"In truth, it was the oyster who made the pearl, not I."

She smiled almost to herself, then ran her finger over the cord of the necklace, which was braided of many long black and red hairs twisted tightly together. "But it was you who found the pearl and made the necklace?"

"Yes."

"And gave it to me as a marriage troth?"

"We promised that we would marry each other. Someday, perhaps farwhen—whenever we could."

"When you had completed your quest, and I had completed mine," she said. "Do you remember?"

"I think it is impossible that I could ever forget."

"And I can't forget how I almost gave the pearl back to you," she said. "I'm sorry, Danlo. That was so wrong. Because in a way, we've been married since the instant we first saw each other."

"I know," Danlo said. "Since that moment—and perhaps even before."

Tamara laughed softly at his strange ideas and his romanticism, which seemed to please her greatly. And Danlo laughed, too, as they locked eyes and drank in each other's delight. Then Tamara rose off her cushion and came over to him. It took her almost forever to unzip his kamelaika, to slip her skilled hands between the fabric and his skin and peel the clothing away from him.

At the touch of her skin, there was a rising heat in Danlo's belly, and he remembered how long it had been since he last lay with a woman. There was a deep presssure in his loins, a surge of blood running up the root of his membrum to the inflamed tip. In truth, he was too full of seed, much too full of himself. Even if he hadn't been dying to die inside Tamara, it had never been his way to refuse the gift of sexual ecstasy when offered by such a beautiful woman, and so he pulled her gently down onto the cushions and kissed her mouth, her neck, the soft golden hair falling down across her breasts. In the way she returned his kisses—fiercely and almost desperately in the fervor of her lips—there was a hunger that had never been there before. There was something new in their love play, almost an awkwardness as if they had never entwined legs or felt the sweat of each other's body before.

Of course, sex was always new, always a plunge into mystery and danger, but not quite in this way. The newness he sensed in Tamara was not so much of touch or technique or even emotion, but rather of being, of the way that she dwelt inside herself. It almost seemed that she was trying to hold on to herself, in the moment, as a child might grasp a beloved doll. She pressed up close to him, and she grasped his long, swollen membrum. She touched the scars there, the tiny blue and red scars that had been cut into the skin during his passage into manhood. The play of her fingers over him was exquisite and almost exactly as he remembered on their first night together. And Tamara, in the heat of her hands and sweet panting breath, was almost the same, too, almost as if she had never suffered the loss of her memories. And this was strange because she *had* once forgotten him and everything about him; this wounding of her soul should have been as much a part of her as her joy in being restored to herself. But—although she had spoken to him in heartfelt words of great loss—in the fire of her blood and flowing muscles, in the voluptuousness of her body, she seemed to have no memory of suffering at all. He sensed that this willful return to innocence was somehow a betrayal of herself. Even as he kissed her lips and touched her between her legs, he sensed that he was betraying her, too—much as if he were a pilot journeying back in time to a younger and more innocent incarnation of herself.

He might have broken away from her, then. He might have caught his breath and stood up into the cool night air, away from the sweat-soaked cushions where they lay. But now, near the heat of the fire, Tamara was moaning and opening her legs, pulling at him. And now he was moaning too, or rather breathing so quickly that the wind escaped his chest in a deep-throated rush of pleasure and pain. He could no more keep himself from sinking down into her than could a stone cast into the sea. He felt her pulling at him, with her hands and her eyes and the fullness of her hips; he felt himself impossibly full with the heaviness of this blessed gravity.

And then he was falling, kissing her mouth and gripping her hand and reaching down with his loins toward the center of her body. As always, in joining with a woman, there was a moment of triumph. The thrill of entering her was intense and lasted almost forever. The anticipation of sliding deeply into her was almost more than he could bear. There was always the promise of new realms of ecstasy, of joining in a cosmic copulation that would leave him empty in the eyes and loins and mind, so utterly empty that only then could he become infinitely full of some deeper part of himself. So beautiful was the pain of this possibility that his whole being concentrated on a single moment of flesh pressing into flesh.

As always, the hot wet shock of her vulva around him electrified his muscles and caused him to gasp for breath and move deeper into her. Such pleasure seemed too perfect to be real, and yet in a way it was almost too real, for he felt the clutch and shudder of it in his hands and his throat and deep in his belly. In rippling waves the rising tide of pleasure spread through his whole body. He couldn't have stopped it if he had wanted to. In his joining with Tamara this way there was wildness and joy, yes, but also a terrible inevitability. It was as if a secret force had fired his nerve cells and seized his muscles. In truth, he was almost helpless before forces that he could not control. Outside, there was wind and ocean, the far-off roar of a tiger. And inside, inside the house, he felt the fire's heat licking at his skin, while beneath him the fierce power and purpose of Tamara's body pulled him ever deeper into sexual frenzy.

He felt himself moving to ancient rhythms, rocking with her and pressing up against her belly, rocking and moving and always moving to the inward roaring of his blood. If he had been able to think, he might have seen that there was something very strange in two people coming together this way to make such pleasure. For a man to lie with a woman in the naked clasp of her body was truly an exquisite madness. With her legs wide open Tamara rocked back and forth beneath him, always rocking and panting and pulling at his hips, wrapping her hands around him and pulling him into her. Danlo felt her fingers lock on to the tight bunching muscles behind his hips, and he felt a deep sense of wonder that any human being would so open herself to another. It was astonishing, too, that his deepest will would drive him in toward the opening of her womb, to enter that blessed place of all danger and desire. He gasped at the incredible audacity of pene-trating her, of disappearing into the soft, clutching darkness in-side her. He was ravishing her, yes, and yet as he moved to the convulsive rocking of her hips and felt her fingernails tearing lightly at his back, it was really she who ravished him. She enrap-tured him; she captured and engulfed him.

In a perfect merging between man and woman, these senses and fears should dissolve into an ecstatic liquid oneness, into rapture, into love. Indeed, much of the joy in swiving each other was in overcoming the ancient opposition and discord between the sexes, and thus allowing two seperate selves to become as one. It was the deepest of paradoxes that the self could find itself only in the other. Danlo, in his plunge into the salty rocking ocean inside Tamara, should have found himself in her, and so found the way to quench the terrible fire tearing him apart. In the sweat streaming down her face, in the sweet liquor of her loins, in her pulsing blood, he should have found the elixir to heal him of the wound that will not be healed.

This urge toward unity was very strong in him. He felt his heart's strong contractions in his chest urging him to move; he felt himself urging in his belly and his hips, urging him into her powerfully and deeply, always urging him toward life, on and on.

It did not matter that out of this urge and ecstatic union would come more life, more suffering, and inevitably, more wounding in separation when their child was born nine months hence and torn away from his mother in blood and pain. The great wheel of life would spin on and on—there was no help for a child's cry, no way to deny life's terrible urgency. And Danlo did not want to deny anything. In the heat of his passion, with his breath coming in hard, quick gasps and his loins trembling to be released of the terrible pressure inside, he was ready to accept all the sorrow and suffering in the universe if only he could die with Tamara into a single moment of screaming, shuddering ecstasy.

Many times before, on Neverness, lying before a blazing wood fire, they had found this blessed place together. Many times since then he had dreamed of kissing her neck as he moved in perfect rhythm with her. Only now, in the light of a different fire, even as she tore at this back and cried out in joy, he knew that on this night there would be no true merging. He knew there would be no oneness, no mystical union of their souls.

He was not, at first, aware of where this knowledge came from. But he had a deep sense of being engulfed against his will, utterly consumed by Tamara's fierce inner fire. He felt this burning all through himself. He felt it in her. He sensed that the temperature of her body was slightly too high, not as in the normal heating up of the flesh in the sexual yogas, but as in a fever. His body was the measure of hers, of her memory, of the true memory that lay deeper than her mind. Once they had joked that their lust for one another was so great that the very cells of his body loved the cells of hers. In his moment of orgasmic release there had always been a sense that his sex cells were returning home to a place of intimacy and utter love. All the cells of his body and hers: in the burning press of skin against skin, in the moisture of her lips, in her vulva's hot silky clasp, he touched her deeply, cell to cell. He licked her neck and tasted the sweat glistening there; it was as salty as blood, and strangely, almost bittersweet like the remembrancer's drug.

He smelled the lovely musky scent of her body, which was redolent with strange hormones and some other bewildering essence of her metabolism that he could not quite identify. In this way, he sensed something about her. Perhaps it was a matter of tender tissues pulling at each other, touching, the life inside their cells sending out signals across thin walls of flesh. Perhaps the nuclei of his cells were somehow open to secret messages encoded in hers. Somehow he sensed this deep cellular consciousness of streaming plasma, energy pulsing through mitochondria, and vibrating DNA.

She moved beneath him quickly, too quickly, and her whole body streamed with an intense consciousness of being. There was something wrong with her consciousness, he thought, something wrong with her soul. In the way she grasped at him with her burning hands, as if she were trying desperately to hold and keep her pleasure all to herself, she seemed intensely self-conscious as she had never been before. She seemed strangely alone with herself, watching herself. And watching him. Although her eyes were tightly closed, Danlo sensed that she was somehow watching him, even as he might study a butterfly delirious with a fireflower's sweet nectar. For a moment, as she screamed in ecstasy and tore at him with her fingers, he stared down at her lovely face. Even as he moved and moved to the quickening rhythm of her hips, he stared at her and something strange, vast, and terrible stared back at him. It looked deeply inside him, drinking in the light of his eyes, devouring the tissues of his soul.

And then he screamed, too, and they entered their moment together. Only there was no true togetherness, just two frantically rocking and thrusting human beings tearing a moment of feverish pleasure from each other's bodies. They cried out simultaneously, not as one voice but as two separate selves, alone with each other. They rocked and they rocked through an endless howling moment, and they writhed and they shuddered, and at last they collapsed in each other's arms, exhausted and completely spent.

Later, as they lay in silence before the dying fire, as Danlo watched the light of the flames reflecting from her sweat-streaked face, he remembered a saying that he had once been taught: *The surfaces outside glitter with intelligible lies; the depths inside blaze with the unintelligible truths.* He touched the scar on his pounding forehead, then. He rubbed the salt water from his burning eyes, and he marveled that the search for the truth could leave him so empty and saddened and utterly alone.

RECURRENCE

Simulations cannot become realizations.
    —Nils Ordando, founder of the Order of Cetics

Simulations must *not become realizations.*
    *—Horthy Hosthoh, founder of the Order of Mystic
Mathematicians and Other Seekers of the Ineffable Flame*

During the following days there were other ecstasy-making sessions in front of the fire, sometimes as many as five in one day (or night). Sometimes they would spend whole nights locked and sweating in the lotus position while Tamara lightly raked his eyelids and face with her fingernails and, like a tigress, bit softly at his neck. Despite the intensity of these dangerous pleasures— and despite a hundred other techniques for smashing the icy inner walls that separate two lovers—there never came the moment of breaking through into that golden realm of oneness and true bliss that Danlo had always cherished. And neither could they penetrate each other's deepest self with mere words. In the morning, they liked to sit by the window in the tearoom sipping coffee and talking as they watched the gulls fetch their meaty breakfasts from the ocean. They talked while taking their stroll at low tide along the beach, and in the fireroom before sleeping they talked in hushed and intimate tones. They talked endlessly and sincerely about everything from the Entity's capriciousness in keeping them prisoners on an unknown Earth to the universal nature of love; they opened their hearts to each other, or tried to, but in some mysterious way they were as strangers to each other.

In those dreadful moments of doubt, when Danlo was alone in the house or down by the ocean's lapping waves, he found that all his thoughts of her had come to involve conflicting images and paradoxes. She was still the most beautiful woman he had ever seen, but all too often her golden face fell dark and deep as space and was terrible to look upon; she loved him with the same burning passion as she always had, and yet sometimes when she touched him in her great need for love, her fingers were like icicles stabbing into his heart.

And then there was the deepest paradox of all. In some way that he could not yet apprehend, Tamara was truly herself, and yet she was not. *She is not she,* he thought. She was not quite the same Tamara that he remembered. Little things about her disturbed him. To begin with, there was the matter of her solitary, nocturnal walks along the beach. As they waited day after day for the Entity to speak to them again and reveal the nature of their respective tests, it became Tamara's habit to leave the house after midnight and wander the moonlit dunes by herself. On Neverness, of course, her profession had required her to make many journeys alone across the city's icy nighttime streets. Danlo knew that Tamara was as brave as any courtesan—as brave as anyone—and yet he had never suspected that she *liked* skating along the Serpentine where it narrows down in the darkest part of the Farsider's Quarter, where the wormrunners and other dangerous men (and sometimes aliens) wait in the shadows of the brothels and whistle at any woman who passes by.

Tamara, he was beginning to see, liked dangerous situations, not for the sake of danger itself, but rather for the sense of personal power that she gained in overcoming her natural fears of the world. Tamara, on Neverness's sometimes deadly slidderies and glissades, had always worn a little finger gun, a spikhaxo, that murderous weapon beloved of warrior-poets and other assassins. In fact, in another age, the warrior-poets and the Society of Courtesans had once been the closest of allies, and it was the warrior-poets who had taught women such as Tamara about ekkana and naittare and other secret poisons.

Like many of her sisters, when Tamara was out on an assignation, her spikhaxo was always loaded with several poison darts that she might fire into the flesh of any man so foolish as to think he might accost a beautiful courtesan and wrest a little grunting pleasure from her for free. And Tamara's darts were always impregnated with the black ink of naittare, a poison so poisonous that within seconds it would penetrate the blood-brain barrier and set off electrochemical storms in the cortex akin to an epileptic fit. Except that the chaos of the brain that naittare caused was worse than any epilepsy, for it always killed, almost instantly, a horrible, hideous death of popping eyes and foaming lips and limbs jerking to the whip of randomly firing nerves. The agony caused by this drug was said to be even worse than that of ek-kana, and for the victim, the dying lasted nearly forever.

Tamara's willingness to use naittare against men had never surprised Danlo because he understood the deterrent effect of such a poison; over the last thousand years only a few courtesans had ever fired a naittare-tipped dart at anyone, and these few instances were well remembered in the stories that the wormrun-ners told in the cafés and had caused even the most depraved criminals to treat the courtesans with respect. But, on the first night that Tamara walked alone by the ocean's edge, Danlo was astonished to see her loading these deadly, black darts into her spikhaxo. And Tamara was astonished at his astonishment. She cited the tigers that hunted the beach at dark as reason enough for such precautions; who knew better than Danlo, she asked, about the tigers who preyed on innocent lambs?

Danlo *did* know about tigers, of course, but he could not understand why Tamara didn't carry a sheshat or some other kind of tranquilizer dart that would instantly immobilize a large predator and render it unconscious but would not kill. After all, there was no deterring one tiger by causing the hissing, scream-ing death of another. And Tamara loved animals, especially cats, whom she regarded as the most graceful and beautiful of all animals. Danlo would have thought that Tamara would do almost anything to preserve an animal's blessed life.

Her response to Danlo's bewilderment was strange. As he watched her carefully slide a black sliver of death into the finger gun's chamber, her face fell lovely and ruthless in intense con-centration at the task at hand. When she was done, she pulled the black spikhaxo glove over her fingers, looked up at Danlo and said, almost jubilantly, "I've always loved your faithfulness to ahimsa, you know, but I've never quite been able to share it. If a tiger hunts me, should I be afraid of killing him? I've always dreaded being afraid. I've always dreaded killing *anything,* but there's always killing, isn't there? Oh, dear Danlo—sometimes it seems that life is nothing but killing and death."

In the fire of her dark brown eyes and the beautifully con-trolled passion of her voice, it almost seemed that she sought the chance to slay a tiger, to experience deeply the extreme peril of life. In a way, this was consistent with her purpose as both cour-tesan and woman. As long as she could remember, she had sought to live more deeply, more truly, and thus to awaken her-self to a new way of being. Unfortunately, her inborn temperament and love of life often worked against this goal. Tamara loved all the things of life, and she could never get enough of it, whether it be sex or food, music, drugs, wine or dance, conversation, maithuna, rock collecting or intellectual gourmandizing.

So keenly did she love the tastes, colors, sounds, and textures of the world that when she was younger, she had often found herself moving from one pleasure to another with all the restlessness and energy of a bee flitting among a field of wildflowers. It was her natural tendency to abandon any activity precisely at the moment when she began to feel tired or bored. Her meditation masters, appreciating her almost bodily hunger for excitement and ecstasy, had warned her that she possessed something of a "monkey mind," a talent for leaping agilely from one branch of experience to another—but never holding any one experience very tightly or very long. They meant this as no insult but rather as an appreciation of the strengths and weaknesses of her wonderful vitality.

Their criticisms, however, had devastated Tamara. From the very beginning of her novitiate as a courtesan, when she was a shy and nervous girl only twelve years old, she had vowed to overcome the flightiness of her mind. She found within herself immense desires for love and ever more life, and yet she found as well an immense will to control those very desires. All through her novice years and even into her time as a voluptuary, with a ferocious discipline that impressed the elder sisters of her Society, she cultivated for herself a new mind, a "dolphin mind" as she called it, a way of diving deeply beneath the waves of her life's experience in order to drink in the essence of whatever task or pleasure engaged her. Whether dancing or washing dishes or memorizing the formulas for the methyltryptamine series of poisons, she learned the art of concentration, the ecstasy of details. She learned to pay attention to things. And most of all, she learned to enter into any new experience with all her natural verve and zest coupled with a marvelously intense awareness of the world.

And so it shouldn't have surprised Danlo to see her strap the spikhaxo onto her lovely hand and step out beneath the full moon onto the beach, but nevertheless he was surprised. The logic of Tamara's life demanded that she experience everything possible as deeply as possible—but human beings are nowise consistent, and their lives are patchwork robes sewn together from various incongruities, whimsies, and passions. And compassion. The real Tamara, Danlo thought, the blessed woman whom he remembered so well, would fight like a fury to save her own life. She would fight a tiger—fight all the demons of hell—to protect those she loved. In truth, she could kill, *would* kill, at need, but she would never seek out fighting or killing for its own sake merely to know what it was like to kill. The real Tamara, he felt certain, in this one instance would hold illogic and compassion closely to herself as tightly as she had grasped his body at their first mating.

After much contemplation and discussion—and the delicate probing of the extreme facility with which Tamara recalled her past—Danlo decided that there must be something wrong with her memory after all. It was not that her memory was not good. In a way, it was much too good. At times, her memory of the moments they had shared was as clear and pure as glacier water, and it was this very purity of memory that disturbed him. For Tamara, unlike himself, had never possessed anything like a perfect memory, and even if she had, her clear recollection of their first meeting or their last all-night dance session bore none of the depth or murkiness or hidden currents of true memory. When he looked into her quick, dark eyes, he saw a vast distance between the things she remembered and her most intimate feelings for those things. She seemed to have all the memories that she should have had, but they somehow failed to connect her with her deepest self or with the most vital and beautiful moments of her life.

It was almost as if she wore her memory too lightly, as if it were nothing more than a glittering golden robe that she might remove at any time and replace with something more pleasing. But real memory, Danlo thought, was more like naked skin inextricably fused with the body, or rather, it was all deeper tissues and bone and nerves connecting every part of one's bodymind. He decided, then, that the Entity had healed her poorly, or at least incompletely. Perhaps it was part of his test that he discover this. Perhaps this strange goddess was testing the depths of his perception and compassion. But test or no, he must find a way to restore Tamara so that she was truly herself again. He had known this since the moment that he first learned her memories had been destroyed. Somehow he must help heal her—and if this was no part of the Entity's test of him, then it must be his test of himself, of his faith, of his prowess, of his ability to love unconditionally and completely despite the flawed nature of Tamara's soul.

One night, as they were sitting by a driftwood fire down on

the beach not far from Danlo's lightship, as Tamara stared into the dancing flames and held his hand beneath the thick red blanket that covered them, Danlo looked at her and asked, "Would you like to practice some of the remembrancing attitudes with me?"

Instantly, her hand tightened in his, the same convulsive squeezing of her finger muscles that would have triggered the spikhaxo glove to fire a dart if she hadn't taken it off before sitting with him. She turned to him in puzzlement. "It's been a long time, hasn't it? But why would you want to remembrance now?"

In the light of the fire, her eyes were dark liquid pools full of doubt and hurt. He thought that he should be careful of what he said. He thought that he should remind her of why she had once taken an interest in the remembrancer's art. Perhaps he should speak of the courtesans' dream of waking up the cells of the human body, of awakening the whole bodymind so that a new kind of human being might be born. In this way, he might ease her into the attitudes of gestalt and imaging and so trick her into remembrancing herself, and thus into healing herself. As he looked into her soft, trusting eyes, he saw that he easily might have accomplished this little deceit. But he could not bring himself to lie to her. His was the guile of guilelessness, and so after a long time of looking at her, he finally said, "Because it would be a way toward the union that we've always talked about."

"One soul," she said. "One soul in two separate bodies."

"Do you remember the night we first breathed each other's soul?"

She nodded her head and smiled. Once, on a brilliant night of snow and starlight after they had promised to marry each other, he had held his mouth over her nose and lips, breathing out while she breathed in. And then she had held her mouth over his. In this way, which was the way of Danlo's brothers and sisters among the Alaloi tribes, their spirits had passed into each other and interfused to become one. "I remember," she said. "But why should we seek backward in remembrance for this union?"

"Because we were . . . so close."

Tamara squeezed his hand more tightly. "I've never been as happy as I am now."

"I think you would remain here forever, if you could."

"In our house," she said. "With you, here, forever—I'd love that."

"Then you would never return to Neverness?"

"No, never," she said.

"Have you forgotten your calling, then? Once a time, you wanted to wake people up, their cells, their . . . souls. You wanted to wake up the whole universe."

At this, she laughed beautifully and looked down toward the ocean shimmering in the moonlight. She breathed in long breaths of salt air and listened to the pounding waves for a moment before saying, "That was before I came here. There's something about this Earth just as it is—it's already awakened, don't you see? And while I'm here, by the forest, by the water, I feel as awake as I've even been, perhaps as I ever could be. I don't care about the rest of the universe, Danlo. How should I care?"

Danlo looked down the beach where his lightship gleamed darkly beneath the stars. During the time since his planetfall, the wind had driven sheets of sand up against the diamond hull, half-burying it in a new dune that built a little higher every day. And every day, upon awakening at first light, he promised himself he would dig his ship free in preparation for the moment when the Entity permitted him to continue on his journey. But he always found other things with which to occupy himself, whether it be cooking elaborate meals with Tamara in her kitchen, or dancing with her in the meditation room, or joining on the floor of the fireroom to work their way through the many hundreds of positions of the sexual yogas. Sometimes his lack of mindfulness and his fading sense of duty alarmed him. Sometimes, on those bittersweet nights when Tamara fed him bloodfruit and tea and cried out in a strange voice during their love play, he forgot about his mission to the Vild, even forgot that the dying Vild stars were part of a greater universe whose boundaries were measureless to man.

"Sometimes," he said, "on this world, after I wake up in the morning and listen to the ocean, it is as if I am still sleeping. Sometimes I look at you, breathing, lying so peacefully next to me, and you seem so far away. And then I feel so strange. So . . . alone. I wonder if I could ever truly understand you."

"I just want you to be happy—is that so hard to understand?"

"But I am . . . almost happy."

"And sometimes when we're together, you're almost sad."

"Yes."

"Is that why you want to practice remembrancing together?"

"There was a moment," he said. "The moment when we first saw each other. That is where everything began. Your eyes, the light, the love, in that moment—it was as brilliant as the sun. Do you remember? I would recapture that moment, if I could."

Beneath their wool blanket, in front of the smoky fire, Tamara turned to face him. She looked at him for a moment, then said, simply, "I've always loved you. I always will."

"Tamara, love is—"

"Love is like the sun," she said quickly. "Like the sun, at first—it's all fire and brilliance."

Danlo looked up into the blue-black sky a moment before asking, "And then?"

"The sun that burns too brilliantly does not burn long. It explodes, you know. Or it consumes itself and dies."

"No, no," he said softly, "love can never—"

"A love that lasts is more like the sunset," she said. "Even as the brilliance fades, the colors deepen."

"But there must be a way to keep the brilliance," he said. "If you look deeply enough, inside the deepness, there is always fire, always light."

"Oh, Danlo, Danlo—if only that were true."

"It *is* true," he said. "Shall I show you?"

"You would take me into one of the remembrancing attitudes?"

He nodded his head as he looked at her face all warm and lovely in the light of the fire. "I would take us into recurrence—we could relive the moment that we first saw each other."

"Isn't it enough that we remember this moment?"

"But . . . to see each other, as we were. To *be* ourselves again, as we truly are—this is everything, yes? If we relive our first moment together, then we can begin truly to live again, to love again, all the moments of our lives."

"I'd love that, only . . ."

"Yes?"

"I'm afraid."

Yes, he thought as he caressed her fingers, she *was* afraid, he could see the dread (or awe) of some terrible thing flickering like fire across her face. He thought he understood the nature of her fear. Once before, out of a vain desire to preserve her memories, she had lost him—and lost as well everything most sacred to her. He thought he understood her secret, then. She, this beautiful woman who sat before him with love pouring out of her eyes like water, had an immense gift for love. But her attachment and identification with this primeval emotion was so great that she was always afraid of losing it. This was the secret of her soul, that despite the ecstasies and little affirmations of her life, it would all be meaningless without love.

"But there is nothing to fear," he said at last. "Truly, in remembrance, nothing is lost."

"Then why do I dread it so?"

"I do not know." He turned to gaze at the fire, and in the flash of the leaping flames a startling thought came to him: *She is afraid because she is not quite herself yet. Because there is always fear inside fear.*

"I dread it," she repeated. "And yet I think I long for remembrance, too. And that's so strange. Because if I already remember everything about us, what more is there to know?"

"But there is always more to memory," he said. "There are always memories inside memories."

She considered this for a while, and Danlo thought that she might be afraid of where her memories would lead her. She was afraid of something that he could not quite see, perhaps something dark and disturbing out of her past that was invisible to her as well.

"I used to love the remembrancing ceremonies, didn't I?" she said.

"Yes, you did."

"Do you think we could make a ceremony together, by ourselves?"

"I had hoped that we could."

"But we've no kalla, have we?"

Danlo smiled at her and said, "Kalla is just a drug. A key that opens the memories. But there are other keys, other ways."

"The ways that Thomas Rane taught you? The secret ways of the remembrancers that you always said you'd show me?"

"And I would have—but there was so little time."

"But now we've all the time in the world."

"Yes," he said. "Time. Time is one of the keys, dissolving time. I would like to take us back to the time we first met eyes. The moment. It was the moment when I fell in love with you."

She removed her hand from the blanket and touched his face. She touched his lips, his eyes, the scar cut into his forehead. She looked at him for a long time. And then she said, "If we remembrance together, if we actually relive this moment of falling, it might be different than you'd hoped. *I* might be different, you know. You might see me as I really was—or as I really am."

"And how are you, truly, then?"

"How could I know? How could anyone ever know?"

"But you will always be yourself, yes? You will always just be you."

"Perhaps, but—"

"And I will always love you," he said. "I always have."

"Oh, Danlo, Danlo—I hope that's true."

The following morning they began their preparations for a private remembrancing ceremony. Of course, they might have tried entering the attitudes immediately and without much formality, but they decided that this would be unwise. Tamara was none too eager to relive her life, and she knew that in remembrancing there was always danger. She knew that the remembrancers, over the millennia, had established many techniques and rules of order to minimize the dangers of delving deeply into the mind; since she was a great respecter of rules, she was quite willing to follow the remembrancing guidelines precisely and with great attention to detail. As for Danlo, although wildness was his wont and he was always ready for extreme states of consciousness and being, he understood that there was always a time for planning and taking exquisite pains with one's work.

In truth, he loved the work of readying himself for remembrance. And he loved rites and ceremonies of all sorts, especially those employing the time-honored technologies of the mind that over the millennia had lost none of their vitality and were often effective in guiding one straight toward the mystical heart of the universe. And so he willingly joined Tamara in the purification of her house. With damp rags he wiped the dust from the stones along her windowsill in the tearoom, and from the lacquered black tea table and from every other object or surface in each of the rooms. He helped Tamara scrub and polish the wooden floors so that they smelled of lemon wax and shone like mirrors. While Tamara went into the forest to gather wildflowers for the blue vase that stood in the meditation room, he set out the candelabra and burned incense, the marvelously pungent buddhi sticks that cleansed the air of positive ions, dirt, noxious chemicals, or any sort of gaseous pollution.

The cleansing of their minds began soon after this. With meditation they purged themselves of anger, fear, hatred, and sorrow—all the doubts and distractions that might keep them from remembrance. For most of three days they tried to hold this deep, quite, clear, meditative consciousness, and they did little other than stare at the burning candle that Tamara set out on the floor of her fireroom. They took little food or drink, they slept little, and they engaged in sexual passion not at all.

With Thomas Rane, on many snowy winter nights, Danlo had studied the more fundamental techniques for entering the remembrancing attitudes. There are sixty-four attitudes, from imaging to eidetics to syntaxis. Over five thousand years, the master remembrancers have devised many formulas for the sequencing of the exercises that prepare the mind for the attitudes. These ancient formulas can be hideously complex. Depending on the initial attitude to be entered and the final attitude desired, according to one's age, sex, personality type, and a hundred other variables, the remembrancer will work out a formula and strictly follow this preparatory program, changing exercises and initiating new ones as often as ten times in a single hour. This, the formalists say, is the soul of the remembrancers' art. However, a second school of remembrancers, known as the constructivists, were always trying to refine the traditional formulas and create (or construct) new ones. And then, of course, there were the radical remembrancers and revolutionaries, who wanted to junk the whole arcane and cumbersome system.

Only a few maverick remembrancers, such as the great Thomas Rane, had ever managed to break free from the ideologies of these schools. It was Thomas Rane's genius to respect the formalists and give them their due, even as he took the best of the constructivists' discoveries and used them with power and insight to go places that the radical remembrancers only dreamed of. It was Thomas Rane who had begun to articulate the mysterious sixty-fourth remembrancing attitude, or the "One Memory," the final attitude that would somehow complete all the others.

Thomas Rane conjectured that the remembrance of the Elder Eddas and the sixty-fourth attitude were really one and the same and had devoted his life to the exploration of this theory. He had sought the entrance to it wherever and however he could, and it was he who had taught Danlo the use of kalla and the more difficult remembrancing attitudes such as recurrence. Thomas Rane, while honoring the ancient formulas as keen insights into the workings of human memory, believed that each remembrancer must find for himself the ideal sequence of exercises to enter any particular attitude. This faith in the individual remembrancer's self-wisdom was his pride and his passion.

So it was that when Danlo prepared Tamara and himself to enter recurrence, he devised his own sequence of exercises. Over most of a day, he breathed with her, and he danced with her, and he played for her the long, deep notes of his shakuhachi—not rigidly according to some dry old formula, but rather moment by moment and paying close attention to the colors of her voice, the fire of her bottomless eyes, the rhythms of her brain and heart. He paid attention to himself. In this way, breathing and moving and inhaling the scent of each other's soul, together they entered deep into the marvelous sixty-first attitude that the remembrancers know as recurrence.

That is, they *almost* entered this attitude deeply. When their time came for remembrance, they sat on the meditation room's beautifully polished floor, which was so warm and smooth that it was like sitting on silk. Before them, on the round table, was a large blue vase overflowing with lovely, pink rhododendrons. Before them, too, arranged in their stand in four concentric rings, almost floating above the floor, there were thirty-three long white candles tipped with red-orange flames. And so before them, as the remembrancers say, there were flowers and fire, but behind them there was only memory. As above so below, inside and out, and it would be their task that night to take that which was behind them and place it before their eyes that they might see a single moment of time as it truly was, as it always would be.

After passing through the attitudes of sequencing and dereism, they entered into eidetics, where the shapes and colors of various remembered things are seen as clearly as a five-pointed eveningstar blossom held a foot in front of one's face. Eidetics is like a key unlocking the door of recurrence, and it opened Danlo to a moment in False Winter two years past when he had stood in a long room full of paintings, sulki grids, wineglasses, and bowls of steaming food. He saw himself eating from a plate piled high with golden kurmash grains while he regarded the beautifully dressed people all around him. Even as he sat on the floor of Tamara's meditation room with his eyes tightly closed, he stood at the far end of this glorious room so distant in space and time.

And then he was no longer watching himself gulp down huge mouthfuls of kurmash. He sensed a break in space, a snapping of time, a vastening of consciousness almost like a light being turned on in a dark room. His sense of himself sitting by Tamara and listening to her slow breathing dissolved utterly, and when he opened his eyes he could no longer see himself because he was suddenly inside himself, as if he had mysteriously incarnated once again into that wonderfully infolded matter behind the deep blue eyes of his younger self. He no longer saw himself regarding fat, old Zohra Bey and the beautiful Nirvelli; he saw these famous people directly, standing before him across a few feet of cool, clear air. It was as if he were truly seeing them for the first time. The intensity of his vision took his breath away. It occurred to him that he was looking upon this room with a much greater clarity and sense of reality than he had possessed two years before. That is the miracle of memory, that even though we stumble through our lives as sleepwalkers lost in a trance, a part of us remembers deeply and perfectly all that we do.

Once again he listened to Zohra Bey tell the young woman standing beside him of his famous journey to Scutarix (he was the first and only human ambassador to have survived a mission to that incomprehensible world), and Danlo saw him finger the hairy mole on his jowly old cheek. Danlo thought that he hadn't paid any mind to this rather one-sided conversation, but apparently he had. He had sensed many things around him that he was sensing truly only now. Before him, a few steps away, the cool and elegant Nirvelli stood surreptitiously watching Danlo through the curved glass of the wine goblet from which she was drinking. The earrings that she wore were wrought of Gilada pearls, perfectly spherical and priceless, and their perfect whiteness made a stunning contrast against her shimmering black skin.

There were sounds all around him: sizzling meats and clicking chopsticks and a waterfall of laughter and bright, bubbling human voices. He noticed that Zohra Bey, for all his ugliness, had a wonderfully mellifluous voice—though in truth, it was really much too sweet, like honey mulled in a fine old wine. And the kernels of kurmash that he crunched between his teeth were really much too hot, seasoned as they were with the flame peppers grown on Summerworld. He sensed other flavors in this marvelous dish, especially the faint zest of quelqueche, which was his first taste of this rare and expensive alien spice.

At that moment, with his eyes watering and the tissues of his mouth on fire, he felt that he could sense everything about everyone in the room, perhaps everything in the universe. Next to him, almost behind him, a vacant-eyed wormrunner was grasping one of the room's many sense-boxes. Danlo suddenly felt moist, hot lips pressing against his face, the coolness of silk in his hands. And this was strange because he knew that he held a plate of kurmash in his hands and his lips were touching only air. Once, this sensory pollution leaking out of the wormrunner's little black box had been almost below his threshold of awareness, but now he was aware of it all too keenly.

And then he looked across the room past all the brilliant men and women, past great pilots such as Radmilla Diaz and the Sonderval, and he knew what it was to be truly aware. A moment earlier he had almost heard the thunder of the dying stars out beyond Farfara and Perdido Luz, but now, for him, the entire universe had narrowed to a single woman standing tall and grace-ful in a sea of faceless people. He had seen Tamara Ten Ashto-reth ten thousand times, in meetings and memories and dreams; and yet he was all too aware that he had never truly seen her before. It was as if a flash of lightning had illuminated her hands, her dark eyes, her lovely face—perhaps even her very soul. She burned with an earthly beauty, and she was nothing but fire and light. Inside her where her heart beat, she was full of animajii, the wild joy of life which she could barely contain. He marveled at her incredible strength and will to life. He felt this primeval hunger of hers like a fire burning in his own belly. Tamara, he sensed, would always hold onto life more fiercely than a tiger gripping a struggling lamb, and yet she inhabited life gently, deeply, as naturally as a fern growing in the forest. And life inhabited her fully, consuming every part of her. She was over-flowing with vital energies like a star bursting with light. It was this rare and splendid vitality of hers that pulled at his heart and fired all the nerve cells of his body. As with her, so with him, he felt himself burning with animajii, too, burning as brightly as any star.

It was the moment in his life when he first became aware of how limitless the possibilities of life might be. And for the first time, he became aware of how very aware other people were of him; he could see it in their faces, in the way they lifted their eyes toward him as if stealing cautious glances at the sun when they thought that his attention was elsewhere. They looked at Tamara this way as well. The two of them were like double stars whose radiance filled the room. Like stars they were full of terri-ble beauty and immense gravities, and it was inevitable that their souls should pull at each other and cause them to seek each other out. There was a moment when she began to look at him across a mere fifty feet of space. It was a moment of blazing awareness almost too brilliant to bear.

Deep in remembrance, in the eternal light of recurrence, he saw something that he had once seen at the very beginning of his love for Tamara—but never allowed himself truly to see: in the moment that they had first touched eyes, he had known that their love for each other would cause them the greatest of suffering. There was torment and death deep inside Tamara's eyes, perhaps inside his own. But in his sudden rushing sense of immortality, in the wild passion of his youth, even as he began to fall, he was ready to endure all the fires of hell for a single moment of love. Love is blind, not innocently and lightlessly blind like a babe floating inside his mother's womb, but intentionally blind, willfully, like a scryer who puts out his own eyes.

All this Danlo saw at last, even as he foresaw that someday all their agony and suffering would be redeemed by love, by life. And seeing this, he almost beheld the true Tamara, she of the terrible beauty, whose purpose was love and beauty, and something more: love inside love, beauty born of ever deeper beauty. But he could not behold her, not yet; he could not quite hold onto the beautiful memories that lived inside him. Now, in this long lovely room that exited only in remembrance, they were beginning to meet each other's eyes again for the first time. This should have been a moment of love, of light, of secret understanding. As she turned her head to look at him, he could almost see the little black circle at the center of her eye that would let in the light of his soul. Only now, as they began their endless and terrifying fall into love, a simple smell destroyed the moment.

In truth, it was not a simple smell at all, but rather the hormones, esters, sweat, sweet amino acids, the essence of tangerines—the essence of Tamara's scent that some part of him had been aware of before he had even seen her. These were the molecues of memory floating in the air, waiting, the hundred different fragrances that a deep part of his brain assembled into a kind of scent-mosaic of Tamara. He had always been keyed into the nuances and subtle colors of this extraordinary scent. And now one color had grown much too strong, much too bright, and he smelled the steely red acridness of sweat and fear. Now this smell was like a red-hot knife being driven up his nostril into his brain. For the ten thousandth time, he opened his eyes. But he was no longer in a faraway room on Neverness two years past, but rather in Tamara's clean meditation room all warm and bright with the burning candles.

He had finally fallen, yes, but not into love. He had fallen out of recurrence. In truth, he had fallen out of remembrance altogether, and so had Tamara. She sat across from him with her eyes wide open, looking at him. Her forehead was beaded with sweat, and her moist neck glistened in the candlelight. She looked long and deeply at him, not in love but in failure and fear. It was as if she had almost seen some deep part of him that she desperately wanted to see, but, like a thallow chick unready to fly away from her nest high in the mountains, had turned away from this terrifying abyss at the last moment. As if she had turned away from herself.

"I'm sorry, Danlo."

"Do not speak. Not yet."

Tamara looked at the blazing candles and wiped the sweat from her face. Softly she said, "I'm sorry, I'm sorry."

"Shhh, be quiet. There might still be a way for us to return."

"But I don't want to return. I can't."

"But we were so close," he said.

"No, no—please."

From Danlo's first night of drinking kalla, he knew that there are always things that a person will not willingly remember. Tamara, he thought, in her plunge into the dangerous waters of remembrance, had finally entered the stage where she couldn't help fleeing herself. All men and women will find in remembrance, somewhere in themselves, some dark and dreadful thing that they must flee from or die—or so it seems. But Tamara was still liminal, still on the threshold of remembrance, though he didn't think that she had achieved full recurrence, as had he. Danlo could see this in her dark, disturbed eyes. A simple word from him or a few moments of silence might move her back into herself, gently back into the current of memories that flowed beneath her surface fears. He could not, however, take her or force her where she would not go. This is the first and last rule for anyone who would guide another into remembrance. Not even Thomas Rane would dare force anyone through the shadows and the writhing worms of memory down to that place of blackness and unknown possibilities where the truly terrible things dwelled.

"It is all right," he said. He moved over across the floor so that he sat behind her, holding her. "It is all . . . all right."

She was quiet for a while as she leaned back into his arms, back against his chest as it rose and fell. Her head was pressed back against his lips, and he smelled the lovely thick fragrance of her hair as well as the bitter sweat that ran down her neck. Then she broke away from him. She stood up and went over to the candles. One by one, with a graceful but incredibly quick pinching motion of her fingers which she had moistened in her mouth, she snuffed them out. Thirty-three times Danlo heard the hiss of water vaporizing, and there came the sickening smell of incompletely burned wax. Soon the room was full of darkness; its only illumination was the starlight streaming in through the windows. In this faint, cold light, Danlo watched Tamara move over to the

vase of rhododendrons. She grasped the stem of the smallest
flower, which she quickly broke off. She took his hand and
pressed this beautiful flower against his fingers. And then she
said, "I'm sorry. I'm so sorry—we *were* very close, you know."

Later that night, as they were sleeping on the soft furs of the
fireroom, Tamara's dreams began. Danlo came awake to the rest-
less turning of Tamara's body next to him; he lay in the darkness
stroking her silky hair and listening to her heavy, uneven breathing. And then she began to whimper and murmur strange words
that he could not understand. As she cried out in her nightmare,
he held his fingers lightly over her lips lest her spirit escape into
the room and wander the world in darkness and confusion and
thus become so hopelessly lost it might never return. He felt her
hot breath against his fingertips, and he bent over her to kiss her
fevered head. And then he whispered, "Shhh, *mi alasharia la,
shantih, shantih.* Go to sleep now, my woman, go to sleep."

But she did not go to sleep, or rather, she did not descend into
the cool, deep, healing embrace of dreamless sleep, which according to the Alaloi way of thinking (and that of the cetics, too),
is the one and only true sleep that a human being can know. She
dreamed vivid, shaking, sweat-streaked dreams; sometime
toward morning she came awake screaming out of one of her
dreams, screaming and gasping and clutching at Danlo as she
held her head against his chest and sobbed. When she could talk,
in a quavering voice, she told him of her dream, of how she had
fought a murderous, slashing knife fight with a man who had no
eyes. She had killed this man, she said. Beneath a sky with three
red moons as full and round as drops of blood, she had stabbed
her killing knife into this terrible eyeless man, and then she had
cut his heart out of his chest.

"It was so *real,*" she said. They were sitting up on the furs,
now, and Danlo was holding her hands. Her eyes were full of
tears, and she said, "I've never had a dream that was so real."

Danlo listened to her talk about her dream, paying particular
attention as she described her feelings of terror and exaltation at
having to fight beneath these three ominous moons. From her
description of the moons' configuration—they loomed low in the
sky and their centers formed an equilateral triangle—he surmised
that she had dreamed of the infamous red moons of Qallar. And
this was strange, because, as she admitted when he told her
of this, she had never seen a foto of Qallar, nor had she known
that this deadly planet was even graced with moons.

"It was as if I weren't really dreaming at all," she said. "Just after I'd . . . after I'd killed this man, I looked up at the moons. I could almost *feel* them pulling at me, the gravity. I could feel the blood on the knife. The wetness. The heat of it—it was really quite horrible, you know. Oh, the whole dream. It was as if I were awake inside my dream, as if I were living this horrible murder moment by moment as it happened and I couldn't wake up because I wasn't asleep, I wasn't dreaming at all. In a way, it as if I were reliving it all again, over and over. I'm not really sure how that's possible. But it was so real, too real—too real *not* to be real, and that's what frightens me because when I squeeze my hands together, I can still feel the heart there all bloody and slippery. And alive—it was still beating when I held his heart in my hands, and I can't forget that Danlo, I'll never forget.''

For a long time she stared into Danlo's eyes, all the while squeezing his hands between her hands as if to reassure herself that she was now truly awake and that he was as real as the hard wooden tiles beside the furs on which they sat. And then Danlo said, ''You know about the sixtieth attitude, yes?''

''I'm not sure.''

''The remembrancers call it dreaming recurrence. It is one of the recurrence attitudes. Like the sixty-first attitude, it is reliving one's memories—only while dreaming instead of being awake. It is possible that you have only descended from waking recurrence into this attitude.''

''But if I was only dreaming,'' she said, ''then what I dreamed wasn't real.''

She looked at him hopefully, searching in his eyes the way someone lost at sea might search the sky for a familiar star. When he saw how full of fear she was, he was almost afraid, too.

''No,'' he said softly. ''No, sometimes dreams are real. Sometimes we dream our memories. And in the attitude of dreaming recurrence, our memories are so real that it seems we are living them again. In a way, we *are* living again. Ourselves. Our . . . lives. There is no time. Truly, no time—what was real *is* real. It always will be.''

Tamara thought about this, then said, ''But I've never been to Qallar. I've never killed anyone—I know I haven't. I *know*. How could this be anything more than a dream? How could this be a real memory?''

''I do not know.''

''Oh, Danlo—it can't be a memory, can it? *Whose* memory? Not mine, please, say you don't think it could possibly be mine?''

But Danlo couldn't say that because it would be untrue. Neither, however, could he quite understand how she had remembered such a thing. For the count of a hundred of his heartbeats he sat holding her hand and stroking her hair. He listened to the ever-present sound of the ocean beating against the beach outside. And then, for the ten thousandth time, he thought: *She is not she*. Over many days he had repeated this phrase in his mind almost as he would a mantra. *She is not she, she is not she*—the sound of these words rose and fell inside him like waves beating through his consciousness. He knew that in these four simple words there was a deep truth. He had known this from the moment that he had first thought them. Only now, watching her as she sat weeping over her terrible dream, he sensed that this terrible thought might be literally true, that she was really *not* she in a way beyond mere metaphor, beyond even the metaphysics of selfness and identity.

She is not Tamara—this thought was like lightning in his brain, and the pain of it was all the greater for his knowing that he had known this all along. For too long his eyes had known this, and his hands, and even the rhythms of his heart. He touched her hair, then. He touched the tears running down her face. He sensed that her flesh was not Tamara's, and neither were her memories or her soul. But if this were true, then who was she? Where had she come from? What was the soul of this strange woman who sat grasping at his arm and looking to him for an answer to the mystery of her life?

She is who she is, he thought. *But she is not a human being, not truly.*

In truth, she was something other than human, something less, perhaps something more—and although this conclusion was hateful to him (and astonishing), logic had led him to believe this as surely as the track of blood upon the snow might lead a hunter to a wounded animal. Danlo had been born with a keenly logical mind, and he loved logic even when he loathed the ways that others sometimes misused this dangerous tool.

"You use a razor to shave with," his Fravashi teacher had once said. "But to smell the essence of a fireflower, it is better that you should use your nose."

Logic was the keenest of the mind's razors, but it could cut at only what the intuition and senses knew to be true. And what did he really know? This Tamara was *not* the same woman he had loved on Neverness, and therefore she was something other. What was she? He did not think that she could be a slel-mime, for if someone such as a warrior-poet had used programed viruses to destroy and replace her brain cells with neurologic circuitry, then surely her memories and sense of herself would be very different from the real Tamara's. If her brain had been truly carked this way, then surely she would have betrayed the robot-like behavior that is the hallmark of this hideous transformation of human being into computer.

Similarly, he thought it impossible that she could be a slel-clone. If someone had slelled her DNA in secret and used this sacred matter to grow a clone resembling the real Tamara, then surely her mind would have been programed for some hideous purpose, as the minds of slel-clones always are. In all his time with her, he had sensed no such purpose or programing. Then, too, a slelled clone would bear the same DNA as did Tamara. The cells of her body would be the same. And they were not the same—whenever he touched her, the cells of *his* body sensed a subtle but vital difference between this woman and the real Tamara, and he trusted the truth of this intuition. For an otherwise rational being such as Danlo to make such an affirmation was quite bold, but it was the time in his life when he was coming into his truth sense, that marvelous faculty of knowing that lies latent inside all women and men much as a shih tree waits to break open from an acorn.

She has been slelled, but not from matter—not from DNA. She has been slelled from my mind.

It was possible that in the forty days that Danlo had waited for his last test to begin, the Entity had created a woman who looked like Tamara. It was surely within Her powers to imprint this Tamara's brain with the various emotions, habits, motor functions, and bits of knowledge that would enable her to function as a mime of human being. Even the warrior-poets and other modern engineers could make this kind of human being—if one considers such soulless creatures human. But the Entity had done something much more than this. She had done something that no modern engineer—or even the god-men of Agathange—could do.

From almost nothing She had created a mind that was almost human. To accomplish this feat of godly carking, She must have imprinted Tamara's brain—not according to some information hologram or computer map of the real Tamara, but almost solely from Danlo's memories. Danlo had a marvelous memory of Tamara's experiences, sensibilities, mannerisms, dreams, and a billion other things about her life—even her pronunciation of certain favorite words, the way she drew out the vowels as if she delighted in prolonging the utterance of these words as long as possible. And the Entity must have known all this.

She is almost she, Danlo thought. *And I have almost remembered her.*

Some time toward morning, after Tamara had finally fallen into a true sleep, Danlo lay awake next to her watching her breasts rise and fall like swelling waves upon the sea. He counted her breaths while he wondered at this beautiful woman whom the Entity had made. It occurred to him that the mind of a woman or a man was infinitely more complex than the dark world that spun silently beneath him, pulling at him with such crushing gravity. The human brain-mind, with its shimmering webwork of a hundred billion neurons and trillions of interconnecting synaptic pathways, was among the most complex creations in the universe—in some ways more complex than even the neurologic components that make up the brains of the galaxy's gods.

He did not think it was possible, even for a goddess, to duplicate perfectly such a blessed creation. Certainly any attempt to mime Tamara as the Entity must have done was doomed to fail. In the harsh light of the new day he could see this, as clearly as he could see salty tear tracks marking Tamara's cheeks. The problem was with his memory. No matter how exactly he called to mind every aspect of Tamara's selfness and soul, the real Tamara, the one and only true Tamara, was much more than he remembered—possibly more than he *could* remember. Once, after Hanuman had destroyed (or stolen) Tamara's memories of their life together, Danlo had offered to imprint her brain from his own memories. He had hoped to heal her memory, thus healing her mind. Out of love and despair he had made this hopeless proposal, never realizing what a terrible thing he was doing.

But now, watching Tamara's breath ruffle the shagshay fur pulled up beneath her chin, he knew. Even supposing that Tamara was a perfect incarnation of his memory of her—and she was not—he realized that his memory was far from perfect. From their first moment together, he had seen her not through the flawless lens of deep reality, but rather as through a million broken bits of glass stained with all the colors of his consciousness. As he looked at Tamara and brushed the golden hair away from her face, he thought of a saying of Thomas Rane's: *We do not remember things as they were; we remember them as we were.*

This Tamara remembered their life together in too much the

same way as he did—he had been blind not to see this earlier. What was wrong with this lovely woman who lay sleeping beside him was that she was too much a reflection of himself, of his own mind. And what he had truly loved about the real Tamara was her otherness, that unknowable essence of her soul that he had sometimes glimpsed but had never quite managed to capture in his memory. Ironically, he had remembered almost everything about her except the only true and important thing, and he realized that he could never quite grasp this mystery any more than he could keep a beautiful bird trapped in his hands without destroying it.

"Oh, Tamara, Tamara," he whispered as he touched her warm, red lips, "where are you? What are you, truly?"

Over the next set of days and nights, Tamara's dreams grew ever more terrifying and strange. There were cosmic dreams unlike anything she had ever experienced before. Once, she dreamed that her body was nothing more than a ball of molten nickel-iron, spinning in space, pulsing in red waves through utter emptiness like an abandoned heart; once she dreamed that her brain was so full of fiery images and agony that it exploded in an expanding sphere of light and death, thus becoming the first of the Vild's supernovas. And there were the more personal and disturbing dreams where she relived the eating of unfamiliar meats and foods, and heard again alien blood musics that she was certain she had never heard before.

She dreamed of men whom she had never seen, hard and beautiful men with violet eyes and quick, sensitive muscles that jumped like electric eels at the slightest stimulation or touch. These murderous men were thought to be smooth between the legs, but she knew that they were not, for once, on a night of strange hot winds and fire wine, she had seduced a young man named Leander and lay with him beneath the three red moons hanging low in the sky. It had been her first time with a man, and nearly the last, for when three of Leander's cell brothers found them together on the grass, they cursed him for breaking his vows and cut him to pieces with their long, killing knives. They would have killed her too, but she was good with her knife, so good that she blinded one of the brothers with a lightning slash to the eyes and disabled the other two before escaping through the towering black thorn trees that surrounded her and tore open her flesh. There was blood streaming from her breasts like red milk, and blood in her eyes, and blood burning its way up between her legs into her womb.

In all her dreams there was blood, especially in her worst

dream, which occurred again and again, sometimes as often as thrice in one night. In this dream, a terrible orange energy ran through her body and brain and twisted her sinews, her nerves, her bones, carking her into the form of a beautiful tiger; dreaming this flaming image of herself, she could always feel her fingernails growing out as long, killing claws, the trembling of her muscles along her belly, the burning hunger to kill that was all torment and desire and was concentrated into a gnawing pain between her shoulder blades. Once, she woke up out of this dream with blood in her mouth and on her lips; she came into consciousness writhing and screaming and biting at her tongue—and clawing at Danlo's face when he came up close and tried to hold her. And then, when she saw that she had scratched open a bloody red gash on his cheek, she wept for a long time, pressing her forehead against Danlo's forehead with such desperation that he wanted to weep, too. After she had stopped weeping—with her tears stinging like sea salt in the little wound that she had made on his face—he looked at her and said, "It will be all right."

"No, no," she said. "I'm afraid to go to sleep at night. And I'm even more afraid of waking up insane."

"You are not insane."

"Sometimes, it's almost as if I don't know who I am."

"You are you," he said simply. "You are . . . who you are."

"Sometimes when I look at myself in the mirror, when I look for myself, there's nothing there. What's happening to me? Oh, Danlo, Danlo—what will I do?"

Danlo took her down to the ocean, then. In the shallows at the edge of the beach, he saw to it that she washed the blood from her mouth and hands. He himself laved handfuls of dark, saltwater over his cut face. The water was as cold as ice but it burned his flesh like fire. They stood on the hardpack for a long time, shivering and watching the waves come and go. It was a day of gray clouds and a mist so fine that it floated down from the sky like an endless silken robe. Looking out through the early morning mist, Danlo could barely see the shape of Cathedral Rock where it loomed all black and menacing somewhere before him. Somewhere, in this soft and impenetrable mist, there were gulls and other birds, for Danlo heard them crying out as if blinded and lost at sea. Tamara, too, was still crying, not obviously in a spasm of voice and breath, but rather in the deeps of her dark, liquid eyes. She was crying for herself, he thought; as all people do, she was crying for what she might have been, for what she someday still might be.

After a while, she said, "Sometimes, when I've stopped sleeping in the morning, I feel as if I've died and my waking life is only a dream. Sometimes I wake up, and I'm afraid I'm only awakening to a new phase of the dream, waking up *inside* the dream, over and over, this hideous, endless awakening. Sometimes I'm afraid there's no way out."

Danlo picked up a flat stone half-buried in the sand and cast it into the ocean. It made a satisfying *plop* and disappeared into the dark water. "There is always a way out," he said. "Or a way . . . farther in."

"Oh, Danlo—I can't live this way."

Danlo looked for his lightship down the beach, but the mist was so dense and gray that he could not see it. "If you would like, I could ready my ship for a journey. We could try to leave this world—I could take you back to Neverness."

"No, I'll never leave this world. I *can't,* don't you see?"

With a snap of his arm, he cast another stone into the water. It skipped three times over the dull, smooth surface before sinking beneath a wave. He looked at her and said, "I . . . do see."

"I can't live anywhere else, not like this," she said. "I feel as if I'm dying."

"No," he said softly. "It is just the opposite."

"Sometimes, after one of the dreams, I feel as if I *want* to die." At this, she looked out at the cold water where he had cast his stones. "Sometimes I want to walk out into the ocean and drown. If I can't live as I have, with love, with joy—why should I live at all?"

"Because," he said simply, "life is everything."

"Once, I thought that too," she said. "Once I wanted to taste every food grown on every world from Solsken to Farfara. I wanted to *see* every world in the universe, if I could live long enough. I wanted to go to Kateken and see the singing caves, and to Agathange. I wanted to love every beautiful man I could. I've always loved love, and I've really lived for nothing else, but how can I love at all when all I want to do is fall down screaming and die?"

Danlo moved closer to her and touched the tiny water droplets clinging to the downy hairs along her cheek. "Please . . . live."

"But I'm not really living, not like this."

"Then live as you will."

"How?"

"Only you will know," he said. "But there might be a way, in remembrance."

"Oh, no—please, no."

"I am sorry," he said. "This will be hard for you."

"You can't really know."

"You have often said that you feel incomplete, that you always are on the verge of discovering some great thing about yourself."

"That's the theme of all my dreams. That's the sense I have, you know."

"I believe that it might help to relive your birth."

"My birth? But why?"

"Because that is where everything began. That is where the secret of your life must lie."

"You sound so sure."

"I am not sure. In remembrance there are never any certainties."

She took hold of his hand and dug her fingernails into the hard calluses that she found there. "I was born in my mother's house—don't you remember? You'd take me back to *that*? I don't know if I could bear to ever see that house again—and I think it would kill me to see my mother."

"I would take you back to the moment of your birth," he said evasively. For a while he watched her shivering in the cold mist. Although he sensed that this birth would destroy this Tamara that he loved, he did not hesitate to propose a second ceremony of remembrance. "I will help you find the way."

"I'm so afraid."

"I will not let you die."

She was quiet for a moment as she looked into his grave, dark eyes. And then she said, "Oh, Danlo—I'm afraid for you, too."

Danlo smiled at her, but said nothing. He listened to the moaning of the whales far out at sea, and he did not tell her that he was afraid for both of them, and for all things that had ever suffered the pain of being born.

SHE

*If you bring forth what is within you, what you bring
forth will save you. If you do not bring forth what is
inside you, what you do not bring forth will destroy you.*
      —*Jesus the Kristoman, from the Gospel of Thomas*

As before, they prepared for remembrance. They brought fresh
flowers into the house and spent several days doing the exercises
that Danlo designed. This time, it was only Tamara who would
relive a part of her life, and so Danlo would be free to guide her
backward through the stages of her ontogenesis from fertilized
ovum to adult human being. Therefore, he selected a different
sequence of exercises than before. He saw to it that she executed
these exercises perfectly. On the evening of her remembrance, he
lit the thirty-three candles and sat with her on the floor of the
fireroom. He looked about them to make sure that he had left
nothing undone. Before them, the rhododendrons were perfectly
arrayed in their blue vase. The wooden beams gleamed with
golden light, and good smells floated all around them: orange
essence and charcoal, warm skin and salt air and silk. It was with
a smell, or rather a taste, that Danlo initiated Tamara's return to
the 61st attitude of recurrence. After guiding her through many
rounds of difficult breathing exercises, he reached into the pocket
of his kamelaika and removed a blue vial filled with plain seawater. He opened the vial and held it up to Tamara's lips. "Drink
this," he said. "Taste the ocean inside; this is what it was like
before you were born."

And so Tamara drank a few drams of water that Danlo had
scooped up earlier from the ocean outside their house, and Danlo
told her that it was time to begin recalling the first conscious
memory of her life, which they had previously discussed in
great detail. Strangely, this memory also involved seawater. In

Tamara's earliest conscious memory, when she was perhaps four years old, she was sitting alone in the kitchen of her mother's house. It was a huge kitchen of stone and steel and other hard things, but it was always warm, always full of the smells of mint tea, honey, spices, kurmash, and roasting bread.

On this snowy winter day, late in the afternoon, Tamara sat on the marble floor playing with jars of water. To her right was a clear jar of distilled water that her mother used in the rather forbidding cleansing ceremonies performed in the facing room deeper in the house. On her left was a blue jar half full of seawater imported from Sahasrara. When Tamara's mother cooked her huge, steaming potfuls of kurmash on feast days, she always added a little of this rare water to enliven the dish and impart the flavor of her family's home world. But on this unforgettable day out of Tamara's memory, Tamara was using the water for a different purpose. It was the day when she had first understood death. As a lively and imaginative child, she had always been terrified of dying, sometimes too terrified to sleep at night, and she had always wondered where she would go when light went out of her eyes and the readers of her church took her body away to be burned at the end of the incomprehensible ceremony of vastening. The idea of simply disappearing like the light of an extinguished candle, of never being again—this utter annihilation and neverness of her life was as inconceivable to her as it was terrifying. Most of all, she couldn't bear the possibility of her love for her mother simply vanishing, for this love was her life, and to be separated forever from her was too terrible to contemplate.

So intense was this love that she didn't realize how much she hated her mother, too, not even when the imperious Victoria One Ashtoreth stormed into the kitchen and caught Tamara playing with her precious water. Tamara, with her little but clever hands, had just succeeded in pouring a quantity of the saltwater into the clear jar. She was sipping from this marvelous mixture when her mother saw what she was doing and gasped in astonishment and betrayal. She spoke no words of rebuke; neither did she strike Tamara as any other astrier mother would have done. She only looked at Tamara with her blazing, scornful eyes, and this single look was enough to tear open Tamara's heart.

And so she was never able to tell her mother of her brilliant discovery. She never explained that when saltwater was poured into the clear jar, it vanished from sight, yes, but the taste of salt spread out and pervaded the distilled water and would never go away. As with salt and water, so with life, and Tamara wanted desperately to tell her mother that although her life's consciousness might someday flow out of herself back into the world, it could never be destroyed. But the practical Victoria One Ashtoreth was not interested in the metaphors or metaphysics of a four-year-old. In a clear and cold voice, she bade Tamara clean up her mess. She told Tamara that it was time that she was taught cooking so that she might learn to be careful with valuable things.

Thereafter, on each feast day when Tamara sat at table with her father and her twelve sisters and brothers, as punishment for her transgression, her mother never failed to thank her for helping to prepare the sacred kurmash that they ate. And with each bite of the faintly salted kurmash that her mother placed in her wide and beautiful mouth, Tamara thought of how she had carefully measured the saltwater into the huge steel pot in which their family's kurmash was always cooked. With each swallow of food that Victoria took, Tamara imagined that her mother was consuming Tamara's love for her, for despite the anger between them, she never stopped loving her mother, and she always prepared the kurmash with infinite care. It was her secret hope that her infinite love would somehow infuse her mother and transform her into a kinder and wiser woman. But it never did. Her mother remained a parsimonious taskmaster who demanded strict adherence to recipes, and Tamara was never able to add enough salt water to the kurmash to flavor it fully.

And she was never able to talk with her mother about love or death or any of life's other mysteries. It was only years later that her mother finally explained that when a worthy astrier was on her deathbed, her mind was encoded as a program and stored within the electron flows of their church's vastening computers. The human mind, her mother said, was a kind of program that could be preserved almost forever this way. Therefore Tamara must continually cleanse herself of evil thoughts and negative programs lest she be found unworthy of this cybernetic heaven and the church elders denied her the grace of vastening. She must continually strive for perfection in her life, her mother told her, or at the end of her life she would have no more life, never again—only blackness, nothingness, neverness.

But Tamara remembered very well the day she had clanked jars and spilled saltwater on the floor of her mother's kitchen. After this, she never trusted anything her mother said, nor did she ever accept any of the doctrines of her church. Somewhere inside her was a deep knowledge that she could never die, even when her heart was pounding inside her chest and she was close to dying—even when she was terrified of death.

"Oh, Danlo, Danlo!" Suddenly, she cried out these three words as she lay on the floor of her meditation room. Her fists were clenched, and her whole body trembled as with terrible cold. Her eyes were tightly closed as she whispered, "No, no—I can't!"

"Shhh, be quiet now," Danlo said. He sat beside her massaging her temples, touching her eyelids. "Just . . . remember."

Gradually, the tremors tearing through Tamara's body subsided. She fell still and utterly silent as she descended down through memories that Danlo could only guess at. Except for her slow, deep breathing, she might have been dead. Once, for a few moments, her breathing stopped altogether, and then despite himself, Danlo began to worry. He placed his hand between her breasts; he worried that her heart was now beating as slowly as the heart of a hibernating snow hare. For a long time he sat this way, feeling the faint thumping of blood beneath his hand. He listened to the sound of the sea beating in waves against the beach outside the house. He listened for the beating of his own heart and his own memories, and he was sure that Tamara had never told him anything about the first years of her life.

If this almost-dead Tamara was now remembering anything at all, it could only be memories that the Entity had imprinted in her. He wondered what strange memories these might be. He was willing to share any of her memories, no matter how false or painful, but the great ocean of remembrance is a private universe in which it is almost impossible for anyone other than the remembrancer herself to live. Danlo was not a god, and so he could not look into the image storm that must be boiling through her mind. According to his criteria and almost impossible ideals, he was not even a full man, let alone what he conceived of as a true human being, and so all he could do was to sit and watch and wait for Tamara to reach her moment.

Tamara, Tamara—you were never really born, he thought. *What must it be like to remember your birth?*

Sometime in that long and timeless night, as Danlo kept watch over Tamara, there came the moment that he had been waiting for. Without warning, Tamara began to whisper, "Yes, yes, yes, yes!" Only her lips moved; she kept her eyes shut, and the rest of her body was as motionless as a corpse. She repeated this word again and again. Danlo supposed that she was remembering the truth about herself and finally making sense of her memories. And then, suddenly, she screamed. Her arms pulled up over her face, and her fingers clawed the air as her mouth opened in agony. She shook her head from side to side with such violence that Danlo was afraid that she might dislocate her neck. This terrible scream broke long and deep from her chest, and it seemed to go on and on forever.

Although Danlo tried to keep Tamara from banging her head on the floor or injuring him with her long fingernails, a terrible power had come into her. The sudden strength running through her arms and body shocked him. In a convulsion of muscle and nerves, Tamara came awake and threw Danlo off her. She sprang to her feet sweating and shaking and still screaming as if some invisible hand had grabbed her body and plunged her into a cauldron of molten iron. When Danlo came closer to help her, she shook her head to warn him away. But Danlo misinterpreted this motion as only that of an uncontrollable frenzy. He tried to touch her face, to cool her momentary madness. And then, with all the ferocity and merciless precision of a warrior-poet, she drove the heel of her hand into the soft space beneath his ribs, beneath his heart. The force of the blow knocked him to the floor. He lay against the hard wooden tiles gasping for breath. Tamara stopped screaming then. She stood looking down at him, and her eyes were wide open and full of light.

"No, no," she said softly, almost to herself.

She looked around the room, drinking in the sight of the floor cushions, the hanging plants, the shatterwood beams glistening above her head. There was an apprehension about her, a terrible awareness as if she were seeing herself in these familiar objects and reliving the first time that she had opened her eyes upon this room. And in this moment of awakening, she must have known that there was something other about the whole house, something more. It must have been as if the doorways connecting the rooms of this mysterious house were like doorways to other dwellings in other places, faraway in space and time. There was starlight in Tamara's lovely eyes, and memories, and sadness, too, for suddenly she shook her head back and forth and murmured, "Oh, no!" She looked at Danlo, who was now up on one knee as he fought to breathe and stand up to face her. And then she ran from the house. She fled outside, down to the ocean, where the starry sky opened like a million doors upon the many-roomed mansion of the universe.

When Danlo finally found her, the sun had just risen above the mountains. From half a mile away he saw her standing down

on the beach where the twelve flat rocks led out through the
shallows to Cathedral Rock. It was a clear and windy day, and
the spray from the breakers sparkled in the early light. The whole
of the world seemed to be sparkling: Danlo's diamond-hulled
ship, and the golden dune sands, and Tamara's beautiful hair,
which was flowing in the wind like a magic robe. The skin of
Tamara's body sparkled like white marble, for she had taken off
her clothes, and she waded naked in the deepening waters. Her
breasts and belly and golden pubes were dripping wet as if one of
the waves had surged up over her. Danlo ran down the dunes and
over the hardpack, but when he reached the ocean's edge, he
approached her warily. He stood in the rising tide at arm's length
from her. The water was so cold that it instantly penetrated the
insulation of his boots and shocked his bones. "Please . . .
come out of the water," he said. "It is too cold."

Tamara reached down into the ocean and scooped up a handful of water. She splashed her face with it and said, "But I'm not
at all cold."

For a while, Danlo watched her playing in the water. In truth,
she evinced no sign of cold. She seemed completely at ease, as if
she had reincarnated as a seal or a hot-blooded whale. Apparently, her madness had left her. She seemed totally aware of the
world around her, of herself, of him.

"Tamara," he finally asked, "what did you remember?"

She looked at him quickly, and her eyes were hot with anger.
"I think you must know," she said.

"I almost know. But how can I *know,* truly?"

"You've known for quite a while, haven't you?"

"Yes," he finally admitted.

"Oh, Danlo—why didn't you tell me?"

"Some things cannot be told. They can only be lived. Or
remembered."

"My birth," she said. "My *real* birth. And then before—
before my awakening in the other house."

"Do you remember this time?"

Tamara looked up the beach in the direction of the house that
was an exact replica of the other house somewhere on this Earth.
She said, "I really remember too much, you know. Too much—
but not quite enough."

"But do you know . . . how you came to *be,* then?"

"I remember certain things," she said. She turned her sad but
lively eyes to look at him across three feet of churning water.
"But there's too much I'm beginning to understand only now."

"Please, tell me."

"But some things can't be told," she reminded him. "My life. My whole, beautiful, short, short life."

"Please tell me about your blessed life," he said.

In truth, her life was no more blessed or beautiful than any other life, although its entire span was much less than that of any other adult human being. It is a mystery of life that it always seems too short, for the mayflies of Old Earth as well as for the golden-winged Scutari seneschals who sometimes live a thousand years. Time, for all living things, is always strange, and Tamara could not quite understand how she had lived so deeply in so little time.

In truth, there were three times in her life. The first time was the longest, though the least remembered. In this time of her quickening, she grew from a fertilized egg to a woman in only forty days. In the blue lagoon near her house on the tropical island—in a nutrient pool that the engineers of Fostora would have called an amritsar tank—the microscopic assemblers of the Solid State Enity accelerated the development of her body and mind. This was a time of floating in dense saltwater and absorbing the sugars, lipids, and amino acids vital to her growth. As with the womb state of a naturally born human being, this should have been a time of love and peace and oceanic bliss. But the cells of her body were dividing explosively and unnaturally, like a barely controlled cancer, and she was growing much too quickly to know a moment of peace. And as for love, where was such a blessed thing to be found in an amritsar tank of cellular-size robots and organic chemicals that the Entity had dumped into a few million liters of saltwater?

During this long and lonely time when the cells of her body knew no connection with any other living thing, it might have been best if she had remained unconscious. Much of the time, of course, she dwelt in this dark state of unknowing, but at other times she dreamed. And sometimes, when her eyes opened on the bright light streaming down through the lagoon's blue waters, she was almost aware of certain talents, sensibilities, knowledge, memories, and purposes that the Entity implanted in her explosively developing brain. Sometimes, in those rare moments of insight that fall upon people like shooting stars, she was almost aware of who she was and why the Entity had called her into life. But she was not quite a human being, not yet, and any awareness of herself as Tamara Ten Ashtoreth of Neverness would have to wait until the Entity imprinted her with the memories of the real Tamara.

This imprinting occurred during the third time in her life, when she had been brought up to the house near the lagoon. In some ways, this was the strangest and most wonderful time she had known. It was a time of love and miracles. In less than a full day, the Entity had imprinted her with all of Tamara's memories, or rather, with the memories of Tamara that She had read from Danlo's mind. Because of the strangeness of this quickened consciousness—because of the time dilations as immense as those of a black hole—it was as if she had lived an entire lifetime in a day. It didn't matter to her that her memory of Danlo's deep blue eyes and his soulful flute playing and all her other memories had never originated with her. It didn't matter to her—then—that she remembered a life that she had never really lived. For when she had awakened in the fireroom remembering this lost life of glass jars and saltwater that the Entity had fabricated, her love for Danlo had been reborn.

This was the miracle of her life, of her *real* life, of all the time she had spent with Danlo since coming to this familiar house above the dunes on this cold and windy northern beach. It was the miracle of love. She truly loved Danlo; in a way, she had been created only for him, to love only him, and she sensed this as one of her deepest purposes. The whole of her life almost seemed one long and secret plot to bring them together so that they might kiss and embrace and create something marvelous out of love. It didn't matter that this third time of her life was a merging of the unreal and the real. To her, the time of her imprinting and the time of love were all as one time: continuous, glorious, and golden. This time *was* time, all the time of her life, and she hoped it would go on and on forever. That is, she had hoped this until her dreams began and Danlo insisted that she try to relive her birth.

All living things, even the strangest and most alien, have a moment of birth. It is the moment of separation from the egg, from the brood-pod, from the silken cocoon, from the mother—or from an amritsar tank full of assemblers and saltwater. It is a time of light and pain, and for Tamara this terrifying time was the second of the times into which her life could be divided. Lying on the floor of the meditation room, with the vase of pink rhododendrons, with thirty-three candles and Danlo's dark blue eyes burning above her—deep in the attitude of recurrence—she had remembered emerging from the amritsar tank many days earlier and walking up to the house near the lagoon. She had remembered the saltwater dripping from her new and naked body; she had remembered her sense of wonder that she *had* a body, that she was really *she,* whoever she really was. With perfect clarity she had remembered and relived the terrible pain of incarnation, and now, standing naked near Danlo in the deadly cold ocean, she was remembering it still.

"It was so strange," she told him. Now the tide was rising higher, washing in waves against her thighs. The sun was a little higher, too, and the gulls were taking their morning flights, screaming above the rocks and the crashing surf. From far away came the barking of seals and the cold wind. The whole beach was alive with sound, and Tamara had to speak with much force so that Danlo could hear her voice clearly. "Life is strange, isn't it? Simply being—and being aware. And it's even stranger to be aware of being aware, and you can't imagine what it's like to have all this terribly beautiful awareness come into you all at once. There was a moment, Danlo. I was *not,* and then I was. Oh, I didn't know *who* I was, not then, but I knew that I was *I.* I suppose in most people, this sense of the self-crystallizing out of pure consciousness takes years. But for me, it happened in a flash. It was like a star coming alive with fire. It was like light bursting inside me. In a way, I *was* this light, this clear and beautiful light that let me see myself as I am. I remember seeing myself as I stepped out of the tank. My bare skin, the drops of water—the beautiful sun falling over my skin like burning drops of light—it was all so new. And I was so ignorant at first. I knew almost nothing. But in a way, I knew everything.

"I had no concept that my skin was made up of cells, the cells of atoms. I had no words for these things. But I knew that I had cells, I could feel them living inside me, almost burning. And deeper inside, the atoms, vibrating like the strings of gosharp— there was this immense sound inside me that I somehow knew was uniquely my own. I knew that I *was* these cells, these atoms. I knew that the atoms of *my* body were somehow different than the atoms of the water or the sand or any other thing. Because I could control it all. This part of the world encapsulated by my skin, I could will to move or not move. I can't tell you what a sense of power I felt when I realized all this. It was like grasping a bolt of lightning in my hands.

"As soon as I left the water and stood on the beach and started walking up toward the house, I wanted to jump back in the tank, even though I knew I *couldn't* do that, I must never do that. It all hurt, you know. The sand was as hot as fire, and it burned my feet. The sunlight hurt my eyes. Just looking at myself hurt—the sun was burning my skin red, and I could feel how fragile the cells of my body really were. Oh, Danlo, why does it all have to hurt so much? It's all so terribly beautiful, and it all hurts so much that I could die. But I can't die, I can never die, and that's the strangest thing of all.''

As the sun ripened the sky into a full and glorious blue, they stood in the ocean shallows holding this strange conversation. The waves were rising higher and higher against Danlo's sodden kamelaika. He shifted his weight from right to left, trying to keep his blood flowing to his cold, throbbing feet.

"Love hurts most of all, you know," she said. "The way love inevitably wakes everything up and causes us to burn for ever more love."

"That is something that Tamara might have said."

"I know."

Danlo listened to the seagull chicks crying from their many nests out on Cathedral Rock. He said, "This must be hard for you. To be . . . and yet not to be. To not know who you really are."

"But I know who I am," she said. "Do you?"

Danlo watched her as she splashed water over herself from her head to her thighs. Her whole body sparkled with this icy saltwater.

"You are not Tamara," he said at last. He winced in pain at the inevitable speaking of this truth. "You are not she."

"Am I not?"

"You are not *just* Tamara. You have some of her memories but . . ."

"Yes?"

"You are something other," he said. "Something more."

"I know—but what?"

"It is hard to put a name to what you really are. You are the Entity's child, yes? Her . . . starchild."

"I'm a woman, Danlo." She rubbed her wet hands over her breasts and belly, then down over her hips. "A woman who loves you."

"Yes," he said. He could hardly hear himself speak above the thunder of the sea. "A part of you is a woman—I can see that you are. But another part is only *my* memory of another woman named Tamara. Which is the part that loves, then?"

"Does it really matter?"

"Yes, it matters," he said softly. "I do not want to be loved by the part of you that is only the ghost of my own memory."

"Because you think it's unseemly to love yourself?"

"No," Danlo said with a sad smile. "Because it is not real. Your memory of the first time we touched eyes, this blessed moment of love never really happened to you. And, therefore, for us, it never really was."

Tamara was quiet for a moment, and then she said, "If I could, I would cark the cells of my body so that I was really she. I'd cark myself—I'd replace all the atoms that compose my heart and brain with new ones. But I don't think there's any power in the universe that could do such a thing."

"No," Danlo said. "But even if that were possible, it would not matter. My memories are still *my* memories."

"And yet when Tamara's memories of you were destroyed, you proposed to replace them with your own."

The cold from the water worked its way up Danlo's legs, and he began to shiver as he nodded his head. "Yes, this is true. And in my life, I have done only one other thing as wrong."

"What did you do?"

"You do not remember?"

"No."

"I wished a man dead. I saw him dying, in my hands."

"You speak as if by such wishing you had actually murdered him."

"I almost did. In a way, this man *is* dead because of me. Just as Tamara would have been dead inside if she had imprinted my memories."

"Oh, Danlo."

"Truly—to cark one's own memories into another's mind is almost worse than murder."

Tamara stepped through the foamy white waves, closer to him. She took his hand and pressed it lightly over her heart. Surprisingly, even though she was dripping icy water, her skin was warmer than his.

"Am I so dead inside?" she asked.

"Most of what you remember about your life is unreal."

"Do you think I can't distinguish the real from what is not?"

"Can you?"

"Oh, I really think I can. I think I've discovered something about the nature of memory."

"Yes?"

"All the memories that were imprinted inside me," she began. "The time in my mother's kitchen when I first wanted her to die, and the first time I saw you in the sun room of Bardo's house and wanted to love you until *you* died—all these things I remember as clearly as I can remember the shape of Cathedral Rock when I shut my eyes. I can remember all these unreal things about my life, even though I suppose I know they never really happened to me—at least to the cells of *this* body. I have all these beautiful memories, but I can't relive them. That is the difference, you know. I found that out in the house. During the ceremony, the second ceremony, when I had finally fallen into recurrence, when I felt myself being born again—I knew that the real memories are those that can be relived, and the imprinted ones cannot."

Danlo pressed his hand into the warmth between her breasts and said, "This is true. The remembrancers have known this for a long time. This is why they forbid their students even the simplest of imprintings."

"You *know* this and yet you still offered to imprint someone with your memories?"

"I had fallen into love. I cannot tell you how much I loved her."

"Oh, I think I know."

"Yes—you have my memories," he said.

"I have *something*," she agreed. "Memory is so strange, isn't it? I can see all these wonderful memories inside me, and yet there is a distance to them. I know they are memories. I'm not really *seeing* them, in the moment as I see you now."

"The way most people remember is not really remembering," Danlo said. "Remembrancing *is* different, truly. Especially recurrence."

"For one's life to recur in a flash—how is this possible?"

"I do not know. But the remembrancers say that matter is really just memory frozen in time. In recurrence, time melts away and we go back to ourselves. And then there is a flowing of our lives again."

She smiled at this and asked, "And what else do your remembrancers say?"

"They say this: that difference between simple remembering and reliving one's life is the difference between seeing a foto of an electrical storm and feeling a bolt of lightning sear one's hand."

Now Tamara was no longer smiling. She took Danlo's hand in her own and turned it palm upward to the sun. Then she ran her finger over the lines and calluses. Finally she said, "I've felt the lightning, too, you know. There was my birth, and before that, the days in the tank. And here in *this* house, all these days we've had together. The flowers and the fire and the love. Do you think I can't remember how your hands burned over me the first time we lay together? Isn't this real?"

"Yes, it is real," he admitted.

"Then at least I will have this part of my life to live and relive again." She shut her eyes, and continued, "As I am reliving it now. All these moments, all this life, all this passion—it's all so real isn't it?"

"Yes."

"And it always will be?"

"Yes, only—"

"And then there is the other thing," she said quickly, interrupting him. She opened her eyes and looked at him grimacing against the icy, wet touch of the sea. "The strangest thing of all."

Seeing that he was now shivering, she took his hand and led him out of the water. They walked up the beach for a while in the direction of Danlo's lightship where it lay almost buried in the sand. Although the wind was up and Danlo remained quite cold, the modest exercise restored the life to his numb legs. When he paused to talk to Tamara on the dunes some fifty feet away from his ship, his legs ached and burned, but he no longer worried that they would freeze and he would have to cut them off.

"What is this strange thing?" he asked.

Tamara stood tall and perfect in the light streaming down from the sun. Her body was now completely dry, and her skin had taken on the lovely white luster of a pearl. Her face was turned toward the ocean as if she was listening to the whales sing their high, haunting songs out along the blue horizon. Or perhaps she was listening to the wind. She seemed to take strength and meaning from the deep sounds of the world all around her, for her eyes grew brighter and she held her head almost preternaturally still. Perhaps, Danlo thought, she was attuned to whispers and vibrations that only she could hear. Her whole being seemed to be trembling as if she were waiting for some great thing to happen. As she stood utterly naked on the windswept dunes watching and waiting and listening to herself, there was something wild and utterly ruthless about her. And there was something vast and splendid, too. Beholding the dazzling beauty of this rare thing, for a moment Danlo felt himself falling as if he had stepped off the world out into the whirlpool of lights that spin through the universe.

"My dreams," she said. "Where do my strange dreams come from?"

"I have wondered about your dreams, too."

"When I sleep and I relive this strange other life of bloody red moons and gleaming knives, where do these memories come from?"

"It is possible," he said, "that the Entity has imprinted you with sleeping memories."

She shook her head at this remembrancing terminology and said, "Sleeping memories?"

"A mountain of memories, yes? Most of these memories would remain unconscious, but through your dreams a few of them would rise up into your mind. As the peak of an iceberg rises above the sea."

"But if these are only imprinted memories, then how is it possible that I've relived them?"

"I . . . do not know."

"I think these are more than just imprinted memories, Danlo. I think my dreams are more than dreams."

"What, then?"

She flashed him a deep, wild look and continued, "The red moons, of course, are of Qallar. Before the Entity grew into a goddess, when She was still human, She was born on Qallar. She was a warrior-poet, you know. The only female warrior-poet there has ever been."

Danlo turned to stare at his ship gleaming in the sun. For the thousandth time, he wondered at the Entity's connection with the warrior-poets. He wondered if She might have slain Malaclypse out of hand merely for his bearing a killing knife and wearing two red rings. After a while he looked back at her and asked, "Then you believe that the Entity has imprinted you with Her own memories?"

"It is more than that."

He thought of her lone walks along the beach at night, and he remembered how she had strapped the murderous spikhaxo glove onto her hand in the event she chanced upon a tiger.

"Her soul," Danlo finally said. "Do you believe that She has made you with a similar soul as She?"

"It is more than that."

"Tell me, please."

"I can hear Her thoughts, you know. I can see Her dreams."

She was quiet while the wind whispered over the ocean, and then she looked at him and said, "I can feel Her pain."

"Telepathy?"

"No, it is something more."

"Are you sure? You wouldn't be the first human being whom the Entity has spoken to in this way."

"But She does not really speak to me."

"In truth? Then where do Her words come from when you hear them inside of you?"

"How can I really know? Where does the wind come from? Where does it go?"

"But your consciousness, itself—"

"You can't understand such things by such simple analysis, you know." She stared at him long and deeply. "You wonder where my consciousness comes from. Does it come from the atoms of my brain? Or from the planet on which we stand? Or does it come from the moon-brains of the Entity? Impossible questions, I think. You really might do better to wonder where your *own* beautiful consciousness comes from."

"Perhaps, but I—"

"These thoughts," she said, "are coming into my mind as my lips begin to move. These words are coming into my mouth. *I* am speaking, Danlo; She does not speak to me."

He thought about this for a moment, and then persisted, "But it would be only natural if She did, yes? She made you of the elements of this earth—in a way, you are a child of Her body."

As he said this, she continued staring at him, and he thought it disturbing the way her eyes were as dark as the empty spaces between the stars. And yet, strangely, they were also full of light.

"I am not Her child, Danlo."

"What are you, then?"

"Just what you have said I am: something other. And something more."

"Tamara, you—"

"That is not my name," she said. Her voice grew cold and deep as the sea. "That is not who I really am."

"Are you not? Who are you, then . . . truly?"

Whether by chance or design, she stood with her back to the sun so that the light framed her head and hair like a fiery golden halo. It was hard for Danlo to look at her. She stood perfectly still, looking at him for a long time. And then she said, "I am She."

Danlo shook his head and used his hand to shield his eyes against the burning sunlight. "No, no," he said softly.

"I am the one you know as the Solid State Entity."

Danlo looked at her dark and bottomless eyes blazing at the center of her brilliant face. At last he said, "Yes, this is true—in some way I have known this since the moment I first saw you. But it is still hard to believe."

"She and I are one. There is nothing in me that is not a part of Her; there is no part of Her that is unknown to me."

"But why?" he asked. "You are the test of me, I think. This love we almost had. This life. If you—if the Entity—only wanted to test me this way, then why not create a Tamara who had no shared consciousness with the Entity? She could have made any woman—any woman in the form of Tamara—and then simply read her mind. It would have been an easier thing to do, yes?"

She was silent while she closed her eyes. She seemed both troubled and deeply desirous of searching for an answer that would satisfy him. Looking at her this way, with her lovely face so full of compassion and vulnerability, Danlo could hardly think of her as anything other than human.

"Because," she said. "Because if She is to accomplish Her purpose, any child of Hers must be the same in the soul. This is the reason Her memories and Her mind are in me. Otherwise all my experiences and apprehension of reality would seem as alien to Her as that of any other human being."

"What is Her purpose, then? What could She hope to know through you that She could not know otherwise?"

She squeezed his hands so hard that they hurt. And then she said, "The Entity wanted to know who *you* really are," she said. "We needed to know."

This response astonished Danlo, who half-shouted, "But why? The Entity read my mind once—I presume She still can."

"There are different ways of knowing, Danlo."

"But why *this* way?" he asked. He pulled his hands free from hers and touched her forehead, her face, her shimmering hair, and then he traced his fingers around the curve of her naked shoulder. "Why *you,* at all, then?"

In answer to this, she ran her own finger across the scar on his forehead. And then she told him, "I was born to touch and feel. From the moment I stepped out of the tank, I knew I had to touch the whole world. To walk the earth again, naked as a newborn child, to feel the sand beneath my feet. To taste the salt of the sea. To touch, to taste, to perceive, to suffer all the senses. To feel, to move, to become what I am. To live, Danlo. To live and live and live again. How can anyone ever have enough life? Or love? I've always wanted so much love. To want to love so badly I could die, all the while knowing I'd do anything rather than die because then there would be no hope for love or anything else. And love is everything, you know. To touch the world, in love, as lovers touch—to watch this love wake everything up even though it all hurts almost more than anything can bear. Only, there's something that you once told me. That pain is the awareness of life. There's so much pain, isn't there? Pain inside pain, and it just goes on and on and never stops. But pain doesn't really matter, does it? I think I'd suffer any pain just to live and be a part of this marvelous awakening. I'd suffer anything if only I could touch your beautiful face and feel what it's like to love and be loved. I'd burn and burn and burn to feel your eyes touching mine the way I remember. *This* is why I am, you know. I'd touch the sun itself if it loved me the way that you once did."

Love, the courtesans say, is the simplest thing in the universe. There was a moment when Danlo looked at her standing all naked and golden beneath the morning sun. There was a moment of touching, when she pressed her hand against his face as if she wanted to catch and hold the teardrops that were almost burning his eyes. There was a moment when he could never love her in the way in which she wanted to be loved, and then, a simple moment later, he was falling into love as inescapably as a stone falls into a star.

"The test continues, yes?" He tried to smile, and he said, "Is this my test, then? To see how much pain I can endure?"

Pain is the awareness of life, he remembered. And then a new thought, *Pain is the fullness of love.*

She came up to him and kissed his lips. Then she told him, "Your tests are over now. This is your reward."

"My *reward*?"

"To love again, if that's what you'll allow yourself to do."

"Is this how you capture me without breaking my soul?"

"We could love each other almost forever, you know."

"No, no—please."

"We could marry each other. Here, on the beach beneath this beautiful sun—we could begin a marriage that would last a thousand years. Isn't this what you've always wanted?"

"To marry, yes. But to marry now, to marry you—how can I do this?"

She smiled at him and asked, "How can you not? We'll marry and mate and make children together."

"Tamara, Tamara, I—"

"A new race, you know. Our children would be the first truly *human* beings. We would teach them how to be human—and something more."

"Our children," he said, considering this. "Our blessed children."

"All our children—someday we would have millions of children and grandchildren. We could fill the whole world with what we create."

"I have . . . always dreamed of having children. You know that I have."

"You've also dreamed of a world without war or evil. A world restored to its original harmony and beauty—to what you once called *halla*."

"I have . . . always wondered if such a dream is possible."

"The whole world, Danlo. We could make it as we will."

The whole world.

He looked east beyond the beach at the forest blazing bright green in the strong early light. There were beautiful birds in the forest, and flowers and tigers. It was all so pristine and almost perfect. No man, he thought, had ever walked through this forest. And the trees themselves—the glorious redwoods and spruce and hemlock—had never know the touch of any man's eyes save his own. He wondered if the trees were only waiting for him to fill the forest with his children. Did these silent trees long for the love of human beings who would worship them as gods? No, he thought. The trees were only trees. They danced almost motionlessly all day in the sunlight, and their millions of long needles shimmered in emerald ecstasy. Their awareness was of photons and water and perhaps the carbon dioxide of his breath, but they had little care for his passions or plans.

"I had thought my reward for surviving the tests was to be the answer to three questions." He turned to smile at Tamara, who was standing patiently in the sun.

"You may have your answer to your questions. Or you may have me."

"But not both?"

"No, not both. It's your choice, you know."

Even though it hurt to keep his eyes fixed in her direction, Danlo could not help looking at her. "How can I make such a choice?"

"How can you not?"

"How can you make me . . . make this choice?"

"Oh, Danlo, Danlo—I've offered you myself, the whole world. What is there to choose?"

The whole world.

Danlo looked southward down the beach where the dune grasses rippled in the wind. Some kind of spider must have woven her web between the strands of grass, for not far from him a lovely silken orb sparkled like silver and diamonds with the early morning dew. There were sandpipers hopping across the sand, and nearer the water, the gulls and the kittiwakes were gliding through the air. The whole beach was teeming with life, and it was a mystery to him how he could ever choose the answer to three questions over the chance to walk this beautiful beach for as long as he lived.

"If I *did* remain here," he asked, "how long would we really have together before we were destroyed? You have said that the Silicon God's attacks upon the Entity are concentrated upon this Earth."

Tamara smiled coldly, ruthlessly, and she said, "Do you think I would let Him destroy what I've created? Do you think I would let Him harm my *children*?"

"I suppose not," he said. "I remember that you . . . would destroy Him first."

"Of course I would, but I promise that no part of this world would be touched by our battles. You would never know that He and I made war."

"And I would remain safe beneath the splendid sky while the gods shattered spacetime and all the stars, yes?"

"Is it so terrible to be safe for a while?"

He kicked at the sand and ignored her question. "I would be safe to remembrance the Elder Eddas, yes? To remembrance the secret of how the Silicon God might be defeated?"

"Is it such a terrible thing to remembrance this?"

"Yes, truly, it is terrible," he said. "War is always terrible, I think."

"But it wouldn't be you who waged war, Danlo."

"Who would it be then? You?"

"I, of course, but not *I*. Did you forget so soon that I have a multiple nature? It would be *She* who warred. In some ways, She's really a terrible goddess, you know, and She loves war."

Danlo was quiet while he ground the toe of his wet boot into the sand. And then he asked, "And you? What do you love, then?"

"I love love," she said. She put her arms around him and embraced him. She pressed her head touching the side of his face while she whispered in his ear. "I love the sky and the trees and the wind. I love you."

He held her touching him while he ran his fingers along her smoothly muscled back. He held her tightly, almost fiercely, and he felt how good it was to be close to her in this way. Her hair smelled of sea salt and sun—good, clean smells that he would never forget even if he must someday leave this world. But holding her as did, with her heart beating so close to his and the breath of her life rushing like a faint wind in his ear, he did not know how he could ever leave her. He looked over her shoulder northward where the mountains rose up and touched the sky. He thought that it would be good to hold her beneath these misty mountains almost forever—as long as there *were* mountains, till the wind and rain eroded them a million years from now and washed them as sand into the sea.

The whole world.

He suddenly broke away from her to face west toward the sea. It was a cold, clear day, and there was a hint of winter in the air. Beyond the offshore rocks, a flock of migrating terns beat their way south to warmer lands. And farther out, almost as far as the horizon, a lone albatross glided along the wind very high in the sky. The ocean was moving as it always did, and he listened to the sound of the cold, deep, blue waters. He watched the great autumn swell rolling in from the open ocean and breaking into sets of white-capped waves as it neared the shore. With the sun slanting low off the water, the whole world shimmered with light. In the face of this impossible beauty, he was very close to agreeing to marry Tamara and remain here forever.

And then he remembered that he had once taken vows as a pilot. He remembered that he had made promises that he must not break. He even remembered his aspiration to become an asarya and all his other dreams, and he stared at the sea so long without moving or blinking that his eyes began to burn. *Words,* he thought. *All my vows and promises are only words.* What were mere words against the marvel of the world that lay before him? How could words ever touch him and bring him love as would this beautiful woman waiting so patiently by his side?

Words were nothing, he realized, and yet all the words that he had ever spoken stood for something, and he could not forget this. He could not forget the tribes of his people dying halfway across the galaxy on the frozen islands west of Neverness. And he could never forget the real Tamara, she of the lost memories and golden soul who must dwell somewhere among the stars. In a shimmering moment of remembrance, as he stared and stared at the motionless sea, his whole life came back to him and rushed into his consciousness like an ocean. This was the moment of choice and decision, the terrible moment of his true test. It was a test, he thought, that the Entity had not consciously designed. Life itself was testing him. Fate was testing him. Or perhaps it was only he who was testing himself.

"Please tell me you'll stay with me," Tamara said.

There was a moment when the whole world was as frozen and still as the deep winter sea, and then a moment later all was crashing waves and sunlight and seabirds crying out to each other in hunger and love.

"Yes, I will stay with you"—he was as close to saying these simple words as the beating of his heart. He wanted to say this almost as badly as he wanted to hold Tamara close to him and feel her sweet breath touching his forever. Instead, he turned to her and told her, "I am sorry. I must go."

Because he could not bear to look at her just then, he began studying the lines of his lightship and calculating how long it would take him to dig it free of sand. The diamond hull, he saw, remained unmarked by the elements of this world, and it glistened all black and beautiful as it always had.

"Oh, Danlo, Danlo," she said.

He could hardly bear the immeasurable sadness with which these words were weighted, though it surprised him that her voice remained calm and unbroken.

"I am sorry," he repeated. "But if my tests are done, I must go."

"I'm sorry, too. I had thought you would stay."

"No, I cannot."

"Of course—you still have your quest."

"Yes."

"Then you still must desire the answer to your questions," she said. "I presume you haven't forgotten your questions."

"No, I haven't forgotten," he said.

"Then you may ask me what you will."

"Now? Here?"

"Why not?"

"Shall I ask you, then?"

"Of course. If you've journeyed twenty thousand light-years from the Star of Neverness to ask the Entity your questions, then please ask now before you lose the chance. But be careful of what you ask."

At last, Danlo made himself look at her, and he was relieved to see that she was smiling. He remembered, then, that the Entity liked to make a game of answering questions mysteriously.

"My first question is this," he said. "Do you know of a cure for the slow evil? The plague that has killed my people?"

Tamara closed her eyes for a moment, then replied, "No, I really don't know. But *you* know the cure. You have always known. Someday, if you complete your quest, you will know it again. *You* will, Danlo—whoever you really are."

While he thought about this strange response, he stamped his cold feet against the sand to warm them. And then he said, "I do not understand."

"I'm sorry that you don't. I really am, you know."

"Then can you tell me what you mean in more simple words?"

"No, I really can't. But you may ask your second question—I promise to answer it as simply as I can."

Danlo blew on his fingers, then held his hands out to the sun. "Where can I find my father?" he asked.

Immediately, she opened her red lovely lips to tell him what he desperately wanted to know. It amused him that her answer was simple, clear, straightforward—and utterly useless. "You will find your father," she said, "at your journey's end."

"And where will *that* be?" he asked.

"Is this your third question?"

"No," he said. "I only wanted to—"

"I understand," she said. "But I've told you that you must take care with your questions."

"I see that I must."

"Then if you will, please ask your third question."

He drew a breath of cold air and thought for a moment. He badly wanted to know if the warrior-poet still lived and would pursue him on his quest like a goshawk following a gull. But if he put this question to Her, his quest might fail here and now. And so he restrained his curiosity, and asked the critically important question: "Where is the planet called Tannahill?"

"I don't know."

"You don't know? Truly?"

"I'm sorry, Danlo."

"But I thought that you knew almost everything."

"No, I'm sorry."

He stood smiling sadly as he stared at the black, mirrored hull of his ship. He had come very far to ask these three questions, and now that he had finally asked them, he was little wiser than when he had begun his journey.

"*I* don't know," she repeated. She looked at him for a long time, and her eyes were bright with compassion. "But it might be that there's one who does."

"Who, then?"

"I am almost certain that Ede the God knew the star of Tannahill."

"But Ede the God is dead, yes?"

"That's true. He is dead. But it may be that he is somewhat alive, too."

"Riddles," he said. "You speak in paradoxes and riddles."

"Then perhaps you should journey to Ede and find the answer to your riddle."

This simple statement of hers amused him, and he laughed gently. "One of the joys of being a pilot," he said, "is that other people are always proposing journeys almost impossible for any pilot to make."

"You wouldn't find this an impossible journey."

"But no one knows where Ede dwells. In a galaxy of a hundred billion stars, it is almost impossible to find a lost god who has never been found."

"*I* know," she said. "I know where He dwells."

She stepped over to him, then. Although she had no real need for secrecy, she cupped her hands to his ears and whispered the fixed-points of the stars where Ede might be found.

"Why have you told me this?" he asked. He grasped her hands and held them lightly between them. "I have had my three questions, yes?"

"I wanted you to know."

"I do not think the Entity would have told me this," he said.

"But I am the—"

"I do not think the person of the Entity who is the Mother would have told me this. The goddess Herself. She of the terrible passions and dreams."

"Oh, don't be too certain of this—She's really a capricious goddess, you know."

"Then why risk defying Her?"

"Because this will speed your return," she said. "Because I love you."

Without realizing what he was doing, he squeezed her hands so tightly that she cried out in pain. When he saw the hurt on her face, he instantly let go. He said, "I am sorry. I am sorry, but I . . . cannot love you. I *must* not."

"I know."

"I will never return here," he said. "I am sorry."

He walked back up to the house, then, to retrieve his chest and stow it in his ship. With a shovel that he made of driftwood and whalebone washed up on the beach, he dug the sand away from the hull. These labors took him most of the morning. During this time, Tamara waited for him in the house. When all his preparations for the continuation of his journey were complete, she appeared on the dunes. She had bathed and washed the salt out of her long golden hair, but she was still naked as a newborn child. She came over to him where he stood by the pit of his ship; she came to give him something and say good-bye.

"You could come with me, if you would like," he said. "I would take you to any star, any world. Any place where there are other people."

"No," she said, "I'll stay here."

"I hate to leave you alone."

"But I won't be alone," she said. She smiled at him, and her eyes were infinitely sad and yet infinitely full of another emotion that seemed very much like wild joy. "I have the whole world."

"What of Sivan wi Mawi Sarkissian and the warrior-poet, then? Have they been tested as I have? Will they remain here, too?"

"I really can't tell you about them, you know."

Danlo bowed his head once in respect for her secretive ways. Then he looked up over the beach. The sun was high in the sky, and the sky itself was a vast blue dome covering the world from horizon to horizon. In moments he must break through this beautiful dome into the roaring black emptiness of the universe, and so he looked at her and said, "I must go."

She stepped closer to him. In her hand, down by her side, she was gripping the pearl necklace, the replica of the one that he had made for the real Tamara. She reached out suddenly and gave it to him. She pressed the teardrop-shaped pearl and the coiled string into his hand. And then she said, "If you ever find the woman you love, you might want to give this to her. If you find her, you might help heal her as you did me."

"But she already has her own necklace," he said. "The one that I once made."

"Then keep this as a token of my love for you. Please remember how I made it for you."

"Tamara, Tamara," he said. With the forefinger of the hand that held the pearl, he touched the tears falling down her cheek. "If I had one more question left to ask, I would want to know if the universe could have been made differently. Halla, not shaida. Without evil, without suffering, without war. Without . . . pain."

Although her eyes were full of tears, they remained bright and intensely focused. She looked at him for a long time with her dark eyes that shimmered like the night-time sea, and then she said, "A better question would be this: Why did God create the universe at all? Why *did* She, Danlo?"

He shook his head slowly back and forth and then bowed to her. "Farewell, Tamara."

"Farewell, farewell," she said. "Fall far and fall well, Pilot."

After this he went inside his ship and sealed himself into the pit. He waited for Tamara to move away before he ignited the rockets. There was a moment of thunder and fire, an intense roaring sound that seemed to well up deep from his belly and shook him to his bones. He left her standing alone on the beach down by the ocean. It took many moments for his lightship to rise up through the sky, and during this time he watched her from the pit's clear diamond window. He had excellent eyes, and he could see her staring up at his ship for a long time. At first he could even see her dark eyes watching him, but soon he had to look very hard just to make out her lovely form among the ocean rocks and the waves breaking over the sand. Very soon she was no more than a point of light as small and white as a pearl. And then, after his heart had beat an uncountable number of times, she was gone.

The whole world, he remembered. *The whole universe.*

He pointed his ship upward where the blue-black heavens opened onto the spaces of the universe. And then he was gone, too, out into the great loneliness, out to the unknown stars and the infinitely bright lights of the Vild.

PART 2

THE GOD

THE DEAD GOD

A man who dies before he dies
Does not die when he dies.
—Abraham a Santa Clara

And so, after too many days spent planetfallen on a lost earth, Danlo returned to the manifold. Of the ten pilots who had made the quest to engage the attention of the Solid State Entity, only he had survived to continue his journey. Li Te Mu Lan, Dolores Nun, Sarolta Sen, Rurik Boaz, Shamir the Bold—it is always fitting to honor the names of pilots who have perished seeking the secrets of the universe—these brave people had been lost into the beautiful but sometimes chaotic space that lies beneath the spacetime of the night. Their lightships and bodies would never be found. And Leander of Darkmoon, the Rosaleen, Valin wi Tymon Whitestone, and Ivar Sarad—they too must be listed among the hundreds of pilots lost to the Vild since Dario the Bold discovered this vast region of exploding stars in the 2539th year since the founding of the Order.

Unknown to Danlo, other pilots of the Second Vild Mission had been lost as well. Eric Rathborn, Alfreda Siri Serai, and Lorenzo Scarlatti never completed the journey to the planet Thiells where Lord Nikolos and the hundreds of lords and masters labored to found a city and second Academy that would be the seat of the new Order. And of the other pilots falling out among strange stars in their quest for lost Tannahill, who knew? Danlo himself knew that he might never set eyes on Thiells (much less again Neverness), for first he must journey to the star cluster where he hoped to find Ede the God.

No pilot of his Order had discovered the slightest clue as to Ede's whereabouts. Many, of course, believed that no such god as Ede existed. These naysayers denied the doctrines of the Cy-

bernetic Universal Church. They believed that long ago, when
the man named Nikolos Daru Ede had carked his consciousness
into his eternal computer, this computer had been destroyed.
There was no way, they said, that a simple computer could expand itself—component by component—until it had grown into a
planet-size machine that called itself a god. Since Danlo had
been given the fixed-points of Ede's star by the Entity Herself, he
never doubted Ede's existence. He never doubted that he could
fall out around this distant star and behold this god of gods—*if*
he could find a sequence of mappings among the strange stars of
the Vild that would lead him to Ede, *if* he could survive the
manifold's twisted spaces and the killing radiation of nearby
stars that had exploded into supernovas.

Many times, while he floated naked in the pit of his ship, he
thought of the soft-faced Li Te Mu Lan and fearless Leander of
Darkmoon and his other fellow pilots; many times he whispered
a requiem for their spirits. As Danlo fell from star to star, passing
through the many brilliant windows of the manifold, he wondered if anyone would ever know if he blundered into an infinite
tree or a Soli-Ringess space, thus never again to pass back
through a window into the world of flowers and starlight and the
golden shimmer of a woman's hair. During many long moments
of memory and desperate dreams, he wondered if anyone would
ever pray for him at his inevitable death.

For one pilot who had journeyed with him into the Entity, he
said neither requiem nor prayer. This was the renegade, Sivan wi
Mawi Sarkissian. Danlo was certain that Sivan and the warrior-
poet known as Malaclypse Redring had somehow survived the
chaos space that had killed Leander and the others. And he was
almost certain that Sivan and Malaclypse had survived whatever
tests that the Entity had put to them: as before on his journey
from Farfara—as Danlo moved farther and farther from the fading stars of the Entity—he detected the composition waves of
another lightship falling through the manifold. Mysteriously, this
ship remained always at the boundary of whatever neighborhood
of stars in which he found himself. It followed him from star to
star toward the star of Ede.

Certainly, Danlo thought, this ghostlike ship must be the *Red
Dragon,* bearing its precious cargo of a ronin pilot and a murderous warrior-poet. Certainly the warrior-poet must still hope that
Danlo would inevitably lead him to his father, and then Malaclypse of the red rings and killing knife might finally put an end
to the ambitious career of Mallory Ringess. But Danlo did not

intend to lead the warrior-poet to his father. He tried many times to elude Sivan's ship. Outside his window were ten billion stars as ancient and luminous as thoughts in the mind of God. He fled into these glorious stars. Once he fell out near the corona of a hot blue subdwarf that nearly resembled the central star of the Ring Nebula in Lyra; once he fenestered through a sequence of a hundred fallaways with such a wild and reckless speed that no sane pilot would want to follow him; once he segued off the plane of the galaxy altogether and passed into a globular cluster of eight hundred million stars that was almost a small satellite galaxy of its own.

But all to no avail. Sivan's ship remained always close to him, wavering like a mirage just at the radius of convergence. Danlo decided that Sivan was a better pilot than he, and so with a smile and a silent bowing of his head in acknowledgment of Sivan's skill, he resigned himself to this relentless and rather eerie pursuit. He turned back toward the distant lights of Ede the God. He tried not to think about Sivan and his ghostlike ship, any more than a man takes notice of his shadow behind him as he races toward the sun. As he plied his art of mathematics and faced his ship-computer's brilliant number storm, he tried to accept the *Red Dragon*'s presence with all the nonchalance of an Alaloi father disregarding the lice attached to his hairy body. He fell on and on past countless stars, and after a time, as all pilots do in the dazzling black neverness of the manifold, he felt very much alone.

In this way he crossed the bright Orion arm. He journeyed ever outward away from the core stars, deeper into the Vild. He fell out around many stars, the yellow and orange and red giants, and the glowering red supergiants as huge and hellish as Antares. There were the blue and white stars and the common yellow stars much like Old Earth's steady, golden sun. Many of these stars he named after the animals that he had known as a child. Berura, the hooded seal; Gauri, the ivory gull; Ahira—he left these names behind him like splendid jewels spinning in the night. Other stars he would never name. These were the remnants of supernovas, the light and dust and elemental matter blasted into space when the great stars died.

The whole Vild was sick with this radiation and matter. Many regions of space were cloudy and opaque to his telescopes. More than once he fell out too near the expanding wavefront of a recently destroyed star, and was almost destroyed by fiery blasts of x-rays and gamma and onstreaming photons. Like a dolphin diving beneath the sea to avoid storm waves, he immediately fell through a random window into the manifold in his instinct to escape this killing light. But he found no peaceful waters there. Beneath the stars of the Vild, the manifold is deadly and strange. He took the *Snowy Owl* through the rare Loudon spaces that slowly melted before him like a scryer's blacking oil spread across deep eye hollows; he fell through the violet, fractalling crystals of the much rarer M-set spaces that possibly no other pilot had encountered before. All these spaces were difficult and dangerous, though none proved so terrible to map through as the almost impossibly chaotic chaos space that he had finessed inside the Entity.

There is really not much to say of this part of Danlo's journey. He survived the many topological traps that opened before him. With ever-growing prowess and grace, he made his mappings and his ship danced like a light beam through the many windows that gave out on the stars.

What Danlo saw when he fell out above the Star of Ede—a pretty blue-white star as hot as Durriken Luz—was utter ruin. Spread out before him across millions of miles of space was nothing but flotsam and jetsam, the remnants of a structure that must have been Ede the God himself. Danlo spent much time with his telescopes scanning this debris, which formed a dark and ugly ring around the whole of the star. At various points, he even risked his ship by rocketing near the ring's outer rim to scoop up bits of matter for analysis. In the samples he took, he found fused neurologics, diamond chips, molecular clary, broken protein chains sometimes pulverized to dust, silicon, germanium, dead assemblers, microscopic rods of spun diamond, and many, many pieces of demolished robots, none of which was greater than two microns in diameter. The ring itself was pocked in many places with glowing clouds of hydrogen, with various ionized gases, and with iron particles polarizing the star's strong blue-white light.

In all this vast wreckage, however, he found no sign of transuranic elements or any kind of manufactured matter. He felt sure that the ring was all that remained of what must have been a vast computer. This black and purple ring around the star was a good two million miles deep and fifty million miles across. After calculating the average density of all this blasted-out matter, he determined that this computer called Ede must have been the largest man-made (or god-made) structure ever fabricated. In truth, the bits of destroyed circuitry that floated beyond his lightship quite possibly represented the greatest and densest collection of matter in the galaxy outside the black hole of the core itself. Ede's eternal computer must have been millions of times as large as any of the Entity's moon-brains, as large, in mass, as a large-size star.

Somehow, in a way beyond Danlo's understanding of the energy requirements of moving matter through the manifold, in order to make the components for his computer, Ede must have swept whole star clusters clean of planets, asteroids, comets— even wisps of hydrogen and other gases blown out from the many Vild stars that had fallen into supernova. Quite probably he had used disassemblers to break all this matter down to its elements, and then, over centuries of realtime, he had used other microscopic robots to build up and fold together the neurologics of his great brain. How this monstrously vast machine had been destroyed he might never know. Possibly the Silicon God had triggered the spacetime continuum's zero-point energies in millions of separate loci inside Ede and so exploded him into trillions of pieces. Or possibly he had undermined the fabric of spacetime itself. Danlo well remembered how the Silicon God's attack upon the Solid State Entity had deformed the manifold beneath and inside *Her*. It was possible, he thought, that if such deformations were great enough, the black silk of spacetime would unravel into an almost infinite number of strands, thus pulling apart any kind of matter folded inside.

However Ede had been killed, it seemed that he must be truly dead. Search though he might, Danlo could find no piece of circuitry or other component alive to the touch of flowing electrons or streams of coherent light. He could not understand how Ede could also be somewhat alive—unless, of course, this ring of cybernetic wreckage three hundred million miles in circumference was only part of Ede the God. If the moon-brains of the Entity were spread across many stars, why not the units of Ede's eternal computer? Because Danlo wanted to know more about this god of gods—and because he still hoped to ask Ede the whereabouts of Tannahill—he set out into the nearby stars to find him.

In the deep light-distances surrounding the Star of Ede, as he formally named it, he found more wreckage. It seemed that a ring of dead computer parts circled each of the stars he explored, though no ring was nearly so large as the first ring he had encountered. As Danlo's ship fell in a huge spiral through this strange neighborhood of stars, the rings became ever smaller.

Some stars shone forth upon no rings at all, but on only dark blooms of floating debris that must have once been no larger than small moons. And some blooms—orbiting stars twenty light-years distant from the Star of Ede—were as tiny as granite boulders that one might stumble over while walking down a mountain path.

But there were very many of them. In the star cluster that was Ede the God, Danlo counted some 670 million rings or pockets of demolished computer circuitry. In a way, Danlo thought, Ede the God must have been something like a starflower opening onto space: the purple-black petals of his brain growing ever smaller and more numerous the farther away from the center. And all of these parts were quite dead. It seemed that the Silicon God's destruction of his enemy was total. In only one respect had the Silicon God's attack upon Ede been less than completely fero-cious: apparently he had spared the many different Earths that Ede must have made. Beginning at a radius of twenty-three light-years outward from the Star of Ede, almost every star was ac-companied by a fat, round, blue and white, water-swollen Earth. This discovery astonished Danlo. He could not imagine why Ede would want to create so many copies of Old Earth. Just gazing at even one of these splendid worlds touched him with marvel and mystery. He thought that these god-made spheres of rock and water and air might somehow hold the secret to Ede's death (or life), and so he turned his lightship to the nearest stars to seek out these Earths one by one.

It was as he was surveying the sixty-sixth of these Earths that he made a thrilling discovery. the *Snowy Owl* was circling the Earth in a low orbit, no more than three hundred miles above the level of the sea. Below him, straight down through layers of ozone and atmosphere, was the great mother continent that had once been called Urasia. Through the breaks in the puffy clouds, he could just see the brown and white folds of the famous Hindu Kush—the mountains of death. And soon, in seconds, his light-ship passed over the first peaks of the Himalaya range. Through one of his telescopes he studied the icefalls of Sagarmatha, the highest mountain and mother goddess of the world.

If Ede truly had created this world, then he had reproduced it almost exactly as Old Earth had been some ten thousand years before the Swarming. In its configuration of glaciers, in its snow-cut ridges and south-facing col, this holy mountain appeared almost exactly as the picture of the ancient and historic Sagarmatha that his computer called up from memory and painted for him with electrons and light. And the surrounding mountains of Pumori and Khumbutse precisely matched this computer-generated map as well. Below him to the north-west was a shining peak called Kailas—also known as Kang Rimpoche to the ancient Buddhists who had regarded this mountain as holy above all others. He easily identified it by the nearby lake, Manasarowar.

It was as he was looking down upon this beautiful lake that his ship intercepted a signal. Surprisingly, it was a simple, and weak, burst of radio waves pulsing once each second like the beating of a man's heart. His computer could decode no information written into these slow, steady waves, and so he concluded that it was nothing more than a beacon, much like the flashing lights on Neverness's Mount Urkel that warn the windjammers and lightships away from the dark and icy rocks below. But why should there be a radio beacon on a pristine Earth where the only flying things were the eagles and the owls and the winged insects that the lesser birds occasionally fed upon?

Before Danlo could pass around the curve of the earth out of range, he fired his rockets and turned his ship through the cold, blue-black space above the mountains. He homed in on the source of the signal: one of the lesser peaks of the Himalayas to the west. He almost decided to explore this peak, and so he took his elegant, diamond-hulled ship down through the atmosphere, the ions, the clouds and the wind, down to a high valley bare of little other than rocks and snow.

He came to Earth on a flat snowfield no wider than the beach outside the Hofgarten on Neverness. He opened the pit of his ship and stepped out onto layers of crunching, old snow. Because he knew it would be cold, he wore his wool kamelaika, his boots, and the black sable furs that he had been given when he first became a journeyman pilot. He also wore a pair of polarized goggles against the dazzling mountain light. The air around him was thin and clear and brilliant with light reflected off the ridges and glaciers all around him. Above him, just to the north, was the peak that he sought. As he squinted at this shining mountain, he made out the unmistakable lines of a building perched on one of its ledges. It was a small building, he thought, a rather simple construction of dark wooden beams contrasted with glittering walls of organic stone. It looked much like the old Architect temples he had once seen on Urradeth. Why Ede would have built such a temple on a high mountain col on a lost Earth deep inside the Vild he couldn't imagine. He was certain, though, that the radio beacon had originated from some source inside the temple. For no good reason, he hoped that this beacon—or the temple itself—might hold the secret of how Ede the God had died. Standing in the cold, rarefied air he was full of hopes and dreams (and memories), and so without further thought, he pulled his goggles tight over his eyes and began the long trek up the mountain.

It took him most of the day to complete this journey. A day, in the manifold, in the superluminal fenestration of a lightship, can carry a pilot six hundred trillion miles through the stars. But to a pilot carrying his own weight up a broken mountain slope, bearing a heavy pack full of food, a tent, extra clothing, and bottles of oxygen, a day is little enough time to cover more than a dozen miles. Although the terrain itself was not very difficult, too many days spent floating in the pit of his ship had weakened Danlo's muscles. He was unaccustomed to exercise of any sort, and this hard hiking in the thin, cold air quickly exhausted him. More than once he stopped to gasp in great lungfuls of oxygen from one of his five little blue bottles. Since many full men had climbed much higher than this without sucking on the nipple of a plastic bottle, he thought it was slightly childish to pamper himself this way.

Danlo, though, was high in the highest mountain range on a planet identical to Old Earth. Two-thirds of the atmosphere lay below him, blanketing the green jungles and the oceans and the far-off dusty plains. Without sufficient oxygen he might have thrown a blood clot and so suffered a collapsed lung or the stroke of death. As it was, his head ached savagely, and as he stepped higher and higher up a sparkling snow ridge, it felt as though a sliver of rock had lodged itself through his eye socket. If he had been prudent, of course, he might have waited several days to acclimatize himself to the thinner air before beginning this excruciating climb. But it was his will and pride to hate prudence, as a man who has been buried alive might hate the cold, clary walls of a crypt. In his blood he could almost feel the signal of the beacon above him beating like a drum clock, and so he panted and pushed his way up the mountain.

His path took him across sunny slopes covered with rhododendrons and other flowering plants. As he plodded higher, there were only mosses and rocks shagged with green and orange lichens. And higher still, there was only bare rock, ice, and snow. By the time he crested the last ridge and stepped onto the broad col on which the temple was built, the snowfields around him were growing gray and cold with the falling twilight. He might have paused to pitch his tent on the freezing snow, but it was his intention to gain entrance to the temple as soon as he could and to spend the night inside.

To look down upon this building out of his memory was very strange. No path led across the snowfield to the temple gates. The temple sat in the middle of a large col, a broad natural bowl scooped out of ice and granite between the darkening peaks to the north and south. As he had first estimated, the temple itself was not large. None of its four walls exceeded one hundred yards in length or in height. Its shape was cubelike, and it rose straight up out of the snow like an overgrown crystal of salt. In truth, except for the organic stone from which it was wrought, it was an ugly building.

In the first cold of evening, Danlo walked straight toward the temple. It did not take him long to cross the frozen col. He walked over the crunching snow straight up to the gates, which were really more like simple doors: two rectangular slabs of wood set into a smooth stone wall. A set of ten shallow stairs led up to them. He quickly mounted these icy stairs and paused before the doors. They were tightly shut, perhaps locked, and he used his ice axe to knock against the crossbeam of one of the doors before trying to open it. The sound of steel against hard old wood rang out and echoed along the glaciers and peaks above him. He knocked again, and then waited for the jarring sound to die.

In the quiet of the mountains, in the clear air so near to the glorious stars, even the steaming of his breath seemed harsh and overloud. For a long time he studied the strange constellations in the sky as he waited before this silent door. He watched the sky, almost expecting to see Sivan's *Red Dragon* fall down from near space. At last, he decided to open the door. With his ice axe, he cleared away the drifts of snow blown up against the base of the door and chipped away at the tough old ice he found below, frozen to the topmost stair. Because he was very tired, these little tasks took quite a long time. When he thought the door was free he grasped the round steel ring that served as the door's handle, and pulled. But the door would not open. He threw off his pack and braced his foot flat against the opposite door. He pulled leaning back hard, while simultaneously pushing his leg straight out to help provide leverage; he pulled with all his strength, pulled so fiercely that his muscles trembled and his spine almost ruptured and his arteries throbbed like snakes beneath his face.

With much shrieking of rusted steel, the door swung slowly open. He might have celebrated this victory by raising his arms to the sky and crying out like a thallow, but instead he suddenly found himself bent over against his knees, gasping for breath in almost utter exhaustion.

It was the wind that revived him. The wind, he remembered, was the wild white breath of the world, and it inspirited him with a power beyond that of mere oxygen to brighten his tired blood. He pushed his pack through the doorway and then stepped into the entrance hall. This high room was much like the halls of other temples that he had visited on Urradeth. There were the various sculptures of Nikolos Daru Ede (as a man) poised on marble stands all along the room's perimeter. There were old steel benches, cold flame globes, a dried-up fountain silvered with spiderwebs and strewn with the husks of dead insects, and hot flame globes suspended high above that no longer radiated either heat or light. On the north wall facing him, someone had made a painting of the important scenes out of the life of Ede. This painting, at least, was still alive. For a while Danlo watched with amusement as Julius Ulric Ede—Ede's father—presented the Ede child with his first tutorial computer on his first birthday.

Then Danlo turned to the handfast at the center of the hall. This was an ominous-looking little black box fused to a bright chromium stand as high as a man's waist. A worthy Architect, upon entering almost any of the Cybernetic Universal Church's various temples, would insert his right hand through the dark opening of this box. He would wait silently and calmly, trying not to sweat while the handfast completed a scan of his DNA. If he was truly worthy of worship—that is to say if he was an Architect in good standing who had recently been cleansed of negative programs and was not in arrears in his tithes to the Church—a pleasing note would chime out, and, for a moment, the Architect's face would appear on the north wall with the face of Ede the God smiling down upon him. But if this Architect had not cleansed himself within the last year, an alarm would sound, alerting the guardian robots that one of the unworthy was about to defile the temple.

On some barbarous worlds such as Ultima, the handfasts were infamous for concealing sharp needles tipped with deadly poisons. Anyone arrogant enough to enter the temple uncleansed would feel cold steel pricking through his flesh, and very soon, the fiery pain of ekkana or some other drug. Although Danlo thought that this handfast might be dead, too, he did not put it to the test. Instead, he set his pack down resting against its stand. Then he bowed to the face of Ede glittering on the wall, and he turned to explore the main body of the temple.

He passed through a small door to his right and entered one of the temple's gowning rooms. Here, in a narrow room of benches and steel closets, the male Architects would remove their street clothes before donning the sacred undergarments known as kardalai. They would pull on their sacred kimonos, too, before fastening a little skullcap to their shaved heads. Thus properly dressed, they would pass out of one of two doors that led into the deeper parts of the temple.

Any Architect in need of a cleansing would submit himself to one of the readers who waited in the many cleansing cells along the temple's west (and east) wall. Beyond the cleansing rooms, Danlo knew, at the very rear of the temple, there was a hospice where dying Architects were taken in to rest before spending their last moments as human beings. There was a vastening chamber where their minds were copied and carked into an eternal computer, and of course, a crematorium to sublime the bodies that had been emptied of true soul. Adjacent to the room containing the great plasma ovens were the chambers of the readers and the elders. Danlo thought this might be a rare opportunity to behold these forbidden chambers, but first he wanted to walk through the temple's two central halls. And so, as if he were a worthy Architect properly gowned and cleansed, he opened the door to the meditation hall and stepped inside.

Immediately upon entering this large, rectangular room, he held his breath in astonishment. The meditation room should have been a stark and vastly serene place. It should have been bare of everything except soft wool prayer mats and the whisper of chants and supplications falling off the glittering stone walls. Instead it was full of things. On stands of some clear, hard crystal that looked like diamond, there were displayed gyres and selduks, mantelets and kevalin sets and the heaumes of various cleansing computers. There were clearfaces and tortrixes and many models of eternal computers. All of these cybernetica were relics and holy objects of the many Edeic sects. On one of the stands, he even saw a set of the Reformed Church's priceless Edeic lights, these once-living jewels wrought of firestones that now appeared to be quite dead.

All through the hall, there were many other things used in the ceremonies of this starflung religion: a babri worn by the elders of the Universal Church of Ede; the staff-computer of the Cyber-

netic Pilgrims of the Manifold; a bottle of holy wine used by the
Fathers of Ede; a replica of Ede's original clearface that adorns
the temples of the Fellowship of Ede as well as those of the
Fostora Separatist Union and the Architects of the Universal
God. Arrayed in no way that he could detect, there were a hundred holy mirrors, perhaps from a hundred different churches,
reflecting the images of the heaps of things gathered in the hall.
One of these mirrors reflected his own lively blue eyes when he
paused in front of it to regard the beard that had grown over his
face during his journey from the Entity.

Next to a glass jar containing a blue rose sacred to the Architects of the Evolutionary Church of Ede, he found a rack holding
a dozen flutes and shakuhachis. He remembered that Nikolos
Daru Ede had been famous for his performances with these
splendid instruments. With a quick smile at his readiness to commit sacrilege, he picked up one of the flutes. He carried it with
him through the grand doorway where the meditation hall let into
the facing room. He thought that perhaps this room would hold
fewer objects and thus the acoustics would be better for the playing of flutes. And so he walked into the Temple's holiest of
holies.

Directly in front of him, in this dead quiet place, was an
upraised altar covered with a square white carpet. As with any of
the very austere Urradeth temples, the only holy object on the
altar was an exact replica of Ede's eternal computer: a large
black cube of neurologics and circuitry resting on mirrored
chrome. Around the altar, across the facing room's glittering
stone floor, there were hundreds of rectangular prayer mats neatly
arrayed in columns and rows. A facing heaume sat gleaming at
the center of each of these mats. It seemed that the room had
been set for an important ceremony. It seemed that at any moment cadres of worthy Architects wearing their glittering kimonos should file into the room and kneel on these mats, there to
pull the chrome-covered heaumes over their heads in order to
interface the eternal computer before them. But there were no
Architects to be found in this lost and ancient temple. There was
only one man, Danlo wi Soli Ringess, who thought to play his
newly found flute to the eternal seeking of human soul.

And then, just as he was about to press the wooden mouthpiece to his lips, he noticed a swirl of colored lights to his left.
There, just outside the facing room's other doorway leading back
into the meditation hall, he noticed a seemingly simple devotionary, a little device that the Architects of the Old Church give to

one another so that they may view the miracle of Ede the Man becoming Ede the God. Devotionaries were little black boxes that projected holograms of the face and form of Ede. Devotionaries were also sanctified personal computers that many individual Architects carried in their hands wherever they went. Many devotionaries, he remembered, could generate and receive radio signals to interface with various planetary communications networks. Because he thought that this devotionary might be the source of the signal that had brought him down to this Earth—and because it piqued his curiosity that of all the cybernetica in the hall, only this little machine still seemed to be turned on—he walked over to examine it more closely.

Immediately, his eyes focused upon the imago of Nikolos Daru Ede. Suspended in the dusty air above the devotionary—a black box bejeweled with hundreds of tiny computer eyes like the compound eyes of an insect—was a faithful replication of the most famous man in the history of the human race. In his first life Ede had not been a large man, and due to the projection limitations of the devotionary, ironically, the hologram display only diminished his dimensions. This luminous, almost evanescent Ede was no more than one foot high from his blue silk slippers to the diamond clearface that he wore on his head. Yet as he had in life, the Ede seemed to usurp and completely subjugate the space that he inhabited, transforming it into something other than mere space. This was the design and purpose of all devotionaries, to show Ede the Man as the one who would transcend all space, all matter, all time.

Because it pleased Danlo—sometimes—to honor the rituals of various religions, he bowed to this imago of a man who had lived almost three thousand years before. Then he circled closer, the better to study Ede's famous face. The imago was turned away as if to look out into the meditation hall and the main body of the Temple—or perhaps only to regard it as a god might look down upon a world that he has created. It was possible, Danlo knew, if he positioned himself just so with his eyes level with those of the imago, to look into the eyelight of this hologram almost as if looking at a real man.

Some of the better devotionaries—those connected with computer eyes and ears—could even process information received from their immediate environment. They could "see" the faces of the devoted Architects who bowed before them; they could "hear" their voices and prayers when spoken to. The devotionaries of the Old Church projected an Ede who could react in certain programed ways according to the words, facial expressions, voice patterns and emotions of the individual devotee. Thus an Architect searching for answers to the problems of her life might be greeted with platitudes or gems of dogma (or sometimes even deep wisdom) out of the Book of God; a doubtful Architect might be gently chastened to return to his faith; a sad and soul-sick Architect might be graced with an unusually long vision of Ede the God: the hologram of His glorious and golden face would suddenly blaze as with an intense inner light and would beam down upon her like the sun. Although Danlo expected the Ede imago to fall into one or another of these almost mechanical attitudes, he was unprepared for what actually happened. At his approach, the Ede suddenly turned his head, arched an eyebrow, and smiled almost wickedly. He looked straight at Danlo and said, *"Di nisti so fayance? La nistenei ito so wahai."*

Danlo did not recognize the language that issued from the devotionary. But even if he had, it always discomfited him to speak to a robot or a hologram generated by some computer, and so he smiled shyly and said nothing.

On wi lo-te hi ne-te il lao-on?

He continued to look at the imago. Ede was not pretty at all but rather striking in appearance. With his coffee-cream skin and his large, sensuous lips, there was a softness about his face that hinted at something deeply feminine inside him. And yet, if this imago were true to life, Danlo thought that Ede must have been a hard man, too, for his features were set with purpose, as if his strong jaws and voicebox and face muscles were only tools in the service of his will. The most memorable thing about him were his eyes, bright and black, full of experience, intuition, acumen. Ede's detractors had always said that he had the cold and calculating eyes of a merchant, but it was not so. In truth, his were the eyes of a dreamer, a mystic, a prophet. Inside his dark, smoldering eyes there were worlds inside worlds. Ede was the man who would contain the whole universe, and everything about him bespoke a hunger for the infinite.

Parang wan i songas noldor ano?

At this, Danlo finally shook his head and sighed out, "I do not understand."

There was a pause lasting little more than a moment, and then the high, tense voice of Ede the Man whined out into the air. Although it was the devotionary itself that generated this famous voice, a set of sulki grids inside this black box convolved the sound so that the words seemed to flow directly from the mouth of Ede. "Are you of the Civilized Worlds? I would think you must be if you speak the Language."

Danlo smiled, then laughed softly. Despite his mistrust of artificial intelligences and the programs that enabled them to communicate with human beings, he was amused.

After staring at the imago awhile, Danlo nodded his head. "Yes, I speak the Language."

"It's curious that you do speak the Language," the Ede imago said, "since we are far from any of the Civilized Worlds."

"Very far," Danlo agreed.

"I'm glad that you speak the Language since this enables us to speak together."

"To . . . speak together," Danlo said, smiling.

"I've been waiting a long time for such a conversation," the Ede said.

Danlo stared long and deeply at the imago of Nikolos Daru Ede. "You have been programed to make conversation, yes?"

"In a way," the Ede said, and his eyes glittered like the organic stone of the walls that surrounded them. "But I might rather say that this devotionary has been programed to instantiate *me* so that I might converse with *you*."

This response almost astonished Danlo. A devotionary's imago of Ede should have been programed to discuss the Doctrine of the Halting or the Eight Duties that were the stepping-stones toward an Architect's vastening—or even the reprograming of an individual Architect's mind following the cleansing of his sins. But it should never have referred to its *own* programing. Danlo thought that there was something strange about the tenor of their conversation, about the very act of exchanging words with this glowing hologram which claimed to be an instantiation of Ede.

"Where were you . . . where was this devotionary programed, then?" Danlo asked. He did not quite know whether he should direct his words to the devotionary or to the Ede imago itself. "On which planet were you made?"

"These are excellent questions," the Ede said.

Danlo waited a long time for the imago to say more, and then he asked, "You . . . do not know?"

Evasively, the Ede replied, "It may be that the answers to these questions will emerge as we converse further."

Danlo slowly circled around the imago to view the face of Ede from different angles. But at each shifting of his position, Ede turned his head, and his shimmering gaze followed Danlo's, never breaking the connection of their eyes. The imago should not have been able to do this. Devotionary imagoes of Ede were never programed with such a range of motion and responsiveness. Devoted Architects must humbly seek out the eyelight of Ede and wait for his benediction, for this god of gods will not otherwise take notice of the all-too human beings who bow before him.

"Why this program, then?" Danlo asked. "I have never seen a devotionary that was programed to hold this kind of conversation."

"It's always interesting to wonder why we're programed as we are."

Danlo said nothing as he listened to his breath steaming out of his mouth. He smiled at the unbelievable idea that he—or any other living thing—could be programed as if he were nothing more than a computer made out of neurons and synapses and the chemicals of the brain.

"Though a more interesting question," the Ede continued, "is who programs us as we are? And more interesting still: who programs the programer?"

This whiff of cybernetic metaphysics annoyed Danlo as much as it amused him, and so he considered turning off the imago. With the Ede hologram vanished back into the neverness of the computer's program, he thought it might be easier to determine if the devotionary had generated the signal that had brought him down to this earth. He circled around the devotionary, searching among its glittering black faces for some switch or power plate to accomplish this end. But he found nothing, just hundreds of computer eyes watching *his* eyes as if he were some strange being impossible truly to comprehend. He concluded that this must be one of the many devotionaries activated by the human voice alone. He wondered if it might be coded to respond to almost anyone's voice. He was about to utter the word *down* when he noticed the imago staring at him. Very quickly, in moments, the Ede's luminous face fell through a succession of emotions: alarm, regret, grief, anger, pride, exhilaration, hope and then alarm again, which was astonishing, since imagos of Ede were usually programed to beam forth only wisdom, serenity, joy or even love.

"Please don't take me down," the Ede suddenly said.

"How did you know that I was considering taking you down?"

"I have many eyes," the Ede said. "And I can see many things."

"Then you can read my *face*? You run cetic programs, yes?"

"My programing is very extensive. And the first algorithm of my programing is that I must ask not to be taken down."

"I see. You must *ask* this."

"My only power is that of words."

"Then it is a simple thing to take you down, yes?"

"It's simple indeed, but one would have to know the right word."

"Then do you know what this word is?"

"I know the word, but I could never say it."

"I see."

"The mere utterance of it, of course, would take me down."

"Then it is futile for me to ask what this unutterable word is, yes?"

"It is futile," the Ede said, "but why would you even wish to take me down?"

"I was hoping to discover the source of a simple radio signal." Danlo watched Ede's face fall into an expression of sudden relief. "I had thought that this devotionary might generate this signal."

"But of course it does," the Ede said, smiling. "Of course I do."

"You speak of the devotionary as if it were identical to yourself."

"Well, it runs my program. Don't you speak of your body and brain as if identical to *yourself*?"

"Sometimes I do," Danlo admitted. He did not want to tell this smirking Ede that he had once thought of his deep self as a fusion of his deathless self with his other self, which happened to be a white bird known as the Snowy Owl. "Sometimes, I speak this way, but I am not a computer."

"And I am not just a computer, either," the Ede said, his face brilliant with self-satisfaction.

"What are you, then?"

At this the Ede smiled wickedly and said, *"Ishq Allah maboud 'lillah:* I am program, programer, and that which is programed."

Danlo, who had once memorized many poems composed in ancient Arabic, smiled at this obvious mistranslation. He said, *"God* is love, lover, and beloved. Only . . . you are not God."

"Am I not? Am I not Ede the God?"

Just then the Ede's face fell through the usual divine emotions of wisdom, serenity, joy, and of course, love. And then his eyes flashed with light, and his whole face seemed to melt into a golden brilliance like that of the sun. It was hard for Danlo to look upon this splendid face. The intense light of it hurt his eyes; the sudden pain that stabbed through his forehead caused him to throw his arm across his burning eyes.

"You are only an imago of Ede as he was as a man," Danlo said at last. "And Ede himself, even as a god, was no more *God* than the dust beneath my boots. No more, no . . . less."

The Ede's face was now a mask of worry. "I notice that you use the past tense in referring to the god."

"For a simple devotionary, you seem to notice many things."

"As I've said, I have many eyes."

"You seem to *know* many things."

"Well, I really know very little," the Ede said. "And tragically, there is space in my memory for very little more information."

"But you know that you are programed to send a signal out toward the stars, yes?"

"Of course I do."

"Why this signal, then?" Danlo asked. He held his hand out toward the meditation hall, pointing at a selduk gleaming on its stand. "Why this temple, as it is? Why should you be programed to lead people here?"

Danlo rubbed his aching forehead as he struggled to breathe the thin, sunless air. Being inside an Architect temple, he thought, was as stifling as being inside a computer. An old, dusty computer.

"Who programed you, then?" Danlo asked. He turned to look at the imago's almost metallic-seeming face. "Was it Ede the God? The true Ede?"

"You ask difficult questions to answer."

"I am sorry."

"It's not that I don't know the answers, of course. But my programing forces me to exercise a certain caution."

"I see."

"If I could ask *you* certain questions," the Ede said, "it might be that the answers to your questions would become clear as we proceeded."

Danlo was now smiling despite his annoyance. He said, "Then please proceed."

"Very well—you are a most reasonable man."

"Thank you."

"My first question is this," the Ede said. "Where were you when you intercepted my signal?"

"I was three hundred miles above this Earth. I was making my fourteenth orbit when I intercepted your signal."

"I see. You intercepted this signal—how?"

"My ship's radio is programed to search for such signals."

"I see. You were orbiting this Earth in a ship?"

"Did you think that I was flying through the sky like a bird?" Danlo asked, smiling.

"I see that you like to answer questions with questions."

"And should I not answer questions with questions?"

"I see that you have a taste for playing with others' sensibilities."

"I am sorry," Danlo said. He looked directly into the Ede's shiny black eyes. "I have been rude, yes?"

"Well, that's the human way, isn't it?"

"Sometimes," Danlo said. "But it is not my way. That is, I have been taught that it is unseemly for a man to speak rudely to anyone—man, woman, or child." Or to an animal, Danlo remembered, or to a tree or a rock or even to the murderous west wind that blows in the night. A true man must speak truly and courteously to all the creations of the world, even one so strange as an imago of a man shining forth out of a computer. "I am sorry. It is just that I am unused to speaking with artificial intelligences . . . so deeply."

At this, the Ede's face hardened into an unreadable mask. And yet there was a brightness about the eyes as if Ede's program, as sublime as it might be, could not conceal his interest in what Danlo had said.

"Have you spoken with many such intelligences?" Ede asked.

"No," Danlo said, "not many."

"Have you spoken with any of these intelligences on your journey here?"

"Perhaps," Danlo said. He thought of the Solid State Entity, and he wondered what kind of intelligence really controlled Her vast moon-brains. "But perhaps not."

"Perhaps or perhaps not," the Ede repeated. He smiled mechanically. "I see that you're a most considerate man. You've remembered that I said I've little room left in my memory, and so you've chosen not to overload me with new information."

"I am sorry," Danlo said. Just then he did not want to tell a hologram—or anyone else—of his journey to the Solid State Entity.

"Sometimes it can be difficult to determine which intelligences are artificial and which are not."

"I suppose that is true," Danlo said.

"But you say that you *have* spoken with what you call artificial intelligences before?"

"Yes, on the planet of my birth. In the city where I was educated, there were many computers. Many ai programs."

"Excuse me?"

"*Ai* programs," Danlo said. "The cetics of my Order sometimes call them *I* programs. In mockery of the belief that computers could possess a sense of selfness."

"I see. The cetics of your Order must be antiquarians."

"That is true—in a way they are. Except the cybershamans. They love computers." Danlo closed his eyes for a moment, remembering. In his mind he saw a diamond clearface molded tightly across a white skull and pale blue eyes as cold as death. Then he said, "Sometimes the cybershamans refer to ai programs as god programs."

"A more appropriate name, I should think."

"Perhaps."

"Your Order—is this the Order founded in the city of Neverness?"

"Yes."

"May I conclude that you are a pilot of this Order?"

"Yes."

"Well, then, you've fallen far, haven't you, Pilot? In your diamond ship that falls faster than light—what is that you pilots call your ships?"

"We call them lightships," Danlo said.

"Oh, I'd forgotten," the Ede said. "But how is it that you were able to take your lightship into parts of the galaxy that have been impenetrable for so long?"

"We have learned to penetrate these spaces. The Vild itself. We have learned to map through the manifold beneath these wild stars."

"I'd thought that the manifold beneath the Vild was unmappable."

"It . . . . almost is."

"Then you have fallen here twenty thousand light-years from Neverness?"

"Yes."

"In your lightship, by yourself? By mappings that you've made alone?"

"Yes," Danlo said. "Pilots always enter the manifold alone."

"Then you've had no help in entering the manifold or piloting your ship?"

"No—of course not."

"But you must have had help in finding this planet?"

Danlo was silent as he stared at the hologram of Ede.

"A hundred million stars in the Vild," Ede said. "Or perhaps thrice as many. Is it a miracle that brought you to this Earth?"

Danlo was aware of the Ede's eyes glowing darkly, practically drilling like lasers into his eyes. He was aware of the devotionary's hundreds of glittering computer eyes focusing on his face. He remembered, then, that cetic programs could enable computers to read truth or falseness from a man's face.

"I was given the fixed-points of a star near this Earth," Danlo said.

"And who gave you this information?"

With a sudden release of his breath, Danlo finally told the Ede imago something of his journey to the Solid State Entity. He made only passing reference to his tests on the beach, and as to his encounter with the Entity's incarnation as Tamara, he said nothing at all. Neither did he speak of his quest to find his father or of the warrior-poet who pursued him. But he revealed that he sought the lost planet called Tannahill. He told the Ede that he sought the Architects of the Old Church, they who were fulfilling their doctrines and prophecies by destroying the stars.

"That is a remarkable story," the Ede said. His face was the very embodiment of the emotion of relief. "You must be a remarkable man to have wrested such information from the Entity."

Danlo looked at hologram's steady lights and said, "You know of the Entity, yes?"

But the Ede, it seemed, did not wish to discuss the Entity just then. He wished to discuss the mystery of Danlo's journey to this Earth, perhaps the mystery of Danlo himself.

"You're a remarkable man," the Ede repeated. "May I ask your name?"

"My name," Danlo said. He did not know which of his names to give to this irksome hologram. Once, he had been called Danlo the Wild; once, a kindly, white-furred alien had bestowed upon him the name of Danlo Peacewise. And then there were his other names: his first name, which his family would call him; the name of his anima, which would play a part in the shaping of the world; and his spirit name, his secret name, which he would whisper only to the wind. "I am . . . Danlo wi Soli Ringess," he said at last.

"Very good," the Ede said. "Then may I present myself? I am Nikolos Daru Ede."

Danlo smiled as he stared at Ede's blazing imago. "Of course you are," he said.

"I've been waiting years for someone to intercept the signal that led you here."

With a sigh, Danlo rubbed his aching forehead. Then he reached down to rub his aching legs. He was very tired from his climb up the mountain, almost as tired as he was from speaking with this strangely programed devotionary. He thought that he should turn away from the devotionary in order to explore the rest of the temple. And soon he must lay out his furs, eat a cold meal of kurmash, ship bread, and dried bloodfruit, and then try to sleep. But something about this ridiculous, foot-high Ede called to him. He sensed that the many-eyed black box generating the Ede might contain much valuable information. Perhaps somewhere in the devotionary's memory—coded as voltages of electrons or on-off pulses of light—was a clue as to the death of one of the galaxy's greatest gods. Danlo needed only to find the way to access this information. He needed only to say the perfect words, and then the devotionary's programs, according to an incredibly complex series of logical decisions, in the way of all programed and otherwise artificial intelligences, would cause the Ede imago to tell Danlo what he needed to know.

As if the Ede could read Danlo's thoughts, he smiled provocatively. And then the Ede said, "I am the door; knock and be opened."

Danlo closed his eyes, listening to the sound of his breath. From the front of the temple, through the cold halls, he heard the wind whooshing faintly through the door that he had left open. And then, suddenly, another door, a door deep inside him opened. And he knew. One moment he was mystified by the presence of this hologram of Ede the God, and in the next moment, a perfect knowledge of the origin of the devotionary's programing shone like a cold, clear light in his mind.

"You *are* Nikolos Daru Ede," he said. "Truly, Ede the God—what is left of him."

As Danlo stood with his hand held over his eyes, he looked through himself to events that had occurred long before he had been born. With a cold and terrible awareness, he looked through the doorway of the memory that lies inside memory. And what he saw was only endless war. It was a war of exploding stars and hydrogen bombs, bullets and information viruses, programed surrealities and bloody knives and weapons of pure consciousness that not even the gods could truly comprehend. The war had begun at least fifteen billion years ago, when the first galaxies had exploded outward from the primeval fireball that the astronomers called the beginning of the universe. Or perhaps the war had no true beginning or possible end, and was as eternal as purposes and passions in the mind of God. Whatever the genesis of this universal conflagration, the phase of the war that would eventually consume much of Danlo's life (and the lives of a hundred billion human beings from the Civilized Worlds to the Vild) could be traced back to a single flash point occurring some eight thousand years earlier at the end of the Lost Centuries. This great event was the fabrication of the Silicon God on Fostora.

The architects and scientists of Fostora built their would-be god on a tiny, airless moon, and they mined this speck of ice and rock with hydrogen bombs should it become necessary to destroy their noble creation. And then they waited. They wanted to see how a computer, initially programed to seek knowledge and control of the material universe, would evolve if given almost complete freedom from human mores and ethical constraints. It was their hypothesis that this unholy machine would develop an ethics all his own and a moral imperative beyond what most human beings understood as simple good or evil. It was their dream to create an entity that understood deep reality, a god, a new form of life as far beyond themselves as they were from worms. They hoped to learn from this god the secrets of the universe—and perhaps the purpose of that tragicomic race of hairless apes who had begun their galactic adventure on Old Earth some two million years before.

But as the first flash of light streamed through the optical filaments of his brain, within the first twenty billionths of a second after he had come into an awareness of himself (if indeed a computer can be truly aware), the Silicon God came to hate the human beings who had made him. He would have made war upon the scientists of Fostora and all human beings everywhere, but this, according to his deep programing, was the one thing that he could never do. And so instead he found a way to escape from his creators. In secret, far below the rocky surface of the moon on which he was imprisoned, he built spacetime engines a thousand times as large as those that are the heart of a lightship. And then he opened a window to the manifold. The Fostoran astronomers, looking out through their telescopes across black space, were astonished to behold the silvery gleam of a window opening, and then, an instant later, to watch as the Silicon God and the moon that contained him vanished from their neighborhood of space.

It would be another fifty centuries before a master pilot of the Order, Ananda wi Suso, discovered that the Silicon God had fallen out and occupied a stellar nebula some six thousand light-years away. There, in the unexplored regions of the Orion arm beyond the Sun—and beyond even the Rainbow Double—the Silicon God had absorbed whole planets and the light of many stars, and he had grown into a true god. There, over five thousand years, he had made war upon the many gods that had sprung from the human race—and many gods such as Solid State Entity and the April Colonial Intelligence had made war upon him.

All this Danlo saw as he closed his eyes and looked deeply into that bright and marvelous place that was neither space nor time nor materiality but rather contained all these things, and everything—everything that had ever been or might possibly ever be. He saw the great battle fought between the Silicon God and the god called Ede. This battle itself could be divided into three distinct phases or acts. In the first act, lasting more than a millennia, the two gods discovered each other across an ocean of stars. Each god, in his program to control the material universe and evolve, was really much like the other, and so it was only natural that each should seek the means of controlling and destroying his rival. For a thousand years of human time, they vied for knowledge of each other. They sent out secret spy ships to infiltrate each other's brains and tap the streams of tachyons by which each communicated with himself. They infected each other with billions of bacteria-size robots that might bore through computer circuitry and reveal the architecture of their logics and their burned-in programming. For a thousand years they fought a war of information viruses and disinformation as each tried to gain control over the other's programing, but neither could prevail over the other.

And then the Silicon God called for a truce. He proposed an alliance with his deadly enemy. He presented Ede the God with a plan for each of them to divide up the galaxy, and then, ten billion years farwhen, to divide up all the galaxies of the local cluster of galaxies, and the superclusters, and someday, the whole of the universe itself. He offered this plan in the form of a surreality: perhaps the most complete and detailed simulation of future events that any god or computer in the Milky Way galaxy had ever run. Ede the God should have been very wary of this surreality, this gift of his rival god. In truth, as a man might spurn a goblet of wine offered by his enemy, he should have rejected it out of hand.

But Ede was flawed by the very hubris that had originally impelled him to transcend from human being into something more, and so he decided to accept the Silicon God's gift. After placing safeguards against poison programs and suchlike, he opened the gates of his light circuits to this seductive surreality that the Silicon God had made. But he underestimated the cleverness of this ancient machine god. As Ede's star-size brain glittered with simulations of an endlessly vast and glorious future, the Silicon God treacherously renewed his attack. He had copied parts of himself and camouflaged these duplicitous programs as God-algorithms hidden within the code of the surreality that he gave to Ede. When Ede opened himself to visions of himself as god of all gods, perhaps even as *the* one and only God of the universe, he found most of his master systems infiltrated by alien programs of what he called the Other.

This was the second act of their battle. In less than a thousand seconds—an eternity in the life of a computer—one by one each of Ede's guardian programs was fracted and then failed. The Other began to seize control of Ede's operating systems. Soon, his last defenses would go down, and then Ede would lose control over the material components of his body and brain, and worse, he would lose control over his mind.

Thus began their battle's third and final act. Because none of Ede's own simulations of the future had ever hinted that such a disaster was possible, he was ill-prepared for what he must do next. But he was neither helpless nor hopeless. Even before his vastening as a god, he had always been *the* master of computational origami, the folding together of many computer parts into a synergistic whole. And now he proved to be a master of the *un*folding. With his mainbrain lost, he decided to abandon it. The Other was chewing through millions of layers of circuitry, converting him to a slave unit, eating him alive. But Ede would not leave the largest and most glorious lobe of his brain to be incorporated into the brain of this treacherous machine god. After pruning his programs and memories and then encoding them as an intense tachyon pulse, he set loose the zero-point energies of the spacetime within his great brain and exploded himself into the pieces of flotsam that Danlo had discovered orbiting the Star of Ede.

He had hoped to destroy the Other and leave not the tiniest diamond circuit for the Silicon God to feed upon. He split the tachyon signal into a million separate beams aimed at a million smaller lobes of his brain orbiting nearby stars. Almost instantly—in less than a thousand nanoseconds—he found his master programs installed in these millions of moon-size brains. But the Other had followed him. In truth, like a leech attached to a man's eyeball (or rather, like a retrovirus stitching itself into its host's DNA), the Other had carked itself into Ede's master programs, into his memory, into his very soul.

Again Ede pruned his programs, coded them as pure signal, and in a flash of tachyons infinitely faster than light, made the almost instantaneous unfolding of his self to smaller lobes of his brain farther out among the stars. Again he destroyed the computer circuitry that he left behind. But he could not wholly free his programs from the Other, and so he repeated this pruning of himself many times. Many, many times. Bit by bit, Ede's soul— his very self—diminished even as his consciousness was blown like the seeds of a dried-out dandelion flower across twenty light-years of space.

At last, when he had pruned himself from a great galactic being into something that could barely be called a god, he found himself installed in millions of separate computer lobes, some of which were as tiny as rocks. And still the Other remained with him. Only now, like a sleekit fleeing a fox into its deepest burrow, Ede was trapped; 99.99999 percent of his great and beautiful brain was destroyed, and no spare circuitry or piece of machinery survived to run his programs or store his memories. And so Ede, the god—what was left of him—made the hardest decision of his life. He destroyed all but one of his brain parts, and then he made a final pruning. In truth, the soul-surgery that he performed on himself might better be called an amputation, but it was really more, much more than even the agony of an animal who gnaws off its leg to escape a trap. At the end of the third act of his battle with the Silicon God, which lasted no more than a millionth of a second, Ede simply erased every program and operating system, every algorithm, virtual, pathway, language, and memory that was not essential to his identity as Ede.

In this last and most desperate of prunings, he thought that he had finally edited out every bit of the Other. And so Ede wrote one final program. He compressed the essence of himself as pictures in a fractal code; in his panic to survive in any way that he could, he carked this core program into a simple radio signal and cast his soul to the black and empty spaces of the universe. It was a hideously crude thing for him to do. But he had no machinery left that might generate tachyons, nor even the high frequency laser light that could hold much more information than any radio signal. In this way, after thousands of years of personal evolution and his ontogenesis into one of the galaxy's greatest gods, after hopes and visions and dreams of infinity, Ede found himself reduced to nothing more than invisible radio waves spreading out through a cold vacuum at the torturously slow speed of light. He was nothing more than information encoded into a primitive pulse of energy of modulating amplitude and moderately low frequency; he was a cry in the night, a lost soul seeking home, the last gasp of breath of a dying man.

It was something of a miracle that this weakened radio signal, after years of crossing the vast interstellar deeps, had fallen down upon the Earth where Danlo now stood. It was a miracle that for centuries, in the lost temple that Ede had once built, the devotionary's radio receiver had remained always turned on, always open to the music and songs of the stars. And so it was a miracle that the program encoding Nikolos Daru Ede, the man, found itself received and installed in the very primitive circuitry of what was little more than a religious toy. It was a miracle, yes, but then all life is a miracle, even the life of a god who is dead and yet remains somehow mysteriously alive.

"You . . . are he," Danlo repeated. He stared at the hologram of Ede, which was staring back at him with an expression of astonishment written across his glowing face. "The core program that survived the battle."

"You know, then," Ede said, reading the strange light in Danlo's eyes. "But how do you know? How could you possibly know?"

Danlo looked down at the dusty temple floor. Six years before, in a dark corridor of the library on Neverness, he had looked into his deepest memory, and this marvelous way of seeing wholes from the tiniest of fragments had first flowered into consciousness. But how could he ever explain such a strange and mysterious sense to a computer?

"How does anything know?" Danlo asked. "How do we know that we know?"

"Do you really wish an answer to this question, Danlo wi Soli

Ringess? My program contains the answers to all the famous philosophical conundrums of man.''

Amused by this impossible offer, Danlo slowly shook his head and smiled. ''I have often wondered what a computer can know. What it truly *means* when the architects and programers say that a computer can know.''

''Then you are not of the school that believes ai programs can render a computer self-aware?''

''I do not like to *believe* things,'' Danlo said. ''I would rather know.''

''Then you must doubt that I am as conscious as yourself.''

''I do doubt. I am sorry.''

''You doubt—and yet here you have stood for a long time conversing with me as if my consciousness were the same as any man's.''

''Yes, that is true.''

Ede smiled his wicked smile, and then asked, ''If you had closed your eyes, would you have known that you were talking with a computer?''

''Is this to be the only test of consciousness, then?''

''Well, it's a time-honored test, isn't it? The ancient turing test.''

''That is true—but there are other tests, yes?''

''What tests?''

With a sigh, Danlo turned and crossed back into the meditation hall behind him. He stepped past the gyres and kevalin sets and the rack of wooden flutes. When he came to the glass jar encasing the blue rose that he had noticed earlier, he smiled at the sacrilege that he was about to commit. After clamping his palms on the cold glass, he lifted off this domelike container and set it carefully on the floor. Then he reached out and grasped the rose's stem. It was narrow and hard, with an almost woody feel to it. He wanted to examine the rose in the light of flame globes, and so, at arm's length, directly in front of his eyes, he held up this symbol of the impossible. Its petals were light blue and as lovely as those of a snow dahlia. He looked at the flower for a long time. Then he returned to the grand doorway of the facing room, where the devotionary projecting the hologram of Nikolos Daru Ede sat waiting on its little stand. Ede was waiting, too. He was floating in the air, watching with intense suspicion as Danlo presented the sacred rose to him.

''Do you see this pretty flower?'' Danlo asked.

''Of course I see it. I see many things.''

"Here," Danlo said, holding out the rose. "Take it."

The hologram of Ede extended one of his diminutive hands, but because his body was not made of flesh, he could not take it. However, the interference of the hologram's coherent light with the flower's blue petals highlighted the rose and caused it to glow brightly.

"I can't hold the flower, of course," Ede said. "I can't touch it."

"No," Danlo said. With a sad smile, he reached out his finger and stroked the flower's many petals. They were as cool as silk and felt as fine as gossamer. "I am sorry."

"Why?"

"Because it will be so hard for you to truly know whether or not this flower is real."

"It *looks* real," Ede said.

Danlo looked at the striations, veins, and the pattern of tiny filaments lining the rose. He said, "Yes, it does."

"But I would deduce that it's artificial. It would have been too difficult to have kept a real flower alive in my temple, even in a clary cold chamber, even in krydda suspension."

Again, Danlo touched the rose. He let the whorls of his fingertip linger over the petals' lacy surface. The cells of his skin slowly slid over the smoothness of gossilk, and instantly he knew that the rose was not real.

"In truth, it *is* artificial," he said.

"You see—we both knew this."

"No," Danlo said. "*I* knew that the rose was not real, but you only deduced it."

"I don't see the difference."

"There is all the difference in the universe."

At this, Ede's face froze into an unreadable mask, and for the first time he fell into silence.

"Talking to a computer's imago is like looking at an artificial flower," Danlo said. "You seem real, only . . ."

"Go on."

"Only, I cannot touch you. Your consciousness. Your . . . soul."

Ede waited a moment before saying, "But I am as real as you."

"No, you are only an ai program that causes electrons inside your brain circuits to move."

"I am as conscious as you are," Ede said.

"But how can that be?"

"I am as aware as any man."

Pain is the awareness of life, Danlo remembered. He stood there staring at the many-hued lights of Ede's little face as he brooded over this saying so close to his heart. He realized, then, that this was his own private turing test of consciousness: the ability to feel pain.

He told this to Ede, who said, "There are many kinds of pain."

"Yes," Danlo agreed as he held his hand over his eye, over the familiar pain shooting through his head. "But pain is always just pain. Pain always . . . hurts."

"Once, I was a man much as you," Ede said in his high, whiny voice. "And I had pains of the body much as any man. When I carked my mind into my computer and left my body behind, I'd thought to escape pain forever. But the pain of the mind is greater than any body pain. Infinitely greater."

"Others have said that to me before."

"Do you think it didn't hurt to cast off my body and become vastened in the light storms of my computer?"

"How could I know?"

"Do you think I haven't suffered for three thousand years at the fear that some essential part of my humanity—of *myself*—was lost in this vastening?"

"I do not know."

"And in my battle with the Silicon God, as I pruned my programs smaller and smaller—do you suppose this diminishment of myself wasn't pure agony?"

"Perhaps," Danlo said. "Or perhaps you are only programed to call it agony."

"Can you imagine what it's like to be a god?"

"No."

"It was like this," Ede said. "In less than a millionth of a second, if I wished, I could have thought all the thoughts that were ever recorded in all the libraries of man."

"I . . . am sorry," Danlo said.

Ede's face fell into an expression of grief. "I've lost almost everything. Even the great simulation with which the Silicon God destroyed me. Especially that. I can't tell you how perfect this simulation really was. The vision. The beauty. The *detail.* It was a surreality of all surrealities: I *saw* the galaxy remade, almost down to the configuration of every molecule. I saw myself transformed, ever vaster. I saw how I would be folded, connected, and how I would build ecologies of information that had never before existed in this universe. I knew what it would be like, someday, *really* to know. To know almost everything. And now I've forgotten it all. Only the faintest memory of a memory remains.''

As Danlo stood there twirling the stem of the blue rose between his fingers, Ede told him about other things that had been lost. Once, Ede said, he had reconstructed the history of the Milky Way galaxy, from the firing of the first stars to the rise of the rainbow star systems and alien races such as the Shakeh and the Elsu and the divine leldra. All that was now forgotten, as was the secret of destroying the Silicon God, which he had apparently learned only toward the end of their battle. Forgotten, too, were the words to a poem that he had been composing for a thousand years. All he could remember was his reason for creating this great poem: It was his fancy to woo a goddess in the center of the cluster of Valda Galaxies some fifty million light-years out toward Yarmilla Cluster. All the words were gone from his memory. This, he said, was not surprising, since each of the poem's sixty-six trillion ''words'' was really a complex of information compressed as beautiful fractal images.

''To lose pieces of oneself is a great agony,'' Ede told Danlo. ''But it is not the worst of it.''

''What is, then?''

''Not knowing is the worst pain there is.''

''Not knowing . . . what?''

''Not knowing if I am really *I*. Not knowing who I really am.''

''I am sorry,'' Danlo said. He studied the rather convincing grimace formed by Ede's facial programs. He thought that Ede certainly looked as if he were suffering a great deal of pain.

''The Silicon God was *killing* me,'' Ede said. ''I had only nanoseconds to write the final program of myself. The program that *is* myself, that must be I, if anything really is.''

As Danlo nodded his head and pressed the petals of the artificial flower to his lips, Ede told him of some of the difficulties in hurriedly writing such a program. He described his frustration in forcing his great self into a personality type that couldn't quite capture the essence of who he really was. But he had had no other choice, he said. From descriptions of various human traits out of sources such as the Enneagram—as well as the cetic system of universal archetypes and the old, Earth-centered astrology—he had cobbled together a persona, an identity, a self. For an ai program, it was a subtle piece of work, even if somewhat incomplete and crude. And Ede, of course, was unhappy with it. He was unhappy with himself, with what he had become.

"Where is the mirror in which I can see my own face?" Ede asked. "How can I ever know that I really *am* I, Nikolos Daru Ede?"

Danlo looked down at the blue rose in his hand and said, "Truly, I cannot know what you are. Conscious or not, aware of your own awareness or only a program running a machine. But you are only you, yes? This is the marvel. You cannot be other than what you are. Isn't this enough?"

"No, it's not enough."

"Then . . . I am sorry."

"There is something I want, something I programed myself to want above all other things."

"And what is that?"

Ede's bright eyes flashed as he looked at Danlo and said, "I want to be human again."

"Oh," Danlo said in astonishment. "Oh, no."

"I want to be a man again, to have a body, to breathe real air."

"But you said—"

"I have said that existence as pure mind is infinitely greater than being a mere human. But what if I am wrong? I want to *know*," Ede said. He looked at the flower clasped in Danlo's hand. "I want to feel myself alive again. I want to smell roses again. I'm afraid that I've forgotten what it's like to really live."

Danlo shook his head, slowly, sadly. "What you desire is impossible."

"Perhaps," Ede said. "But on Old Earth, blue roses were also an impossibility until the botanists engineered the first one at the end of the Holocaust Centuries."

"A human being is not a rose."

"I believe that the Solid State Entity has learned the secret of incarnation." Ede's face, as he said this, was full of hope. "I believe that She can incarnate human beings as easily as a cartoonist creates his characters."

"Perhaps," Danlo said. He looked down at his hands. He did not want to tell Ede of the Entity's failed incarnation as Tamara.

"And there might be another way. It is a far possibility, but still possible nevertheless."

"Yes?"

"You've said that you seek the planet Tannahill. The Architects of the Old Church."

"Many pilots of my Order seek Tannahill."

"The Architects have always worshiped me as God," Ede said. His smile was now as radiant as the sun. "At my vastening, when I carked my mind into my eternal computer, what do you suppose became of my body?"

"I do not know."

"Shall I tell you?"

"Yes, if you would like."

"The Architects, of course, usually burn their dead after the vastening ceremony. But I believe that my body was preserved. On Tannahill, displayed in the temple there—it lies frozen in a clary crypt."

"But your vastening occurred nearly three thousand years ago!"

"Has it really been so long? My followers must be very faithful."

"But why?" Danlo asked. "Why this shaida burial?"

"Because the Architects revered everything about me, in life and in death. Even my old and very human flesh—it serves as a perfect reminder that the body is just an empty husk without the program of the soul to animate it."

"But three thousand years!"

"To me it seems like yesterday. Only a moment ago."

"But the freezing, over the centuries, the molecular drift . . . and then there is the process of vastening itself. The scanning of the brain, of the synapses—this destroys the brain, yes?"

"Perhaps."

"In vastening, the pattern of the brain's synapses is modeled as a computer program—but the brain itself dies. This is the price of carking one's mind into a computer, yes?"

Ede smiled wickedly for a while, then said, "It would seem so. But in any brain that has been vastened, it may be that molecular traces of the synapses remain. It may be that the synapses, and thus the brain itself, could be reconstructed."

"Do you believe this, truly?"

"It's my hope."

"Then you hope somehow to recover your body?"

"I do."

"To raise the dead," Danlo whispered. He pressed his hand to his navel as a sudden shiver ran through his belly. "You would cark your consciousness back into your old body, yes?"

"I want to live again. Is that so wrong?"

Danlo closed his eyes a moment before saying, "But you are here, on this lost earth. And your body lies on Tannahill."

"*My* body, Pilot," Ede said.

"And Tannahill lies . . . farther into the Vild."

"I would like to see my own body again. To touch it, from inside."

"Do you know where Tannahill is, then?"

"No," Ede said. "Once I knew, but I have forgotten."

"I am sorry."

"But I know of other peoples who may know of Tannahill."

"These peoples are human, then?"

"Mostly—most of them still are."

"And these human beings live where?"

"At the center of the Vild. Where the stars are wildest, on other Earths that I once made."

"Do you know the fixed-points of these stars?"

"I know them."

"Will you tell me where these stars are?"

"Only if you promise to take me with you."

"In the hold of my ship? As cargo in a lightship?"

"No, as a passenger. As a fellow seeker of the ineffable flame. And of other things."

Danlo rubbed his head and sighed. "All right—if you would like, you may share the pit of my ship."

"And you must promise one other thing," Ede said. He was smiling now, and it seemed that he was reading the emotions from Danlo's face.

"What is that?"

"You must promise that if we find Tannahill, you will help me recover my body."

"That will be hard to do."

"Hard to promise or a hard promise to fulfill?"

"Both."

"I'm only asking you to help me—is that so wrong?"

Danlo rubbed his aching head, remembering. "The dead . . . are so very dead when they die. It is shaida for the dead to live again."

"But I am not dead at all," Ede said. His eyes twinkled, and the hologram manifesting his shape flared as brightly as a flame globe. "I am as alive as you are—almost."

"Even if you do not reveal the fixed-points of the stars that I seek, I might find them anyway," Danlo said.

"Possibly."

"I may find Tannahill without you, but you will never leave this lost Earth without me."

"It would seem that you hold the superior negotiating position," Ede said.

"Yes."

Ede's eyes were now as hard to look at as black holes, and they seemed to drink in the light falling off Danlo's face. Ede said, "But I would think that you don't like to negotiate."

Merchants, Danlo thought, haggled over the price of a Fravashi carpet; wormrunners argued with whores over the cost of sharing their tattooed bodies for a night. "Truly, I hate negotiating," he said.

"Then help me. Please, Pilot."

For a long time Danlo stared at Ede's face burning in its computer-generated colors, and he lost himself in Ede's sad gaze. There came a moment when Danlo's face was burning, too, his forehead and his eyes and the blood rushing beneath his skin. And then another moment, fearful and strange, when all the world was nothing but fire and pain and a wild white light shimmering through the cold space between them and all around. "If you would like," Danlo finally said. "If I can, I will help you."

"Thank you."

"And now," Danlo said, looking about the floor of the temple cluttered with all the cybernetica and other things, "I must find a place to sleep."

"Of course you must. And in the morning?"

"In the morning I will explore the rest of the temple. I have always wanted to see the chambers where the Architects are vastened."

"And then?"

"And then we will return to my ship. To the Vild. To . . . the stars."

So saying, Danlo bowed politely. It amused him to watch as the little hologram of Nikolos Daru Ede—with his emaciated body and huge bony head—returned his bow with an other-worldly grace, as only an imago floating in the air might accomplish.

"Good night, then," Danlo said.

"Good night, Pilot. Sleep deeply and well."

With another yawn (and with a strange smile that Ede could not see), Danlo turned to walk back through the temple and retrieve his pack from the entrance hall. Soon he would eat his shipbread and taste the acid tang of dried bloodfruit. Soon he would be asleep on soft furs, while in another part of the temple, the hologram of a man who had once been a god would keep a vigil all night. Danlo wondered what it would be like to be a ghost haunting the light circuits of a simple devotionary computer; he wondered at the consciousness of a machine that was as cold and constant as the light of the oldest stars. Most of all he wondered a simple thing: If Ede never slept, how could he ever dream? And if he never dreamed deep and lucid dreams, how should he ever want to be a man again, how should he want to be marvelously and terribly alive?

THE SANI

The longest journey begins with the first step—unless you can fly.

—Justine the Wise

To say that the universe is vast is as simple as breathing fresh air, and yet truly to comprehend its infinite deeps is another thing altogether. The Milky Way galaxy is only a tiny part of the known universe—no more than a snowflake spinning in the wind along the world's endless fields of ice—and yet to a man crossing its cold fields of stars in a lightship spun of diamond and dreams, the galaxy is very large indeed. It is recorded that once a star exploded. Ninety thousand years ago, in the far part of the Perseus arm, at the very edge of the galaxy where the stars fade off into the intergalactic void, a hot blue giant supernova fell and cast its blinding light to the universe. Light is almost the fastest thing there is; light is so fast that in the time it takes to affirm its fastness, in simple words, it will fall through space a million miles—and yet it took fifteen thousand years for the light from this dead star to cross only a small part of the galaxy and rain down upon the icy forests of Old Earth. Men and women, living in houses of sewn animal skins or in snow huts or dark cold caves, beheld this strange new star and marveled at the terrible and beautiful nature of light. They wondered at the secrets of the universe, even as the radiance faded to a point and then died, even as they evolved into a race of near-gods who built pyramids and cathedrals and great shimmering lightships to fall among the faraway stars. And in all these tens of thousands of years, even as human beings swarmed outward from Old Earth and built their great stellar civilizations and dreamed of an infinitely glorious future, the light from the supernova continued falling across the galaxy. To this day, it is falling still. Soon, perhaps in a few more millennia, the light will break free from the Milky Way at last and continue its journey on to the Canes Venatici and Ursa Major Cloud and the millions of other galaxies of the universe. Bound into wavelengths of simple light will be images of a people who once wore animal skins as clothing and ate the flesh of animals for food. Someday farwhen this is the reflection of human beings that the universe will first behold. It is a primeval and somewhat savage face—but full of promise and possibilities. By the time the alien peoples of the Sakura Sen have looked upon human beings as they once were, some say that men long since will have evolved into gods who are far beyond the horrors of meat or matter. Humanity, the scryers say, will exist only as numinous beings who finally will understand the secret of light. Someday they will transcend light altogether—and then the doors to infinity will be flung open and all the universe will be theirs.

In a way, of course, certain human beings had already gone beyond the limitations of lightspeed. And Danlo, as a pilot of the Order in his diamond ship named the *Snowy Owl,* fenestered across the twinkling stellar windows of the Vild with all the speed he could command, but relative to the lifetime of simple man his journey was slow, for he had to find mappings among strange new stars, and the spaces of the Vild are as twisted and tortuous as they are immense. Somewhere along this long journey into loneliness—perhaps it was near the remnants of supernova that he named Shonamorath—he found himself welcoming the companionship of the little devotionary computer and the hologram that called itself Nikolos Daru Ede.

Danlo had stowed this computer in the pit of his ship. It floated with him in silent darkness. Or rather, the light of Ede's glowing face and the words he spoke often dispelled the darkness and the silence that are the usual companions of a pilot falling through the manifold. Other objects from the temple had also found a new home in Danlo's ship. With a willful and strangely reverent sacrilege, Danlo had plundered the blue rose from the meditation hall, as well as a kevalin set and five of Ede's wooden flutes. He might even have taken an eternal computer from the facing room, but he doubted the wisdom of bringing such a device anywhere near the electromagnetic field generated by the devotionary.

Often, among the brilliant and deadly Vild stars, he wondered if Ede had a secret reason for wanting to join his quest to find Tannahill. He wondered if Ede might be hiding a secret program to cark his soul back into another eternal computer and thus retrace his old path toward godhood. Perhaps Ede hoped that the Architects of the Old Church would once again aid *this* most ancient and secret quest.

Once, in an attempt to glean some hint of Ede's true motivations, Danlo asked him if he would ever consider remaking the journey from man into god. Ede's response was immediate and direct—and perhaps an evasion of the truth. With a sincere expression that the Ede hologram often programed to hide uncertainty, he smiled at Danlo and said, "How should any man ever want to become a god? Haven't I lost enough myself on that dream already? And if I succeed in becoming human again, how much more will I lose in regaining my body? Enough—I've had enough of transcendence. No, Pilot, once I wear my own flesh again, I shall be content."

In truth, the hologram of Ede was as far from contentment as a man is from a worm. In the pit of Danlo's ship it floated like one of the bioluminescent Ik demons who are said to haunt the forests outside the temple on Jacaranda. This Ede was always awake, always aware—and always tormented by problems of both a practical and philosophical nature. For instance, one of his confessed reasons for wanting to fall human again was so that he could remembrance the Elder Eddas. This ultimate secret of the universe was known to be encoded into human DNA. It was said that only human beings, deep in remembrance, could unveil and bring into full consciousness the ancient memories locked inside the human genome.

Ede believed that the purely machine gods of the galaxy such as the Silicon God and Ai Mind (and once a time, himself) could never find the Eddas. And so he would cark his consciousness back into blood and flesh and living chromosomes, but to do so he must face once again the soul-sick terror of losing all of himself, instantaneously and forever. When the time came for him to cark the pattern of his mind from the devotionary computer's light circuits into the electrochemical synapses of a living brain, what would it mean to say that he continued to live on in a new form? Even if he exactly duplicated the pattern of himself, in atoms of carbon, hydrogen, oxygen and nitrogen, would he retain a continuous consciousness, as a man is certain of his own marvelously continuing life from one heartbeat to the next?

As a thought experiment—Ede was as susceptible to this kind of mental excess as the princes of Summerworld are to eating rich and sweet foods—he considered the duplication of a man. Suppose that some god such as the Solid State Entity could duplicate a man perfectly, down to the configuration of his body's every atom. Never mind the quantum uncertainties, the impossibility of ever knowing both the exact position and velocity of the electrons and other subatomic particles of which atoms are made. Suppose that the Solid State Entity, through godly technologies that Ede no longer remembered, could exactly duplicate the substance and mind of a man. Suppose further that at the precise moment of duplication, the thoughts and feelings and fears, the very consciousness of the two men were identical. Now, according to the logic of this dreadful and impossible experiment, let the Entity through starfire or antimatter or some other means, instantaneously annihilate the first and original man. Or better, let this man be asked to annihilate himself. The question must then be asked: What will be lost?

If the man has been perfectly duplicated, the answer must be: Nothing will be lost. If the logic of the experiment has been true to the deeper logic of the universe, of stars and atoms and living neurons, this original man should not hesitate to destroy himself. He should be secure in the knowledge that he would continue on as his second self, exactly as before. And yet, in the real world of doubts and dark dreams, of blood and pain and the neverness of the soul, the original man would hesitate. Even knowing that he somehow lived on in his double, to destroy himself would be suicide. It would *feel* like dying. In the truest sense, it would be dying, for the secret of life is not in its pattern or form, but only in the continuous flow of consciousness from one moment to the next.

"This is the problem," Ede confessed to Danlo one day after they had passed through a particularly desolate region of blown-out stars. "If I become a man again, will I still be I? If I say the word that will take this devotionary down, what will happen to *me*?"

Ede, of course, as a man, as his original self before he had dared to become a god, had deeply felt the logic of the real universe. Like any man, he had felt doubt. But he had scorned his fears and his uncertainty as most ignoble emotions. He was after all Nikolos Daru Ede, the founder of what would become man's greatest religion. He must always be a man of genius and vision and, above all, faith. It was his genius, as an architect, to find a way to model his mind in the programs of what he called his eternal computer. It was his vision, as a philosopher, to justify the carking of human consciousness from the living brain into the cold circuits of a machine. And it was his faith, as a prophet, to show other men how they could transcend the prison of their bodies and finally conquer death.

He, himself, had been the first man willingly to give up the life of his body so that he might find the infinite life of the soul. He had allowed his fellow architects to destroy his brain neuron by neuron so that the pattern of synapses might be perfectly preserved. He had died the true death so that he might not die. He had committed this brave (and mad) act out of pride, out of fundamental misunderstanding, and finally, out of a misplaced belief in a rather curious idea that he had come to love. Despite all deeper logic, Ede finally convinced himself that the soul of man might live on forever as pure program inside an eternal computer—and this soon came to be the fundamental doctrine of the Cybernetic Universal Church. Sadly, tragically, a part of Ede always doubted this doctrine. And so for three thousand years, even as a god, his original suicide had haunted him. It haunted him still. And yet even realizing this, Ede could not escape from the flaw that had led to his tragic first death. This flaw was in his thinking; he knew very well that there was a flaw in his personality, in his mind, perhaps even in his very soul.

"For me," he confessed in the privacy of Danlo's lightship, "an idea has always been more beautiful than a woman, a theory of nature more sustaining than bread or wine."

All his life he had been in love with ideas. But not, as he implied, merely because of their beauty or their power, but rather because ideas were like comfortably furnished rooms in which he could always take refuge when the universe itself, with its cold, hard edges and uncaring ways, threatened to hurt him. Although he was loath to admit it, his deepest motivation was fear. He was always searching his environment for dangers. In truth, this was his real reason for wanting to become a god. It was always his dream to control the universe in order to protect himself. And so he always sought theories that would explain the universe. He was always trying to reduce the universe's infinite complexities into simpler computer models of reality. The Holy Grail of his life was the finding of one, single theory or model that might encompass all things.

This was why he had accepted the Silicon God's gift, the simulation of the future universe that had ultimately destroyed him. It was his hope to elaborate and refine this simulation and make it his own. In the time since then, a million times a million times, he had lamented his attachment to ideas and theories, which was really just an attachment to himself. Although he

longed to be a true visionary, to behold the universe just as it is,
this he could not do. For he could never free himself from himself—from the original program that he had written when he had
carked his human selfness into his eternal computer.

"I made a mistake," he told Danlo one day. "Out of fear, a
fundamental mistake."

According to Ede, his mistake was to write the program encoding his personality too narrowly. Because he feared that the
infinite possibilities of godhood might annihilate his sense of
self, much as a sprouting plant destroys the seed from which it
springs, he carefully searched the Enneagram for a personality
type that might define and preserve the pattern of his selfness no
matter how great a god he eventually became. And so in the very
beginning he had codified all his human traits and faults and
bound them into a simple form. He had then carried these faults
godward. This mistake was exacerbated during his battle with the
Silicon God when he had to compress himself, to prune his
memory and programs down to the very simple remnants of Ede
who haunted the devotionary computer.

And now, three thousand years later, like a bonsai tree that
had been pruned and repruned into its final, twisted shape, he
was fixed in himself. He was stunted and constrained and nearly
dead. And this was one reason for his wanting to become human
again: He wished to become unfixed. He wished to transcend his
personality type, and thus finally to become what he called a true
person.

"Although I can reprogram myself," Ede told Danlo,
"there's a master program controlling which programs I can edit
and which I cannot. Unfortunately, as I am now, this master
program is untouchable. But once I'm in the flesh again, I shall
finally discover the answer to a question that has been bothering
me for a long time: just how mutable is man? I want to know,
Pilot. I want to know if a man can touch any part of himself; I
want to know how matter moves itself. These new programs, new
minds, new life—how does it all move itself to evolve?"

Ede's need to know all manner of things ran his life. As he
and Danlo fell among the brilliant Vild stars, Danlo often thought
that the defining statement of Ede's life might be: I know, therefore I am. Once, after Danlo confessed that their escape from an
incandescent Triolet space had been rather narrow, Ede asked to
interface the ship-computer so that he might know what kinds of
dangers that the *Snowy Owl* encountered. As a good pilot of the
Order, Danlo would rather have pulled out his own eyes before

letting any other person (or computer) interface the brain of his ship. But he was also a considerate man, and even for a devotionary-generated hologram he could feel a kind of compassion. And so, with the help of his ship-computer, he made a model of the manifold. Using his ship's sulki grids, he projected glittering images into the dark air of his ship's pit. This projection of the pathways and embedded spaces that they fell through was not very much like the deeply mathematical way in which Danlo himself experienced the manifold. But it was good enough for Ede, who had lost most of his mathematics during his battle and the tragic diminishing of his selfness. Like an itinerant historian first beholding the rings of Qallar, he gaped in astonishment at the colors of a fayway space, at the sparkling lights and the lovely, fractaling complexity. In this manner, viewing the models that Danlo's ship made for him, Ede came to know things that few except the Order's pilots have known. In this way, too, viewing the rippling distortions at the radius of convergence around their ship, he discovered that they were not alone.

"I believe another ship might be following us, Pilot," he said to Danlo. "Perhaps it's an emissary of the Silicon God sent to ' destroy us."

It was then, within the silken web of the manifold, some thirty thousand light-years out from Neverness, that Danlo finally told Ede about the warrior-poet named Malaclypse Redring. He told him of the warrior-poet's quest to find a god and destroy *him*.

"Then ever since your planetfall on Farfara this ship has been following you? This *Red Dragon,* you say?" Ede's face was a glowing mask of apprehension, and he seemed to doubt what Danlo told him. "I don't understand, Pilot. If the warrior-poet expects you to lead him to Mallory Ringess, why didn't he follow you to my temple? After all, he couldn't have known that you would find me there and not your father."

As it happened, Danlo had been brooding over this very question for at least a billion miles. But he had no answer for Ede, or for himself. And so he built an icy wall of disdain around his doubts, turned his face to the strange star, and fell deep into the heart of the Vild, where the darkness of space was filled with light. There were dead stars and supernovas everywhere. Falling through these blazing spaces, Danlo thought, was something like approaching a dragon. Beyond the edge of the Orion arm, the supernovas grew more dense, and the breath of the stars grew ever hotter. As he fenestered among thousands of stellar windows that seemed almost to melt and fuse into one another like sheets of molten glass, this fiery breath built into a raging wind. Often, when he fell out into realspace for a moment, his ship was blasted by a stream of atoms, photons, and high-energy particles. In a few places the radiation was so intense that it might have seared away the diamond skin of his ship if he hadn't quickly made a new mapping and taken the *Snowy Owl* back into the manifold. There he fell through spaces both deadly and strange.

After many days of such journeying Danlo came across sights unknown to any man or woman of his Order. Usually a pilot delights in making such discoveries, but the things he saw caused him no joy. He found tens of dead stars and hundreds of burned-out planets. Some of these blackened spheres must have once been as beautiful as Tria or Old Earth, but now their great shimmering forests were burned to char, their oceans vaporized, and their very soil melted to magma or fused into rock. On other planets the biospheres had not been totally destroyed, but rather purged of all life much larger than a bacterium or a worm.

Farther into the Vild, Danlo discovered other death worlds. Many of these were covered with human remains, with bleached white bones whose shape he knew so well. For the first time, he appreciated the very human urge to go out among the stars and fill the universe with life. Few races had ever felt this driving force so deeply as *Homo sapiens*. In truth, no other race had swarmed the galaxy for a million years. And now human beings were safely seeded on perhaps ten million natural or made worlds—not even the gods could count humanity's numbers. Danlo thought it ironic that of all the living species in the galaxy, the most dispersed and secure were human beings, they who were destroying the security of the galaxy's other races, perhaps even destroying the galaxy itself.

"We're a mad, murderous people," Ede confided after Danlo had explored his thirty-third death world. "We murder others so that our kind can swarm the stars like maggots on a corpse. Why do you think I felt compelled to escape my flesh and transcend into something finer?"

This, Danlo thought in his more contemplative moments, defined the essential tension of the human race: human beings' genius for living life successfully versus their desire to transcend all the blood and the breathing and pain. Possibly no other species was so secure in life and yet so dissatisfied with it. Man, the eschatologists said, was a bridge between ape and god. According to their very popular philosophy, man could only be defined as a movement toward something higher. While Danlo always appreciated this desire to be greater, he felt that man's destiny lay not so much in a heightening or a quickening or even a vastening of the self but rather in a deepening. His own true quest, he told himself, must always take him deeper into life. He must always journey further into the heart of all things where the sound of life is long and dark and deep—as infinitely deep as the universe itself. And so he could never quite believe in the kinds of transcendence for which human beings have strove for so long. He could never quite affirm humanity's mad and marvelous dream of becoming as gods, and perhaps something more.

Toward the center of the Vild, out near the star-shrouded Perseus arm of the galaxy, Danlo discovered a succession of Earths that Ede the God had once made. The radiation from various supernovas had scorched two of these doomed planets, but the other nine were untouched, as pristine and wild as any planet Danlo had ever seen. It was on the eleventh Earth that Danlo made the acquaintance of a people who called themselves the Sani. The ten thousand people of the Sani lived in a rain forest at the edge of one of the northern continents; the rest of the Earth, it seemed, was uninhabited. Danlo found the Sani to be a sad, philosophical people—as well they should be considering their tragic past and uncertain future. In fact, their very name for themselves meant something like "the Damned."

"It is my fault," Ede confessed to Danlo after the *Snowy Owl* had come to rest on the sands of a wide, windswept beach. "I made these people as they are. I *made* them, you see, and perhaps it was wrong for me to experiment with human beings in this way."

What Ede the God had once done, according to Ede's very incomplete memory, was to seed this eleventh Earth with people. He had done this many times as part of his experiment to grow supposedly innocent human beings from frozen zygotes, to imprint a carefully designed culture onto them, watch how their society developed, and then to destroy them and begin anew. Ede told Danlo that on this eleventh Earth, there had been at least five such human societies in the last millennium. No society—no tribe, city-state, or arcology—had lasted more than two hundred years. And the Sani knew this. It was part of Ede's experiment that they should live out their lives in their rain-drenched forests, all the while knowing of the doom soon to befall them. This is why they called themselves the Damned, and looked to the starry sky in despair rather than awe, for they lived in fear of the hand of God.

Danlo had little difficulty meeting with the elders of one of the Sani's largest bands. Deep in the forest, along the banks of a fast-running river, he found an encampment some three hundred people strong. The Sani built their houses out of great, sturdy logs and roofed them with sheets of bark; they made their living from the salmon they fished from the rivers, from the abundance of berries, roots, and pine nuts that they gathered from the forests. Theirs appeared a rich, easy life of roasted fish-feasts and thanksgiving and drinking their holy blackberry beer. But the Sani did not allow themselves to revel in their earthly paradise: displays of spontaneity or animal joy, they believed, mocked man's spiritual nature. Their way in the world was simple if exacting: they must perfect themselves and all their actions beneath the glittering eyes of God. To accomplish this, they must suffer infinite pains. As Danlo would soon learn, the thirty-two tribes of the Sani therefore suffered the harshest of spiritual lives.

"Our ways are not easy, but we must ask you to respect our law until it is time for you to leave."

This came from an old woman named Reina An, who sat with Danlo before a blazing fire at the center of the Sani village. Beside her were other elders: her first husband, Mato An, and old Ki Lin Shang along with his wives, Hon Su Shang, Laam Su, and toothless, white-haired Jin Joyu Minye. Because Danlo's visit was a singular event, most of the tribe had abandoned their work for the day. They crowded around the fire, though taking care not to press too close lest their naked bodies inadvertently touch Danlo or the strange-looking devotionary computer that he carried. Although Danlo could not know it, upon his arrival Reina An had sent messengers to the elders of the other bands. Later that day they would make their short journeys through the dripping forest in order to meet Danlo and honor him—that is, if Reina and the others hadn't already decided to execute Danlo as a dangerous hsi tuti who might break their law and thus bring the wrath of God down upon them.

"Your law is sacred to you, yes?" Danlo looked at Reina An even as he directed his question toward the devotionary. The Sani spoke a variant of High Westerness Chinese, a language with which Danlo was unfamiliar. Once, of course, in his study of the universal syntax, he had learned the characters of Old Chinese, but this was little help in understanding the strange words that fell from Reina's mouth as easily and musically as a soft rain. Fortunately, the Ede, acting as translator, quickly made sense of what Reina and the other elders said. If the sight of a glowing, talking, foot-high hologram astonished any of the elders, they gave no sign. Even when Nikolos Daru Ede spoke in a clear if somewhat stiff Sani, they did little more than cock their heads and squint their eyes. Danlo immediately guessed that they had never seen a devotionary computer. Perhaps they had never seen Ede the God, their creator and destroyer who could never touch them again.

"Your blessed law—this was given to you by . . . God?"

"No, of course not," Reina said. She was a quick-minded and crabby women whose soft brown eyes missed nothing. Although it was wet in the forest, with the sky gray and misting, she was naked like everyone else. She sat on a new bear fur, and the bones of her rigidly straight spine stuck out beneath her skin like the rungs of a ladder. If the fire heating her withered old chest was too hot or the rain drizzling down her back was too cold, she gave no sign. "It is we who give our law to Him."

There was a moment of silence before Ede translated this. And then Danlo asked, "To . . . God?"

"To the Master of the Universe," Reina said. "To Him who makes the sun and the rain. To our creator and sustainer. He gave us life, and so we must give him every devotion of our lives, every moment. This is why we made our law. This is why no Sani must ever break the Yasa, which we give to Him with all the gladness of a mother giving her daughter to be a bride."

Although Reina spoke carefully and precisely, it was as if she were reciting a formula. Danlo thought that there was little real gladness in her voice.

"Your law, the Yasa, is complex, yes?"

After Ede had translated Danlo's question, Ki Lin Shang smiled sadly and said, "Our law is actually quite simple—even a child knows our law."

At this, Ki Lin Shang turned and beckoned to a pot-bellied little boy who stood behind him. Ki Lin pulled the frightened boy onto his knee and asked, "Child, can you tell us the Yasa?"

The boy—Ki Lin's bright-eyed grandson who could have been no more than four years old—seemed immediately to understand that he must speak to the Ede hologram if Danlo was to understand him. "We must take pleasure in the world and in all that we do; all that we do must be pleasing to God."

He paused a moment while Ede translated this, and then, quite shyly, he said, "May all our thoughts be beautiful."

Here Ki Lin Shang smiled proudly as he brought his fingertips to his temples. Slowly, gracefully, he then spread his arms outward in a gesture of giving and intoned, "Hai!"

Emboldened by his grandfather's chanting of the sacred syllable of affirmation, the boy continued: "May all our words be beautiful."

As if a signal had been spoken, the elders sitting on their bearskins touched their fingers to their lips and gave their formal blessing to the world. "Hai!" they said as they held their hands outstretched over the black, loamy earth of the forest.

Now all the people standing around them were ready to take up the chant. They held their arms crossed over their chests, waiting. Danlo, too, sitting across from the ever-watchful Reina An, placed his fingertips on either shoulder. Once, he had loved ritual as fiercely as he did fresh meat, and so he fell easily into this last of the Sani's prayer postures. Almost before the boy could speak, Danlo found himself reaching his hands outward to the sky and whispering, "May all our actions be beautiful."

And then, a moment later, along with the other three hundred men, women, and children, he chanted, "Hai!"

After the Sani had closed their eyes in silent affirmation of their sacred law, Reina An turned to Danlo and cast him a strange, piercing look. She stared at him for quite a long time, and then said, "You knew. While the boy recited, even before, you whispered the last verse of the Yasa."

Danlo, who was suddenly uncomfortable in his wet woolens, looked around at all the naked people staring at him. "It . . . seemed the right thing to say."

"You *knew,*" Reina An repeated. "Without hearing first, you knew."

In truth, Danlo *had* known exactly what the boy would chant. The words had suddenly appeared on his tongue like mushrooms sprouting up in a wet forest. Before any of the others had begun the blessing, he had seen their arms—and his own arms—outstretched to the sky. He did not want to ascribe this sudden foreknowledge to any special skill such as scrying or that mysterious way of seeing whole patterns from single parts that had first come over him in the library on Neverness six years before. It was logic, he thought, simple logic that had moved him to whisper the words of the Yasa.

Reina An moved her hand to her tired eyes as if to rub them, but then, thinking better of such a weak-willed action, she stroked her thick white hair and smiled instead. She looked at Danlo and told him, "It is well that you understand the spirit of the Yasa, for it is difficult to know the law's many applications unless one is Sani.''

Here, at the end of Ede's translation, the little hologram of the man who would be God floated in the misty air and almost smiled. He caught Danlo's eye and said, ''I confess that I haven't given a full rendering of the word *Sani*. I should tell you that it means not only 'the Damned' but 'the Chosen.' ''

Because Ede's confession went on much too long to be a simple translation of Reina's words, she glared at the devotionary computer with dread and loathing, as if Ede's glowing hologram were some kind of poisonous snake.

''It is always difficult for strangers,'' Reina An said, ''to understand that everything must be given to God.''

Ede, in his translation of this simple sentence, hesitated a moment because the Sani word for ''stranger'' was the same as ''enemy.'' It was this way with many of what he called the primitive languages. Indeed, since the Sani had come into existence only two hundred years before as an isolated people on a lost Earth, it was curious that they should even have a word for ''stranger.''

Ki Lin Shang nodded his head in agreement with Reina An. ''Once,'' he said, ''my beautiful wife Laam Su found a blue rose growing in the forest. She wanted to pick it for me, but instead she left it on its stem as a gift to God.''

This statement of Ki Lin's piqued Danlo's curiosity for two reasons. First, because of Ki Lin's assertion that blue roses grew wild on this Earth. And second, because Ki Lin had referred to Laam Su as beautiful. Certainly, it was hard for even Danlo to see much beauty in Laam Su. Like Reina An, she tried to sit straight before the fire, but due to some bone disease (or perhaps just old age) her spine was bent and deformed. She huddled at her husband's side, hunched over and squinting at Danlo with her good eye. Her other eye, he saw, had been mostly destroyed in some kind of accident. Indeed, the whole left side of her face was twisted with a patchwork of scars as if she had been burned by a lightning stroke or had perhaps stumbled into an open fire pit as a child. She sat in the drizzling rain, shivering like a dog and silent in her concentration upon her own miseries. She would not meet Danlo's eyes, nor did she look at any of the other Sani surrounding her. She seemed to hate the necessity of sitting in council on such a cold and ugly day; in truth, she seemed to hate everything about her life. And most of all, she hated the requirement of the law that she hate absolutely nothing in the world—or at least that she hide these forbidden hates from other people and the eyes of God.

Beauty is only skin deep, but ugliness penetrates to the bone— Danlo remembered his friend Hanuman li Tosh saying this about another woman they had known in Neverness years before. And then, while Danlo stared through the dead gray air at poor Laam Su, her husband turned to see what Danlo might be looking at so intently. Suddenly, as if someone had thrown a heap of dry sticks into the fire, there was a flash of light. Laam Su's tired old face suddenly came alive and shone with a deep and lovely light. Danlo finally saw her, then, as her husband saw her, perhaps as she really was: she was beautiful because she loved Ki Lin and he loved her, and more, because she had survived some seventy years of a hard and uncertain life. In truth, she was beautiful simply because she existed at all, as one shining part of God's marvelous and infinitely various creation. All things, in their secret nature, shimmered with a terrible beauty, and the beholding of this truth was the essential part of the Sani's sacred law.

The way to look at all things is with a naked eye, Danlo remembered. *With the mind's eye naked to the universe.*

Danlo's eyes played over the weathered old skin of Laam Su's body, and he suddenly understood why the Sani went about their lives unclothed in such cold and rainy clime. The only way to look at the human form—and everything—was in nakedness. To clothe oneself was to hide one's beauty, and thus to scorn God's loveliest handiwork.

"There is nothing we must not surrender up to God," Ki Lin Shang affirmed. "Especially pride and the layers of the self that separate us from Him."

Without further pause, Danlo bent low to pull off his leather boots. Then he rose up and removed his glittering black rain robe; he dropped this rather sophisticated garment on the steaming earth below him. Lastly, he freed himself from his black, wool kamelaika and the undersilks that he always wore close to the skin. When he was finished divesting himself of his layers of clothing, he stood naked in front of the fire. His skin shimmered with a golden light, and he felt the heat of the flames licking at him. At the same time, though, it was cold—a wet, drizzly cold pinging at his heated flesh and rolling down his back in long, snakelike tracks.

"May all the Sani be beautiful"—he heard a young woman say this even as Reina An nodded her head in approval of his act of disrobing. The Sani, then, crowded closer to get a better look

at Danlo's body. He had a truly beautiful body: long, lean, graceful, and yet quickened with a terrible power like that of a young
tiger. Now, at last, some of the bolder Sani dared to touch him.
Two boys and an old women pressed close and ran their fishy-
smelling fingers over his shoulders. All the Sani, he suddenly
noticed, seemed to smell of old salmon. The smell wafted from
the smoke pits and pervaded the village; it called his memory to
similar smells that had comforted him as a child. It was the smell
of life, a good, pungent, organic smell, though somewhat hard to
take if one was unused to it. Although Danlo had vowed never to
eat meat again, he never minded its smell, not even when a young
woman rubbed her hand over him, thus rubbing her greasy fish
essence into the fine black hair covering his chest and belly.

That hair of any sort grew from Danlo's body seemed to
astonish the Sani, who were as smooth in the flesh as dol-
phins. They were astonished, too, by Danlo's scars. The young
woman—her name was Kameko Luan—boldly ran her finger up
the long, white scar on his thigh where the silk-belly boar had
once wounded him. Others were looking at his burned knuckles
and the chin scar he had earned during a particularly vicious
game of hokkee. For a moment, Reina An caught his eyes and
then stared at him strangely, at the lightning bolt scar that he had
once cut into his own forehead. Most of the Sani, however, were
staring between his legs. They obviously wanted to know how
(and why) Danlo's membrum had come to be circumcised and
decorated with tiny, colored scars. If they found this sign of
Danlo's passage into manhood to be beautiful, they did not say.
For a long time everyone stood there in silence, and the only
sounds were the rushing of the river, the hiss of the fire, and the
soft silvery music of the falling rain.

"May God behold our beauty and smile always upon us,"
Reina An said. She beckoned for Danlo to rejoin her on her
bearskin, where he had left the devotionary computer silently
flickering in its colors.

"Will you tell me more about God?" Danlo asked. He sat
back down on his heels with his spine straight, in the position of
formal politeness that his masters had taught him as a novice in
Neverness.

"I *could* tell more about God," Reina An admitted as she
nodded her head. "About the Master of the Universe, there is
always more to tell."

"The Master of the Universe," Danlo said softly. "Then you
believe that the universe was created by God, yes?"

Reina An shook her head. "No, the stars and all that we see on a clear night have always been and will always be. How is it that you, a man from the stars, do not know this?"

It surprised Danlo to hear Reina An speak so easily of his origins among the stars. He had wondered if the Sani would even know of other stars and other worlds—and the many other human beings who lived elsewhere.

"I do not know why . . . I do not know," Danlo said. "It is hard to know about the universe, yes?"

Danlo was uncertain as to what the words *stars* and *universe* actually meant to Reina An. After all, as a child, he had once thought that the stars were the eyes of his ancestors watching over him.

"It is God," Reina An said, "who was created by the universe."

"And yet you refer to Him as the creator of the world."

"Of course—God created our world."

"Your . . . world," Danlo said.

"Our beautiful Earth that spins around our star."

At first, Danlo had supposed that the Sani might use a single word for both "universe" and "world," that Ede was merely translating in context for his benefit. But clearly, Reina An understood these celestial concepts in quite a sophisticated way.

"It must be a difficult thing to create a world," Danlo said. Here he looked at the Ede imago, whose glittering face was as silent as stone.

"Well, God is *God,*" Reina An said. "He is the Master of the Universe."

"Has God created other worlds, then?"

Reina An bent her head over to confer with Ki Lin Shang. They whispered furiously back and forth to each other for a while, then Reina An straightened up and said, "God has created many Earths. Twelve times twelve is their number. Someday He will create new stars, whole oceans of stars. At the end of time, when all the universe acknowledges Him as Master, he will create other universes—twelve billion times twelve billion in number."

"Your creator must be almost impossibly powerful," Danlo said. He continued to look at the hologram of Ede, who translated his words mechanically, as if he were nothing more than a simple language program running the circuitry of a common computer. He did not look at Danlo, nor did he betray any emotion—or any sign that his computer-generated face was even capable of displaying such a human trait. "Your God—he is splendid, yes?"

"God is beauty," Reina An recited. "All that He creates is beautiful, and yet . . ."

"Yes?"

"God is our Creator and Sustainer, but God is the Destroyer, too."

At this, Ki Lin Shang nodded his head and intoned, "May all that is not beautiful perish from the Earth."

Although most of the men and women near Danlo immediately repeated this line from the Yasa, he thought that there was little enthusiasm in their voices. Indeed many of the Sani—particularly the children—seemed fearful and disturbed.

"May all worlds that are not beautiful perish from the stars," Ki Lin said.

After Reina An had repeated the obligatory "Hai!" she smiled sadly. To Danlo she said, "The Master of the Universe destroyed a world to make our beautiful Earth."

"He is Destroyer of All," Ki Lin Shang said.

"He is Destroyer of All that is not beautiful," Reina An corrected.

The two elders of the Sani tribe traded pained looks as if they had disputed the exact words of the Yasa many times before. But clearly neither wished to pursue theological fine points in front a stranger. Ki Lin Shang cleared his throat, looked at Danlo, and recited, "May all stars that are not beautiful perish from the universe."

Danlo, who had fallen across thirty thousand light-years of space encompassing millions of stars, wanted to cry out: "But each star *is* beautiful—the stars are splendid with light!" However he kept his silence and waited to hear how Reina An would respond.

"God is Destroyer of Stars," she said. "He must destroy to create."

"God is Destroyer of People," Ki Lin said. "All the peoples of the Earth rush into God's fiery jaws like moths into a burning flame."

Danlo was unsure of Ede's translation of this last, and so he looked at Ki Lin Shang and asked, "Does God destroy all people, then, or all . . . peoples?"

"Certainly he destroys all people," Ki Lin said. "All must live and all must die."

Reina An nodded her head, then added, "All peoples must die, too. All who are not beautiful."

Danlo, kneeling silently on his bearskin, wondered if the Sani word for "beautiful" and "perfect" were one and the same. He would have asked Ede this, but he did not want to interrupt the flow of conversation.

"Other peoples have walked the Earth before the Sani," Reina An continued. "And now they are gone."

"Gatei, gatei," Ki Lin said. "Gone, gone."

"And that is why the Sani must always be beautiful—or else we will be gone, too." As Reina An told Danlo this, there was a note of terrible sadness in her voice, and something other, as well.

After a long pause, the standing Sani crowded even closer to hear what Reina An and Ki Lin Shang might say next to this beautiful stranger, who sat naked as any other man beneath the beautifully misty sky.

"You seem to have . . . a rare knowledge of God," Danlo said to Reina An.

"Well, I am old and I have had many years to learn the Yasa," she said. She smiled nicely at Danlo's compliment.

Danlo hesitated for a moment, not wishing to utter words that the Sani might regard as blasphemy. Finally, he drew in a breath of air and said, "It is almost as if you had spoken to God."

But Reina An took no offense at his statement. She only sighed and told him, "Once when I was young girl, when my mother took me down to the sea, while listening to the waves I almost thought I did. But no. God does not speak to the Sani any longer."

"Any . . . longer?"

"Once God spoke to us, but that was long ago."

"Do you mean before you were born?"

"Before the life of any Sani who now walks the Earth. But when my mother's grandmother's great-grandmother was first born—her name was Niu An—God spoke to us. Niu An remembered His words to tell the rest of the tribe."

"I see," Danlo said. "Then God spoke to Niu An when she was a newborn child?"

"It seems strange, I know, but Niu An was not born of a mother as you or I."

"How was she born, then?"

"She was born from the breath of God."

"Truly?"

"She was born out of the Earth, from the clay and seawater that God shaped with His own hands. When God breathed the breath of life into her, she came alive and took her first step upon the Earth."

"That is a beautiful story," Danlo said. In truth, he didn't doubt what Reina An had told him, remembering as he did how the Solid State Entity had created an incarnation of Tamara in an amritsar tank on another Earth far away.

"All the firstborn came into life in this way," Reina An said. "Niu An was born as a full woman—she never knew what it was like to be a child."

"But she knew God?"

"She talked with God."

"She heard his voice, then?"

"She saw His face."

"His . . . face?"

Reina An nodded her head. "On the beach, out over the waters, the sea was burning and there was a great flash of light. And God appeared to Niu An."

"I have always wondered what God would look like," Danlo said. He glanced down at the impassive face of Nikolos Daru Ede, and he almost smiled.

"God's face blazes like the sun," Reina An said. "His eyes shine like stars, and his lips burn with fire."

"I see."

"When God opened his glorious mouth to tell Niu An about beauty, he gave the fire of speech unto her lips."

"Then it was God who taught Niu An to speak, yes?"

"It was God," Reina An said. "God taught all the firstborn what they needed to know to be Sani."

"I see."

"And the firstborn taught our grandmothers and grandfathers everything they needed to know to be beautiful."

"I see," Danlo repeated. And then, as he turned his face to the hot fire before him, after a moment's reflection, he said, "And now God is watching and waiting—waiting to see what kind of beauty the Sani bring forth out of the Earth, yes?"

Reina An turned to stare at Danlo for a long time. Ki Lin Shang, too, and his wives, Hon Su Shang and Laam Su, fell silent as they stared at this tall, strange man from the stars. Danlo drew in five slow breaths, and now all the Sani were staring at him, through the mist and the cold air of astonishment rippling through the village, silently staring.

"Again, you speak the words of the Yasa," Reina An said.

"Truly?"

"Without hearing them—and yet you know."

"Perhaps."

"How is it that you could know this?"

"I do not know."

"How is it that you could know what none of the others knew?"

"What others?"

"The other people who came before you."

Again, Ede's translation frustrated Danlo. He did not know whether Reina An meant "people" or "peoples."

"Do you mean the other peoples who walked the Earth before the Sani?"

"No," Reina An said. "The others. The other people from the stars."

Danlo sat completely still, staring at the fire. His heart began thumping in his chest like a bunda drum, and he wanted to jump up and dance around the fire—and yet he remained as motionless as a snow tiger watching a sleekit through the winter woods.

"How long ago did these others come to your Earth?" Danlo asked at last.

"Oh, perhaps five years ago—when I was a new great-grandmother."

"They came here from where?"

"From their Earth, I suppose."

"You never heard these people call their world by a name, then?"

"No, but they had a name for themselves. A strange and ugly name."

Danlo watched the flames dancing along the logs of the fire, and he said, "Yes?"

"An ugly, *ugly* name—they called themselves the Architects of God."

Now Danlo finally moved, slowly turning his head to look at the devotionary computer that projected Ede's hologram into the misty air. Danlo finally understood why none of the Sani had shown much curiosity over such a magical-seeming piece of technology: not long ago, it seemed, the Sani must have grown used to the sight of these ugly, little computers.

"Where are these Architects, now?" Danlo asked. He looked off through the dark forest, where he could almost hear the rush of faraway voices. "Do they still dwell upon your Earth?"

"Oh, no," Reina An said, looking down at her hands. "They are gone."

"Gone . . . where?"

Ki Lin Shang, who had remained silent for quite a long time, suddenly broke in, "*Gatei, gatei*—gone, gone. Why do you wish to know where they have gone?"

"I was only curious," Danlo said.

While Ki Lin Shang and Reina An traded significant looks, Danlo caught the faint sound of a Sani woman whispering something. It almost seemed that she was saying: "*Gatei, gatei, para sum Edei*—gone, gone, into God."

"They have gone home," Ki Lin finally said.

"To their world?" Danlo asked. "Have they returned to their star?"

Again, Ki Lin Shang and Reina An looked at each other, but they said nothing.

"Does their star have a name, then? Do you know which is their star?"

Reina An looked up at the impenetrable, iron gray sky for a long time. And then she said, "I know. It is a star of the Fish constellation. If it were a clear night, I could show you."

Danlo grasped the devotionary computer with such force that its sharp edges cut into the palms of his hands. At last, he thought, he might be close to completing his quest to find Tannahill—as close as the fall of night, as close as a good clean wind that would blow away the clouds and reveal the Vild's millions of beautiful stars.

Just then, however, there were voices from the forest and everyone turned to watch three old men make their way down the muddy main street of the village. Like the rest of the Sani, these elders from the nearest band were brown of skin and utterly naked. Their feet and legs were spattered with mud, and they moved very slowly as if they had been walking through the cold for a long time. They walked past the smokehouses and the barking dogs; they walked among the excited children right up to the edge of the fire pit where Danlo sat with Reina An and Ki Lin Shang. After Reina An had made the introductions, two of the three men bowed low and turned to smile at Danlo. The third elder, a stern-faced man who was known as Old Fei Yang, would not meet Danlo's eyes. He would not sit on the bearskins near Danlo, nor would he accept the cup of blackberry beer that young Toshu Luan offered him. Instead, he scowled down at the devotionary computer glittering in Danlo's lap. He fingered the deep wrinkles marking his small, toothless mouth. And then, in an ancient voice that sounded like two pieces of dried bone rubbing together, he shrilled out, "Have we forgotten our manners? Is this the way to honor a stranger? We should make a feast to honor this man's journey."

"A feast!" someone suddenly called out. And then, many others, "Let's make a feast!"

"A beautiful feast," Old Fei Yang said. "Let this poor tired man rest while we prepare our most beautiful foods."

Old Fei Yang then suggested that the Sani elders meet together to organize the feast while a young man named Ten Su Minye and his two strong and beautiful brothers escorted Danlo to the guest house at the very edge of the village. For a moment, it seemed that Reina An and Ki Lin Shang might dispute this rather rude and preemptory decision of Old Fei Yang's. But after all, Old Fei Yang *was* the Oldest of the Old, and his word carried a great weight among all the Sani, even here in this little village that was not his own. And so in the end, things went as he had said. Ten Su Minye and his brothers—big men with muscles bulging from the logs they cut and hauled through the forest everyday—showed Danlo to a little log house sitting in a huge puddle of mud. They held the heavy log door open while he stepped inside. Instantly, Danlo smelled the terrible nearness of dank bearskins and stinking old fish, and then the door banged shut leaving him alone with his devotionary computer. He began pacing around the room like a caged tiger as he awaited the feast and the sight of the star that he had sought for so long.

THE FEAST

*Know, O beloved, man was not created in jest or at
random, but marvelously made for some great end.*
                                        —Al Ghazzali

After their first moments together in the house, with the rain
beginning to patter on the roof above them, the Ede hologram's
face screwed up into the very embodiment of confusion. "I had
thought that we were about to learn the location of Tannahill.
And now we're supposed to wait here while the Sani prepare a
feast! Who can understand such a people?"

For the time, Danlo paid the devotionary little attention. He
set it down on one of the many bearskins spread out over the dirt
floor and walked about the house. Like all the Sani houses it had
no windows, but the fireplace was ablaze with sweet-smelling
spruce logs and there was a low table set out with dried salmon,
walnuts, and bowls of fresh blackberries. Danlo did not know
how long he would be required to wait for the Sani's feast, but at
least he would not be too cold, nor would he starve.

Ede seemed annoyed by Danlo's silence, and so he said, "I
confess that I don't like waiting in this village for the sky to
clear. There must be another way for the Sani to describe the star
of Tannahill."

Danlo examined the house's walls, then, the tightly fitted logs
chinked with dried clay as hard as stone. He looked up at the
sloping, solid wood ceiling, wondering if he might find some
place where the beams were loose or rotten. But the ceiling
seemed as well-made as the rest of the house. In a way, it had a
kind of simple, sturdy beauty, as all the Sani houses did.

"If only we'd come here five years ago," Ede said, "then we
might have simply accompanied the Architects back to Tannahill."

At last, Danlo sighed and sat down cross-legged facing the devotionary computer. He looked at Ede's brooding, little hologram, and said, "The Architects did not return to Tannahill."

"What?" Ede's face was as featureless as a bowl of mud, and then, a moment later, the alarm program took control of the light beams composing Ede's cheeks, mouth, and eyes.

"The Sani killed them." Danlo closed his eyes while he rubbed the lightning scar cut deep into his forehead. "They invited the Architects to a feast beneath the stars. And then they murdered them. With knives, each man and woman, they murdered."

"How do you know this?" Ede asked. His face fell through a series of emotions: doubt, fear, hate, awe, resentment, calculation, and finally, doubt again. "How *could* you know?"

Danlo sat listening to the rain falling through the forest outside, and he wondered how he could ever explain to Ede how he knew what he knew. How could he explain it to himself, this way of seeing that was beyond logic, beyond all space or time? Once, he had called this mysterious vision by the Fravashi term *yugen,* but how could any word ever encompass the terrifying (and lovely) cascades of images that sometimes rushed through his inner eye with all the power of a waterfall? How could he describe the connectedness, the utter strangeness—like the cold, clear joy of beholding a distant seascape from a single shell sparkling in the palm of one's hand? From the fear and hate written on Old Fei Yang's face, Danlo had seen the death of the Architects. Even now, as he closed his eyes, he could still see this little tragedy as if it were occurring at the moment. As if it always *would* be occurring.

In Old Fei Yang's village, deep in the forest some miles away, the Sani sat feting a group of Architects. There were nine of these strangers, five men and four women, each dressed in the traditional white sikon kimonos, each holding in his or her hands a devotionary computer similar to Danlo's. At the height of the feast, when the Sani and their guests had filled themselves with fish and bread and blackberry beer, the Sani smiled to see their guests so relaxed and comfortable. As was their custom at any gathering, they recited lines from the Yasa. They talked with the Architects about the mysterious nature of God. And then they surprised the Architects with fish knives that they had hidden beneath their bearskins. Men, women, and children, they fell upon the Architects in a fury of slashing and stabbing and high, terrible screams that pierced the quiet of the dark woods. They made quick work of their murder, hoping that the souls of the nine Architects would eventually understand that in all those things that must die, the sight of blood was always beautiful to God the Destroyer.

"I *know*," Danlo said. "The feast occurred five years ago. Five years and thirty-three days."

"But why did the Sani make such perfidious murders?"

"You truly do not understand, then?"

"I suppose they didn't want to be proselytized by a group of religious fanatics."

"Yes, of course—but it is more than that."

The Ede hologram formed up a sarcastic face. "Please tell me."

"The Architects had no love of beauty."

"And for this they were executed?"

Danlo sat there in silence, listening to the beat of the rain on the roof and the beating of his own heart. He smiled sadly but did not speak.

"And now the Sani are preparing another feast."

"A feast," Danlo finally said. "Yes."

"To murder you?"

"Perhaps."

"Perhaps?"

Danlo smiled down upon the alarmed hologram of Nikolos Daru Ede. It amused him that Ede, who was always alert for dangers in the environment, who fancied himself as a master cetic and reader of minds, could so easily misread the human heart.

"There is an even chance that I will be executed or . . ."

"Or what?"

"Honored. Even as we speak, the Sani are making their preparations. It will either be a blood feast or . . . a welcoming."

"Then you don't believe that Old Fei Yang has determined your fate?"

"No," Danlo said. "He is full of fear and anger, even hate, but there is something other, too."

"And what is that?"

"Beauty," Danlo said. "He loves all that is beautiful in the soul of man."

"Do you believe this?"

"Yes—truly."

"Then you don't believe Old Fei Yang will argue for your execution?"

Danlo shook his head. "Oh, he may argue for it, but it will not be his choice to make."

"Then what will determine which kind of feast we attend tonight?"

"I will," Danlo said. "There will be something I must do—or not do."

"And what is that?"

"I am not sure yet. I cannot . . . quite see it. We will have to wait."

Ede's face was now all alarm and calculation. Finally, in a low voice he said, "If there's a fifty percent chance of your being executed, then surely you should try to escape."

"Do you have a plan, then?"

"Of course," Ede whispered. "I'm good with plans. You could pretend that you've eaten bad fish, and ask to void yourself outside. When Ten Su Minye and his brothers open the door, you could overpower them."

"Overpower three strong men?"

"You're a pilot of the Order," Ede reminded him. "Haven't you trained in the fighting arts?"

Danlo slowly nodded his head. "The *killing* arts, they are called on Neverness."

"Surely you can't think it's wrong to kill others who are about to kill you?"

Danlo bowed his head as he touched the scar above his eye. He breathed deeply, saying nothing.

"It would actually be quite easy," Ede said. "You could use one of the logs from the fire to break open Ten Su Minye's brains. And then you could run down to the beach, to your ship."

With his eyes closed, Danlo tried not to envision what Ede had suggested. He tried not to see their little house at the edge of the forest or the broad, sandy beach, which he might attain after only half a mile sprint though the giant coastal trees. Most of all, he tried not to look upon his mind's creation of a nightmare, the vivid colors: the blackened log still glowing from the fire, the scattered white ashes, the redness of blood upon Ten Su Minye's forehead, upon the bearskins and walls, upon Danlo's trembling hands. Never killing, never harming another, not even in one's thoughts—Danlo had made this vow long ago, and so he desperately tried not to see what any other man might have seen so easily.

"No," Danlo said at last. "I cannot escape this way,"

"But why not?"

In a slow, halting voice, in whispers and sighs and occasional silences, Danlo told Ede of his vow of ahimsa.

"But the Sani may kill you—aren't you *afraid*?"

Danlo nodded his head, then smiled. "Yes, I am afraid."

"And so," Ede asked, "is it your plan just to wait here for the Sani's feast while you sit breathing like a buddha? Toward what end?"

"Toward truly living," Danlo said. "Toward being more alive."

"But what good is that if you're to be killed?"

"Being truly alive is good simply because it is good," Danlo said, smiling. "And more practically, it prepares the heart, the spirit—the whole bodymind. So that when the moment comes, I will know what to do."

Ede was quiet while he processed this. And then he asked, "And to which moment do you refer?"

"The . . . moment," Danlo said. "There is always a moment."

"And now you sit speaking as mysteriously as a Buddha, too. I'm afraid I don't understand."

Danlo sighed as he looked down at the flickering lights of Ede's face. Then he said, "I am only speaking of the now-moment. It is when the door opens. When nowness becomes thenness, and the future is always and now. When one chooses, yes or no, which future will be. When there is nothing in the universe except one's will: to act or not act, to see, to know, to move—to move the universe. There is always this moment, yes?"

But Danlo's explanation did little to ease Ede's perplexity. "I'm not sure. For me, time is as continuous as the atomic clock built into this devotionary, and I must act according as my program runs. If you're executed, what will happen to me?"

"I do not know."

"I might be marooned on this Earth forever."

"Perhaps another pilot of my Order might rescue you someday."

"That's unlikely. Your finding me in the temple was the rarest of chances."

"Still, there is a chance. And you are immortal, yes?"

"Immortal, in a way, but not indestructible."

Danlo smiled sadly to himself. "There is nothing in the universe that cannot be destroyed."

"I suppose," Ede said, "that I might eventually convince

these savages that I am their God, after all. They might build me an altar, set me upon it and worship me.''

Danlo thought about this while he stared at the thick wooden beams of the door. He breathed evenly, deeply, and then he said, ''Is this what you truly desire?''

For a moment, the Ede program hesitated, and then Ede said, ''Of course not.''

''I have wondered if we should tell the Sani about you,'' Danlo said. ''About you . . . as God.''

''Why not? Don't you believe in telling the truth?''

''Yes, but . . . the truth that is not heard is not the truth.''

''The Sani's God is dead,'' Ede said bitterly. ''*That* is the truth.''

Danlo shook his head. ''No, their God is still alive. For them, marvelously and beautifully alive.''

''I should tell them how the Silicon God murdered me.''

''If you told them this, they wouldn't believe you. And if they *did* believe you, it would leave a hole in their soul.''

''And through this hole would enter logic and reason.''

''No, only madness would enter. When a people believe nothing . . . they will do anything.''

''Such as murder?''

With a long sigh, Danlo said, ''Murder is the least of it.''

''I think you're quite fond of these Sani people, aren't you, Pilot?''

''Yes, I am,'' Danlo said. For a moment he closed his eyes, and the cold currents of time swept him into the future, and he saw the Sani as they one day might be: their tribe of some ten thousand strong would multiply a thousand times over and fill the Earth. And in this time—perhaps a thousand years—the strict and stern Sani religion would mutate, evolve, and spread in many different forms to every continent of the world. There would be doctrinal heresies, schism, and abandonment of faith. Perhaps there would even be holy wars. But there would be religious revivals, too, and even though the Sani religion might be riven into a thousand different sects and wholly new ways of worship, the pure and luminous core of their faith might remain. Even after ten thousand years, when the Sani were no longer the Sani, they might still revere beauty. Halla, Danlo remembered, was the beauty of life. It was his hope that the Sani, of all the peoples of the race of man, might someday find a way to live on the Earth in harmony and beauty.

"Well," Ede said, "I don't understand how you could be in love with a people who are about to kill you."

"It is the same way . . . that I love the world."

"I think we should escape," Ede reiterated. "Now, through the door—it's open, you know. The Sani don't have locks on their doors."

Danlo smiled and picked up his flute. "There is always a time for going through a different doorway."

"Are you so eager to die?"

"No, truly I am not. But I am curious to know if I will die . . . or live."

Danlo returned to breathing upon his flute, then. For a long time he sat on the bearskin with the shakuhachi's ivory mouthpiece pressed to his lips. Without making a sound, he fingered a long, meditative song that the alien called Old Father had once taught him. His belly fluttered with the nearness of death, but he let his breath fill him and force his fear into a tiny pocket deep within himself. When he finally grew tired, he lay down and slept in front of the fire. Once, he awoke hungry and ate the entire bowl of blackberries as well as most of the walnuts. And then he slept again until dawn when he picked up his flute and silently played throughout the whole day—until the cracks around the door began to darken with the fall of night.

Then, outside the guest house, there were voices. The door suddenly opened, and a very tired Ten Su Minye greeted Danlo politely. His brothers and five other men were there, too, waiting to escort Danlo to the center of the village. Danlo walked slowly in the procession of naked men with the devotionary held in his right hand and the flute in his left. Sometime during the day the rain had stopped, but it was colder than it had been the preceding day, clear and cold with the first stars of the evening showing bright in the sky. Danlo lifted his eyes to the brilliant heavens, wondering which group of stars might be the Fish constellation. He might have asked Ten Su Minye this if they hadn't first arrived at the village's central fire pits, which were stoked with freshly cut wood and fairly roaring with orange flames.

It was between the two largest fire pits that the Sani had laid out their feast. All the Sani except for one sick old man named Wan Su had turned out to greet Danlo. Ki Lin Shang and Reina An—and their husbands and wives and children and cousins and nieces and nephews—all stood formally around the fire pits waiting to greet their guest. Old Fei Yang was there, too, standing as rigidly as his withered old body would allow. He would not look at Danlo, nor did he exchange pleasantries with any of the other thirty-nine elders who had arrived from the faraway villages during that day. Instead he stared down at his hands, as if he hoped to find a bit of beauty in the swollen knuckles and clawlike fingers misshapen from a lifetime of slitting open the bellies of salmon and other animals that he had killed. According to good Sani etiquette, he bowed to Danlo and motioned for him to sit beside him on the bearskins to his left. As Oldest of the Old, of course, Old Fei Yang had the position of honor at the center of the elders. On his right, were Ki Lin Shang and Reina An and Miliama Chu, one of three elders from the Owl Sani farther up the coast. As if a signal had been given, all the other Sani around the other fire pits sat on their bearskins, and the feast began.

Because Danlo was very hungry (and because all his senses were marvelously awakened), he tore into the colorful dishes before him with a rare joy of eating which he hadn't felt in a long time. There were many dishes to choose from. On great wooden platters before the fire were cuts of roasted venison and bear steaks, wild duck and goose, and the mashed brains of various animals. The Sani relished salmon above all other foods, and so they were proud to serve up slices of smoked salmon in dill sauce, baked salmon with herbs, and salmon fried, grilled, poached, and braised into half a dozen different kinds of stew.

Danlo, of course, would eat no meat; he had wondered if the Sani might find this dietary stricture to be strange or offensive. But when he explained his vow of ahimsa, the Sani immediately seemed to understand, even Old Fei Yang, who reluctantly said, "To respect the lives of the animals is beautiful." It was beautiful, too, to respect the lives of plants, but Danlo had to eat *something,* and so he gladly partook of the vegetable dishes passing from hand to hand all around him. The Sani women had baked a delicious cornbread spread with blackberry preserves, and Danlo filled himself with slice after slice before turning to the sweet potatoes, honeyed carrots, and wild rice with pine nuts. And then there was a surprisingly spicy walnut salad and pickled cabbage and roasted chestnut meats. If he had wished, he might have sampled twenty different squash dishes or gorged himself on bowls of raspberries, elderberries, pawpaws, or baked apples. But Danlo did not want to gorge. Although he had once been taught to "eat for a season" whenever the opportunity presented itself, he did not want to fill his belly so full of food that there would be little room left for the proper intake of breath. Very soon, Danlo thought, it would be important that he be able to breathe properly and deeply.

"You *still* might escape," Ede said. He spoke in a low voice amid the clamor of conversation and clacking plates. Danlo held the devotionary computer in his lap, and he smiled because Ede had taken to whispering witticisms or warnings to him in between his translating duties. "Look how these people eat—their bellies are as swollen as blood ticks! If you ran toward your ship now, who could catch you?"

Indeed, most of the Sani had now eaten as much food as human beings could possibly hold. Many lay sprawled on their bearskins, holding their bellies and groaning. Many more were belching politely as they picked at their teeth with little slivers of wood and visited with family or friends. Reina An, looking out among the cooking fires at her well-fed people, decided that it was time for drinking the sacred blackberry beer. She conferred a moment with Ki Ling Shang and with Old Fei Yang, who nodded his head in agreement. And then she summoned her grandson, Kiyo Su, a young man with a nervous face, which he tried to hide by smiling as often as possible. Kiyo Su then went off to gather up his brothers and friends—all the young men of the village. Soon they returned bearing skinsful of blackberry beer. The Sani were more than ready to taste this sacred drink. As Kiyo Su and his brothers went around the fires, each Sani—man, woman and child—held out his wooden cup to be filled. When this was done, Kiyo Su and the others filled their own cups and turned toward the elders to await the recitation of the Yasa.

"We drink the beauty of God," Old Fei Yang called out in his raspy voice. "May all God's works be beautiful."

Following Old Fei Yang's example, all the Sani put their lips to their beer. Danlo took a sip and tasted the strongly alcoholic liquor, which was at once sweet and thick and bitter. He held his cup beneath his nose, inhaling the essence of wild blackberries, all the while watching Old Fei Yang, and waiting.

"We drink the beauty of the world," Reina An said. "May all the world be beautiful."

And then it was Ki Lin Shang's turn, and he sang out, "We drink the tears of God. May all our tears be beautiful."

And so it went, each of the elders on Old Fei Yang's right reciting from the Yasa while the Sani sipped their bittersweet beer. When the last of them had finished, it came time for the other elders to make their libations. Since Danlo was sitting to Old Fei Yang's immediate left, it fell to him next to say the sacred words. No one expected him to know what to say: Danlo wasn't even a man of the Sani, much less an elder, and so everyone was surprised when he raised his cup and called out in a clear, strong voice, "We drink the music of the world. May all our songs be beautiful."

Danlo held his breath for a moment, feeling the weakness return to his belly as he watched Old Fei Yang. All the Sani sat there stunned. Nobody drank their sacred beer. Then Ki Lin Shang quietly said, "These are not the words of the Yasa."

"Truly, they are," Danlo said. "I have spoken truly."

Here, Old Fei Yang snapped his head in Danlo's direction, and with much anger, he said, "The others who called themselves Architects—they, too, thought that they could tell us about God."

All through the village, men and women sat frozen on their bearskins, looking intently at Old Fei Yang as if awaiting a signal.

"But I would never hope to tell anyone about God," Danlo said.

"Then you haven't come to our Earth to tell us about your God?" Reina An asked.

"No."

"You haven't come here to tell us about this man named Ede who became God and Master of the Universe?"

"No—truly I have not."

Reina An pointed at Danlo's lap, down at the hologram of Nikolos Daru Ede. The imago, Danlo saw, had frozen into motionlessness as had the Sani. For the moment, Ede neither spoke nor looked at Danlo.

"Then you don't believe this ugly idol is God?"

Danlo looked at Ede's sensuous lips, his crooked teeth, his black eyes blazing out of a bald head that was much too big for his body. He sensed that Ede's programs must be running furiously, even as Ede was forced to translate this last slur against himself.

"He is no more God than you or I," Danlo said, smiling. "He is no more God than the mud on my feet."

No more, truly, Danlo thought. *But no less.*

This response seemed almost to mollify Old Fei Yang, who nodded his head sagely, then asked, "If you haven't come to our Earth to tell us about God, then what is the reason for your journey?"

Whatever answer he might have been expecting, he seemed

fairly astonished when Danlo said, "I am making a quest. My people are dying of a disease, and I must find a cure."

As Danlo told something of his people, the Alaloi, and the virus that was killing them, Old Fei Yang's whole manner began to soften. As Oldest of the Old, he had seen much suffering, and he had lost grandchildren to lung fevers and other afflictions. Then too, like any of the Sani, he could appreciate how easy it was for a whole people to be suddenly destroyed.

"I'm sorry, but I know of no medicine that could help your people," Old Fei Yang said. "I've never heard of such a disease."

"I am sorry, too," Danlo said.

"Not even the Yasa tells of any medicine that might be useful."

Danlo was silent while he stared at the flute in his hand.

"Nor does the Yasa speak of music—as you have spoken."

"No?"

"Do you think that I don't know the Yasa?" Now Old Fei Yang's anger was returning, and sinews along his neck stretched as tight as the strings of a gosharp. It was a dangerous moment, but still not the moment that Danlo had been waiting for.

"Does anyone know the Yasa?" Danlo asked softly.

"What do you mean?" Reina An broke in. And then, from the other elders and the rest of the Sani, as if in chorus: "What does he mean?"

But Old Fei Yang did not ask this question. He sat very still, like a lost hunter awaiting the rising sun.

"May the Yasa always be beautiful," Danlo chanted. He closed his eyes, then. Once, during the previous night, these words had come to him like fireflowers opening in his mind, and now he prayed that they were true. "May we always find new beauties; may we make our sacred Yasa as God makes the world and always keep it beautiful."

Now the whole village had fallen silent, even the noisome dogs who were busy gnawing at their feast bones. No one seemed to understand how Danlo had known these last lines of the Yasa. No one could explain how Danlo seemed to know the most basic thing about the Yasa: that the sacred law was perfect but incomplete.

"We drink the music of the world," Danlo whispered. "May all our songs be beautiful."

He looked at his flute's beautiful ivory mouthpiece, and he remembered a line from the *Song of Life* that his grandfather had once taught him: *Halla is the one who brings music into the world.*

"My people," he said to Old Fei Yang, "had a Yasa, too. In spirit . . . the sacred words of all people are really the same."

Old Fei Yang held his cup of blackberry beer trembling in his right hand. What Danlo had said must have been very different from the Architects' universal condemnation of all such "false" revelations as the Yasa.

Danlo breathed deeply a moment, then continued, "If all people were to look long enough for God's beauty, it may be that they would discover the Yasa, too."

"That itself is a beautiful thought," Old Fei Yang said. He reached out, then, with his trembling left hand to touch Danlo's bamboo flute. It was obvious that he had never seen such a beautiful thing before. "I'll always remember this thought."

Danlo, feeling his belly tighten as hard as baldo nut, seeing that his moment had almost come, lifted up his flute and began to play a song. Old Fei Yang and all the other Sani sat rapt on their bearskins for they had never heard such music before. They knew only the lullabyes that the Sani mother hummed to their children on stormy nights—that and the natural music of wind and rain and the chirping of the songbirds.

The melody that Danlo breathed into his flute recalled all these things, and more. Danlo played to the distant whales out at sea and to the stars; he played to the pain that he could see filling up Old Fei Yang's shiny eyes. Like Danlo's music, this pain was beautiful in its depth and purity. It connected the two men to the memories of their childhood—and to the beauties of the living world all around them. This was the whole inspiration of Danlo's song, to open the heart to the world, to seek out the secret beauty in the depths of the human soul. Danlo played and played, and each note that fell from his flute was like a numinous golden arrow aimed at Old Fei Yang's heart. He played for a long, long time, until the moon was high in the sky and the fires had burnt low. When he was finished at last, he put down his flute and looked at Old Fei Yang. There were tears in the old man's eyes, and something more. There was the other thing, the splendid and beautiful thing that Danlo had seen when Old Fei Yang had first walked into the village.

"That was very beautiful," Old Fei Yang said. His voice was as dry as sandstone, and he had trouble getting the words out. "I hadn't thought such sounds were possible."

This is the moment, Danlo thought. *The forever and now.*

Until now, Danlo hadn't known what he would do when his moment came. That was the terror (and beauty) of the future, the not knowing—the not seeing of that dark, unknown land of ice crystals and fire where all things are possible. Once, though, he had been taught that there was always a way to choose one's future, a way to act, flawlessly, in total affirmation when the future arrived. This way required one to be truly alive in the present moment, utterly awake and aware of every sound, every vibration, every ray of light—of the shimmering interconnectedness of everything in the world. Only then was it possible to know what to do when one didn't know what to do. And now it was *now,* as it always would be. Now the fear in his belly melted away before an onstreaming rush of pure, luminous energy. Beneath him—beneath the bearskin on which he and Old Fei Yang sat—there was a knife. Beneath the old black fur there was a spot where the knife lay; it was almost between the two of them but farther in toward the fire pit near the edge of the bearskin. Danlo had seen this spot in his waking dreams. He knew it from Old Fei Yang's pained looks whenever the gaze of his tired old eyes chanced to fall anywhere near it. In truth, Danlo knew this spot the way a wounded tiger knows his death spot, only now he was seeing it as if for the first time. He saw that he might easily shift his body about to forestall Old Fei Yang's reaching the knife when the time came. But suddenly he saw another thing, and so he remained sitting where he was.

Slowly, as if only stretching his muscles after a long meal, he straightened out his leg. He let his heel fall onto the bearskin where the knife was secreted. As if accidentally discovering a rock beneath him, he forced a frown to his face and then bent over and grasped the edge of the bearskin, and peeled it back to reveal the knife. It was a fisherman's knife: small and curved and as keenly sharpened as obsidian could be, which was very sharp indeed. "Look," Danlo called out, "Someone has lost his knife." He stood up and held the knife above his head. "Has anybody lost a knife?" he called out.

Now the eyes of everyone in the village were focused upon this deadly little knife. Nobody spoke. Nobody moved.

And then Old Fei Yang broke the silence. "It's my knife," he said, holding out his hand. "I must have dropped it while making preparations for the feast."

"Oh," Danlo said. He looked at Old Fei Yang's outstretched hand. "May I borrow it for a moment?"

Without waiting for a response, he sat back down on the bearskin. From a wooden bowl in front of him, he picked up a fat, red apple. He used the knife quickly to cut out a crescent-shaped wedge, which he offered to Old Fei Yang.

"Your voice is very dry," Danlo said to Old Fei Yang. "Here, this will help against the dryness."

Old Fei Yang exchanged a quick and puzzled look with Reina An. And then he shrugged his shoulders, took the slice of apple and bit into it as if he feared it might be poisoned.

"My mouth is dry, too," Danlo said. "It is hard to play the flute when one's mouth is dry."

Here, suddenly, he handed both the apple and the knife to Old Fei Yang. Then he picked up his flute and said, "Would you please cut me a slice of apple while I wipe down my flute? There is a song that I would teach you, if you'd like."

There was a moment. Old Fei Yang sat holding the apple in his left hand, the knife in his right. He stared at the knife for an uncomfortably long time. Then he stared at Danlo, at his dark, wild eyes, his beautiful smile, his naked throat. He watched as Danlo polished his golden flute against the bearskin. This was Old Fei Yang's moment of choice and fate, and it seemed to go on and on forever. And then, at last, Old Fei Yang smiled mysteriously. He cut off a section of apple. He gave it to Danlo and asked, "You would teach me a song?"

"Yes, if you'd like."

"You'd teach me how to play this beautiful instrument?"

"Yes."

"Oh, I'd like that very much," Old Fei Yang said. "Is it very hard to play?"

"Truly, it can be," Danlo said. "But why don't we begin with a song that my teacher once gave me. It is a simple song. A beautiful song."

There on the bearskins by the fire of the Sani village, Danlo taught this fierce old man how to play the flute. The sight of Old Fei Yang, Oldest of the Old, blowing into a piece of bamboo amazed the Sani. Despite all the rules of decorum, they crowded around Danlo's bearskin to watch Old Fei Yang place his fingers on the shakuhachi as Danlo had shown him. Old Fei Yang played neither long nor very well, but he played quite beautifully—which is to say with all the power of his breath and heart and soul. When he was finished, he wiped off the mouthpiece and returned the flute to Danlo. He wiped his eyes and then picked up his cup of blackberry beer. "We drink the music of the world," he said. "May all our songs be beautiful."

The Sani women and men needed only the slightest of reasons for drinking their sweet, purplish beer, and so together all the Sani lifted their cups and chanted, "We drink the music of the world. May all our songs be beautiful."

"I believe these truly are words of the Yasa," Old Fei Yang said. "We must thank Danlo of the Stars for bringing us these words."

Old Fei Yang went on to promise that when the season of the rains was finished, he would take Danlo's words to the elders of even the farthest Sani tribes. In the spring, they would decide whether or not to add them to the Yasa.

"Will you stay with us?" Old Fei Yang asked. He motioned to Reina An and Ki Lin Shang and Jin Joyu Minye—and then to all the Sani standing about or sitting by the fires. "We made this feast to welcome you."

Danlo tried hard not to look at the hologram of Nikolos Daru Ede. This was the possibility that he had foreseen while silently playing his flute in the guest house. Like a master chess player (or a warrior going into battle), he had laid his strategy and made his moves according to the requirements of the moment. And he had won. For the time, he had won his life. But he did not stop to celebrate or congratulate himself, for soon, in only another moment, there would be other possibilities and a new battle would begin.

"I would like to stay with you," Danlo said. "Only . . . I must complete my journey."

At this bad news, Old Fei Yang seemed sad and almost angry again. "You could teach the children to play your sacred music. They would learn much more beautifully than a foolish old man."

"Perhaps I could stay," Danlo said. "But only long enough to show you how to carve new flutes. Only until the children learn the notes."

"But there are so many songs you could teach them."

"It would be better if they made their own songs."

"I had hoped you might come to my village. You might even marry my granddaughter, Sunlian—she is a beautiful woman."

"I am sorry," Danlo said.

Old Fei Yang sighed, then forced a smile. "I understand. You must find a cure for your people."

"Yes."

"Then you'll seek this cure among the stars?"

"Yes—among the stars." Danlo breathed deeply a moment,

then said, "In truth, I seek the star of the Architects. It is they who made the disease that is killing my people. It is said that they know of a cure."

Old Fei Yang scowled and plucked at the tendons of his neck as he considered this. He said, "I didn't know human beings could make a disease."

"Truly, they can."

"The only true cure for disease is beauty. If you'd stay with us, you might find how this is so."

"I am sorry."

"The Architects are evil," Old Fei Yang said. "They know nothing of beauty."

Danlo remembered that the Architects were destroying the stars, and he thought, *shaida eth shaida.*

"You should not make a journey to these people," Old Fei Yang said.

"Nevertheless, I must." Danlo waited a moment, then asked, "Do you know which is their star?"

Old Fei Yang shook his head. "No."

"I do," Reina An said. She pointed a bony finger upwards high above the spruce trees at the sky. "That is their star."

Danlo moved close to Reina An, close enough that he could smell the salmon grease in her hair as well as the essence of wild roses that she rubbed over her body in order to smell more beautiful. With his eye, Danlo followed the line of her finger where it led out to infinity. There, in the deeps of the Vild, out in the light-distances, there were fields of brilliant stars. Danlo watched as Reina An's finger described the arc of stars forming the Fish's backbone. He watched as she pointed out the three stars of the Fish's tail. (Three-In-A-Row, as she called them.) There was one star, brighter than the others, that she called the Eye of the Fish. This was the Architects' star, she said. This huge star shone a faint salmon pink, and Danlo thought that it might be a red giant. He stared at it for a long time, fixing it in his mind. Later he would stare at it through his ship's telescopes and apply the theorems of probabilistic topology, and with luck he would determine its fixed-points. And then, soon, in only a few more days, he must take his lightship out into stars and journey there.

"Do you see it, Danlo of the Stars? Do you see it?"

"I see it," Danlo said.

Ever since coming to the Sani village, Danlo had wondered if he should tell these people about the stars. Although Ede the God was truly dead, the Sani could never be safe from sudden destruction, for they lived in the light of the Vild stars, which the Architects were destroying one by one. No people anywhere could ever be safe, and that was a truth of the universe almost too terrible to face. Even if the Order's mission to the Old Church succeeded and the Architects finally saw the light of reason, the deadly light of once-killed stars might at any moment fall upon the Sani and annihilate them. Danlo stared and stared at the Eye of the Fish, and he thought that even this magnificent star could explode as suddenly as any other. It was to stop this massacre of the stars, Danlo remembered, that the Order of Neverness had made a mission to the Vild. This was why he had journeyed to the Earth of the Sani. And this was why he must say good-bye to these tragic people and leave them to their fate.

"The stars," Danlo said at last, "are the children of God alone in the night."

He sat on his bearskin with Reina An and Old Fei Yang, and they both complimented him on the beauty of his words. Danlo silently prayed that one day the Golden Ring would grow around this Earth and protect the Sani from the Vild's fury. Many women and the men sat around them drinking their blackberry bear and asking Danlo for more words and more songs. And so far into the night he chanted from the Song of Life, and he played his flute to the wild and beautiful stars.

ALUMIT BRIDGE

*The computer is the bridge that will carry man on his
journey from animal to god.*
                                    —*from Man's Journey*, Nikolos Daru Ede

Every journey must have its end. Even the purest of pilots—they
whose only gladness is the luminous falling from moment to
moment and star to star—will look forward to their homecoming.
And so they lay their plans and go out into the stellar wastelands
of the universe; they think always of great treasures to be won,
secret knowledge, triumph, the glorious completion of their
dreams, their quests, their lives. Sometimes, their longing to fulfill their purpose is so deep and terrible that they will tremble
to seize the joy of victory prematurely only to find empty air
trapped in their hands. This is the moment of broken hope, the
moment of doubt, disillusionment, even despair. For Danlo it
came when he fell out of the manifold near the star that the Sani
had named the Eye of the Fish.

  There he found an alien world all emerald and violet with
some of the strangest plant life that he had ever seen. He had
hoped that this lovely world would be Tannahill, for the finding
of lost Tannahill, if not the end of his journey, would be the
beginning of his achieving various goals. He would make a mission to the Architects and tell them of the Order and the Civilized
Worlds; he would ask if they possessed a cure for the disease that
was killing the Alaloi people; and last, if fate presented the opportunity, he might keep his promise to the ghost of Nikolos
Daru Ede and recover his frozen, three-thousand-year-old body.
All these things (and more) he might accomplish if only his luck
and courage ran true. Although in reality he knew that his
chances of success were not great, after his feast with the Sani,
he was as drunk with optimism as a seagull that has gorged on

fermented blackberries. He thought that anything might be possible. And so when he learned that this long-sought world was *not* Tannahill, but Alumit Bridge, he fell so swiftly into hopelessness that all the colors of the world below him darkened to black and he could hardly breathe.

"Pilot—are you all right?"

Ede's powerful voice spoke out of the stale air in the pit of Danlo's ship. Except for the glowing hologram of Nikolos Daru Ede, this mostly empty space would have been as lightless as a cetic's box. Danlo, floating naked as a babe in his mother's womb, was stricken with the lightlessness of the universe. For the moment, he was wholly unaware of the devotionary computer that he always kept near him.

"Pilot? Pilot?"

"I am too tired," Danlo finally said. "I have been away from home too long."

"Perhaps you've miscalculated this star's fixed-points," Ede said.

Danlo smiled at this, amused despite his dark mood. Even a journeymen pilot, having been shown the Eye of the Fish, could not have failed to find its fixed-points.

"Perhaps," Ede said, "you misunderstood which star that the Sani woman was pointing to."

"No, this is the star."

"Then perhaps the Sani misunderstood which was the Architects' star. Before they killed the missionaries at their feast."

"Perhaps," Danlo said.

"Of course, it *is* a coincidence that this star is circled by such a rich world."

"A . . . coincidence," Danlo said.

"And to find this world peopled with human beings—surely this is a coincidence, too."

Danlo's mind was almost as murky as an abandoned cave, but when Ede said this, he suddenly remembered something—and it was as if a torch had been lit inside him. "A *rare* coincidence, yes."

"You don't believe in pure chance, do you?" Ede asked. As a man—as a good programer and cybernetic architect—Ede had always reviled tychism, the school of philosophy teaching that absolute chance underlies all of reality. But now, as the remnant of a ghost of a god, he was not so sure.

"I do not believe . . . that God plays dice with the universe,'' Danlo said, quoting the Einstein. ''All coincidences are intriguing, yes?''

''Perhaps—but are they meaningful?''

''Everything is meaningful,'' Danlo said.

Ede sighed in a rather mechanical way, as he was programed to do, and he asked, ''What is the meaning of finding a world named Alumit Bridge where you had hoped Tannahill would be?''

Immediately upon falling out in orbit above Alumit Bridge, according to the rules of his Order, Danlo had sent a radio signal flashing down to the world below him. And almost immediately his greeting had been answered. The people of Alumit Bridge spoke a language apparently evolved from ancient Istwan, and Ede had little trouble translating it, and ascertaining that these people—they called themselves the Narain—claimed to know nothing of Tannahill.

''You truly do not know?'' Danlo asked.

''No, I don't think I do.''

''You do not remember that Nikolos Daru Ede was born on the planet Alumit?''

Ede was silent while he processed this. His face froze into a glittering attitude of thoughtfulness, and the jeweled eyes of the devotionary seemed as unfocused as a baby's. Then he said, ''I must have pruned the memory of my birth planet by accident. But it's strange that I wasn't aware of this pruning.''

''Memory itself is strange,'' Danlo said. ''Until you spoke of coincidences, I too had forgotten about Alumit.''

Ede looked straight into Danlo's eyes then, and he said, ''I suppose that you've also noticed the coincidence of the Narain speaking a derivative of Istwan?''

As he floated in the murky air in the pit of his ship, Danlo nodded his head. ''Istwan *was* the language of the Old Church, yes?''

''This is true,'' Ede admitted. ''But two hundred years after the Great Schism in 1749, at the end of the War of the Faces, there were fifty Architect sects. And all of them revered Istwan as their holy language. The Architect missionaries spread Istwan everywhere.''

''But it was the Old Church that established itself in the Vild.''

''Well, perhaps other churches did as well.''

''Perhaps,'' Danlo said.

"Or perhaps the Old Church's missionaries taught Istwan to the ancestors of these Narain."

Danlo smiled at the Ede hologram and said, "We could invent a thousand hypotheses as to why the Narain seem to know nothing of Tannahill."

"I notice," Ede said, "that you use the word *seem* in relation to the Narain's knowledge of Tannahill. Do you think these people have lied to us?"

"I do not know," Danlo said. "But there is something strange here. Something strange in the Narain naming their world Alumit *Bridge*. A bridge to what?"

"Who can say? There must be a thousand bridge worlds in the galaxy."

"I would like to explore these strangenesses," Danlo said.

"We could speak with the Narain again. We could interface the radio."

"I would like to speak with them face to face."

"Do you mean imago to imago?"

Slowly, Danlo shook his head.

At this, Ede's program generated something like alarm, and he asked, "Do you mean you'd make a planetfall here?"

"Yes."

"But it's too dangerous," Ede immediately said. After his witnessing the Sani's feast, he was most wary of placing himself in further jeopardy. "An unknown world—an unknown people."

"Pilots must take chances. Everyone, everything . . . always must."

"Perhaps this is true," Ede said. "But shouldn't the risk be in proportion to the possible gain?"

"Now you are arguing like a merchant," Danlo said. And then, ashamed of speaking so rudely, even to a computer, he said, "I am sorry. But the Narain *might* know of Tannahill. Isn't this gain enough?"

Ede was silent while he considered this, and his soft, glowing face was almost unreadable. "But there might be a hundred other peoples in the Vild who know of Tannahill. People who wouldn't hide their knowledge."

"People such as the Sani?"

"Perhaps," Ede admitted. "If we could find another such people, somewhere among these stars, we could make precautions and preparations."

"I see."

"The Sani had practically no technology. With a little foresight, it would be rather easy to protect ourselves from such savages.''

''The Sani were not savages.''

''Still, they had no—''

''I will never arm myself, if that is what you mean,'' Danlo said.

''But if you go down to this planet, how will you protect yourself? The Narain are quite sophisticated, aren't they?''

In truth, the Narain were perhaps as technologically fluorescent as any peoples of the Civilized Worlds. The continents of Alumit Bridge were dotted with cities, all of which were great, glittering arcologies built on many levels high into the sky. They had radio and hologram displays and a planetary communications network; from one brief conversation with some man or cybernetic entity who called himself Abraxax, Danlo suspected that the Narain interfaced this network in very sophisticated ways. Some of the cities were graced with light fields that could accommodate jets and jammers—and probably even shuttles capable of rocketing up to deep ships and other vessels as they fell out above the planet in near space. Such a people would no doubt possess a sophisticated weaponry: perhaps lasers and eye tlolts and dreammakers, as well as a thousand kinds of poisons and genotoxins. According to Ede, for Danlo to fall into the hands of such unknown people would be madness.

As Danlo moved about his ship's pit, dressing himself in preparation for a planetfall, he considered what Ede had said. He took his flute into his hands, and he might have held it up to the devotionary's thousand computer eyes as if to say, ''This is all the protection that I will need.'' But this would have been pure arrogance, perhaps even hubris. In truth, he did not really believe that his flute could keep him from harm when his time had come. Nothing could—and it was this open-eyed acceptance of his fate that vexed Ede so completely.

''You don't care about yourself,'' Ede said as Danlo pulled on his black pilot's boots. According to Ede, the preservation of one's own life was every man's fundamental program. But in Danlo, the writing of this deep program had somehow gone awry. ''You don't care about your life.''

''But truly I do,'' Danlo said as he zipped up his formal black robe. ''To live truly is everything.''

''You're a dangerous man,'' Ede continued. ''Perhaps even a madman—why should my fate be interwoven with such a mad, wild man?''

Danlo smiled at this and asked, "How else should your fate have been woven, then?"

"Why must you always answer my questions with questions?"

For a moment Danlo was silent, and then he asked, "Is there a better way to answer questions that have no answer?"

"Is there nothing can I say to dissuade you from going down to this planet?"

"How can I know the answer to *that* question?"

"Then you'll take your ship down to this world?"

"I must," Danlo said. "If you'd like, if you believe the risk to yourself is too great, I could make a fall to one of this star's other planets. I could leave you there and then return to this world."

For a while, the Ede imago simply stared at Danlo, and neither of them made a sound. And then Ede said, "If the Narain were to kill you while I was stranded on bare rock on some airless planet, what would happen to me?"

"I do not know."

"Unfortunately," Ede continued, "my best chance for success lies in promoting *your* success. Thus I must translate for you and advise you; I must go wherever you go."

"I am sorry."

"Then, too, I must tell you that I'm growing fond of you. I feel the need to protect you from your own wildness."

"Truly?" Danlo asked. He was now amused almost to the point of exaltation, and he couldn't help smiling.

"You don't believe me?"

"I do not know what to believe," Danlo finally said.

"Well, you should believe me," Ede said. "You must believe me—I would never lie to you."

"I . . . would like to believe that."

Ede forced a mechanical smile and said, "There is another thing. If Malaclypse has followed us here, he may follow us down to the planet."

"I do not believe he will do that," Danlo said. He closed his eyes for a moment, and it seemed that he could almost see the warrior-poet's thoughts. "I think that he will wait until I find Tannahill. If I find it."

"Why, Pilot?"

"It may be that he seeks my father to slay him, truly. But I think that he seeks Tannahill even more. He follows the purposes . . . of his Order."

And, Danlo thought, perhaps the purposes of the Silicon God as well.

So Danlo took the *Snowy Owl* down to the world called Alumit Bridge. He fell down through layers of dense white clouds, straight down toward the city of Iviunir and its single light-field. He fell blindly down toward the field's landing pads and long glittering runs that he could not see. In little time, his diamond ship broke free from the lowest clouds. And there, directly below him, was a city built a quarter of a mile into the sky. It was something like the domed cities of Yarkona, only Iviunir's outer skin was not translucent and lovely like clary but rather opaque like the shell of a turtle and flattened at the top. Indeed, the city's superstructure seemed to be made of some kind of grayish green plastic. Upon seeing this, Danlo's belly immediately tightened. Life inside Iviunir, he realized, would *not* be like wandering the Yarkonan parks beneath a great golden dome. It would be more like living inside a plastic beehive, and as soon as Danlo considered this, he felt the burn of acid in his throat and his head began to ache. He might have turned his ship back to the stars, then, but he was scarcely a thousand feet above the light-field, which occupied the city's topmost level. And then the *Snowy Owl* fell down to one of the many runs as gently as a butterfly alighting on a flower, and it was too late.

As had been arranged, he was met near the end of the second run by a man named Isas Lel Abraxax. Danlo opened the pit of his ship and climbed down to the run's grayish surface, which indeed proved to be one of the transkerine plastics. Although it was raining slightly, the air was almost as warm as blood soup. He caught the whiff of unpleasant smells, plastics and aldehydes and ozone, certainly, but also that of fungi and decaying plant matter—and perhaps some other kind of organic life that he could not quite identify. The light-field itself was strangely quiet. He had expected thunder and rocket fire, jets and jammers and lullcraft, the usual bustle of ships being met and attended to. Instead, but for the falling rain, there was only silence. It was almost as if all such activity had been interrupted or suspended in honor of his arrival.

"*Che dai so,* Danlo wi Soli Ringess!" a voice called out from the rain. A good hundred feet away from Danlo's ship, a thin, bald-headed man stood next to some kind of wheeled robot. The rain would have soaked his thin garments, but one of the robot's arms held out a plastic red umbrella covering the man's head. He bowed to Danlo and continued his greeting: *"Che dai sova Ivi-unir ji Alumii Vrarai."*

Although there was little need for translation of this, Ede faithfully rendered the words into the Language of the Civilized Worlds. Danlo carried the devotionary computer in his left hand while he strode down the wet run toward the bald-headed man. He came up close enough to see the irises of the man's eyes, and then he bowed formally and said, "I am Danlo wi Soli Ringess. And you are Isas Lel Abraxax, yes?"

The man agreed that he was indeed Isas Lel Abraxax, though it seemed that he claimed this identity without enthusiasm, almost as if he were unsure of his name. He had ugly blue eyes shot with flecks of orange, strange and distant eyes whose light it was difficult for Danlo to hold. In truth, Isas Lel would not meet eyes with Danlo; instead he gazed at the devotionary computer in Danlo's hand. He apologized for the inclement weather, and when the Ede hologram translated his words, he seemed amazed and perhaps a little scandalized to see the imago of Nikolos Daru Ede programed to perform such a lowly function.

He knows of Ede, Danlo thought. *He has seen such computers before.*

Then, momentarily, Isas Lel's eyes fell dead to the world. Danlo guessed that he was interfacing the computer that covered his head. Like all the Narain, Isas Lel's head was as smooth as a seagull's egg; like all the Narain elite, he wore shiny clearface molded to the shiny skin around his skull.

"Aqavai nui harima?" Isas Lel asked. "Shall we go inside now? It's bad to be out overlong in the world."

He climbed onto the robot and dropped down into the single seat built above the wheels. Because a bright blue canopy covered this seat and most of the robot's hard plastic body, he had no further need for his umbrella, which the robot folded up and stowed in one of its compartments. At last Isas Lel seemed to notice his guest waiting patiently in the rain. With a wave of his hand, he invited Danlo to sit beside him. Although Danlo had never liked entrusting himself to any kind of robot, he did as Isas Lel bade him. And then Isas Lel smiled faintly and spoke to the robot. *"Vato,"* he said, and instantly the robot accelerated across the wet plastic of the runs.

Danlo listened to the rain drumming against the plastic canopy above him; he listened to the *suss* of the robot's soft plastic wheels squeezing the water out of their way as they rolled on and on across the nearly silent light-field. Soon they came to a building. Or rather, they came to that part of the city where the arcology rose up like a wall around the perimeter of the field's southern half. Inside this grayish plastic wall, Danlo supposed, would be the caverns where the Narain worked on the vessels that flew from city to city, or from the city to the stars. There he would find programmers and tinkers and watchmen, and all the tools and machinery needed to attend the arrival of a lightship or the lesser ships of the cities of Alumit Bridge whose names Danlo did not know.

He realized, then, that he was too eager for the sounds and sights of human activity. He was too eager to leave the desolation of the light-field behind him—although in truth his dread of entering such a soulless city was worse than that of a child who stares at the dark opening to a snow tiger's lair. For a moment—a long moment—he looked down at the misty hills below the city, at the lovely alien forest shimmering purple and green in the morning light. And then, perhaps at some silent signal of the robot's, a door in the great wall before them slid open. In hardly any time at all they rolled through this doorway into the city of Iviunir.

"We'll proceed to another level," Isas Lel said. "The others are waiting for us there."

"The . . . others?"

"The other Transcendentals. And the other, oh, others. You'll soon see. Please be patient."

Whatever Danlo had been expecting of this great, squat city, the reality of it was worse than he had feared. The robot bore them down endless empty corridors, turning this way or that according to its program. No natural light illuminated these corridors. The walls, while not the ugly green of the city's exterior, were composed of some unusual plastic glowing with various muddy colors. In many places, some kind of bluish, alien fungus had infected these walls, spreading out over the plastic like mold on bread. The air that Danlo breathed was dank and dead and reeked of toulene and sulfur and other kinds of chemical pollution. Somewhere below him, in the bowels of the city, there dwelled perhaps twenty million people. He could almost feel the echoes of their many voices vibrating up from the bare, plastic floor. Danlo could never understand why human beings would choose to live inside such structures—unless they did so purely for the sake of protection. Iviunir, like other arcologies that Danlo had seen, was built as sturdily as the castle worlds of the Astaaret. Its tough, composite plastics could withstand the blast of a hydrogen bomb, as well as shielding against the radiations of distant supernovas. For a people living in the center of the Vild, this last consideration must have been the critical one.

At last the robot came to one of the city's great gravity lifts. It stopped and waited while Isas Lel spoke of little things such as Danlo's unique diamond pilot's ring and the strangeness of the black silk robes that Danlo wore. The lift's double doors opened. The robot wheeled them into the lift, where they were its only passengers. With a sickening jolt, the lift began falling. Down and down into the arcology it fell for many moments. Danlo could not guess how many levels they had descended. Somewhere outside this plummeting plastic chamber would be apartments and restaurants full of people. There would be shops and libraries and dream parks—as well as factories fabricating everything from the Narain's plastic clothing to the food that they ate. In most arcologies, the food factories are spread out across the topmost level to take advantage of whatever natural sunlight might fall upon the various plants growing in their vats. But in Iviunir, it seemed, these floating farms must be located on some level deep inside. Danlo supposed that the Narain must employ artificial light to trigger the photosynthesis upon which most life ultimately depended. Perhaps this light would be generated by hot fusion cells, or even by dirty fission reactors. Once, on Treblinka Luz, Danlo had come across such barbarisms. Once, too, as a wild young man, Danlo had loathed eating any food grown by such unnatural means. And now, falling into a the bowels of this unholy city, he smiled at his childhood inhibitions, which in truth were still as much a part of him as the scars of his thigh and forehead. For the thousandth time, he reminded himself that light was only light, that "artificial" light was as real as the radiance of any star. This light was not at all like other man-made and artificial things which were truly unreal.

"We won't be long," Isas Lel said to Danlo. Now the lift was falling so fast that Danlo almost felt the uneasy freedom of weightlessness in his limbs and belly. He remained seated on the robot, holding the devotionary computer tightly against him for fear that it might fly away. "We're almost there."

The lift pulled to a stop at the fifteenth level. Again the robot signaled for the lift's doors to open. Then it wheeled them down several empty corridors, the last of which gave out onto a narrow street. Actually, this plastic-paved way through the city was more of a tunnel than a street. On either side of their rapidly rolling robot were shops displaying everything from clothing to selduks

to holograms of imprinting services. Above them, stacked like
unseen blocks, where the street's ceiling practically pressed
against their heads, there would be apartments where people
lived. According to Isas Lel, most of the levels in the city were
divided into sublevels—sometimes as many as three or four.
Space was precious, he said. On the fifteenth level, only the great
boulevards allowed an unobstructed view from level to level.
Because Danlo was sweating in the stale, conditioned air, he was
very eager for a more open space, however closely bounded it
might really be. And then the robot suddenly debouched onto
Boulevard Nine, as it was called, and his wish was granted. And
almost immediately he forgot about his sweaty silks or the dull
pain in his head. He almost forgot to breathe the city's lifeless
air, which he shared with twenty million other people.

"So many," he said to Isas Lel. "So many people. So many
robots."

As precisely as the hands of a clock coming together at midnight, the robot merged with a great stream of other robots rushing down the center of the boulevard. All these robots were made
of blue or yellow plastic—or pink, magenta, flame red, or a hundred other bright colors. All the robots bore human beings on
their single seats, and they all rolled at dangerous speeds packed
too closely together. Although Danlo loved speed as he did fresh
wind, he couldn't keep from wondering how long it would be
before one of the robots stopped too abruptly or veered into
another robot too close beside it. But, of course, none of them
did. Danlo marveled at the perfect coordination of so many ugly
machines. He could only suppose that they were all interfaced
with some master computer that controlled their movements.

Likewise with the people of Iviunir. On the boulevard's bright
white walks—between the rolling robots in the middle of the
street and the shops at the edge—swarms of human beings
moved as with great purpose. They passed to and fro at a fast
walk, issuing from the many side streets as if some unseen master clock were calling them to their individual appointments.
There was something machinelike in their motions, and yet
something very human, too: an excitement as if they were march-
ing to war or being called to some great religious event.

High above them—sixty feet above their hairless heads—the
blue plastic of the next level hung like an artificial sky, but no
one seemed to mind that he lived inside such a stifling place.
Hardly anyone even noticed Danlo, who was the only human
being on this vast street dressed in black. Almost everyone else

was dressed in white kimonos or robes of glittering chatoy. The Narain appeared to be a soft people whose thin bodies and age-less faces had never known the touch of wind or sun. Most of them were indeed as pale as maggots; though in truth, their skin was more of a pinkish white, an unusual mutation suiting its sufferers to live in cold, rainy climes such as once had existed in the far western forests of Urasia on Old Earth—or perhaps to a life inside the plastic worm mounds of the worlds of the Vild. With their shaved heads and shapeless bodies, they seemed an-drogynous, as sexless as freshly hatched Scutari nymphs.

"Are there no robots on your world?" Isas Lel asked. He fingered the water droplets still clinging to the umbrella by his side. With the wind whipping at their faces—and the unbeliev-able noise of the street—he had to talk very loud for Danlo to hear him. "Is it possible that the people of Neverness don't use robots?"

Here Isas Lel called for a bit more comfort, and their seat began to recline. He called for the robot's wind windows to be raised, and suddenly they were enclosed in what seemed a clear plastic bubble. Danlo looked out through this bubble. Among the manswarms on the street, he saw many personal robots accompa-nying their human masters. There were robots washing the win-dows of the shops and robots sticking plastic blocks together as they fabricated new additions to the many high apartments that lined Boulevard Nine. One robot—a fearsome construction of wheels, tubes, and mechanical bassinet—attended a newborn baby, one of the few children Danlo was to see in Iviunir. Every-where, it seemed, robots of every possible design crawled and creeped and rolled. Even outside the restaurants, where minis-trant robots served iced drinks and various strange-looking dishes, other insectlike robots were digging in the soil of the pretty flower fields. When Danlo remarked that this work would be better accomplished by a man or woman, Isas Lel seemed confused.

"Perhaps there is a problem with *your* robot," he said as he pointed to Danlo's devotionary.

Although Ede's expression did not change, his hologram lifted its little finger slightly and traced out a half-moon for Danlo's keen eyes—and his eyes only—to interpret. After their experience with the Sani, both he and Danlo had deemed it wise for them to have a secret language between them, and so Danlo had taught Ede the cetic's language of signs.

"What problem?" Danlo asked.

"A problem in translating. You can't really believe that people should plant flowers."

"But why not?"

"Oh, because it is *work,*" Isas Lel said. He spoke this word, *falke,* as if it were dirt in his mouth—as if its meaning should be obvious to anyone. Work was work; work was a worldly affair. Only robots or madmen worked. For evolved human beings such as Isas Lel or any of the Narain, no matter how low their rank, their time was to be spent on more transcendental pursuits.

"I planted flowers once," Danlo said. He closed his eyes as he recalled a brilliant day in False Winter when he had abandoned his mathematical studies to plant fireflowers with Tamara in the dirt outside her house. "I never counted it as work."

Isas Lel regarded Danlo as if he were some kind of alien insect. Then he said, "But you used your *hands,* didn't you?"

"Yes—how not?"

"Then it was work."

"Then you consider everything one does with one's hands as work?"

"Almost everything."

Danlo sat as straight as a zanshin master on the seat of the rolling robot. As de facto ambassador to the Narain people, he should not have allowed himself to argue with Isas Lel. But he was a pilot first, and even more a man, and so he said, "I saw a robot feeding a baby. On the street, in front of a restaurant. Surely the mother cannot consider it work to feed her baby."

"Surely she would—if this child had a mother."

For a moment, Danlo did not breathe. All his life, he had heard of worlds whose children were born out of artificial wombs and listened to the jokes about slelniks, these human abominations who had neither father nor mother. As a journeyman in Neverness, he had even met one of these unfortunate yet seemingly perfect human beings so flawless in the flesh and haunted in the eyes. The thought that Isas Lel—and everyone else in the city—might be slelniks stunned Danlo. He sat in silence, and he did not know what to say.

"Surely," Isas Lel continued, "it's work to grow an infant inside oneself. And even more work to care for it."

"But that is just life!" Danlo finally gasped out. "Life itself. Truly—how else are we to live?"

Isas Lel sighed as if he were arguing with a child. His face was full of disgust and scorn. And then he said, "Live? Our robots can do *that* for us."

After that, for the rest of their brief journey through the city, neither of them spoke. Soon they came to a large white structure that rose seamlessly from the boulevard's plastic. Danlo would have thought that they would need to climb down from the robot in order to enter this structure, but at Isas Lel's command, the robot moved into the rightmost lane of the boulevard, decelerated, and then exited neatly onto the walkway in front of the structure. Although the robot was now creeping along almost as slowly as an old man might hobble, the men and women swarming the walk were careful to avoid any kind of collision, and they hurried out of their way. For most of the Narain, walking was the single exercise they permitted themselves, but no one expected a Transcendental to stoop to this kind of labor. More than a few people cast envious glances at the clearface glittering on Isas Lel's head and bowed to him as if he were a god. Then the robot broke free from the manswarms and rolled up to the building's shiny doors. They opened, allowing the robot to move inside.

This is madness, Danlo thought. *If I remain here very long, I will fall mad.*

While the robot rolled down a long white corridor, Danlo used his fingers to make a sign that only the devotionary computer could detect. He looked down at the Ede hologram floating above the jeweled box on his lap. Ede's attention, it seemed, was concentrated on Isas Lel. Perhaps Ede was trying to read the man's unreadable face. When Isas Lel's eyes momentarily fell vacant in some private communion with the computer he wore on his head, Ede responded to Danlo's sign. With his fingers made of light, he warned Danlo of the precariousness of their situation. "You wished for difficulty and danger—well, you should be careful of what you wish for lest you receive it in abundance."

"I know," Danlo signed.

"This man is in almost continual interface with some cybernetic field," Ede signed back. "Very likely everything you do and say will be scrutinized by any others who share face with this field."

"Yes, I know," Danlo signed. "But what would you advise I do?"

"Look at his eyes! Kill him now while he is faced—you could appropriate his skullcap and command the robot to return to our ship. Our chances of escape might never be so great."

Danlo smiled at this impossible suggestion and then, with his hands, he asked, "What would you advise me to do . . . that I can *do*?"

Ede's answer came immediately. "Be mindful, then. Guard your face—guard your thoughts, Pilot."

During their brief time in the corridors of this nameless structure, they passed few other people, all of them Transcendentals much like Isas Lel, wearing clearfaces over their bare skulls and riding on wheeled robots. They all seemed intensely interested in Danlo; they all looked at him openly as if he were some rare alien animal that Isas Lel had brought back from the forests outside the city to amuse them. It was as if Danlo had entered some sort of private club where Transcendentals—and only Transcendentals—met each morning to while away the endless hours of their workless lives. Danlo wondered what pursuits might lure such a cold-eyed people, and then Isas Lel's robot rolled right up a cold little room that had been prepared for Danlo's arrival.

"Here we are," Isas Lel said. "We've been waiting to meet you."

At this, Danlo exchanged finger signs with the Ede hologram, promising to guard the face of his being. Then he smiled at the danger before him, and he gazed at the doors to the room where the Transcendentals of Alumit Bridge were waiting for him.

THE TRANSCENDENTALS

*The central paradox of Edeism is this: that God is
eternal, infinite, transcendent, ineffable, formless, faceless,
omnipotent, and omnipresent, but He is also Nikolos
Daru Ede, the Mahaman, the man-who-will-become-God.
All Edeic theology and the doctrines of the different sects
derive from the attempt to explain this mystery.*
                              —from the Encyclopaedia Britannica,
                                1,754th ed., 10th rev., Standard Version

The doors to the room slid open, and as the robot rolled forward,
Danlo found himself in what Isas Lel called a meeting chamber.
The floor of this windowless room was a dull white plastic un-
adorned by rug or carpet; its walls and ceiling were a single half
dome of pure chatoy or some lustrous material very like it. Upon
Danlo's entrance, the dome's chatoy surface flared into colors.
Streaks of crimson, ocher, jade, and orchid pink flowed all
around him, and then, as he watched, the colors began to mutate
and form up into a recognizable scene. It was a sunset, he saw.
Here, deep in the belly of the city, in the middle of the morning,
he watched Alumit Bridge's huge sun drop behind hills glowing
with a bright emerald light. The sky was ablaze with bands of
violet and rose, and it was all very beautiful—if wholly unreal.
That the Narain preferred such simulated sunsets over beholding
the world directly troubled Danlo. He was troubled, too, by the
vases of freshly cut flowers near the room's center, and by a
gleaming chromium tea service that a ministrant robot had apparently rolled into the room. It was as if Isas Lel, from little things
that Danlo had said during their brief journey from the light field,
had somehow ordered this room prepared for his comfort.

At the room's exact center point, some robot had set down a
plump red cushion. Isas Lel invited Danlo to sit on this cushion.

He himself remained seated in his robot, as did the other Transcendentals, who were sitting on their robots, watching and waiting as the light of the false sunset reflected off their golden clearfaces. There were six of them, and they had arrayed their robots in a half circle around Danlo's cushion. As Danlo sat cross-legged before them—beneath them—their glassy eyes fell upon him like cold blue stones that crushed his heart.

"May I present Lieswyr Ivioss?" Isas Lel asked, holding out his hand toward a thin woman whose classically formed face was almost as smooth as a baby's. Lieswry Ivioss seemed almost as young as Danlo, though in truth she had been born in the city ninety years before.

"And may I present Kistur Ashtoreth?" This was a man—or a woman—whose pale, pink skin and fine features bespoke a fragility common to the people of Iviunir. At being presented, Kistur Ashtoreth bowed his head and smiled at Danlo, which surprised him greatly. Of all the Transcendentals, he was the only one to favor Danlo in this way.

"And Patar Iviaslin, and this is Yenene Iviastalir," Isas Lel continued as he waved his hand around the semicircle. With the exception of Kistur Ashtoreth, Danlo found the Narain's names to be strange, especially of the last two women (or men) that Isas Lel presented. These were Diverous Te, a frail-faced being who seemed wholly absorbed in some other world, and Ananda Narcavage, she of the trembling lips and half-closed eyes that would not quite look at Danlo eye to eye. These, then, were the nobility of the city, the princes and lords and maharinis. Danlo supposed that they might also be the masters of the world of Alumit Bridge, and in this he was almost right.

"May we offer you tea?" Isas Lel asked.

With a wave of his hand, he beckoned to a plastic ministrant robot who poured out seven steaming cups of tea. The robot served these cups to the Transcendentals and to Danlo. He sat holding this cup near his nose, drinking in the tea's strange and spicy aroma. On the floor by the cushion, where he had set down the devotionary computer, the Ede hologram surreptitiously made signs for Danlo to see. "Beware of poison!" Ede signed. "Beware of truth drugs—these Narain will want to read your mind!"

Smiling at this, Danlo took a long sip of tea. There was nothing else he could do.

The inquisition that he had been awaiting began at once. Isas Lel brusquely said, "You claim to be a pilot of an Order on a world named Neverness. What Order is this? Which star lights your world?''

Danlo set his tea cup down against the floor. He let his hand fall against the trousers of his robe where he kept his flute tucked into the long pocket. Through a thin layer of black silk, he gripped the flute tightly, drew in a breath of air, and said, "In truth, Neverness is the name of the city where I was educated. The planet's name is actually Icefall—though many call it by the city's name also. The star . . . is known as the Star of Neverness."

"And you were born in this city?"

"I was born . . . near it."

"An open city, you said when we talked by radio—Neverness is open to the light of its star, is that true?''

"Yes."

"And where is this Star of Neverness, then?"

Almost instantly, Danlo reached out and pointed at a steep angle upward slightly to the right of Ananda Narcavage's head. It was Danlo's pride that no matter where in the universe he might fall, no matter the eccentricities of orbit or spin of any planet on which he found himself, no matter which way he might turn in the artificially lit tunnels of a soulless city—no matter how he was spatially oriented, he could always find his way home. "It is there," he said simply. "My star is there."

For a moment, Isas Lel seemed confused. As were the other Transcendentals. They sat on the reclined seats of their robots, and their eyes were so vacant they seemed almost to disappear from their heads.

"I meant," Isas Lel said, "where is this Star of Neverness in relation to the Known Stars?''

Danlo smiled to himself as he considered the implications of this question. He wondered how many stars these hive-dwelling humans might truly know. As for himself, he knew ten thousand stars by name, and perhaps a million more by sight—by their constellation within the galaxy's billions of jeweled lights.

"And which are the *Known* Stars?" Danlo asked.

"Is it possible that you don't know?''

"Truly I do not know."

Isas Lel shut his eyes then. A moment later, the sunset scene died from the room's walls, its pretty colors sucked away like paint down a dark drain. For a while the meeting room was almost as black as space. And then there were stars—or rather thousands of points of white light that appeared as stars, glittering out from the chatoy walls around Danlo. He almost instantly recognized the Sani's pale blue star and the Eye of the Fish and Medearis Luz, and all the other stars in this neighborhood.

"Can you tell us which of these stars is the Star of Neverness?"

"None of them," Danlo said.

"But these are the *Known* Stars," Isas Lel emphasized as if Danlo might be either deaf or blind.

"The Star of Neverness burns elsewhere."

"But these are all the stars within a radius of fifty *light-years*!" Isas Lel said this word, *light-year (lignia-toh),* as if it represented an unimaginable distance. As indeed six trillion miles almost is.

"The Star of Neverness burns far away."

"Farther than a hundred light-years?"

"Yes."

"How far, then?"

"Far . . . very far," Danlo shut his eyes for a moment, then continued, "If one were to measure a straight light distance from your star to mine, it would be perhaps thirty thousand light-years."

Although Danlo had spoken softly, as he usually spoke, this number fell out into the room like a thunderclap. For a long time, no one said anything, and there was deep silence.

"That's impossible!" Diverous Te blurted. His (her?) voice was almost as low as the lowest tone of Danlo's shakuhachi, and it was the only time that morning he would be graced with hearing it.

"Thirty *thousand* light-years, impossible," Ananda Narcavage agreed.

"No, no," Lieswyr Ivioss said in her dulcet voice, "that can't be true."

But of course it was true. Danlo had fallen far across the lens of the galaxy, perhaps farther than any other pilot in the history of his Order. Thirty thousand light-years was indeed a far, far way—so far that even the master pilots of Neverness, safe by the fires of their houses, would have been fairly astonished had they known of this feat.

Suddenly, there in the twinkling darkness of the meeting room, the eyes of Patar Iviaslin and Kistur Ashtoreth and all the other Transcendentals focused on Isas Lel as if he had spoken to them. And then Isas Lel actually *did* speak, in words, in waves of dark air that could be heard as sound.

"It may be," he said, "that this Danlo wi Soli Ringess of Neverness actually is telling the truth. Or that he believes that he is."

Just then the sunset scene returned in a torrent of blinding colors, and Danlo suddenly knew the truth about this "meeting" room. Behind the chatoy finish of the domed walls would be purple neurologics or some other kind of scanning element sensitive to the electrochemical events of his brain. Sensitive, perhaps, to his slightest thoughts. The whole room was like a computer—like the clearface skullcaps that the Transcendentals wore on their heads. Even more, the room was like the pit of Danlo's ship. Only it had not been built as an interface between a pilot's brain and the logics of a lightship, but rather as a place where the Transcendentals might examine the minds of the lesser Narain, who needed help in entering into the cybernetic space of the Field. In the literal sense, the room was a facing chamber where one's mind might be peeled apart like the layers of an onion. Danlo had heard of such places before: the Yarkonan truth chambers, the blacking cells of Qallar—as well as the secret null rooms in the cetics' tower on Neverness.

"If this is the truth," Lieswyr Ivioss said, "then we should like to know how it can be true."

Danlo sat very straight, feeling the holes of his flute beneath his silk robe. Silently, almost casually, he moved his fingers against these holes. And in his mind, a deep music played, and it was this intensely melodic inner music that would help to confuse the scanners of these Transcendentals' mind machine. Since Danlo first had entered the room, he had been listening to this secret song, and now he began to employ certain other techniques that his cetic friend Hanuman li Tosh had once taught him.

"Danlo wi Soli Ringess," a voice called out of the darkness all about him, "can you tell us how to find this Star of Neverness?"

But, of course, Danlo could not tell Isas Lel this. As a pilot, he was forbidden to reveal the fixed-points of this star—or of any star.

"Can you tell us how you piloted a ship across thirty thousand light-years of space?"

"I . . . can," Danlo finally forced out. In his mind, the notes to a song that he had once made for his teacher appeared like drops of flaming crimson and chrome. It was very hard for him to speak. "But . . . I . . . must . . . not . . . tell . . . you. I . . . *will* . . . not."

"Can you tell us more about your ship that carried you such an impossible distance? This ship that you call a lightship?"

The words in Danlo's mind were like the reek of cinofila and skrix and all the other smells of an alien zoo. He moved his lips, but the only sound to emerge was like an expanding blue-black balloon. *"No."* At last he heard himself say this, as a recognizable sound made with his tongue almost pressed against his teeth. "No," he said, but with his senses confused as they were, in a moment of time, this simple utterance sounded almost like yes.

"This is enough," he heard someone say. He opened his eyes to see the lavender gush of sound waves falling from Kistur Ashtoreth's mouth. "We should never have brought him here."

For a moment, all the Transcendentals seemed to disappear like dry ice evaporating into air. Danlo thought that they must be simultaneously interfacing with each other. And then, a moment later, Isas Lel and the others fell out of the space above their robots like lightships from the manifold. They all looked at each other, and Isas Lel turned to Danlo and said, "There's something very strange about you, Danlo wi Soli Ringess of Neverness. You seem almost as naive as any naman, and yet you have such extraordinary skills."

The word *naman* Ede translated as "unadmitted." Danlo knew that he should know this word—its significance—but for the moment it escaped his mind.

"If you wish to relax your mind," Isas Lel said, "I promise that there will be no more interface with this room unless you desire it."

Danlo looked down at the hologram of Ede, who was furiously signing to him, "It's a trick! Don't let them see your face! Don't let them see you!"

But Danlo had heard the truth in Isas Lel's voice, and he trusted this truth. Slowly, he smiled and said, "I do not desire interface."

"Please relax, then."

Danlo nodded his head. "If you'd like." Very slowly he drew a breath of air and let it out.

Isas Lel continued looking at him and asked, "Where did you learn these mind skills of yours?"

"From a friend," Danlo said. "From a cetic."

"And what is a cetic?"

While Danlo explained something of the cetic arts and the Order's quest for knowledge about the nature of mind in the universe, Isas Lel's cold blue eyes seemed to melt and flow until they were almost human.

After Danlo had finished speaking, Kistur Ashtoreth said, "We've never heard of this Order. No one has."

"I . . . am perhaps the first pilot to have journeyed this far into the Vild."

There was a moment of confusion among the Transcendentals because the word *Vild* did not translate into their language.

"And what is this *Vild*?" Kistur Ashtoreth asked.

While Danlo explained about the region in the galaxy where the stars were exploding into supernova one by one, none of the Transcendentals moved. They seemed almost uncomfortable sitting in their plushly cushioned robots. Patar Iviaslin, with her little glasslike eyes, seemed not to be able to look at any other thing in the room except the vase of orange and purple flowers. Diverous Te was as silent as he or she ever would be, and Lieswyr Ivioss actually blushed so that her whitish pink skin actually fell full red.

"My Order has made a mission to the Vild," Danlo said. He did not think it necessary to explain how the Order—ever rife with factionalism and competing visions of how its purpose should be fulfilled—had divided in two. "We seek the planet Tannahill. We seek the people who are called, or once called themselves, the Architects of the Infinite Intelligence of the Cybernetic Universal Church. The Old Church. Is it possible that anyone in this city might know of this planet or these people? Is it possible . . . that anyone might know of anyone who would know?"

Isas Lel nodded his head as if deeply considering what Danlo had asked him. And then, even as Danlo himself might do, he answered his question with a another question, "Why would your order seek the Architects of this religion?"

"Because we. . . ." Danlo began to speak, but just then he remembered the meaning of the word *naman*. In Istwan, a naman was an outsider, or more literally, one who was "unadmitted" to the graces of the Cybernetic Universal Church. It was strange, Danlo thought, that in referring to him, Isas Lel should have used this word from the sacred language of the Old Church.

"Because the stars are dying and we would ask the Architects . . . ." Again, Danlo began to speak, but suddenly in his mind, like a new star appearing in the sky, there was a certain knowledge about these Narain people.

"What would you ask them?"

"The Architects of the Old Church," Danlo said. He looked at the golden clearface glittering like a halo atop Isas Lel's head. It seemed to catch the light of clearfaces of the other Transcendentals, who sat rigidly in their robots as they stared down at Danlo—and he stared steadily back at them.

"Please continue."

"You are they," Danlo said at last. "Truly, you are—but you are not, too. You, all the Narain people . . . you were *once* Architects, yes?"

There was a moment of silence, broken only when Lieswyr Ivioss snapped out, "Why should you think this?"

"Because it is the truth."

"But how could you possibly know this?"

"I . . . just know."

At this, Kistur Ashtoreth exchanged looks with Isas Lel, then said, "We should tell him, shouldn't we? We shouldn't keep this information from him."

Isas Lel stared at Danlo for a long time, and then nodded his head as if he had come to a momentous decision. He said, "*We* are the Architects of the Cybernetic Church. The true Architects. The true Universal Church."

"I see," Danlo said. He held Isas Lel's eyes as Isas Lel told him the truth about the Narain people.

In truth, the Narain were the followers of Liljana ivi Narai, a strong-willed woman who had once been a respected Elder of the Old Church on Tannahill. But she was also a visionary and a mystic, and more, a revolutionary who challenged the stale doctrines and suffocating theocracy that ruled the Old Church. A scarce two hundred years before, she had called for a revival of the true spirit of Edeism. She preached the rejection of all doctrines that were outworn by time or actually damaging to the soul, and she led her many followers in secret facing orgies and other ecstatic rites designed to bring her people closer to Ede the God. Her people claimed that they were the true Architects of God; they believed that they had rediscovered the spirit of the True, Eternal, and Universal Church. They were heretics, of course, and the Old Church orthodoxy had immediately persecuted them as a danger to all that was holy. In the second year of Liljana ivi Narai's apostasy, there were tortures and the deep cleansing of many heretics' minds; there were banishments, reprogramings, and even executions.

Finally, in the year 2541 since the Vastening of Ede, Liljana ivi Narai negotiated an exodus. She was given ten deep ships with which to leave Tannahill. She led her people to an alien planet with turquoise oceans and landscapes of emerald and lavender, an untouched world whose sunrises and sunsets were a glory unto God—only the Narain cared nothing for these natural splendors. They worshiped at the altar to a different deity, and they named their world Alumit Bridge to symbolize their hope of a spiritual return to the birthplace of Nikolos Daru Ede. They immediately set their robots to dig minerals out of the ground and build the many arcologies that dotted the continents. There, inside these great heaps of plastic, they would be safe at last to transcend themselves and draw ever closer to the eternal Ede. In them—especially in their prophets and most accomplished Architects who called themselves the Transcendentals—would live the true spirit of Edeism. They would make something truly holy, something truly new and yet as old as the stars.

When Isas Lel had explained all this, Danlo took a sip of his spicy tea and said, "Then your ancestors came here from Tannahill. You must know of this world, yes?"

"We know of Tannahill," Kistur Ashtoreth admitted. He was clearly ashamed of the deception that the Transcendentals had put forth, and it seemed almost as if his delicate face was about to break into tears. "Some of our eldest remember Tannahill—they were born there."

Danlo nodded his head slowly, saying nothing as he inwardly shuddered at the idea of men and women living more than two hundred years. And then he asked, "Can you tell me where Tannahill is? Can you tell me which of the Known Stars is its star?"

"Perhaps we can," Isas Lel said. "But why would you wish to journey there? As you've been told, Alumit Bridge is the home of the true Church. Why not make your mission here?"

In the time it took for the Ede hologram to translate this question, Danlo thought quickly. He did not wish to insult these people, and so he let the truth work his will for him. "You have said that Liljana ivi Narai spoke against all of the Old Church's harmful doctrines, yes?"

"This is true," Isas Lel said in a guarded voice. "Over the centuries, the Church had formulated many false doctrines—we call them programs—that mocked the spirit of Edeism."

"And the Narain, your people, when you founded Alumit Bridge—you cast off these programs, yes?"

Isas Lel smiled almost for the first time, and he said quite proudly (but not altogether accurately), "We freed ourselves of *all* programs. No one should circumscribe another's path toward God. Nothing should—we should all be free to enter the Field and find God where we may."

Danlo returned his smile, for he was now truly amused at Isas Lel's hidden assumption that God could be found in some cybernetic space—and only there. But then, for a moment, his face fell serious, and he said, "Then it must also be true that the Narain have been freed from the Program of Totality, yes?"

For the count of ten of Danlo's heartbeats, Isas Lel only stared at him. The Program of Totality, according to the Order's historians, was the ancient imperative that the Architects should expand into the universe and fill it with their offspring. And more, that they should ensoul as much human life as possible. It was their dream to cathect dead matter with consciousness. To do this they should regard all the material elements of the universe as food. They should fall through the galaxy and find lush, untouched planets; they should farm these worlds and convert their carbon, hydrogen, oxygen, and nitrogen into protein to nourish their children's growing bodies. And when they had stripped the biospheres clean, they should destroy these worlds. They should set their robots to pulverizing them into dust and minerals, down to their very atoms in order to free all their elements to nourish ever more human life. World upon world they should dismantle in this way, and then, ultimately, they should destroy the stars. For it was the supernovas themselves that were the galaxy's greatest creative force. The supernovas were like vast, brilliant gods who made new elements—oxygen, silicon, iron, gold—in the incredible heat of their dying bodies.

Someday, farwhen, all the galaxies of the universe would be full of nothing but these freed elements—and an uncountable number of human beings whose souls had been carked into eternal computers. And, of course, with Ede the God. Ultimately, at the end of time, Ede would feast upon these elements and absorb the entire universe into His infinite body. He would incorporate the trillions of eternal computers into the Universal Computer that was only Himself and nothing more. The minds and memories of all the Architects who had ever lived would at last be at one in Him.

And then would come the miracle that every Architect

dreamed of with all the fervor of lovers who have been apart too long. Beyond the end of time—when time and beingness began again—there would be a new creation. A second creation: Out of His infinite love for man, Ede would sacrifice Himself and re-make the universe from the material elements of His body. He would make trillions of new Earths, perfect worlds whose lovely green gardens and blue oceans knew neither suffering nor evil nor death. He would fill these worlds with human beings. He would make new bodies for all the faithful who had ever suffered in his name. And then he would then cark their consciousnesses from his computer's memory spaces back into living flesh, incar-nating their purified souls into these golden, perfect, immortal forms.

Some of the Old Church theologians held that this golden state of man reunited with God would last through eternity; oth-ers claimed that each man and woman (and child) would live forever, and someday, far beyond farwhen, even as Nikolos Daru Ede had once done, would go on to become God—creator of his or her own universe. But all the most orthodox theologians be-lieved that the universe of rocks and comets and stars was funda-mentally flawed and must therefore totally be remade. And it was man's glory—his purpose in life—to be a partner in God in this holy remaking of the cosmos.

"It's the madmen of Tannahill who are destroying the stars, not we," Isas Lel finally said. "But how is it that a pilot of Neverness has heard of the Program of Totality?"

Danlo looked up to see that the Kistur Ashtoreth and the other Transcendentals were curious about this, too.

"The Old Church had its beginning on Alumit," Danlo said. "And Alumit lies near the spaces of the Civilized Worlds."

As Danlo went on to explain, in the year 1749 since the founding of Neverness, there had been a schism within the Cy-bernetic Universal Church. The Old Church had waged war with the heretical Reformed Church, and this War of the Faces grew to become the longest and greatest war that human beings had ever suffered. In the end—after two hundred years of bloody slaugh-ter—the Old Church had been defeated. Its surviving Architects had fled into the spaces that were to become the Vild, while the Reformed Church went on to expand and make missions to Yarkona, Neverness, and a thousand other Civilized Worlds. In truth, Edeism had nearly become *the* Civilized Worlds' universal religion. If not for the resistance of the Order's infamous and implacable Timekeeper (and the Order itself), the youth of

Neverness might have grown up making the Eight Duties of an Architect rather than dreaming of becoming cetics or scryers or pilots.

"It's long been forgotten which star shines upon Alumit," Isas Lel said. "But, of course, we remember the War of the Faces."

Danlo reached down to grasp the flute in his leg pocket. He gulped in a huge breath of air and said, "During this war, a virus was made. A bioweapon. It is known that the Old Church Architects, with the help of the warrior-poets, engineered a virus that killed billions of people."

That killed my people, Danlo thought. *Haidar and Chandra and Cilehe and . . .*

"And who were these warrior-poets?" Yenene Iviastalir asked.

After Danlo had explained about the Order of the Warrior-Poets, he stopped breathing almost forever and thought: *And now the warrior-poets seek to renew their connection with the Old Church.*

He pressed his fist to his forehead, then asked, "Is it possible . . . that any Architect of the Old Church might know of a cure for this virus? Might any of the Narain have heard of a cure?"

Isas Lel slowly shook his head and then suddenly, in Danlo's own head, on the left side, there was a deep and terrible pain as if someone had driven a knife into his eye. "The Plague has no cure," Isas Lel said, and these words fell upon Danlo with all the force of a great stone crushing the air from his chest.

"The Plague has no cure of which we *know,*" Kistur Ashtoreth corrected. "We Narain are not biologists."

"I see."

"I've never heard of a cure," Ananada Narcavage said.

"Nor have I." This came from Lieswyr Ivioss, who tapped the clearface on her head as if it held all possible information in the universe. "But why would you seek the cure for a disease that has killed nobody for a thousand years?"

"Not a thousand years," Danlo said. He pressed his fist hard against the lightning bolt scar cut above his left eye. "The Plague has killed, *is* killing . . . so many."

Haltingly, in between breaths of stale air reeking of carbon dioxide and plastic, he told the Transcendentals of the death of the Devaki people. The Plague virus was not extinct, but rather, like an assassin's siriwa thread woven into a death robe, it had become embroidered in the human genome as a passive segment of DNA. That is, in human beings possessing the appropriate suppressor genes it was passive. In others, in isolated peoples such as the Alaloi, the virus at any moment might explode into billions of lethal bullets of protein and DNA that would fract the neurons of the victim's brain into a warm red jelly.

"The Devaki were only one tribe of Alaloi," Danlo said. "But there are many others."

"And you would bring them a cure for this dormant Plague virus?" Isas Lel asked.

"If I can. Truly, I . . . must."

Isas Lel looked at Kistur Ashtoreth, and then said, "We would help you find this cure, if we could. We would gladly give you this information. Also, you ask the location of Tannahill's star. We would like to give you this information, too; however . . ."

"Yes?"

"It's difficult to give information to one who doesn't give freely in return."

Danlo clenched his jaws together so tightly that his teeth hurt. The Narain, it seemed, despite their pretensions toward transcendence, were really just as acquisitive and stingy with their possessions as merchants.

"All that I could give to you . . . I would give," Danlo said.

"But we've already asked you where the Star of Neverness lies, and you haven't given us this information."

"But it is not mine to give!" Danlo almost shouted. For a moment, he almost considered telling Isas Lel the star's fixed-points, which would have been completely useless information to anyone except a pilot trained in the mathematics of probabilistic topology. But he could not reveal this secret, and so he said nothing. "I have taken vows."

"Oh, you've taken vows, of course," Isas Lel chided.

"I do not see . . . why you would wish to know where Neverness lies."

"Oh, we don't really care where your world lies. But we would like to know how you've fallen so far across the stars."

"I have been lucky," Danlo said truthfully as he thought of the manifold's many twisting spaces that he had barely escaped. "I have had such rare good chance fall upon me."

"Oh, luck, perhaps—but there's also a great deal of skill in being a pilot, isn't there? If you would give us anything, we would ask for these skills."

"It is not easy to be a pilot," Danlo said.

"But would you teach us what you know?"

As Danlo spoke with Isas Lel and the other Transcendentals, it became clear that the piloting skills of the Narain and the Architects of the Old Church were quite crude. It had taken years for Liljana ivi Narai's deep ships to cross the few light-years from Tannahill to Alumit; in the last ten centuries, the Old Church's pilots had barely managed to establish pathways among the seventy-two worlds of what they called the Known Stars. In part, this was because they had the bad luck to live within the Vild, where the manifold was as dangerous and deranged as a Scutari shahzadix in heat. But Danlo attributed most of their ignorance to the Old Church's age-old contempt and fear of pure mathematics. In this, of course, they were not alone. In truth, of all the peoples among the stars of whom Danlo had ever known, only the cantors and pilots of Neverness had loved mathematics so fiercely that they freely gave their lives to their art. In the icy spires and towers (and lightships) of Neverness, alone of all the cities of man, mathematics had reached its fullest and most beautiful flowering. This love and deep knowledge was the Order's true power, and as with all power, it was not easily acquired nor given away.

"To become a pilot takes many years," Danlo said.

"We Narain are a patient people," Isas Lel said as he stared at Danlo.

"In this becoming . . . there are many dangers."

"On our journey to Alumit Bridge, we Narain have known many dangers."

"I . . . am no teacher," Danlo said.

"But you could teach what you know, couldn't you?"

"No—my Order allows only master pilots and other masters to teach." Danlo neglected to tell Isas Lel that after the accomplishments of his journey into the Vild stars, upon returning to the new Academy on Thiells, he would almost certainly be elevated to his mastership.

"Your Order lives by its rules, doesn't it?"

"Yes," Danlo admitted.

And then, when he saw Isas Lel's face begin its fall into defeat and anger, he knew that he might have a rare chance to win this difficult man's goodwill.

"If you truly desire your people to be pilots, there might be a way."

Now Isas Lel's eyes fell upon Danlo like laser lights.

"Please tell us," Isas Lel said.

"My Order has always made new pilots," Danlo said. "Many peoples of the Civilized Worlds send their children to Neverness to complete their education."

For a while Isas Lel played with the plastic fabric of his robot's seat while he thought about this. "Are you saying that we should send our children thirty thousand light-years across space to this Star of Neverness?"

"No," Danlo said with a sad smile. "That would not be possible. But on the planet Thiells, very soon, there will be a new Academy. You could send your children there."

This, too, was the power of the Order. For a long time, the elite of the Civilized Worlds had sent their brightest children to Neverness to be educated. They always hoped that their daughters and sons would return bearing jewels of knowledge wrested from the Academy's cold stone halls. And sometimes they did return. But the spires of Neverness and the Order's ineffable spirit almost always worked a deep magic upon them. The once-parochial children of the Civilized Worlds returned as Ordermen in their hearts, and not as Yarkonans or Silvaplanaians or Thorskallers. In its way, the Order had always been as subversive as it was sublime. However, Danlo neglected to tell Isas Lel this. As an emissary to the Narain, it was Danlo's duty to practice diplomacy, even if he hated the hidden lies that this required of him.

"To send our children to your new Academy—that is a great opportunity," Isas Lel said.

"Yes," Danlo agreed. "Many have found it so."

Isas Lel's face fell rigid with control, and his eyes were now as hard as sapphires. "And if we were to tell you the location of Tannahill's star and you were to journey there—would you also offer this opportunity to the Old Church?"

"I might have to."

He fears the Old Church, Danlo thought. *And even more he fears letting his fear be seen.*

"It's not possible that the Church Elders would ever allow their children to be educated by namans of some unknown Order," Lieswyr Ivioss ponted out, acidly.

"I agree," Isas Lel said, after some thought. "But that does not imply that they would be uninterested in this young pilot's art."

He fears that the Architects will torture me for this knowledge, Danlo thought. For a moment, he sat perfectly still, feeling what it would be like for some Elder Architect or master torturer to

twist a needle knife up the optic nerve of his eye into his brain.
But why should he fear this so?

"But clearly," Kistur Ashtoreth added, "it would be almost
impossible for the Elders to learn much of this art unless they did
send their children to this Academy on Thiells—wherever Thiells
actually lies."

"Can we be sure of this?" Ananda Narcavage asked.

"Can we be sure of anything?" Kistur Ashtoreth replied.

Although Danlo appreciated the Transcendentals speaking so
freely, with him sitting there on a little red cushion before them,
he knew that much remained unsaid.

"How can we be sure?" Isas Lel added. "That's a difficult
question."

"Of course, Patar Iviaslin said, "if the Old Church *did* send
their children to this Academy, it's impossible that they would
excel in the pilot's art as would *our* children."

"To enter this manifold that Danlo wi Soli Ringess has spoken of so eloquently must be something like interfacing the
Field." This came from Yenene Iviastalir, who liked to speculate
on metaphysics as well as practicalities. "I should think our children would have an advantage here."

They must doubt whether they should trust, Danlo thought.
*They must doubt that the rewards of trusting me to journey to
Tannahill would be worth the risk.*

"Perhaps our children would also have much to learn from
the Order's cetics," Isas Lel said. He fingered the clearface
above his forehead as he smiled at Danlo. He seemed to be still
somewhat awed by Danlo's display of cetic virtuosity.

But what risk? Danlo wondered. *What is their true fear?*

Once, years before, Hanuman li Tosh had taught Danlo the
cetic's art of face reading; he had taught Danlo that the body's
conditioned responses of muscle and the deeper nerves always
betrayed the secret workings of the mind. An arching of an eyebrow, a pursing of the lips, a twitch of a finger—any of these
motions could tell the tale of what one was thinking. Thus, if a
cetic knew how to interpret the tells, as these subtle body signs
were called, he could read one's true fear. But Danlo was no
cetic, and even for a master cetic such as the dreaded Audric Pall,
these Transcendentals would have been hard to read.

"Our *children,*" Isas Lel said. "Sometimes hard choices
must be made."

And then, suddenly, like a drop of supercooled water crystallizing into a snowflake, Danlo knew. This was no simple reading

of the tells of Isas Lel's smooth and empty face, but rather a revelation out of some strange inner sense, as immediate and compelling as if he had suddenly been plunged into the icy sea.

He fears war, Danlo thought. *Ever since the Narain fled to Alumit Bridge, the Old Church has threatened war.*

For a moment, as Danlo wondered what it would be like to live under the threat of war, his deep blue eyes were full of light and compassion. And then he said, ''The lords of the Civilized Worlds have chosen to send their children to Neverness for three thousand years. And in this time, there has been no war.''

Isas Lel looked at Danlo strangely. ''Why do you speak of war?'' he asked.

''Is it possible,'' Danlo asked, ''that war between the Narain and the Old Church . . . is possible?''

''Why would you think that?''

All the Transcendentals were trying hard not to look at Danlo, and all guarded their faces as a wormrunner might hide a firestone.

''War . . . happens,'' Danlo said. He did not wish to explain the mysterious callings of his truth sense, and so he fell back upon the logic of human religious history. ''Whenever there is heresy or schism within a religion, war is always possible, yes?''

''Perhaps,'' Isas Lel said. ''But why should you so suddenly call our attentions to this possibility?''

Danlo was silent while he stared at Isas Lel, and his eyes were like liquid, blue-black jewels.

''How do you know so much?'' Isas Lel finally asked. ''How do you know what you know?''

''This pilot *does* know things,'' Kistur Ashtoreth added. ''I think this Danlo wi Soli Ringess of the Order of Neverness knows about people.''

For a while, no one spoke. Isas Lel and Kistur Ashtoreth, Lieswyr Ivioss and Patar Iviaslin all sat on their motionless plastic robots staring off into some other world that only they could see. Danlo sensed that they were discussing him, perhaps even deciding something of great importance. After his heart had beaten a hundred and twelve times, Isas Lel finally broke the silence. He bowed his head to Danlo and said, ''It's true, for two hundred years we've lived with the possibility of war. But it was only five years ago that the Old Church sent home our ambassadors and asked theirs to return to Tannahill. They've broken off all exchange of information.''

What Isas Lel told of, then, was a common enough story,

repeated countless times since the rise of humankind's first religion millennia ago on Old Earth. A group of once-faithful believers, having grown alienated by their mother church's suffocating ways, comes to doubt its doctrines and authority. There is then schism, exodus, a founding of a new church, new beliefs, new rituals—an intensely new religious experience of the bodysoul that is thought to be only a return to the church's original spirit. If these heretics possess enough vision and fervor, they will gain converts, even as an avalanche gains power on its explosion down a mountainside. They will gain confidence, too, casting off all doctrines and taboos, creating new theologies, feeling divine joy rush through their veins as if they had drunk the sacred wine of the gods. They have taken the first steps upon a path for which there is no return, and thus their heresy intensifies.

The old church is at first tolerant of these heretics—even if they call themselves Transcendentals. After all, they are the church's sons and daughters, and it would be an act of grace to bring them back to the true way toward God. But no heretic, having tasted the sweet liquor of infinity, will be satisfied with holding only an empty cup in his hands. And so there is no going back to the old church, and as with a woman whose love is spurned, the church grows angry and hateful. Relations between the church and its heretics deteriorate; perhaps they even break off altogether. If this break happens to coincide with the rise to power of the church's extreme orthodoxy, then the threat of war becomes very real.

"The Iviomils have called for a facifah," Isas Lel said. "A holy war to return us to the Eight Duties—either that or to return us to Ede."

As Danlo would appreciate in the days that followed, the calling to "return one to Ede" was a euphemism for Church-sanctioned murder.

"It is difficult to reason with these Iviomils, yes?"

"It's impossible," Isas Lel said. "They despise reason."

Danlo let his hand rest against the bamboo flute in his leg pocket, and then he sat very still. At last, sensing that Isas Lel and the others hoped that he might help them, he said, "But there are Architects other than the Iviomils—it is possible to reason with *these* people, yes?"

"Faith without reason is blind," Isas Lel said. "The Elders of the Church have appreciated this for three thousand years."

No, for at least thirty thousand years, Danlo thought. *Faith*

*and reason; reason and faith—the right and left hands that make
all religions what they are.*

"The Church Elders are open to reason?" Danlo asked.

"Some of them are," Isas Lel said. "The High Architect,
Harrah Ivi en li Ede, is an exceptionally reasonable woman."

"But since you no longer have an embassy on Tannahill, it is
no longer possible to reason with her, yes?"

"That is the way things are."

Danlo looked deeply into Isas Lel's pale, wavering eyes. He
thought that there was the beginning of an understanding between them. "If I were to journey to Tannahill," Danlo said, "it
is possible that I might be presented to Harrah Ivi en li Ede,
yes?"

"It's more than possible."

"I might gain her confidence," Danlo said. "I might . . .
reason with her, yes?"

Isas Lel almost smiled, then, though his eyes were still wary.
"Harrah has many enemies, and it wouldn't be easy to converse
with her openly."

"I see."

"And she has a brilliant mind. Like the diamond of your
lightship, Pilot, it's clear and almost perfectly ordered, but not
easily penetrated."

Here Danlo smiled as he thought of his lightship abandoned
on the uppermost level of the city somewhere high above him. If
the Narain had tried to open it or scan its contents, they almost
certainly would have failed. Nothing much less than the blast of a
hydrogen bomb (or a supernova) could open a sealed lightship.

"If one knows the right words," Danlo said, "it is always
possible to open another's mind."

He remembered, then, something that his Fravashi teacher had
once said to him: *The human mind is made with words. And that
which is made with words, with words can be unmade.*

"It's possible," Isas Lel said, "that you could find new words
to open Harrah Ivi en li Ede's mind. You have a way a way of
opening people to themselves, Pilot. I think we've all seen that."

Danlo, sitting straight on his cushion, looked up at the half
circle of Transcendentals safe in their robots. Each man and
woman (and manwoman), he saw, was now smiling at him.

"Kistur Ashtoreth was right," Isas Lel said. "You know
about people. And you know things that should be impossible for
you to know—perhaps you might know how to help us avoid this
war."

Danlo's heart was now beating quick and light, like a spar-rowhawk's. He was very pleased with the turn of the conversation; in truth, he was almost pleased with himself. But he should have been wary of this pleasure and pride. The greater the heights of emotion, the more terrible the fall.

"If we were to tell you of Tannahill's star," Isas Lel said, "would you speak for us with the Church Elders?"

"Yes," Danlo said.

"You have your mission, your calling to your Order, too," Isas Lel said. "We wouldn't ask you to compromise this—but if you journeyed to Tannahill, would you also be our emissary?"

"Yes," Danlo said. And then he thought, *I have almost accomplished what I must accomplish.*

"An emissary of peace," Isas Lel repeated. "All we want is peace."

Danlo bowed his head in silence for a moment. He remembered, then, that his Fravashi teacher had once bestowed upon him the name of Danlo Peacewise.

"We'd *like* to point out Tannahill's star for you to see," Isas Lel said.

With the warm flush of triumph spreading like coffee-wine through his veins, Danlo looked up at the dome beyond the Transcendentals. He expected to see the star scene return in a flash of brilliant lights, but this did not happen.

"We'd like to show you this star, but unfortunately, we can't."

"You . . . cannot," Danlo said. He drew in a breath of air and held it until his lungs began to burn.

"It's not our decision to make."

The scene on the chatoy walls, Danlo saw, was still that of the sunset. In all the time they had spent talking, the bloody red sun of Alumit bridge had dropped scarcely an inch below the glowing horizon.

"I do not understand," Danlo said. He looked at Lieswyr Ivioss, all haughty and self-willed beneath her glittering clearface, and the shy, quiet Diverous Te, and all the others. "You call yourselves the Transcendentals, yes? Of all the Narain, are you not the ones to make this decision?"

"We are the ones," Isas Lel said, "but we are not."

"You are, and you are not," Danlo said. "You—"

"I," Isas Lel said, interrupting, "am only one of many. As with the others."

Danlo looked at the pretty sunset, the streaks of amethyst and carmine burning across the low sky. He said, "Yes, one of many. I had thought that all of you, together, speaking together within the interface of what you call the Field would make this decision."

Isas Lel shook his head. "I must explain myself more clearly. I am one of many who are one. But none of the others whom you have met today are of this one."

"What . . . one?"

"My name, *our* name, is Abraxax. Only Abraxax is the Transcended One."

Just then Danlo remembered their initial conversation by light radio, with Danlo and his lightship floating in space some three hundred miles above the planet. This proud Transcendental had first identified himself by the full name of Isas Lel Abraxax.

"And *my* name," Kistur Ashtoreth said, "is Manannan."

As Isas Lel then explained, each Transcendental was part of a group self, and each of these selves had a name. For instance, Isas Lel's transcended self, as he called it, was a sevenplex: across Alumit Bridge, in Megina and Kelkarq and other cities there lived six other Transcendentals with whom he shared selfness. In the cybernetic space of the Field, which was as timeless and locationless as a dream, they would choose a moment to meet and merge. From their many talents and personalities—Isas Lel's sense of purpose, Omar Iviorvan's kindness, Duscha li Lan's imperturbability, and so on—they would assemble a single cybernetic entity.

Thus each Transcendental was one of many who were one—a Transcended One. Lieswyr Ivioss was one of a triad named Shahar; Diverous Te shared selfness with the famous Maralah quad. Although a few maverick Transcendentals in the other cities of Alumit Bridge entered the Field as only singletons, this was uncommon. The ideal, as Isas Lel explained, was to go beyond and transcend the single self. And so the Transcendentals claimed to have done. If Isas Lel could be believed, these higher cybernetic selves were as real and complete as ordinary human beings limited by existence in the everyday world—only they were almost as powerful and intelligent as gods.

"It is the Transcended Ones who are the lords of the Narain," Isas Lel explained. "We may meet with you in this facing chamber to tell you what they decide, but it is *we* as *they* who must meet within the Field to come to a decision."

"I see," Danlo said. Though, in truth, he could not understand what it might mean to merge with another as a higher cybernetic entity. "Then you are interfacing your higher self, this Transcended One, almost continually."

For a moment, Isas Lel's little eyes seemed almost to disappear from his head. And then he told Danlo, "Yes, almost."

"Then this meeting of selves, this conclave of your higher ones—this also is occurring almost continually, yes?"

"Even as we speak, Danlo wi Soli Ringess."

"You must decide if you can trust me, yes? Are you close to a decision, then?"

"No, we are not close. There are many Transcendentals, many Ones."

According to Isas Lel, in all the cities of Alumit Bridge, there were exactly 16,609 Transcendentals who had surrendered themselves to merge into 4,084 higher entities. Of these, the most prominent were Abraxax, Manannan, Tyr, Shahar, Maralah, El, and Kane. That the Transcendentals in the facing chamber shared selfness with one or other of these entities was no accident. Iviunir was the first and most prominent city on the planet, the city to which all Transcendentals aspired to live if they were worthy.

"How could I help you to your decision?" Danlo asked.

"I'm sorry, Pilot, there's nothing you can do now."

"Nothing . . . truly?"

Isas Lel Abraxax, who had come to suspect something of Danlo's wild spirit during their brief time together, looked at him sharply and asked, "What are you thinking?"

Almost casually, Danlo drew his shakuhachi out of its pocket in his robe. He held it lightly between his hands, but he did not play it. "If I could speak with Abraxax and Manannan, these Transcended Ones, perhaps I could help them make their decision."

"But you *are* speaking to them," Lieswyr Ivioss reminded him. "Now, through us, the Ones hear your every word."

"Yes, but if I could speak with them face to face, I might give them more than just words."

"Face to *face*?" Patar Iviaslin choked out in a high, outraged voice. "What do you think you mean by this?"

And then Ananda Narcavage, she of the El twelve, looked at him and demanded, "Are you asking to enter the Field and interface the Transcended Ones?"

"Yes," Danlo said, quickly, boldly, wildly. "I would face them if I could."

In the dead silence that followed Danlo's astonishing proposal, all the Transcendentals could only stare at him. He might as well have suggested taking part in the warrior-poets' knife ceremony or helping a Scutari shahzadix with her multiple matings and the ritual cannabalism that concluded this sacred blood orgy.

And then Isas Lel cleared his throat and sucked some water from a clear plastic tube that his robot dangled in front of him. He said, "Well, sometimes the common people may face with Transcended Ones. We must never become unapproachable."

"Yes, of course," Ananda Narcavage said. "But this Danlo wi Soli Ringess, a pilot of unknown star, a naman—"

"A naman, enter the Field and face a Transcended One?" Lieswyr Ivioss exclaimed. "No, no—that would be impossible."

But, of course, it *was* possible, and Isas Lel reminded the others that this was so. "To pilot his ship across the stars, Danlo wi Soli Ringess must enter the field that he calls the manifold."

At this Danlo almost smiled, but the pain above his eye, where his headaches came, drove all amusement from his face. He thought that Isas Lel couldn't truly understand about the manifold. In truth, the manifold wasn't merely just another cybernetic space or surreality; it was something much, much deeper—perhaps even deep reality itself.

"And Danlo wi Soli Ringess has been trained by his Order's cetics, by these cybershamans who are said to be masters of the cybernetic spaces."

This, at least, was true. Danlo was pleased that Isas Lel should champion his proposal to enter the Field. And then Lieswyr Ivioss, who had seemed antagonistic to Danlo and all his hopes, abruptly changed her manner. "Perhaps," she said, "Danlo wi Soli Ringess *should* be allowed to face a Transcended One. If he proves worthy, perhaps we should allow him to enter the Field."

For the twentieth time that morning, the eyes of Isas Lel and Lieswyr Ivioss and the others hardened, as of clear water freezing into cloudy white ice. And then, some moments later, they returned to full consciousness of the facing chamber and of Danlo, who was still sitting patiently before them.

"It has been decided," Isas Lel finally said. He seemed ill at ease, almost embarrassed.

Danlo waited for him to say more, then asked, "Yes?"

"It's been decided that telling you the location of Tannahill requires a decision of all the Transcended Ones."

"I see."

"Some believe that this decision would best be made if you could enter the Field and face the Ones."

"Truly?"

"Unfortunately, however, others do not."

"I see."

"The decision as to allow you to enter the Field is itself difficult. But we have decided that this decision must be made."

"You have decided . . . only this?"

"I'm sorry, Pilot. But we Narain have no single ruling lord, as does your Order. We make our decisions well but not easily."

"No," Danlo said. "Not easily."

"And so we must ask you to wait while we decide if you're to enter the Field. Will you wait a while longer, Danlo wi Soli Ringess?"

All the Transcendentals were watching Danlo, waiting to see what his decision would be. Danlo bowed his head and told them, "Yes, if you'd like, I will wait."

"Very well," Isas Lel said. "An apartment has been prepared for you. A robot will take you there."

So saying, Isas Lel looked at the facing chamber's red plastic doors, which suddenly slid open. A empty robot wheeled into the room and stopped only inches short of where Danlo sat. Danlo understood that his meeting with the Transcendentals was over. He rose up from his cushion, slid his flute back into its pocket, and reached down to grasp the devotionary computer. He held this miraculous translating machine close to his belly. As he settled into the robot's softly cushioned seat, his back was turned to seven very curious men and women. And so, for a moment, with his body shielding the Ede imago from their watchful eyes, he was able to look down and behold the signs that Ede was flashing him. Ede's hands and little fingers of light fluttered like flying insects. And the meaning of these cetic signs was clear: "Beware any invitation to enter this space they call the Field. Beware of Lieswyr Ivioss and her Transcended One called Shahar."

"Yes?" Danlo whispered.

And Ede signed back, "There are many who wouldn't want you to journey to Tannahill. And so they will try to trap you within the Field. Like a bee is trapped by the nectar of a fireflower. Like a moth is trapped by light."

Danlo closed his eyes for a moment as he considered this. And then he whispered, "Yes, I see."

"Let's leave this place while we can, Pilot. Before it's too late."

"No, I will not leave yet."

"Then let the Transcended Ones make their decision without you. Don't face them within the Field."

Danlo smiled to himself as rubbed the scar that marked his aching head. "But I must face them," he whispered. "If I can, I will."

After that, almost without a sound, the robot began to roll away from Isas Lel and his transcendent friends. They quickly rolled through the open doorway, into the bright, plastic corridors leading to the streets of the city of Iviunir.

THE FIELD

*There is no matter without form, and no form not
dependent upon matter.*

— *saying of the cetics*

While awaiting the decision of the Transcendent Ones of Alumit
Bridge, Danlo was given a small apartment on the city's seventeenth level, overlooking a huge and busy street called Elidi Boulevard. As he would soon discover, of course, it was actually no
smaller than any other apartment in Iviunir; like Scutari nymphs
in their feeding boxes, the Narain required little living space. His
five rooms were tiny, separated from one another by thin walls of
white plastic: there was a bathing room where he might cleanse
his body, a multrum barely large enough to allow for squatting
and voiding oneself of wastes, a facing cell almost the same size,
a sleeping chamber, and—barbarically—a kitchen.

Danlo had always regarded the private consumption of food to
be a shameful and barbaric thing, but the Narain lived according
to different sensibilities. They preferred convenience to company; it was their way to voice their immediate hungers to their
ministrant robots, to wait silently a few seconds while these
semisentient machines lit the light ovens in the kitchen, and then
to recline on soft white carpets of spun plastic in their sleeping
chambers, there to swallow their meals of tasteless factory foods
in solitude. It was a bad way to live, but then, as Isas Lel had
warned Danlo, the Narain preferred to let their robots live for
them.

In Danlo's free moments, he searched the city for signs of
true human life. He found few instances of that warm, earthy,
marvelous quality he thought of simply as livingness. The Narain
did not gather in restaurants to talk about the events of the day;
they did not meet friends in public squares or in cafes or in

shops. In the whole city, he could find no park or agora that served to focus the Narain's appreciation of one another. Many times, on the streets, he sought to engage men or women (or womenmen) in conversation, but it seemed that no one wanted to talk with him. They hurried past him as they hurried past each other.

Theirs was a cold and terrible isolation from one another, and yet Danlo never sensed that the Narain disliked each other or were fundamentally misanthropes, as were, for instance, the exemplars of Bodhi Luz. In truth, Danlo attributed the Narain's unsociability to shyness. It was almost as if they had never learned to meet each other eye to eye, to inquire as to a friend's well-being, to smile and laugh and open their hearts to the sounds of their lovers' hearts—to take joy in the light of each other's soul. An alien (or a stranger), proceeding down the plastic walkway of the Elidi Boulevard, might have thought that the thousands of single-minded human beings rushing by in their plastic kimonos were not really human. He might have thought that they were not really alive, or worse, that they were more robotlike than any robot. In a way, this was true. To be in the world, *sar en getik,* for almost any good Narain, was to be not truly alive. In truth the Narain lived only to return to the cleanliness of their apartments, to pull their silver heaumes over their heads and lie down in their facing cells.

And there, in their dark apartments, in their millions, stacked one atop the other like corpses in a funeral ship, they would close their eyes and enter into the many glittering spaces of the Field. There they would merge and be as one. Some pursued the bliss of cybernetic samadhi; some sought union in the integration into higher selves; a few desired little more than the exchange of information with other minds.

It was only after Danlo had risked his life talking with a gang of young rebels whose tattooed faces proclaimed them the Assassins of Ede that he began to understand the Narain people and to perceive the paradox of their way of life. As great as was their isolation from each other out on the streets, their sense of common purpose within the Field was even greater. This purpose remained for Danlo unclear. Once or twice, however, as he might make out the shape of a great white bear stalking him across miles of sea ice, he thought that he had caught sight of the Narain's dream. If he had been allowed to enter the Field freely like any of the common Narain, he might have entered this consensus hallucination and beheld all its hubris and horror. But in the facing cell of his apartment there was no heaume for him to place upon his head. The Transcendentals, it seemed, had allowed him every freedom in the city except the only one that really mattered. They had told him that he must wait for the decision of the Transcendent Ones, and wait he must.

And so Danlo began to study the syntax and words of modern Church Istwan. He had much time in which to learn this rather difficult language and much need to learn it. While walking the city streets and boulevards, of course, he could—and did—use the translating program of his devotionary computer to converse with the rare individuals who consented to talk with him. But if he were to journey to Tannahill this wouldn't do. To employ the hologram of Nikolos Daru Ede as a mere translator would be sacrilege.

"You would probably be killed on sight," Isas Lel had warned Danlo. "The Worthy Architects would rip the devotionary from your hands and swarm upon you and tear you into pieces."

To learn the syntax of Istwan was no great problem as it was one of the hundreds of granddaughter languages of Ancient Anglish, which Danlo had once studied as a novice. Then too, Danlo had a phenomenal memory, and it was no great feat for him to learn a thousand new words each day. Soon he found himself able to converse with the Narain without the aid of his devotionary computer.

But still Ede almost begged Danlo to accompany him on his outings into the city, and out of a strange loyalty, he acquiesed. As Danlo grew more confident of his ability to speak Istwan, however, he found himself ignoring Ede's translations—and especially Ede's neverending and very tiresome premonitions of doom.

One day, the Transcendentals sent a bright yellow robot to the doors of Danlo's apartment. It bore him through the tunnel-like streets between blocks of old buildings, back along the great Elidi Boulevard and the city's other thoroughfares. Eventually, it brought him to the Transcendentals' sanctuary. There, as before, the robot rolled through long hallways blighted with various strains of bluish mehalchins growing from the pitted plastic walls. It was almost as if the meeting chamber hadn't changed in the many days since Danlo's first audience with the Transcendentals. The domed chatoy walls still ran with the colors of Alumit Bridge's violet-red sun that never set; at the center of the room sat the chromium tea service and fat red cushion; the Transcendentals, with their golden clearfaces gleaming on their hairless skulls, sat waiting eyelessly in their robots. Only the flowers were different. In the two plastic vases near the cushion, the brilliant orange and azure alien flowers had wilted and dried to a dead black. The Transcendentals—Isas Lel, Kistur Ashtoreth, Diverous Te, Yenene Iviastalir, Lieswyr Ivioss, Ananda Narcavage, and Patar Iviaslin—apparently had overlooked this little death. Although they must have returned to their apartments for bathing, food, and rest since meeting Danlo, they seemed not to have moved for many days.

"Danlo wi Soli Ringess of Neverness—welcome," Isas Lel said. He invited Danlo to remain seated on his robot as if he had suddenly become an equal with the Transcendentals. But Danlo preferred the cushion on the floor, and so he stepped over to it and sat there cross-legged, waiting as straight and silent as a yu tree.

"We've good news for you," Isas Lel said. "A decision as to your request to face the Transcended Ones has been reached."

Danlo looked from Isas Lel to the vacant-eyed Diverous Te, from Transcendental to Transcendental, face to face. Already, it seemed, most of these seven had entered the Field to interface their higher selves.

"Yes?" Danlo asked at last.

"You will be allowed to enter the Field," Isas Lel said. Of all the Transcendentals present, he seemed the only one even half-aware of Danlo. "It has been decided—you may plea your mission with the Transcended Ones."

"Thank you," Danlo said.

He looked down at the many jeweled eyes of the devotionary computer that he had set upon the floor and wondered about the optics of these glittering, insectlike eyes, how the shapes and colors of the world must appear to this programable machine. He might have wondered, too, how the Transcendentals appeared to the hologram of Nikolos Daru Ede, but of this nonmystery there could be little doubt. *Don't do it!* the Ede hologram signed to Danlo. *Don't let these spiders trap you in their cybernetic webs and suck away your mind!*

Danlo smiled at this very organic metaphor. And then he looked at Isas Lel and asked, "When may I face the Transcended Ones?"

"Now," Isas Lel said. "This is why we've brought you here. But first we must acquaint you with the Field's topography. We will guide you where you must go."

They can't allow themselves to trust you, Ede signed. *There is much that they would hide from you, and so you mustn't trust them.*

"You will share thoughtspace with me, yes?" Danlo asked.

"Well, I *will* be able to exchange thoughts with you," Isas Lel said. "But only those thoughts that you—and I—encode as words."

"I see."

"Shall we begin now, then?" Isas Lel asked.

"If you'd like."

"Very well. Then if you'll close your eyes, I'll take you to the Transcended Ones."

Just then the room began to darken, and Danlo closed his eyes. As a novice in Neverness, in the dark, steamy cells of the library, Danlo had often immersed himself in tanks of warm saltwater as he reached out with his mind to interface the Order's great information pools. He had lain naked beneath the deep purple neurologic scanners that read the electrochemical events of his brain. In many ways, sitting on the floor of the meeting room was similar in experience. There was the darkness and the quiet—though this was not nearly so profound as the almost total suspension of the body's outer senses that one felt while floating in one of the library's cells. Danlo supposed that the computers behind the meeting room's chatoy walls must generate a much more powerful logic field than did the library's little, organic cells. In truth, the whole meeting room was much like a librarian's cell, and even more like a cetic's heaume that encased one's head—only much, much larger. This was an evolved technology that the Order could scarcely afford, except perhaps in the null rooms of the cetic's tower. But it was not a wholly unfamiliar technology. Already, a moment after Danlo closed his eyes, the computers of the meeting room infused images directly into the visual cortex at the back of Danlo's brain. In the meeting room, around his face and eyes, all was darkness. But inside him, *behind* his eyes, suddenly, there was light. There was sound and shape, direction and color, and the cybernetic space of the Field opened before him.

—Are you all right, Pilot? Is this comfortable for you?

The meeting room's scanning computers read the words of Isas Lel, formed up in the language centers of his brain. Other computers encoded these words as electrical impulses and stimulated the nerves of Danlo's inner ear. And so Danlo "heard" Isas Lel's raspy voice whispering inside his head.

—Yes, thank you, I am all right.
—Can you move? If you can, why don't you begin with an information pool. Any one will do.

In the silent meeting room, sitting on his cushion with his eyes tightly closed, Danlo realized that he was being tested. He smiled to himself, for the movement through information pools was the most fundamental of cybernetic skills. The cetics of his Order called this sense of motion "seeking." Even a child, he thought, knew how to face a data space and seek for information.

—Are all your pools open to me, then? Or are any of them forbidden?
—All are open, Pilot. We believe in free information.
—I see.
—But I must ask you not to enter any of the astronomy pools.
—If you ask this, then I will not.
—Otherwise, you may choose whichever pool you wish.
—I may drink of any pool, but only those that I can find.
—What do you mean?
—The easiest way to hide a pool . . . is by locating it inside an ocean.
—You're clever, Pilot.
—No, it is just the opposite.
—*Very* clever. But are you clever enough to find whatever you might seek? We shall see, Pilot. We shall see.

With his mind, Danlo moved forth toward the information that he sought like a thirsty man crossing the desert; it was as if he had crested a dune of sun-baked soil and stone, all the while hoping to find a pool of clear, cool water on the other side. But the information flowing before him was less like a pool than a raging ocean. And the water was turbid with sediments, salty and undrinkable.

—Well, Pilot?

No one—no human being—can absorb very much information. Can a man drink the sea? No, and neither can he find his way across it unless he has a compass or bright stars to light his way. Even a master cetic would be helpless and blind if cast adrift on a chaotic information space. However, no human society has ever gathered up trillions of random bits of information and simply dumped them into one, huge collective pool. Information, to be useful, is always selected, interpreted, weighted, encoded, processed, organized. And human beings, with their very human brains that are much the same from the exemplars of Bodhi Luz to the Ihrie Nebula god-men, all seem to organize information in only a few basic ways. As the master librarian Elia Jesaitis had once taught Danlo, all information systems have their own logic, and being a pilot of the Order, Danlo was nothing if not a logical man. Logic was the key to unlocking whatever informational secrets one sought—logic and also the various cybernetic senses that Danlo's masters had helped him to develop when he first came to Neverness as a wild young man so many years before.

—You hesitate, Pilot. It's overwhelming, isn't it?

For a moment, Danlo *did* hesitate. Before him were endless information flows encoded in various ways. Some of this information had been organized to be accessed by the physical senses. With his eyes still closed, Danlo saw the building of the first arcology on Tannahill and countless other images out of history; he saw a face-painting of Liljana Narai as well as molecular fotos of deadly Trachang viruses. There were sounds of people praying in swarm inside an Architect temple. He heard voices, a cacophony of hundreds of voices crying out as of prisoners chained into a dark cave. These voices were each trying to explain something, from the engineering of information viruses to the Program of Transcendence.

And there were smells, too, the scent of roses and garlic and burning plastics. These were the simulated sensa of a surreality, and Danlo had long since learned how to apprehend this kind of information. He had learned, too, that immersing himself too deeply in simulation was a very slow and inefficient means of seeking knowledge. To move quickly among the data pools, one must be able to kithe information encoded as symbols. Perhaps the greatest glory of the Order was the development of the Universal Syntax, a way of representing all possible knowledge by arrays of three-dimensional mental symbols that the grammarians called ideoplasts.

But the Narain, it seemed, had no such art. In the Field of Alumit Bridge, symbolic information appeared as words strung together in sentences, in truth, as whole sets of sentences falling one after another linearly much as an orator might speak. And each word was represented not by its own beautiful ideoplast but rather by symbols encoding the word's different sounds. It was a simple way to convey words and ideas, but primitive, barbaric. Compared to the sublime art of kithing ideoplasts, it was like trudging along on snowshoes across the frozen sea when one might sail a hundred miles per hour in an ice schooner. But it was also quite easy; if one could *see,* even a child or a cybernetic cripple could still read information written this way.

—Pilot?

Like a thallow perched atop his mountain aerie, waiting, Danlo exulted in his powerful sense of sight. Before him, below him, the collective knowledge of the Narain people and a hundred generations of the Cybernetic Universal Church lay glittering with all the depth and clarity of a frozen seascape. For that is the beauty of organization, that when one reaches out to logically arranged data with the proper senses, the flowing information pools fall into form and become more like snowflakes, frozen waterfalls, crystal mountains.

And in Danlo, these inner, cybernetic senses were deep and keen. There was his sense of shih, a sort of master sense allowing him to perceive the relationship between information and knowledge, between knowledge and wisdom. With shih he might drink in the information crystals and know by the tastes of sweetness or bitterness which paths through the Field's data space that he should seek. There were his senses of iconicity and syntaxis, and gestalt, where information would just "pop" into his mind with all the suddenness of a soap bubble swelling into its colors. And, of course, the senses of fractality and fugue, and above all, fenestration. In the Field, as in all cybernetic spaces, there would be windows to pass through, clear arrays of information opening onto ever new arrays, window after window, layer upon crystalline layer sometimes hundreds of panes deep. A cetic—or even any Orderman whom the cetics had trained—might fenester through these windows with all the speed of a pilot falling through the manifold.

—Perhaps you aren't ready to face the Transcended Ones.

Suddenly, Danlo moved. In truth, he almost flew along the frozen rivers of information, swooping here or there as a Snowy Owl might follow an elusive kitikeesha chick. In clumps of two or ten, the thirty-one different letters of the Narain alphabet passed before his inner eye at a blinding speed, like millions of bright shells strung along the tide line of a frozen beach. And so he raced above the field of biological history, reading, looking, seeking. He ached to cry out in discovery, to close the talons of his mind around a single fact or clue that might lead to a cure for the plague virus that had killed his people. But he found nothing. He fenestered through many windows, seeking in such unlikely areas as heuristics and biographies, and still the knowledge he sought escaped him. Perhaps, he thought, a cure did not exist. Or rather, perhaps Isas Lel had told the truth in saying that the Narain knew nothing of such a cure. Although it is impossible to prove the absence of information until every window of every subsubfield of knowledge has been opened and all the data searched as carefully as a kitikeesha picking through snow for a worm, with every reference to the plague virus's etiology that Danlo read, he became more and more certain that the Narain were as baffled by this terrible disease as were the Order's biologists.

Perhaps some outlaw virologist had once recorded a description of the effects of an array of alien drugs on the virus's embroidery within the human genome. Perhaps this knowledge existed in some lost informational pocket in some far field within the greater Field itself. If so, then Danlo might search for years and never find it. Even a master librarian might be pressed to uncover such esoterica. With this in mind, after a long time of soaring across icy mountains of information, Danlo abandoned his search. He came to rest on a branch of a decision tree high above the fields and streams of brilliantly formed information below him.

—Oh, Pilot, there you are.

Isas Lel's voice rang inside Danlo's mind. Although the sound of it was only a computer simulation unaffected by the workings of Isas Lel's heart and lungs, there was almost a breathless quality to this disembodied voice as if he had found much trouble in following Danlo on his wild flight.

—Are you lost, Pilot? It seemed that you were falling un-
controllably through the windows.

—I . . . was falling. But I am not lost.

—No? Are you sure? It's impossible for anyone to read so
quickly.

—If your people know of a cure for the plague, I could not
find it.

Danlo went on to describe the many pools to which his seeking had taken him. When he was done, Isas Lel seemed convinced that he was indeed not lost after all.

—You surprise me, Pilot. Does everyone in your Order
have this talent with information?

—Many do.

—It seems that your Order has much to teach us, then.

—Yes, this is true. And you've much to teach us.

—We can only hope so. You haven't joined in the conversation of my people yet, much less faced a Transcended
One. Are you ready to leave the information pools and see
where we Narain really live?

—Not yet. If it is all right, there is more that I would know.

So saying (or thinking), Danlo sprang forward with his mind
and spent a long time skimming above the Field's thousands of
information pools. Here and there, like an osprey fishing the
ocean waters, he dipped down to taste some tantalizing bit of
knowledge. Sometimes, he dived deeply into ancient Narain poetry or eschatology or any other art where here might find wisdom or insights. And so he understood at least a part of the
dream of the Narain people. For them, God was not only a transcendent reality outside the universe, but also a living force that
had emptied itself into the universe at the moment of its birth. It
was their purpose to recreate God after this cosmic disintegra-
tion; in this they saw themselves as partners with Ede, and perhaps more, as the very Architects of His divinity. How this could
be so—how the Narain hoped to transcend themselves in creating
Ede the God—Danlo would soon learn.

—Pilot?

Danlo learned other things as well. Of particular interest to
his quest was an Oredolo, a formal epic detailing the Narain's

exodus from Tannahill. And an ancient child's poem. And above all—Danlo found this almost forgotten in one of the fantasy pools—a light painting of the Known Stars made on Iviendenhall, when the Narain had paused near this hot blue giant two hundred years before on their journey to Alumit Bridge. From these three sources, Danlo hoped that he had all the information he needed to fix the location of Tannahill's star. In his mind, deep within his visual field, where there burned all the colors from cobalt to crimson, he was about to illuminate this light painting and fix it in his memory. He could almost *see* the stars, and then, suddenly, there was a brilliant burst of light as if one of them had exploded into a supernova.

—Pilot!

And then there was only darkness. Inside Danlo's mind, the Field was as dark as the space of the Old Morbio. He knew, then, that he had lost interface, that he had been expelled from the Field as soldier bees might eject a wasp from their hive. He opened his eyes to the lesser darkness of the meeting room. There on the floor, the hologram of Nikolos Daru Ede beamed like a mother seeing her son return from war. There, too, in the twilight, the chatoy dome glowed a pale orange as if the simulated sun had finally just set. He saw the Transcendentals sitting in the half circle atop their robots. All except Isas Lel had their eyes closed; it seemed that they all continued to interface the Field. Isas Lel, however, had his eyes fixed on Danlo with all the trepidation of a man beholding a Scutari alien for the first time.

"You're very good, Pilot," he said.

"I almost had it," Danlo said. "The viewpoint, out of the light-distances, the stars, another moment and—"

"You promised not to enter any of the astronomy pools! And so you didn't, did you?"

"No."

"Can you tell me where you found the light painting, then?"

Danlo explained about the forgotten fantasy pool and his plan to reconstruct a star map from the sources that he had discovered. And then he said, "The information was not forbidden, only hidden."

"Hidden, not forbidden—I must remember that," Isas Lel said.

"I am sorry."

"But why should you be sorry? You kept your promise."

"But I was not true to the spirit of the promise."

Isas Lel's soft brown eyes almost shone out of the meeting room's darkness. "You're a strange man, Danlo wi Soli Ringess. So fierce with yourself."

"The truth is the truth."

"So fierce *within* yourself."

"How should I not be?"

"Oh, there are many ways of being with oneself. And with other selves, as you'll soon see."

"What do you mean?"

"When we return to the Field, you may see how it is to be one of many who would cherish one such as you."

"You would allow me to interface again? Truly?"

"It's already been decided," Isas Lel said. "Of course, this time there will be no need for you to explore the information pools, will there?"

For a moment Danlo was silent, and then he said, "No."

"Very well, then. Why don't we go on to the association space? It would be good for you to take part in the conversation of my people before facing the Transcended Ones."

Danlo nodded his head and smiled. "If you'd like," he said.

As before, the lights of the meeting room faded to blackness. As before Danlo entered the Field, only this time there was no clear light behind his eyes or mountains of information but only voices. There were many voices—how many Danlo could not say. Perhaps there were a billion of them. The voices were too loud; they shrieked and shouted and reverberated almost as one single sound, almost like the roaring of a great swarm of people crowded together in a public ice ring.

And yet there were words, too, individual words almost as clear as the notes of a bell and strings of statements that ran together like paints spilled into water and almost made sense.

. . . *of God Ede in the system where the Elidis say yes the assassins would take the seventeenth level mehalchins flowers infolding the One at the omega point to share all mind the conversation of the true Narain Ones who go to One have you heard the many lives patterns the beauty of God facivi facilah for in what sense is Tadeo Aharagni mad or divinely mad for assassinating this naman Danlo wi Soli Ringess of Neverness in the Sagittarius arm of stars when they die the Old Church Iviomils would destroy all things are beautiful when faced with lives of God instar I*

*know nothing of God who the Fanyas said the Jurridik said
do not believe the family is killed when the mothers of Ede
and the mothers bear their own and keep them calling this
the only threat they must go to God to Ede on and on
and . . .*

—Pilot?

In Danlo's mind, the voice of Isas Lel sounded loudly, and it
was as clear as the notes of a gosharp ringing out above lesser
instruments.

—Pilot, you're too high.
—Yes, I know.

Danlo fell back upon his sense of fractality, then. He moved
lower in the association space, down to where the great conversation of the Narain people began to divide and redivide into separate streams. It was rather like viewing the ocher green
wholeness of a planet's continents from space and then falling
down to an Earth. Gradually, the single sound of the conversation
began to break up, and Danlo was aware of many conversations,
as of an Earth's many different lands. Each land, it seemed, sang
with its own sounds, its many separate conversations all associat-
ing and connecting to a major theme.

In one land, the Narain doomsayers (or dreamers) might concentrate on eschatology, while in a nearby land, aspiring Transcendentals talked about nothing except the ineffable nature of
Ede the God. One land was all waterfalls, flowers, and songbirds,
and there music was being discussed or played. Another land,
almost as barren and dry as a desert, was inhabited only by a few
thousand hardy linguistic police. These eccentrics were expert in
peeling back the words of common speech to reveal various species of *nibwaw,* a term used in the Algorithm for pointless or
frivolous theological debate. Every millisecond or so, one of
these linguists might journey to nearby lands to monitor the
many streams of the Conversation and warn their fellow Narain
to speak more carefully. Few, however, paid them any attention,
especially the dwellers of one strange-looking place (it was all
stunted with conversational vegetation like bonsai trees) who
spent all their time telling jokes.

Within any of these lands—and across the Field of Alumit
Bridge there were thousands of them—countless symposiums,

soliloquies, and debates went on continually. And at yet a lower level of individual voices, there were musings, arguments, laughter, cries, confidences, whispers, murmurings, lamentations and prayers. A Narain man or woman (or child), upon entering the association space, might choose to visit any of these lands and simply listen to the brilliant wordplay, much as a butterfly might float through an open window into a room full of people and eavesdrop on a conversation.

—Where would you like to go, Pilot?

It had always been Danlo's dream to go everywhere, or rather, to journey to the center of all things so that he might see the universe as it truly was. But in this universe of the Field, in the millions of people spinning out their silvery words and weaving together the great Conversation, he could find no true center.

Then Danlo became aware of other conversations, all of which formed around a single topic of moment: the arrival on Alumit Bridge of the pilot called Danlo wi Soli Ringess. The Narain, it seemed, were very interested in discussing his life—not the stylized and formal life of one who has interfaced the Field, but rather the real (or unreal) life of a man who has lived since childhood en getik, who has sat in caves before blazing woodfires and skated down icy streets and piloted a diamond lightship across the stars.

For a long time, as time is measured within electron-quick exchanges of information within the Field, Danlo listened to the Narain discussing his quest to find Tannahill. After a while he became aware that Isas Lel was listening, too. And then Isas Lel spoke to him, or rather directed his thoughts to the Field computers so that they might generate words that only Danlo could hear.

—You're now a luminary, Pilot. Almost everyone on Alumit Bridge knows your name.
—Truly?
—There are so many who would speak with you. Would you care to speak with them?

Danlo was silent as he considered talking with the Narain people. To do this, as Isas Lel advised, he should not simply open his mind's mouth and let his words rain down like the voice of God out of the clouds, but rather he would do better to create a persona and cark out his selfness into the Field's onstreaming information flows. In other words, he must instantiate as a cybernetic entity, a kind of symbolic being who might possess as much presence and reality—within the Field—as a tiger who has leaped from a misty forest into a room crowded with people.

—You have instantiated before, haven't you?
—Yes.
—Then why not instantiate now?

As Danlo sat on his soft cushion in the meeting room, he listened to the almost countless voices keening across the Field that opened through his mind. He listened for the sound of his heart and breath, and he smiled to remember the etiology of the verb *to instantiate.* Once a time, as far back as the Anglish language spoken on Old Earth, *to instantiate* meant "to represent an abstraction or a universal by a concrete instance." Thus a sculptor, dreaming of the Holy Mother, might instantiate this beatific vision as a splendid ivory carving or a statue chiseled out of marble. Or a poet such as Narmada might instantiate the ideal of cosmic love in the *Sonnets to the Sun* and sing his verses to swarms of aficionados across the stars. Over time, however this meaning had changed. In truth, like a Scutari zahid shedding its skin, the meaning of this verb had been turned inside out. Now, on the Civilized Worlds, in most languages touched with the influence of the Cybernetic Universal Church, *to instantiate* meant "to represent a concrete instance of the material world as an abstraction having a reality all its own." In many peoples, but especially among the Narain Architects, this abstracting process meant representing real world objects as programs or as models in various kinds of cybernetic spaces. Thus the green and violet jungles of Alumit Bridge might be simulated as a light painting or as brilliant colors in the mind of a man interfacing the Field. Or a man himself—all the colors of pride, love, and hate that made up his very soul—might be encoded as a computer program and allowed to run with all the other millions of personhood programs running and interacting simultaneously within the Field. For the Narain, this was the very meaning and ideal of instantiation. What was reality, after all?

To the Narain, the Field's information flows, and the icons and encoded personae of human beings, were much more real than Alumit Bridge's swollen rivers or the many millions of people lying eyeless and alone in the tiny facing cells of their apartments. And so this inversion and the modern meaning of instantiation made good sense. To instantiate oneself in the Field was to make an appearance as an imago or icon, to cark out and come alive as a cybernetic entity possessing various degrees of presence. Indeed, the Narain programers have identified at least nine basic degrees of instantiation. (The cetics of Neverness define only seven degrees of instantiation, but their classification system is quite different, deriving as it does from the neurologicians of Simoom.) At the first degree, there is simple designation where one is identified by a name and where one's communications to others appear as words encoded alphabetically. There is voice and facement and personification. According to the programers, the degrees of instantiation are in fact degrees of realness or reality. There is the rather vegetable-like existence of full icon as well as the electrified animation of cathexis. And there is the blinding, blazing reality of facing a Transcended One in transcendence. Ultimately, of course, for any Architect, even the Narain, there is the timeless and ineffable state of vastening, where one's selfness is carked out into a computer's information field as pure glittering program and memory and nothing more. One day—and soon—Danlo would be the first man ever to interface the realm of vastened souls and return to the real world to tell of what he had seen.

—Pilot? Would you care to instantiate?
—If you'd like.
—Why don't we begin with facement, then? I believe that this would be the proper degree for envisaging so many people.

Quite formally, then, Danlo asked the Field's computers to instantiate him in facement. In only moments, an icon of his face—his fine, strong forehead cut with the lightning bolt scar, his hawklike nose, the childlike smile of his full lips, his deep blue eyes—would appear before anyone who wished to speak with him. There was a one-to-one correspondence between this icon and his real face. As he moved within the realspace of the meeting room so would his icon move and change expression; as he spoke, so would his icon speak, in words that were as clear as the utterances that poured forth from his marvelously human face.

"It . . . is an honor to be here."
Danlo spoke the first timeworn greeting that came to mind.

Even as the words left his lips, he smiled in embarrassment, for he knew that copies of his icon and these trite words would be instantly distributed to many thousands of people. All across Alumit Bridge, women and men lying in their facing cells would behold the icon of Danlo wi Soli Ringess and wonder why the Order had sent such a foolish man to meet them.

"It is we who are honored to meet you at last."

In the visual field of Danlo's mind, an icon appeared. It was the face of a young woman (or a womanman), soft, smooth, hairless—and wise in the ways of finding her path through cybernetic spaces. This icon spoke to Danlo about Ede the God and the exploding stars of the Vild; she told Danlo that she wished to cark out as a persona in a facilah painting and share a lifescape with him. In truth, she spoke for a great many people. In Iviunir and hundreds of other cities, there were many millions who instantiated as icons and hoped to meet Danlo face to face. While all of these people were privileged to view Danlo's bold and wild face, only one person at any moment might instantiate and appear in Danlo's presence.

This is a limitation of facement, in its distributive degree. It is the cost of being a luminary. Even though Danlo might wish to meet all who wished to meet him, common wisdom held this to be impossible. And so the Field computers' powerful sorting programs selected a few icons from all the millions of icons who wanted to share space with Danlo, and it was the cleverness of the Field programs to select icons that would ask a comprehensive array of questions. If the program was well written (as most of the Field programs were), then nearly all the Narain instantiating with Danlo should feel as if they had spoken with him directly:

"Is it true that most of the people on your world are strictly either men or women?"

"Doesn't it make people fall mad to live in a city open to the stars?"

"Can you tell us the doctrines of the Reformed Cybernetic Churches?"

"Do they cleanse the mind of memory and negative programs?"

"Are they a power among the powers of the Civilized Worlds?"

"What is it like to grow inside your mother's belly? What is it like to be born?"

"Have you ever sexed a woman?"

"Have you ever sexed a womanman?"

"Can you tell us about the whales?"

"Are the orcas truly mad?"

"Are there other religions in the city of Neverness?"

"Can you tell us more about the Way of Ringess?"

"What *are* the Elder Eddas, really?"

"Then many believe that your father became a god?"

"And others believe they too can transcend by following his path?"

"Can this be possible?"

"What path did he pursue?"

"Did he really cark his brain with computers?"

"Then was he in constant interface with his own private Field?"

"Did he fall mad facing himself?"

"What can it mean to be a god?"

"What can it mean to be a human being?"

"What can it mean to be God? What can anything mean?"

One by one, as the icons of women and men appeared in his mind, Danlo tried to answer these questions, insofar as they were answerable. After a while, however, he grew tired of this distributive degree of facement. Since, at any moment, many, many people could envisage his icon, he thought that it only fair that he should be able to behold each of theirs. In the contributive degree of facement, this would be so. It was an easy enough thing for the Field programs to allow various people to contribute their icons as a group with whom Danlo might converse. Among the Narain, this was often done. Of course, the human mind being limited as it was, these groups were rarely larger than seven or ten people. And so when Danlo faced the Field computers and requested a moment of full contribution, Isas Lel must have thought that Danlo was joking—or else that he had fallen mad.

—Pilot, do you know what you're asking?

Just then, Isas Lel's voice broke the flow of icons and the series of questions sounding in Danlo's inner ear.

—Yes, I think I know.

—*Full* contribution? No, no—that can't be allowed.

—But why not?

—Did you know that there were nine hundred seventy-six

million people in the facement space with you? Almost a
billion people, Pilot.
—So . . . many?
—Too many. More than a million times too many. No one
has ever faced so many people simultaneously in full con-
tribution.
—Then this will be the first time, yes?
—You don't understand.
—Is there a limitation in your computers, then?
—Of course not! But the arrays, the icons, the impossible
resolutions—it's dangerous to play with instantiation in
this way.
—Truly?

Isas Lel paused for such a long time that the silence in
Danlo's mind was like a sigh.

—The truth is, Pilot, since no one has ever faced so many
icons before, no one knows what the danger really is.
—Then there might truly be little danger.
—The danger is in not knowing.
—No . . . that is the joy.
—A billion people! Who would want to face so many?
—Then you will grant my request, yes?
—If that's what you really wish, then prepare yourself.

As Danlo sat in the darkened meeting room, he could see
neither the Transcendentals in their robots, nor the flowers in
their vases, nor the colors of the chatoy walls. In truth, he could
see nothing at all, outside or in, and neither could he hear any
voice or sound—save the breath moving through the inner flute
of this throat and escaping from his mouth. And then there came
a moment. His visual field was as dead and black as iron, and a
moment later there were lights. At first the lights were few in
number and soft, as of the pinks and lavenders of a flame globe.
And then the lights grew in intensity, and there were many more
of them. Each light was an icon of a human face, bright and
unique and full of expressiveness, and yet so tiny that it almost
vanished into a glittering point. Danlo gasped to behold this cube
of lights, arrayed in icons a thousand across and down, and a
thousand shining faces deep. There was a moment when he could
almost distinguish each of these brilliant points from every other,
and more, could almost see the hubris and hope and many other

emotions cut into each individual face. He could almost hear the
plaints and perplexities of a billion people asking him their questions all at once. And all this directly, from their minds to his,
without the filter of Field computers' ai programs to select and
display—and thus to subtly distort—the spirit of what they would
ask of him.

And then vastness of information overwhelmed him. The cube
of faces, the billion points of light, dissolved into a single, blinding flash that burned through his brain; the voices welled up into
a single voice that deafened him and swept over him and
drowned him in a great tidal wave of sound.

But only for a moment.

—Pilot, are you all right?

Again, in Danlo's mind, there was darkness and silence. Or
rather, there would have been silence except for the whine of Isas
Lel's worried voice.

—Pilot?
—I am all right.
—Are you sure?
—Yes, truly I am.
—I was afraid that you might have temporarily fallen mad.

At this Danlo smiled to himself. He directed a reassuring
thought at Isas Lel.

—I am not mad.
—Full contribution! What a dangerous, useless exercise
this was!
—Dangerous perhaps. But not useless.

In all the millions of questions that people had asked of him,
Danlo had sensed an underlying theme. If all the Narain's extra-
neous words could be boiled away, much as the tyfwi medicine is
extracted from the sap of yu trees, he thought that a single, essential question would remain: Is it really possible for human beings
to transcend to godhood, or is this merely the cybernetic dream
of a strange people isolated from the rest of the human race?

—Have you found a use for full contribution, Pilot?
—Perhaps.

—Please tell me.

—Perhaps I understand your people more deeply now.

—And what do you understand?

—It is hard to say.

—Please say it. Or think it.

—If you'd like. Your people want so badly to become more.

—You didn't **need to** experience full contribution to learn this.

—No, but . . .

—Please continue.

—There is this irony, then. When one lives only for the impossible, the possibilities of life become . . . so finite. So hideously limited. Your people fear this finity. Deep in their bellies, beneath the Field's dazzle, they fear that they are wasting their lives.

This observation of Danlo's, heartfelt though it might be, could not be expected to please Isas Lel. And so it did not. His words blazed in Danlo's mind like the flash of a laser canon.

—Do you believe that transcendence into godhood is *impossible?*

—Perhaps the movement godward is possible. I . . . truly do not know. But your people dream of something more.

—What, then?

—Transcendence itself. To be freed of their bodies, free of themselves. To live . . . free from life.

—But how should anyone want to live en getik when there is so much more?

—Is there? Truly?

—You'll soon see. If you're ready, it's time you faced a Transcended One. Your request, Pilot. Unless you've changed your mind, we'll instantiate at the transcendence degree.

—No, I have not changed my mind.

—Can I assume that you've experienced full simulation before?

—Yes. Many times.

—Very well. Then I must go away now. When we next meet, I shall be only a part of the One called Abraxax.

—The . . . Transcended One.

—Just so. Follow his voice. Please prepare yourself, Pilot.

Just then Danlo fell out of interface with the Field. He returned to his perception of the meeting room. He opened his eyes upon the seven dead-seeming men and women sitting in their robots, and at last he prepared to meet their higher selves, the Transcended Ones of Alumit Bridge.

CHAPTER 14

HEAVEN

*Once a time, I dreamt I was a butterfly, fluttering
hither and thither, to all intents and purposes a
butterfly. Suddenly I awakened. Now I do not know
whether I was then a man dreaming I was a butterfly, or
whether I am now a butterfly dreaming I am a man.*

—Chuang Tzu

As before, Danlo remained seated on the cushion in the meeting
room. As before he closed his eyes, and there was darkness,
stillness, silence. And then, inside him along his spine, there
came a faint vibrating as of electricity passing through him. It
was an unfamiliar, uncomfortable sensation. Did the Narain's
computers generate stronger logic fields than those of the library
in Neverness? He did not know. He surmised, though, that this
was the work of the neurologics behind the meeting room's
smooth walls. He fell into interface with the Field then, and its
powerful computers began to stimulate the nerves along his arms
and legs. He felt his liver and lungs and other organs begin to
tingle and burn, almost as if his body were being remade from
the inside out. There was a fire in his belly, a bright light in his
brain. He felt at once nauseated and exalted, almost trembling in
anticipation of some great change about to take place inside him.

. And then the Field computers touched his brain. They infused
him with shapes, colors, smells, textures, sound. He suddenly
opened his eyes to look down at his hand. And what he saw
astonished him. Although his hand still possessed the same structures of palm, knuckles, four fingers and a thumb, his skin
seemed to have transformed itself into some bright iridescent
substance as beautiful as chatoy or gossilk. He peered carefully
at his fingertips to make out the familiar whorls and lines that
should have been there. But there were no lines, no familiar print

patterns, only streaks of amethyst and scarlet and a hundred other
colors all swirling and dazzling him with their beauty.

This discovery so excited him that it seemed he could no
longer sit in stillness. He felt himself flying up from his cushion,
standing up straight as a man should stand. Only, he did not
really stand at all, but rather floated up to an erect, vertical posture. He felt as light as a thallow's feather in the wind; it was as
if the Field computers had cancelled gravity, utterly discon-
necting his bones and muscles from the pull of the Earth. In
truth, his body moved with such a lightness of being that it
seemed far beyond the limitations of common matter. He saw
that his clothes—his black pilot's robes—were gone. He was as
naked as a newborn child. And as with his hand, his whole body
sparkled like a diamond, from the fiery flecks of color flashing
within his feet to the deep violet hues of the hair hanging down
over his forehead.

To see himself transfigured in this way as a luminous being
was to recall a time when he had once smoked a huge pipeful of
triya seeds, one of the more visual psychedelics. Only the Field
computers' recreation of himself was much more total. This was
the power of full simulation. It was the power of creating a total
cybernetic self (or surreality) and tricking the brain and the
body's sensory organs into experiencing it as real. As a young
man, Danlo had feared mistaking the unreal for reality almost
more than he did death. And so he had sworn to master the
complexities of computer simulation. And so once again, gladly,
rashly, he dared to instantiate as a cybernetic entity, this time
carking out into the degree of full transcendence and entering
into an unknown world.

"Danlo wi Soli Ringess!"

He heard a voice calling him. He turned his head, trying to
determine its source. The radiance of his lovely new body was so
intense that it illuminated the meeting room. He could see all of
its surfaces quite clearly. The chatoy walls were now glowing a
dull red, and the desiccated flowers in the vase were as black as
dried blood. The seven Transcendentals sat in their robots with
their eyes tightly closed. Their skin was as white as marble, and
they seemed almost dead. No sound could have escaped their
motionless lips. "Danlo wi Soli Ringess!" the voice called
again. Danlo turned to see that the door of the meeting room was
suddenly—and mysteriously—open.

A golden light streamed through this doorway. It was so beautiful that he began to walk toward the light—and toward the

many voices that he heard whispering and calling from just beyond its threshold. He stepped closer, and then he realized that
he was not really stepping with his legs at all, but rather floating
in some weightless manner as a man drifting through space. Just
as he was about to pass through the doorway, he felt something
move deep inside him. It was almost like the rushing of his
blood, almost like the intense connectedness of tissue pulling
against living tissue that he remembered feeling as a child growing in his mother's womb so long ago. And even more it was like
music: deep, rhythmic, melodious, sacred, as if each cell in his
body were harmonizing in a marvelous, inner song.

He knew then that he was not really floating toward the open
doorway but still seated in the meeting room on the cushion that
he could almost feel beneath his knees. The powerful surreality
generated by the Field computers had almost completely seized
all his senses. He was blind to all but computer-painted colors,
deaf to all but the sound of voices that sophisticated programs
simulated and poured into his open head. With his tactile senses,
he should have been able to feel only what the Narain's powerful
computers programed him to feel. And this was almost so, for his
fingers tingled with intense luminousness, and they seemed to be
outstretched to the brilliant light pouring through the doorway.

But it was *not* really so. In reality, he sat holding his bamboo
flute tightly against his thigh; his fingers made of flesh that he
could not quite feel were wrapped around the flute's hard, round
finger holes. He sensed the truth of this. Deeper than his senses
of sight, hearing, smell, taste and touch lay his proprioceptive
sense, the inner body knowing of its own existence in space and
time. Proprioception was way the body sensed its own internal
stimuli, the firing of nerves, the movement of its cells, the deep
feeling of its own reality. In many ways it was the very sense of
the self, the deeply physical self of blood and bones which lay far
below the awareness of the mind. Of all the senses, it was the
most difficult to confuse. But the Narain were masters of simulation, and they had found ways to perturb even this marvelous
inner sense. Only because Danlo had honed his proprioceptive
powers as he would a diamond chisel was his sense of reality so
strong and keen. Many of his fellow Ordermen, upon entering the
saltwater cells of the library, had lost themselves in magnificent
surrealities, floating through these unreal cybernetic spaces as if
sucked into a dream. It was Danlo's pride, however, always to
know where in spacetime he was (and who he really was), always
to keep sight of the bright inner stars that guided his way. And so

now, here, in the meeting room of the Transcendentals, he moved toward the open door, but he did not really move at all. In truth, he was aware of existing in two ways of being at the same time; he fell into the dual consciousness of a hunter who enters the dreamtime of the altjiranga mitgina and sends his other self (his dreaming self) seeking seals or other animals across the frozen sea.

"Danlo wi Soli Ringess—this is where we really live."

At last Danlo stepped through the doorway. Before him, beneath him, a vast plain glittered like an endless sheet of gold. He gazed outward, looking for the horizon of this brilliant new world. But there was no horizon. Neither was there a sky above him, only a harsh white light glaring like a cold flame globe that has been turned on too high. The plain seemed to open into infinity in all directions.

Arbitrarily, he called the direction that he was facing north, while behind him—where the doorway opened into the meeting room—was south. The east was off to his right, and his left hand was held out against the glare of the western plain. As a child he had often prayed to the world's four points, and now he thought to turn slowly in a circle to reverence *this* world, no matter how surreal and strange it seemed. He began to face east, but in turning he noticed that the doorway behind his back was suddenly gone. He turned more quickly now, looking for this lost doorway, turning south, west, north, and east again in his urge to orient himself. And again he turned, and yet again, and now he was whirling about almost like a Sufi dancer, turning and seeking the way back to the meeting room where his real body lived and dwelt inside itself. But he could not find the doorway. At last, breathless and dizzy, he stopped his spinning. He had lost his sense of direction; the golden, featureless plain before him gave him no clue as to how he should proceed.

"Danlo wi Soli Ringess, we are waiting for you. You know the way."

From out of the east (or perhaps the west, north, or south) came a low, serene voice. Danlo decided to follow this voice. He turned to face the sound of it, and he began walking forward, step by step. Soon he grew impatient with his progress for he seemed not to be drawing any closer to the voice, which had now been joined by many others: "Danlo, Danlo, come, come—we are waiting for you."

Wishing to move more quickly, Danlo wished for skis to slide across the nearly frictionless golden substance beneath his feet.

He wished for any means to reach the source of the lovely voices reverberating in the distance, and with this wish he found himself suddenly fluttering like a butterfly above what he called the ground. He began to fly, slowly at first, but then faster and faster, as a goshawk might race through the sky. The wind blew fiercely at his face, whipping his long black hair behind him. If not for this cool wind, he could not have sensed that he was moving, for the plain below him was only an endless plate of gold and it bore no features by which he could measure the distance he traversed. And although he had no way to determine his true speed, he felt that he was still flying too slowly.

Then suddenly he began to accelerate. He shot across the golden plain like a rocket. The wind was now almost like a solid wall slamming against his face; he had to cup his hands over his nose and mouth in order to breathe. He remembered his first journey to Neverness then, calling to mind how the wind called the Serpent's Breath had frozen his face and almost killed him. He found himself wishing that there was no wind to impede his progress and steal his breath away. And suddenly there was no wind. All around him was only coldness and silence as if he were high in a planet's stratosphere. He thought that he must be soaring ten miles above the golden plain, but since it was as smooth as clary and as endless as the Greater Morbio, he might have been a million miles high—or only a few hundred feet.

After a while—perhaps it was an hour or only a few seconds—far off in the distance he noticed a slight swelling in the golden surface of the world. It was as if the intense light of the sky (or what he called the sky) had caused the ground to melt and buckle and heave itself upwards. Soon, in less time than it took to draw in a breath, he flew over this swelling. And now beneath him, there were other swellings, low and round like the domes of snow huts. As he flew, the swellings rose higher and there were many more of them. Hundreds of mounds pushed up above the glittering plain. Some were conical in shape like volcanoes; some were great heaps of gold cut with crags and cols, and these seemed almost as jagged as the snow-capped mountains of his childhood. He flew over broad valleys flowing with silver-gold glaciers. He flew and he flew, and the golden mountains grew higher and higher.

And still he heard voices calling him from far off in the hazy distance, and so he wished for yet more speed, and he moved faster still. Now the mountains melted into a golden blur below him. There were so many that he could not count them. He thought that he was moving quickly, very quickly, perhaps even faster than light. His body was all streaks of violet and maroon and flaming red. He felt limitless and marvelously quick, as light as light. In some sense, he could scarcely feel his body at all, for it was almost as numinous and insubstantial as a prayer in the mind of a saint. He might have continued this impossible flight forever, but then he remembered that his purpose in entering this cybernetic space was something other than pure, soaring ecstasy.

"Danlo wi Soli Ringess—you have almost found the way."

The sound of the voices now fell before him. In another moment, if he moved quickly enough, he might discover the source of these golden voices. And then, in the distance where the light of the world streamed off into infinity, perhaps a million miles away, there was a mountain higher than all the others. In the far light, it was all scarlet-gold and pointed like a spear cutting the heavens. So vast was this glorious mountain that it seemed the whole of the plain beneath it had been created merely to support its weight. It took Danlo only a few moments to draw nearer the mountain. He was moving much more slowly now. Once again he felt the wind smothering his face. Once again he could make out the ridges of the individual peaks of the lesser mountains below him.

"Danlo, Danlo, you are so close, come closer!" a voice called to him. Now he could clearly see that a range of high peaks lay between him and the great golden mountain. In only another moment he would crest this range of shield mountains and possibly discover who was calling him. Although he hated aspects of this surreality—its flatness of space and almost monotone colors—he felt curiously grateful that it didn't seem more real. He never forgot for a moment where he really was. And then with this thought, something strange happened.

All around him the plain of the world began to bend, curving down in on itself as of a hand closing into a fist. The sky, so even and hellishly white, suddenly popped outward and changed color. Now the sky looked like a true sky; it was domed like the vault of an Aslamic mosque and as blue as cobalt glass. The mountains— the shield mountains lined up like a great wall before him—were suddenly cut with sheer rock faces and capped with fields of ice and snow. Miles upon miles of broadleaf trees and evergreens carpeted their lower slopes. And then, a few moments later, he soared over these mountains. He dropped lower, down into a lovely valley. Now there were many colors, not only the green, white, and blue of vegetation, snow and sky, but the gray-brown tree trunks, red and purple flowers, orange fruits, and stones veined with turquoise, amethyst, and rose quartz.

Through the middle of the valley ran a swift, crystal-colored river fed by many streams which ran down from the shield mountains—and from the great mountain standing alone across the valley. This mountain no longer glittered like gold. Like the other mountains, it was covered with thick green forests and glazed with ice fields. But it was so vast and high that even its lower ridges disappeared into the clouds. Danlo wondered if it would be possible to climb this mountain; he wondered if its sharp rocks would cut his hands or if its deep snows would freeze his feet. Did a real summit of rock and ice lie pointing skywards somewhere far above the puffy clouds? He wondered if anything about this lovely valley would seem real if only he might touch it. In truth, he worried about this.

And then, as lightly as a butterfly, he floated down to a grassy meadow atop a low hill. The long green grass rippled in the wind and swished against his naked legs. It tickled his strange new skin that still shone with sparks of crimson and chrome and was as smooth to the touch as a pearl. The sun—high above the valley, high above the white mountains of the world—felt as warm upon his skin as any natural sun. It was a clean yellow sun, much like the bright sun that shined down upon Old Earth. As with any real sun, it was so brilliant with light that it was almost impossible to look at. For a long time, Danlo stood with his luminous hand outstretched to the luminous sun. He felt the hot, liquid joy of light pouring into him, running along his veins. And then, through the woods below the hill, he heard a deep voice calling him. It seemed very close, very familiar, very real.

"Danlo, Danlo—come to us, come to the mountain!"

Almost without thought, Danlo turned toward the great mountain across the valley. In that direction, below the meadow where the long grass gave way to the forest, there was an opening into the trees that looked like the beginning of a path. He decided to follow this path. He walked down the meadow, into the trees, and he felt the path's hardpacked soil beneath his feet. It took him winding through the thick woods, over streams strewn with boulders. The variety of trees and other plant life astonished him. He recognized elders and elms, thorn trees and mahogany and ailanthus, and many kinds of fruit trees: apple and olive and lemon, as well as cherry and papaya, mango and apricot and almond. There were shrubs such as oleander and mountain lilac and rose of Sharon. And magnolia and ninebark and photinia and coffee bushes and a hundred others. The smells of spearmint and hore-hound and other herbs were everywhere. And the flowers! There were so many flowers it seemed the whole woods had broken open in wild displays of color. Marigold, rhododendron, Afari-quian violet, lotus blossoms, cornflowers, fireweed, dahlia, blu-ets, orchids, snowdrops, roses—he thought that every flower that had ever blossomed might somewhere be growing in this magical forest. The perfume from these thousands of flowers was so in-tense that breathing was both a torment and a joy.

After some hours of walking, he came to the river running fast down the center of the valley. He was wondering how he might cross this beautiful river when he remembered that all through his childhood he had walked or skied upon the frozen waters of the ocean. Might it not be possible that the molecules of water before him would crystallize at need or somehow cohere to bear his weight?

And so almost without pause, he stepped out onto the river. The touch of the water upon his naked feet was wet and cold, and yet there was a strange feel to it, almost a resilience or tension to its surface. He seemed as light as an insect stepping across a still pond. In only moments, he made the crossing of the river. There the path continued through the woods, making its way upward through stands of teak and tamarind. It climbed higher and higher, occasionally bending or dipping down through orange groves or pines, but always cutting in the direction of the great mountain. Now the voices seemed to spill out from behind every bush, to float up from the lemongrass or the sorrel or the patches of pansies beneath the pretty rosewood trees.

"Come, Danlo, come—you are almost there."

The path grew suddenly steeper; for a mile or so, climbing up it was almost difficult. And then it crested one of the mountain's foothills. There the path finally gave out into a huge natural bowl scooped from the side of the mountain. Danlo loved the sense of openness all around him; he loved the clarity of the air, the clean smell of water spraying over stone. At the far side of the bowl, sheer granite rock faces glittered in the sunlight. Many waterfalls plumed down the rocks to the clear pools below.

It was here, around these deep and lovely pools of water that a group of luminous beings had gathered. They lay sunning them-selves on shelves of water-polished rock, or sat serenely in the nearby grassy meadows. A few of them stood below the trees of an apple orchard, picking heavy, round, red fruits. Each man or woman (their sex was hard to determine) looked much as Danlo looked, naked as a starchild, with long, lustrous bodies dancing with light. At the sight of Danlo's appearance among them, they held out their their long hands and beckoned to him. "Come, come," they called to him. "We've been waiting for you."

Danlo climbed up toward these wonderful beings, over sun-drenched rocks that burned his feet. Strangely, although he could feel this burning in his luminous flesh, there was no pain. Strangely, too, there was a quiet in the air. The impact of water falling onto the rocks and into the pools made much less sound than it should have. From the orchards and meadows and fields of bellflowers came a sweet singing—from the golden lips of beings such as Danlo as well as from the throats of larks and nightingales and other songbirds. He listened for the buzz of bees or perhaps grasshoppers chirping, but in all the woods that he had passed through, in all the emerald forest sweeping up the sides of the great mountain, he had heard no insect sounds. Neither, on his journey, had he seen any rabbits or snakes or other animals. He sensed that even in the deepest part of the forest, no tigers watched or waited. He thought that this was sad and strange, but he had no time to dwell on this strangeness for just then one of the luminous beings walked across a gleaming pool of water and came up to him.

"Danlo wi Soli Ringess," she said. "I am Katura Daru, of the city Iviohahn."

Her eyes were a lovely green, as bright as emeralds, and it seemed that a liquid red heat poured off her body. She laced her arms around Danlo's back, drawing him closer. She—with her wonderous skin wrapped around him like an electric eel, he had no trouble telling that she was a full woman—she kissed his mouth and opened herself to him. In truth, she invited him in. Everything about her pulled him deeper into the moment, calling him to an escatic merging of their flesh, perhaps even their minds and souls. He could almost feel what it would be like to go inside her, to flow in between her legs and disappear into the slip and glide of their glorious bodies. She would surround him and engulf him in the soft numinous tissues of her being, and he would cry out in indescribable passion, and it would almost be like mating with a woman whom he loved deeply, from the heart.

Almost.

He remembered, then, who he really was and why he had come to this impossible place. He was almost certain that he still sat alone on his cushions in the meeting room, holding his bamboo flute between his hands. With some difficulty, he broke away

from the woman who called herself Katura Daru. He stood naked
on a flat granite rock, marveling at her otherworldy beauty. For a
long time he looked at her—and at all the other luminous beings
who were standing about the flowers and the pools looking at
him.

"Katura Daru, I am Danlo wi Soli Ringess of Neverness," he
said, formally presenting himself. "You are a Transcended One,
yes?"

At this there came a soft laughter from the beings all around
him. Katura Daru laughed, too. Her smile was as bright as the
sun and her teeth gleamed like moonstones.

"No, oh, no," she said. "I'm only a woman as you are a man.
I've only instantiated here in the degree of transcendence as you
have, too."

"Then you are a Transcendental, yes? Only one . . . of
many who are One?"

"No, I'm not a Transcendental, either. Not quite yet."

"I am afraid . . . that I do not understand."

Again Katura Daru laughed, as did many of the others. Beneath the waterfalls there were hundreds of luminous beings
standing alone on the rocks or gathered into groups of two or
four or more. They laughed with clear, wonderful voices, and
there was no ridicule in them, no malice.

"I've been chosen to come here so that you *do* understand,"
she said.

She explained to Danlo that on the world of Alumit Bridge, in
Iviunir and Iviohahn and a hundred other cities, there dwelt many
Narain who had earned the chance to transcend themselves. And
so they were invited to instantiate as luminous beings and cark
out into this most highly sought of all the cybernetic spaces.
They too had found their way here across the golden plain and
the many thousands of paths through the forest. They too had
been called to the sparkling pools below the waterfalls. And here,
beneath a fine yellow sun, they met and talked and touched and
joined, one into one, one and one into two, the twos into fours,
and if they were skillful enough in the ways of overcoming themselves and merging into the higher wholes, someday after years
of soul work, they might claim at last to have transcended their
humanity. In their separate selves, as they wheeled about the dark
tunnels of their cities in their robots, these Narain would be re-
nowned as Transcendentals. But in their instantiation in the Field,
especially in this exclusive space called Heaven—in the union of

their many selves into something greater, someday it would be their triumph and glory to live only as the Transcended Ones.

"We're only human," Katura Daru said as she held her hand out to the others standing around the pools. "But someday we'll evolve."

"I see. You will evolve into Transcended Ones, yes?"

"That is our work."

"And do the Transcended Ones help you with this work?"

"Oh, yes—that is part of *their* work."

"I had thought that it was the Transcended Ones who called me to this place," Danlo said.

"But of course it was."

"Truly?"

"The Ones call all who are ready to come to them."

"They call people here, but they do not live here themselves?"

"But of course they live here. We all live here, if we can."

"Are the Transcended Ones invisible, then?"

"No, they aren't invisible."

Danlo looked to the right, then to the left. He looked at the trees, the rocks, the fine mist thrown up into the air from the crash of the waterfalls. He saw the sun burning through this mist, and lovely rainbows, but there were no beings who appeared any different from Katura Daru or himself.

"And where are these Transcended Ones, then?"

"They live higher up the mountain."

"I see. Then is it possible to go where they live?"

"No, it's not possible."

"I see."

"We must wait for them to come to us."

"Wait . . . how long?"

"Not long, Danlo wi Soli Ringess. They're coming now, to meet you."

"Truly?"

"They're coming here."

"Will I know them when I see them?"

"Of course."

"What do these Transcended Ones look like then?"

"They look like themselves," she said. "They look beyond themselves."

"I see," Danlo said, though he did not really see at all.

"They look like *that*. Do you see? Over there—*that* is what they are."

So saying, Katura Daru pointed above the waterfalls higher up the mountain. Danlo turned to follow the line of her finger, and his eyes drank in an astonishing sight. There, from over the rim of the rock faces, from out of the forests and the lower clouds, many beautiful balls of light appeared and began falling slowly through the air. They floated down without wings, as light as butterflies, as lovely as pearls. There were thousands of these lights. Some of them seemed the size of a dolphin, though a few were almost as large as the whales that swam through the cold oceans beyond Neverness Island. All were spherical in shape, and all shone like rainbows as if the substance of their beings was the same as Danlo's own luminous body. But even the dullest of these Transcended Ones shone more brightly than did Danlo or Katura Daru or anyone else waiting by the pools. To look at them was to marvel at the colors, the bands of purple and orchid pink, the flaming crimson whorls, the unique striature of diamond blue or lavender or ultramarine that marked each ball of light as different from the others. In truth, some of the larger lights were almost impossible to behold. They burned as brightly as starbursts, and looking at them was like looking at the sun. Down the mountain they came in their thousands of colors, floating down near the rock faces, touching the cold water of the falls. It seemed that they were coming straight toward Danlo. Their sudden appearance caused great excitement in Katura Daru and the others. They gathered by the pools and turned their faces toward the spheres of light falling down from the sky. They faced the Transcended Ones of Alumit Bridge: their sisters, their brothers, their fathers, their mothers, their masters, their gods.

"He has come," Katura Daru said to them. She stood with her hand half-covering her eyes as she spoke to the Transcended Ones. "Danlo wi Soli Ringess has come here to face you."

Now the lights fell down and converged in the space above the pools. They hung in the air like flame globes packed too closely together, but Danlo saw that none of them actually touched any other. Just above the pool at Danlo's feet, nine of the largest and brightest of the Transcended Ones gathered in a half circle that shone like a crescent moon. The light of their beings burned his eyes. Because he could not look at them directly, he stared down at the mirror-like pool before him and studied their glorious reflections.

Wecome, Danlo wi Soli Ringess. We meet again at last.
May I present myself? I am the One called Abraxax.

A strong, deep voice rolled over the pools and filled the air. It might have been difficult to determine the source of this golden voice, but as it sounded, one of the spheres in the crescent near Danlo flared almost like a star-falling nova. This, then, he thought, must be the higher self of Isas Lel Abraxax. Somehow, the flame of Isas Lel's mind had joined with those of his meld mates to form the ball of light floating above the pool.

And may I present Maralah, Tyr, Manannan, and Kane?

At the mention of these Transcended Ones' names, the lights nearest Abraxax flared more brightly for a moment. It was their way of bowing, Danlo thought. He remembered that the quiet Diverous Te was one of the Maralah quad while Kistur Ashtoreth shared transcendence in Manannan.

And Orunjan, El, Inari, and Shahar?

One of the Transcended Ones, to the far left of Abraxax, sparkled with a lovely display of cobalt and crimson lights. This was Shahar, an elevenplex who was almost as famous as Abraxax himself. Lieswyr Ivioss was of Shahar, and Danlo could almost feel her presence in the way the lights flickered on and off, making unique patterns that beguiled him and somehow called him closer.

And this is Aesir, Narsinh, Varah, and Arawn, and Sha-mash, Rahu, Ninlil, Rhea . . .

Danlo scarcely listened to these names as Abraxax presented each Transcended One hovering above the pools. As there were some 4,084 of these glorious beings waiting to meet Danlo, the presentations took much time. But time, in the cybernetic space called Heaven, is strange. Danlo spent most of this time staring at the splendid lights of Shahar, and hours were as minutes, and in only moments, it seemed, each of the Transcended Ones had been honored and named.

We are gathered here to decide if Danlo wi Soli Ringess should act as our emissary to Tannahill. Or, failing that, whether we should aid his journey there in showing him Tannahill's star. We have asked Danlo wi Soli Ringess to instantiate here so that he might face us directly and make his plea.

With this, the voice of Abraxax fell silent. Above the pools facing Danlo each of the thousands of light spheres floated patiently. And Katura Daru and the other luminous beings such as Danlo stood or sat or reclined on their rocks, and they were silent, too. They waited for Danlo to speak. They had come to hear his words, and more, they waited for Danlo to blaze with an inner truth and reveal the naked face of his being.

"The starfields of the galaxy are vast," Danlo began. For a moment, it seemed that he was almost a true man, almost an incarnate being of flesh and bone. As he spoke, he could feel the sounds of his words vibrating in his throat. His voice left his lips and carried out across the rocks and the pools; it was almost as if he were standing in a public ice ring on Neverness addressing a swarm of real people.

"Vast are the light-distances, and the number of stars is almost uncountable, and yet the death of a single star casts a terrible light on all the others. A splendid light, truly, but a killing light, too—a light that someday will fall on every city of every planet, everywhere. And in the Vild, so many stars. There may be millions of them. Millions of stars, dying, exploding, falling into supernovas. All these stars being killed. We now know why. We know of the Old Church, on Tannahill. It is there that my Order would make a mission. It is there that I must journey if I can."

Danlo went on in a like manner for a long time. Most of what he said to the Transcended Ones was not new. And all of what he said, in words, might have been spoken while he knelt on his cushion in the meeting room, with Isas Lel and Kistur Ashtoreth and Shahar and all the other Transcendentals watching him. They easily—and faithfully—might have transmitted his message to the Transcended Ones gathered here. But Danlo had wanted to face the Transcended Ones in the flesh, so to speak. He had wanted to give them more than just his words. It had been his hope to stand before them much as a man, to look at them eye to eye and open his heart to them. Only, these Transcended Ones were as eyeless as firestones, and they burned so brightly that he could not even look at them. And he himself, as an instantiated and luminous entity, had no heart. Search though he might in the center of his new being for the heart rhythms so familiar to him, he could feel almost nothing.

"And the rate of increase of the Vild's spaces is possibly

exponential. If the Vild were to expand into the galactic core where the stars are densest, possibly a chain reaction of supernovas might be set off. It is possible that the whole galaxy . . ."

As Danlo continued, he sensed that the thousands of Transcended Ones were indeed concentrating on more than just his words. Somehow, he thought, these brilliant and eyeless beings were staring at *him*. He looked down at his long, naked hands, then. The bits of color flashing there continually changed both in pattern and intensity. Was it possible that information as to Danlo's cybernetic self was encoded in these shifting patterns? Might not the Transcended Ones penetrate his thoughts and emotions as easily as a cetic reading fear from the sweat on the palms of a man's hands?

Often, ever since entering the Order, Danlo had wondered how much of one's deep self might be preserved in the programs and the process of instantiating into the cybernetic spaces. How could such essential qualities as the terrible coldness of snow or a mother's fierce love for her child (or a man's hatred of himself) ever be rendered into symbols, models, or instantiations carked out into the glittering neverness of the Field?

The Narain, of course, believed that instantiation as a cybernetic entity was *the* way to free the essential self from all those parts of their being that they reviled as carnal, animal, illusory, limited, and much too alive. Their collective dream was one of higher life, a truer life, and they held that it was *only* the truest and realest self that survived instantiation into facement or full icon or any of the higher degrees. A man's feeling for his own life and his deepest consciousness, they said, was mostly a fiction. Could this truly be possible, Danlo wondered? Could it be that his deepest self was truly faceless like an ice sculpture melting in a warm wind or a hibakusha caught looking at a nuclear blast?

I cannot see them, Danlo thought. *And if I cannot see them, how can they truly see me?*

After Danlo had finished making his plea to the Transcended Ones, Maralah, Rhea and a fourplex named Bodhideva asked him about his Order, his education, his childhood among the primitive Alaloi tribes. They wanted to know the feeling of his love for mathematics, as well as his deeper love for the woman Tamara Ten Ashtoreth. Carefully, almost gently, they questioned his hate of killing, his hate for his former friend Hanuman li Tosh, and most of all, his hate of the act of hatred itself. In truth, they wanted to know everything about him. Danlo sensed that these Transcended Ones could hear his thoughts almost before he spoke them. Their computers could look into the language centers of his brain and record the patterns of the neurons as they fired in clouds of crimson light. Some of the time, they might identify individual thoughts in these pretty patterns. And their computers could track the electrochemical impulses as they ran along the nerves leading from the brain into the muscles of the tongue and throat, and thus they could predict which words he would speak.

And so they could read the surface of his mind, but Danlo sensed that this electronic telepathy could not penetrate to his deeper thoughts, or touch his memory in any way. This willful limitation of scanning technology was part of the Transcendent Ones' ethics. For each of them—indeed for any of Narain instantiating into the Field—one's mind was as sacred as a temple. A man or woman should share with others only those parts of himself that he wished to share. And these parts were most often only the virtuous ones: the clever ideas, the noble thoughts, the harmonious emotions, the three essential elements of the self that the Narain identified as goodness, truth, and beauty.

How little they see of me, Danlo thought. *How little they truly wish to see.*

Some of the Transcended Ones, however, saw him perhaps more clearly than he might have imagined. Or rather, they saw him more hopefully; they focused upon those aspects of his character and talents that they hoped would make him an ideal emissary to the Architects of the Old Church. They argued for telling him the location of Tannahill. But other Transcended Ones seemed undecided. To entrust their fate to this strange man from the stars was almost beyond their powers of affirmation.

For a long time, the Transcended Ones engaged in a vehement debate as to what they should do. Some—such as Aesir, Ninlil, and Shahar—vehemently opposed telling Danlo anything about Tannahill. Their strong emotions could be perceived as pulsings of ruby color that rippled just beneath the surface of their round, radiant bodies. And then Shahar, who had hitherto almost shrieked her objections to pointing Danlo's way toward the Old Church, seemed to make an abrupt turn of heart. She decided to display her reasonableness. And so she turned the light of her being so that it shined upon Danlo's face, and made an astonishing proposal.

We invite Danlo wi Soli Ringess to share in our One. We

would like to know him better, from the inside of his
mind and ours. Only then will we know if we should
show him the star that he desires to see.

Shahar further promised that if Danlo could persuade her of
his worthiness, she would champion his cause to the other Transcended Ones, particularly to Ninlil and Siva and their numerous
confederates who strongly opposed telling him *anything* about
Tannahill. Although in many ways this suggestion made obvious
sense, her openness toward inviting Danlo into herself shocked
the usually serene Transcended Ones. It was almost as if she
were a singleton woman proposing to mate with an alien—or a
dog.

Will you share with us, Danlo wi Soli Ringess?

For a long moment there was silence above the pools, and
Katura Daru and the many luminous beings who had not yet
gone beyond themselves looked upon Danlo with both envy and
awe. The 4,084 Transcended Ones, however, did not move; they
hung in the air as motionlessly as stars on a winter night.
Abraxax and Maralah and Manannan and Tyr—they each waited
in a brilliant silence that fell over Danlo like a net of woven of
light.

"Yes," Danlo said in his bold, clear voice. But his belly felt
queasy, almost as if he had eaten a piece of bad fish. "I will
share your One."

Then please come in.

Danlo, dwelling in his luminous body above the rocks of a
bubbling pool, stared at Shahar for a long time. Then he smiled
at the strangeness of what he was about to do, and he bowed
before taking his first step toward this glittering Transcended
One.

THE ONE

The unreal never is; the real never is not.
—from the Bhagavad Gita, 2.16

The ball of light that was Shahar separated itself from the other Transcended Ones and floated closer to Danlo. It hovered in the air only inches above the surface of a large, flat, wet rock. Somehow Danlo understood that he was to walk toward this light as he would move toward an open doorway. This he did, stepping carefully over the slick rock. The light of Shahar was so intense that he approached her with his hand held over his forehead to shield his eyes. Closer to her he came, and something about this great Transcended One opened, even as a whale's mouth might open. In truth, Shahar was as large and lovely as a killer whale, and perhaps she was as fierce, as forceful, as wild.

Is it so hard to share, Danlo wi Soli Ringess?

Danlo took the last step toward Shahar, and it was like stepping down into a clear pool of water. Or rather, it was like flying upward into a rainbow. In truth, as Danlo stepped into the blazing being called Shahar, his metaphors almost failed him. For a moment, the luminous tissues of his body melted into hers, and it was as if he had drunk from a wine bottle full of liquid light. He might have become lost in this intoxicating rush of light, but then he remembered who he really was and how he had come to be here.

This is the trap that the Ede warned me of, Danlo thought. *This golden light is the honey, and I am the bee.*

Danlo closed his eyes, then, and struggled to remember that his true self was still sitting on the little red cushion in the Transcendentals' meeting room. And there on the seat of a bright plastic robot, the true self of Lieswyr Ivioss sat too, and as for the other Transcendentals who shared the Shahar eleven, somewhere on the planet of Alumit Bridge, they each sat in other meeting rooms or lay in their apartments' darkened cells, thinking their individual thoughts, feeling their individual feelings. And even as Danlo had instantiated in the Field as an individual entity, so it was with them. But since they were each one of many who were One, upon carking out into this golden cybernetic space, their individuality had instantly melted away. On the great mountain above the waterfalls, they had met and melted and merged into the One called Shahar. They shared their thoughts, dreams, emotions. They *completed* each other's thoughts, even as they sculpted their individual selves to complement each other's temperaments. And so their sense separateness vaporized like icicles under a hot sun, and they fused together into this glittering sphere of light.

Shahar is devious, Danlo thought. *But she would rather conceive of herself as subtle, brilliant, sublime.*

At last, Danlo opened his eyes. He beheld Shahar from the inside, where the light of her being appeared less brilliant and no longer blinded him. Indeed, now that he could see again, he became aware of the other beings who made up the substance and soul of Shahar. There were eleven of these Transcendental beings, each one instantiated into a form as luminous and varicolored as his own. He recognized Lieswyr Ivioss from the blazing scarlet hues of her passion and pride. Other Transcendentals were associated with other names. These were Germana Pall, Sul Iviastalir, Ivria Tal, Maral Astroth, Adal Dei Chu, Husmahaman, Atara ivi Chimene, Duncan Iviwich, Ananda ivi Sitisat, and Ordando Ede.

Names, however, within the burning boundaries of Shahar's oneness, were not important. What mattered were the higher qualities of the self, the various strands of goodness, truth, and beauty which each one could bring here and weave together to create their Transcended One. This making of a higher whole from many parts was a continual work of art. In some sense, Shahar would never be finished or complete; she was an evolving entity whose soul could only grow like a Fravashi tapestry, infinitely in all directions, strand by golden strand.

And I am here to add to this weaving, Danlo thought. *For a moment or forever.*

Lieswyr Ivioss and her ten meld-mates seemed to be weaving Shahar's brilliance with the movements of their glittering bodies.

They flitted about like butterflies, darting, whirling, diving, hovering, and always flying together in a cloud of light. Theirs was an intricate dance: wingless, weightless, almost timeless. At any moment, two of them such as Ivria Tal and Maral Astroth might be mating. This sharing did not occur sexually and animalistically, as of a man's lingam entering the yoni in the heat of passion, for none of the luminous beings—including Danlo himself—seemed to bear between their legs anything so crude as sexual organs.

Rather, they joined body to wraithlike body, the evanescent tissues of their beings running together as if they were amoebas who had opened their outer membranes to each other and let their cytoplasm flow together and merge into a single fluid. When a mating was successful, the two (or sometimes three) actually disappeared into one: a single womanman enlarged and deepened and blazing ever more intensely, whose iridescent hands were as long as a Bodhiworld exemplar's, whose eyes radiated light like double suns. Thus, at any moment, within the blazing sphere called Shahar, there might exist only ten individual beings, or nine, or sometimes only eight or seven or six. When Shahar was most completely herself, her eleven separate ones would merge utterly into One—the Transcended One that called to Danlo with a voice like honeyed wine and pulled him inward, as if he were only a lost pilot falling down toward the almost infinite gravity of a blue giant star.

How can I be with so many? Danlo wondered. *How can I be one with so many who are already One?*

Indeed, it is always hard to join with others. The Narain Transcendentals labored for a lifetime to achieve their desired unities. In the sculpting of the soul—in the complementarities of goodness, truth, and beauty—the complexities of union increased almost exponentially with each new being who came into a One. Thus the difficulty increased, too, but so did the joy. And joy, he thought, was what the Narain really lived for.

They will try to trap me with joy, Danlo thought.

Because Shahar and other Transcended Ones did not trust him to journey to the Architects of the Old Church, they would try to keep him on Alumit Bridge (or rather, seduced within its glittering Field) in the only way that they could.

But what kind of joy?

Almost certainly, he thought, there was the joy of the meeting room's very real logic fields pulling at his brain. Its computers would be programmed to stimulate his neurons, to trigger the

release of endorphins, epinephrine, serotonin, and the other manifold chemicals of consciousness. Soon, perhaps, would come a
moment of neurotransmitter storms and mind-lightning and that
wholly artificial bliss that he knew as electronic samadhi. Or
perhaps the Narain would not need to rely on such crude and
mechanical techniques. Danlo sensed that the telepathy they
shared through Shahar would be intoxicating and profound and
would induce the most melting of ecstasies.

—Danlo of the stars, you must let us in.

—I have nothing that I would hide.

—You must let *yourself* into us.

—Like this?

—Almost. But first you must let go of yourself.

—My self?

—You must let go of your fear. Your deep hatreds and your
pull toward despair. All your negative emotions—you must
let these go.

—But aren't these passions part of myself?

—They're only part of Danlo of Neverness. They must
never be part of Danlo of Shahar.

—Truly not?

—We must keep Shahar pure. Only when goodness, truth,
and beauty are perfectly integrated may we achieve the
highest quality.

—This quality is just pure joy, yes?

—Almost. But joy is really part of beauty; it's only one of
the higher qualities.

—Then you seek a transcendent quality. Higher than joy.

—Infinitely higher.

—The quality that is beyond all qualities?

—You almost understand.

—You seek the quality that is . . .

— . . . beyond itself and all things that are . . .

— . . . perfect in itself and reflects . . . .

— . . . worldly things for it is . . .

— . . . love . . .

— . . . only pure love . . .

— . . . within itself like a mirror . . .

— . . . that is beyond love . . .

— . . . held up to itself and reflecting only love . . .

— . . . love love love . . .

For a moment, as Danlo lost himself in electronic telepathy with the One called Shahar, he became aware of someone swimming in the same stream of consciousness as he. This other—or others—added to his thoughts and sometimes completed them. Likewise, he touched her thoughts as well. And yet, while his thoughts remained *his* thoughts even as those of the other could only be other, together they created a unity of mind beyond their separate selves. This fusion of their mentations reminded him of a Fravashi fugue, in which many Old Fathers would gather to sing their beautiful songs, continuously interweaving melodies as they might the golden and silver threads of a tapestry. And what would emerge—almost miraculously—was a single, splendid song, rich in individual colors and motifs, and yet complete in itself, in its movement toward one overarching and transcendent theme.

Love is the secret of the universe, Danlo thought. At least, he *thought* that he thought this, all of himself, of his own mind. Though, in truth, with the consciousness of eleven others pouring into him like streams of golden light, it was growing almost impossible to know which thoughts were truly his own.

Love is the purpose of life.

Somewhere above the pools and the waterfalls cascading down the great mountain, the shining sphere called Shahar floated in the air. And *inside* Shahar, Danlo floated, too, and eleven other beings of light flew all around him and near him (and through him), touching his arms and chest, slipping their luminous fingers across the pearly smoothness of his body, his neck, his face. It was hard for him to see these beings just as they were, for the colors of their flesh flowed in iridescent pulses, red into violet, orange into gold, and nothing about their tone or form held still for very long. One of them he thought he recognized as Lieswyr Ivioss.

But as for the others, as he drank in the radiance of their subtle, quicksilver shapes, it was impossible to tell what they looked like in real life. Of course, in the real world, in the lesser world of rocks and trees and plastic rooms, this embarrassment of eating and excreting and breathing that they called the getik, how they looked scarcely mattered. They might be young or old, thin or fat, ugly or fair—but here, in the Field, in this glittering cybernetic space called Heaven, they would instantiate only as brilliant and beautiful beings.

As *perfect* cybernetic beings. They were perfect in their forms, yes, but more important, they had pruned and purged

themselves so that only the purest inner qualities remained. It
was only these qualities, these refined selves that they allowed to
instantiate into the Field. And so in a sense, the Lieswyr Ivioss
who floated near Danlo touching his sable and scarlet hair was
not the same hard, angry, scornful Transcendental of the meeting
room. She was something less, but also something more. Gone
was her diffidence, her penchant toward violence of feeling. She,
as her cybernetic self, had transcended these baser emotions.
Anger had become willfulnesss, and scorn elevated to discern-
ment. Her hardness of character had deepened into strength.
These last were the positive, approved qualities.

In the ancient downs system of organizing the positive aspects
of the self, there were many, many qualities, and all of these
could be located on a great wheel divided into thirds, as of
sections of a pie. One section (this was usually color coded as
yellow or gold) was given over to those qualities related to goodness, while the other trisections arranged the component qualities
of beauty and truth. The wheel was a metaphor for the perfecting
of the self. Looking inside the fiery emotions and genius of one's
own soul was like moving within this wheel. The farther out on
the wheel one drifted, the farther away from the quintessential
qualities that all the Narain strove for. But as one moved inward,
various subqualities such as responsibility and authenticity would
fuse into full qualities such as trustworthiness. And trustworthiness, fairness, and integrity would in turn come together into the
higher quality of honesty. And honesty, along with wisdom,
courage, faith, and freeness, was only one element of truth.
Goodness, beauty, truth—these were the three highest qualities,
and together they encircled the wheel's core like the coils of a
serpent winding around a tree. Or a heart. At the wheel's mystical center, as red as blood, was just pure love. Love was the one
quality beyond all qualities, the pure essence of being that all the
Narain hoped to realize within themselves.

Love is the purpose of love.

As Danlo floated near the center of Shahar, the fingers of
Lieswyr Ivioss and the others brushed his body like so many
fronds of seaweed. He touched their minds, and waves of love
swept through him. He couldn't tell whether this powerful emotion was the result of merging minds or its cause. He couldn't tell
if it was real or only the effect of the meeting room's computers
manipulating the chemicals of ecstasy within his brain. He almost didn't care. So intense was his feeling for Germana Pall and
Ivria Tal and all the others of Shahar that his body burned as if

he had been plunged into a vat of molten gold and his brain was afire as with starlight. He was very close to letting go of himself, to merging completely with Shahar, even as a block of ice melts into a warm tropical sea.

Love beyond love beyond . . .

—Danlo of the Stars, let yourself in.

Deep in the throes of a love beyond human love, Danlo realized a thing. If he were to win Shahar to his mission of journeying to Tannahill, he *must* let himself into her utterly, to let his dream become one with hers. But in so doing, the pleasure and the temptation to remain forever would be too great. Like the ancient lotus eaters of Old Earth, he would lose his will toward his fate; he would lose his very purpose.

I will lose my dream, he thought. *I will lose myself.*

He realized another thing, then. Lieswyr Ivioss and Husmahaman and Adal Dei Chu and all the other Transcendentals of Shahar (and of Alumit Bridge) were afraid of becoming lost, too. The surrender of their separate selves was their greatest joy but also their greatest terror. And so in merging into a Transcended One, like a Summerworld merchant holding back a handful of gold coins from the tax collector, each Transcendental would always secrete some vital part of herself.

This was the failing of their ideal of perfection. Goodness, truth, and beauty all women and men sensed within their souls, but they were also full of flaws, and they lived the worst of lies, and sometimes it was a terrible beauty that called to them from deep inside. In truth, it was almost impossible to rid oneself of only the negative qualities. The very act of the self-slashing at the self and willing itself to go away only reinforced it, redefined it, made it stronger. This was why no group of Transcendentals had ever merged completely.

They do not truly expect me to lose all of myself, he thought. *Only enough so that I become love-drunk and lost within the One.*

It was clear that if Shahar had her way, he would be like a foolish young man who opens the door and stumbles into a room stocked with an infinite number of wine bottles. And helplessly he would drink bottle after bottle, remaining always drunk (and always a fool) forever.

If a fool would persist in his folly, he remembered, *he would become wise.*

He closed his eyes, then, and a perfect picture of the downs wheel in all its colors came into his mind. He could clearly see that foolishness was not one of the positive qualities. Nor was wildness. Once, he remembered, his friends had called him Danlo the Wild for they supposed that he lived without fear and would dare almost any act no matter how reckless or dangerous. But his friends had been wrong. He had his fears as did any sane man. And of these fears the deepest and perhaps only *true* fear was that of mistaking the unreal for the real. Thus his prowess in entering any computer-generated surreality and never becoming lost. Thus his pride that he of all men always knew exactly where he was and who he was—and what he really was.

Truly, I am afraid, he thought.

Somewhere, inside his real self, his belly quivered with acid and fear. But a true wild man, he told himself, would feel his way through this fear by facing it to see what was there. A true man must always face himself, must always look fearlessly on the wildness that blazed inside. This he promised himself he would always do. And so at last he opened his eyes. Out of pure wildness, he let go of himself. He watched the luminous tissues of his body pulling apart and separating into colors, as of light shined through a prism. He felt himself as ten thousand strands of light, unravelling, spinning away from himself, onstreaming, interfusing with the brilliant inner illumination of Shahar.

The pleasure was indescribable. And so was the terror. He was breathing hard and sweating, and somewhere, inside his chest, he could feel his heart pounding like a fist upon an iron door. He was dying and willing himself to die, but worst of all, when he was reborn, it would be as a glittering, cybernetic being who might or might not be real.

To live, I die—even as he began to dissolve utterly into the light of Shahar, he remembered these words of his father. To become himself he must first lose himself. This was the paradox of his existence. This was foolishness or deep wisdom, he couldn't tell which.

I am not I.

There was a moment when he was less than a steamy breath of air vanishing into the wind—and yet almost infinitely more. All that he was as pilot and man he brought into Shahar. He brought his honesty, his courage, his playfulness, his verve. He brought goodness, truth, and beauty; he brought his love. In utter wildness he brought his darker emotions, even as an owl might clutch a writhing snowworm in its talons. He brought his memories. Of course all Transcendentals, when they merge into a One, carry with them the record of all that has happened to them as instantiated entities within the Field. It is considered bad form, however, to burden one's meld mates with memories of their other life of the getik. And more, all the occurrences of this mundane life are thought to be irrelevant to the much vaster life of a Transcended One.

But Danlo did not know this, and so he brought to Shahar diamonds and rubies and firestones and pearls. Freely, he gave her his memory of the first time that he had seen snow; he gave her his memory of loving fire and wind and sky and the woman named Tamara Ten Ashtoreth whom he thought was forever lost. He gave her his hatred of Hanuman li Tosh, too, along with his hatred of himself in falling into hate at all. Once a time—it seemed long ago—he had dived deeply down inside himself into a clear remembrance of the Elder Eddas, and he gave these genetic memories to Shahar as well.

And when he had given all this emotion, mind, and memory, there was nothing left of him. He could no longer feel his body, neither his luminous instantiated form nor his real body seated on the red cushion in the meeting room. He no longer knew what was real. He no longer cared. All about him was a dazzling white light which floated motionless like snowflakes frozen in space-time. And then he realized that this light was not outside him at all, but rather *inside,* where he and all the terrible radiance of Shahar were finally one.

I am not I.

He realized that this was true, and yet the very fact that he could make this realization meant that his consciousness had not completely gone away. Strangely, he seemed to be more intensely conscious of himself than he had ever been. In some ways, he seemed to be more truly himself, like a flame that has found its home in a sun-dried forest. His purpose in journeying to Tannahill and finding a cure for the disease that was killing his people still remained. Or rather, he became aware that this purpose was only part of a greater cosmic imperative to journey to all places in the universe and to find the cure for the suffering of all things.

A word came into his mind, then. It struck like a lightning bolt through him, and lit up the minds of Lieswyr Ivioss and Adal Dei Chu and the others who were part of the greater mind of Shahar. The word was *ananke*. This was a Fravashi term for the universal fate to which even the gods must yield. Of course,

all beings rush toward their individual fates like moths into a
flame, but this was not ananke—not unless a man had completely
surrendered his life to the fate beyond fate. Only then would his
purpose be one with the greater purpose of the universe. Only
then would his true purpose (and himself) eternally remain.

I am only I, Danlo remembered. *I am always I.*

There was a moment of blinding light when Danlo died into
Shahar and all the others of this Transcended One died into him.
There was a moment when he knew that he was still alive and
that he would always live. He knew other things, too. In giving
everything to Shahar, he received everything in return. As if the
lid to a treasure chest had suddenly been flung open, all that was
in her mind was revealed to him. All at once there were silver
cups and glittering gold rings, and he suddenly knew the minds
of Atara ivi Chimene, Duncan Iviwich, Ordando Ede—and eight
other Transcendental women and men. One of them—Ananda ivi
Sitisat—knew precisely where in the Field's information pools
the location of Tannahill might be found. Each of the ones of
Shahar were masters at delving through the Field's information
spaces. All the knowledge of the Narain people was Shahar's;
this was her collective memory, which she might access whenever she needed to solve a problem or contemplate the mysteries
of the universe.

I am a god.

Danlo would never be able to tell how much time he spent
merged with Shahar. It seemed almost like years. For countless
moments he lived the life of a Narain god, and he suddenly knew
that he could move about this cybernetic space completely at
will. He had memories of these cybernetic movements. He could visit any
land of the golden plain at a thought, instantaneously, discontinu-
ously, much as a light ship can fall from star to star without first
passing along the line of endless empty space. Unlike the luminous beings who only visited Heaven in hopes of someday going
beyond themselves, the Transcended Ones were unconstrained by
any natural (or unnatural) laws. Indeed, Shahar and Abraxax and
Manannan and Kane *made* the laws by which Heaven existed and
was sustained. They made and remade the very substance of
Heaven. This is what the gods of Alumit Bridge did for amusement when they weren't busy thinking. They created impossibly
high mountains and waterfalls and forests and butterflies and
birds—all in the spirit of play. They played for the sake of play
alone, and their only concern was the ultimate evolution of their
game.

I am Danlo wi Soli Ringess.

Danlo remembered himself, then. Having accomplished the almost impossible feat of keeping true to himself while in full transcendence, he remembered that it was time to return to his existence as a man. And so, with all the force of his will, he separated himself from the brilliance of Shahar. It was almost the hardest thing that he had ever done. But as he had come, so must he go. He willed the sphere of Shahar to open to him, and like a hole puncturing an iridescent water bubble, or like a hole in his soul, an opening appeared. He willed himself to walk through this hole. To walk, to fly, to be expelled outward with all the terrible force of an exploding star—there was a terrible moment of confusion, separation, darkness, pain. After a while, when the pounding agony in his head had gone away and he opened his eyes, he found himself standing on a flat rock beneath the waterfalls of the great mountain. The forests around him were as green as emeralds, and the sky above him was a perfect blue that only a computer could paint. Standing on other rocks by the silvered pools were Katura Daru and all the other luminous beings such as himself. And, of course, there were Shahar and Abraxax and Maralah and all the Transcended Ones of Alumit Bridge. These lovely spheres floated above the pools like thousands of bubbles of light. In all the time Danlo had spent merged with Shahar they seemed not to have moved.

I am only Danlo wi Soli Ringess, Danlo remembered. He looked down at his blazing hands, at all the colors of his long, lightsome fingers. *But I am also still a luminous being carked out into the Field.*

He had instantiated into the Field in order to face the Transcended Ones and ask them the whereabouts of Tannahill. This he had done. This he was still doing, standing on his rock and letting the light of the four thousand spheres fall upon his face. Just in front of him, Abraxax and Shahar and seven other gods still waited in a half circle. Because they burned almost as brightly as suns, Danlo again turned his eyes downward toward their reflections in the pool. He waited to see if they would tell him what he needed to know.

Danlo wi Soli Ringess—what have you done?

The powerful voice of Abraxax moved the air and drowned out the sound of the waterfalls. This was not a reproof, but rather a demand for simple information. Apparently, neither Abraxax nor any of the other Ones truly understood what had happened when Danlo merged with Shahar. Their only hint was what they had seen at the moment when Danlo entered full transcendence: Shahar had momentarily flared up through the colors of the spectrum, red into orange, blue into violet, until finally she shone with a pure white light more intensely than any other One.

"What is it possible to do?" Danlo asked, answering Abraxax's question with another question.

For a moment, no one moved. There was a vast stillness above the pools, and even the waterfalls ceased their plunge down the mountainside. And then Abraxax spoke again.

We will come together now to decide if Danlo wi Soli Ringess should be shown the star of Tannahill. We will come together here. Please cover your eyes.

Danlo understood that Abraxax was speaking to him, to Katura Daru and to all the other luminous beings around the pools who still remained somewhat less than gods. He watched as Katura Daru and her friends threw their hands over their faces. And then Danlo did the same, pressing his palms against his eyes so hard that he saw stars where only blackness should have been.

Please wait for our answer.

There was light, then. Even through the flesh of his hands, the lovely, luminous flesh that ran with its own colors but wasn't real, he sensed this light. It burned his skin and radiated through blood and bone. He might have kept his eyes covered as did the others, but because he was still in a wild way, he flung his arms to the sky and lifted up his head. He opened his eyes. And in the moment before the terrible light blinded him, he saw an incredible thing. Abraxax and Manannan and Aesir and Ninlil and Shahar—all 4,084 of the Transcended Ones—these flaming scarlet spheres rose up high above the pools and came together like a cluster of stars at the galaxy's core. They merged into a single sphere as bright as Rigel or Alnilam. As bright as a supernova: there was a moment of wild, white light that burst through the air with so great an intensity that the forests and the sky and even the great, golden mountain vanished into its illumination.

Danlo felt a terrible fire in his eyes then, and he should have been afraid. But he remembered that he was not really *he*. This luminous being who stood beneath such an impossible light was only a computer model carked out into the surreality of the Field. His true self, his *real* self, still sat on the plastic cushion in the meeting room. He remembered this self. Now that he was no longer merged with Shahar, he could almost feel himself panting and gripping his bamboo flute and sweating inside the black silk robes that covered the limbs of his real body. He remembered that nothing that occurred in the Field could harm this body or touch his true self in any way.

Of course, it would be a simple thing for the meeting room's computers to target nerve cells within its field, thus burning out the retinas of his deep blue eyes or destroying the visual centers of his brain. It would be simple, yes, but it would be criminal programing, and the Narain were not criminals. They were something other. Now that Danlo stood by a quiet pool looking up into the brilliant sky, he could finally see this otherness. In truth, this deep quality of the Narain was almost all that he could see for he was now completely blind. The beautiful light of the Transcended Ones had found his eyes and had melted them until they ran like liquified jewels over his temples and neck. He stood on his rock as eyeless as a scryer, and like those self-blinded and farseeing women of Neverness—like his mother—he beheld a vision of the future. He finally understood the dream of the Narain people in all its hope and horror.

Someday, farwhen, the Narain would fall across the stars and build great plastic cities like Iviunir to dwell inside. Perhaps on *every* world where it was possible for human beings to carve out a habitation. And here, in these plastic people mounds, the Narain would crawl into their trillions of separate apartments and lie down in darkness inside their separate cells. Their pale white bodies, like snowworms, would never know the touch of a real sun. They would breathe stale, conditioned air and close their eyes as they pulled silvery heaumes down over their heads. And then they would instantiate into cybernetic space. On each world they would program their great computers to generate a Field, millions of separate Fields sucking up the souls of the Narain people on millions of worlds. And someday, when they learned the secret of casting signals faster than light, they would interface all these separate computers to generate a single, omnipresent Field. This creation was their great hope, and they called it the One Field. Here all the common Narain—they who had not yet gone beyond themselves—would finally come together into many, many Transcended Ones, the Great Ones, the hundreds or the thousands or even the seemingly impossible millionplexes.

And then, in turn, like shards of glass fusing into a crystal ball, *these* Ones would merge into yet Higher Ones, on and on, until at the end of time every Narain man and woman was finally united in a single Transcended One. Their name for this One was God. Some called this union Ede, and this was the Narain's deepest dream, to be united at last in Ede the God. The Narain thought of themselves as the true Architects of the Infinite Intelligence of the Cybernetic Universal Church, and as Architects it was their glorious destiny to come together and create the One they called God.

Danlo wi Soli Ringess.

The voice of Abraxax fell like a nuclear blast over Danlo's face. Danlo would have opened his eyes to look upon this Transcended One, but then he remembered that he had no eyes.

Danlo wi Soli Ringess—although you have looked upon the unseeable, we give you back your sight.

Danlo felt a burning near his brain, and then a wetness as if his eye hollows were full of tears. He began blinking away these tears, and he touched his fingers to his eyelids. Beneath these twin slips of skin he felt the resilience and roundness of new eyes grown where moments before there had been only blackness and char and empty space.

Danlo wi Soli Ringess—you may open your eyes if you wish.

Danlo opened his eyes. He found that he could see again: streams and clouds and the sparkling spray of the waterfall crashing against the rocks. The trees were green, and the mountain was gold, and all the colors of this glittering world were his. Because the light above him in the sky was still blindingly bright, he stared down into the mirrored waters of the pool. And then he remembered something that he had learned while merged with Shahar. He remembered that he didn't need Abraxax or the other Transcended Ones to give him sight or even to bestow upon him new eyes.

Now, standing beneath the light of the gods, he knew the way to program changes in his luminous body. Miraculous changes: now, after a moment of will and thought, he lifted up his head and let his new eyes fall upon the Transcended Ones. He could see them quite clearly. A hundred yards from him, Abraxax and Shahar and their friends floated in the air, and they still shined, but now like common flame globes rather than suns. He could see that they had not, after all, merged in full union as might the starlight of a distant globular galaxy. In truth, they seemed more like fish eggs stuck together into a single, glistening mass. And even now, they were pulling apart, separating, and arraying themselves above the pools into their Ones. Danlo smiled to see that he could look at each of 4,084 Transcended Ones directly, boldly, painlessly. He understood that they had come together only temporarily in conclave to decide what should be done with him. And now this conclave was at an end. Now Abraxax and Manannan and El and Maralah and Tyr and Shahar gathered again in a crescent just in front of him. When Abraxax spoke, it was with the voice of decision.

Danlo wi Soli Ringess—you are truly a man who has gone beyond himself. We invite you to remain here with us in Heaven and be a mere man no longer.

Danlo smiled in amusement and vexation (and in a terrible longing to merge again with Shahar), but he just stood there and shook his head.

So it must be, then. Shahar has told us that you are a man of rare purpose. No one else has ever been able to give all of himself to a One and yet retain all of himself as well.

Danlo rubbed his forehead, and his fingers could feel no trace of a scar marking his luminous skin. He asked, ''How could I be other . . . than who I am?''

But who **are** *you, really, Danlo of Neverness?*

''Who is anybody?''

What *are you?*

''I am a man,'' Danlo said in a clear voice. ''Truly . . . only a man.''

And then he closed his eyes, remembering: *I am almost a man. Always almost a true man.*

You are part of Shahar now. And she is part of you.

As Abraxax continued speaking, Danlo discovered that the Transcended Ones were confused as to whether he had merged with Shahar, or somehow—mysteriously, impossibly—she had merged into him. Not even El or Kane, the wisest of the Narain gods, could understand how a One could be absorbed into a mere man who was only one. But all were agreed that a remarkable transformation had overcome Shahar. In the conclave of the Transcended Ones, Shahar had extolled Danlo's goodness, truth and beauty, his love of love, his love *beyond* love—even his love of life. Wildly, boldly, playfully, and very uncharacteristically, she had persuaded even Aesir and Ninlil to embrace Danlo in all his liveliness and passion. And while the Transcended Ones could never quite condone Danlo's more painful emotions—his hatred so dark and deep that it was like a black rent in his soul—they were moved that in touching him from inside himself, *she* was moved so profoundly.

We're agreed as to what you may be told, Danlo wi Soli Ringess.

Danlo waited on his rock, watching the interplay of lights among Abraxax and Shahar, Manannan and Kane. He felt his body tremmbling with anticipation, and he smiled but said nothing.

Shahar has told us that a warrior-poet named Malaclypse Redring pursues you. It would be dangerous if he were to reach Tannahill, too.

Danlo held his breath as he considered all his thoughts that he had shared with Shahar. If the Narain hadn't known about the warrior-poets, they certainly knew now. And perhaps they had learned more of his pilots' art than he would have liked them to know—though without him to act as a teacher, they would never be able to make much use of this knowledge.

But there are dangers in whatever path we choose. And so we will tell you where Tannahill may be found.

Now Danlo bowed his head in thanksgiving for the efforts that the Transcended Ones had made on his behalf. He felt his heart beating with all the speed of a clock in quicktime, and he could scarcely keep himself from crying out in triumph.

Are you still willing to act as our emissary to the Church Elders?

Danlo smiled uneasily and nodded his head. "Yes—if you'd like."

Shahar has argued that you would be the ideal emissary.

With a strange foreboding, Danlo gazed at the sphere of light that was Shahar. It was almost like gazing at himself. In truth, he could now see himself as *she* saw him: soon he would meet the Old Church Elders and draw them into his consciousness as he had with her. With his sheer goodness and the strength of his truth (and all his wild beauty), he would win Harrah ivi en li Ede and all the Elder Architects to his purpose. Clearly, Abraxax and the other Transcended Ones shared this hope of Shahar's. But Danlo was full of doubt that touched on despair. When he closed his eyes and looked into the future he could see something dark and dazzling and deadly, something as terrible to behold as a black hole or a dying star. Sometimes, when he faced these faceless Transcended Ones, it was almost as if they *had* no future. Truly to apprehend the glitter of their unreal forms was almost like trying to capture a light beam in one's hand. When Danlo opened his fingers and looked down through the whorls of time, he descried only nothingness and blackness, like the void between galaxies. Perhaps he had been too long in this computer-made surreality. Perhaps it was time to return to himself and leave his instantiated form as well as his sense of desolation far behind him.

Shall we show you the star to which you'll journey as our emissary?

Again, Danlo shook his head. "Not yet. First, I would like to return to the meeting room."

Do you know the way back?

"Yes—I know the way back," he told Abraxax.

Then we must say good-bye now.

At these words, Maralah and Tyr and Manannan drifted through the air and took turns in passing in front of Danlo. And Aesir and Ninlil and Orunajan and El—one by one, the four thousand Transcended Ones of Alumit Bridge passed by him in a great glittering parade of lights. Each One paused a moment to shine its full radiance upon Danlo's face. And then almost all the Ones were gone, floating like clouds up the mountain until they disappeared into the gleaming white layers of the real clouds—or rather, into those instantiations of cumulus clouds that were only as real as anything in the Field. The last of the Ones to leave was Shahar. She spent many moments simply hovering near Danlo, glowing inside herself with a lovely blue light the color of Danlo's eyes. Then she flared brightly in making her farewell, and she too was gone.

Now I am alone, Danlo thought.

But, of course, he was not really alone. Katura Daru and many of the other luminous beings standing about the pools came over to him. They touched their luminous fingers to his face almost as if *he* were a Transcended One and not just an instantiation of a common human being such as themselves.

"Good-bye," Danlo said to her, and he bowed to the others.

Then he turned so that he stood facing away from the great mountain. He smiled once, and above the pool nearest him, wavering in the air, a rectangle of golden light appeared. This was his portal, his doorway back into the meeting room. He looked down at his hands and his naked limbs, and found himself still instantiated into his luminous body. His real self—his true self made of carbon and oxygen, breath and blood and wild dreams—sat cross-legged on the floor. Silently, this self held a long bamboo flute to his lips, and his long black hair spilled down across the yellow shaft. For a while he floated there staring at himself. He took note of his dark blue eyes so grave and deep.

There was something strange about his eyes, the way that they were still locked open upon the infinities of the Field and yet sparkled with light and laughter as if greatly amused by the paradoxes of his dual existence. Looking at himself this way through the blue-black windows of his eyes, he beheld all the fires of his life blazing inside him. He knew then that he must always return to himself. There was a moment when he thought that the path inward would take him streaking like light through these lovely windows. And then he remembered that there was another way home. He gazed down to where his black silk robe stretched tightly over his chest. There, where his heart beat once each second with all the force of a pulsar—this was the way back into life. With this thought, a circle of golden light appeared over the center of his body. Through its shimmer he could see his heart contracting, throbbing, quickening his true self with streams of lifeblood.

Through this doorway he must pass if would become himself again, and yet he hesitated a moment while he looked at Isas Lel and Lieswyr Ivioss and the seven other pale Transcendentals who sat on their robots watching him. He looked at the meeting room's chatoy walls that still ran with the scarlets and rubies of the sunset scene. There was a curious flatness to these colors as if the essence of redness had been sucked out of them. He remembered then that he was viewing this false sunset only through the eyes of his instantiated self. If he would see the meeting room just as it really was, he must leave the computer-painted mindscape behind him and return to his own true and blessed vision.

I am the door, he remembered. *Knock and be opened.*

And so, at last, he stepped through the doorway into his heart. Into himself—there was a moment of rushing breath, intense realness, the wild joy of life feeling itself so marvelously alive. At last he opened his eyes. That is, his eyes which had been dead to the room's curves and colors, suddenly came into full sight. He could see the seven Transcendentals watching him with all the awe that children of an artificial world might have for a real-life tiger. He looked at them and smiled. Then he looked down at his fingers touching the holes of his shakuhachi. How vividly he remembered the print patterns on the palms of his hands! How good it was to feel the air currents falling across his real flesh again! With a clear and natural laugh he stood up suddenly, and strands of red showed brightly among his rippling black hair. He stretched his cramped arms, legs and back, feeling how good it was to feel the burn of muscles moving deep inside his body.

"Pilot, are you back? Have you broken free of the spiders' web?"

Danlo looked down at the devotionary computer that he had placed on the floor much earlier. The hologram of Nikolos Daru Ede was signing to him, frantically trying to determine his state of consciousness.

"You've broken interface, haven't you?"

This question came from Isas Lel, who sat drinking from a plastic cup that his robot had given him. That he seemed unsure whether or not Danlo was still facing the Field seemed strange.

"Yes," Danlo said with a smile. "Now I am facing . . . only you."

At this, Lieswyr Ivioss tried to catch him with her lovely eyes. She returned his smile, and it was almost as if they could see the light of each other's thoughts.

"We'll show you Tannahill's star, if you wish," Isas Lel said.

He was quiet for a moment, and the sunset scene glowing on the walls faded to darkness. Now, inside the meeting room, it was night, and the stars came out. There were millions of stars twinkling against the black chatoy dome. Danlo recognized Alumit Bridge's red sun and many others in the immediate neighborhood of stars. One of these bright lights, he supposed, must be the star of Tannahill that he had sought for so long.

"No," Danlo said as his eyes flicked from one light to another. "Please, not this way."

"What do you mean?" Isas Lel asked. He looked at Diverous Te, then at Patar Iviaslin and Kistur Ashtoreth, and it was clear that the Transcendentals were puzzled by Danlo's refusal to accept this immediate information.

That is, all save Lieswyr Ivioss were puzzled. Danlo saw that this elegant woman was still smiling at him. She bowed her head as she waited for him to say the words that she knew he would say.

"I . . . would ask you a favor," Danlo said. He bowed to Lieswyr Ivioss, and then in turn to Isas Lel and each of the Transcendentals.

"Very well," Isas Lel said. "And what would you ask?"

Danlo held his breath for a moment and listened to the sound of his heart. "Outside this meeting room, outside the walls of the city, it is night, yes?"

Isas Lel, who could instantly dive down into the Field's deepest pool in order to retrieve the daily weather records on Alumit three thousand years ago and other arcane bits of information, seemed almost stymied by this question. He closed his eyes, taking a long time to answer it.

"It *is* night," he finally said. "It's actually close to middle night."

"And is it a cloudy night or clear?" Danlo asked. "Are the stars out, then?"

"It's a clear night. But why would you ask?"

"I would like to return to the light-field now. To return to my ship."

Danlo looked at the Ede hologram, which was busy making signs with its luminous fingers: "Yes, yes—let's leave here while we still can!"

"But why?" Isas Lel asked, genuinely puzzled.

"I would like to stand beneath the stars again. I was hoping that you could stand with me and point the way to Tannahill's star."

"I suppose I could do that," Isas Lel said, frowning. "But what then?"

"Then I must complete my journey."

"So soon?"

"I must take my lightship back into the stars."

"You'd leave in the middle of the night before you've slept or rested?"

"Yes."

Isas Lel paused a moment to look at the other Transcendentals. Information passed from eye to eye and from brain to brain via the pathways of unseen cybernetic spaces. After Isas Lel had spent an unusually long time staring at Lieswyr Ivioss, he said, "Very well, if that's your wish, we'll accompany you to the light-field."

With this pronouncement he called for another robot to carry Danlo in comfort on their short journey to the roof of the city. Moments later, the doors to the meeting room slid open, and a bright yellow robot rolled through the room. It came to a stop directly in front of Danlo, who returned his flute to its pocket in his pants leg before bending to pick up his devotionary computer. "Thank you," he said, bowing politely. Then he sat down on the robot's red plastic seat, and he was very glad to leave the meeting room behind him.

Their journey through the streets of Iviunir was short and memorable. Word of Danlo's departure had immediately spread through the Field's association space and men and women had broken interface with this planetary communion to bid Danlo farewell. They had taken off their heaumes and left their thousands of separate apartments to swarm the city streets. There, along the broad boulevards, they lined up to watch Danlo and the Transcendentals in their shiny robots roll past them. The sound of their many voices cheering him along was almost deafening. They stood ten deep in their shiny white plastic garments, and Danlo counted ten thousand well-wishers before he gave up counting. It was then, looking out at these swarms of hopeful Narain, that he felt the full weight of being chosen as their emissary.

I must speak for all these people, Danlo thought. *Truly, then, I must speak well.*

At last, after many streets, corridors, and the crushing weight of the gravity lifts, they returned to the light-field. There Danlo found even more people on either side of the long run where his ship lay like a silver-winged bird waiting in the night. The robots rolled down the run between these rows of people, right up to his ship and stopped suddenly. Because Danlo was very glad to see the *Snowy Owl* once again, he fairly jumped out of his robot. He stood looking over his ship's lovely lines, the way her diamond skin shimmered in the starlight. As Isas Lel had said, it was full night and there were many stars. For a moment, Danlo gazed up into the heavens. He drank in the radiance of Medearis and the Trao Double and Valda Luz and many other stars that he knew. He drank in as well the clear, natural air and all the scents of the forest far below the city. For the first time in many days he became aware how good it was just to stand beneath the sky breathing deeply the dreams of the night.

"I've never seen the stars this way," Isas Lel said. He sat motionless in his robot looking out into the Vild. In all his life, in all the times he had greeted luminaries from other cities or worlds at the light-field, he had never been outside at night.

"The stars are the children of God," Danlo whispered.

"What did you say?" Isas Lel asked. With a heavy sigh, he climbed down from his robot and walked over to Danlo. The other Transcendentals took this as a sign that they should do the same. They came over to where Danlo stood almost beneath the great sweeping wing of his ship.

"The stars are the children of God alone in the night," Danlo said. "It is a line from a song that I once learned."

"I never thought that there could be so *many* stars," Kistur Ashtoreth said.

Ananda Narcavage nodded his/her head. "Let's show Danlo wi Soli Ringess the star that he desires to see and go back to our apartments. It's not good to be outside this late."

The Transcendentals of Alumit Bridge stood in their separate selves like naked children and watched the beautiful stars, and they felt vulnerable and alone and completely exposed to the terrible nearness of the night.

"Shall I show you Tannahill's star?" Isas Lel asked. He

stepped over by Danlo's side, and he frowned as if it had been many years since he stood so close to another human being.

"Please . . . yes."

With a trembling finger Isas Lel pointed up toward a well-known constellation in the eastern sky. There, some forty degrees above the horizon, a bright triangle of stars twinkled against an inverted triangle approximately the same size. Both triangles were nearly equilateral and configured so as to make a nearly perfect hexagon. Or a star. Danlo immediately saw that if the six points of light were connected as a child might connect dots in a puzzle, then they would make a six-pointed star. To himself, he immediately named this strange constellation as the Star of Stars.

"Do you see the six hex stars?" Isas Lel asked. "We call this group the Stars of David. I'm not sure why."

Danlo watched these splendid stars giving up their faint illumination into the night. He waited in silence for Isas Lel to say more.

"Do you see the star at the apex of the upright triangle? It seems almost blue doesn't it? *That* is the star of Tannahill."

At last, after years of his journey, after falling trillions of miles across the galaxy's stars, Danlo finally laid eyes upon this brilliant blue sphere that he had sought for so long. He let all the stars in the immediate neighborhood of stars burn their pattern into his mind. And almost immediately he understood why Reina An, in guiding him toward the Architect's star, had pointed out Alumit Bridge's star rather than that of Tannahill: as arrayed from the Earth of the Sani, the two stars lay along a straight line. Thus Alumit Bridge's bloody sun would block out the light of Tannahill's star. Reina An had pointed truly after all. Danlo need only fall a few tens of light-years farther upon the infinite line made by her bony old finger, and he would fall out upon the world of Tannahill.

"You're leaving now, aren't you, Pilot?"

This question, which was not really a question, came from Lieswyr Ivioss. She stood up from her robot and came over to where Danlo and Isas Lel were watching the stars.

"Yes," Danlo said, lowering his eyes to meet hers. "I must complete my journey."

"Your *mission* to the Old Church."

"Yes, my mission," Danlo agreed.

"And when you've succeeded, will you return here?"

Danlo stared into her brilliant eyes, then looked at Isas Lel and the hundreds of others who were watching him. "I will return. I will tell you what the Elders of the Old Church have said about the Narain people—and about the stars."

"And then?"

"Then I must fall on to Thiells. I must tell the Lords of my Order about Tannahill."

"Will you ever return to Iviunir after that?"

Danlo looked down at his hands, and he answered her question with another question. "Who can see the future?"

"Will you ever return to Shahar?" she asked.

In her voice there was a terrible longing that called to Danlo with all the urgency of a bird lost at sea. For a moment he felt this longing, too. He brooded upon all the joys of creating a higher, cybernetic self and merging with other instantiated entities. But in the end, this joy was illusory. In the glittering mind-scapes of the Field, what could it mean to know real joy or sorrow? What could it mean to be brave in the absence of real threat or to call oneself alive when totally disconnected from the pain and cold of the real world?

What does it mean to truly live? What does it mean to love?

As the stars burned in the night sky above them, Danlo stared at the sudden burning wetness that filled up Lieswyr Ivioss's eyes. He knew her secret, then. Earlier that night, in merging into the One called Shahar, he had seen the surface of her mind, but now he looked into the depths of her heart. She, this glorious creature of blood and tears and love, this very human being, would never die for Shahar. In playing the game of transcendence, she might momentarily sacrifice the lesser parts of herself to cark out as a surreal Transcended One, but in the *real* world, she would never lay down her life for this One.

Danlo looked at the other Transcendentals and all the people standing along the run; none of them, he thought, would be willing to die for an abstract entity programed by a computer. Someday, perhaps, when they came out of their dark apartments and their surrealities and they saw each other as they really were, *then* they might die for each other—for that marvelous, streaming life that they shared as a people. But until that time, they would be as Lieswyr Ivioss: forlorn and fearful and very much alone.

"Will you return to us?" she asked again.

Danlo, who did not like to tell untruths, smiled sadly and shook his head. "No," he forced out. "I am sorry."

"I'm sorry, too," she said. Then she called up her courage and smiled at him. "Nevertheless, I wish you well. We all do."

At this, she bowed to him, as did the other Transcendentals still sitting in their robots. And all the men and women waiting along the run bowed deeply, and they called out, "We wish you well."

The last of the Narain to say good-bye was Isas Lel. He bowed and said, "We all wish you a safe journey, Danlo wi Soli Ringess. You are our emissary as well our friend."

After that, Danlo called for the doors to his lightship to open, and as he climbed up to the dark pit where he would once again face all the perils of the manifold, he felt a terrible dread of the future. He looked down at the dark plastic of the run, down through the city of Iviunir and the soil and rock of the darkened planet below. He looked down through the sands of time, and there he saw the bloody star of Alumit Bridge burning brightly among all the stars of the Vild.

PART 3

THE CHOSEN OF GOD

TANNAHILL

*And so Ede faced the universe, and he was vastened, and
he saw that the face of God was his own. Then the
would-be gods, who are the hakra devils of the darkest
depths of space, from the farthest reaches of time, saw
what Ede had done, and they were jealous. And so they
turned their eyes godward in jealousy and lust for the
infinite lights, but in their countenances God read hubris,
and he struck them blind. For here is the oldest of
teachings, here is wisdom: no god is there but God;
God is one, and there can be only one God.*
　　　　　　　　　　　—from the Facings *of the Algorithm*

In the vast distances of the galaxy, two stars separated by only
three dozen light-years of space are almost as close as two stars
can be, and yet to pass from one blazing orb to another is often a
difficult feat. In a ship traveling through realspace at half the
speed of light, this journey would eat up some seventy years of a
man's life. To a pilot mapping almost instantaneously from star
to star, however, such a fallaway might take only a moment—or
forever.

As Danlo lay inside the lightless pit of his ship, the *Snowy
Owl*, he thought about this problem. He fell through the shimmering manifold, making his mathematics and searching for a
mapping that would enable him to open a window upon Tannahill's not too distant star. Often he thought about the Great
Theorem of the pilots. Years ago his father had proved that it is
always possible to fall from one of the galaxy's stars to any other
in a single fall. It is always possible, yes, but it is always difficult
to find such mappings. Distance alone is no determiner of this
difficulty. The topology of the manifold is strange, and it can be
easier to map across ten thousand light-years of space, from the

Detheshaloon to the Rainbow Double, than to fall on to a nearby
sun so close that it is like a blue-white flame globe alight in a
neighbor's window. Although Tannahill's star was almost close
enough to touch, Danlo might reach out with his hands (and his
mind) for a very long time before he closed in upon it.

Once, he remembered, there had been a pilot returning from a
long journey to his friends and family. This was more than five
thousand years ago on Arcite before the Order had moved to
Neverness. The pilot—Chiah Li Chen—had fallen out of the
manifold around a neighboring star. He looked across only eight
trillion miles of realspace to see Arcite Luz blazing like a beacon
in the distance. He was so happy that he might have wept. When
he fell back into the manifold, he was certain that he would reach
his star in only a second or two of realtime.

Only, by bad chance, his lightship blundered into a rare Gallivare tube that had borne him twenty thousand light-years halfway toward the galaxy's core—like a piece of driftwood swept
along by an ocean storm. It had taken Li Chen more than a
hundred years to return across the dense stars of the Cygnus arm
to his home. There he had found his wife long dead and his
children's grandchildren scattered upon a dozen other worlds. It
is said that the broken-hearted Chiah Li Chen was the first pilot
to kill himself by willingly mapping his lightship into Arcite's
dangerous red star.

All pilots must return home, Danlo remembered. *But where is
home?*

Often, during Danlo's dangerous passage to Tannahill, he
thought about the ice-glazed spires of Neverness and the woman
whom he had loved. Often, he thought of returning home. In
truth, it can be the easiest thing in the universe for a pilot to
return to the City of Light. The cantors, in their gray robes and
their mathematical arrogance, have proclaimed the Star of Neverness as the topological nexus of the galaxy. Because many billions of the manifold's pathways converge in the thickspace near
its cool yellow sun, Neverness has always been at the center of
man's greatest stellar civilization. "All pathways lead to Neverness"—this is a saying of the pilots. Deep in the black belly of
his lightship, Danlo remembered this. He remembered each of
the many thousands of pathways that had carried him deep into
the stars of the Vild. It would be almost possible, he thought, to
retrace his way along these many twisting paths. Or he might find
new mappings, new pathways—or someday he might blaze with
marvelous insights into the secrets of the Great Theorem, and

thus he might see how he could always return to Neverness in a single fall.

But now, as he sought a mapping through the violent and beautiful spaces that underlay the Vild, he prayed only that Chiah Li Chen and he would not share the same fate. He prayed that he would reach Tannahill's star after only a few quick falls. And so it happened. There was one bad moment when he almost opened a window upon an infinite tree and another when his ship began slip sliding into an inverted serpentine. Apart from these near disasters, however, his journey was easy. Ironically, as Danlo would later muse, he had a much easier time reaching Tannahill than leaving it.

The greatest excitement of his passage among the stars came not from danger but from mystery. Not far from Alumit Luz he came across a red giant that he named Haryatta Sawel, which meant "the raging sun." It was there, just after Danlo had mapped free from the spinning thickspace associated with this star, that he once again descried signs of another ship following him. As before, in his wild flight toward the Solid State Entity, this ship remained always at the threshold of the radius of convergence. He wondered if this ship was real—if it really fell through the manifold in such an impeccable manner that it remained always at the exact boundary of the neighborhood of stars surrounding the *Snowy Owl*. It seemed as insubstantial as smoke in a cold wind or an icon instantiated into some cybernetic surreality.

Perhaps, Danlo thought, this mysterious second ship was only a reflection of his own. The perturbations a lightship makes in passing through the manifold are hideously difficult to read, and such mathematical mirages and illusions are always possible. *Could* Malaclypse Redring, in Sivan wi Mawi Sarkissian's ship the *Red Dragon,* really have pursued him halfway across the galaxy? This miracle of piloting seemed truly *im*possible, and yet Danlo sensed that it must be so.

His sense of others watching him was primal, animal, and very keen. He remembered back to a sight he had witnessed during his childhood, the way a hungry gull would sometimes follow a Snowy Owl in order to scavenge any leavings from the rare white bird's inevitable kill. Danlo could only think that the warrior-poet still pursued him in hope of being led to his father. (And for other more bellicose purposes.) He dreaded this eventual meeting as he might look with horror at two pieces of plutonium slammed together. Strangely, though, for himself he still had little fear.

And so perhaps inevitably Danlo came to Tannahill. One bright, happy day, he fell out far above this lost and fabled world. With his telescopes and his keen eyes, he looked down through space, down between the patchy clouds of the atmosphere upon an unbelievable sight. Tannahill was a fat world of great oceans and bulging landmasses; but the waters of the world, as Danlo saw, were nearly dead. In many places, the shallows were choked with sludges and grayish green mats of some weedlike marine plant, while the deeper seas bore the taint of acetylene and benzene and ten thousand other man-made chemicals. So pervasive was this pollution that oceans fairly ran with ugly colors as if smeared with blacking oil: metallic greens and muddy pinks and a dark, dirty gray that reminded him of a piece of frozen skin that has fallen into necrosis. The atmosphere, too, was horribly polluted. There was too much carbon dioxide, of course, and the oxygen: nitrogen ratio was dangerously out of balance. Danlo's computer analyses showed much sulfur and halogens and even the traces of fungicides. At first, Danlo wondered how the animals walking through Tannahill's forests could ever get their breath; but after he had painstakingly scanned the whole of the world, he realized that on all the surface of Tannahill there *were* no forests. Neither did there live any animals—at least none much larger than the worms or the insects that infested the rare patches of exposed soil.

Tannahill's three large continents girdled the world's equator, and each of them had been given over wholly to the purpose of human habitation. And what dwellings these people had built! In all Danlo's journeys he had never seen anything like what the Architects had made of their world. Except for the slopes of the highest mountains and the great gorges cutting the deserts, the Architects had covered almost every area of earth with great plastic cities. It was as if they long ago had set out to build a few hundred arcologies of the design copied in the cities of Alumit Bridge—and then their architecture had exploded out of control, growing like cancers until their edges had met and melted together into a planetwide smear of plastic.

The transformation of Tannahill was the most total unbalancing of the natural order that Danlo had ever beheld. For such a criminal and insane act he knew only one word, and that was shaida. He remembered, then, a line from the *Song of Life* that his grandfather had once taught him: *Shaida is the cry of the world when it has lost its soul.* Only, Tannahill had lost much more than its soul; it had lost trees and rivers and rocks and the fresh, clean wind that was the breath of the world. In truth, this plastic-covered habitat of twelve hundred billion human beings had lost its very life.

Shaida is he who kills what he cannot give back into life.

For a long while Danlo dwelled in remembrance of other peoples and other places, even as he orbited Tannahill in his lightship and studied the world below him. He might have spent many days of intime in such contemplation, but soon enough the Architects in their planetary city sent a laser-coded signal beaming up through space.

Please tell us who you are and whence you come.

To the Architects of Tannahill, it would be obvious that Danlo had his origins elsewhere than the seventy-two worlds of the Known Stars. All these worlds, as he knew, had been seeded by Architects of the Old Church, and none of them, with only their Church-sanctioned technologies, could produce anything so marvelous as a lightship.

All these stars—all these worlds so similar to Tannahill, Danlo brooded. *The pressure of their population must be truly terrible.*

After Danlo had explained that he was a pilot of the Order and an emissary of the Narain of Alumit Bridge, there fell a long pause in communication with the world below him. Danlo waited as wary and watchful as a zanshin artist who slowly circles his opponent and expects any possibility.

"Surely they will invite you to make planetfall, Pilot."

Out of the blackness in the pit of Danlo's ship there came an unholy glow, almost as of a swarm of phosphorescent kachina flies lighting up a cave. The hologram of Nikolos Daru Ede moved its mouth and spoke according to the programs of the devotionary computer that projected his familiar human form into the air. According to his master algorithm, Ede could not help but warn Danlo of danger.

"Surely the Architects cannot harm you unless you *do* fall down to their world."

After a while, from an unknown voice coded into the signal that the Architects aimed toward his ship, Danlo received a request for more information concerning the Order of Mystic Mathematicians, Neverness, and the Civilized Worlds. Danlo spent much time describing his journey across the Sagittarius and Orion arms of the galaxy. He told of his stay among the Narain of Alumit Bridge and that he had come to Tannahill in order to plea for peace between the peoples of these two estranged worlds.

Eventually, the voice of a man who identified himself as the Dedicated Honon en li Iviow of Ornice Olorun invited Danlo to take his ship down to a light-field near the coast of Tannahill's largest continent. Danlo homed in on the signal that was provided. Although it was twilight, with the edge of the world spinning into darkness, he had no trouble piloting the *Snowy Owl* down through the layers of the atmosphere. Soon he saw that the zone of Tannahill known as Ornice Olorun covered a fifty-mile-wide swath of land caught between a range of mountains and the poison sea.

Once a time—a thousand years before—Ornice Olorun had been Tannahill's first city, a beautiful jewel of a city overlooking the white sand beaches of a beautiful ocean. Over the millennia, however, it had grown north and south, three hundred miles up and down the coast, and toward the west, sending out great plastic tentacles between the mountains to connect with Eshtara and Kaniuk and other cities of what used to be called the Golden Plains. It was near these white-capped mountains that Danlo found the light-field.

As with the fields of Iviunir and the other cities of Alumit Bridge, it was built of composite plastics above the roof of the city almost half a mile into the sky. The Architects had called Danlo to earth during a clear evening; far off in the distance he could see other light-fields of other cities and the red flash of rocket fire. These flashes lit up the night in a shower of sparks that never stopped, for many Worthy Architects from the Known Stars tried to make the pilgrimage to Tannahill, and many more Architects fled Tannahill for new worlds around new stars. And who could blame them? Out over the sea, he saw, the air was discolored by the hues of toluidine purple and other chloride chemicals. The mountains to the west—lit up by the setting sun—glowed a hellish orange madder. All Danlo's life he had loved traveling to new and distant lands, and ever since he had become a pilot, it had been his joy to walk upon the earth of strange new worlds. But tonight his head throbbed with foreboding and despair, and he sensed that his feet would touch only hard gray plastic.

As he was directed, he flew his ship down to a well-lit run

near the center of the field. For a while, he rocketed slowly along this run, casting his eyes left and right at the other runs, looking at the skimmers and jets and jammers—all the many crafts crowding the spaces of this busy light-field. He moved straight toward a white structure that rose up from the field like an immense plastic bubble a quarter mile in diameter and almost half as high. The doors to this guest sanctuary, as Honon Iviow had called it, were open. As the *Snowy Owl* passed inside and the huge doors slammed shut behind him, Danlo wondered whether his status among the Architects was to be that of honored guest or prisoner.

You may debark from your ship now.

Danlo opened the diamond doors of his ship's pit, and he climbed down to the smooth white plastic that made up the sanctuary's floor. He sealed the ship behind him. For a while he stood quite still, squinting and pushing his palm against the pain that stabbed through the left side of his head. Somewhere above him, high up against the curving roof, incandescent globes blazed with a terrible, sick light. When his eyes had adjusted to the brightness, he turned in a slow circle to survey his surroundings. In a way, this strange guest house reminded him of a snow hut, for it was windowless and white and built into the familiar shape of a dome. But it was monstrously huge and lacked the intimate and organic feeling of a snow hut's interior. In this soulless room, there were no sleeping furs, or fish pit, or drying rack for his clothes. There were no oilstones burning with a soft yellow flame, filling up the space around him with a soft lovely light.

Instead there were machines or objects that were the fabrications of machines. There were grids and assemblers and hinun wheels. Various robots, some half as large as his ship, were rolled up near the room's circumference, awaiting servicing instructions from some unseen master computer or controlling entity. Normally they would be employed to tug, lift, open, fuel or repair any of the shuttles that came down from near space. One kind of robot merely unloaded the exotic cargoes or human beings that these shuttles carried. the *Snowy Owl,* however, required no such servicing. It fairly filled the center of the dome, a great shimmering sweep of diamond always waiting to fall back to the stars. It was Danlo's pride that of all the thousands of vessels to be dragged into such domes, in a thousand years, this was the first

time that Ornice Olorun or any of Tannahill's other cities had
been graced with the arrival of a lightship.

**We must ask you to remain in the sanctuary for a few
days while tests are being made. We hope that you are
comfortable.**

Danlo stood looking at the devotionary computer that he held
in his hands. The familiar form of Nikolos Daru Ede had temporarily vanished, to be replaced with the imago of the Dedicated
Honon en li Iviow. Honon, if this glowing imago were true to his
real-life person, was a small, suspicious man but also, perhaps,
urbane, proficient, and shrewd. His voice was sweet and quick,
and it issued out of the devotionary computer like high notes
from a flute.

**You will find that food and refreshment have been pre-
pared for you. If you require conversation or information, you may call for a face-to-face with me at any
time.**

At the far end of the sanctuary, Danlo found a large area
where the plastic of the floor rose up like a shelf overlooking the
rest of the cavernous room. Here the Architects of Ornice Olorun
had built something like an apartment. Set atop this higher level
was a bed, bathing chamber, sense box, dining table, and various
statues of Nikolos Daru Ede sculpted out of some kind of dense
black plastic. There was a golden-stringed gosharp on which one
might play lovely music, and a spare devotionary to supply melodies of a more spiritual nature. And other things. Unlike the
Narain, the Architects took care to maintain their physical selves,
and so they had provided various ways for their guests to move
their bodies. Adjoining the sleeping area was a moving walkway
on which he might trudge for days without progressing more
than an inch and a plastic climbing tree whose many jointed
branches reached nearly to the dome's curving roof. There was
also a pool. But as much as Danlo loved splashing through cool,
clear water, he did not swim in it for it reeked of chlorine and
other chemicals. The air in the dome was bad, too. When he
concentrated on the odors assaulting his nose, he could pick up
the traces of hydroxyls, propylene, styrene, and various ami-
noplastics. There were obnoxious smells such as ketones and
mercaptans, and dangerous ones such as benzene and toluene

and other aromatic hydrocarbons. If it were possible, he would have held his breath for all the time that he dwelled in the cities of Tannahill. But he had to breathe as he had to live, and so he climbed the stairs to the sanctuary's apartment, and he settled in to play his flute and to eat the peculiar-tasting food that the ministrant robots served him.

After he had bathed and rested, other robots came with needles to draw his blood. As well they collected skin scrapings, saliva, ear wax, lymph, urine, even the dung that he left steaming in the dark hole of the multrum. He balked, however, at providing these noisome machines with the semen samples that they requested. And it was only with the greatest difficulty that he allowed them to cover his mouth with a piece of soft, clear plastic and procure the exhalations of his lungs. The breath, he remembered, was sacred and blessed; a man's breath shouldn't be sucked into a sealed plastic bag, but rather it should leave his lips to flow over earth and snow and be rejoined with the greater breath of the world.

When Danlo had done all that he must do to begin his mission to Tannahill, the imago of Honon en li Iviow appeared out of his devotionary to thank him.

You will understand that we must be careful of strangers, Danlo wi Soli Ringess. We must be careful of contamination.

A few days later, when the biologicals had determined that Danlo harbored no bacteria, viruses, or DNA fracts harmful to the people of Tannahill, the Dedicated Honon en li Iviow invited him to address the Koivuniemin, or the Assembly of Elders, the ruling body of the Cybernetic Universal Church. In preparation for this long-awaited moment, Danlo trimmed his beard and combed out his thick black hair, which had grown long and wild during his journey into the Vild. Then he dressed in the black pilot's robe that his Order required upon all formal occassions. He polished his black leather boots until they shone like mirrors, and he cleaned his black diamond ring of oils and dirt until it shone brightly, too. Because he disliked going anywhere without his shakuhachi, he secreted the long flute in an inner pocket of his robe's flowing pantaloons. Thus armed to face these unknown men and women who might hold sway over his fate, he took the devotionary computer into his hands. Like any other

Architect of Tannahill, he would carry this little jeweled box with
him wherever he went.

We will call a choche for you.

True to his word, Honon Iviow called to life one of the sanctuary's five old choches. It rolled right up to the stairs beneath
Danlo's apartment, and it opened its gull-winged doors so that
Danlo might step inside. Danlo hated being inside this mobile
plastic box, for it was not brightly colored and open as were the
similarly functioning robots of Iviunir, but rather made of an
ugly gray plastic and wholly enclosed. The doors suddenly
locked shut around him, exacerbating his sense of being imprisoned.

The choche *was* graced with windows, however, and as Danlo
sat on his soft plastic seat, inhaling molecules of silicone and
nylon, he found that he could look out at the scenery passing by.
At first, of course, there was little to see: only the robots and
furnishings of the guest sanctuary. But then the choche rolled
through an airlock and a series of doors out into a corridor that
led to a gravity lift. After falling away, they debouched onto one
of Ornice Olorun's side streets. Here there were people wearing
white or brown kimonos, and because Nikolos Daru Ede had
been a devotee of the sacred jambool—a drug known to cause
baldness as well as visions—all Architects had shaved heads in
memory of all that Ede had sacrificed in bringing the truth to
humankind. But, ironically, because too close an emulation of
Ede was blasphemy, most covered their shiny pates with a little
brown skullcap known as a dobra.

It troubled Danlo that although he could see all these people
in their kimonos and funny little hats, they could not see him.
The windows of the choche were made of a mirrored plastic that
let in the light of the world but permitted no visual information
from the interior to escape into the prying eyes of gawkers or
passersby. Nor could anyone easily get at the choche's unseen
occupants: its body was molded from one of the kevalin plastics
almost impervious to laser fire, missiles, or explosions. Such is
the construction of any choche employed to carry an Elder Architect, ambassador, or other luminary about the uncertain streets
of Ornice Olorun.

"You must beware assassins."

The Ede hologram signed this warning to Danlo as they
looked at each other through the semidarkness of the choche's

interior. Although the choche felt quite private, Danlo thought it unwise to risk verbal conversation.

"Anywhere that there are armored robots." Ede signed, "there are assassins."

This was true, Danlo mused. But then assassins haunted the history of almost all human societies, especially one so distressed as that of Tannahill. As Danlo rolled in safety toward his appointment with the Koivuniemin, he saw signs of misery and disquiet everywhere. First and last, there were too many people. They swarmed the streets in their millions like ants through tunnels in the earth. Indeed, the streets of Ornice Olorun were dark and narrow and cut off from sunlight, very much like tunnels or underground passageways.

Once, perhaps, a thousand years ago, they had been as open and airy as the broad boulevards that Danlo had seen in Iviunir. But the Architects, ever spawning great broods of babies, ever hungry for space, had been forced to make use of every cubic inch of their endless city. Over time, they had torn up commons and parks and playrings, even as they synthezised great blocks of new plastic and added on to their apartments and other buildings. Everywhere Danlo looked, the Architects had actually expanded their buildings out *over* the streets.

There, a scant fifteen feet over the heads of Architects making their daily errands, building fused into building, filling in what should have been open space between the many levels of the city. In some parts of Tannahill—in Ivi Olorun, for example—the streets were so twisting and tunnellike that it was impossible to gain a clear line of sight much greater than four hundred feet. The effect of this terrible constriction was that many Architects had never beheld distances. Although their religion taught that it was man's destiny to expand into an infinite universe, they, in their everyday lives, had known only closed horizons. Thus they experienced a terrible conflict between sensibility and sense, between their most sacred beliefs and what their eyes and heart knew to be true.

But what is really true?

Danlo wondered this as his choche forced its way through the many people teeming down the street. Of all the thoroughfares in Ornice Olorun, this strip of gray plastic running between the light-field and the great Temple where the Koivuniemin met was the broadest and straightest—but still inadequate to move the manswarms of the city. Most of the Architects that Danlo saw bore this crowding bravely. Dressed in their clean white kimonos, cradling their devotionaries protectively against their bellies, they did their best to flounder through the raging river of humanity that swept them along like so many bits of protoplasm. If they made no apology at being jostled or elbowed or bumped by another, it was because the reality of living inside their arcology had forced them to abandon the normal social graces. In such a crush of people, where collisions occurred with the frequency of heated gas molecules inside a sealed jar, to say "excuse me" every three seconds would quickly grow as tiresome as it was pointless. Although many Architects had accepted this necessary rudeness as their fate, others had not. The faces of many men and women were full of grievance, bitterness, and resentment.

Once, when Danlo's choche stopped before the bombed-out front of a restaurant, an angry young man spat at his window and hurled a piece of plastic so that it went skittering over the choche's roof. He made a crude sign in Danlo's direction and screamed an obscenity, a slang word for a forbidden interface with one's computer. Danlo wondered at this astonishing act. Could this man have known that the choche carried a pilot of the Order and an emissary of the Narain of Alumit Bridge? Could the Architects in the mob around him have known this as well?

But while many women and men and children regarded this rabid man warily as they might an armed plastic bomb, they made no move to rebuke him or restrain him in any way. They merely stood staring at the choche as if the fire of their eyes might melt the mirrored windows. Although they could not see him, Danlo felt his eyes touching theirs. In truth, something about their wild spirit touched him deep inside.

These were a people who had suffered privation and pain. Although there had been no actual starvation on Tannahill, many people looked hungry and much too thin. Some were afflicted with diseases. Danlo thought that these diseases must be rare and unique to Tannahill for he had never seen such death signs before. One little boy, clinging to the folds of his mother's kimono, had been blinded by some kind of fuzzy, alien fungus sucking at his eyes. Many men bore a blue taint to their skin as if this very same infection were only waiting to erupt and consume their bodies. Perhaps, Danlo thought, this was some mutant strain of the mehalchins that pitted and discolored the facades of the buildings along the street. If an alien organism could eat hardened plastic, why not the flesh of men whose faces were already eaten up with dreams and despair?

The terrible pressure of their numbers, Danlo thought. *Such people would make terrible enemies.*

After a long time of rolling past endless shops and endlessly zealous faces, the swarms of people grew even denser, if that were possible. Danlo sensed that they must be approaching the Temple. There came a moment in his journey to meet the Koivuniemin when the streets around him were dark and pressed close on either side like the walls of a crevasse. And then his choche broke free into the New City, and the streets at last opened up.

Here there were real buildings, as Danlo thought of buildings. These great white structures did not flow into each other, as of plastic melted together in continuous slag heaps. Rather they were laid out on well-ordered blocks, each block set off by fine, tree-lined boulevards. Danlo marveled at these trees. He hadn't expected to find such treasures in this dread city. Nor had he expected the brilliant light which poured down upon the triangular leaves of the alien murshim trees.

He looked through his choche's windows up at the great dome that enclosed the whole of the New City. Probably, he thought, it was made of clary or some other transparent plastic. It reminded him of the domes that enclosed the havens of Yarkona and other cities of the Civilized Worlds. Through this dome he saw the sulfur-tainted Tannahill sky, and far off, in the east, the steely glint of the ocean. Despite the discoloration of these once-splendid vistas, Danlo was grateful for any sight of the natural world.

This is the best of a bad place, Danlo thought. *Truly—this must be the soul of Tannahill.*

But even here, on the zero level of the New City, beneath the clear dome letting in the light of the sky, Danlo saw signs of discord: at the edge of a little park, he came across a statue of Kostos Olorun that some criminal or blasphemer must have recently scorched with a laser, melting out the eyes and deforming the bulbous nose. The terrible smells of ozone and burned plastic still hung in the air. And in the streets there were still too many people. Most of them, of course, in their crisp white kimonos and wide-eyed wonder, were pilgrims from distant zones on Tannahill or other worlds of the Known Stars. But more than a few were Readers and Dedicated Architects and even the grim-faced Elders of the Koivuniemin who had business in the Temple.

This famous building, as Danlo saw, was much the largest in the New City. It rose up from the center of the huge square somewhere at the end of the endless boulevard down which Danlo traveled. Even at this distance, he could see it clearly. Built in the overall shape of a cube, it was all angles and points and many-faceted like a diamond cut to catch the light. The Architects, ever fearing assassins' bombs, had ordered it made of pure cut-white kevalin, a plastic almost as rare and hard as diamond.

Other buildings of the district—with the exception of the High Architect's Palace—were less expensive as well as less grandiose. For five miles in any direction, these buildings were constellated around the Temple like lesser heavenly bodies around a star. Here were the houses of the Dedicated Architects, the low estates, the hotels, halls, spas, villas, and many offices of the ancient Church institutions. On the blocks closest to the Temple, surrounded by purple bene trees and lawns of real grass, were the Elders' residences, the High Estates, the House of Eternity, Ede's Tomb, and the Palace itself. This, then, as Danlo had observed, was the soul of Tannahill—as well as the seat of an ancient Church that was destroying the stars.

They must dream of Old Earth, Danlo thought. He looked at the grass and the violets and all the other earthly flora that had been made to grow throughout the New City. *All men dream of Earth.*

The boulevard down which Danlo rolled—like eleven others—gave out onto an avenue that made a huge square around the Temple grounds. A wall made of cut-white kevalin surrounded the Temple itself. Although there were twelve gates set into this wall, to the north, west, east, and south, it was not easy for any common choche or pilgrim to pass through them. But as Danlo's choche rolled up to one of the western gates, it was not stopped, and neither was Danlo questioned by any of the robots or the quick-eyed Temple keepers that guarded it. He passed unimpeded though this outer gate and then through an inner light-fence meant to burn anyone so foolish as to try to gain entrance to the Temple grounds by force or stealth.

His choche rolled down a pleasant path cutting among the lawns and the bene trees; it rolled onto a little lane that led right up the steps of the Temple. Here it finally stopped. The doors opened, up and out, and once again Danlo was reminded of the way a seagull lifts up its ivory wings. As he stepped from the choche, setting his black boots down upon the white walkway, a cadre of keepers immediately swarmed around him. They were each strong, tall men, almost as tall as Danlo, and they each wore a flowing kimono woven of spun-white kevalin. Thus protected by these layers of laser-proof plastic and human flesh, Danlo was invited to walk up the steps into the Temple. One of the keepers, a one-eyed man whose face was a patchwork of old burn scars, introduced himself as Nikolos Sulivi. Then he said, "Welcome, Danlo wi Soli Ringess of Neverness. We will take you to meet the Koivuniemin now."

And so Danlo passed inside the great Temple of Tannahill. When he stepped inside the entrance hall, its vastness overwhelmed him. Like the entrance halls of the Urradeth temples (and the temple that he had found on the Edeic Earth), this room was filled with sculptures of Nikolos Daru Ede. There were plastic benches on which one could sit to watch the wall paintings of Ede's glorious life; there were fountains and cold flame globes and various species of holy computers. There were many handfasts, of course, for scanning the DNA of all the Worthy Architects who sought entrance to the Temple. And there was much more: oredolos depicting the Old Church's exodus into the Vild, holograms stands and mantelets, prayer rings and remembrance stations and holy relics of Alumit's first temple, which were encased in huge clary vaults.

Danlo's sense of space was very keen, and he was almost certain that even the largest of the Urradeth temples could fit into this single hall. Its air of sanctity disturbed him, just as the air itself—heavy with molecules of hydroxyls and kevalines—was like a plastic blanket thrown over his face, blinding him, smothering him. He remembered, then, the cathedral that his friend Bardo had purchased on Neverness. Standing on real floorstones cut from a mountain's granite was very different from being inside a building synthesized from plastic. Here, there was no organic feel at all, and even the sound waves of his voice fell off the angles of the walls in an unsettling manner. Once again, he was overwhelmed by a sense that he was entering a monstrously large computer. The glittering lights, the information pools, the programed looks of awe on the white-robed Architects' faces—it all seemed so artificial and unreal.

But what is real? Danlo wondered. He looked into the eyes of the Temple keepers who escorted him through this unbelievably large room. There was a grimness in the way they continually scanned the manswarms for signs of danger, as well as duty and determination in the face of death. *Truly, life is real. Life and death.*

At last, the keepers bore him into the main gallery that served as a waiting area for anyone invited to witness the deliberations of the Church's ruling body. Here Danlo paused to wait like any of the pilgrims or readers called before the Koivuniemin. He stood enduring the stares of the various Architects who waited with him, and then he looked down to see the Ede hologram staring at him, too. As he might have guessed, the little Ede was fingering a cetic sign at him, which he read as, "Beware, Pilot, beware." Danlo smiled at his devotionary computer. And then he began counting his heartbeats as he turned to look at the doors to the room before him and waited for them to open.

THE KOIVUNIEMIN

They call themselves the Iviomils, the chosen of God.
We call them the Faceless because they scorn the truth
that we can come face to face with Ede our God. They
would excoriate all mystics and anyone who does not
share their beliefs. They preach a return to the purity of
Edeism's beginnings. They would abolish the facing
ceremony as blasphemy, for they say that we can only
interface an image of Ede, but never the essence of God
Himself. We must be very wary of these Faceless. I
believe that in the years to come, they will be the
greatest danger to our Eternal Church.
                         —from the letters of Liljana ivi Narai

It did not take long for Danlo's escort to speak with the Temple
keepers who guarded the doors of the Hall of the Koivuniemin.
These six wary men had expected Danlo's arrival. They asked
him for his name, and then bowed to him. Without bothering to
scan him for weapons (Danlo presumed that the choche's computers had already performed this vexing function), they opened
the doors and ushered him inside.

This is a place of death.

Immediately upon entering the Hall of the Koivuniemin,
Danlo felt the eyes of thousands of people fall upon him. The
northern third of the room, through which Danlo now passed,
was a kind of loggia built on three levels. This viewing area was
swarmed with pilgrims standing shoulder to shoulder so that they
might be privileged to witness the great events occurring in the
rest of the Hall below them. There, laid out in many concentric
arches, were the long, curving, devotional tables where the Elder
Architects sat and decided the Church's fate. The tables all faced
south and encircled a red-carpeted dais at the very end of the

Hall. The whole design of this vast room was calculated to draw one's eyes toward this dais—toward the reading desk of the High Architect that sat there like some holy relic on display. In truth, this glittering piece of furniture was really more of a throne than a desk. It was wrought of cut-white kèvalin and etched around its sides and arms with purple neurologics; it was a colorful, eye-catching thing, and the faces of all the Elder Architects should have been lifted up toward it, waiting.

But as Danlo entered the Hall, each of the thousand Elders sitting at their tables turned in their chairs toward the north to study this naman of an unknown Order beyond their neighborhood of stars. Down the central aisle through the devotional tables Danlô walked, and as he passed by row upon row of Elders, they pointed their old fingers at him and shook their heads and voiced their outrage at his long, black hair and his otherworldly black pilot's robe. Many of them, with their shaved heads and ugly brown skullcaps, were plainly jealous when the keepers escorted Danlo almost to the very front of the Hall. The keepers held out his chair while he moved up to a little white table almost within whispering distance of the High Architect's reading desk. This was one of two tables to hold the position of honor at the front of all the many rows of tables in the room. Across the aisle separating the Hall, east and west, the other table of honor faced Danlo's. Here, in their shining white kimonos, sat twenty men and women, the highest ranking of all the Elders: Bertram Jaspari, Jedrek Iviongeon, Fe Farruco Ede, Kyoko Ivi Iviatsui, Sul Iviercier and others whom Danlo would come to know. They each stared at Danlo as he set his devotionary computer on the table and took his place in a hard plastic chair facing them. All his life, he remembered, he had hated sitting in chairs. And even more, he hated sitting at a long, white table whose nineteen other chairs remained empty. There, in the vast uncertainty of the great hall, beneath the reading desk of the High Architect—and beneath the stares of two thousand hostile strangers—Danlo felt almost naked and very much alone.

There are those here who would murder me as I once would have speared a tiger who stepped into my tribe's cave. With this thought came a memory of a poem that he had once spoken as a prayer: *Only when I am alone am I not alone.*

When the thousand Elders of the Koivuniemin at last had turned back in their chairs to face Danlo (and thus to face the reading desk of the High Architect) at the front of the Hall, one of the Temple keepers moved over to the front of the dais and called for silence. "You will all please stand," he suddenly announced. At each of the devotional tables, the Elders rose to their feet almost as a single body moving against the pull of gravity. Then, from behind the dais, on the south wall of the Hall, a door opened. Ten keepers escorted an old woman into the Koivuniemin's presence; they led her a short distance across the white plastic tiles right up to the dais's steps. With their help, she climbed up the red carpet and took her place at the holy reading desk. Of all the men and women present, she wore the only white skullcap and hers was the only kimono embroidered with gold crewelwork. "We welcome our highest Architect," the first keeper announced. "God's Architect, Keeper of the Eternal, our Eternal Ivi, Harrah Ivi en li Ede."

As one, all the Architects in the hall clasped their fingers beneath their chins in a prayer mudra and bowed to the High Architect of the Cybernetic Universal Church. Danlo bowed too, but according to the protocols of his Order. He kept his hands down by his side, and he dipped his head only so far as it was still possible to keep his eyes fixed on the woman whom he honored. And Harrah Ivi en li Ede, he saw to his delight, kept *her* eyes fixed on him. She had big, soft, brown eyes, beautiful eyes that betrayed a deep vulnerability. Danlo stared at this beautiful old woman across twenty feet of space, and he instantly loved the boldness of her gaze. He sensed that she possessed the rare strength to live within her vulnerability and turn it to her advantage. She was a proud woman, he thought, proud and powerful and yet almost selfless in her devotion to what she conceived of as the truth. Although Danlo instantly trusted her—insofar as he could trust any religionary bent on blowing up the stars—he did not look forward to matching his reason against her will.

"My Elder Architects of the Koivuniemin!" Harrah suddenly said. Her voice was as old and dry as the strings of a Yarkonan gosharp—and as sweet sounding and profound. Even though she remained seated, her words needed no amplification, and they carried out clearly into the Hall, even to the loggia's upper level. "My Dedicated Architects and all the Worthy from the cities of Tannahill and the worlds of the Known Stars, we are met here today to welcome Danlo wi Soli Ringess of Neverness. He is—"

Here, Harrah paused to push the fingertips of each hand against her temples. She was 128 years old, and she couldn't call her memories to mind as quickly as she once had done. "He is a Pilot of the Order of Mystic Mathematicians and Other Keepers of the Ineffable Flame, Emissary of what he calls the Civilized

Worlds—and strangely, an emissary of the Narain heretics of Alumit Bridge. A heavy burden for one so young to carry. He has come far to give us his words and salutations of distant peoples. We must decide if we should accept his gifts.''

For the count of five of Danlo's heartbeats, no one spoke. Danlo turned to look at the thousand Elders sitting silently in their rows. The Elders had set their devotionary computers in their proper places on the tables in front of them. A thousand imagos of Nikolos Daru Ede beamed their holy countenances upon the Elders and cast colors of brown or violet or ocher upon their old faces. A vast tension vibrated through the Hall, and Danlo smelled the bitterness of old sweat and fear that made his belly clutch.

''Holy Ivi!'' one of the Elders finally called out. Across the aisle, at the other table of honor, a little man stood up with great force as if his chair suddenly had been electrified. Although at sixty-one he was very young for an Elder, he was so humorless and grim that he might have been born with the dead. His face was cut with the deep lines of some terrible inner discord and was all edges and angles. Indeed, Danlo thought that he had never seen a face so sharp and narrow, like an ax head chipped out of a piece of flint. Unlike a well-made tool, however, there was an asymmetry about this man that hinted of inherited deformity or perhaps the exposure to some teratogenic chemical while he had been a babe developing in his mother's womb. The bones of his bald head seemed misshapen and slightly out of joint; this caused the crown of the skull to swell out like the point of a volcano. To cover this disfigurement, he wore a padded dobra embroidered with much gold thread and much larger than the skullcaps of the other Architects. His name was Bertram Jaspari, and Danlo immediately sensed that he was a shrewd and implacable man—as well as devious, fervent, tireless, and utterly lacking in grace.

''My Holy Ivi,'' Bertram repeated when he had gained the attention of all the Elders of the Koivuniemin. ''My views on this question are well shared. This Danlo wi Soli Ringess is a naman of an unknown Order. And worse, he is an emissary of the Narain heretics. Do not the *Logics* say that 'as a husband picks flowers for his bride, a man should choose which thoughts will best adorn his mind?' *We* say that the Pilot should not be allowed to speak. Who knows what negative programs run his naman's mind? When a naman speaks, his words may be as viruses that will infect all *our* minds. He is unadmitted; he sits here uncleansed before the eternal face of Ede; he should not have been brought into the Temple, much less allowed to address the Koivuniemin and our Holy Ivi."

Having completed this diatribe, the Elder Bertram Jaspari looked at Danlo as if to say, "We will pull the teeth from your voice before you even open your mouth."

For a moment, Harrah looked at Bertram carefully, and then she turned her piercing gaze toward his confederates who sat with him at the table of honor. These were Jedrek Iviongeon, Oksana Ivi Selow, and Fe Farruco Ede, all Elders of reknown and influence. "We must thank you for sharing your doubts," Harrah said.

Danlo looked up at the south wall behind Harrah where a great icon of Ede the God gleamed from its chatoyant surface. He understood that when Harrah used the pronoun "we," she spoke for the eternal Church as well as for the spirit of Nikolos Daru Ede.

"Holy Ivi," Bertram said. "Doubt implies uncertainty, but the *Logics* are quite clear as to the danger of namans such as this pilot."

"How certain you seem of this," Harrah said.

"We *are* certain," Bertram said. He looked over at Jedrek Iviongeon, a fierce old man with bristling white eyebrows and bloodshot blue eyes, and at the cunning Oksana Ivi Selow and then turned to look in the rows behind him for those many Elders who supported him. At last he looked back at Harrah. "Aren't *you*?"

While Harrah sat at her reading desk unperturbed (or perhaps stunned) by the insolence of Bertram's question, Danlo smiled at Bertram as he remembered the words of an old admonition: *I wish that I could be as certain of anything as he seems to be of everything.*

"*We* are certain of only one thing," Harrah said as she looked down at Bertram. "And that is, that for man, in this universe, all must always be uncertain. The truth is in Ede and only in Ede."

"*That* is certainly true, Holy Ivi," Bertram said. "And that is why Ede has given us His holy Algorithm, that we might be certain of his truth."

"We have always looked to the Algorithm for truth."

"As have we, Holy Ivi."

At this, Harrah beamed a smile at Bertram. There was neither irony nor condescension on her face; to Danlo, this benediction seemed utterly sincere. "If we look with a pure mind and love in our hearts," Harrah said, "the truth shines from Ede's words like light from the sun."

"The truth is the truth, Holy Ivi."

"If we open our ears and listen, the truth will sing inside us as a holy song."

"We must once again disagree," Bertram said. "The truth does not shine *from* what Ede has said; His words, themselves, *are* the truth, and we must simply obey His Algorithm and live by the Law."

"We would not wish to live any other way."

"But do not the *Logics* say: 'A naman is as dangerous as an exploding star'?"

"Indeed they do," Harrah said. "But do they not also tell us that we must be masters of the stars and lords of light?"

Here Bertram stepped into the aisle almost over to Danlo's table. He pointed a finger at Danlo, and Danlo saw that Bertram's ugly little hands sweated in times of duress. "But this man is a naman! And you have brought him into God's temple uncleansed!"

"We have brought him into the Hall of the Koivuniemin."

"Do not the *Logics* say that a man must be cleansed before he may face Ede in His holy house?"

Harrah looked at Bertram for a long time. Again she smiled at him, this time as if he were only one of her many grandchildren who wasn't quite old enough to understand the true spirit of Edeism. She asked, "And is it not said in the *Facings:* 'Whoever truly looks upon Ede's face, and looks truly, he shall be cleansed of all that is negative in his deepest programing and dwell in the eternal house of Ede until the end of time'?"

"But he is a naman! Has he, for one moment of his unclean, naman's life, ever given any thought to Ede or turned his eyes toward an *image* of His glorious face?"

At this, Danlo, sitting straight in his hard, plastic chair, couldn't help but think about the ruin of the great god called Ede whom he had discovered out in the galaxy's wastelands. He looked down at the hologram of Nikolos Daru Ede floating in the air. He looked at Ede's glowing face, and suddenly—but very slightly so that only Danlo could see—the Ede hologram winked at him and called up a smile to play across his sensuous, ruby-colored lips.

Strangely, Harrah chose that moment to smile at Danlo. Then she said, "Who can know what this pilot has thought or seen if we will not let him speak?"

"There are other ways of knowing," Bertram said.

Danlo thought that he had a sharp, irritating voice full of spikes like a Yarkonan thornbush—and full of threat as well. And he suddenly knew that this prince of the Church took great pleasure in causing others pain.

Again, Harrah stared at Bertram. "We should suppose that you would welcome the opportunity to hear the pilot's words," she said.

"How so, Holy Ivi? We have Ede's words—do we need others? Why should we pay heed to what a naman has to say about his journey across the universe?"

He pays great heed, Danlo thought as he looked at Bertram. *But like a merchant-prince with his treasures, he wishes to keep this information for himself.*

"And why," Bertram continued, "should we welcome the opportunity to listen as this naman brings us the words of heretics? We all know what must been done with heretics and their emissaries."

Bertram was a clever man, and he often triumphed at discourse and debate. But for all his glittering intelligence, like gold paint peeling off a lead ring, there was something shabby and shallow in his appreciation of other people. Because he was blind to the true power of Harrah Ivi en li Ede's mind, he completely overlooked the trapdoor that she held open for him.

"We should all welcome this pilot's words," Harrah said from her reading desk. Her voice was spirited and strong and it carried out into the Hall of the Koivuniemin. "Are we not all Elders and Worthy Architects of our Eternal Church? Haven't all our minds been cleansed of that which is negative or unworthy of the divine? And does not it say in *Meditations* that an Architect who has been cleansed is like a perfect mirror that can reflect nothing but Ede's perfect light? What do we see when we look out today in the sanctity of this Hall? Nothing but mirrors, a thousand perfect mirrors. We look out at all your perfect faces and see nothing but His glorious face reflected there. No particle of dust or bit of disinformation could mar the brilliance of such mirrors. Who among us has not spent a lifetime polishing and reprograming himself so that the words of a naman, however harmful or heretical, could not simply be reflected back into the darkness from which they came? The Elder Bertram Jaspari? How should he fear this young man from the stars? Has not the Elder Bertram been cleansed of such negative programs as doubt and fear? We see that he has. How he has polished himself! How perfectly he shines!

"Therefore, it cannot be fear that runs him—it must be something else. What could this be? Looking at him, we see nothing but devotion. He is devoted to the truth of the Algorithm. He pursues this truth more fervently than a suitor does a wife. Who could fault such zeal? Who could blame him for allowing himself to be run by such a divine desire? We are not here to blame or to find fault. We are here only to serve as an architect of Ede's divine Program for the universe. It is upon us alone, as High Architect, to be the final reader of this code. The truth is the truth, as Elder Bertram has reminded us. But the truth cannot be possessed or seized by force; it cannot be taken easily by merely mouthing the appropriate words. We must prepare ourselves to be worthy of the truth. We must program ourselves to shine with goodness and beauty and to bring these gifts to our beloved. Truth, like a woman, must be wooed and won—and this only through the purity of mind and the heart's deep love. It is upon us to remind the Elder Bertram of this. It is upon us to remind him that he must not approach the holy Algorithm as a merchant buying the services of a harlot, but rather in reverence, as a man bearing flowers in his hand."

When Harrah Ivi en li Ede at last had finished speaking, the Elders sat at their devotional tables dumbfounded and breathless. Never in memory of the Koivuniemin had any Elder suffered such an astonishing reprimand. Bertram Jaspari, whose white kimono now showed dark circles of sweat down the sides, stood fused to the floor of the Hall. He stared up at Harrah where she sat calmly at her reading desk. His eyes were as dark as dead moons; the muscles had popped out along his jaws as if the trigeminal nerve of his face had been touched with a jolt of electricity. Although Elder Architects were supposed to have evolved far beyond such base emotions as anger, Danlo could see that it was not so. Danlo thought that if the Temple keepers were to allow Bertram near Harrah's person, so great was his rage that he might tear at her with his clawlike hands and try to rip out her throat.

"Holy Ivi," Bertram finally managed to choke out. Now that he had regained his voice, he fell back upon that menacing quality of character that had served him so well in his rise to his Eldership. "We agree that it is upon you to be the final reader of the Algorithm. Therefore, we implore you to read it literally as it was written. The truth is there for all plainly to see. If Ede's words are misconstrued or interpreted according to mystic fancies, the damage to our Church could be incalculable. As Elders, we have taken a vow to be protectors of the Church. If you would see the truth as it is, Holy Ivi, look into the mirror that we hold before you and know that we will defend our Eternal Church no matter the cost."

With this, Bertram glanced over at Jedrek Iviongeon, who returned a knowing look and reflected a pure ferocity and faithfulness to the doctrines in which Bertram Jaspari believed. Then, while Jedrek cast his bloodthirsty gaze at his fellow Elder Fe Farruco Ede, Bertram let his eyes fall upon Oksana Ivi Selow, a dour old woman with many friends among the Koivuniemin. These Elders, in turn, shared eyespace with others sitting at their tables, and in this way, their zeal passed through the Hall as of mirrors reflecting the light of many mirrors.

"We implore you to see the truth before it's too late," Bertram Jaspari said. Then he sat down at his table of honor, folded his hands beneath his chin, and looked up at Harrah Ivi en li Ede almost as if to say: "We await your answer."

Danlo remembered, then, many things that Isas Lel Abraxax and the Transcendent Ones of Alumit Bridge had told him about the power struggles within the Old Church. He was almost certain that the "we" to which Bertram Jaspari referred was a sect of Architects known as the Iviomils. These were the orthodox of the orthodox. Iviomils were evangelists, missionaries, inquisitors. More alarmingly, the Iviomils thought of themselves as soldiers of God who must wage a facifah, a holy war to fulfill their faith's promise and glory. That this war might begin on Tannahill, within the very Hall of the Koivuniemin, seemed not to distress Bertram Jaspari or any of the other god-minded Architects who exalted themselves by the name of Iviomil.

"We thank you for speaking so truthfully," Harrah said to Bertram. And then, naming her enemy, she looked out at the rows of Elders and told them, "We thank all you Iviomils and any others who would defend our Church. Is it not written in the *Iterations* that whoever will die for the truth is an iviomil beloved of Ede and will not truly die when he dies? But is it not also written that truth is a many-faceted marvel, like an infinite diamond? And that to live with a pure mind is the only way to behold the terrible beauty of the universe's truth? Therefore, we implore *you* to have the courage to live your faith and listen for any truth in what this Danlo from the Stars will tell us here today."

While Harrah broke off talking to lock eyes with Bertram, Danlo remembered something else that Isas Lel had told him about the Old Church: that perhaps as many as a third of the Elders of the Koivuniemin were either Iviomils or sympathetic to the Iviomils' call for a purification of the Church. Harrah's two most recent predecessors, the High Architects Maveril Ivi Ashtoreth and Hisiah Ivi en li Yuon, had weakened the architetcy by acquiescing to many of the Iviomil's demands. The founding of a new college for training missionaries and enforcing the law requiring every married woman to bear at least five children were only two of the many items on the Iviomils' ambitious agenda.

It was said that only Harrah's diamond-hard will and her devotion to the renewed strength of the architetcy had kept the Iviomils from seizing control of the Koivuniemin. But it was said, too, that Harrah was very old and that no other Elder possessed the stature to replace her. Many spoke of Bertram Jaspari as the next High Architect. If this elevation were ever to occur, he would be the first Iviomil to be so exalted. It was a measure of Bertram's baseness that he lacked the patience simply to allow Harrah to age naturally and to die with grace.

"We will now hear from Danlo wi Soli Ringess, Pilot of the Order of Mystic Mathematicians and Other Keepers of the Ineffable Flame," Harrah announced. "We would ask him to explain, if he might, why the lords of his strangely named Order have sought our world."

Thus bidden finally to begin his mission to the Architects of the Old Church, Danlo stood up to address the Koivuniemin. He set his black pilot's boots firmly upon the white tiles of the floor; with his long fingers, he combed back the wild hair hanging down over his eyes. During his journey across the stars, he had memorized twenty speeches that he might blindly recite to these rapt and rabid fanatics of a waste-laying Church. And now, here, in the Hall of the Koivuniemin, beneath the great, glittering face of Nikolos Daru Ede, looking out over a thousand faces as empty of their own true thoughts as so many silver mirrors, he suddenly decided to forget his prepared words. What good were an emissary's words against minds so perfectly polished that they already reflected Ede's perfect truth? Danlo had hoped to bring the clear light of reason to them, but he could see that in order to touch them, he would need much more than rhetoric, no matter how brilliant or shining with the arguments for peace that he had formulated. Today, he needed the spear of compassion to pierce their hearts; a hammer he needed to smash the glass imprisoning them inside the very limited way in which they viewed the universe.

But where to find such rare and splendid weapons, he wondered?

"Eternal Ivi Harrah en li Ede," he began. "Elder Architects of the Koivuniemin, Dedicated Architects, and all the Worthy who have journeyed so far from home, I would like to tell you of all the marvels that I have seen." Here he paused a moment to draw in a deep breath of air; he felt the faint burn of ozone as a deep pain in his lungs. He took in another breath, and he smelled aldehydes and ammonia, halogens and cooked plastic, and perhaps even a trace of mercury vapors, and the pain jumped up to his left eye as of a spear stabbing into his brain.

"But I . . . must tell you of the tragedies that I have seen as well," Danlo continued. "We pilots seek the marvelous, truly. But on any such quest there will be much that is tragic and sad. I must tell you of these sadnesses. I must tell you of my life."

So saying, Danlo touched the lightning-bolt scar above his left eye. He looked across the room at Bertram Jaspari and Kyoko Ivi Iviatsui and other Elders sitting near them, and he told the Koivuniemin of his birth and of his strange and wild childhood among the Alaloi peoples who live on the frozen islands west of Neverness. He told of the death of his found-father and found-mother—the death of the whole Devaki tribe. This tragedy had been the work of a virus, he said. The slow evil had slain his people just as it had once taken the lives of billions of humans throughout the Civilized Worlds. It was the Architects of the Old Church, he reminded them, who with the help of the warrior-poets had manufactured this virus as a bioweapon during the War of the Faces.

"When my found-father, Haidar, went over to the other side of day, there was nothing left in his eyes. The light. It . . . flees so quickly. It can take a long time to die of this disease, but when the moment comes, there is nothing left of life, not even pain."

Especially not pain, he remembered.

He told of his deepest friend, Hanuman li Tosh, a sweet-natured boy whose terror of the Church's cleansing ceremonies had almost destroyed his spirit. He described his own journey into the Vild, and he told of the supernovas that he had seen. The radiation of these exploding stars, he said, fell everywhere. The killing light had burned the biospheres of many worlds to char.

"So many worlds," Danlo told them. "So much death. The trees, the flowers, the alien plants all burning like twists of toalache in a pipe. The animals, all blinded just before they went over. The people, too. How many human beings have died this way? Who will ever count their numbers? Who will ever say their names or pray for their spirits?''

Danlo paused to look up at Harrah Ivi en li Ede. He saw pain in her lovely brown eyes as well as a kind of bitter regret. If all the Elders were as compassionate as she, Danlo thought, he might possibly win them to the truth of his quest.

He told them of marvels, then. He told them of the Solid State Entity and the ringworlds out around Barakah Luz; he tried to describe what it was like to pilot a lightship through the many-colored spaces of the manifold. Many pilots of his Order, he said, at this moment were daring these shimmering spaces in hope of finding the Architects of Tannahill. At the edge of the galaxy's Orion arm, on the planet named Thiells, the Order was establishing an Academy to train new pilots to go out among the peoples of the Vild. The Order would invite many youths from many worlds to learn the pilots' art—as well as the arts of the cetics, the scryers, and all the other disciplines of the mind. The Order would do this because it was part of their purpose to bring peace to the Vild.

"That is why I have agreed to act as an emissary for the Narain, as well as a pilot of my Order, to bring peace. All peoples wish for peace. It is the dream of my Order that soon there will be peace among people, peace on every planet and throughout the stars. And someday, across the infinite circle of the universe itself. This is why I stand here today, in hope of peace.''

After Danlo had finished speaking, he bowed to Bertram Jaspari and Fe Farruco Ede and to many Elders of the Koivuniemin. He looked up at the High Architect's reading desk and bowed, deeply, to Harrah Ivi en li Ede. Then he made a fist and pressed his diamond pilot's ring into the palm of his other hand. As he sat back down at his table of honor, each pair of eyes throughout the Hall was turned upon him.

After Danlo's heart had beat nine times, Harrah Ivi en li Ede smiled at him and said, "Blessed are the peacewise, for they will dwell eternally at the center of the universe.''

"You understand,'' Danlo said.

"As you say, all peoples pray for peace.''

"And yet peace is so rare.''

"All people are born with negative programs,'' Harrah explained. "But we can learn to reprogram ourselves.''

"Often I have thought that the universe itself is flawed.''

"But of course it is. And that is why our Ede came into life, to bring a new program to the universe."

Danlo bowed his head for a moment, remembering. Then he said, "There is a word that my father once taught me, *shaida*. This is the world when it has fallen into disharmony. All the suffering, the evil of the universe. I would find the cure for this evil if I could."

"And you hoped to find this cure on Tannahill?"

"I . . . once hoped to journey to the center of the universe. Where, as you say, all is peace. This is why I became a pilot. Because if I could find that perfect place, I might see how shaida breaks out of the stillness like a tidal wave from the ocean deeps."

"You speak so metaphorically, even mystically." Here Harrah paused to smile again, and turned to look straight at Bertram Jaspari. "You must appreciate that many of us present here today have no sympathy with mysticism."

"As you have said, the name of my Order is strange," Danlo explained. "I am a pilot of the Order of Mystic Mathematicians. Through our blessed mathematics we seek . . . the mysteries of the universe. We seek the ineffable flame. The light. The light inside all things, that orders all things. That *is* all things. It shines everywhere the same, yes? Here on Tannahill as well as in the stone halls of the Academy on Neverness."

With a slow and stately bow of her head, Harrah honored Danlo's forthrightness. And then, at last, she said, "We thank you for speaking so freely. We're sorry for the death of your family. We know this disease that you call the slow evil. Since the War of the Faces, the Great Plague has killed many Architects, too. Though you are wrong to suppose that it was the Church who engineered the virus. It is well-known that it was the Reformist heretics who were responsible for this abomination. We know little about the warrior-poets—a name out of history. Perhaps they were associated with the Reformists. If so, this was only one of the tragedies of the war."

Harrah went on to lament the treacherous victory of the Reformed Church in the War of the Faces. Danlo sensed that, although she did not lie concerning her knowledge of the warrior-poets, neither was she telling the full truth. He felt this as a tightness in his belly and a burning behind his eyes. And then Harrah continued her history lesson, recounting the Old Church's flight into the unknown regions of the Vild. It had been a long and dangerous journey into darkness, she said. The Architects, at first wholly ignorant of the pilots' art, had resorted to blowing up the stars in their crude attempts to fracture spacetime and open windows to the manifold. Many of the Church's ships had been lost in wild spaces for which the Architect mathematicians had no name.

Of the 326 deep ships that had begun the Long Pilgrimage, as it was called, only one survived to fall out near Tannahill. Ten thousand Architects were few enough to populate a virgin world covered with lovely alien trees and sparkling oceans—or so they had thought at the time. But as with sleekits and other extremely fecund mammals, the reproductive powers of the Architects were phenomenal. In less than a thousand years, the Architects had filled their planet and had begun sending seedships full of fanatic, planet-hungry Iviomils to other stars. In their time on Tannahill, the Architects had found ways other than creating supernovas to enter the manifold. But these ways were not reliable. The Architects had learned only the barest rudiments of the pilots' art. It was possible, Harrah said, that the Iviomils of the Vild had come across spaces that they could not penetrate. It was possible that these faithful Architects had fallen back on their star-destroying techniques in their zeal to bring God's Algorithm to unadmitted peoples and faraway worlds.

"It is possible," Harrah told Danlo and the thousand Elders of the Koivuniemin, "that the lost Architects of the Long Pilgrimage also never learned to move through the manifold. Who can know how many lost Architects there really are? They might be causing the stars to fall into supernovas—they might know of no other way to complete Ede's program to populate the universe. We are sorry that this must be so. We mourn all those peoples who have died the real death without any hope of being vastened in Ede. We had thought that the number of supernovas was less than a hundred. Now we are told that there are probably millions. So many stars. But in the making of a supernova, so many new elements, too. Oxygen and nitrogen, hydrogen and carbon and iron. Are not our bodies made of this starseed? Are we not children of the stars? And is it not written that 'upon the light of the stars you shall turn your eyes and feast?' Each man and woman is a star—that, too, is written. It is part of Ede's Program that we Architects must shine. We must create the elements for new life and remake the universe. Now, and always, we must follow Ede's Program in utter faith."

Does she truly believe what she says?

Danlo wondered this as he gazed at Harrah across a few

dozen feet of the Hall. He sensed a terrible conflict behind her soft, brown eyes and her perfectly unreadable face.

Or does she defend this doctrine only to placate Bertram Jaspari and her enemies?

"And now," Harrah continued, "we must invite the Elders to speak. We invite them to ask Danlo wi Soli Ringess anything they would know concerning his quest."

The first of the Elders to question Danlo was, of course, Bertram Jaspari. He stood up from his table of honor and pointed at Danlo. "This pilot speaks words that border on blasphemy. He accuses our Holy Church of engineering the Plague virus! He tells of an unspeakable hakra whom he calls a god and dignifies by the name of the Solid State Entity! He has consorted with the Narain heretics! As a naman, what else could we expect of him? But we must never forget that he *is* a naman. We must never forget that his words are full of negative programs—the very *shaida* evil that he would seek a cure for! Must we listen to these words? Our Holy Ivi has said that we must, and therefore we shall. But we must question all that the pilot has told us. There is much in his account of his journey—and his very life!—that is unbelievable."

For what seemed a long time, Bertram asked Danlo questions. Neither he nor many other Elders could quite accept that Danlo had grown to manhood among a people who had long ago engineered themselves into the forms of primitive Neanderthal human beings. That Danlo and his tribe had once hunted living animals for their meat revolted Bertram. As with all the Architects of Tannahill, for his whole life he had eaten only cultured plant foods—and these produced in armored factories down in the levels of Ornice Olorun that no one was allowed to visit. He could scarcely imagine the icy islands of Danlo's childhood, much less envision Danlo gripping a spear and skiing after a shagshay bull through the great, green yu trees of a primeval forest.

Although these details of Danlo's life in the wild fascinated Bertram, he was obviously much more interested in Danlo's career as a pilot. He wanted to know everything about the Order; he asked about the relationship of Neverness to the rest of the Civilized Worlds. And many other questions. Had the Reformed Cybernetic Church really established itself as an authority in Neverness? Had they really spread their heresy to Yarkona and Larondissement and a thousand other worlds? How many pilots and lightships could the Order send out into the galaxy? And of this number, how many had joined in the Second Vild Mission and journeyed to Thiells where the Order was establishing a new Academy? Most of all, as with the Narain Transcendentals, Bertram Jaspari desired to understand how a pilot could fall so far across the stars. But this Danlo would not reveal. He then told the Elders of the Koivuniemin why he was not permitted to speak of his blessed pilots' art. To most of Bertram's other questions, however, he responded as truthfully as he could—sometimes too truthfully.

"You say that this hakra that you call the Solid State Entity has expanded into a region of space at the edge of the Orion arm. What, would you estimate, is this hakra's size?"

"She is spread out across many stars. Perhaps a whole nebula. Her body and brain are vast."

"But how vast is vast, Pilot?"

"Perhaps the measure of Her physical self would be six hundred thousand cubic light-years."

"What? But that's impossible!"

Bertram traded a quick, dangerous look with Jedrek Iviongeon as if to ask why they must suffer the lies of a troublesome naman. Throughout the Hall, however, the Elders buzzed with excitement like bees who have discovered a new source of honey.

"What is truly possible?" Danlo asked. He spoke softly, almost to himself. He sat at his table of honor, and Bertram's doubt both vexed and amused him.

"Why are you smiling, Pilot?"

"I was only remembering something."

"And what is that?"

"It was something that I once asked my Fravashi teacher."

"Would you care to inform the Koivuniemin what this question was?"

"Yes, if you'd like, Elder Bertram."

"Well?"

"I asked him how it was possible . ... that the impossible is not only possible but inevitable."

"What? But that's absurd!"

As Bertram stood across the room staring at Danlo, his hard little eyes were a dead gray color like old sea ice.

"It *is* a paradox," Danlo agreed. "I am sorry."

"I think you are fond of paradoxes, Pilot."

"Sometimes, yes."

"Then you should understand that the only way to save the universe is first to destroy it."

"Do you believe that the universe can be destroyed? Truly?"

With a wave of his hand, Bertram brushed this question aside. He turned to his fellow Elders and said, "As for the people who have died in the light of the supernovas, we must remember that they were only namans. At the end of their lives, they would have died the real death anyway. Should we mourn people who turn away from the possibility of being vastened in Ede? We must remember the missions that we sent to Ezhno and Masalina—rejected without even the opportunity to tell of Ede's Vastening and the Algorithm that He gave us. And what of those brave Iviomils whom we sent to Matopek? Lost in the manifold—or perhaps murdered upon reaching the namans' world. Such murders have happened before. How many Iviomils have given their first lives to bring the truth to such murderous namans? If a naman should reject the truth, should we mourn his inevitable death? Is it not written that he who turns away from Ede is like a flower hiding from the sun? Should we be surprised when these flowers wither and die?"

He is confusing his metaphors, Danlo thought. *So many people, so many children—all these splendid flowers facing their own truths and dying into light as their suns died.*

"Others have turned away from Ede, as well," Bertram reminded the Koivuniemin. "Even Worthy Architects who were once our own. We find it more than disturbing that Danlo wi Soli Ringess should act as an emmissary for the Narain heretics. He has said that he prays for peace, but we must wonder if peace is really his purpose!"

As if a signal had been given, one of the Elders behind Bertram—a jowly old Iviomil named Demothi Iviaslin—struggled to his feet and wheezed out, "Let us ask the Pilot if he has entered any of the forbidden cybernetic spaces that Narain are known to face in complete disregard of the instantiation rules of the *Logics*?"

Danlo told the Koivuniemin, then, much of what had occurred during his time on Alumit Bridge. Although he was reluctant to describe his ecstatic merging with that sublime being known as Shahar, he admitted that he had entered the Narain's computer-generated Field and had faced the Transcended Ones.

"Truly, they were as bright as stars," Danlo said. "I tried not to turn away from them."

"That is blasphemy!" Bertram suddenly shouted. "The Pilot blasphemes, and we might possibly forgive him his crime, for he is only a naman. But we cannot forgive the heretics. They have surely left the Church. And so they are not only heretics but apostates! We must decide what should be done with them. We must seek a solution to the Narain problem before it is too late."

Just then another of the Iviomils behind Bertram called out, "What should be done with the Narain?"

And, across the Hall, another of Bertram's confederates loudly demanded, "What should be done about the problem of Alumit Bridge?"

"Let's call a facifah!" cried a red-faced Elder.

"Yes, a holy war!" Then, several voices called out at once, "Let's make a holy war upon the heretics!"

For a while, the Hall of the Koivuniemin rang with shouts and calls for war. And, from other Architects such as Leo Tolow and Varaza li Shehn, calls for reason as well. At last Harrah Ivi en li Ede called for quiet. She looked down at Bertram and the many other Iviomils bent on bringing violence into the Hall. Then she reminded the Elders, "This is not the time to debate the merits of a facifah. We are here only to speak with Danlo wi Soli Ringess."

"Then I must ask the pilot a question," Bertram Jaspari said. In the light falling down from the Hall's glittering ceiling, his face seemed as gaunt and grim as the bones of an old skull. "Did any of the Narain call themselves gods? Did any man or woman ever claim to *be* God, in mockery of all that is holy?"

Danlo stared at the point of Bertram's misshapen head pushing up beneath his brown skullcap. It reminded him of the peak of Mount Urkel that towered above Neverness. He remembered then, the Narain madman named Tadeo Aharagni, who had indeed claimed to be Ede the God. Because Danlo could not help but tell the truth and because he suspected that Bertram already knew the answer to his own question, he spoke to the rapt Elders of this man.

"Tadeo Aharagni calls himself as Ede the God, truly. But he means only that he and Ede the God are of the same substance. That they share the same spirit. This sharing occurs between all the Narain and the Architects of the Church, yes? I believe that the Narain of Alumit Bridge have remained true to the spirit of Edeism."

"*You* believe this?" Bertram shouted in outrage. "A naman wishes to tell us about the spirit of Ede the God?"

"Spirit . . . is always truly spirit, yes?"

"But the heretics mock Ede! In trying to make a new religion, they mock the Holy Algorithm!"

"But does not your Church teach that—"

"What can a naman know about our holy Church?"

Danlo was silent for a moment as he pressed his fist against his forehead. "What do *you* know about your Church, then?" he asked.

"What! What do you mean?"

And Danlo told Bertram, "If you cannot see what is holy in another's religion, you cannot see . . . what is holy in your own."

"I see a heretic sitting before us in our holy Hall telling us lies!" Bertram shrieked. "That is to say, you *would* be a heretic if you had ever had faith in the only true religion."

"And you would kill all heretics, yes?"

"We would save them from themselves! We would cleanse them of their negative programs. As fire burns away fungus in a diseased face."

"Is this the same fire that has fallen out of the murdered stars?"

Bertram stood staring at Danlo. Then he said, "We shouldn't be surprised, I suppose, that a naman is concerned over the fate of other namans doomed to die."

"They were *people*!" Danlo, who rarely evinced anger toward other men, felt the beginnings of black wrath as a pounding of his heart and a terrible heat behind his eyes. "Mothers and fathers . . . children who played with flowers in the sun."

"No, namans, only namans."

"But they of Alumit Bridge—they are not namans! They are your far-cousins! They are your granddaughters and great-grandsons!"

"They are heretics and apostates."

Danlo looked at Bertram for a long time. "How is it that you hate so deeply . . . people who seek only love?"

"I'm afraid that you could never understand how we Iviomils feel toward the heretics who have betrayed us."

Danlo, who knew almost all there was to know about hatred, said, "No, it is just the opposite."

I understand too well, Danlo thought. *The orthodox always hate prophets and new revelations. The godless always hate the godful.*

"Please, tell us, Pilot, what you think you understand," Bertram said in his most mocking voice.

Danlo bowed his head slightly, and said, "If you'd like. You Iviomils are like merchants who have hoarded gold for a thousand years and set a guard around your wealth. But all your coins are cold in your hands. You seek the true gold—everyone does. This is the gold of flowers and sunlight. It shimmers inside all things. It is just life itself. The wild joy of life finding ever greater life within itself. It is as warm as a newborn child. It is as splendid and rare as a blue giant star. You look across the stars at Alumit Bridge, and you see the Narain dancing in that loveliest of lights. Do you fear that they have found what you most deeply desire? Truly, you do. And so you covet their gold. And so you hate them, and hating, you speak so easily of making a holy war. But even if you call a facifah, you cannot make their treasure your own. All you can do is to destroy it. All you can do is to hate —and in the end you will only hate yourselves for killing that which was most precious to you."

After Danlo had finished speaking, a vast silence fell over the Hall. His words had shocked and shamed many of the Elders. Many stared openly at Bertram as if to ask why he had shown the Church so poorly to this pilot and emissary from the stars. But the Iviomils sitting at their curved tables stared at Danlo in silent rage. As did Bertram. His sweaty hands were clenched into fists, his blue-tinged skin flushed red.

"This naman," he said, pointing at Danlo, "is a dangerous man."

There was menace in his voice, rising hatred in his eyes.

"And perhaps something more," he continued. He smiled grimly and looked over at cruel, old Jedrek Iviongeon; he looked at Fe Farruco Ede and Oksana Ivi Selow and many of his other friends. "Something I am reluctant to put a name to."

Danlo sat straight in his chair counting the beats of his heart. All his life he had tried to speak the truth. Only now, as he watched the dark angels of violence pass eye to eye from Bertram to Jedrek and then on to the Iviomils who sat near them, he wondered how well truth had served his purpose. With men such as Bertram Jaspari, would not a carefully constructed lie be a much more effective tool? He watched Bertram staring at him, and he remembered something that his friend Hanuman had once told him: that bad things always happen to those who think they must bring the truth.

"If I may," Bertram said almost softly, "I should like to ask the pilot one more question."

From her reading desk at the front of the Hall there came a stirring and a swish of silk as if Harrah had awoken from a bad dream. Slowly she nodded her head. "You've already asked many questions. But if you wish, you may ask one more—as long as you're careful of what you ask."

"Thank you, Holy Ivi," he said, bowing. Then he turned to Danlo and said, "You seem to have a love of the heretics—have the dreams of the Narain become *your* dreams? Is it your wish to try to become a god?"

"No," Danlo immediately replied. He couldn't help smiling at Bertram. "I wish to become . . . no more than I was born to be."

"That is no answer, Pilot. You've told us nothing."

For a moment, in the light flashing from Danlo's deep blue eyes, there was everything. And then he said, "I want only to be a true human being."

"But what does that mean?"

"There is a word that my Fravashi teacher once gave me," Danlo said. "The *asarya*. This is a man who could say yes to everything about being human."

This answer seemed to satisfy many of the assembled Elders, who nodded their heads and fell with buzzing voices into a hundred separate conversations. But Bertram looked out at the Elders of the Koivuniemin and then turned to Harrah Ivi en li Ede. "Our Holy Ivi has said that this Danlo wi Soli Ringess has spoken truly. Has he indeed? If we are to consider all that he has told us, we must be certain that he really is who he says he is. Perhaps we should invite him into a cleansing cell that we might read the truth or falsity of his words. I—or many other Elders—would be honored to offer my services at such a reading."

Bertram's little mouth puckered as with the anticipation of sucking on a bloodfruit. He looked at Jedrek Iviongeon and several other Iviomils who shared his cruel intentions.

"At this time," Harrah Ivi en li Ede said, "that will not be necessary."

"But we must know the truth!"

"We, also, desire to know the truth about the pilot," Harrah said. "And the truth about all that he has told us."

"There is only one truth, Holy Ivi."

"But there are many paths toward this holy place," she reminded him.

So saying, she turned to look at Danlo sitting alone at his long plastic table. Her face was thoughtful, provocative, and sad—but otherwise wholly unreadable. Danlo watched the eyes of a thousand Elders looking back and forth between Harrah and him, and he sensed that he was about to be tested yet again.

CHAPTER 18

THE PROPHECY

A similar problem concerns the Doctrine (or Program) of the Halting. This is the teaching that the halt state of the universe will occur when Ede has absorbed and become coextensive with the universe. But according to the ancient mathematics, there can be no universal algorithm for deciding whether or not a turing machine will ever reach its halt state. Therefore, it is impossible to know scientifically that Ede will in fact become the Universe-as-God. There can be no proper reconciliation of this vital doctrine with scientific theory unless God is seen as an infinite being outside space and time. The cybernetic theologians usually have seen God in this way. When Ede becomes God at the end of the universe, time will stop and Ede will exist in eternity. In some sense, Ede already is eternal, and thus He exists in all times at once. Since this is so, he is privileged to foreknow the halt state of the universe and all states leading to this singularity in time. Thus his pronouncement, "I am God," can be seen not merely as a prophecy of the future and a visualization of the halt state, but as a present validation of Ede's eternal being in the omniscient and the divine.

—from the Encyclopaedia Britannica, *1,754th ed., 10th rev., Standard Version*

While the world of Tannahill turned slowly on its axis and Danlo sat patiently watching Harrah Ivi en li Ede, she bowed her head to one of the keepers who stood ready to minister to her desires. The keeper—a handsome young man who might have been her grandson—bowed his head in return. Then he left the dais and walked over to the rear door by which Harrah had entered the

Hall. With the strong, crisp motions of one who is certain of his body, he opened this door. He beckoned to the two men who waited in the anteroom behind it, then led them out into the Hall right over to the table of honor where Danlo was watching them with all the intensity of a thallow searching the skies for a brother bird.

Although the sudden appearance of these men caused the assembled Elders to crane their necks and gasp in astonishment, Danlo remained clear-eyed and calm. He smiled at these newcomers and bowed his head in acceptance of the logic of their presence. For he knew these men. They were, of course, Sivan wi Mawi Sarkissian, the renegade pilot, and the warrior-poet, Malaclypse Redring of Qallar. They had followed him thousands of light-years across the stars, and Danlo watched with great amusement (and not a little dread) as the keeper pulled out their chairs and sat them at the table of honor almost next to Danlo.

My fate, Danlo thought. *My beautiful and terrible fate.*

At least one of the Elders, however, was not even slightly amused. The Elder Bertram Jaspari jumped up from his chair, astonishment and outrage upon his implacable face.

"Who are these men?" he demanded. He pointed at Sivan. "Namans, obviously—this one is dressed as barbarically as the Pilot! From what world do they come? Why weren't we informed that they had made planetfall? How is it that they are brought into the Koivuniemin's Hall, and no mention of this event is made on today's agenda?"

The other Elders shifted in their chairs to look at Sivan and Malaclypse. Danlo looked, too. In truth, he never took his eyes off the warrior-poet, who, in turn, stared deeply into Danlo's eyes as if to say: "No matter where in the universe you may journey, Pilot, no matter how far you fall, your fate is joined to mine."

According to the warrior-poets' ways, Malaclypse wore a long kimono in honor of the Architects' style of dress. But because he was a warrior-poet of great accomplishment, this singular garment was not white, but rather woven of scarlet and sapphire and gold—and a hundred other colors. Everything about the warrior-poet fairly shimmered with colors. He wore a red ring on the little finger of each hand. His eyes were the same deep and vivid violet that Danlo remembered so well. With these marvelous eyes, the warrior-poet searched the room, looking first at Danlo, then at Bertram and moving quickly over to Harrah Ivi en li Ede poised so mysteriously behind her reading desk. As always, there was death in the warrior-poet's gaze. As always, he waited ever ready either to die himself or to bring any man or woman whom he must assassinate to his moment of the possible.

These Architects fear the warrior-poet, Danlo thought. *But they do not truly know why they fear him.*

With a wave of her hand, Harrah Ivi en li Ede motioned for Bertram to sit down. Then she introduced both Sivan and Malaclypse Redring. Although she apologized for not informing the Elders that she had called these two namans to the Hall of the Koivuniemin, she clearly did not regret her decision. Danlo understood immediately that this was a display of her power.

"It would seem that Malaclypse Redring of Qallar comes to us on a mission, as does the pilot," Harrah said to the Elders. "The Order of Warrior-Poets, it seems, desires to reestablish relations with our Church. What an extraordinary coincidence that representatives of two such venerable Orders should find our world at the same time after fifteen hundred years of being lost to us. What a coincidence that the warrior-poet seems to know this pilot. We have asked Malaclypse Redring into our Hall that you may explore these coincidences. Here they sit, at the table of honor, so that you may honor them by asking them questions. As Our Eternal Ede has said, there is always a way toward the truth."

At this, Danlo locked eyes with Sivan wi Mawi Sarkissian, who sat at the warrior-poet's right. Sivan was dressed as Danlo had first seen him at Mer Tadeo's party on Farfara, in plain gray garments of no distinctive cut or style. Years ago, when he had forsaken the Order, he had surrendered his pilot's robes. But he had not surrendered his black diamond pilot's ring; a pilot and his ring, as the saying goes, are forever. With this almost indestructible ring Sivan now rapped the edge of the table. He bowed his head to Danlo, an acknowledgment of Danlo's great feat in piloting his lightship through the Vild and finding Tannahill. In turn, Danlo touched his own ring to the plastic table. He smiled and bowed to Sivan. For Sivan to have followed him halfway across the galaxy was an almost impossible accomplishment.

The two pilots stared at each other for a long time. Between them there was an immediate understanding. They shared memories of the terrors of the manifold as well as the spires and the icy streets of Neverness. They were both strangers and outsiders on this lost world. And yet, despite their strange camaraderie, Danlo could never forget that this renegade pilot served Malaclypse Redring—the great warrior-poet who was his nemesis, his shadow, his enemy.

"I should like to question the warrior-poet."

This came from an Elder Architect named Nashota ivi As-taret, a big, stern woman well-known to the Koivuniemin for making long and boring speeches as to the duty of all women fulfilling the obligations laid down in the *Logics*. She was also, as everyone knew, a prominent Iviomil, the confidante and mouth-piece of Bertram Jaspari. "I should like to ask him how he knows this pilot."

At first it was not easy for Malaclypse to make his responses understood. Although the warrior-poets are noted for their silver tongues, Malaclypse had only learned the language of the Archi-tects in preparation for his journey into the Vild. Unlike Danlo, who had absorbed this language from living men and women on Alumit Bridge, the warrior-poet had learned the ancient Church Istwan spoken at the time of the Long Pilgrimage. Over fifteen hundred years, the language had changed greatly. And so Mala-clypse's speech was stived with misinflections, malapropisms, and archaic terminology. His accent was very thick. However, as Nashota ivi Astoret continued to question him, he listened care-fully. He was very quick, very smart. Moment by moment, it seemed, the words flowing out of his mouth like liquid silver were articulated with more modern rhythms and a shift in the sounds of the vowels. He abandoned such locutions as "Holy Exalted Elder" in favor of more proper forms of address. With both charm and aplomb, he spoke of many things to the Elders of the Koivuniemin. After he had told of Danlo's and his meeting on Farfara, he recounted his Order's ancient enmity with the Order of Mystic Mathematicians, of how the warrior-poets had once sided with the Old Church. He implied that the warrior-poets had indeed aided the Old Church in designing the virus that had caused the Great Plague. This news caused near-havoc among the Elders. From dozens of curving tables came cries of disbelief and outrage. At last—and yet again—Bertram Jaspari pushed his chair back and took the floor. He pointed his finger at Malaclypse and said, "We must ask the warrior-poet a ques-tion."

Reluctantly, Harrah Ivi en li Ede nodded.

"By your own words, your Order has been the enemy of the pilot's Order for thousands of years. Why should we believe what you say?"

At this, Malaclypse let his marvelous violet eyes play across Bertram's face. And then, in a deep, clear voice vibrating with utter certainty, he said, "We warrior-poets are taught three things: how to kill, how to die, and how to tell the truth."

The Elder Architects sat quietly in their chairs, and no one moved.

"Why have you come to our world?" Bertram asked softly.

"The simple answer is that my Order would like to renew its ancient relation with your Church," Malaclypse said.

"Is there a more complicated answer?"

"As with an onion, there are always layers of complication," Malaclypse said. "The universe is infinitely complex."

He comes to make enemies between my Order and the Church, Danlo suddenly knew. *That is the first of his purposes.*

"Perhaps we could peel back these layers to uncover the truth," Bertram said.

"There is always a way toward the truth," Malaclypse agreed, saying nothing—and perhaps everything, too.

Bertram stared at Malaclypse as if he had suddenly acquired the skills of a cetic and could read the warrior-poet's face. "From what we understand of your Order, you warrior-poets share nothing in common with our Holy Church."

"Nothing?"

Bertram hesitated. "We can think of nothing."

"Then we must indeed perform some more onion peeling," Malaclypse said. "For both my Order and your Church share one crucial purpose."

"And what is that?"

"We, as well as you, are disturbed by the growth of the galaxy's gods."

"There are no *gods*!" Bertram said immediately and angrily. "No god is there but God; God is one, and there can be only one God."

"And the name of God," Malaclypse said, "is Ede, the Eternal, the Infinite, the Architect of the Universe."

"You are familiar with the Algorithm?"

"We warrior-poets always seek the poetic. In the Algorithm we have sometimes found the most sublime poetry."

"It's a mistake to hear the words of the Algorithm as mere poetry," Bertram said. Despite the rebuke in his voice, the warrior-poet's words obviously pleased him. "Poetry, however sublime, is made by man. But the Algorithm was given to us by Ede the God."

" 'He will hammer the heavens and the stars will ring,' " Malaclypse said, quoting from *The Birth of Ede the God.* "It's difficult to hear this as other than poetry, is it not? Surely you can't picture Ede as some sort of infinitely vastened human being floating out in the cosmos with a gigantic hammer in his hand?''

"But He *will* hammer the heavens," Bertram said. "We must take these words in truth as they were given to us."

"But in what way are these words true?"

"We must accept this verse literally without asking in what way it is true."

"But wouldn't many in your Church dispute this? Don't your Elidis teach that the Algorithm must be read like poetry if the voice of Ede is to be heard inside the heart?"

Here, Bertram looked over at a nearby table and snatched a quick, poisonous look at Kissiah en li Ede, the most prominent Elder Architect of the Elidi sect. Kissiah, whose bright, black eyes burned with the same mystical intensity of his far great-grandfather, sat smiling like a buddha as if he agreed with all that Malaclypse had said.

"You seem to know much about our Church," Bertram observed as he looked at the warrior-poet.

"I know that you do not countenance the galaxy's gods," Malaclypse said. And then, uttering the hated word, he continued, "I know that you would cleanse the universe of all hakras."

"What do you know of the hakra devils?"

"Don't many women and men aspire to the godhead? Aren't there would-be gods everywhere?"

"Not on Tannahill," Bertram said. "Not among the worlds of the Known Stars."

Malaclypse looked at Bertram sharply. Then he said, "But other worlds know other ways."

"Naman worlds."

"From Solsken to Farfara, there are a thousand of the Civilized Worlds," Malaclypse said. "These are not wholly naman worlds. Many branches of the Cybernetic Church have established themselves there for a thousand years."

"The Reformist heretics," Bertram spat out. "They are no longer of our Eternal Church."

"And yet they too would forbid the rise of the would-be gods, if they could."

"You imply that these so-called Civilized Worlds have allowed the hakra devils to live?"

"It can be hard to keep a man from moving godward."

"Which worlds?" Bertram wanted to know. "Which hakras—do they have names?"

"It's said that the Solid State Entity of whom the pilot has spoken had its origins on one of the Civilized Worlds."

Her true name is Kalinda of the Flowers, Danlo remembered. *It is known that She was born of Qallar—and once a time She was the greatest warrior-poet there has ever been.*

"Are there other hakra devils?" Bertram asked.

"None so evolved as this Entity."

"But there are those who have turned their eyes godward in lust for the infinite lights?"

"It's possible," Malaclypse said.

Danlo turned to look at Malaclypse's beautiful hands. They were folded beneath his chin almost as if he was ready for prayer. The two red rings encircling his fingers touched each other in a figure eight, thus forming the ancient symbol for infinity. The light from the rings shimmered crimson, and Danlo remembered that Kalinda had been the only other warrior-poet ever to wear two red rings. But in the end She had betrayed the Order of Warrior-Poets to become a goddess. Might Malaclypse be planning revenge? Did he somehow hope to slay the goddess, She whose vast brain and being was spread across thousands of stars? No, that was not possible. But it *was* possible, he thought, that Malaclypse could hurt the Entity in another way. Twenty-five years ago, Mallory Ringess had befriended the Entity and had made an alliance with Her. Some said that this union had been almost a marriage. Perhaps Malaclypse hoped to wound the Entity by finding Mallory Ringess and slaying him. If Mallory Ringess truly had tried to become a god, Malaclypse was bound by the new rule of the warrior-poets, to slay all hakras and potential gods.

But why, Danlo wondered, *did the Entity not slay him when he fell out above the Earth? Did She spare his life simply because he wore two red rings?*

"Do you know the names of these other hakra devils?" Bertram asked Malaclypse again.

"I know *a* name," Malaclypse said. He stared at Bertram, and it seemed an immediate understanding passed between them as if he had handed Bertram a bloodfruit to eat.

"And what is that name?" Bertram asked. He spoke loudly and with calculated purpose, letting his voice carry out to the Elders around him.

"There is a man," Malaclypse said, "who may have attempted to become a god. He was a pilot who lived in Neverness."

"A pilot?"

"A pilot, indeed. He was the Lord Pilot of the Order of Mystic Mathematicians."

This news, dropped into the Hall of the Koivuniemin like a bomb, caused the Elders to explode into shouts of disbelief. The vast room shook with the force of a thousand voices. For a long time, Danlo watched and waited, counting the beats of his heart. Then Harrah Ivi en li Ede called for quiet. She looked down from her reading desk, and to Malaclypse she said, "Please tell us this Lord Pilot's name."

Now a thousand Elder Architects were watching the warrior-poet and waiting, too.

"His name," Malaclypse said, "is Mallory Ringess."

"Mallory *Ringess*?" Bertram immediately asked. He cast Danlo a long, venomous look.

"That was his birth name, the name by which he was commonly known."

"Then does he have another name?"

"His proper name is Mallory wi Soli Ringess."

Bertram continued to stare at Danlo. "Does this Lord Pilot bear relation to Danlo wi Soli Ringess?"

"He is his father."

Again, the Hall erupted with protest and shouts of anger. One of the Elders, pointed her trembling finger at Danlo and cried out, "He is the son of a hakra!"

And an old man near her shouted, "What if he aspires to be a god, too?"

"He should be cleansed of his hubris!"

"But what if he is himself a hakra?"

"Then he should be cleansed completely. The universe must be cleansed of all hakras."

For some time the Elders of the Koivuniemin discussed the urge to move godward, which was programed inside all human beings. Some said that his was man's original program, a wholly negative program that must be rewritten and overcome. Then, from her reading desk, Harrah spoke to the Elders, reminding them that no man was to be held accountable for the programs or actions of his father—or of anyone else.

Malaclypse then told of Mallory Ringess's astonishing career, from his strange birth to his discovery of the Elder Eddas, and finally, his ascension as Lord of the Order. He told of how, on a dark, deep winter day, Mallory Ringess had climbed into his lightship one last time and had left Neverness, possibly to go out into the galaxy and become a god. From this great example, he said, a new religion called Ringism had blossomed like a fireflower almost overnight. The Ringists of Neverness—and now many other Civilized Worlds—taught that Mallory Ringess became a real god and would one day return to the city of his birth. They taught that all human beings could become gods, too, and that the path toward godhood was in remembrancing the Elder Eddas and following the way of the Ringess. These teachings were called the Three Pillars of Ringism, which were also the deepest of heresies against the tenets of the Old Church.

The Elder Architects sitting at their tables listened in horror to his every word. When he finished speaking, there was silence in the Hall. Then, all at once, the Iviomils jumped to their feet and called out such condemnations as, "Heretics!" "Blasphemers!" "Hakras!"

Finally, Bertram Jaspari, greatest of the Iviomils, pointed at Danlo and demanded, "And what role did this pilot play in the making of the cult called Ringism?"

"He was close to the founders of Ringism, a former pilot called the Bardo and the cetic, Hanuman li Tosh."

"Is that all?"

"No. It's said that Danlo wi Soli Ringess drank the kalla drug and gained a great remembrance of the Elder Eddas. It's known that he shared this knowledge with other Ringists at a gathering that attracted a hundred thousand citizens of Neverness."

"And what are these Elder Eddas of which you speak?"

So Malaclypse told the Koivuniemin of the deep, genetic memories that an elder race of gods had supposedly implanted inside all human beings. So great was the disbelief in the Hall that even Bertram had trouble speaking. "You say that these Elder Eddas are supposedly programs designed to guide humanity into *godhood*?"

"That is one part of the Elder Eddas, as I understand it," Malaclypse said. "We warrior-poets do not lose ourselves in remembrance."

"But you imply that there are other parts?"

"It's also believed that the Eddas is pure information, pure memory—the collective wisdom of the ancient gods known as the Ieldra."

"But there are no gods!" Bertram reminded Malaclypse. "No god is there but God, and Ede the God was the first and only god."

"The Ringists, it would seem, do not share this theology."

Bertram looked at Malaclypse, looked at Danlo, and then turned to look out at the many Elders sitting tensely at their tables behind him. "The Narain heresy is a denial of our holy Algorithm and an affront to God," he said. "But this Way of Ringess is far worse."

Perhaps he is right, Danlo thought.

As Danlo studied Bertram's sharp, fanatical face, he wondered if he should tell the Elders that the greatest of gods, the Solid State Entity, had once been a warrior-poet, even as Malaclypse Redring. And he wondered if he should explain that he had separated himself from Bardo's new religion long before he had left Neverness and had made enemies of Hanuman li Tosh even as he had set himself against the Way of Ringess and its dangerous doctrines. But Danlo did not wish to be seen as spiteful or defensive. He sensed that he still had the goodwill of Harrah and many of the Elders—perhaps even most of them except the Iviomils.

"We must ask ourselves," Bertram said to his fellow Elders, "what should be done about this Ringism cult? What should be done about this pilot and emissary of heretics, Danlo wi Soli Ringess?"

So adroit had been the verbal dancing between Bertram and the warrior-poet that Danlo wondered if Bertram was performing a play for the Koivuniemin. Had Bertram truly not known of Malaclypse's presence on Tannahill until Harrah had summoned him into the Hall? Perhaps Bertram somehow had contrived to meet with Malaclypse in secret; perhaps these two dangerous men had made a secret alliance.

Looking at Malaclypse sitting so calmly at the table they shared, Danlo thought that this might be possible. For a moment, the whole of Danlo's awareness concentrated on the warrior-poet. He drank in the peppery essence of the kana oil perfume that Malaclypse wore as well as the intense light of Malaclypse's eyes. As always, Malaclypse seemed marvelously alive; he seemed always to be poised on the edge of eternity, waiting for some critical moment. Danlo wondered how well the Temple keepers had searched him for weapons. A warrior-poet, he knew, always kept weapons secreted about his person: hidden knives, false fingernails, poisoned darts disguised as toothpicks—and especially explosive siriwa thread woven into the fabric of his garments. Had Malaclypse conspired with Bertram to slay Harrah Ivi en li Ede? *It is possible,* he thought, and he stared at Malaclypse for what seemed forever.

And even as his eyes burned with the beauty of Malaclypse's deadly form, he saw Malaclypse reaching his red-ringed hand into an inner pocket of his kimono. He saw Malaclypse moving, and yet he was aware that Malaclypse moved not. It came to him that he must be scrying, that this was a prevision of moments yet to be. Because of Danlo's intense concentration, he took no notice of the other movement that came from behind his table.

But just as Bertram pronounced the words, *What should be done about Danlo wi Soli Ringess?*, a large, fleshy-faced Elder named Janegg Iviorvan rose from his chair. He had the end position at a table two rows back behind Danlo, and it took him little time to bluster forth into the center aisle as if it were his calling to address the Koivuniemin. But his purpose that day was neither speech nor communication. In his large, fleshy hand he brandished an ugly weapon. At the sight of this terrifying thing, several nearby Elders shouted out, "He has an eye tlolt!" And then, like a wave spreading through row after row, others picked up the panic until the farthest reaches of the Hall echoed with the warning.

"Death to heretics!" Janegg Iviorvan cried out. "Death to namans!"

In the moment that Danlo heard the hatred in Janegg Iviorvan's voice and turned to behold his assassin, many things happened at once. Many Elders tried to flee, their bodies jamming the narrow aisles. Danlo was distantly aware of how the men and women around him reacted according to their deepest programs—whether for self-preservation or some other purpose. Across from him, at the other table of honor, Bertram Jaspari threw his hands across his face and fell shaking beneath his table and Jedrek Iviongeon, too, sought what little protection the plastic tabletop afforded him. Twenty feet away, the keepers standing around Harrah's reading desk jumped into motion as if they had been touched with nerve knives. In such situations it was their duty to swarm Harrah, to cover her with their bodies and bear her with all speed out of the Hall. This they tried to do, but Harrah confounded their efforts. As it happened, one of the Temple keepers was indeed her grandson, a young man named Leander en li Daru Ede. When Harrah perceived the threat of Janegg Iviorvan's eye tlolt, almost without thinking, she arose from her chair and threw herself in front of Leander. So great was the force of her fierce old body—and so unexpected her action—that she crashed into Leander, throwing him off balance and so that she fell protectively across his face and chest onto the red carpet of the dais. And all the while, from the devotionary computer on the table in front of Danlo, the hologram of Nikolos Daru Ede flashed out finger signs, warning: "Cover your eyes! Use your chair as a shield and cover your face!"

If Malaclypse Redring took any notice of these events, he gave no sign. Of all the people present, save one, he retained the greatest presence of mind. Even at the moment when Janegg Iviorvan's eye tlolt was brought to bear in his and Danlo's direction, Malaclypse reached his red-ringed hand down into his kimono's inner pocket and with blinding speed he pulled out a red needle-dart and sprang to his feet. And yet, as fast as he moved, he did not fling the dart into the madman who stood before their table.

Janegg Iviorvan pointed the tip of the eye tlolt directly at Danlo's face. His trembling, red thumb held down its catch. The instant that he released his grip, or was struck down by Malaclypse or one of the Temple keepers, the eye tlolt would fire a missile that would seek out Danlo's eye and break through the iris, retina, and bone and tunnel into his brain. There it would explode, instantly destroy each of his hundred billion neurons, liquefying his brain much as a bloodfruit is pounded into red jelly.

I must not fear, Danlo thought. *I must not return hatred with hate.*

That Janegg Iviorvan had not immediately released the eye tlolt's catch seemed strange. It gave Danlo hope for life. While his heart hammered in his chest like a pulsing star, he looked at Janegg. Janegg stared at him with his madman's eyes as if he were looking for something much more than a mere target for his weapon's missile. Danlo was no cetic, and yet it was not hard to read Janegg's anguished face. Like all men who hate so terribly, his deepest wish was to love. Like all who set their hearts to kill, he secretly desired life.

Hatred is the left hand of love, Danlo remembered. *And joy is the right hand of fear.*

With a deep breath and emptying of his lungs, Danlo let the fear run out of him like a sighing wind. He felt something deep in his belly, then, a hot rush of life, animajii—the wild joy of simply being alive. He felt oxygen brightening his blood, and blood flowing to every tissue of his body. Although he was always aware of the eye tlolt pointing at him, he concentrated on holding Janegg's intense gaze. He smiled at Janegg. Everything that he was, as a man and more than a man, went into this smile.

In the way he looked at Janegg—openly, sadly, and yet with the joy of infinite possibilities—there was no contrivance of gesture or falsity of emotion. Danlo's deep blue eyes were as wild as Janegg's, and they shimmered with a shared pain.

I, too, have hated a man and wanted to kill him, Danlo thought. *But I must never hate.*

The cries of fear in the Hall around him seemed as distant as the farthest galaxies. Danlo heard Janegg sucking desperately for air, and the inrush of his own breath, and then he heard himself say, "If you kill me, you kill yourself."

The Elders sitting frozen at their tables nearby, he supposed, might hear these words as a threat of retribution. But he did not mean them so. He only hoped to convey to Janegg the truth of ahimsa, which is that all beings were connected to each other in the deepest way and thus it was impossible to harm another without harming oneself. And so he gave this truth to Janegg. He held Janegg's fearsome gaze, and freely he gave him all his strength, his compassion, his wild love of life. This was *his* eye tlolt, and he fired it at Janegg's eyes with all the force of his soul. He watched as it went in. Then the terrible hatred frozen within Janegg's face began to melt like an ice sculpture beneath a warm sun. He licked his lips, coughed, and looked down at the weapon in his hand almost as if he couldn't understand who had put it there. Danlo chose this moment to remove his shakuhachi from the pocket of his robes. He brought the bamboo flute up to his lips and began to play a melody that was full of suffering and sadness—and yet full of hope, too, in the way that these darker emotions transformed themselves and ultimately gave birth to sheer joy. Poised on the edge of death, he played and played, and the notes rushed from his flute like a thousand tlolts, these little arrows of sound that found their way into Janegg's ears and those of Harrah Ivi en li Ede and the astonished Elders all around them.

What happened then was both marvelous and tragic to behold. Janegg's face was finally free of fear, and he began to smile, grimly and with anguished self-understanding. His arm relaxed and fell toward his side. The tip of the eye tlolt dipped down toward the floor. "I'm sorry," he said. It seemed that he was speaking to himself, perhaps to Bertram Jaspari, to Harrah Ivi en li Ede and all the thousand Elder Architects of the Koivuniemin. "I'm sorry—I can't kill him."

And in that moment, the warrior-poet named Malaclypse Redring moved. He crossed the table and struck like a bolt of lightning. So quick was the flash of his kimono and limbs that it was difficult to make out what occurred between Janegg and him. But this is what Danlo—and many others—thought they saw: Malaclypse closing with Janegg, grappling with him hand to hand as he tried to disarm the eye tlolt and rip it away from him. It *seemed* that the shock of their struggle must have caused Janegg's thumb to fall off the eye tlolt's catch. For in a flash of crimson light, the eye tlolt fired even as Danlo cried out, "No!"

Instinctively, most of the women and men witnessing this event covered their eyes. Janegg Iviorvan did as well. But before his hand reached his face, the tlolt missile burned through the air and found the opening into his head as surely as a hawk homes in on his prey. All he could do was to claw at his eye as he cried out and writhed in sudden agony—and this only for an instant before the tlolt exploded inside his skull. His arms fell away from him even as he began to fall. And Danlo, who had jumped to his feet in a wild attempt to stop the warrior-poet, saw the little red hole at the center of Janegg's left eye and saw the cold ice of eternity fall across Janegg's other eye, and then Janegg's dead body was pulled to earth with a thud by the terrible force of gravity.

For a long time there was chaos in the Hall, frightened cries, open weeping, shouts of confusion. Bertram continued to crouch beneath his table, but the braver Jedrek Iviongeon grunted and groaned as he struggled to regain his chair. Malaclypse Redring stood over Janegg's corpse like a thallow guarding his kill. The Temple keepers, true to their duty, were still trying to bear Harrah Ivi en li Ede away from the dais. But Harrah commanded them to help her back to her reading desk and so great was the aura of her authority that they obeyed her wishes. She calmly took her seat while other keepers, grim-faced men in their clean white kimonos, rushed into the Hall and fairly swarmed Janegg's body.

They were in a panic to spirit it away to deeper parts of the Temple where the vastening chamber and crematorium awaited all dead Architects. In these dark and secret rooms, the programs and patterns of the brain—the very soul—could be lifted away from the flesh and preserved forever in the cybernetic space of an eternal computer, or so it was said. For all Architects in good standing with the Church, this vastening of one's mind occurred at the end of the process of dying or at the moment of death itself. But for Janegg Iviorvan, Elder Architect though he was, there would be no salvation. And not because he had fallen mad or tried to assassinate Danlo, but because his brain was completely gone. This was the horror of eye tlolts and other synapse-searing weapons. When a man's hundred billion neurons were reduced to a blood soup, there were no brain patterns to preserve. All Architects lived in dread of such a death. And so when one of the keepers knelt over Janegg's body and announced, "Nothing can be done for this man," there was a terrible silence in the Hall. Many Elders sat dumbfounded in their chairs staring at Janegg. Danlo stared at him, too. He stood almost still, grasping his shakuhachi while he pressed his hand to the scar above his eye.

After that, the keepers took Janegg's body away. Harrah Ivi en li Ede asked the Elders to return to their seats, and they did as she bade them. However, there was no attempt to resume the day's agenda. Only with difficulty could Harrah quiet the Elders and keep them from pointing at Danlo as they whispered fearful interpretations of the afternoon's events. Many condemned him as a heretic and potential hakra and blamed him for Janegg's horrible death. But others more devoted to truth—and the Elidi master, Kissiah en li Ede, was one of these—had tried not to turn away from terror. And so they had witnessed what had really happened between Janegg and Danlo. They had seen Danlo calmly playing his flute in the face of death, and they had watched the madness fall away from Janegg's eyes. Harrah Ivi en li Ede had beheld this marvel, too. In her clear, powerful voice, she told the Koivuniemin of what she had seen. And then she reminded them of the ideal of Architect virtue and accomplishment. She bowed her head toward Danlo. And then she quoted from *Visions,* saying, " 'A man without fear who will heal the living.' "

When the Elders had absorbed this astonishing connection between Danlo and the well-known lines from the Algorithm, Harrah's impassioned gaze fell upon Bertram Jaspari. Here, her eyes seemed to say, was a man with much fear who couldn't even heal himself of his criminal ambition. It was to Bertram Jaspari, no less than to the entire body of the Koivuniemin, that Harrah addressed her next remarks.

"We have heard that Danlo wi Soli Ringess is the son of a hakra and has spoken at a gathering of the Ringist blasphemers. But it is no crime to be related to a hakra, and none of us have heard what he said at this gathering. We should rather concern ourselves with what we have seen here today. This much is clear: the pilot faced his assassin without fear and played a music that healed him. Such music he played! We have never heard its like!

We have never felt such power and beauty. Elder Janegg felt this, too. He was mad with hatred for the Pilot—mad enough to murder, and we must ask who programed this passion into him? Was it himself only? Perhaps. Perhaps not. This much is clear: we have seen Elder Janegg put aside his weapon and turn within himself to a new program. Was it not Danlo wi Soli Ringess who effected this reprograming? Did he not, in the end, cure Janegg of his madness with the 'passing of his breath and the brilliance of his eyes'? Who has ever beheld such a miracle? Who does not remember the prophecy?''

Here Harrah paused to stare at Bertram as if he remembered little of the true spirit of the Algorithm, much less the requirements of being an Elder Architect or even a man. Then she continued, ''We must now recite the whole verse from the *Visions*. Please abide with us for a moment.''

Harrah motioned to her grandson, Leander en li Daru Ede, who handed her a cup of water to drink. After she she had moistened her lips, she cast Danlo a long, deep look, and she smiled at him strangely.

'' 'One day,' '' she said, quoting from words that Nikolos Daru Ede had spoken to his followers just before His vastening, '' 'One day, when you are near to despair, a man will come among you from the stars. He will rewrite your worst programs with the passing of his breath and the brilliance of his eyes. He is a man without fear who will heal the living, walk with the dead, and look upon the heavenly lights within and not fall mad. This man will be only a man, as all men can only be. But he will be a true Architect of God; in him, God's Program for man will be perfectly realized. In a dark time, he will be a bringer of light, and like a star he will show the way toward all that is possible.' ''

These ancient words, directed at himself, amused Danlo and caused him to smile. But they did not amuse the Elders of the Koivuniemin. Along with Kissiah en li Ede, many women and men were staring at him with new hope as if they were truly seeing him for the first time. But many of the Iviomils took great insult from Harrah's suggestion that Danlo might be the man of whom the *Visions* had once spoken. Bertram Jaspari, in a rather childish display of energy and outrage, banged his table with his fist and suddenly called out, ''He is a naman and possibly a hakra! How dare our Holy Ivi suggest that he could possibly be the Lightbringer?''

''How dare *you*!'' Harrah Ivi en li Ede said as she glared at this graceless man who would bring down her architetcy and lead the Church to ruin.

Almost all the Elders in the vast room looked back and forth between Bertram and their Holy Ivi.

"You have brought this Danlo wi Soli Ringess into our Hall and that alone is—"

"You will be silent now," Harrah said. Like a sword sheathed in gossilk, beneath the politeness of her voice, there was keen-edged steel.

Bertram sat with his mouth open, his words cut off in mid-sentence. His little eyes were full of deviousness, impatience, hatred. For a moment, it seemed that he might not keep silent after all. But then, perhaps sensing that the shocked Elders were not yet ready to support him, he deferred to Harrah. He lowered his eyes and bowed his head, as all Architects must do when they face their Holy Ivi.

"We cannot know," Harrah said, "if this pilot is the Light-bringer who has been promised to us. But we can put the prophecy to the test."

She waited while the Elders absorbed her intent, and then she continued, "We must also discover how Janegg Iviorvan could have passed into this Hall bearing a such a horrible weapon. We must discover how a fully cleansed Elder could have fallen into such a murderous program that he would attempt to assassinate our guest."

"Yes, an inquest!" someone shouted. "Let's call an inquest!"

"There *must* be an inquest."

From the many rows of Elders in the Hall came many voices, "An inquest! Let there be an inquest!"

Harrah Ivi en li Ede bowed her head in honor of the Elders' desire for justice. Then she held up her hand to motion for silence. "While these matters are being settled, we will ask the pilot to be a guest in our house. The warrior-poet as well. The keepers will escort them after the Koivuniemin is adjourned. And now we must pray for Janegg Iviorvan's soul. Although he ran the worst of programs, in the end he was cleansed of negativity, and so we must pray that he finds his way on toward Ede the God."

After that Harrah led the Elders in a rather long and convoluted prayer concerning the indestructibility of information and its ultimate concentration in Ede the God at the end of time. Then she bowed her head in silence. With a sigh and a groan as if she might have injured her frail old body in her attempt to shield her grandson from Janegg's attack, she slowly rose from her reading desk. This was a signal that the Elders of the Koivuniemin should rise, too.

Danlo stood straight and tall, very relieved to be free of his chair. He looked over at Bertram Jaspari almost bent over the other table of honor. With his dead gray eyes, Bertram was staring at him, firing at him silent missiles of hate. Danlo did not know if Harrah's inquest could reveal the truth of what had occurred in the Hall of the Koivuniemin that day, but he sensed that if Bertram had his way, he would bring to Danlo, and many others, nothing but darkness and death.

IN THE PROPHET'S PALACE

*Whole civilizations have spent their spiritual wealth
asking where the soul goes after death. A better
question would have been: Where was the soul before
you were born?*

—*a Fravashi koan*

Harrah Ivi en li Ede provided Danlo with a room in her house at
the very easternmost edge of Ornice Olorun. In truth, with its
hundreds of guest rooms, chambers, halls, and labyrinthine
passageways, her "house" was much more like a palace—the
grandest palace that Danlo had ever seen, grander even than Mer
Tadeo's mansion on Farfara. But neither its size nor its splendor
was its main attraction; because the palace was built on the zero
level of the city overlooking the ocean, many of its rooms had
windows allowing a view of the sky and the waters of the world.
Due to Tannahill's polluted atmosphere, of course, it was impossible to open these windows, but Danlo loved sitting near the
great skylights as he played his flute and stared out at the sandy
beach far below. Sometimes he would pass whole days in this
manner. Sometimes, at night, he would lift his eyes to the stars or
wonder about Tannahill's eerie, noctilucent clouds: blue and
white waves glowing high in the atmosphere, phosphorescent displays of radiation that were the result of the planet's excess carbon dioxide and methane reacting with sunlight. These death
clouds, as Danlo thought of them, reminded him that he was only
a stranger on an alien world—alien not so much because of its
flora or unusual landscapes, but because of what human beings
had done to make a natural paradise almost completely uninhab-
itable.

And so Danlo dwelled in Harrah's house while he waited for
the next phase in his embassy to the Architects to begin. After

three days of being confined to his room while Harrah conducted
an inquest as to Elder Janegg's bizarre death, he concluded that
he was something less than a guest though perhaps more than a
prisoner. No necessity of life or luxury of whim was denied him.
His room was a marvel of rich furnishings, sacred art, cybernetica, and most surprisingly, flowers and green potted plants. Unlike the Narain, who were content to live within the surrealities
of the Field, the Architects of Tannahill dreamed of Old Earth as
it was thousands of years ago, before the Swarming Centuries—
as it would be again at the end of time when Ede the God recre-
ated countless pristine and unsullied Earths for His chosen people to inhabit.

It was the great paradox of the Architects that even as they
destroyed nature they longed for it and came to love it the more
they were denied its glories. Thus they had graced his room with
hanging ananda blossoms, all white and splendid and shining like
stars, and most marvelously, a parrotock bird whose feathers
fairly exploded with reds and blues and other brilliant colors. It
saddened Danlo to see this lively animal kept in a little steel
cage, though he supposed it was no worse off than most of the
people who lived in the apartments of Ornice Olorun.

He remembered the riddle that his grandfather had once posed
him, and which he, in turn, had posed to the Solid State Entity:
How do you capture a beautiful bird without killing its spirit?
And though he still could not answer this question, he took delight in tossing the bird fat mawi nuts and seeing its spirit soar
whenever he approached its cage to look into its bright golden
eyes. Often he would play his flute, giving it music from deep
inside him, and the bird would return this gift by warbling and
whistling and singing the loveliest of songs. Often he wondered
if the parrotock was imakla, a magic animal possessing great
powers.

One day, as he voiced his doubt in words, he was astonished
to hear the bird answer him. "Are you imakla?" the bird
squawked, answering his question with a question. "How can a
magic being live inside a cage?"

At first he wondered if the bird could truly talk, but in little
time he discovered that it was only a clever mimic, repeating and
permuting his words with less sophistication than even the most
basic computer ai program. If Danlo wished for conversation, he
would do better to spend his time listening to the imago of
Nikolos Daru Ede that floated above his devotionary computer

and mechanically sounded out warnings such as, ''Be careful of the bird. Its eyes might be soft-wired to spy on you.''

It was at such moments, in painful awareness of the limitations of the devotionary's program, that Danlo despaired of ever communicating with this glowing Ede. As well—but for different reasons—he found that the Palace keepers who came every day to clean his room and bring him hot meals would not talk to him. After restocking the cage's feeder with fresh mawi nuts and disposing of Danlo's bed linen as if they dreaded touching any object that had come in contact with a naman, they silently collected the dishes from his previous meal. With eyes cast downward, but stealing glances at this strange man from the stars who might be the Lightbringer, they hurried from his presence, leaving him very much alone.

Inevitably, out of curiosity and loneliness, Danlo turned to the holy heaume that sat gleaming on the altar in his middle room. When he pulled it over his head, he found that he could interface various cybernetic spaces. None of these were so profound or well articulated as the Field generated by the Narain's computers on Alumit Bridge. There were no free information pools, nor was there anything like an association space where the Architects of Tannahill might come together in a single planetary conversation. And with one important exception, there were no surrealities and no degrees of instantiation higher than that of voice or facement.

The Elders of the Church believed in restricting both information and communications; they saw themselves as protectors of the people and thought that it was their duty to keep dangerous technologies out of their hands. Indeed, in this district of Ornice Olorun—called the New City—among the Temple buildings, palace and high estates, there were whole institutions where hard-eyed men and women met to determine which technologies were in harmony with the Church doctrines, with the *Logics* and the holy Algorithm. It was their belief that they should change the conditions of life to fit the human soul rather than mutilate human nature in service of arbitrary new technologies.

And so as Danlo sat cross-legged beneath the glittering holy heaume, he found that he could not communicate with the Architects as he wished. But he could *commune* with them. One day as he closed his eyes and attempted various degrees of instantiation, he came across a space known as cybernetic communion, and this discovery both amused and alarmed him.

Every morning, it seemed, after the first bell, Harrah Ivi en li Ede would make the short journey from her palace to the Temple.

There, in the facing room where Ede's eternal computer sat on the altar, surrounded by row upon row of holy heaumes and the four mirrored walls, Harrah would conduct a facing ceremony. The greatest Elders of the Church such as Bertram Jaspari would join her, as well as many lesser Architects and the lucky pilgrims who had won the day's lottery and were deemed worthy to enter into the Church's holiest physical place. Although the facing room was huge, it could accommodate only a few thousand people, the tiniest fraction of all the Worthy who lived on Tannahill, much less the worlds of the Known Stars.

Therefore, at the very moment when Harrah Ivi en li Ede placed the holy heaume upon her head and turned to face the Ede's eternal computer, even as all the Elders present followed her example, Architects in their billions of apartments all across the planet would take up the heaumes from their own private altars and face into cybernetic communion.

Danlo would always remember the first time that he joined the multitudes of Tannahill in their sacred cybernetic space. He sat cross-legged on the prayer mat of his room, holding the cold, hard heaume in his hands. For a while he gazed at his reflection in the heaume's mirrored surface. It troubled him to see how wild his eyes looked, almost as if he didn't care if he died or fell mad with computer-induced dreams of God. He put the heaume on his head. Because he had a large head, long and well shaped, the fit was too tight and the metal squeezed his temples. There was a moment, then, of surreality when he instantiated into a communion space. It seemed that he had suddenly fallen through a hole in the floor, and then he found himself carked out into the facing room of the great Temple. In the many rows before him and behind, thousands of Architects knelt on their prayer mats wearing holy heaumes identical to his own. At the center of the room, near the massive, glittering altar, Harrah Ivi en li Ede stood by Ede's eternal computer. She wore a flowing kimono of pure white perlon, and on her head, her white dobra stitched with intricate gold crewelwork.

The simulation of this holy place, Danlo thought, was very good, though not quite perfect. Although the colors and textures of real life held true—the fiery bronzes of various sculptures of Ede the Man, the blue roses in their vases, the lovely brown pools of coffee that were Harrah's eyes—the sounds of the men and women breathing all around him seemed ragged and strangely muted. And there were no smells. Or rather, there were no *bad* smells, none of the amino plastics and ketones and the stench of unhealthy bodies that Danlo had found almost everywhere on Tannahill. Instead he drank in the fragrance of lilacs and honey, of wind and waterfalls and of freshly washed women's hair.

He sensed that the billions of Architects across the planet were simultaneously experiencing the facing ceremony just as he was. He was aware of many other people (or icons) kneeling all about him, many of whom must have instantiated in this brilliant surreality just as he had. And they were aware of him. Their eyes were wide with wonder and outrage that a naman had found his way into this forbidden space. They must have supposed that Harrah had given him a special dispensation to instantiate in their presence—either that or perhaps she had cleansed him of his negative programing and led him to utter the Profession of Faith that all newly converted Architects must make when they become children of the Cybernetic Universal Church. For none of them voiced objection to Danlo's sudden appearance. They merely stared at his long and graceful form, his black pilot's ring, his wild, blue eyes.

And then Harrah, who was staring at Danlo, too, commanded their attention. From the altar, she grasped a holy heaume in her hands and placed it on her head as might a self-crowned king. And then she faced the Worthy Architects of the Temple and all of Tannahill, and said, "We all come from the Father; and to that place we shall return like a drop of rain flowing to the ocean."

At that moment, fifty-billion human beings—whether present in the Temple in the flesh or alone in their private rooms ten thousand miles away—entered the same place. They entered the same consciousness, the same apprehension of Ede the God and all that He had made. For Danlo this experience of the divine was like liquid cobalt dropped into the center of his brain. Instantly, like an artist's paint suffusing a glass of water, the color spread out until it touched his mind with the deepest and loveliest blue light that he had ever beheld. There came a moment of cybernetic samadhi, then. His bliss was so intense that he could not feel his body, or the memories behind his eyes or the beating of his heart. He was like a strange and alien being lost in an ocean of light, and then, at the end, he was light itself, all brilliant and clear and perfect within itself.

He would never be able to say how long this moment lasted. After what seemed an eternity, the heaume surrounding his head began to generate a different kind of field, and a stream of images poured into him. There were words, too, sounds and smells, the hot, red gush of love in his throat. And so like any Architect, he entered into that holiest of holies, the cybernetic space containing all the books of Ede's sacred Algorithm. Of course, the Algorithm's "books" were nothing like the two leather-bound volumes of paper that Danlo kept in his chest; they were more like surrealities or pictorial histories or even the lifescapes of the Narain facilah artists. Some said that the Algorithm was in reality its own space or, as an uncreated vision of God, was beyond the spaces generated by any computer. Of the Algorithm's true nature, Danlo did not know. At the moment neither metaphysics nor theology interested him. He found that the words pouring like music through his mind were too hard to ignore, and the images of Ede called to him. That morning Harrah was guiding the multitudes through the final level of the Algorithm's *Last Things*. These well-known words sounded inside him: "He will fall across the stars, and He will fill the universe with Himself."

Just then Danlo felt himself falling once more. He was like a meteor plunging through cold space or like a bird diving through the night and coming to earth by the shore of a tropical ocean. The world beneath him was like no world that he had ever seen, for he stood on an endless beach without limit or horizon. A billion Architects stood there with him. Or perhaps there were a billion billion men and women in their perfect white robes, off to his right and left, swarming the sands of this impossible beach. They were each looking up at the sky, watching and waiting. Danlo looked heavenwards, too.

And there, amid the faint stars of the universe, the story of Ede's ontogenesis from man into God exploded into light. Danlo watched as the now-familiar face of Ede—with its sensuous lips and black, blazing mystic's eyes—appeared like a moon floating in the sky. He watched as Ede transcended himself into something new. It was like watching a museum hologram unfold, only infinitely vaster and more profound. A million miles above him, against the black wall of the night, a brilliant golden light began to shine within Ede's coffee-colored skin until it had totally consumed Him in a dazzling sphere, and Ede the Man became Ede the God. Suddenly, however, this splendid light vanished as of a star's radiance being sucked into a black hole. For a moment, the sky was dark. As Danlo would learn, this was symbolic of Ede's Dark Night of the Soul, his time of supreme despair, just at the moment when He had carked His selfness into His eternal computer. It was a reminder that supreme victory may follow utter darkness.

Then, at the center of the sky, far out over the ocean, a tiny cube appeared. At first, Danlo thought, it looked something like an ancient communications satellite. After a while, though, it glittered as if faced with ten thousand jeweled lights, and Danlo instantly recognized it as an icon of Ede's eternal computer. Quickly, it began to grow. The cube, like a seed crystal dropped into a supersaturated salt solution, instantly added to itself along each of its six faces. It grew until it filled the space around it and burst across the sky. The effect was of black space being devoured by all the brilliance and informational expanding capabilities of a holy computer. Indeed, as this scene from the *Last Things* neared its cosmic conclusion, the tropical air around Danlo seemed to fall full of the coldness of space itself. He realized that the beach upon which he stood—and the whole world—was falling through space, following Ede on his great journey out into the universe.

All about him there were many stars, and then whole nebulas full of stars. Many of these, such as the Rainbow Double, Danlo recognized. With a terrible fascination, he watched as Ede's eternal computer grew without bound until it filled nebula after nebula and its ten thousand jeweled lights outshone and obliterated the light of the stars. And then these little lights actually *became* the stars. Their number multiplied from ten thousand to ten million—and soon there were billions of glittering lights, and Ede the God grew to consume all the stars in the lovely spiral arms of the galaxy known as the Milky Way.

The logic of the rest of Ede's destiny was compelling and total. Danlo watched as Ede's sacred cybernetic body grew forty million light years through space to absorb Andromeda and Draco and other galaxies in the local cluster. And then Ede gobbled up Virgo and the Canes Venatici Cloud and many other clusters, and then whole clusters of clusters. These were great, glittering spheres of stars half a billion light years in diameter, and it seemed that the universe contained an infinite number of them. But finally, at the end of history, as Ede grew ever outward through black drears of space and time, he had consumed every star, every particle of matter and bit of information in the universe. At last, as was written in the Algorithm, Ede and the universe were one.

And Danlo—and many billions of Architects standing on this surreal beach outside of space and time—witnessed this ultimate miracle. He watched as the whole universe took on the form of a glittering black cube, a truly eternal and cosmic computer that was Ede the God and nothing more. He knew this must be so, for then there occurred the final transcendence. This almost infinite cube of matter began to glow with a light from inside itself. It glowed and glowed ever brighter, and then there was a terrible flash too brilliant to behold. After the dazzle had left Danlo's eyes, he saw that the universal computer that was Ede the God was gone. Or rather, it had been transformed into a familiar form, the great, glowing face of Nikolos Daru Ede that now filled all the universe. The face that *was* the universe. As had been written in the Algorithm long ago: "And so Ede faced the universe, and He was vastened, and He saw that the face of God was His own."

The rest of the facing ceremony was brief. Harrah guided Tannahill's Architects through other readings from the Algorithm, though none so profound as the one that Danlo had just experienced. Soon Danlo returned to the Temple's facing room, and he (or rather his icon) resumed his posture of kneeling among the rows of the Worthy in their clean white kimonos. Then Harrah, in her strong, clear voice, discussed the Eight Duties of an Architect, which were devotion, obedience, meditation, mission, pilgrimage, cleansing, facing, and vastening. She reminded them of the Four Great Truths that Ede had discovered: the truth of evil and suffering, the truth that evil arises from the negative programs inherent in the nature of the universe, the truth that this evil can be overcome through writing new programs, and the truth that these programs can be written only through an Architect's completing the Eight Duties, and thus through Ede Himself.

The last part of the facing ceremony consisted of nothing more than a repetition of the vow of obedience and the profession of faith. These words, of course, Danlo did not speak. But he joined the others as Harrah guided them in a prayer for peace and a moment of silent meditation. And then the ceremony was over, and he once again found himself sitting cross-legged on the prayer mat of his room. With interface finally broken, he pulled the heaume from his head and sat wondering at the terrible power of this religion known as Edeism.

It was early the next day, after the facing ceremony, that Harrah Ivi en li Ede summoned Danlo to join her for breakfast in what she called her morning room. Two kind-eyed keepers who might have been Harrah's grandsons appeared at Danlo's door and escorted him down various hallways to a lovely room full of flowers and sunlight. Harrah, still dressed in her formal kimono, greeted him with a nice smile just inside the doorway. After they honored each other with deep bows, she led him over to the eastern windows where a small plastic table had been set for a light meal. Harrah dismissed the keepers, then, telling them that she wished to dine with Danlo alone. The keepers looked at Danlo as if they might have invited in a tiger from the wild, but at last they bowed politely and left the room. Danlo pulled out Harrah's chair while she sat down, and then joined her at the table.

"We love this time of morning," Harrah said.

Danlo looked out of the window, down at the ocean. Except for the ever-present pollution, the day was clear and bright. The waters just beyond the beach shimmered in a river of light that led straight out to where the blazing sun hung low in the sky.

"It . . . is splendid," Danlo agreed.

"Would you care for some juice?" she asked. Politely she waited for him to say yes, and then with her steady old hands picked up a plastic pitcher and poured a strange green juice into two plastic cups. She moved in a precise yet smooth manner, as if she were watching herself and judging her gracefulness—or lack thereof—according to the most exacting of measures.

"Well," she said, "those nice young men have left us alone, but we are in no danger, are we?"

Danlo did not know if the *we* to which she referred included both of them or only herself as the Holy Ivi. So he smiled and asked, "Can one ever truly be free from danger?"

"We notice," Harrah said, smiling, too, "that you have answered our question with a question."

"I am sorry, Blessed Ivi," Danlo said.

" 'Blessed Ivi,' " Harrah said thoughtfully. "All the children of the Church address us as 'Holy Ivi' or 'Ivi Harrah,' but we like the way you say *blessed*."

"Truly?"

"How not? You say it with your heart while your eyes sing. If you would like, you may address us this way—but only when we're alone."

"Then are we to be alone more than this once, Blessed Ivi?"

"Why shouldn't we be? Are you as dangerous as some of my counselors fear?"

"I think that you, too, Blessed Ivi, like to answer questions with questions."

At this, Harrah laughed softly, then closed her eyes for a moment before taking a sip of juice. It seemed that she might be saying a silent prayer. "That may be true. But we notice that you still have managed to avoid our original question."

" 'Am I dangerous?' "

"Yes—that we would all wish to know."

"But Blessed Harrah, how should I answer a question when you already know the answer?"

"We do?"

"Truly, from the moment we first met eyes in the Temple, we have trusted each other."

"And isn't that strange?" Harrah mused as she nodded her head. "We *have* trusted you, but now we must decide if we should trust our initial trust."

"I am no danger to your physical self," Danlo said.

"No, we think not."

"But I am probably a danger to your public self. To your architetcy."

"How clearly you see things no naman should see!"

"And I am certainly a danger to your religious self. In this, Bertram Jaspari spoke the truth."

Harrah took another sip of juice and smiled at Danlo. "We have sensed this, too. Your beliefs are very different from ours."

"But, truly," Danlo said. "I have no beliefs. One should be able to face the universe naked in the mind without beliefs, yes?"

"And *that*," Harrah said, "is perhaps the most dangerous belief of all."

"But that is not a simple belief. It is a belief . . . about the nature of belief itself."

"Oh, indeed, yes—you *are* a dangerous man," Harrah said, almost laughing. "Perhaps that is why we have invited you here."

"To test your beliefs?"

"How clearly you understand! How fragile faith in one's religion must be if it breaks at the first testing."

"I do not believe that your faith is fragile."

"We shall see," Harrah said.

And then, noticing that Danlo's cup of juice remained untouched, she encouraged him to drink. She was the High Architect and God's Prophet of the Cybernetic Universal Church, but she was first a grandmother who liked to see that all her children were well fed.

"It's juice from the tasida fruit," Harrah said. "Do you like it?"

"Yes, very much" Danlo said, after taking a sip from his cup. The juice was sharp and acidic and very sweet.

While Danlo drank his juice, a robot bearing a platter of food rolled into the room. It set various bowls and dishes on the table and refilled Harrah's juice cup before rolling away. Almost as if she was preparing a plate for one of her great-grandchildren, Harrah used a pair of tongs to serve him slices of a hot bread called jinsych. She spread the bread with a black protein paste made from one of the plants native to Tannahill. Aside from a thin, cool, herb soup and a few sections of some scarlet-fleshed fruit, this was all they had. The *Logics* prescribed a spare breakfast, and in any case, Harrah did not like to eat much better than her fellow Architects, many of whom had only bread for their morning meal. Although Danlo was relieved to discover that no one of Tannahill ate meat or any substance that came from an animal, he had noticed that many Architects were too poor to afford the variety of plant foods necessary to good health. This sad estate of her people obviously distressed Harrah. No matter how many new food factories that the robots constructed, she said, no matter how deeply into the earth the robots mined for minerals and new space to grow green plants, there never seemed to be quite enough for her children to eat.

Danlo never doubted Harrah's sincerity. He loved the kindness he saw in her soft, dark eyes, her rare grace and vulnerability. As he would learn, she had advanced to the architetcy not only because she possessed a superior intellect and strength of spirit but out of her great reverence toward Ede and her willingness to care for others, even those who scorned her and treated her as an enemy. Possibly no other High Architect since Edeism's beginnings would have tolerated Bertram Jaspari's open disrespect. But Harrah regarded him, as she did all her people, as a child of the Church—and, therefore, a child of Ede, a child of God.

"We must apologize for the Elder Bertram's words. The line between true passion for God and mere zeal is as thin as the edge of a razor. Sometimes it's difficult to know when one has crossed over."

"Yes, it can be," Danlo said.

"And we must apologize for the Elder Janegg's actions. We're still trying to discover how he might have smuggled an eye tlolt into the Koivuniemin's Hall."

"Perhaps he had help."

"We do not like to believe that any of our children might have conspired to assassinate you," Harrah said.

"But men have always murdered, yes?"

"Oh, indeed, yes. However, although murder is a terrible program to run, there are worse ones. You were our guest in our holy Temple. A conspiracy to murder you in this place is a conspiracy against *us*. Against our architetcy, against the architetcy itself—and therefore a hakr against God."

"A . . . *hakr*?"

"This is willfully embracing a negative action. To run a program contrary to God's Program for the universe."

"I see."

"We would like to believe that Elder Janegg acted alone. And that his actions ran only from a talaw."

"I see. This . . . talaw—this is a flaw in one's personal program, yes?"

"A flaw, indeed. All of us may run these negative programs that lead us into error."

Into madness, Danlo thought, remembering Janegg's hellish eyes—and other eyes that he had seen. *It is always possible to fall mad.*

"It remains a mystery, however," Harrah continued, "how Janegg could have entered the Temple uncleansed, running a talaw. Or a hakr."

Danlo chewed a piece of bread for a long time as he remembered the fate of his grandmother, Dama Moira Ringess. Then he asked, "Is it possible that the warrior-poet might have programed Elder Janegg to kill?"

At this simple question, Harrah's eyebrows arched in surprise. "We are not sure what you mean when you say *programed.*"

After Danlo had swallowed a piece of a bitter fruit called a tilbit, he explained how the warrior-poets long ago had developed the art of slel-mime as a tool of assassination and control. The warrior-poets, he said, were famous for infecting their victims with bacteria-size robots that would migrate through the blood into the brain. There, these tiny assemblers would replace neurons with millions of layers of organic computers, thereby miming the mind and creating a slave unit in the place of a man. The warrior-poets were also adept with secret drugs, many of which they used to control people. Was it possible, Danlo asked, that Malaclypse Redring had either mimed Elder Janegg or injected him with one of these terrible drugs?

"We don't believe so," Harrah said. "Before Elder Janegg saw Malaclypse in the Temple, they were never in contact."

"Still, it is strange, yes? Malaclypse appeared ready to murder Elder Janegg just after Janegg had murdered me. To assassinate the assassin—this is an ancient strategem. At least as ancient as Al-Ksandar's murder of his father, Philip of Macedon, on Old Earth."

"We know little of Old Earth," Harrah said with a sigh. Again she closed her eyes as if in prayer. Carefully, almost daintily, she took a bite of the tilbit fruit. And then she said, "We would like to believe that Malaclypse killed Elder Janegg only out of error."

"Some might think it strange that this error might make it impossible to know the truth."

"Please tell us what you are thinking."

"The eye tlolt, the explosion inside Elder Janegg's head—this made it impossible for his selfness to be saved, yes?"

"Indeed, his brain was totally destroyed," Harrah said. "And so it was impossible to save the programs of Elder Janegg's self inside an eternal computer. He has been denied vastening, and that's a terrible fate. But we believe that he still might be saved."

"Truly?"

"At the end of time, at the omega point when Ede has become the entire universe—then all the Worthy will be saved. In Ede's infinite memory, He will absorb all matter and energy—and thus He will have downloaded all information that is or has ever been. And so He will remember Elder Janegg. He will run the program that is his selfness and soul. And Elder Janegg, as with all Worthy Architects, will be once more forever."

Danlo tried not to smile as he rubbed the scar above his eye. He said, "Then in a hundred billion years we might know the truth of why Elder Janegg wanted to murder me. But now it is impossible to read his programs from his ruined brain."

"Indeed," Harrah said, finally admitting that she understood Danlo's point. "We *have* considered this. If there was a conspiracy to assassinate you, if someone had programed Elder Janegg to kill, if this secret assassin immediately had Elder Janegg killed—then any means of murder leaving his brain intact would leave the conspirators vulnerable."

"Your scanning computers can read the memories from an untouched dead brain, yes?"

"From a *dying* brain, at least," Harrah said. She took a sip of tea. "But we do not want to believe that Bertram Jaspari or anyone else might have programed Elder Janegg with enmity and hatred toward you.''

"Anyone can hate,'' Danlo said. A sudden pain flashed through his head, and he clasped his hand to his eye. It was as if a tlolt had burst through his own eye into his brain. "Anyone can hate . . . of himself, from inside himself.''

"Anyone can hate,'' Harrah agreed. "But the miracle is that you cured Elder Janegg of his hatred.''

"But I—''

"With the passing of your breath and the brilliance of your eyes, you cleansed him of this terrible negativity. We have *seen* this, Pilot. With our own eyes, we have watched you rewrite this terrible program.''

"But truly it was Janegg who cured himself. I only played him a song.''

As Harrah held her hand over the teapot to warm herself, she looked at Danlo for a long time. " 'A man without fear who will heal the living.' ''

Danlo smiled to think that Harrah and other Architects might look to him as the one who would fulfill their ancient prophecies. And then his face fell grave. "But I have healed no one. And Elder Janegg is dead.''

"We believe that you are a rare and remarkable man.''

"No, I am only—''

"And such remarkable things you have accomplished! Who would have dreamed that you would take up the holy heaume in your chamber and find your way into our Temple.''

"But wasn't the heaume placed upon the altar so that your guests could join your facing ceremony?''

"Indeed, it was. But we have never had a naman for a guest before.''

"But even namans,'' Danlo said, smiling, "may find their way through the cybernetic spaces.''

"No namans that we have known. And even a child of the Church takes many years to learn the protocols for facing a computer.''

"But I am a child of the stars,'' Danlo said. "I am a pilot of a lightship—we pilots live facing our computers.''

"Then you are adept at interface and all degrees of instantiation?''

"More so than any others of our Order except the cetics.''

Harrah took a sip of tea and sighed. "There are those who

will say that we should have ascertained this before allowing you to take up a holy heaume."

"Bertram Jaspari?"

Harrah nodded her head. "There are those who will say that no naman should be allowed to look upon a holy heaume, much less the opportunity to place one on his head."

"I . . . am sorry."

"No, this was our oversight. We never dreamed that you would instantiate into the facing room."

"You mean the heaume's *simulation* of the facing room, yes?"

Again Harrah nodded her head. "Almost all of Tannahill was present with you in that room, Pilot. A hundred billion of the Worthy—and they all saw you there, kneeling to face Ede's eternal computer in your black pilot's robe."

Like a raven among kitikeesha birds, Danlo thought as he remembered kneeling among all the men and women in their immaculate white kimonos. And then he said, "Yet I was aware of only a few thousand Architects."

Harrah smiled at him. "That's one of the paradoxes of instantiation, isn't it, Pilot?"

"Yes, I suppose it can be," Danlo said.

After they had finished their breakfast, Harrah said yet another prayer in blessing of the food they had eaten. She stood up from her chair, then, and she moved about the room. She seemed all full of life and boundless energy, like a bird. And like a bird—a hummingbird or an anakoon—she flitted from place to place, here and there, straightening a mirror upon the wall or using her strong fingers to prune a dead leaf from one of her many potted plants or touching the face of a sculpture of Nikolos Daru Ede.

Danlo loved watching her move. He loved the grace with which she invested each of her motions, and more, the intense consciousness of herself as a realization of one tiny part of God's Program for the universe. This consciousness colored all that she did. Before she had become the Holy Ivi, she had been an exemplar of the Juriddik sect, and she believed in an exact adherence to the programs for living as set forth in the *Logics.* But she did not obey these rules blindly as might an Iviomil. She did not constrain her actions out of fundamentalism or fear, but rather from her reverence for life.

All that an Architect did—the foods that she ate or shunned, her prayers, her words and thoughts, the way that she sexed with

her husband—every detail of her life should reflect her love of
God. In truth, it was the Edeic ideal to bring God into every
aspect of life, to behold Ede's infinite face in such finite things as
a flower or even a plastic cup. Where the Iviomils and even many
of the Juriddik valued the *Logics* only because they prescribed a
way that human beings might live contentedly as human beings
in a universe of vast and bewildering technologies, Harrah rever-
red them for their own sake. Each *logic,* each prayer before interfacing or ritual words spoken at one of her grandchildren's
births, was a symbolic gesture designed to bring her into a
greater awareness of God. Each of the many religious objects in
her room, from her devotionary computer to the Ede figurines to
the holy heaume, was a sacred work of cybernetica that the *Logics* suggested all the Worthy should display. For each individual
logic—and each physical representation of the *Logics'* ideals—
was a point of contact with the divine. It was Harrah's hope that
her people would regard Ede's Program for man even as she
regarded Ede's mysterious face which glistened on the far wall:
with obedience, with thankfulness, with faith, and above all, with
wonder.

"We've lived a long time," Harrah said thoughtfully as she
returned to the table and sat back down. "We've seen many
strange and marvelous things. But in all those years, the strangest
of all, we believe, is that a pilot named Danlo wi Soli Ringess
falls out of the stars seeking the center of the universe."

"I seek other things, too."

"Of course—the cure for the Plague that you call the slow
evil. Well, we're afraid that you won't find it here."

At this Danlo was silent as he stared down at his pilot's ring
gleaming black at the edge of his clenched fist.

"And we don't believe that you'll find your father on Tannahill."

"I have not said that I seek my father."

"No," Harrah said, and her old face was aglow with kindness. "You didn't need to. But from all that the warrior-poet told
us, from all that we have seen of you, we believe that you *do* seek
this man—if indeed he remains only a man."

"I . . . have never known him."

"If you seek your father, you seek yourself," Harrah said.
"But who are you, really, Danlo wi Soli Ringess? This we would
all like to know."

Again Danlo said nothing, and he stared out of the window at
the ocean.

"Perhaps, then," Harrah sighed out, "we should discuss those things that you seek on behalf of your Order. Or as an emissary of the Narain."

"I seek only peace. Should that be so impossible to find?"

"We, too, would seek a peaceful solution to the problem of the heretics."

"Truly?"

As Harrah took a sip of mint tea, she slowly nodded her head. "But as for the other objectives of your Order, those might prove more difficult to achieve."

"I am only a pilot," Danlo said, and he picked up a cup of lukewarm tea that Harrah had poured for him. "I have vowed only to find Tannahill—perhaps I should return to the lords of my Order so that they might send you a true ambassador."

"In time, that might be. But now it is *you* who sits in my house, no other. It is you who have cured Elder Janegg—*your* brilliant eyes, Pilot, the passing of your beautiful breath."

Danlo looked at Harrah's wise old face as he took a sip of tea. He said, "But the songs that I have played on my shakuhachi— what could this music possibly have to do with why I was sent to find your world?"

"Possibly everything," Harrah said. She, too, took a sip of tea, and she favored him with one of her mysterious smiles.

"The stars are dying. All these millions of marvelous lights— and men are murdering them, one by one."

"But you don't really mean 'men,' do you? It is we Architects who are destroying the stars."

"Yes."

"And your Order would simply ask us to desist in these cosmic murders, isn't that so?"

"Yes."

Harrah let out a long, sad sigh. "We *do* wish that it could be so simple. But although Ede's love for his children is the simplest thing there could be, it would seem that His Program for the universe is just the opposite."

"What do you mean?"

"Have you considered, Pilot, who these Architects are who destroy the heavens?"

"They are of your Church, yes? Men and women who wear white kimonos and seek Ede's face in the light of the shattered stars."

"They are *of* the Church," Harrah admitted, "but they are not *with* the Church."

"I do not understand."

"We speak of the Architects of the Long Pilgrimage—they who have been lost to us for more than a thousand years. And all the Iviomils and others who have been sent out from Tannahill, out into what you call the Vild."

"But they are *Architects,* yes?"

"Oh, yes, we believe so. However, we can't simply face them and speak to them as we can our other children here on Tannahill—and even the other worlds of the Known Stars."

"I see."

"In all their journeys, in their fargoing pilgrimage toward Ede, they've had to carry the Church with them in their hearts." Here she smiled sadly, then added, "And in the holy computers installed in their ships."

"But they still carry the doctrines of the Church, yes? All those sacred commandments and beliefs that your Church calls programs?"

"We can only hope so," Harrah said.

"Then they carry with them the Program of Totality, yes? Like children carrying torches into a dry forest."

"The Program of Totality is part of Ede's Program for the Universe."

"To destroy the universe . . . in order to save it?"

"No, Pilot—to *remake* the universe. To be a part of this glorious work of architecture all around us."

"I see."

Harrah, beholding the despair on Danlo's face, smiled and reached across the table to touch his hand. "We must tell you, however, of our understanding of the Program of Totality. We don't believe that it necessarily requires us to destroy the stars."

"Truly?"

Like a condemned prisoner who has received an unexpected pardon, Danlo felt wave upon wave of aliveness rippling through his blood.

"We must warn you that this is only our understanding."

"But you are the Holy Ivi of the Cybernetic Universal Church!"

"In time, it may be that the Church will share our understanding."

"I see."

"But now other Architects—the stargoing Iviomils and they of the Long Pilgrimage—understand the Program differently. And we lack all means to face them, to speak with them."

Danlo removed his shakuhachi from his pocket. He sat staring at the flute's glossy golden surface as he considered all that Harrah had told him.

"My Order has always trained pilots," he finally said. "We are making a new Academy on the planet Thiells. There you could send your children. We could make a thousand new pilots. In time, ten thousand, and more. We would make ten thousand lightships and bring your understanding of the Program to every star in the Vild."

"Are you proposing an alliance between the Church and your Order?"

"Why not?"

"We wish that it could be so simple."

"If you look deeply enough," Danlo said, "all things are simple."

"Perhaps—but we're afraid an alliance would be impossible."

"Bertram Jaspari would oppose this, yes?"

"He and all Iviomils would call such a union with namans an abomination. A hakr, even. But we believe that Elder Bertram secretly desires the benefits of this union, if not its form."

"I see. He desires the power to fall among the stars, yes?"

"Indeed. We believe that power is his purpose."

"The power to expand the Church out into the stars?"

"And more," Harrah said, taking a sip of tea. "He believes, as do we, that the Architects of the Long Pilgrimage would respect the authority of the architetcy."

"But *you* are the Holy Ivi."

"But we will not live forever, in this form. You must know, Pilot, that it's Elder Bertram's hope to become the Ivi after we have died and gone on to our vastening. He hopes to be Ivi of all the lost Architects of the Vild—and all the Iviomils sent forth from Tannahill over the last thousand years. So many people. So great a power."

"And do you have such hopes of your own, then?"

"We dream of a unified Church, of course. The true Church is in all people, in all places—we would see all peoples take joy in Ede's infinite Program. We would bring the power of God to everyone, everywhere."

"I see."

"We would like to believe that a part of Elder Bertram still hopes for this, too."

Danlo smiled at Harrah and said, "I have never known anyone who tried so hard to find the good even in bad men."

"But there are no bad men. There are only negative programs."

Again, Danlo smiled. He said, "Negative programs, then, if you'd like."

"All this points to why it's unlikely that Elder Bertram would have wanted to assassinate you."

"Truly?"

"If you were killed, Pilot, how could Elder Bertram ever hope to send Architect pilots into the Vild?"

"But you have said that he opposes sending Architect children to Thiells."

"Perhaps he hopes that there are other ways of training pilots."

Danlo blew very softly on the ivory mouthpiece of his flute, then said, "I think I see. But I have taken vows, Blessed Ivi. I would never try to train pilots myself, for Bertram. Or for anyone else."

"Perhaps Elder Bertram hopes that there might be other ways of utilizing your pilot's skills."

"I do not like the way you say this word *utilize.*"

"We're afraid that Elder Bertram is a very ambitious man."

"And I am afraid . . . to be afraid of this man," Danlo said. "This would give him an even greater power than he already has, yes?"

For a while, Danlo and Harrah sat in the morning sunlight discussing the problems and politics of the Cybernetic Universal Church. A robot came to clear their dishes, while another one brought a pot of toho tea, all cool and bitter and sweet. They returned to the hope of finding the lost Architects who were destroying the Vild stars. Harrah believed that, while it was presently impossible to send children to Thiells to train as pilots, the pilots of the Order might carry missionary Architects in the holds of their lightships.

"These missionaries," Danlo said, "would bring to the lost Architects your understanding of the Program of Totality, yes?"

"We're afraid that it's not as simple as that."

"But it *is* simple, truly. Why can't your missionaries simply say that the stars are blessed and must be looked upon with all the love of a child for his mother's eyes?"

Harrah smiled and then laughed softly into the sleeve of her kimono. "We believe that you're a very romantic man, Pilot."

"Truly, I am."

"But of course we can't simply send missionaries into the Vild to proselytize people with our understanding of the Program. First we would have to redefine it."

Harrah went on to explain that the Program of Totality was no part of the holy Algorithm. In truth, few of the programs of the Church really were. In the Algorithm, like a wise father addressing his children beneath a sabi tree, Ede had spoken many words concerning the nature of life in the universe and how it should be lived. Men and women had come to interpret, debate, and formalize the imperatives implicit in these words. And so, over fifteen hundred years of falling across the stars, the greatest minds of the Cybernetic Universal Church had come to formulate many programs. These statements of the Church's fundamental beliefs were gathered in the *Commentaries,* which, after the *Logics* and the Algorithm itself, was the most sacred body of Church literature. As Danlo would discover, the *Commentaries* were well named, for their full elaboration had been a historic and evolutionary process: a great Architect such as Yurik Iviongeon would put forth his understanding of what Ede had meant when He had said: "The universe is like a universal turing machine." And then others would make comments concerning Elder Yurik's inspiration, and over time, there would be comments concerning arguments made about the comments of some obscure theologian of little name or accomplishment. In this way, the programs of the Church came to be formatted and defined. And although it was the prerogative of all Holy Ivi's to add to the *Commentaries,* editing or redefining the Church's most ancient programs was always difficult. And always dangerous. For a Holy Ivi must always act with her finger on the pulse of her people. Above all she must win the Koivuniemin to her vision rather than merely commanding dissident Iviomils to obey her pronouncements, as her exalted rank permitted her to do. A High Architect who ignored the zeal or sanctimony of the Elders risked disharmony in her Church—or divisiveness, schism, and even war.

"You must understand," Harrah told Danlo as she stirred some sugar into a new cup of tea, "that it's the Elders who elect a new Ivi. And those programs that the old Ivi has redefined may be completely undone by the new. It's *our* duty—as with every Ivi—to give our people programs not just for a year but for all time. Until the end of time, until the architecture of the universe is complete."

Here she clapped her hands once as she looked at the far wall of the room and intoned, "First scene, please."

At the sound of her voice, the image of Nikolos Daru Ede glittering on the wall's chatoyant surface began to dissolve and fade. In moments, in its place, there appeared the likenesses of three newborn babies, two girls and a boy. Their fat little faces were pink and round, and they were frozen into expressions of empty-eyed wonder as if they had just attempted their first look at the marvels of the world. Each baby wore a new white kimono of precious cotton cloth; each wore a knitted white dobra snug over her or his bald head.

"Do you see my babies?" Harrah asked. "My great-grandchildren. Tirza Iviertes and Isabel Iviorvan en li Ede— these are the girls. The boy is, ah, give me a moment, please."

Harrah shut her eyes, then, as she folded her hands over her heart. Danlo thought that she had beautiful hands, with long, strong fingers still adept at plucking a gosharp's strings.

"The boy is Mensah Iviercier, of my fourteenth daughter's line—she is Valeska Iviercier en li Ede. I have another daughter, Katura Iviercier, and I'm afraid I sometimes confuse their lines."

Danlo, not quite knowing what to say, responded with a commonplace. "They are beautiful children."

Although, due to the trials of birth, Mensah Iviercier's head seemed almost as pointed as Bertram Jaspari's, Danlo spoke the truth. To him, all babies were beautiful.

"Indeed, they are," Harrah said.

She told him, then, something of her marriage to the Elder Sarojin Eshte Iviastalir, who had died of the mehalis infection many years since. She said that during the first part of her marriage, she had borne fifty-three children, one child each year until she had begun her rise in the Church hierarchy at the age of sixty-eight. Over the past sixty years since then, her line had increased so that she counted 1,617 grandchildren as her direct descendents, many of whom still lived in her birth city, Montellivi. So far, she had more than ten thousand great-grandchildren; there was no day of the year, she said, in which one or two new great-grandchildren did not come forth to change the face of the universe.

"We try so hard to remember their names," she said to Danlo. "But now, even my great-grandchildren are bearing their own children."

Over yet another cup of tea sweetened with sugar, Harrah

confided that she spent part of each morning memorizing the names of her vast family and sending birthday presents.

"There are mnemonics and other attitudes of recall that the remembrancers of my Order teach," Danlo said. "If you'd like, I could help you with some of these attitudes."

"That's a gracious offer, Pilot, and we believe that you're a man of remarkable grace. We've also heard that you have a remarkable memory."

Danlo did not tell her that when he was only four years old, he had memorized the names of his grandfathers and thousands of his far great-grandfathers back some fifty generations. He chose not to explain that once, as an exercise, he had envisioned the names and faces of half a million of his *own* descendants, should he ever be so blessed as to father children.

"Truly, the problem is not how we remember," he said. "It is why we ever forget."

Harrah smiled sadly, and she turned to face the far wall. "Next scene, please," she said. Almost immediately the chatoy surface of the wall glittered with new colors, and a new scene appeared. At least ten thousand Architects, as tiny as dots, stood shoulder to shoulder and face to face in a very crowded portrait of Harrah's family.

"*We* cannot forget that each of our children is a star," Harrah said. "Each of us is a child of Ede, and we were each meant to shine."

"Yes, to shine," Danlo said, not yet seeing where Harrah was leading him with all this talk of memory and children.

"Are you familiar with the Program of Increase, Pilot?"

"This is the imperative that women should bear many children, yes?"

"Indeed it is. And it's a good program, a sacred program in which we all believe. Has not Ede told us that we should increase without bound and fill all the universe with our children's children? And yet . . ."

Danlo waited a moment then said, "Yes?"

"And yet there was a time, at the beginning of the Church, when this natural increase was left to the passion of each husband and wife."

"I see."

"We have all time to fill the universe, you know. And all time is in Ede, and we must remember that the Program of Increase is part of His Infinite Program, which will run in its own time until halting at the end of of all things."

Danlo smiled as he squeezed his flute. He said, "I am no Iviomil, Blessed Harrah. You do not need to convince me."

"No, we suppose not," she said, laughing softly. "And yet we do wish we could reason with the Iviomils. Bertram Jaspari willfully forgets that it was men and women such as ourself who once defined this program."

"This definition occurred at the time of the Great Plague, yes?"

Harrah looked up suddenly and nearly dropped her tea in surprise. "How is it, Pilot, that you know what so many Elders of our Church have forgotten?"

"I have been studying Church history," Danlo said. He explained that he had spent a part of every morning sitting beneath the holy heaume in his chambers, exploring various cybernetic spaces. "I have found your archives, your history pools. Those that were not forbidden. There is much information there."

"At the time of the Plague," Harrah said, "nine of ten children died. In some places ninety-nine of one hundred. Therefore, it was necessary that a woman should bear as many babies as she could."

"But your people outlived the Plague."

"Indeed we did, as many other peoples did not. But we believe we paid a price. It was Ivi Sigrid Iviastalir and the Elders of her Koivuniemin who defined the Program of Increase as it reads today."

"That a woman *must* bear at least five children?"

"Every married woman."

"And that a woman *should* bear ten times as many?"

"Or more, if she is so graced. This is the ideal."

"So many children," Danlo said.

"Too many," Harrah said, almost whispering. "Too many of our people don't have enough food to eat."

For a moment, Danlo bowed his head as he remembered what it was like to be hungry. Once, as a young man, during his journey to Neverness, he had nearly starved to death out on the ice of the frozen sea.

He asked, "But doesn't the Algorithm say that whoever is vastened will take sustenance in the infinite body of Ede?"

"But whoever is *not* vastened must still eat, you know."

"But wouldn't Bertram Jaspari say that the sufferings of this world are only a test to determine who is worthy of vastening and who is not?"

"Indeed he would."

"And wouldn't all the Iviomils say that the sufferings of this life are redeemed when an Architect dies and his selfness is vastened in an eternal computer?"

Harrah pointed at the portrait of her family glistening on the wall. "These are my *children,* Pilot! My babies. And they are hungry. The truth of evil and suffering is one of the Four Great Truths, but to seek needless suffering is a hakr against God."

"The Program of Increase causes the greatest of suffering."

"And this is why," Harrah said, "we must always take utmost care in formatting and defining a program."

"Because it is harder to redefine a program that to define it in the first place, yes?"

Harrah nodded her head. "An error written into a program as a mere reaction to a temporary problem, however grave, can lead to great harm."

"An error," Danlo said, deep in thought. "Like a virus."

"What do you mean?"

Danlo suddenly looked up at Harrah. "Like an aberrant virus infecting one's DNA, it can become impossible to get rid of."

At this terrible metaphor, Harrah smiled sadly and said, "We're afraid our Holy Church is inherently conservative. But unfortunately we conserve the negative as well as the positive."

"Isn't this the nature of orthodoxy?"

"Indeed it is."

"But even so, your Church has always provided for change, yes?"

"What do you mean?"

"I have learned that the Holy Ivi may receive new programs."

"And how do you think we may do this?"

"I have learned that the Holy Ivi is the guardian of Ede's first computer. The first eternal computer, into which he carked his soul."

"You've learned almost too much," Harrah said, smiling at him.

"It is said that Ede's Program for the universe is written in this computer. It is said that the Holy Ivi—and only the Holy Ivi—may interface with it."

"And what else is said?"

"It is said that the Holy Ivi alone may read Ede's Infinite Program and determine which programs of the Church are in accord with it."

"Oh, may she indeed!"

In Harrah's dark, almost black eyes there blazed a light of

pure faith. She looked deeply at Danlo for a long time. In the unspoken communication flowing like water between them, Danlo understood that she would never interface Ede's eternal computer merely out of expediency or political needs.

"*If* the Holy Ivi is truly inspired," Danlo said, "if her vision is true, then it is said that she might thus redefine old programs. Or install programs that are wholly new. This is her power, yes?"

Harrah took a long drink of tea and then sighed. "Is it also said that no Ivi has used this power in five hundred years?"

"I do not know."

"We're aware of our power, Pilot. But power is not a simple thing. We have the *ability* to interface Ede's Eternal Computer. We pray for the grace always to realize this ability in receiving new visions."

"I . . . see."

"And we have the *authority* to receive a new program and install it in the Church canon. To change the Church, as you say."

"This is what it means to be the Holy Ivi, yes?"

"So we would hope," Harrah said. "But we are uncertain as to whether we have the *influence* to make the entire Church accept a new program."

"You believe that the Iviomils would not accept a new Program of Totality?"

"They *might* not."

"And you believe that they would not accept a redefinition of the Program of Increase?"

"The Elder Bertram Jaspari has said that they certainly will not."

"Then you must fear schism, yes?"

For a long time, as Danlo clutched his flute between his hands and looked into Harrah's sad brown eyes, she looked at him. At last she took a drink of tea and said, "We *do* fear schism. Above all things, almost, we fear Architect falling against Architect in what the Iviomils would no doubt call a facifah—this unholy holy war that Elder Bertram is dying to loose upon the universe. And yet . . ."

"Yes?"

"There might be a great possibility here. This could be a critical moment for the Church—or even in Ede's Infinite Program itself."

Yes, infinite possibilities, Danlo thought as he looked at Harrah. He pressed his flute to his lips, but he said nothing.

"To install these new programs would be dangerous," Harrah said. "Yet there's danger, too, in the Church stagnating under the weight of wrongful programs. Which is the greater risk?"

"I do not know. But if *you* know, Blessed Harrah, that these new programs are in accord with Ede's Infinite Program, then mustn't you try to install them no matter the risk?"

"We're afraid that we must."

"Then . . ."

"But we don't know this yet. All we have, at this time, is our own personal understanding of what Ede's Infinite Program requires of us."

"Truly?"

"We haven't dared to interface the Eternal Computer seeking knowledge in these matters."

"Because you were afraid of what you might find?"

"No, because it wasn't time. Doesn't the Algorithm say that when hope is darkest, then like a star falling out of the night, a sign will be given? We've been waiting for such a sign, Pilot."

Danlo did not like the way that Harrah was searching his eyes just then, so he looked down to where his fingers silently pressed the holes of his flute. "What . . . sign?" he finally asked.

"We believe that your coming out of the stars might be this sign."

"But it might *not* be, yes?"

Again Harrah smiled and quoted, " 'One day, when you are near to despair, a man will come among you from the stars. He is a man without fear who will heal the living, walk with the dead, and look upon the heavenly lights within and not fall mad.' "

"But surely," Danlo said, "the congruence between this prophecy and what occurred between Elder Janegg and myself was only chance."

"You've just spoken heresy, you know. All that we do occurs according to Ede's Infinite Program. It's a grave error to believe in chance."

"I am sorry."

Harrah bowed her head as if forgiving him his error, and then she continued quoting from the Algorithm: " 'In a dark time, he will be a bringer of light, and like a star he will show the way toward all that is possible.' "

"Do you truly believe that I am a lightbringer?"

"All people are lightbringers insofar as they are part of Ede's Program to illuminate the universe. But are you *the* Lightbringer, out of the prophecy? We should like to put this to the test."

Danlo, remembering too well the ways that the Entity had tested him on the Earth that She had made, was not eager to agree to Harrah's suggestion. He sat gazing at her as he silently fingered the holes of his flute.

"If you passed these tests," Harrah said, "this would be a sign that we might interface the Eternal Computer and seek a divine understanding of the programs that we've discussed.

"I see."

"We believe that it would also be a sign that the Church was entering a new era—perhaps even the Last Days before the Omega Point. We believe that almost all Worthy Architects would regard it this way."

"I see."

"It's possible that we could make the greatest changes. Perhaps we could even send our children to Thiells to train as pilots."

"The impossible *is* truly possible, yes?"

Harrah smiled quickly, betraying a rare moment of impatience. And then she asked, "Will you agree to be tested, Pilot?"

Danlo closed his eyes as he blew a low, almost inaudible note upon his flute. In his mind's eye, he could see the future sweeping toward him all white and wild like the inevitable advance of a winter storm.

"To be tested how?" he finally asked.

"The first test is already done," Harrah said. "A man without fear who will heal the living. We've all seen this in you, Pilot. Your fearlessness, as well as your compassion in curing Elder Janegg of his madness."

"But this was an accidental test, yes?"

"As we have said, there are no accidents."

"But your other two tests—you must have a format for these."

"Indeed we do."

"Please tell me."

"A man without fear who will walk with the dead."

Danlo felt his heart suddenly beating hard inside his chest, and he asked, "But what can this mean, to walk with the dead?"

Harrah looked nervously down at her tea as if what she was about to say verged upon sacrilege. "It can only mean that the Lightbringer is he who will interface an eternal computer. One of the computers that holds the souls of all dead Architects who have been vastened."

"You are asking me to face a space into which dead minds are carked?'' Danlo would almost rather have been buried alive in a mass grave full of old corpses.

"Only if you are the Lightbringer. Only if you would walk with the dead."

Danlo blew another note on his flute, this time long and ominous. He said, "This is very dangerous, yes?"

"Indeed, it *is* dangerous."

"Not even a master cetic of my Order would interface such a space."

"Nor would any Architect of our Church. You would be the first."

"I see."

"A man without fear, Pilot."

"Assuming that I was alive afterward, what is the last test, then?"

"A man without fear who will look upon the heavenly lights within and not fall mad. You must be able to see yourself as a reflection of God and not let the light destroy you."

"I see."

"Do you?"

Danlo considered this a moment as he put down his flute. He said, "No, truly I do not."

"There is a ceremony that we Architects make," Harrah said. "We call it the light offering. This is a simulation of one's mind. Of our selfness and soul. We paint a picture of the mind with a hologram—with a billion sacred lights. An Architect wishing to make a light offering displays the patterns and the programs of himself for all to see. If he is worthy, he will have purified himself of his negative programs. And he will have written new ones. This makes for a beautiful offering indeed. The light, the colors—all the colors of consciousness. There's no greater beauty than a consciousness focused on the splendor of Ede the God."

"Then you wish me to make such an offering, yes?"

"Only if you would do so freely, of your own will."

"And you wish me to look upon the display of lights? These . . . heavenly lights within?"

"That would be the essence of the test."

"This, too, is dangerous, I think."

"We're afraid that it's very dangerous, Pilot."

"Others have viewed the models of their own minds, then?"

"They have."

"They viewed their own minds at the same moment that their minds were engaged in this self-viewing?"

"Indeed, they tried to see the reflection of the infinite in their own light."

Gazing at the bright black sky, Danlo remembered, *you see only yourself looking for yourself.*

He blew a single, high, piercing note on his flute, and his dark eyes filled with the fierceness of his will toward the unknown.

"But there are dangerous feedbacks," Harrah said. "Depersonalization, loss of identity—the nausea of pure existence. The deep programs of the mind, itself. To see what makes oneself run can be a terrifying thing."

The terrible fires of the self that burn and blind, Danlo thought. He played a strange and deep song upon his flute, then. He played and played while Harrah stared into the deep blueness of his eyes.

"All who have attempted to look inside this way," Harrah said, "have fallen mad."

Danlo put down his flute for a moment and asked, "Then why should you hope that I would succeed where others have failed?"

"If you are the Lightbringer, then you will succeed."

"And if I succeed then I am the Lightbringer, yes?"

"Indeed."

For the count of nine of his heartbeats, Danlo held his breath and stared at the dark mirrors that were Harrah Ivi en li Ede's eyes. Like a sword suspended on a silken strand above his head, all time seemed to hang upon what he said next.

"I will take your tests, then," he told Harrah. The easiest decisions, he thought, were those in which one had no true choice.

"We hoped that you would."

"I will take your tests, only . . ."

"What is it, Pilot?"

Danlo turned and pointed out the window, far below the zero level of the city—down to where the ocean broke against the beach in great waves of water and foam. He said, "You must promise me that if I, too, fall mad, I will be taken down to the sea. You must leave me there, alone."

"But you'd be in danger of drowning!"

"Yes."

"You'd have no food, no drink. And the air is bad to breathe—you'd die there, we're afraid."

"Yes, possibly I would," Danlo said. "But it would be far

worse to be shut away in one of your hospices down on the thirteenth level of the city. I'd rather die beneath the stars.''

This talk of death obviously distressed Harrah, for she wrung her hands together and smiled at Danlo in terrible sadness. For any Architect, the fate that Danlo proposed he might suffer was the worst possible: to die the real death alone, violently, painfully, without any hope of being vastened in an eternal computer.

"Is this what you really wish, then?''

"Truly, it is.''

"Very well. But you must promise us that you won't dwell upon this future. You must think only of success.''

"I . . . promise.''

Harrah bowed her head in honor of the promises that they had made to each other. Then she reached behind her neck and undid the clasp of the necklace that she wore. For a moment, she held the steel chain between her fingers. The little black cube of the devotionary computer swung back and forth, describing a lovely arc through space.

"This belonged to my husband,'' she said. She placed it in Danlo's hand, then, and smiled kindly. "Would you wear it?''

"If you'd like,'' he said, even though the giving of this unusual gift astonished him. With a few deft motions of his fingers, he snapped the strand of steel behind his neck. "Thank you, Blessed Ivi.''

"You're welcome. Please wear it as a token of all the trust and hope that we have in you.''

Danlo bowed his head, then looked at Harrah in deep silence.

"As soon as the tests are arranged,'' she told him, "we will call for you to come to the Temple.''

"Until then, Blessed Harrah.''

"Until then, Danlo wi Soli Ringess.''

Their breakfast having been successfully completed, Harrah walked him to the door and bade him farewell. All during Danlo's return to his room, as he walked down the silent halls lined with paintings of the most famous Holy Ivi's of the Cybernetic Universal Church, he brooded upon the nature of these strange tests and wondered what it would be like, once again, to walk with the dead and look upon the blessed light inside himself.

IN THE HOUSE OF THE DEAD

From the unreal lead me to the real.
From the darkness lead me to the light.
From death lead me to immortality.
    —*from Brihadaranyaka Upanishad*

The communication of the dead is tongued with
fire beyond the language of the living.
    —*from "Little Gidding," T. S. Eliot*

For the next few days Danlo kept to his rooms, doing little other than eating, meditating, and playing his flute. Sometimes, when he wished for conversation, he would turn to the devotionary computer that he had set out next to the facing heaume upon the room's altar and talk with the imago of Nikolos Daru Ede—if such a tiresome and mechanical exchange of words could be dignified as true "talk." More than once, however, this glowing ghost of the man who had become Ede the God surprised him. After plying Danlo with the usual questions concerning the recovery of his frozen body and warning Danlo of possible plots against his life, the Ede imago forced a smile to his luminous lips and observed, "These Architects have made a mockery of all that I once discovered. Of all that I once taught them. It's enough to make me sick. If I could vomit, I would."

The only real person with whom Danlo spoke during this waiting time was a man named Thomas Ivieehl, one of the many keepers of the Holy Ivi's palace. Thomas was a spare, suspicious man, and at first his communications with Danlo were guarded. Every day he would appear in Danlo's rooms after the evening meal to make sure that the altar and the tabletops and all plastic surfaces were spotless and that Danlo had every possible comfort. At first he wouldn't deign to exchange more than a few words with a naman such as Danlo, but as the days wore by and Danlo always greeted him in generosity and kindness, his attitude softened. It was from Thomas that Danlo learned that Malaclypse Redring, the deadly warrior-poet, was a guest in another wing of the palace. Danlo learned something else as well. It seemed that Bertram had demanded the right to visit Malaclypse in his rooms, and Harrah Ivi en li Ede, out of fear of prematurely alienating the Iviomils and much of the Koivuniemin, had assented. Five times Bertram had called upon Malaclypse. What the two men discussed together, no one knew—not even Harrah, who refused to hide listening robots in Malaclypse's rooms or otherwise spy upon him.

One day, on a day of stale air and artificial lights much like any other day in the city of Ornice Olorun, Harrah sent word to Danlo that he should prepare himself for the second of his tests. Her keepers escorted him through the palace, and a choche met him outside on the palace steps. She, the Holy Ivi met him at the foot of these steps and announced that she would ride with him. To share space with the Holy Ivi was a great honor, and the throngs of Architects lined up outside the palace cheered to see Danlo take his place by Harrah's side.

News of Danlo's test seemed to have spread much more quickly than the choche could travel. All along their short journey through the city, Architects crowded the streets in order to view the astonishing spectacle of Harrah Ivi en li Ede sharing a choche with a naman who might very well be the Lightbringer. Architects seemed to issue out of the nearby buildings like termites, a great swarm of pale men and women dressed in their pale white kimonos. When the choche rolled slowly past Ede's Tomb and the Temple to the place where Danlo might live or die, the surrounding grounds for a mile in any direction were packed with people. Danlo counted half a million of them before he gave up and concentrated on the building before him.

This was a large black cube made of nall, a plastic so dense and hard that it was far stronger than steel. The walls of this building, it was said, were thirty feet thick. Thus had the Architects built their House of Eternity, to withstand the slow fire of time no less the blast of hydrogen bombs. For the House of Eternity held the greatest treasure of the Church, greater than gold or firestones or Gilada pearls. In its cold, dark vaults were stacked many banks of cold computers, the Cybernetic Universal

Church's eternal computers that held the souls of all Architects who had ever died and been vastened. The Architects on the streets called this terrible building the House of the Dead, and they dreaded it even as they longed to take their places in the cybernetic heavens believed to exist eternally inside.

When Danlo stepped outside his choche, he was greeted with an immense cheer issuing from hundreds of thousands of throats. Twelve keepers from the House of Eternity greeted him as well. Two hundred grim Temple keepers formed a cordon around Danlo and Harrah and escorted them up the House's long, black steps. The fear of assassination hung in the air, as heavy as the smells of death and disease that Danlo found wherever he went in this endless city. It seemed that not everyone welcomed his arrival. Almost drowning out the voices of acclamation (and the sound of his own pulsing heart) were catcalls and jeers and demands that he should leave Tannahill forever: "Naman go home! Death to namans! Pilot man, die the real death in the House of the Dead!"

Along either side of the House's steps, the keepers had set up a light-fence of blazing ruby lasers designed to keep back anyone so foolish as to attack the Holy Ivi. Behind this fence, at the very edge of the black nall steps, stood Bertram Jaspari and Jedrek Iviongeon—and Fe Farruco Ede and Honon en li Iviow and many other Elders. Although Bertram, with his sour, little face and pointed head, remained deathly silent, he did not discourage any of the swarms of Iviomils standing behind him from casting threats at Danlo. Some of these desperate men even cast at Danlo rotten fruit or wads of spittle, which burned up in the laser light in quick hisses of steam. Their blue-tinged faces were ugly, their mood bellicose, perhaps even rebellious. Danlo thought that in proposing his tests, Harrah skated a dangerous path on thin ice. While his survival today truly might empower her to make sweeping changes in the Church, the very act of suggesting that he might be the Lightbringer could give the Iviomils a cause for schism. Danlo well remembered how many billions of people had died when the Cybernetic Universal Church had last fallen into schism and war; he could never forget that as a result of this war, *his* people, the Alaloi tribes in the wilds west of Neverness, were dying still.

At the top of the nall steps, on a portico too narrow to accommodate very many people, the keepers had set up Harrah's reading table—a massive thing of ironwood, inlaid with gold—from the Hall of the Koivuniemin. With slow, studied motions, Harrah took her place in the chair behind this table. Danlo stood before her clutching his shakuhachi in his left hand; on his right hand, around his little finger, his diamond pilot's ring shone with a fierce, dark light. He wore his formal black pilot's robes, black leather boots, and around his neck, the little black cube of a devotionary computer that Harrah had given him. And he wore something else as well.

Once a time, years ago during his passage into manhood, he had won the right to display the wing feather of the Snowy Owl. Once he had thought of this rare, white bird as his other self, the magic animal who held half his soul. Now he was far from such primitive beliefs, but strangely, even so, he sensed the rightness of wearing this relic from the past. And so that morning while dressing, he had fastened Ahira's white feather to his long, wild hair. As he readied himself to enter the dark building before him, he reached up to touch the imakla feather. Silently he called to that part of himself that he had turned away from for too long. *Ahira, Ahira,* he whispered inside himself. *Lo los barado.* He stood before Harrah's golden desk listening for the answer that he had sought for so long. There were no owls on the planet of Tannahill, or even any wild birds, but even so there was a moment when he heard a high, deep cry. And then, coming to his senses, he realized that this sound was only the screeching of a hundred thousand voices calling his name. Or perhaps he was scrying, turning his face toward the future and hearing himself scream in madness and pain.

Ahira, Ahira, he prayed. *Ahira, Ahira.*

Just then Harrah nodded at one of the keepers and the man suddenly called out for silence. Such were the programs and the discipline that the Church wrote into one's spirit and flesh that the manswarms crowding the Temple grounds obediently fell silent. Not even Bertram Jaspari or any other Iviomil dared to shout down the Holy Ivi when she wished to speak. And speak Harrah Ivi en li Ede certainly did.

In truth, she chose this occasion to make a rather long speech. In her clear and compassionate voice, she reminded all the assembled Architects of their duty toward God, as well as their dream of a future in which the universe would be remade and all worthy men and women redeemed from the black and bottomless depths of time. "This is a time of great changes in our Holy Church," Harrah told the multitudes gathered below her. "Perhaps this is even the beginning of the Last Days when all the universe will be new. We Architects must always be ready for the future, even for such astonishing and unforeseen events as a naman pilot falling out of the stars. We are met here today to determine if this man, Danlo wi Soli Ringess of Neverness, is truly the bringer of the future. Is he the bringer of light who will show the way toward what is possible? Is he the man without fear who will walk with the dead? We shall see.''

So saying, Harrah nodded at two old keepers who opened the nall doors behind her reading desk. Danlo looked into the building where he would spend the next few hours—or perhaps the rest of his life. It was dark inside, almost as black as the air deep within a hole in the ground. As had been arranged, Harrah would keep a vigil at her reading desk while Danlo underwent his test inside the building. One last time, Danlo bowed his head to Harrah, then smiled. He looked out into the huge crowd below him. There, just to the side of the nall steps, standing next to Bertram Jaspari, he saw Malaclypse Redring staring up at him. Malaclypse wore a bright, rainbow kimono around his body and an intense curiosity on his face. Danlo stared into his deep, violet eyes, and it seemed as if the warrior-poet were telling him that to prepare for death, he must first learn how to live. Danlo remembered a saying of his father, then. *To live, I die.* He touched the feather in his hair, touched his pilot's ring and grasped his bamboo flute tightly in his hand—and with these little affirmations of life, he turned away from the city of Ornice Olorun and walked into the House of the Dead.

When the doors banged shut behind him, Danlo found himself in a space that seemed as black and vast as the Greater Morbio. But of course it wasn't. In truth, the interior of the House of Eternity was not at all expansive and open, but rather packed full of many stacks of eternal computers. There were thousands of these little black boxes, each built exactly into the shape of a cube and no larger than the devotionary computers that all Architects carried with them wherever they went. So dense were these stacks of computers that there was little room for walking about the black floor. The House of Eternity was the one Church building closed to most Worthy Architects and the millions of pilgrims who swarmed into Ornice Olorun each year; it was a cold, dark place constructed more for the care of computers than the comfort of human beings. Indeed, it was so cold that one of the House keepers met Danlo at the door and gave him a babri, a cloak of a soft, quilted plastic, probably some kind of furine or ester. After Danlo had swaddled himself up like a newborn babe, the keeper led him through the stacks of computers deeper into the building.

It was very quiet in this strange place. Although he tried to step softly, the slap of his leather boots against the floor seemed almost as loud as the crack of an iceberg breaking away from a glacier. Once again he heard the beating of his heart, and he smelled cold sweat and ketones and dust, as well as the close, oily reek of nall. At the center of the building was a square area almost completely enclosed by four walls of computers. Entering this area was like stepping into a little room. There the keepers had thrown together a thin, old mat and a few babris and had prepared a kind of bed upon the floor. One of these keepers—an old man who introduced himself as Cheslav Iviongeon—bade Danlo to lie down on this bed. Any other man would have been insulted at these mean preparations for such an important test. But Danlo was only estranged. As he settled himself down on the hard floor, he knew immediately that he did not want to be there. Although he tried to lay as still as a corpse, the coldness of the nall floor below him instantly penetrated his body and caused him to shiver violently.

"Would you please bring another babri?" Cheslav Iviongeon said to one of the other keepers. "We don't want the pilot to be too uncomfortable."

It was dark in this little room, and Danlo could almost feel the dark blue irises of his eyes dilating to let in more light. He stared up at Cheslav Iviongeon and considered Cheslav's last name; he remembered Harrah warning him that he was Jedrek Iviongeon's brother and one of the city's most prominent Iviomils. It seemed that the old man suffered from the mehalis, for his skin betrayed the telltale cyanine color of that disease. He was cadaverously thin, and his shaved head gleamed like a skull. In truth, he was nothing but loose flesh and bones; when he motioned with his hands and spoke to Danlo, it was as if a skeleton had come to life and was clacking around above him.

"Welcome, Danlo wi Soli Ringess," he said. His voice was strained and hoarse as if he'd been coughing at the cold air. He was a grim man with a grim and gruesome sense of humor. "Most people only enter the House of Eternity after they've died, but we haven't quite reached that glorious state, have we? Soon enough, though, we'll leave the blood and bones behind. You even sooner than I, Pilot."

Here he shook his old hand at Danlo and laughed, and so loud was the creaking of his joints, it was almost as if he were shaking a rattle.

"When do we begin?" Danlo asked, looking up at the black ceiling.

"Soon, soon," Cheslav said. "But first we must make a copy of your soul."

As Danlo watched the various keepers moving about the building intent on their various duties, he thought about the Architect word for "soul." In modern Church Istwan, this was the *pallaton,* that almost indestructible form of the self that could be preserved in an eternal computer. The pallaton was pure program and information; the pallaton was a model of the mind encoded as bits of ones and zeros and stored as perfectly arrayed electrons frozen onto diamond discs. When a man—or woman—died, he would enter into a vastening chamber, a cold room full of computers and robots, drills and lasers and microscopes and needle knives. There his brain would be pulled apart, neuron by bloody neuron down to the webwork of once-living wires called dendrites and axons. Scanning computers would then make a model of the brain's trillions of interconnections. After this model had been stored on a diamond disc (and after the body had been consigned to the crematorium's plasma fires), the disc would be taken to the vaults of the House of Eternity.

Danlo, lying in his makeshift bed, turned to watch the many keepers scurrying about, tending to these very diamond discs. Each disc was the size of a shih leaf, though perfectly round in shape. It was the keepers' task to bear the glittering discs from the vastening chamber to their place of permanent storage inside the black, eternal computers. Although the discs were mostly made of diamond, the keepers carried them as if they held living eyeballs in their hands. In truth, a single disc could hold the pallatons of thousands of dead Architects, and so the keepers bore the discs as if they were the most precious objects in all the universe.

"A copy of my soul," Danlo said. "My selfness, my pallaton, you say."

One of the keepers—another unhealthy old man—brought Cheslav Iviongeon a glittering silver heaume. Cheslav, who was a master programer as well as Elder Keeper of the House of Eternity, looked at Danlo and smiled coldly. He said, "We'll try to create a temporary pallaton. Unless, of course, you're willing to make the Profession of Faith, be cleansed, and die the real death?"

"No," Danlo said, smiling. "Not yet."

Cheslav rattled his knuckles across the heaume's metallic surface. "Then will you allow me to place this computer on your head? It will scan your brain while still alive."

Danlo considered as his heart beat ten times, then finally said, "Yes."

For a moment, Danlo sat up to allow Cheslav to perform his dreaded task of enclosing his head inside a computer. With much puffing and grunting, Cheslav managed to force the heaume down over Danlo's thick black hair. In the closeness of the room, Danlo smelled the old man's fetid breath coming in huffs and spurts.

"Ah, there—you've a large head and long," Cheslav said. "You may lie back, now."

As if a signal had been given, five of the other keepers gathered around Danlo's bed and stood staring down at him. Their faces were as pale as the flesh of snowworms; their unfriendly eyes were like black holes sucking at his soul. These men, and one woman named Ramona Iviessa Ede, were all programers who believed in the teachings of their Church. They were curious to see what would happen when the workings of Danlo's living mind were modeled and copied by their scanning computer. If they had been permitted to gamble, they might have made wagers as to whether Danlo would live or die right then. Three of them thought that nothing would happen. Because Danlo was not truly dead and this scanning computer could only paint a rudimentary picture of his mind—at least when compared to the eternal pallatons written by the much more powerful scanning computers of the vastening chambers—they argued that a temporary pallaton was not a true pallaton, and therefore, this procedure posed Danlo no risk at all.

But the others, including Cheslav Iviongeon, were not so sure. They looked down at Danlo, three death's-heads fairly floating in the dim light, and a terrible uncertainty marked their grim faces. It was almost as if they were afraid that the mere modeling of Danlo's mind would somehow "steal" his soul and render his flesh lifeless and cold. If a man's very selfness could truly be copied onto a diamond disc, then what life of the body could remain? Could a man have two souls? Or two times ten thousand—as many copies as a machine could make? Could a man simultaneously exist both as mind in the flesh and as informational bits and pulses of light inside an eternal computer? Surely, Danlo thought, these were questions for the theologians.

But even as he lay back on his mat and felt the hard heaume crushing his head, he wondered for the ten thousandth time in his life about the nature of consciousness. He wondered about himself, about his own soul, and the coldness of these thoughts, no less the icy chill of the floor, sent waves of fear shivering through his body.

"This will take some time," Cheslav Iviongeon told him. "From time to time, I may ask you questions, and you must please tell me what you feel."

In truth, during this part of Danlo's test he felt almost nothing. He lay against the hard floor trying to control the violent tremors tearing through his body. After some time had passed— perhaps two tenths of an hour, he thought—he succeeded. There were bad smells in the air, ketones and sweat, the faint reek of the mehalis disease as well as the black thickness of nall, but he tried not to concentrate on these. He lay with his eyes closed, clutching his flute against his belly. He breathed steadily and deeply as he tried to remember all the songs for the shakuhachi that he had ever composed. Thus engaged, time seemed to flow swiftly but invisibly, like water rushing through a glass tube. He waited for Cheslav Iviongeon to ask him questions, and he was surprised when the first words out of Cheslav's mouth were a request to sit up.

"Would you please let us remove the heaume now, Pilot? It's done."

Danlo sat up straight and two of the keepers grasped the heaume with their bony fingers and pulled it from his head. With great relief Danlo felt the cold air as it found his sweaty, matted hair.

"So soon?" Danlo asked. "Then your attempt to model my mind was a failure, yes?"

Cheslav shook his head as he smiled grimly. "We've been here two hours, Pilot. And no, I don't believe our attempt was a failure. We'll soon see, however."

With this, he nodded to one of the keepers, a thin man who bore the heaume away into the darkness of the building. Danlo was given to understand that this keeper would entrust the heaume to a cadre of programers in the vastening chamber. There its information would be downloaded into a great compiling computer. There, in this huge black machine almost the size of a house, a model of his soul would be encoded and put together. His pallaton—or rather a temporary realization of his selfness, which would then be copied onto a diamond disc.

"How long must we wait?" Danlo asked. Usually he was as patient as stone, but he dreaded the next phase of his test, and he wanted to begin it as soon as possible.

"Soon, soon," Cheslav told him. His creaky old voice fell off the banks of computers like metal against metal. He suddenly turned and looked over his shoulder. "Well, then, the Worthy Nikolaos returns now."

Danlo looked up to see the same gaunt-faced keeper make his way toward them down the dark aisle. Soon, the Worthy Nikolaos approached Cheslav Iviongeon, and into his outstretched hand he placed a diamond disc.

"Here we are," Cheslav said, holding up the disc. "Or should I say, here *you* are?"

With a tight, unreadable smile, he held the disc toward Danlo. Danlo put down his flute and carefully took the disc.

"We made this just for your test. Yours is the only pallaton on it."

"I see," Danlo said. The little slice of diamond in the palm of his hand was cold and glittering and hard, and he stared at it for a long time. In its gleaming surface, he could see—faintly—the reflection of his own face.

"As far as I know, no Architect has ever held what you hold, Pilot. Or seen what you see."

"I . . . see," Danlo said again.

"Of all the acts of our Holy Ivi's architetcy, this has been the strangest. And the most dangerous."

"Many people have objected to this test, yes?"

"Many times many, Pilot. To be vastened while one is still alive—I can't tell you how offensive such covetousness is to any Architect."

"I see."

"Such an act is really unthinkable—the Algorithm explicitly warns against such acts."

"I am sorry."

"Of course, there is one exception to this rule."

"Yes?"

"The Algorithm permits such a vastening in times of facifah when the Worthy might be killed in battle. As a safeguard against one dying the real death."

"Have I truly been vastened, then?"

Cheslav Iviongeon looked at Danlo sharply, coldly. "Some will say that you have. But I think not. We've only made you a temporary pallaton."

Danlo looked away from Cheslav and stared back at the mirror in his hand. His reflection was so faint that he could not see his own eyes, the deep blue inside blue color that had always astonished him. "But you believe that my selfness has been carked onto this disc, yes?"

"Many people believe many things," Cheslav said evasively. "But those most faithful to our Holy Ivi will distinguish between a temporary pallaton and one that is eternal. Indeed, they'll leap to grasp at the difference. They'll split words like the theologians. Thus they'll argue that no abomination has been created here today; they'll proclaim that the spirit of the Algorithm has been observed. This, I believe, is what our Holy Ivi will hope. This is her gamble, her plan."

"Then you believe that I have been vastened only temporarily, yes?"

"We do not speak of vastening as merely the creation of a pallaton."

"No?"

"One is not vastened, properly, until the disc containing the pallaton is loaded into an eternal computer. And then, when the program runs, the pallaton comes virtually alive. It's said that heaven opens up, and there is lightning and light and all information, and . . . and it's really impossible to speak of such things, Pilot, because only the dead know what it's like to be dead."

"How am I, then, to know . . . what only the dead truly know?"

At this, Cheslav Iviongeon smiled grimly and said, "Because you'll behold the alam al-mithral. That is, we will create a simulation of our cybernetic heaven. And you will interface this holy space."

Cheslav stroked his bony head, and then he explained that the alam al-mithral space of the dead Architect souls was cut off from realspace and that there was no way to enter it easily. But there *was* a way. He, Cheslav Iviongeon, master programer and Keeper of the House of Eternity, had discovered how a mortal man such as Danlo might walk with the dead. All that Danlo was—his curiosity, his recklessness, his playfulness, his verve and valor, and his love of truth—all of these traits and much else had been carked into computer code. His essence had been transformed and transcribed into a program called a pallaton. Soon, very soon, his pallaton would be downloaded into one of the building's eternal computers. There it would join the pallatons of all the trillions of Architects who had ever died and been vastened. In this way, the essence of Danlo's mind and soul would enter the pallatons' universe as burning bits of information. The other pallatons would perceive him as one of their own; they would exchange information and interact with him as if he were just another pallaton.

"Who are you, really, Danlo wi Soli Ringess?" Cheslav Iviongeon pointed at the diamond disc in Danlo's hand. "We'll see if we haven't captured your real essence. Your deepest programs. We'll cark them into an eternal computer. The pallatons of all the vastened will interact with the pallaton of Danlo of Neverness. If you'll consent to entering a virtuality, we'll make you a simulation of these interactions."

For a long time Danlo stared at the disc that he held in the palm of his hand. In its diamond surface, he could see little bits of color, violets and blues and gold. "I will interface the virtuality that you call the alam al-mithral. This cybernetic heaven. This is the soul . . . of my test, yes?"

With this understanding, Danlo gave the disc to the Worthy Nikolaos, who bore it away toward one of the eternal computers. With a quick motion of his hand, he snapped it into an opening of this little black cube.

"There, it's done," Cheslav Iviongeon announced. "You've been vastened. Temporarily vastened, I should say. Even as we speak, your pallaton is experiencing wonders. Every computer in this room is linked to every other. And to all the eternal computers on Tannahill. And now, Danlo of the Stars, it's time that you experienced this heaven, too."

Danlo did not like the way Cheslav smiled just then, with his cracked, yellow teeth and a look of grim necessity clouding his eyes. He wondered how a mere computer program could experience anything. And then he saw Cheslav holding a new heaume in his blue-tinged hands, and he wondered what experiences the old man thought that he would soon suffer.

"This will create for you a simulation of the alam al-mithral," Cheslav told him. "May we put it on you?"

"If you'd like, I suppose you must," Danlo said. And then, more willfully: "Yes."

With the Worthy Nikolaos's help, Cheslav forced the heaume over Danlo's head. As before the fit was too tight, and the heaume's metal hurt him. Danlo wondered why they couldn't find a larger heaume. *Small heaumes for small heads,* he remembered one of his teachers once saying. It amused him to think that thousands of years of daily facing ceremonies and the blind following the Church's doctrines had bred human beings with brains stunted like bonsai trees, but he knew this wasn't really true.

"Please lie back now, and we'll begin," Cheslav said.

With a painful bow of his head, Danlo lay back against his cold blankets. He pressed his wooden flute against his belly; he closed his eyes and began to pray: *Ahira, guide me. Ahira, Ahira.*

In truth, he did not know what to expect of this virtuality that Cheslav Iviongeon and his programers had made for him. Once, when he was a child, his grandfather had told him to expect of life only the unexpected and he would never be disappointed. Even so, as he took a deep breath and stepped through the doorway into the cybernetic heaven called the alam al-mithral, he had expectations. Try as he might to experience the virtuality with all the freshness of a child playing in his first snowfall, the weight of a thousand journeys through one surreality or another pulled him down into old habits of the mind.

Almost at once the room's sensa—Cheslav's raspy voice, the reek of nall plastic, the dark glitter of thousands of computers stacked one atop the other—vanished. Danlo opened his eyes to find himself carked out into the unknown spaces of the other-world. He was floating in the midst of what seemed to be dark, heavy clouds. All about him lightning bolts rent the grayness, and flashes of light illuminated the mist. He smelled ozone and sweat and the fragrance of alien flowers. Various shapes and colors flickered wherever he looked. Once or twice, he thought he saw faces. In their ghostly whiteness and shades of copper and pink, they seemed almost familiar, as if well-known images and objects were trying to take form—either that or else some quirk of the eternal computers' master program was causing everything to break into pieces and bits of light and swirl around him like snowflakes in a winter storm. Such chaos sent waves of nausea pounding through his body. His belly burned with a dull, acid pain, and his head was on fire. He knew that he must make sense of these images, and soon. If he did not, he might fall mad. And so, almost immediately, he began to seek the rules and methods for moving through this strange space. In every surreality into which he had ever instantiated, there was always a way to master the rules and move deeper into structure and meaning.

This is truly overwhelming, he thought. *But it is not real.*

As he floated through the violet clouds of chaos, he was seized with a fear that in *this* surreality there might be no rules. Or, at least, no rules that he could discover and manipulate. The alam al-mithral, he remembered, had been created neither as an entertainment nor as a pedagogic tool for teaching the mathematics of the manifold. Perhaps he was not meant to discover how to move through this space; perhaps he was not meant to move at all.

You are here to walk with the dead, he told himself. *Nothing more.*

Off in the distance—it might have been ten feet away or a mile—he thought that he saw the face of a famous Architect, Mendai Iviercier, who had been the greatest Holy Ivi to succeed Kostos Olorun in the early days of the Church. He wanted to come closer, to study this plump, pink face more closely, but he couldn't move his arms or legs; his neck was as stiff as if he'd suffered a paralytic stroke, and even his eyes remained frozen forward, locked open upon whatever images fell before him. In little time—it might have been a second or a millionth part thereof—Mendai Iviercier's face broke up into glasslike pieces: chin, cheeks, ears, forehead, nose, and eyes, and then even these still recognizable structures shattered into a grayish pink dust. And then, as if touched with some terrible inner force, the dust exploded outward, a billion billion points of glittering silver dissolving into the essential nothingness of the alam al-mithral.

Ahira, where am I? Danlo wondered. *Who am I—Ahira, Ahira?*

He remembered, then, that he was here to experience a simulation of what was occurring to his pallaton inside the House of the Dead's eternal computers. Only this and nothing more. The program of these computers would determine all his experiences in this dead-gray underworld. He would have no freedom to move; he would have no free will at all. Suddenly, all around him in the mist, there appeared faces. Many of these faces seemed familiar and Danlo desired to view them more closely, but he had no power to move his eyes. Once, he had witnessed men from the Order of True Scientists using chemicals to immobilize alien beings and then dissect them with lasers and glittering needle knives. Now, he himself felt as helpless as a Scutari nymph pinned to a board. Although his eyes were tightly closed (the eyes of his real body shivering beneath stacks of cold computers), Cheslav Iviongeon's master program had pinned the eyes of his pallaton open. There was nothing he could do, he thought, except to let the program run.

If I must, I, myself, can always run. Truly, I can. I can rip the heaume from my head and run from this terrible building.

And then, to his horror, as he tried to feel the smooth bamboo of his flute, he found that he could not. He could not move the fingers of his real body, or his arms or legs, and therefore, he could not move to pull off the heaume and run away from this awful test. The heaume's dislocation of his senses—even his deep proprioceptive sense of his own cells—was almost total. Its powerful logic field had stripped him of sight, sound, and touch, and had programed for him a powerful new reality.

I am not I, he thought. *I am only a program running inside a machine.*

As faces appeared all around him in the cold mist, he knew that he must fight this thought with all the force of his will. That he still possessed a will both fierce and free he knew deep inside himself just as he knew that sunlight on a clear day is warm and good. The conflict between his own inner sense of selfness and freedom and the experience of existing as a pallaton caught in some dread eternal program was enough to make him fall mad. It was one of the terrible moments of his life. He wondered if even his thoughts would soon fall under the control of this program. Perhaps his memories would, too. Perhaps he would remember a life that he had never truly lived; perhaps he would fall forever into a cybernetic reality that wasn't truly real.

I am Danlo wi Soli Ringess. I must not be afraid.

At the very moment when Danlo was wondering what kinds of interactions Cheslav might have programed for his enlightenment, new faces appeared in the mist just before his eyes. Faces and forms: seven Architects with their shaven heads and white kimonos took shape seemingly from the substance of the clouds themselves. Sounds issued from their dead lips. It seemed almost like speech. Danlo caught the vowels and consonants of words and then whole segments of sentences. These seven dead souls— or rather simulations of pallatons—seemed to be holding a learned discussion.

A famous theologian named Ornice Narcavage, who had been dead some five hundred years, was discussing the divine nature of the Algorithm. Only, her words sounded more mechanical than even the utterances of the Ede hologram of Danlo's devotionary computer. And the responses of the other six souls were much like programed dialogues out of some boring history lesson: long sequences of information masquerading as true conversation. This amused Danlo, and he might have laughed, but he couldn't move his lips or open his mouth.

This is not so bad. I can survive this.

Almost with this thought, the face of Ornice Narcavage turned toward him and seemed almost surprised at his black robes and wild hair. She herself was as bald as a stone, and her eyes were a dead black, like slate. "We have a visitor," she said to the others. "He knows little of the Juriddik."

"Or the Iviomils," a pallaton named Burgos Iviow said.

"But he must know about yarkonah," a third one said.

"Let's ask him about yarkonah."

Danlo wanted to tell them that Yarkona was a harsh but beautiful world a hundred light-years coreward from Neverness, near Simoom and Urradeth. But to his astonishment, he found his mouth suddenly moving and strange words pouring out like wine from a cracked vat. "The Fravashi teach the truth of ananke, which is a universal fate to which even the gods must submit. This idea has been used in support of the Church's Program of the Halting, which states that . . ."

For quite some time, against Danlo's volition, his pallaton went on lecturing about the various doctrines and programs of the Cybernetic Universal Church. At the same time, he lay remembering that Yarkona was not only the name of a planet and the name of one of the Order's great pilots who had discovered it, but also a term for the theological attempt in the 300s to interpret Edeism in terms of Holism and Fravashi philosophy. In truth, Danlo knew little of this other "yarkonah," but he had once been a student of a Fravashi Old Father, and so it wasn't too difficult for him to extend pure and simple Fravashi concepts to the incredible muddle of thought that passed as Church theology. That is, it wasn't difficult for his pallaton to do this. Danlo listened in awe and dread as he felt his mouth moving in ways that he couldn't control. He listened to the words of his pallaton, this clever but ultimately unalive computer program, and he knew that he himself would never say such clever but lifeless things.

They have tried to make me a robot. But I am not. I am only I. And I know that I know that I . . .

As Danlo's pallaton lectured on and on about the Fravashi reconciliation between free will and fate, he noticed that this glittering projection of a computer program was talking faster and faster. Now words began to spill from his mouth like marbles from a wooden box. He could scarcely understand what he was saying. And the pallatons of Ornice Narcavage and the others floating in the clouds spoke in response, and it was as if a recording of voices had been speeded up into a high-pitched babble. In any cybernetic space, of course, accelerations of information were always possible. Indeed, in the simulation of the alam almithral that Cheslav Iviongeon had made, he must have programed tremendous time *decelerations* so that Danlo could grasp the lightning-quick information exchanges taking place between the pallatons. What if, Danlo suddenly wondered, these time decelerations were relaxed? What if he were made to view the pallatons' heaven in realtime—in the real nanoseconds in which the eternal computers generated the space of the alam almithral?

It would be like hell, he thought. *The quick fires of computer time would burn my mind.*

Danlo wanted to cry out, "No, no, I will not let it happen!" But he could not speak, and the sound of his pallaton's voice was like the shriek of a rocket plummeting to Earth. When the other pallatons answered him, the collective noise they generated was so intense that it felt more like heat than sound. The clouds in which he was floating began to move, not slowly as clouds might in a warm false winter wind, but violently, furiously, as a mushroom cloud might boil up over a sleeping city at night. Bursts of carmine and pink and puce colored the air in great glittering bands. There was too much light. The intense illumination hurt Danlo's eyes. But he could not turn his head or shut his eyes; he could only gasp at the terrible fire lancing through his brain. And all the while his pallaton talked on and on, and he looked out upon the many other pallatons who were now carking out to speak with this pilot named Danlo wi Soli Ringess.

It hurts, it hurts! Oh, Ahira, Ahira, how it hurts!

As the program accelerated, thousands of faces flickered before his eyes, one face following another with all the speed of a wormrunner using his thumb to rifle a pack of pornographic Tantra cards. The effect of viewing so many silver-gray mirrors of the human soul was almost blinding. In truth, just then Danlo wished that he were as eyeless as a scryer. But even if he were blind, he realized, it would have been of no help. The heaume crushing his head like an iron fist would still infuse images directly into his brain. He could no more stop this image storm than he could contain a supernova explosion inside his cupped hands.

They will try to kill me with images. Or make me fall mad.

It was no mistake, he realized, that the program encoding his pallaton had suddenly accelerated. A rage of images was as dangerous as a lightning storm, and it would be possible to destroy a man's mind in this way. And this was Cheslav Iviongeon's design. Somehow, Danlo knew that this was true. Harrah had warned him that Cheslav was an Iviomil, perhaps even one of Bertram Jaspari's most faithful followers. He had accepted the risk that Cheslav might try to harm him. It would have been simpler, of course, for Cheslav to assassinate Danlo by directly destroying his brain. All heaumes are dangerous, and it is all too easy to burn out the neurons and synapses with an overpowered logic field. But Harrah's inquisitors would easily have discovered such a crude and murderous strategem, and therefore, Cheslav and his programers had been forced into more subtle means for disposing of such a dangerous naman as Danlo.

It is written that whom the gods would destroy, they first make mad. Although Cheslav Iviongeon dwelled far from the godhead, with his shiny heaume and black eternal computers, no less his mind-killing program, he truly possessed the means to move Danlo into madness.

I am flesh I am not I am I—I am I am I am . . .

Danlo was almost helpless before the images blazing in his mind's eye. He must have beheld the pallatons of a million dead Architects in a moment. Or perhaps a million times a million. After a while—as the pain in his head grew white-hot like heated steel—the faces of these dead souls began to change. In truth, they mutated into shapes that were at once heartbreakingly familiar and utterly strange. Long brown hair exploded like feather moss from their bald heads. Their jaws lengthened and broadened, while their face bones grew stronger, bolder. Everything about them seemed strong, especially the heavily muscled limbs of their bodies, which also sprouted a dense matting of hair. But it was their eyes that drew him inward with all the force of the sun capturing a comet. Their eyes shone like golden pools of light. Each pair of eyes was deeply set beneath prominent browridges; they were watchful, soulful, eyes that he had seen in dreams. And eyes that he had once beheld in real life, too. He marveled at the primeval beauty of these new forms. And he marveled that the dead, in his mind, could come so suddenly to life.

Haidar eth Chandra eth Anevay eth Choclo eth—no, no, no, no!

Danlo, floating in the blazing nothingness of the alam almithral, blinded by the light, could no longer make out the faces of dead Architects. Instead he beheld the shimmering forms of men, women, and children whom he remembered too well. They stood in a great circle all around him, holding out their hands, beckoning. He knew without counting that there were eighty-eight of these blessed people. He remembered, then, the cold and terrible day when he had buried the eighty-eight members of his tribe, the mothers and fathers and sons of the Devaki, whom he had loved more than life itself.

Oh, God, please, no! No, no, no, no.

Was it possible, he wondered, for his people to be truly alive in the way that all life lives even after death? Was it possible that in the One memory, there truly was no time? Was there only the eternal Now-moment where all things and people who had ever looked upon the glories of the world still lived? If this were so, then Danlo's people might still be watching him, now and forever. Perhaps the shock of the images had somehow unlocked a secret door in his brain. Perhaps, at last, in the fever of near-madness, he had somehow stepped through the doorway into this blessed universal memory where life and death are as one.

No, no—I am not. I am not, I am not, I am . . .

He suddenly knew that he was not remembrancing but only hallucinating. The shock to his brain had been very profound. The images now haunting him were only ghosts from his own memory, not the essence of the One memory itself. Although the forms of Haidar and Chandra and all the others of his tribe seemed utterly real, he knew that they were not. They were only vivid shapes and shades—shadows out of the deepest part of his mind.

No, no, please, no.

Somewhere in the heaven of the alam al-mithral—or in the hell that each man carries inside himself like a burning stone—a woman came nearer to Danlo. She was short and round with a beautifully animated face and brown eyes always full of love and compassion. She was Danlo's found-mother, Chandra, and in life she had always liked to sit by the soup skins, telling the other women stories of Danlo's daily adventures and always laughing. But now, here in this dark, dread space blazing like fire inside Danlo's heart, she was not smiling. Her once-soft face was full of suffering, pain, death. For an eternity she looked at him with her sad, lovely eyes, which he had seen too often in his dreams. And then in a voice as deep and moist as the ocean, she asked him, "Why did you leave me, Danlo?"

"But, Mother, I never left you!" he heard himself say.

"Why did you leave me to die?"

"No, no, I would never—"

"Why, Danlo, why?"

"No, never, never, I . . ."

Then Haidar, with his black beard and great, bearlike shoulders, came up to Danlo. He held out his huge hand, which was covered with blood. "A man," he said, "does not leave his family to die. Not a true man."

"But father," Danlo heard himself say, "I made you tea and rubbed hot seal oil on your forehead. While you were still alive, I never slept. I prayed until my voice flew from my mouth like a bird. I never left your side, unless it was to gather herbs or wood for the fire."

"Then why did I die, Danlo?"

"I do not know."

"Why did you let us all die?"

Now the others of his tribe gathered close to him in a circle. There was Choclo, with his impish grin, and Mentina and Cilehe and his near-sisters and near-brothers. Choclo was not grinning now, but rather grimacing in terrible pain with his palm clasping his ear. When he drew his hand away, his fingers dripped blood. There was blood in his hair, blood staining his white shagshay furs. "I loved you as I did all my brothers," Choclo said. "But why did you bring the slow evil to our tribe?"

"Oh, God, I . . ."

"Why did you live, Danlo? Why did you live when we all died?"

"I do not know!"

Because Danlo's head ached with a terrible pain, he pressed his hands hard over his eyes. After a while, he felt a burning moisture there, and he let his palms fall open before him. And in the deep bowl of his hands, there were no tears, but only blood. He began to sob, then, and drops of blood welled up in his eyes and seared his face like the touch of acid wire.

"Danlo!"

"No, no."

"Oh, Danlo, Danlo!" This came from his found-mother, Chandra, who reached out to take hold of his hand. Her fingers were cold, and she gripped him with all the power of a coiling snake. "Do not leave us again."

"Stay with us," Haidar said. "We are your people, and we love you as the trees love the sun. Please stay with us."

And then Choclo and Mentina and all the others of his tribe crowded still closer. They each held out their hands to touch him, and love flowed from their fingers like hot oil rubbed over a wounded body. It warmed Danlo inside, bringing him to the edge of deep joy. "Stay with us, Danlo. Stay with us and be loved."

Danlo noticed, then, that the terrible pain splitting his head was gone. For the first time in many years, no pain lurked like a tiger behind his eyes; he felt only peace, pleasure, and a contentment as deep as the cavernous black spaces between the stars.

I will stay with you, Danlo thought. *I will stay with you here, always.*

Madness, he knew then, need not be a descent into some fiery, screaming hell. Rather it could be like falling into a nurturing pool of love, as warm as blood, gently falling and falling forever.

"Yes, Danlo, fall into our arms," Chandra said. "Fall into our hearts. Look into the ocean of love we hold in our eyes, and fall forever."

"Danlo," his found-father, Haidar said. "We are your family, and families are forever."

And Rafael, his near-brother, and all the others cried out, "We are your family! Stay with us, Danlo. Oh, Danlo, Danlo!"

Yes, I must stay. I, too, must die now. Yes, yes.

"No!"

Danlo heard himself cry out this single word, and the suddenness of the sound shocked him. It tore through his being like thunder, and yet it haunted him like the call of the Snowy Owl far out over the frozen sea.

"No," he said again, "I will not stay."

In the end, it was his will that saved him. He remembered that many other tribes of the Alaloi people had been touched with the slow evil. They would surely die of this disease, he thought, if he did not return someday soon to save them.

I will return. I will.

He willed himself, then, to see himself just as he really was. There came a moment of stunning clarity as of stepping from a smoky cave outside into the bright winter air. He was falling mad, truly, but his very power to reflect upon this falling meant that he hadn't yet plunged into total madness. He realized an important thing. His hallucinations of his family, as terrible and beautiful as they were, might be the key to unlock the door to this insane inner prison that Cheslav Iviongeon had programed for him. If these ghosts from his memory could drive out the images of the dead Architects, then he himself held the power to create an interior world far more vivid and "real" than any computer-generated surreality—even one so profound as the alam almithral. If, in his falling madness, he had unconsciously called up phasms of his dead family, why not then concentrate the whole of his awareness on a vision of his own choosing?

The whole art of journeying into the unknown, he remembered, *is in knowing what to do when you don't know what to do.*

Once, Leopold Soli—pilot, hunter, warrior, and the blood father of his true father—had taught him that when a man goes out into the wild (or inside to that dark and strange land of the soul), he must do three things. First he must learn to see the snowstorms and chaos of the world as signs of the unknown rather than as a call to panic. A true warrior, Soli had often told him, never fell into panic. And then, like a thallow winging his way skywards, he must shift to a higher state of awareness, both of himself and of the infinitely various seascapes below. Last, and most important, no matter how lost in darkness he might feel, he must trust that he held inside himself the brilliant constellations of light that would always point his way home.

I do know what to do. Truly, I do.

For a while, he let his adoptive mother and father speak to him and touch him as they would. He accepted the uncertainty and anguish of his feelings; he accepted the uncertainty of reality itself. He let all his senses fall free like a handful of feathers tossed into the wind. Choclo was telling him something now, reminding him of the first time they had ever hunted seals together. Something inside called out to Danlo then, and he knew that he should pay close attention to what Choclo was saying. No, that wasn't quite right; rather he must see in his memory every nuance of snow and cloud of their journey out onto the sea's ice. Somewhere in his marvelous memory, he knew, shined the one star that would lead him from this place of madness.

That day with Choclo, out beyond the Twin Sister Islands— that was the day in which I first saw Ahira.

As Danlo had waited on the cold sea ice, just before twilight with the wind rising and first stars showing silver over the mountains, he had caught sight of a wild white bird streaking into the sky. It was Ahira, Choclo had told him, the graceful Snowy Owl who could fly higher than even the blue thallows of the Ten Thousand Islands. For a long time Danlo had stood frozen to the ice, utterly ravished by the beauty of this bird. It was a moment in his life he could never forget.

Ahira, Ahira.

This glorious image of winged whiteness, along with the faces of his family, blazed in Danlo's mind. He could see Choclo as he was now, leaking blood from his ears and tormented in death, but he could also see the other Choclo of years past when he had first pointed to Ahira soaring above the sea. He let all his senses fall upon this younger, happier Choclo. He let his eyes drink in the sight of the Snowy Owl climbing ever higher into the sky. This magic animal drew all his awareness. All other images faded away and vanished from his vision. The whole of his world, and of all worlds, became this single bird and the twilight sky beyond. The whiteness of Ahira was as pure as snow and as lovely as starlight. Only two colors lit his awareness now, this dazzling white and the deep blue of the sky. Ahira flew ever higher pulling Danlo into blueness, into that marvelous blue beyond blue, so cool and perfect that it was like falling slowly into the clearest of ocean waters. There, in this endless sky, where all was silence and light, he could see only one color. There shimmered only one substance, true and flawless and blue-black like a liquid jewel or cobalt glass melting into the sky's infinite deeps. And now Danlo himself melted. Higher and higher he flew, and he felt his whole being vibrating at the frequency of blue light and dying into a blue inside blue inside . . .

Danlo wi Soli Ringess.

He would never be able to measure how much time he spent in this whisperless place. But he knew exactly how long he dwelled there: forever. A little while beyond forever, with the afterglow of perfect blueness still warming his tightly closed eyes, he fell back into time. He fell back into space and felt himself come into a more familiar consciousness. He was aware of himself breathing too slowly, lying back against his cold blankets inside the House of the Dead. His eyes and temples felt free of the weight of the crushing heaume. Someone, he thought, must have removed it. He could not imagine why Cheslav Iviongeon would have allowed him this escape from his mind-killing prison. And then, far off it seemed at first, from twenty feet away, he heard voices. He knew that he should pay close attention to these voices.

"Danlo wi Soli Ringess," someone murmured. "The naman pilot is dead. Or as good as dead—his mind is totally gone. Did you see the computer model, where his brainwaves fell flat?"

Slowly, with infinite care, Danlo opened his eyes. Slowly he turned his head. There were other colors now: the black of nall plastic, sweat-stained white kimonos and dead gray light hanging heavy among the stacks of computers. There was scarlet, too. Sometime during his journey into the alam al-mithral, he must have bitten his tongue, for his throat burned and his lips were caked with blood. Neither Cheslav Iviongeon nor the other keepers, it seemed, had bothered to clean his face. He saw them standing across the room with their bald heads bowed, gazing at a display of lights, perhaps a model of his brain that some computer had made.

"The pilot," Cheslav Iviongeon said, holding up the diamond disc inscribed with Danlo's pallaton, "was faced into the alam al-mithral for two hours after the accelerations began. Two hours! He should have fallen mad after the first two minutes."

One of the other keepers whispered something, then. Danlo, with his keen sense of hearing, gathered that Cheslav Iviongeon had let the murderous program run for a good hour more after Danlo's mind had melted flat, as an insurance of his madness. Only after it had become impossible that Danlo would ever walk clear-eyed in the world again had Cheslav allowed one of his keepers to remove the heaume.

"When a naman walks with the dead," Cheslav told the other keepers, "he should expect to die. It seems that he was not, after all, the bringer of light whom our Holy Ivi hoped for."

Slowly, with much struggle and pain, Danlo kicked his blankets away. Slowly—but quietly—he sat up. He sat cross-legged, as his found-father had once taught him. Cheslav and the others had their backs to him, so they did not see him. During all the time of his journey into the alam al-mithral, he had held his shakuhachi close against his belly. He was holding it still, gently but firmly, as a Snowy Owl might clutch a nesting stick in his talons. This blessed flute was warm from his body's heat and ready to play. After wiping the blood from his mouth, he touched the flute's ivory mouthpiece to his lips and drew in a deep breath.

"It's time we told the Holy Ivi what has happened," Cheslav said. "She must decide what to do with his body, whether it should be kept alive for others of his Order who might search for him or cremated in the ovens."

Suddenly, with all the power of his belly, Danlo blew a single, high, shrill note upon his flute. The effect of this otherwordly sound on the keepers was cruel. As if the House of Eternity had been struck with a hydrogen bomb, one of them clasped his hands to his ears and dived to the floor. Another—the Worthy Nikolaos—threw up his hands as if he himself had faced the ghosts of the alam al-mithral and screamed in sudden terror. Even Cheslav Iviongeon was unnerved. He whirled about to sense the source of the terrible music rushing through the air. In so doing, when he saw Danlo sitting up fiercely playing his flute, the diamond disc slipped from his sweaty fingers and spun crashing against the base of one of the computers. The hard nall plastic—harder than diamond—caused the disc to shatter. All that remained of Danlo's pallaton were bits of diamond glittering on the cold, black floor.

"You—you're alive!" Cheslav cried out. "That's impossible!"

"Yes, I live," Danlo said, lowering his flute. "I am sorry."

As quickly as he could, Danlo struggled to his feet. He held his flute straight out in his fist as if to warn Cheslav and the keepers away. He didn't think that they would try to overpower him and force the dreaded heaume back over his head, but he had cheated death once that day, and once was enough.

"Pilot, you're shaking. After such an interface, you're not yourself, so if you would only stay here with us for—"

"No."

Danlo spoke this single word softly, but with all the force of the wind. For a long time he stared at Cheslav as he might a boy who liked to pull the wings off flies. And then he turned his back on him and walked out of the House of the Dead.

When he opened the doors of the building, he found that it was late afternoon. Sunlight streamed down through the dome high above the zero level of Ornice Olorun. He stood for a moment in this golden light, and he felt all the goodness of life spreading through his body like fire. There was sound, too, a thunderous roar like the ocean in storm. He became aware, then, of many people crying out his name.

"He lives!" these voices shouted. "The pilot lives!"

Below the nall steps of the House of Eternity, spread out across the street and the nearby lawns, there still waited thousands of people, though not quite so many thousands as earlier that morning. Behind the light fence guarding the steps, Bertram Jaspari stood scowling as if one of his Iviomils had served him vinegar in place of wine. He exchanged a venomous look with Jedrek Iviongeon, who was Cheslav's second brother. Next to these two princes of the Church waited Malaclypse Redring, calmly, with infinite patience, as if he would have waited a million years for Danlo's return. He looked up at Danlo standing on the steps, and his violet eyes shone with a strange longing.

"Indeed, Danlo wi Soli Ringess lives," Harrah Ivi en li Ede announced. She still sat behind her reading desk on the portico where Danlo stood. "We must ask if he has indeed walked with the dead."

Now, behind Danlo, from out of the dark building, Cheslav
Iviongeon appeared followed by the other keepers. Their once-
white kimonos were gray with sweat. They stood near to Danlo—
but not too near. Although the Worthy Nikolaos hung his head in
shame as if he'd been made to participate in some evil program,
Cheslav held his head high and glared at Danlo. He waited for
him to speak.

"Yes," Danlo said at last. His voice sounded distant and
strange. "I have walked with the dead."

"You must please tell us what this was like," Harrah said.
Her pleasant old face beamed triumph at Danlo, and she waited
to hear what he might say. Bertram Jaspari and Malaclypse Redring and the brothers Iviongeon—and tens of thousands of Architects—all waited to hear what Danlo might say.

It was like walking into a room full of drill worms, he thought.
It was like walking into a lake of fire.

For the count of twenty heartbeats, Danlo stood silent not
knowing what he could tell these people. And then he chanced to
remember the words of an ancient poem. He smiled sadly, and
his eyes burned with tears. "The dead know only one thing," he
said. "It is better to be alive."

Then he tried to move forward toward the steps, but his legs
could no longer hold against gravity's crushing weight. He collapsed to the portico's hard surface and lay fighting for breath.
His last thought before falling into unconsciousness was that he
had learned only the tiniest part of all there was to know of death.

PREPARATIONS

*All are rushing into your terrible jaws; I see some of
them crushed by your teeth. As rivers flow into the
ocean, all the warriors of this world are passing into
your fiery jaws; all creatures rush to their destruction
like moths into a flame. You lap the worlds into your
burning mouths and swallow them. Filled with your
terrible radiance, O Vishnu, the whole of creation bursts
into flame.*

—*from the Bhagavad Gita, 11*

It took Danlo two tendays to recuperate fully from his ordeal in
the House of the Dead. The keepers of the Holy Palace, at Harrah's bidding, ordered a special choche for Danlo, and they bore
him back to his rooms, where Harrah's personal physician attended him. Although Danlo came awake later that night, it was
another day before he could eat any food or indulge in conversation. Fierce pains crackled through his head, coming and going
with the unpredictableness of ball lightning. He tried to sleep as
much as he could; he tried to play his flute and remember all that
had happened to him in the alam al-mithral.

During this waiting time between tests, he wished that Harrah
would call for him or perhaps even visit him in his richly furnished rooms. But she never did. From Thomas Ivieehl, the
sharp-eared palace keeper whom he had befriended, he learned
that the Holy Ivi was kept busy with important matters. In truth,
Danlo's entrance into the House of Eternity had precipitated
earth-shaking events.

Half a world away, in the city of Bavoll, the news of Danlo's
success had set off riots, and at least three Elder Architects loyal
to Harrah had been murdered. And in Iviendenhall, on an island
just off the coast on the other side of the continent, it was said

that a cabal of Iviomils had seized control of the local temple and had cut communications with the rest of the planet. Even in Ornice Olorun, where the Iviomils held much less sway than in the western arcologies, there were plots against Harrah Ivi en li Ede as well as random terror. One man, a keeper whom Thomas Ivieehl had known since boyhood, was caught trying to smuggle plastic explosives into the palace itself. But before Harrah's readers could question him, he had set off a heat charge implanted in his ear, thus destroying his own brain as surely as the eye tlolt had caused Janegg Iviorvan to die the real death. On the fourth and seventeenth levels of the city, plasma bombs destroyed five apartment cubes and killed at least thirty thousand people.

And so it went. Every hour, it seemed, new reports of disaster and outright religious disobedience arrived from every corner of Tannahill. It was the greatest crisis of Harrah's architetcy—perhaps even the greatest since the time of the two High Holy Architects five centuries earlier.

Bertram Jaspari, of course, tried to seize the advantage that all this chaos provided. Not only did he involve the Koivuniemin with his usual intrigues and coercion, but he attacked Harrah's planetary proclamation of Danlo's triumph. Danlo wi Soli Ringess, he said, the naman pilot, had not truly walked with the dead. He had only tried to face the terrible beauty of the alam al-mithral, and he had failed. At the first sight of the dead Architect souls, he had fallen mad and had fallen into a coma as might any other mortal man. For a time, many Architects across Tannahill believed this lie. Many men and women began turning to Bertram Jaspari and listening ever more closely as he spoke of the Church's corruption and the need to return to the purity of the past.

And then, seven days after Danlo's fateful Walk, as it came to be called, Danlo dealt a fierce blow to Bertram's growing authority by making a simple announcement. He told of a piece of information that he had gathered in the alam al-mithral: a secret that the ghost of Morasha Ede, Nikolos Daru Ede's second daughter, had shared with him. In Ede's Tomb, it seemed, in the clary sarcophagus that housed his frozen body, the first Architects had built a secret compartment. For three thousand years, Ede had lain dead over a little cube of space containing a treasure. What this treasure was, Danlo didn't say for he truly didn't know. But he told of how this compartment might be found and the secret words whose utterance would open it.

Bertram Jaspari and his Iviomils would have liked to have

scoffed at such a wild prediction. But they dared not. On the day after a riot on Ornice Olorun's twelfth level nearly destroyed two minor food factories, Harrah Ivi en li Ede sent her keepers into Ede's Tomb to test the truth of Danlo's "prophecy." And they spoke the secret words encoded by Ede long ago: "I am the door; knock and be opened." And to the astonishment of all present, on the side of the glittering clary crypt, a hidden panel slid open. There Harrah's keepers found a single diamond disc very much like the ones in the House of the Dead. Only it held not the pallatons of deceased Architects, but only the sacred words of Nikolos Daru Ede, the man who had become God. If the theologians who evaluated the disc's information were correct, they had discovered Ede's love poems to his third wife, Arista Miri. These were the beloved *Passionaries,* one of the five lost books of the Algorithm. That this priceless treasure had been recovered due to the valor of a naman from Neverness embarrassed and infuriated Bertram Jaspari. If he had possessed the smallest grain of shame, he might have apologized to Danlo and begged Harrah's forgiveness. But, as events would soon prove, he only redoubled his efforts to program people's minds against Harrah and to destroy her architetcy.

"If Bertram were to incite the people against Harrah, they might riot and try to storm the palace."

These words of warning issued from the Ede devotionary set atop the altar of Danlo's room. As it often did, the hologram of Nikolos Daru Ede illumined the silver heaume and sent a glowing light out over the sacred art and cybernetica as well as the ananda blossoms hanging halfway down the wall. If Danlo had counted right, it was the 1,719th time Ede had warned him of imminent danger since they had come to Tannahill.

"I can only hope," the Ede imago said, "that these barbarians don't storm my tomb searching for other treasures. If they broke the sarcophagus by accident, my body would prove impossible to redeem."

The following day, an unexpected visitor came to the palace to ask for a meeting with Danlo. This was Malaclypse Redring, and Danlo could not guess why he would seek so urgently to see him. He wondered if Bertram might have sent him to the palace as a secret emissary. But, in truth, it was hard to imagine anyone *sending* a warrior-poet anywhere, for any reason. Although Danlo was still weak from computer interface and his head throbbed like the beating of a drum, he received Malaclypse in his altar room. There, beneath the ananda blossoms, they sat on soft white cushions on the floor. Danlo wore only a worn black kamelaika from Neverness, and he held his bamboo flute gently against his lap. Malaclypse, however, sported a glittering rainbow kimono woven on Qallar. His two red rings glittered on the fingers of either hand. The warrior-poets, he remembered, most often dressed to blind the eye, the better to distract their victims while they plied their needles and knives and struck with all the quickness of poisonous snakes.

"It's good to see you again, Pilot," Malaclypse said. "We've come very far since Mer Tadeo's garden, haven't we?"

Danlo realized then that the two of them hadn't spoken face to face since the night of the supernova on Farfara.

"Oh, truly very far," Danlo said. "I had thought that I would never see you again."

"You don't seem entirely pleased."

"No," Danlo said. "I am not."

"But we have a mutual mission to Tannahill, don't we?"

"No—everywhere you go, you bring violence and murder."

"Is it I who have walked with the dead? Is it I whom half of these Architects would assassinate while the other half proclaim as the Lightbringer?"

Despite the seriousness of the situation, Danlo smiled. "You know who I am," he said.

"Do I, Pilot?"

Malaclypse regarded him strangely with his blazing violet eyes, almost as if in their journey across the stars, Danlo had grown from a young man into some terrible angel of light. Almost as if he feared him.

"I am only who I am—Danlo wi Soli Ringess."

"But the essential question remains unanswered," Malaclypse said. "Are you the son of the father? Are you of the same substance as Mallory wi Soli Ringess?"

Danlo smiled, then touched his lips to his flute. He asked, "Why have you come here?"

"Do you wish to know why I've come to Tannahill?"

"No," Danlo said. "I think I already know that. Even if you have not found my father, you have found what you seek in Bertram Jaspari and the Iviomils. In the weakness of the Church itself."

"I only serve my Order as you do yours."

"Yes, truly you do. And so I would ask why you have come *here*, to my rooms tonight?"

Malaclypse fixed his marvelous eyes on Danlo, but he said nothing.

"Do you serve your Order?" Danlo asked. "Or do you serve only yourself?"

"You're very clever, Pilot."

"There is something that you would ask of me, yes?"

"Yes."

"Something that you would like to know."

"Something that no one knows except you," Malaclypse said.

"Please ask, then."

Malaclypse paused a moment and turned to look at the door. It seemed as if he were trying to drink in the little sounds around him and discover whether any of Harrah's keepers might be spying upon him. But except for his and Danlo's soft breaths and the occasional squawk of the parrotock bird in its steel cage across the room, the palace was almost silent.

"What is it like?" Malaclypse suddenly whispered. "What is it like to be dead?"

Danlo never let his eyes fall away from the intensity of Malaclypse's dark gaze. Although his question had not surprised him, it disturbed him deeply. "You warrior-poets worship death," he finally said.

"Not so, Danlo wi Soli Ringess. We worship life."

" 'How do I learn to live?' " Danlo asked, quoting a saying of the warrior-poets. And he supplied the answer: " 'Prepare to die.' "

At this, Malaclypse smiled and whispered, " 'How do I prepare for death? Learn how to live.' "

"Life," Danlo said mysteriously, "is all there is. Live your life, Warrior. Write your poems, Poet. You will know soon enough what it is like to be dead."

"Do you threaten me, Pilot, or are you making another prophecy?"

"Neither," Danlo said. "It is only that all people die . . . so soon. A heartbeat and we are gone. In a breath, our spirits are lost to the wind. Life is so infinitely precious. Why seek to cast it away before it is time?"

"Do you try to persuade me of this wisdom or yourself?"

"I have no wish to die," Danlo said.

"Is that true?" Malaclypse asked. "I've followed you across the galaxy. Into the Entity. You live your life like a warrior-poet: flawlessly and fearlessly. I think you, too, seek death. This is what haunts you about your walk with the dead, isn't it?"

For a while Danlo stared out the window at the evening lights playing over the ocean far below the city. Because he didn't wish to answer Malaclypse's question, he picked up his flute and began composing a slow, deeply melodic song. Finally, he wiped his lips and looked over at Malaclypse. He said, "Whatever I seek for myself, I would bring only peace for others."

"Peace and light," Malaclypse said. "*If* you are the Lightbringer."

"Yes, truly, light," Danlo said smiling. "It is the opposite of darkness."

"Do I bring only darkness, then?"

"You bring war. You ally yourself, and your whole order, with the Iviomils . . . and why? You would set one Architect killing another."

"But I am a warrior, am I not? And war is the way of the world. Of the universe itself. Someday you may come to appreciate this."

"No, there is always peace," Danlo said. "There . . . *must* be."

"Pilot, Pilot."

"Somewhere, at the center, even in the heart of man, there must be peace. The harmony of life, this blessed halla."

Again Danlo looked out the window at the shimmering ocean. He sat very still, and his eyes fell far away into the cold deeps at the edge of the world. He drank in the waters' dazzling darkness and then gazed up at the sky. There, only the fire of the brightest stars could penetrate the layers of pollution enveloping the planet. This was the killing radiation of supernovas somewhere in the Vild, and it called him out of himself, scrying, on and on, out into the vast light-distances of the universe.

"Is it peace you're seeing now?" Malaclypse asked.

Danlo shook his head. "No—it is just the opposite."

"Please tell me, if you will."

The Entity, Danlo remembered, had told him that the Silicon God sought the death of the entire galaxy. Was it possible that this shaida being might somehow be using the warrior-poets to this end?

"I see people," Danlo finally said. "Who would ever have dreamed the universe would bring forth so many of our kind? So many people. So terrible and beautiful we are. I see all these people dying for a dream. And dying for delusion. And for one man's desire for power. But always . . . dying. Only dying. Bertram Jaspari. He is ready to send his millions of faithful to their deaths. All the Iviomils. All the Architects. I see all the robots, all the factories, all the deep ships, the lasers and viruses and eye tlolts and bombs. And something else. A terrible weapon, these great engines the Architects make to unravel the threads of spacetime. The star killers, the streams of graviphotons flowing into the sun. The light that blinds. I see the whole planet, the whole galaxy—all the people preparing for war and death.''

Danlo fell once more into silence, and he pressed his flute against the scar cutting his forehead. Malaclypse looked at him almost fearfully, which was strange because warrior-poets must fear nothing in all the universe, least of all other men. ''You can't stop it, you know,'' he said.

Danlo put the flute's ivory mouthpiece to his lips, and he said nothing.

''You can't change the world, Pilot.''

Danlo blew a single, low, soft note, which moved out into the room like the sound of the wind.

''You can't change the nature of the universe itself.''

''No,'' Danlo finally said, putting down his flute. ''But I can change *my* self. This is the nature of my next test, yes? We shall see if I can truly change myself.''

Danlo bade farewell to Malaclypse Redring of Qallar and then sat playing his flute and reflecting upon this most disturbing visit. If he had been more mindful, he would have asked the Palace keepers not to admit anyone else wishing to see him. But now that it seemed that he might indeed be the Lightbringer, many sought words with him. And so, during the following days, Danlo sat to tea in his rooms, speaking with the greatest princes of the Church. They discussed the Order's founding a new Academy on Thiells and the possibility of sending the Church's brightest youths there to learn the pilots' art. There was talk of great change, which would begin in the temples of the Church and spread like a wildfire across the stars. Many of Danlo's visitors prided themselves on being theologians, and these argumentative men and women loved to discuss Fravashi philosophy or the Program of the Second Creation or Three Pillars of Ringism, that explosive new religion founded on Neverness only a few years before. Danlo grew so used to these daily (and nightly) visits that he would answer his door at the first knock without bothering to ask who might wish to see him.

And so, some twenty days after his almost fabled Walk with the Dead, on the night before his last test, he heard the sound of human knuckles rattling against wood, and he opened his door expecting yet again another round of pointless theological debates. Or perhaps he hoped that Harrah herself had come at last to advise him and to wish him well. He was very surprised, therefore, to see the most prominent of all the Church Elders standing in the doorway scowling, as if he hated having to wait for Danlo to ask him inside. At the best of times Bertram Jaspari was an impatient man, and that night he was sweating in an unusual hurry.

"Danlo wi Soli Ringess—may we come in?" Bertram formally asked.

Danlo looked down the hallway to see if some other Elder such as Jedrek Iviongeon accompanied Bertram. And then, remembering that Bertram often spoke in the "we" case as if he were already the Holy Ivi, Danlo smiled in amusement.

"If you'd like, please come in," he replied, holding the door open for him. "May I make you some tea?"

"No, thank you," Bertram said, casting Danlo a quick, cold look as if he thought he might try to poison him. "We don't have time for that."

Danlo invited Bertram to sit with him in the altar room, as he had with Malaclypse Redring and the other Church illuminati. Bertram carefully let himself down onto the white cushions set on the floor; with his sharp face and sticklike limbs, Danlo thought he looked like a ratri bird settling down over a nest full of eggs. As he always did, Bertram wore his gold embroidered dobra to cover his pointed head. He was sweating as if he'd eaten tainted meat, and his face was ash blue with the mehalis fungus that infected him. Danlo stood in awe of this man's incredible ugliness, but he never let these surface blights obscure the even deeper deformities of Bertram's soul.

"You're surprised to see us here, aren't you, Pilot?"

In truth, on any other world ruled by one of such extensive power as the Holy Ivi, Bertram would have been either banished or imprisoned for his rebelliousness—or worse. But Bertram, with all the skill of a jewfish slipping out of a net, had managed to avoid attaching himself to any of the plots against Harrah or the riots of the Iviomils. Then, too, Harrah was the most forgiving of Holy Ivis.

"I am not wholly surprised," Danlo said. Because he was in playful mood—playful in the fierce way of a Fravashi Old Father who inflicts upon his adversaries the angslan, the mind pain leading to the light of heightened awareness—he used his flute to point out the window at the blue-black ocean. "This is a splendid view, yes? Perhaps you would hope that this view from the Holy Ivi's palace might be yours . . . forever."

Bertram's face fell purple with fury, for a moment, and then like a snake shedding its skin inch by inch, he seemed to shrug off this dangerous emotion.

"There's no need to insult us, Pilot," he said. "We've come here tonight in faith, in the hope that we might work together toward a common purpose."

Danlo, remembering the hell of the alam al-mithral that Bertram's fellow conspirators had programed for him, listened in astonishment to Bertram's words and wondered if he might not be hallucinating again. "Truly?" he asked. "Do you truly believe that we share a purpose?"

Bertram smiled then, for him a wholly unnatural exertion that seemed most unsuited to his implacable face. "Does not the Algorithm say that all men share the purpose of moving toward the one light of Ede the God? Please, may we tell you something of *our* purpose, and then we shall see if we can help each other?"

Slowly Danlo nodded his head. "If you'd like, then."

While Danlo rolled his flute slowly back and forth between his hands, Bertram cleared the phlegm from his throat and began to speak. "First, we would like congratulate you on your triumph in the House of Eternity. We admire your courage, your ingenuity in the face of falling madness. What a mind you have, Pilot! We've been a Reader for thirty years, and we've never had the pleasure of reading out the programs of such a mind as yours. Did you know that many people are already calling you the Lightbringer? They believe your last test will be the easiest and that the program of your success is already written."

"You do not appear as disturbed by this possibility as you were in the Hall of the Koivuniemin."

"These past days, we've had much time to reflect upon your coming to our world," Bertram said. His voice was sweet now— too sweet, like a blood tea overladen with honey. "We confess that at first, it seemed impossible that a naman could be the Lightbringer out of our holy Algorithm. But you are no common naman. The Elders whom you've entertained in your rooms attest to your unusual knowledge and appreciation of our eternal Church. Many are saying that you're already an Architect in spirit. It only remains for you to make the Profession of Faith and submit to a cleansing, and you would be one of us."

"I . . . am not ready to do that," Danlo said.

And then, remembering his tragic involvement with the Way of Ringess on Neverness, he thought, *I will never again join my life with any religion.*

"Very well," Bertram said, "but we believe it's not impossible for you to be a great presence in our Church. As Lightbringer, of course, if that is written, but possibly as a Reader, yourself, or even someday an Elder."

Danlo pressed his flute to his lips to hide his amusement at this bizarre suggestion, and he tried not to smile. "My Order," he said, "forbids any pilot or academician to hold a formal position in any religion."

"But you were not born into your Order. And it is not necessarily written that you will die a pilot."

"Do you suggest that I abjure my vows, then?"

"Others have," Bertram said.

"Sivan wi Mawi Sarkissian?" Danlo said, naming the renegade pilot who had ferried Malaclypse Redring across half the galaxy. And then, shaking his head, he said, "No—I would never."

"You can't imagine how many Architects across Tannahill are calling for you to succeed tomorrow," Bertram said. "You can't imagine how they hope you are the Lightbringer."

"I am sorry."

"A man must follow the program written for him," Bertram said.

"I am sorry, but I must . . . follow my star."

At this, Bertram's sweaty fingers formed themselves into two tight little fists. Hatred flashed across his face, to be replaced a moment later by condescension and a glittering friendliness as false as plastic pearls. He said, "Only a naman would speak so poetically."

"But I am a naman, yes?"

"Did you know, Pilot, that in the year 1089, when our missionaries reached Durriken, ten million namans simultaneously made the Profession of Faith and became Architects?"

"No."

"Did you know that one of these former namans, Vishnu Harith na vio Ede, the forty-first Holy Ivi, rose to the architetcy itself?"

"No, I did not know that."

"Such miracles are always possible," Bertram said. "If a

common programer such as Vishnu Harith could rise to be our Holy Ivi, why not the man who would be Lightbringer?"

For a moment—but only a moment—Danlo sat on his cushion wondering what it would be like to be the spiritual master and ultimate religious authority for untold billions of people. Because such a fantastic dream amused him, he wanted to smile. But because Bertram Jaspari, with his sweaty little hands and dead eyes, sat waiting for an answer, he only bowed his head politely and said, "I am sorry."

"You're *sorry*!" Now the hatred and envy burned across Bertram's face again, filling up his neck veins as a drill worm swells with blood. "Naman—you could be the High Holy Architect of the Cybernetic Universal Church!"

No, never that, Danlo thought. *The Iviomils would murder me first.*

"Well?"

"I am only a pilot," Danlo said. "It is all I ever want to be."

"Namans!"

Now Danlo finally smiled. "Across the stars, there are so many of us, yes?"

Having failed at falsehood, Bertram decided to share with Danlo part of his real purpose. "Indeed, you namans are everywhere. But it's written in the Algorithm that each naman is a seed of an Architect as a child is the beginning of a man. Give the seed the correct amount of water and sunlight, and what a worthy tree will grow! It's written in God's Infinite Program for the Universe that all men and women will someday be trees worthy of Ede's infinite light. Even if you don't believe this, Pilot, you must appreciate our Church's mission to water these seeds and fill the stars with such forests."

"I would never have dreamed," Danlo said, smiling, "that a Church Elder such as yourself could speak so poetically."

This compliment of Danlo's seemed only to irritate Bertram, for he scowled and said, "I only repeat what is written in the Algorithm. This isn't poetry—it's just the truth, Pilot."

"All right, the truth, then, if you'd like."

"You must appreciate our problem," Bertram said. "So many Iviomils we've sent forth into the stars. So many who would bring God's program to the namans. And so many Architects of the Long Pilgrimage who have been lost to our Church. All these Worthy, Pilot. They've either never known Tannahill or will never see it again. How are we to ensure that they remember the Program and do not inadvertently seek to alter or edit it? How do we save them from falling into negative programs? You think of us Iviomils as mindlessly rigid, but we are not. We merely return to the purity of the past and the exact remembrance of Ede's sacred words. If we did not, the Iviomils we've sent to Lenci and Zoheret and all the other worlds might fall into error and bring a stained light to the namans. We can't and won't allow any Architect to fall into false programs.''

''I see.''

''Do you, Pilot? Do you also see that the Holy Ivi must someday find a way to reestablish contact with all the Iviomils we've sent forth into the stars?''

Danlo drummed his fingers along the holes of his flute, then asked, ''Do you truly mean contact or . . . control?''

''All Architects must make a vow of obedience,'' Bertram said.

''I see.''

''Will you help us?'' Bertram asked. ''You know our need. You could train our ships' programers to pilot through the stars.''

Danlo shut his eyes, then, remembering what it was like to take a lightship through the strange and fiery spaces of the manifold.

''It would be possible,'' Bertram said, ''for us to send our Iviomils as far as Tarrus, and for them to return in a few years, rather than a few lifetimes.''

''If I could train your Iviomils, it *would* be possible,'' Dano said.

''Well?''

''I am sorry—I cannot train another to be a pilot.''

Bertram's face tightened as if he had lockjaw, then he said, ''Oh, you *could* help us, Pilot. But you *will* not—this is all your will, you know.''

''No—my order does not permit solitary pilots to give away the secrets of our art.''

''Your godless, programless order.''

''I have made *my* vows,'' Danlo said. ''But even if I were willing to break them, it is hard to make pilots.''

''But not impossible.''

''The finest genius of my order is plied toward making people into pilots,'' Danlo said. ''So many are called. But so few are chosen. And fewer of these become journeymen, much less full pilots.''

Journeymen die, Danlo remembered. *In the manifold, it is so easy to die.*

"But you've said your Order would train the Narain children to become pilots."

"Yes."

"The Narain heretics!"

"We would also train Architects from Tannahill. But you would have to send your children to the Academy the Order is building on Thiells."

"That will never happen," Bertram snapped. "Do you think we would place our children in the hands of namans? Our *children*? No, no—never."

Danlo blinked his eyes at the hatred he saw pouring out of Bertram like gouts of sweat. He said, "Isn't that for the Holy Ivi to decide?"

"Exactly," Bertram said, and his eyes fell as dead as stones dropping out of the sky. "The Holy Ivi."

"The Holy Ivi, Harrah Ivi en li Ede," Danlo said, staring at Bertram.

Bertram nodded his pointed head. "A very dangerous woman. We've said this before. We believe that she might attempt to redefine the Program of Totality. And the Program of Increase."

Danlo sat very still as he looked into dead gray ice of Bertram's eyes. He touched his lips to his flute, but he said nothing.

"We believe that she might be ready to receive a *new* Program. And to install this Program as a final monument to her architetcy."

Danlo felt a rare burst of hatred blazing through his own eyes, and he stared at Bertram until the older man looked away.

"As yet," Bertram said, somewhat nervously, "we believe that she lacks enough support with the Koivuniemin to dare receive a New Program. But she seeks only a sign, Pilot. Your success tomorrow as the Lightbringer would enable her to ruin the Church with this new Program."

For the count of five heartbeats, Danlo did not move. And then he asked, "Why did you come here tonight?"

Bertram suddenly turned his head and looked at the blue and red parrotock bird perched in its steel cage. He looked at the room's plastic door and at the flowers hanging down the wall; he looked at the altar where the hologram of Nikolos Daru Ede floated above the devotionary computer like some disembodied angel of God watching him, waiting for him to say something. Last, as the sweat leaked from pores of his face, he braved looking at Danlo once more.

"You have the power to save our Church," Bertram said. "You, Pilot."

"Please, go on."

"If you were to fail your test tomorrow, you could say that you were still ill from your Walk with the Dead. You wouldn't be permitted to undergo a new test, of course, but you would still have your pride."

Danlo closed his eyes for a moment as he slowly shook his head. He did not want to believe what Bertram was asking of him; so great was his bewilderment at these words that it seemed Bertram might have been speaking an alien language.

"You wish me deliberately to . . . dishonor myself?"

"Not dishonor, Pilot. Only the pride of doing what you must. The pride of a worthy man who would submit to God's Infinite Program."

This is his true purpose in coming here tonight, Danlo thought. *All his other proposals were only as an illusionist's sleight of hand.*

"Will you help us, Pilot?"

Danlo shook his head as he brought his flute to his lips. He played a long, lonely note which filled the room like the cry of the Snowy Owl.

"We would like so much to help you," Bertram said. "Perhaps we could help each other."

Danlo stared at Bertram, and then he put down his flute. In a soft voice that was almost in a whisper, he said, "Yes, I would like your help."

For the second time that evening, Bertram smiled. "It's the duty of all Elders to help their children toward the truth."

"I would like you to help me to be alone," Danlo said. He bowed his head toward the door. "Please go."

Instantly, Bertram's face fell back into its cyanine scowl. Although he tried his best to force a smile, other programs inside him were doing their work. "You misunderstand me!" he said, outraged at Danlo's request.

"No—it is just the opposite."

"Listen to me, Pilot!"

"No—I am sorry."

"We've asked for your help in great matters," Bertram said. He rubbed his sweaty hands together like a Trian merchant about to propose an exchange of goods. "And so, in return, it would be only fair for me to offer you a gift."

"I desire no gifts."

"Really?"

"I want only to be alone. It is all that I ask."

"But it was not all you asked on the day that you addressed the Koivuniemin."

A sudden pain blossomed inside Danlo's head with all the brilliance of a fireflower opening to the sun. "What . . . do you mean?" he said. But as Danlo sat remembering his words to the Koivuniemin on that terrible day of eye tlolts and death, he suddenly knew very well what Bertram would say next.

"You came to our world seeking favors for your order," Bertram said. "But you also sought something for yourself."

"Yes," Danlo said. Now the pain behind his eyes swelled huge and red like a star falling nova; his throat ached with the hard knot of hope.

"You sought a cure for the Great Plague. You said that this disease was killing the tribes of Alaloi people who had adopted you."

"Yes."

"And you hoped that we Architects might know of a cure."

"But there is no cure. Harrah herself believed that it wasn't the Architects of the Old Church who had engineered the Plague virus. She knows of no cure."

"Our Holy Ivi doesn't know everything," Bertram said.

For what seemed a long time, Danlo held his breath. There was a huge knot in his throat that no amount of swallowing could dislodge. It felt as if his heart itself were stuck there, throbbing in pain. "If you will," he finally said, "please tell me what the Holy Ivi does not know."

Quickly, because Bertram still had need of great hurry, he told Danlo of a quest that he himself had completed. As an Elder, he said, he was permitted entrance to certain Church archives forbidden to mere Readers or any of the Worthy Architects. And in one of these ancient information pools, he had discovered many records from the War of the Faces. Of particular interest was the testament of Radomil Ivi Illanes, one of the Holy Ivis who had led the Old Church through the final phases of the War. Although this testament was incomplete, its information having been lost or expurgated over the last thousand years, a few of Ivi Illanes's words drew Bertram's attention as a new star captures the eyes of all who behold her:

> *We have done a terrible thing. It was a great error for
> my predecessors to ally the Church with the Warrior-*

Poets. And it was madness for them to accede in the making of the virus. It has slain our enemies in their billions as the engineers foretold, but now this virus has mutated. It afflicts even the Worthy, they who remain faithful to the Program and to our eternal Church. Our engineers have made a cure, but it already may be too late to save many of my children from a terrible death.

Bertram sighed as he fingered the dobra covering his head, and he finished telling his story. "Ivi Radomil ordered his engineers to build an antivirus. He saved the Church. But so many of our Architects did indeed die that we were forced to flee into the darkest part of the galaxy. Here, on Tannahill, we live on, Pilot. And here, in our holy archives, lives the information that you seek. It seems that the antivirus is complex and hard to assemble, but I've already spoken to several engineers who are certain they could synthesize a cure."

"Truly?" Danlo asked. Because his eyes burned with the water of his terrible hope, he covered them and stared out the window. Then, after a while, he turned to see Bertram staring at him. The Elder's face was tight with impatience and guile. "I do not believe you," Danlo said.

"To lie deliberately is a hakr," Bertram smugly said. "We Elders have been cleansed of such programs. We don't lie."

And that itself is a lie, Danlo thought. And then, *Could it be that he tells the truth? Ahira, Ahira—what should I believe?*

"You've come so far, Pilot. You've waited so long. And now the cure that you seek is almost in your hands."

Danlo squeezed his flute so tightly that he feared it might break. He said, "Out of compassion for the fate of my people, then, you have come here tonight to offer me this cure?"

"We are an Elder of the Church," Bertram said. "And so we must have compassion for many people. All our Architects, here on Tannahill, and those lost among the stars. All namans who would be Architects."

"I see."

"You desire to save your people. And we desire to save ours."

"I see."

"Will you help us, Pilot? Will you let our engineers synthesize a cure?"

"No—I do not believe you know of a cure. I do not want . . . to believe you."

"Pilot!"

After taking in a deep breath and feeling his heart beat five times, Danlo said, "Yes?"

"Can you afford to doubt the existence of this cure? Are you really willing to disbelieve me?"

Truly, do I have the will? Danlo wondered. *Oh, God—do I have the will to do what I must?*

Danlo shifted on his cushion so that he could look out the window at the stars. There should have been millions of these brilliant lights, but because the sky that evening was particularly heavy with pollution, he counted only ten stars—and nine of these supernovas from the far reaches of the Vild.

"Please, Pilot—it grows late. We must have an answer."

Danlo closed his eyes, remembering the faces of Haidar and Choclo and Chandra. They had each bled from the ears before dying, and Choclo, late one desperate night with the fever burning his skin like fire, in a terrible screaming pain, had bitten off most of his tongue. This, then, was the fate awaiting the other tribes of the Alaloi. In Danlo's youth he had set off with dogsleds to visit the Patwin and Olorun tribes, but farther to the west of Neverness Island lived whole tribes of his far-cousins whom he had never met. He knew their names, however: The Honovi and Raini, the Wemilat and the Paushan and Turi. And all the others. So many tribes; so many of the blessed People. But even as he tried to recall the stories of the very distant Jyasi tribe of the Fifty Islands of Uttermost West, the eyes of all his ancestors blazed in his mind like stars. In truth, inside him there were many stars, those of the galaxy's Orion arm, of course, and all the countless stars he had left behind him on his journey into the Vild. He knew their names, too: Saralta and Munsin and Kalanit and Kamala Luz—and perhaps ten thousand others. How many of these splendid spheres of light would die if the Cybernetic Universal Church did not redefine its Program of Totality and stop blowing up the stars? How many billions of human beings from Ihle Luz to the Morbio Inferiore would be lost if Danlo did not give Harrah Ivi en li Ede the sign that she so desperately sought?

"Well, Pilot?" Bertram's voice fell out into the room like a glass ornament dropped against a rock. "We must have an answer tonight."

How many thousands of his Alaloi sisters and brothers, Danlo wondered, still lived to the west of Neverness? He didn't know, for no one had ever counted them. But certainly, somewhere in the Vild, billions of men, women, and children dwelled and built their great cities to the glory of God—perhaps five million billions against only thousands of the Alaloi. Looking out the window at the stars, a terrible thought came over Danlo: The value of a human life was not simply multiplicative. The pain of losing someone you loved was a million times greater than hearing of the deaths of a million unknown souls. In truth, it was infinitely greater. Knowing this, feeling this truth as a blinding flash of pain that tore like lightning through his head, how could he refuse the gift that Bertram offered him? If there was the slightest chance that Bertram truly had discovered a cure for the slow evil, how could he deny the blessed Alaloi the gift of life?

"We must go now," Bertram said. "We've much to do before midnight. Please say that you'll help us, and then you will leave Tannahill with the cure for the Plague. But we can only offer you this gift now—tomorrow will be too late."

"No."

"*No,* Pilot?"

"My answer is no, then." Danlo pressed his flute against his aching forehead, but his eyes fell clear and cold upon Bertram, and they didn't move. "I cannot help you. I will not."

"Consider well what you're saying!"

"Tomorrow, I will submit to the last test."

"But you mustn't!"

"I will look upon the heavenly lights within and—"

"God damn you, Pilot!"

"And I will not fail."

"God damn all you faithless, filthy namans!"

Very quickly, considering his age, Bertram pushed himself to his feet, and he stood clutching his cushion in front of him as if it were a shield.

"The stars, themselves, are alive," Danlo whispered. "They are the eyes of God, the blessed stars."

"You're mad!" Bertram shrieked. He waved his hand at the expanse of plastic above the altar. "But your madness won't save you tomorrow. And neither will Harrah. You may think these Palace walls protect you, but your program is already written, and it halts, Pilot—how very suddenly and soon it halts!"

"Please go," Danlo said softly. "Please go away."

Bertram cursed again and shook his cushion in Danlo's face. Then he screamed in frustration and rage, and he turned to hurl the cushion at the parrotock's cage across the room. But his old arms were feeble and his aim poor. The cushion missed the cage entirely, and it was only by bad chance that one of its corners caught the steel stand and unbalanced it. With a terrible squawking of the parrotock and an explosion of brightly colored feathers, the cage crashed to the floor. Although Danlo leaped to catch it, he was too late. For a moment, he feared that the beautiful bird was either injured or dead. But then the parrotock squawked with life, and he hopped about in his overturned cage as if he were only glad to attract Danlo's attention. He called out for a nut as he always did when he hoped to be fed.

"Why did you do that?" Danlo asked, looking at Bertram.

"We didn't like the way it looked at us."

"He . . . is only a bird. A blessed bird."

"You're more concerned about a filthy bird than you are your own people!"

Something almost broke inside of Danlo then. Despite his vow never to harm another living being, he grabbed up the steel cage stand in his hand. With the hatred that he feared above all other things almost blinding him, he wanted to swing the heavy steel rod against Bertram's head.

"You're a murderer, aren't you, Pilot? Like all your filthy family—the warrior-poet told me about your father. We see that *that* program is written for you, too."

"Go away!" Danlo stood with the steel rod in his right hand and his shakuhachi in his other. He used the flute to point toward the door. "Please go."

"This all is upon you, you know," Bertram said. His face was full of hurt—the very wilfull hurt that he loved inflicting upon others. "You think you came to our world seeking peace. You think you bring light, and you hope to stop the stars from exploding. But no star is untouchable. Not even the Narain's. Not even the star of Neverness."

Because Danlo did not want to believe what he was hearing, he dropped the steel stand and put his flute to his mouth where he blew a long and terrible sound.

"Good-bye, Pilot. We'll see you in the Hall of Heaven tomorrow."

With that, Bertram Jaspari, the greatest Elder of the Cybernetic Universal Church, turned and walked out the door. After Danlo had put the stand and the parrotock's cage back together and rearranged the cushions, he sat down and drank a cold cup of tea. And then he picked up his flute. He played for the parrotock, to gentle him and because the bird always loved any kind of music. He played for his people, the Alaloi, but this was no requiem or dirge, but only a song of hope. He faced the sky outside the window, and he played for the stars. He played and played, and after a long time, the hatred left him, and his eyes were full of nothing except light.

THE HEAVENLY LIGHTS

*You use a glass mirror to see your face; you use works
of art to see your soul.*
    —Bernard Shaw, Holocaust Century eschatologist

> *I do not know a man so bold
> He dare in a lonely place
> That awful stranger consciousness
> Deliberately face.*
>
>   —source unknown

The next night, in the Hall of Heaven, Danlo faced his last test.
The Hall was one of the many lesser buildings surrounding the
Temple, and it was unique both in its function and its shape. The
House of Eternity, Ede's Tomb, the Elders' Dining Hall, and the
great cube of the Temple itself—all these structures bespoke the
symbolism of the Church with their planes and angles and their
relentless rectilinearity. But the Hall of Heaven was different.
Davin Iviei Iviastalir, the eighty-eighth Holy Ivi and a visionary
different in many ways from all his predecessors, had ordered the
Hall built as a domed amphitheater. Unlike the windowless
House of Eternity, with its dense and dreary nall plastic, a great,
gossamer bubble of clary wholly enclosed the Hall without en-
gendering in its visitors a sense that they were being closed in.
Because the dome was as transparent as glass, the thousands of
Architects who swarmed the Hall could look out upon all the
other buildings of the New City of Ornice Olorun. And tens of
thousands of their churchmates could look in. When a light offering was being made, pilgrims and other people from all across
the Temple grounds would pause and watch the flashes of color
illuminating the dome.

On the day that Danlo wi Soli Ringess promised to make a

light offering to Ede the God, many Architects crowded around the Hall of Heaven in hopes of discovering if this naman pilot from Neverness might truly be the Lightbringer. And many more filled the Hall itself. When Danlo entered the Hall, he counted some twenty-eight thousand three hundred people huddled together on plastic benches, waiting for him. The rising tiers of these benches were arrayed about a circular open space perhaps two hundred feet across. At the exact center of this space, the Architects had built a chair.

In truth, with its massive golden arms and strange, silvered headpiece, it looked more like some barbaric throne than a place for a mere man to sit. When Harrah's keepers led Danlo across the floor and bade him take his place before the thousands of watchful Architects, he couldn't help feeling that all these people expected great and godly things of him. But he was only a man. And more, he was a man who had always hated sitting in any kind of chair, especially one that would surround his brain with an intense logic field and display the innermost workings of his mind for all to see.

"My brothers and sisters, will you please come to silence!"

On the floor beside Danlo's chair stood a portly old man with a big nose and big, boisterous voice. His name was Javas Icolari, the Elder Javas who was one of the most prominent theologians of the Juriddik sect and one of Harrah Ivi en li Ede's closest friends. Harrah had asked him to say a few words before Danlo began his test, and the affable Javas was glad to oblige.

"Emissaries and namans from the Known Stars, pilgrims, Worthy Architects, Readers and my fellow Elders, you are welcome here today." Javas turned and bowed deeply to Harrah Ivi en li Ede where she sat in the first tier of benches directly facing Danlo. "My Holy Ivi, welcome, welcome—you do us all great honor with your eternal presence."

Harrah returned Javas's bow and smiled at him encouragingly. Javas then explained the importance of the marvels that everyone would soon witness and gave a rather long and boring account of the history of this strange ceremony called the light offering. As he rambled on, Danlo held himself straight and silent in his chair. He looked across the central circle at Harrah. She had the position of honor, sitting as she did in the middle of the first bench of the Hall's western quadrant. For all other ceremonies, of course, the position of honor was located directly across the Hall opposite Harrah, on the first bench of the eastern quadrant. But because Danlo would be making a light offering like no other, his chair had been turned around facing west. And because the Holy Ivi wished to look at Danlo face to face and eye to eye—at least before his test began—she had seated herself at a bench normally reserved for the lesser Elders of the Koivuniemin.

That morning, however, on Harrah's bench and those near to her, sat the greatest men and women of the Church. To Harrah's right were Varaza li Shehn, Pilar Narcavage, and Pol Iviertes. To her left, Kyoko Ivi Iviatsui and Sul Iviercier carefully folded their white kimonos as befit the oldest Elders of the Church. Next to them waited Kissiah en li Ede, the Elidi master, the inscrutable mystic who had favored Danlo's mission to Tannahill from the first. Ten benches toward the south, as far away as protocol would permit, the Hall's keepers had sat a few of the Iviomils. There Jedrek Iviongeon exchanged wary looks with Fe Farruco Ede and Oksana Ivi Selow while at the bench's center, Bertram Jaspari scowled and sent darts of hatred shooting across the room at Danlo. By no accident, Malaclypse Redring had been placed next to him. The benches between Harrah and Malaclypse were full of her keepers, quick-faced men and women who kept a fierce watch over the Iviomils and any others who might wish to harm Harrah. But everyone else in the hundreds of surrounding benches sat looking at Danlo all alone in his golden chair at the center of the Hall. Soon, when Javas Icolari finished his speech, they would crane their necks to gaze at the lights above Danlo's head, up into the air.

"Danlo wi Soli Ringess!" Javas turned toward Danlo to address him. "Do you desire today to make an offering to Ede the God?"

As would any worthy Architect, Danlo had brought his devotionary computer into the Hall. Upon sitting down, he had placed it on the massive arm of his chair. There the hologram of Nikolos Daru Ede glittered in the air as did thousands of others throughout the Hall. The little glowing Ede betrayed no signs of running the remnant programs of a dead god but only smiled beatifically as did all the other Edes floating above their devotionaries.

"Danlo wi Soli Ringess—will you make a light offering today in honor of Ede's quest to write the Infinite Program?"

Danlo realized suddenly that Javas Icolari and everyone else was waiting for him to give his assent. "Yes," he said, finally remembering the correct response that Harrah's keepers had taught him. "It is my desire—I will make an offering."

"He will make an offering!" Javas Icolari shouted this out

even to the topmost tiers where the common Architects strained to take in what transpired on the floor below them.

"Being clean in his mind and free of negative programs," Javas said, "Danlo wi Soli Ringess wishes to show that he is worthy of being vastened in Ede our God."

Although this last assertion of Javas was only a formality, it troubled Danlo. Five days earlier, in the silence of his altar room, he had placed the holy heaume upon his head, and he had faced one of the history pools. There, waiting cool and clear in the eternal information flows of a vast cybernetic space, he had found many records concerning the evolution of the Church's most scared ceremonies. The light offering, it seemed, had not always been a public event.

It had begun nearly three thousand years earlier, during the architetcy of Wallam Mato Iviercier—long before the War of the Faces and the Old Church's flight into the Vild. Originally, in the first days of the Church, the offering had been nothing more than a visual aid to Readers hoping to free their brethren from negative aspects of themselves. A Worthy Architect would enter the Temple (the first and original Temple on Alumit), and he would step into a dark, little cell where he would greet his Reader and submit to a cleansing. The Reader would place a silver heaume on the Worthy's head; this scanning computer would read out the brain functions and make a model of the mind. The Reader would then study the projection of this model—the many-colored hologram similar in size to the devotionary imagos of Nikolos Daru Ede that were just becoming popular. If one believed the mythos of the Church, a well-trained Reader could descry in the glowing hologram lights the patterns and master programs of the human mind.

It was the duty of every Architect, of course, to submit to such cleansings that he might one day be free of the negative programs that caused man so much woe. All Worthy Architects hoped thus to purify themselves before their old age and certainly before death. Because only the pure in mind could have their pallatons vastened into an eternal computer, no one could afford to ignore his spiritual refinement.

In actuality, of course, almost no one was denied this cybernetic salvation. Some said that this proved the power of the Church to rewrite people's flawed personal programs. Others, such as the Elidis, cited it as evidence of the Church's corruption. For almost all Architects to be pronounced perfectly clean before death, they said, defied all probability and all evidence of most people's imperfection. Only seven hundred years earlier, they observed, the Readers who certified an Architect's worthiness to be vastened were themselves flawed with the most negative of programs. Many of these Readers were proud, ambitious, venal. They traded favors with each other and with important Architects seeking an Eldership in the Koivuniemin. Sometimes they sold outright the much-coveted black badges of purity that the Architects of that time wore on the sleeves of their kimonos. Their power over people's lives had grown very great. But as the Elidi master Gabriel Mondragon had accused, such readings were at best imprecise. In truth, it was almost impossible to read the mind's programs from a display of colored lights, much less make judgments as to which were positive, negative, or divine. In these ancient readings of one's inner radiance, there was much sham, self-delusion, vanity, and overweening pride. It was pride, above all other things, that had led to the evolution of the modern light ceremony.

"Having meditated upon the mysteries of Ede's Infinite Mind," Javas continued, "Danlo wi Soli Ringess wishes to show that the glories of the human mind are only a reflection of the divine."

Once a time, the greatest princes of the Church, upon being pronounced free of negative programs, wished to prove their perfection to people other than their personal Readers in their private cells. And so they had invited whole conclaves of Readers to witness the glittering holograms of their minds. Because the reading cells could only accommodate a few men or women, the readings had been moved to the facing room of the Temple. But still these proud princes of the mind coveted greater glory, and so they demanded that all Worthy Architects be allowed to view the triumph of their readings.

And this was done, and because the facing room was too small for the swarms of Architects who desired to behold a model of a perfectly programed human brain, the Church built their first assembly halls exclusively devoted to this evolving ceremony. They called these cubical buildings the Houses of Heaven, and those Architects most adept at showing the divine light within were called the Perfecti. They were artists of the mind, masters of their brains' deepest programs. They were masters of moving their minds. Originally, the light offering had been a static model of the brain, as frozen in time as colored ice or a foto of a man's face. But the Perfecti, wishing to show the mind's true beauty, had taken to composing luminous movements of pure thought akin in grandeur to man's most compelling music. Thus, over the centuries, the light offering had evolved from a private and purely religious duty into a very public art form. While no one could ever forget that the Perfecti's glittering compositions were made in honor of Ede the God, most people attended the light offerings not as witnesses to perfection but because they liked to be dazzled and awed.

"And now," Javas told the assembled Architects, "our Holy Ivi, Harrah Ivi en li Ede will describe the nature of today's unusual ceremony."

Having completed the formalities preceding all of the most important light offerings, Javas Icolari took his place on the bench nearest Harrah's. And then, with Pol Iviertes holding her flowing white kimono off the floor, Harrah stood to address the throngs in the Hall of Heaven. "My children," she called out in a clear voice. She paused for a moment to look at Danlo waiting all alone in his chair, and she favored him with a smile. "My children, we must remind you that we are here today not merely as viewers of an offering but as witnesses to the words of our holy Algorithm. Is it not said that one day, when you are near to despair, a man will come among you from the stars? Is it not written that he will be a man without fear who will look upon the heavenly lights within and not fall mad?"

Danlo, sitting by himself on a golden chair before nearly thirty thousand people, tried to keep a smile of amusement from his lips. Although Harrah had implied that he was as fearless as light, he felt his heart beating up through his neck arteries with all the force of a man rhythmically hammering two rocks together. He looked at Harrah standing so solemnly in the Hall's exact west. He remembered something about directions, then. In his tribe a man would die to the west. When his time came to make the journey to the other side of day, his sons and daughters would wrap him in furs and place him against a yu tree so that he could look out over the frozen sea and listen to the wind calling him.

"We must remind you," Harrah continued, "that Danlo wi Soli Ringess is no Perfecti, and we are here today not to comment upon the beauties of his mind. We are here only as witnesses to his test. *Will* he look upon the heavenly lights within and live to tell us what he has seen? *Is* he indeed the bringer of light who will show the way toward all that is possible?"

Again Harrah paused, and she let her gaze fall upon Bertram Jaspari and Malaclypse Redring of Qallar. Then she said, "We shall pray that he is the Lightbringer, for this is indeed a dark time for our eternal Church. We would ask you all to pray for Danlo wi Soli Ringess, for whether Lightbringer or not, he must face today the heavenly lights that even our most accomplished Perfecti dare not look upon lest they fall mad.''

Harrah bowed her head in silence, and as robots moving to a single program, 28,345 women and men followed her example. But in the Hall that evening, there were 28,348 people. Bertram Jaspari sat stiffly on his bench refusing to pray. And next to him Malaclypse Redring, being a warrior-poet, was permitted neither prayer nor any other observance of religious practice. And Danlo wi Soli Ringess, as he gripped his flute in his hands, kept his eyes open and his head erect. As his found-father, Haidar, had once taught him, a man could pray for his family, pray for his tribe, and pray for all the people of the world. In private, he could even pray to the one animal who was his other self. But it was unseemly for a full man to pray for himself in sight of others who were praying for him so fervently.

"We wish you well, Danlo wi Soli Ringess of Neverness." Harrah had finished her prayer, and she lifted her hands toward the thousands of Architects at their benches around the Hall. "We all wish you well. May you behold His Infinite Light in your own."

With a brilliant smile revealing her infinite faith in Ede the God (and perhaps in Danlo wi Soli Ringess, the man), Harrah sat back down on her bench. Then the lights of the dome gradually dimmed. The open spaces around Danlo and over the tiers of benches grew dark, almost black. For a moment, a deep silence swept over the Hall. Danlo listened to the inward rush of his own breath. It was as if his heart and the whole world were filling up with a cold, icy wind. The metal seat and arms of his chair felt cold to the touch, and he wished that he had worn a wool kamelaika instead of his formal black silks. To either side of his face, the chair's silver headpiece flared out like the wings of a seagull, enclosing his brain in a logic field so intense that he could almost feel it humming. He sat watching and waiting, counting his heartbeats as the scanning computers within the headpiece made a model of his brain.

Ahira, Ahira, he heard himself thinking, *this will be my last test.*

In truth, he did not anticipate that this light offering would be nearly so difficult or dangerous as his Walk with the Dead. Of course no sane man would willingly look upon a model of his own mind. In viewing the visual cortex alone, there were possibilities for wild feedbacks, the building of intense bursts of light that could burn out the brain. And whether the offering be sham or show, it was certainly dangerous for anyone, even a master cetic, to look upon his own consciousness. But it was a danger of a lesser degree than letting a Temple keeper infuse images directly into his brain. He would not be interfaced with a computer. The scanning computers in the silver headpiece could only read the firing of his brain's neurons; they could not hurl him into a raging surreality and make him face the demons of his soul. And if the lights in his visual cortex grew too intense, he could always close his eyes, breaking the feedback. At the worst, Danlo expected his always lurking head pain might explode into a few bad moments of agony. Or, for a few moments, he might lose himself in the terror of pure consciousness. He remembered, then, what his grandfather had taught him once on a day of blizzard and terrible cold: that the whole art of journeying into the unknown was in knowing what to do when you didn't know what to do.

I will look within myself and behold myself smiling back at me. And then, after recalling a favorite old poem, he thought, *I am the eye with which the universe beholds itself and knows itself divine.*

Suddenly, in the black air above him, out of the empty spaces curving beneath the dome, a great cube of light appeared. The light was immense and deep beyond the measure of his eyes, and suddenly he knew that this test would be more wildly dangerous than any he had ever faced. He sat almost frozen to his chair, holding his flute in his right hand while with his left he touched the white owl's feather in his hair. Somewhere in front of him, in the dazzling darkness, Harrah Ivi en li Ede sat not far from Jedrek Iviongeon and Bertram Jaspari and thousands of other waiting Architects. But they were far from Danlo's field of vision, and he did not see them. His eyes were only for the light above him, the manifold colored lights that shone as one single, terrible light. He could look upon its brilliance all too easily. The cube of light floated over the western quadrant of the Hall. For excellent reasons, the golden chair beneath him was usually turned toward the darkest part of the dome in the east. Danlo wished he could gaze into the nothingness of that direction, but instead he had promised to face what the greatest Perfectis of the Cybernetic Universal Church were never permitted to behold.

It is only a hologram, he thought. *In my life, I have seen ten thousand holograms.*

The cube of light was only a holographic model of his brain, truly, but it was two hundred times as large in dimension. And it was not an exact model. The human brain is curving bundle of neural structures, fissures and folds, molded together like a ball of snowworms. But the light offering glittered high in the Hall as a perfect cube. It was as if Danlo's cerebral cortex, cerebellum, and brainstem had been squeezed into a box. And yet no part of his brain—not even the hippocampus or the tiny, nutlike amygdala—was missing. One hundred billion neurons quivered within the walls of his skull, and the offering represented each of these cells as a tiny colored light. Whenever one of his neurons fired, a corresponding light in the offering would flare brightly for a moment and then fade into quiescence.

All through the hologram, from its center to its eight corners, waves of lavender or aquamarine light rippled outward in hideously complex swirls almost too quick for his eyes to follow. He tried to perceive the crackles of carmine or emerald or rose marking out the various neural pathways. But nothing in this model of his brain would hold still for more than a moment. With this thought came an immediate response, a movement of maroon pulses through his cerebral cortex, or rather, that topmost and front part of the cube where the thinking center of his brain glowed in colors from ruby to puce. He observed these pulses, and this act of apprehension generated new thoughts, which boiled through the hologram with the speed of superheated steam.

It occurred to him that thought was motion, and motion light. His eyes swept the cube back and forth, from side to side, up and down. He almost expected to see light reflecting off each of the six faces, everywhere filling up the cube with its brilliance. But, astonishingly, much of the hologram was dark, even black. At any moment, perhaps, no more than a fifth of the individual neurons in his brain were firing. Because he knew it was dangerous to do so, almost without thinking, he looked toward the rear of the cube where his visual cortex glowed a dull red. But the very act of fixing on this disturbing color caused many other neurons in his vision center to fire. The offering modeled this as intense bursts of radiance, which in turn, as Danlo drank in the light with his eyes, caused yet greater bundles of neurons to flare into activity. In scarcely a moment, the whole of his visual cortex exploded into a bright violet flame. The pain of it burned like a hot knife thrust through his eye to the back of his brain. He could almost see this pain: it looked like a black tunnel surrounded by walls of fire. He might have fainted in agony, but his will toward consciousness was strong. He continued to stare at the terrible light of his own vision for a long time—at least for a count of three heartbeats, which was quite long enough to make the watching Architects gasp in amazement and fear.

I will not fear, Danlo thought, gasping for breath. Fear, he knew, was like an icy water so cold that it burned inside every cell of the body. There were five ways of living with fear. Some fled from fear as they might a slavering bear, and some sought to cover it up with a blanket of false emotions and pretend to fearlessness. A zanshin master, fighting a duel to the death, tried to let his fear flow through him like water, neither grasping at it nor trying to dam it up, but only noticing its path as if he were looking through a clear glass. The warrior-poets, of course, were said to be beyond fear. If true, then in some important way it was impossible to think of them as still being wholly human. Likewise, the gods of the galaxy had supposedly transcended all such base programs, but the oft-quaking hologram of Nikolos Daru Ede glowing on the arm of Danlo's chair gave the lie to this conceit. Possibly, he thought, if his father had truly become a god, then he had discovered how to outlive his essential dread of death. But Danlo still lived as a man, as he always would, and to him fell the fifth way of facing fear. He dared to look upon his worst terror eye to eye and to change it—much as his retina might transform the killing radiation of the sun into an inner light illuminating his brain. It was his way to feel fear as thrill. And so, even as a child playing with bear cubs, he had always sought out danger and death. Once, on the night of the three moons, his grandfather had warned him that this deep wildness would always be his most glaring weakness and his greatest strength. Harrah Ivi en li Ede might proclaim him to be a man without fear, but in truth, he was only wild—wild like the wind, wild like the white thallow who dives through the air only for the joy of testing his wings.

I will not fear. I will taste the fear inside myself, and it will only bring me greater life as if I had drunk the blood of a bear.

After the pain had almost blinded Danlo, he finally looked away from this part of the light cube. There was a moment when he thought that he might be truly blind, for all that he could see was blackness. And then he realized that his eyes had only fallen upon a section of the hologram representing his motor cortex.

Because his body was frozen into motionlessness, the neurons here were mostly as dark as bits of black ice.

Most of the universe is dark, he remembered. *But out of the darkness, light.*

Upon realizing that he was neither blind nor mad, Danlo felt a sudden flush of heat spread throughout his belly. He imagined that he saw this in the light offering as a scarlet glow suffusing all his neurons—much as a drop of blood might stain a glass of water. With greater confidence now, he faced the many-colored streams of his thoughts. Although he was no Perfecti, he had undergone disciplines of the mind that no Architect had ever dreamed possible. As a young man, he had learned difficult language philosophies and the states of plexure from a Fravashi Old Father. He had sat around fires with autists as they fell together into full lucidity and explored the thoughtscapes of the realreal. And with the help of Thomas Rane, the greatest of the Neverness remembrancers, he had nearly mastered the sixty-four attitudes of that most difficult art. By nature he was a mathematical man, and more, a pilot of the Order of Mystic Mathematicians. He had survived the broken spaces of the manifold by proving difficult mathematical theorems—by thinking calmly and clearly in the face of death. He decided to think such thoughts now. Out of playfulness and pride, he would look upon his mind in all its splendor of mathematical inspiration.

The greatest theorem I know is the Continuum Hypothesis.

Indeed, this was the so-called Great Theorem of Danlo's Order, and Danlo's father had proved it true: that between any pair of discrete Lavi sets of point-sources there exists a one-to-one mapping. This proved that it was possible for a pilot to fall from any star in the galaxy to any other in a single fall—if only he were genius enough to discover the right mapping. Because Danlo thought that his father's proof fairly shimmered with the cool light of elegance, he decided to work through it in his mind. And so he called up the crystalline diamond ideoplasts representing the theorem's general statement. He began working through the five Gadi lemmas, and he marveled at their power and the inevitable unfolding of their logic. At last, when he showed that the Justerini subspace was embedded within a simple Lavi space, an array of diamond and emerald ideoplasts built up within his mind's eye more lovely than even the fabled cathedrals of Vesper. And all this beauty within him was reflected in the light offering. The whole of his cortex, it seemed, had come brilliantly alive with rings of tangerine and scarlet, with luminous cobalt spheres embedded inside those of topaz, auburn, and jade. In a far part of Danlo's consciousness, he became aware that many of the Architects in the hall were gasping at the loveliness of this display. Almost certainly, he thought, they had never beheld the secret fire and order of pure mathematics.

The light, the light—the beautiful and terrible light.

And neither had Danlo—at least not in this way. For a while he gazed at the lights of his own mind, and he played with logic and number. He flew through ancient proofs of the Zassenhaus Butterfly Lemma and the Fixed-Point Theorem; he spent a few long moments exploring open theorems that had never been proved. And he never let his eyes fall free of the offering's hundred billion lights, at the way the correspondences built and formed and fractured into lovely colored patterns. Soon he began thinking new thoughts; he played with ideas for a strange, new mathematics that would incorporate paradoxical logics and a rather mystical apprehension of the orders of infinity. As he gained skill in controlling his mentations, he took delight in conjuring fantastic thought arrays and sparkling, almost iridescent sequences of concepts and abstractions. In his best moments, a powerful idea storm might rip through the light cube like lightning, dazzling Danlo and thousands of others with the shock of its brilliance. To listen to the sudden cheers of the astonished multitudes was to understand the pride of the Perfecti who had developed this subtle art. And more, it was a calling for Danlo to face his own hubris, that terrible pride beyond pride that some men carry in their hearts like ticking hydrogen bombs. In Danlo, pilot and would-be Alaloi shaman, this took the form of a wildness that would drive him to any place in the universe where it was possible to go. Wildness, as his grandfather had once warned him, would be either his path toward God or the doorway to his doom.

I am free, he thought. *My mind is free. My will to move my mind is truly free.*

For a few exhilarating moments, he felt the thrill of being able to summon many-splendored thought patterns solely according to his desire to behold them. He moved about his mind creating and recreating these patterns with the ease of a painter daubing colors on a canvas. And then he noticed a terrible thing. When he concentrated on a certain area of his brain where he wished a certain pattern to unfold—perhaps in the occipital lobes or in the body sensory areas just behind the central sulcus—he noticed a slight delay between the time his neurons fired and the moment in which he became aware of the corresponding thought. This delay seemed to last about half as long as a heartbeat. That there should be any delay at all touched him with terror. For a while he tried to think faster than the light offering could model his thinking. But he might as well have tried to dance faster than his own reflection in a mirror. No matter what beauties he brooded upon or where inside himself he looked, his awareness of his thoughts always lagged behind the brain processes that generated them. If this were truly so, then the storm of chemicals leading to the firing of his neurons completely determined all of his mind and memory—including this despairing thought itself. Where, then, was the freedom of his will to think, to act, to move, to breathe? To hate or to love—how could he ever be free to choose one deep passion over the other? And worse, what could it mean to say he loved life or anything at all when he was nothing more than a chemical machine programed to react according to the terrible quick fire of his brain?

I am not I. I am the light that dances faster than light. I am the light that ignites the fire.

As Danlo sat sweating in his metal chair, he heard a murmur of disquiet roll across the rows of benches. Most of the Architects present were aficionados of the mind, and in the lovely violet and gold structures of Danlo's deepest programs, they began to detect disharmonies—the broken symmetries and dangerous, quicksilver reflections of a mind looking too closely at itself. Now, as Danlo sought the true source of his selfness, he began to perturb the secret rhythms of his brain. He generated new rhythms unconnected to the self-regulating mechanisms and cycles of his body. Thus he began to think with ever greater speed. And now the time between the firing of his brain and his awareness of his thoughts was no longer half a heartbeat, not because he had discovered a way to transcend the limitations of his brain, but only because his heart was beating much faster. He continued to stare at the light offering. He began to hate the way it seemingly anticipated his thinking. This hatred he saw modeled as a violet-black glow spreading like ink from his prefrontal lobes to his cerebellum, coloring almost every cluster of neurons. Almost, he could not help himself. He began to see the light offering as more than merely a model of his mind. It was almost as if his soul had been stolen and projected out into black air for all the people in the Hall to see. In a moment of despair, he wondered how these billions of glittering lights had captured his anima—

that part of man's spirit that was his will and his life's quickest fire.

I am almost I. If I look deeply enough, quickly enough, I will see that I see that I . . .

If Danlo had dropped his eyes away from the heavenly lights, then, his test might have been over. If he had stood up from his chair, and turned east away from the great, glowing cube, many of the Architects whispering to each other in their seats might have proclaimed him as the Lightbringer. But he had yet to bring himself to the source of his own light. Until he found the place inside himself where the energies of his consciousness broke out of his own secret heaven (or hell), he would not will himself to look away. No one knew this except him. Where Harrah Ivi en li Ede and perhaps Kissiah en li Ede and a few others saw that he was dancing on the knifeblade's edge of madness, most others only pointed at him and exclaimed upon his courage and tenacity in looking at the light offering longer than he needed to look.

I am the eye with which I behold myself. I am the I, the I, the I . . .

Danlo knew that he could look away from the light offering any time that he chose. But he also knew that he could not choose such a cowardly path. He both could and he could not, and that was the hell of his existence. He was like a man carefully balanced on the rocky ridge of possibility, and only the slightest puff of wind would suffice to unbalance him and cause him to fall. The paradoxical nature of choice itself drove him to discover the source of his freedom of will. (Or perhaps the iron chains of his own enslavement.) It drove him ever deeper into himself, into the most mysterious and wildest part of the universe. He became aware of many things, then. Even as he rushed into the storm of consciousness raging through his brain, his exterior senses intensified. It was as if his ears had grown arms and fingers, and he could reach out into the Hall to grasp even the faintest of whispers. And so he heard Bertram Jaspari tell Jedrek Iviongeon that the cursed naman pilot had finally fallen mad. Danlo wi Soli Ringess had crossed the threshold from which there is no return, and so they needn't fear that he would ever again walk through their holy Temple bearing a smile upon his lips and light within his hand. Harrah Ivi en li Ede, as well, was thinking of him. He could almost hear her murmuring a prayer. A great tension, like a piece of pulled steel, ran between her and Bertram Jaspari, connecting them to a shared fate. With a new sense for which he still had no name, he could feel this force pulling at him, too. He sensed the warrior-poet; it was as if he shared a cage with a tiger. Malaclypse of the two red rings, he who worshiped death and other cosmic mysteries, sat staring at him in awe, almost in love. He fairly trembled with a terrible hunger for the infinite. With his dark violet eyes he urged Danlo inward, deeper into his own marvelous consciousness toward death or ultimate triumph—or perhaps both. Malaclypse's passion, as with all his breed, was to apprehend the nature of eternity. He looked to Danlo for signs of divinity, and on his beautiful face burned the old question: was Danlo truly the son of his father? Would Danlo's pride drive him to, storm the heavenly heights of godhood, as had Mallory wi Soli Ringess?

He would still slay all would-be gods, Danlo thought. *With his killing knife or poisonous darts, he might slay me, here, now. Only . . . can a man truly become a god?*

He suddenly knew that his father had once made the same journey that he made today. All beings, whether man, snowworm, or god, blaze with their own inner lights. Each man and woman is a star, he remembered, and Mallory Ringess as a man had burned with a need to face the truth of his own soul. If Danlo willed himself to continue staring at the light offering and complete his journey into the wild, then in a way he would not be alone. Like a star, his father would be there inside him, watching him, waiting for him—and always guiding him inward toward the fiery center of the universe.

Father, Father.

There came a moment of brilliance and burning when Danlo did not know whether he was still looking at the great cube or at the shimmering lights of his own mind. He felt himself falling, not as a wingless bird might plummet toward the hard ice of a planet's surface and certain terminus in time, but rather falling into infinity, endlessly falling, faster and faster, as a lightship pulled into the heart of a black hole. He felt this falling as a nausea in his belly and a terrible acceleration of his mind. There were tremendous time distortions. He could see his brain lights; they flickered faster, ever faster. An Architect, upon facing death, spoke in glowing words of being vastened into an eternal computer. But now, in sensing the almost palpable programs of his brain, Danlo felt himself being infinitized, being fractured into a hundred billion waves of light moving at infinitely accelerating speed. There came a shattering of himself. He looked at his mind ever more closely, as through a diamond lens increasing its power of magnification from ten times to ten thousand. The waves of his own consciousness, at first as seemingly smooth and undulant as the body of a snake, now appeared as jagged as a tiger's teeth. The closer he looked, the more the waves split apart into yet smaller waves, fracturing and fractalling down to infinity. How delicate and beautiful they appeared! The waves were as perishable as ice crystals in a fiery wind, and he could hold them only for a moment before they broke up and vanished into the black neverness inside himself. He knew, then, that he *was* these waves of light, and nothing more, vibrating and shimmering and always dancing down into that dazzling darkness at the center of his soul.

Father, Father—I am afraid.

He remembered a time when he was ten years old and had become lost out on the sea's ice after a day of hunting seals. Just as night fell, a great white bear had leaped at him out of the darkness, rising up like a mountain over a ridge of drifted snow. The bear easily might have killed him before he could have raised his spear, but as it happened he only wanted to play with Danlo. Sometimes bears were like that. He only wanted to frighten Danlo into a desperate dance of survival, and this he had done. Danlo still remembered his shocked surprise as a clutching of his belly and a scream that had had no time to form upon his lips. It had been a moment of supreme fear for his life, and yet the terror he felt now at falling into himself was infinitely greater. For it seemed that he could never escape. He felt himself losing control of his thoughts; each burst of mentation raced by him with a heart-stopping speed. It was as if he were strapped into a rocket sled and forced to view the flickering reflections of the stars in the glossy ice beneath him. The reflections of his mind appeared with all the suddenness of a man discovering fire. There were mathematical concepts and worries and old faces; there were attitudes toward fear and counterideas and countless memories. Many of his thoughts, he noticed, came in pairs. One moment he might think that life sang with joy, while in the next infinitesimal of time the opposing idea would tear through him like a flash of lightning. Such thoughts flashed inside him, the affirmative and the negative, his need to affirm all things and say yes (even to this terrible opposition driving him mad), coupled with the terror and the great no of existence itself. In the time it took to draw a breath, ten thoughts might form, oppose each other, shatter, and reform into new thoughts. One thought might call up a thousand others, and each of these, a thousand more. Like a seed ice crystal dropped into a supercooled cloud, the simplest thought might touch off a chain reaction of thinking, thoughts crystallizing thoughts a billion billion times over in a quickly building storm. There was no end to these thoughts. There was no following them, beholding them, or controlling them, for they exploded outward or inward infinitely in all directions.

I know that I know that I know that yes is yes and no is no and there is no yes without a no and no no but that yes follows no as day follows night and darkness light is yes and no is not nothing but only the neverness from which comes selfness and light bright sight and seeing all myself I know that I will say no but no I mustn't say no, I know, no, no, no no . . .

Like a thallow flying into a sarsara, he was caught in the thoughtstorms raging through his brain. There was whiteness, wildness. Here, as ice crystals swirl together into clouds, waves of consciousness shimmered and flowed together, always moving and dancing, always forming patterns that were both terrible and beautiful to behold. He saw bright bands of violet and flaming streamers of scarlet and gold—all the colors of the spectrum and others which were wholly new. A Perfecti, viewing these lights from the safety of one of the Hall's many benches, might have said that Danlo at last was apprehending the deep programs of his own mind. But this would have implied a detachment and freedom of will that Danlo no longer felt. In some sense he wasn't apprehending himself at all but only simply being—existing as the chemical storms of tryptamine and serotonin causing his neurons to fire. He *was* this fire. He burned and he burned, and he couldn't keep himself from burning.

At last he understood the pain of his friend Hanuman li Tosh, the cetic who once had gone inside himself and returned to recount the nature of hell. This was the pain of pure existence, matter forming and rushing and combining, endlessly, decaying and shattering and recombining without meaning or purpose, on and on until the end of eternity. It was the pain of the gods, those tragic beings who felt themselves cut off from this onstreaming flow of atoms and photons and yet caught up in a fire that they could never quite control. Perhaps it was even the pain of God, terrible and deep, for if God was being in itself and the substance of all things, then this infinite body was continually ageing, dying, decomposing and separating from itself, on every world and piece of dust in the universe, on and on throughout space and time.

God, he thought, consumed God in this eternal flame. The

burning could never stop. Knowing this, Danlo felt a terrible fear of being trapped forever in his own fire. He hated himself for fearing at all, and he hated his own hatred with such wrath that he might have destroyed himself then if only he could have willed himself to die. But now, in this moment, he was nothing but a red, raging flame, and he had neither desire nor will, but only despair. This terrible emotion was more absolute than that of a pilot returning from the stars to discover his birth world blackened by the killing light of some supernova. It was greater than that of a god who watches a whole galaxy of stars dying and collapsing into a singularity made by one of his enemies.

Danlo, himself, now began collapsing into himself, into the darkest depths and the burning cold neverness of his soul. He fell like a stone dropped into a bottomless pool. He fell and fell, and all his being was in this endless falling and endless time, the infinities downward, fire inside fire, pain inside pain, the blackness deepening into an ever more vast and total blackness. In the time of a single heartbeat—in only a moment—he lived ten thousand years.

To live, I die. To live, to live—no, no, no, no . . .

There came a moment when he did not think that he would live much longer. In truth, he did not *want* to live if it meant falling forever into madness. If his brain was connected along many-silvered nerves to every part of his body, then he could send messages to all his muscles and organs. If he tried hard enough, he could find the way to make his heart stop beating. In the black pathways of despair winding through his brain, he could almost see this way. Somewhere inside him, like a diamond inside a black velvet box, shined the secret of life and death. He looked and looked, deeper and deeper, and he trembled to open this box. The key was almost within his grasp; it gleamed like a golden shell buoyed on the cresting wavefront of his consciousness. For ten billion years, he lived with this most terrible of desires. He could will himself to die. He could do this almost as easily as holding his breath. He remembered, then, Leander of Darkmoon and the eight other pilots who had died trying to find their way toward the Solid State Entity. Like him, they had sought the secret of the universe, but they had found something else. They had been too afraid to die, and so they had died—this the goddess Herself had told him. If, then, he faced his own death fearlessly with open hands and eyes, did that mean that he was fated to live? Or was there, after all, truly a choice?

For in the end we choose our futures, he remembered.

These were the words of his father, his mother, perhaps even the meaning of the wind or the Snowy Owl's cry on a moonlit night. It was the sound of himself, whispering, weeping, laughing. As he fell deeper into the long, dark, roaring ocean inside, he heard the calling of his consciousness. *His* consciousness. His will—he sensed that he still surged with a will toward life as wild and free as a thallow flying toward the sun. He knew this must always be so, and this sudden knowledge astonished him. For he had thought himself a slave to the chemicals burning through his brain. He *was* these chemicals, truly, this exquisitely tuned orchestration of blood, body, and brain, but what did this mean? He willed himself to see himself just as he truly was. It was like looking into a mirror reflecting a mirror reflecting a million more mirrors shimmering with the far-off brilliance of his own face. In this inward gazing down through the well of darkness to the distant light, he caught a glint of blue-black; perhaps this was the color of his eyes or the color of infinity or even the color of consciousness itself.

Gazing at the bright black sky, you see only yourself looking for yourself. When you look into the eyes of God, they go on and on forever.

When Danlo looked through his own eyes into his brain, he saw starfire and light. A hundred billion neurons fired in quick, deep rhythms that he was only now beginning to apprehend. The brain's inner workings, of course, consisted of much more than the firing of all these separate cells. In truth, no part of the brain existed in separation. Many neurons intertwined their synapses with ten thousand others—sometimes with as many as three hundred thousand other nerve cells. The brain as a whole organ generated an electromagnetic field that pulled at every single cell. And each one was as perfect as a diamond. Inside the clear cell walls were dense-cored vesicles, neurotubules, and mitochondria tearing apart phosphate molecules to free up life's energies—and a thousand other structures. Motilin, dopamine, and taurine and many other neurotransmitters cascaded in a neverending flood. He saw lipids and amino acids combining, glucose burning and ions swirling through the water of life in an incredibly intricate and beautiful dance. What ordered these chemicals of consciousness, he wondered? What made matter and organized it into such subtle and marvelous harmonies?

I am that I am. I am only carbon and oxygen and nitrogen and hydrogen and potassium and iron and . . .

He was only these elements of the earth, nothing more, nothing less. These elements of the stars. For every part of him—every atom of carbon in his eyes, every bit of iron in his heart—had been once fused together in the fire of a long-dead star. The stars, in truth, made the atoms of the universe, but what made these atoms come together in consciousness and life? What made them move? For move they did, almost quicker than he could imagine, pulsing and resonating, vibrating billions of times in a moment, seeking out other atoms with which to spin and dance and sing their cosmic songs. In one mad, marvelous moment beyond time, beneath time, he looked into the center of a carbon atom sparkling somewhere near the stem of his brain. He needed to know the secret of matter, and he saw a fiery cloud of electrons—and protons and neutrons exchanging energies, hugging each other in a terribly compelling love beyond love, binding themselves to themselves in a single, ball-like nucleus. And deeper he looked, and he saw the quarks, like infinitesimal sapphires and emeralds and rubies, all full of charm and strangeness. And deeper still, the strings and infons and the splendid noumena, which could be grasped only by the mind but never sensed—or rather sensed only in the fire of madness or in that marvelous, mystical clarity that befalls a man when he discovers his inner sense of the infinite.

What was matter, truly? Matter, he saw, was magical stuff. Matter shimmered. All the matter of the universe was woven of a single, superluminal tapestry of jewels, the light of each jewel reflected in the light of every other. Matter was holy, matter was alive, matter was but consciousness frozen in time. For as far down the great chain of being as he looked, down and down through the infinities, he could see no final form or bit of matter but only light. This was not the light of the sun or stars, not the photons or the flashing wavelengths of visible radiation by which he might behold the distant galaxies or the blueness of his own eyes. Rather it was a light inside light, purer and primeval, the light inside all things. In some ways, it seemed more like water than light, for it flowed and surged as a single, shimmering substance. It moved itself. It had will, *was* will itself. This deep consciousness that some called matter knew how to come together into ever more complex forms. It evolved; ultimately, as with man, it evolved to perceive itself and cry out with wonder and wild joy. This, he saw, was the essential nature of consciousness, that it was always aware of its own splendor, even as a cresting wave of water reflects the light of the entire ocean beneath itself.

I am this blessed light.

Knowing this, Danlo suddenly realized that he could move himself. His selfness, he saw, consisted of more than the firing of his neurons, and his consciousness was much more than the patterns or programs of his brain. For he could feel it flowing through every blood cell and atom of his body—his heart and hands and every part of himself ablaze with nothing but this pure light. At last he understood how the Solid State Entity and other gods might possibly manipulate matter through consciousness alone, and how they might create terrible weapons of consciousness with which to destroy each other and rip open gaping holes in the fabric of the spacetime continuum. This was the true nature of consciousness and the meaning of matter, that ultimately both were one substance without cause or control outside itself. Although he was no god, and he couldn't directly touch Bertram Jaspari or any of the other Architects watching him, he could move his own mind. *His* will—truly, it was as free as the wind, as free as his desire to say yes or no to the madness devouring him. He could live as a blind man wandering forever through the black caverns of his mind, or he could see himself just as he was: a luminous being who might bring the light of pure consciousness to himself and show thirty thousand watching Architects that they, too, could blaze like stars.

Yes—I will.

There was a moment. From the dark rows of benches facing Danlo, he heard Bertram Jaspari calling in his whiny voice for the offering to be concluded. He heard Bertram Jaspari calling for Harrah's physicians to take Danlo away. For Danlo wi Soli Ringess had fallen mad, Bertram said, as any aficionado of the light offerings could see by looking at the hologram floating high in the Hall of Heaven. As Danlo himself could see—if only he would look at himself as a vast cubical array of colored lights and nothing more. Now the light cube had mostly fallen dark, with a few glowing clusters of ocher and puce signaling the disturbed brain patterns of a madman. From time to time, bursts of sapphire and smalt rippled from Danlo's cerebral cortex to his brainstem, but other than these seemingly random movements, his mind appeared to be lost in its own blackness.

Danlo heard a sigh of disappointment and dread whoosh from thousands of lips almost as a single sound. He heard Harrah Ivi en li Ede praying softly for him—and for herself, for her grandchildren, and possibly even for the future of her Holy Church. Even the imago of Nikolos Daru Ede, glowing from the devotionary computer upon the arm of his golden chair, betrayed its concern. Subtly, quickly, so that almost no one could see, the Ede flashed desperate finger signs in front of Danlo's face, but to no avail. The Ede kept staring at Danlo, and almost no one noticed that his usually beatific countenance had darkened in despair.

Of all the men and women in the Hall save Danlo himself, perhaps only Malaclypse Redring of Qallar understood that the light offering might not be finished. Although Malaclypse was almost as silent as a tiger crouching in the snow, Danlo could hear his breath moving in a slow, steady rhythm strangely synchronized with his own. He could almost feel the warrior-poet's eyes burning across his face, watching and waiting, searching in Danlo's blue-black eyes for any sign of life—or that tragic death-in-life that Bertram Jaspari acclaimed as Danlo's fate.

Danlo might have looked through the dark Hall for the warrior-poet, then, but he still could not move his head. He still stared at the glowing cube of lights; in all the time he had sat motionless in his chair, he had willed his eyes to remain open upon them. And now there came a moment when these lights began to quicken and change color. From his frontal lobes to his vision center to the brainstem, all at once, points of dark blue light flared into life and spread their deep fire from one corner of the cube to another. Soon the entire cube shone with a single, blue-black light quickly brightening to cobalt. For a moment Danlo looked upon this lovely blueness, this marvelous blue light growing ever more brilliant and wild.

As from far away, he heard thirty thousand Architects gasp in astonishment. Through their urgent whispers and sudden cries, he heard Harrah Ivi en li Ede's voice choke with emotion and Bertram Jaspari cursing with bewilderment and disbelief. It seemed that Malaclypse Redring had stopped breathing; Danlo could almost feel the paralysis of the warrior-poet's belly as a deep pain in his own. A deep joy. For now Danlo moved his mind with all the gladness of a thallow soaring into the sky. Then the great offering that he made to Ede the God and all the Architects of the Cybernetic Universal Church leaped into light. All fiery and splendid it shone, like the blue-white light of the brightest stars. In Danlo's splendid brain, a hundred billion neurons blazed with their own beautiful fire, and for a moment each of the corresponding lights in the great cube came alive in the most intense illumination. This dazzled the eyes of all the men and women sitting on their benches. (And created an unprecedented show of

lights for the tens of thousands of Architects still waiting on the
Temple grounds outside the Hall's flashing dome.) It was as if
Tannahill's sun had exploded in their faces for all to behold. But
now many people threw their hands over their eyes and turned
away, and no one in the Hall could look upon this beautiful and
terrible light, and that was the hell of it. But that was the heaven,
too. For in all the thousands of years since the Church had insti-
tuted this ceremony, in all the thousands of thousands of offerings made by the Church's most accomplished Perfecti, no one
had ever succeeded in lighting up more than a fraction of his
brain. In truth, no one had ever thought it possible. For a man to
look upon the heavenly lights within and not fall mad was miracle enough. But for Danlo to come into such a wild and glorious
consciousness meant that he truly must be the Lightbringer foretold in their prophecies, and possibly something more.

We are all bringers of light, he thought as he listened to the
cries of acclamation ringing through the Hall. *I am only the spark
that ignites the flame.*

At last Danlo looked away from the light offering. He let his
eyes fall upon the bamboo flute that he had held in his hands all
during the time of his test. In the intense illumination pouring
down from above, it gleamed like gold. He smiled as a thought
came to him. Almost instantly, the lights of the offering flickered
to reflect this thought, but he did not look upon them. Instead he
suddenly stood away from his chair. With his mind's connection
to the computer's field suddenly broken, the light offering indeed
had come to an end. The great cube instantly fell dark and quiet.
The whole of the Hall, for a moment, seemed as black as the
ocean at night. Then Danlo smiled again and laughed softly,
almost sadly. He stood alone on the floor of the darkened dome,
and he listened to thirty thousand Architects calling his name.
"Lightbringer!" they shouted. They were clapping their hands
together, jumping down from their benches to the floor of the
Hall. "Danlo of Neverness is the Lightbringer!"

*Truly, I am the spark, but what flame have I lit? Oh, Ahira,
Ahira—what have I begun?*

As the lights of the Hall came back on (the common clary
plasma lights, that is), Danlo stood scrying and letting visions of
the future blow through him like a fiery wind. He beheld a splendor brighter than the brightest star and colors inside colors and a
terrible beauty. A single sound ripped him out of his reverie. It
was the quick suss of a knife being drawn from its sheath. He
turned to look across the few tens of feet separating him from the

first row of benches. There Bertram Jaspari stood shouting at
Danlo, shaking his little fist at him and shrieking out that Danlo
was *not* the Lightbringer, after all, but only a filthy naman cetic
sent from Neverness to trick them and to destroy their Holy
Church. Next to him Malaclypse Redring waited calmly with his
long killing knife held up high for anyone to see. The steel blade
caught the glare of the dome lights and reflected their burning
rays into Danlo's eyes. Danlo couldn't guess how the warrior-
poet had smuggled this knife into the Hall. And neither could the
keepers protecting Harrah, for upon seeing that Malaclypse was
armed, these grim-faced men cried out in dismay and fell over
the Holy Ivi to shield her.

A few of the keepers rushed the warrior-poet, but these were
met by Jedrek Iviongeon and Lensar Narcavage and many other
Iviomils loyal to Bertram Jaspari. They formed a wall of living
flesh between Harrah and the warrior-poet, and for the moment it
seemed impossible that he could harm her, much less assassinate
her. And it was far from certain that this was his purpose. He
gazed across the floor of the Hall, and his violet eyes met
Danlo's. Death was as near as the eyelight reflected back and
forth between them, as near as a steel knife that at any moment
might be hurled spinning through the air. For a moment, Danlo
held this gaze while he listened to the roaring voices and the
stamp of thousands of feet coming closer. He knew, then, that
even if the knife were to find his throat, he would die as a martyr,
for the people still would proclaim him as the Lightbringer, and
Harrah Ivi en li Ede would then install the new programs that
would forever change the Church. If the warrior-poet killed him,
it must be for the other reason, because Danlo was truly the son
of his father, and he had dared to shine more brightly than any
human being ever should.

And so with a smile on his lips, Danlo picked up his flute and
began to play. He never stopped looking at Malaclypse, and he
aimed a song like a golden arrow straight at Malaclypse's heart.
For only a moment, Malaclypse hesitated almost as if he were a
tiger wondering at the wisdom of hunting an armed man. But this
was enough time for a sea of jubilant Architects to close in
around Danlo—to reach out toward him with their hands as if
warming themselves by a fire or beckoning to the sun. When
Malaclypse saw that it would be impossible for him to harm
Danlo, he too smiled. He kissed the haft of his knife as he
touched the long, steel blade to his forehead. Then he held up the
knife to salute Danlo, and he quickly bowed his head.

Terrible beauty, Danlo thought. *The terrible beauty.*

Quickly, as Bertram Jaspari jerked on the sleeve of Malaclypse's kimono and cried in panic, Malaclypse turned to fight his way from the Hall. The skirmish between Harrah's keepers and the Iviomils had deepened into a full battle. The terrible sounds of hatred and rage and crunching flesh filled the air. Fanatic-eyed men cursed and shouted and flailed and kicked, and more than once, Malaclypse's killing knife slashed out to lop off a few fingers or to open some unfortunate Architect's throat. So ended the great light offering. Through sprays of bright red blood and the chaos of men and women crying in confusion, Bertram Jaspari led a few hundred of his Iviomils from the Hall of Heaven where the swarms of Architects waited for them outside.

It has begun, Danlo thought. *Truly, it is impossible to stop— like trying to put back the light into a star.*

He could no longer play his flute. A dozen Architects in their white kimonos swarmed near him, clutching at his hands, his hair, his face. He felt their hands closing on him, pulling him upward, lifting him into the air. They bore him high upon their shoulders and cried out, "Lightbringer, Lightbringer!" They never stopped shouting his name. And Danlo listened to the thunder of their voices and looked up toward the heavens in the direction of the shimmering stars. In a silence as vast as the Vild, he wept inside himself as he reflected upon the terrible and beautiful nature of light.

C H A P T E R 2 3

THE LIGHTBRINGER

Who would bring light must endure burning.
—from *Man's Journey*, Nikolos Daru Ede

War came to Tannahill the next day. Or rather, men brought this organized mayhem to the Architects of the Old Church, for war is never some cosmic accident descending upon a people with all the chance and inevitability of asteroids falling like fire out of the heavens, but only the will and work of man. As for the War of Terror, which it would soon be called, the Church historians laid its cause before the will of a single man: the Elder Bertram Jaspari. It was Bertram Jaspari, they said, who denounced Harrah's enchantment with the naman pilot, Danlo wi Soli Ringess. It was Bertram Jaspari who attacked Harrah herself and her architetcy, claiming that she had fallen into negative programs and was therefore unworthy to be the High Holy Ivi of the Cybernetic Universal Church. On the very night after Danlo had looked upon the heavenly lights, it was Bertram Jaspari who called together Jedrek Iviongeon and Nikos Iviercier and many Elders loyal to himself. After fleeing the Hall of Heaven, they met in secret conclave at Jedrek Iviongeon's estate. There, in Jedrek's private meditation hall, these hundred rebellious Elders, most of whom had long been Iviomils, proclaimed themselves as the true Koivuniemin.

In their first act as the ruling body of the True Church, they deposed Harrah Ivi en li Ede as Holy Ivi and elected Bertram Jaspari in her place. It was Bertram Jaspari—and no other—who accepted the title of the Holy Bertram Ivi Jaspari and called for Iviomils across Tannahill to follow him in a facifah that would purify the Church. All true. But it is also true that many millions of men and women *did* follow him. And many millions more remained faithful to Harrah and the Old Church, and only out of their willingness to oppose each other in violence and death was war truly made.

Although this latest schism of the Church had been building for centuries, neither faction was prepared for full war. Bertram, apparently, had decided upon open rebellion only on the night before Danlo's test, when he had visited him in Harrah's palace. And so his Iviomils, while very well disciplined and organized, had little enough time to stockpile the lasers and tlolts and poisons and bombs so useful in fighting a war of terror through the many levels of a planetary city. Harrah, who loathed the very idea of war as she might some explosive alien fungus, hadn't thought that Bertram would move so quickly; perhaps she had hoped that he wouldn't dare to make war at all. Of course, she had planned to await Danlo's proclamation as Lightbringer before redefining the Programs and Increase and Totality that were destroying the Church. (And the stars of the Vild.) She had planned to enter the facing room of the Temple and kneel before Ede's eternal computer where she would receive a New Program for the Church and all the universe.

It was her plan, as well, to install this New Program during a planetary facing ceremony—but only after her Readers had prepared all Worthy Architects across Tannahill for a great event. She had calculated that Bertram Jaspari would wait until this ceremony was done before denouncing her. Bertram Jaspari, she supposed, would need to cite this New Program as evidence of her unworthiness before leading his Iviomils into schism and almost certain war.

But she was wrong. She was no warrior—at least not in the sense of one experienced in warfare. In truth, she would never be a natural strategist of killing, but only a woman who loved flowers and grandchildren and God. The first fundamental of war is to strike quickly with utter ruthlessness; he who deals death upon the first blow may need no other. Bertram Jaspari, that vain and shallow man who saw so little of humankind's true possibilities, at least understood this much. And he had Malaclypse Redring of Qallar to guide his hand. With the warrior-poet's help, he struck immediately, with terror and great cruelty.

At the same minute, at the end of the morning facing ceremony, in every city across Tannahill, cadres of armed Iviomils moved to seize power. Some fell against such obvious targets as light-fields, food factories, tube trains, and the many light-nexi connecting the planet's billions of computers into a single entity. Some contented themselves merely with controlling their fellow

Architects with the threat of death: from every corner of Tannahill came reports of Architects denouncing Architects as agents of the Order or of the Narain heretics, followed swiftly by beatings, unauthorized cleansings, and even summary executions.

These murders—to give them their true name—shocked everyone from child to elder, for they were public, bloody, and final, in the sense that those put to death had no hope of ever being vastened in an eternal computer. Some cadres, as in Niave and Karkut, occupied local temples that were of little strategic importance but of immense value as symbols of the majesty of the Eternal Church. In Ornice Olorun, too, the Iviomils concentrated their attacks upon the great Temple itself. For Bertram's followers to capture this ugly cubical building would be not just a symbolic victory but a direct blow to Harrah's power. From the first, it must have been Bertram's plan to cleanse the Temple of all Architects loyal to Harrah. He must have hoped to fill the Koivuniemin's Hall with Elders such as Jedrek Iviongeon and thus to enter the Hall in triumph and acclamation as the Church's true Holy Ivi. More critically, he must have dreamed of entering the holy Facing Room and taking his place before the altar on which rested Ede's eternal computer. From this holiest of holies, he would lead the Architects of Tannahill in a restored facing ceremony truer to the Church's most venerable traditions and the strictures of the Algorithm. Thus the people would have no choice but to accept him as the one and only Architect empowered to interpret Ede's Program for the Universe.

Bertram might have succeeded in usurping the architetcy from Harrah if he had captured Ede's Eternal Computer, and more, had captured or killed Harrah herself. But Harrah, who had little taste for attacking her enemies, proved to be very good at defense. From the first moment of the schism after the morning facing ceremony, she showed a diamond-hard will and a coolness of decision in the face of crisis. Upon seeing that Bertram had begun massing an army of Iviomils on the streets and grounds outside the Temple, she quickly chose to abandon this very central building. She reentered the facing room, and much to the shock of all the Worthy gathered there that day, she lifted Ede's glittering Eternal Computer from the altar and fled into a choche waiting outside the Temple.

While her keepers fought to hold back the swarms of Iviomils surging through the streets—while they fought hand to hand with tlolts and knives, and quickly died—Harrah fled across Ornice

Olorun to her palace at the edge of the city. There she gathered together keepers summoned from every level of the city, and from the adjacent cities of Astaret and Dariveesh. She called for all Worthy Architects to join her in facifah, this holy war that they tragically must fight against their brothers and sisters. Within the hour, all those who could find or fight their way to the Holy Ivi's palace formed themselves into the army.

Harrah herself would have led these Worthy of God, but she was too old, too valuable as the High Holy Ivi, and the Elders Kyoko Ivi Iviatsui and Pol Iviertes begged her to remain in the palace. From her altar room she might face Ede's Eternal Computer, and thus reverently face Tannahill's billions of Architects who would need all her courage and faith in the days to come. And so Harrah left the Iviomils to occupy many important Church buildings, including the House of Eternity, the Hall of Heaven, the Temple, and Ede's Tomb. Bertram Jaspari counted the capture of this last as a great victory. The sacred, frozen body of Nikolos Daru Ede, the man, he announced, lay safely in his hands. But if Harrah had abandoned much of the city to the Iviomils in their newly dyed red kimonos (Bertram himself had donned the first of these dreadful garments as a symbol of his willingness to shed blood), she never abandoned her people. And although Bertram might possess Ede's ice-hard body, Harrah guarded the computer that had been a vehicle for the vastening of His eternal soul.

It would be impossible here to chronicle all the events of the War of Terror, even as limited in time as the killing proved to be. The truly critical events of this war, at least, were the individual decisions of countless Architects and all the little acts of courage or cowardice, heartlessness, or faith—for this was a fight for men's and women's souls, perhaps for the very soul of the Church itself.

On the second day of the war, a terrible battle raged over the possession of Ornice Olorun's light-field, but on that same day, in the distant city of Montellivi, a woman named Marta Kalinda en li Ede stood before a cadre of Iviomils and pleaded for the release of her husband, the Elder Valin Iviastalir, whom they had captured as a hostage. The cadre might have beheaded Marta or exploded open her brain with a tlolt, as they had done with dozens of others in this doomed city. Instead, through the sheer force of her faith, she shamed the Iviomils into doing as she asked, and more, into releasing the thousands of children being held for cleansing and reeducation as to the literal meaning of the Algorithm.

In Amaris, one of the Worthy underwent torture rather than reveal the name of a friend who had poisoned one of Bertram's lieutenants, while his wife betrayed this very same man in exchange for food to feed her nineteen children. And from the thirteenth level of Ornice Olorun, almost right below the floor of Harrah's palace, came the shocking story of an Iviomil who had sewn a plastic bomb into his abdomen in order to slip this barbaric weapon past the detectors in the local food factory. And then, with a quick prayer to the Holy Bertram, he had detonated the bomb, blowing up himself and the entire factory—along with at least twenty-six Worthy Architects who had sworn to keep Harrah's army supplied with rations of beanbread and yeast.

And so it went. The Architects, both Iviomils and the Worthy, were natural soldiers. Although their martial traditions were only a memory a thousand years past, they were disciplined and obedient and brave, but for their fear of dying the real death. At first, this fear gave the Iviomils great power. Almost immediately after claiming the architetcy, Bertram held that any man or woman who opposed him to be in abandonment of the True Church. His enemies were therefore apostates and heretics, or naraids, to use the slang word quickly becoming popular. A *naraid,* according to Bertram, was one who had turned away from God and was therefore unworthy of vastening. And so any Iviomil could slay any of Harrah's followers without fear that they were committing a hakr, this crime of denying an Architect his ultimate salvation. This they did, piling up the bodies of the Worthy (or naraids) like dead fish. But, during the dark days following the fall of the Temple, the Worthy used their lasers and nerve knives against the Iviomils only with the greatest reluctance, for as Harrah reminded them, the Iviomils were their sisters and brothers, their cousins and daughters and great-grandsons. All Architects, she said, were children of Ede who would someday be vastened in Him.

And then Bertram, under tremendous pressure to honor the Church's ancient canons of war, issued an order to Cheslav Iviongeon that soon would undermine his advantage. Henceforth Cheslav—and the other programers of the House of Eternity— would use the compiling computers to create pallatons of all Iviomils before they went into battle, much as they had done with Danlo for his Walk with the Dead. It gave the Iviomils great courage to know that even if their bodies should be vaporized in the blast of a hydrogen bomb, their souls would be forever safe graven on to an eternal diamond disc.

Ironically, however, this certainty of salvation made it easier for Harrah's Worthy to kill them. And when Harrah invited her followers likewise to preserve their pallatons, the Worthy found it much easier to risk their lives in the suicidal attacks their Elders began asking of them. As one of the ancient generals once remarked, war is progressive. So it was with the War of Terror. By the seventh day of Bertram's false architetcy, the people of Tannahill fell into the frenzy of killing almost as easily as sleekits starved and forced together into a cage.

Only two people refused to have pallatons made in counterfeit of their true selfness. The first, of course, was Malaclypse Redring of Qallar—he who sought the very opposite of cheating death. And Danlo wi Soli Ringess, too, only smiled when one of Harrah's readers invited him into the vastening chamber that they had hastily constructed in the west wing of the palace. It vexed him to consider his fate should one of the Iviomils' missiles evade the palace lasers and explode in his face: one of Harrah's programers would cark his pallaton into an eternal computer, and the Architects would say that the Lightbringer at last had become a part of the eternal Church, as all men and women must someday do.

Although there was no chance of Danlo changing his mind, the Ede hologram glowing out of Danlo's devotionary computer constantly spoke in favor of salvation. Whenever Danlo was alone with this glittering machine, the Ede reminded him just how desperate their existence truly was. On the first day of the War, when the bombs began exploding and Harrah had taken refuge along with two hundred Elders and Danlo inside the palace, the Ede had calculated that one of Bertram's first moves would be to attack Ornice Olorun's light-field and to capture Danlo's lightship. Bertram certainly would try to capture Danlo himself, to torture him or to cleanse him into acting as a mouthpiece for the Iviomil cause.

"It would be best if you'd let the programers make a pallaton of your selfness," the Ede told Danlo after a particularly bad day of bloodshed. It was the ninth day of the War, with the third battle for the light-field just beginning. And, according to the rumor passing around the city, Malaclypse of Qallar had managed the assassination of Sul Iviercier and Pilar Narcavage and two other Elders who had been unable to take refuge in Harrah's palace. "As I know only too well, preserving part of one's program is better than nothing."

Danlo, who had spent most of the day tending the wounded Architects who filled the rooms and halls of the palace, was almost too tired to respond. He did not want to tell this little hologram that the very survival of Nikolos Daru Ede as a bit of program carked into a devotionary computer was reason enough to discourage him from seeking a similar fate.

"Of course," the Ede continued, "if Harrah's people succeed in winning the light-field, it might be possible for us to escape."

In the privacy of his altar room, Danlo rubbed his eyes, which still burned from all the horrors that he had seen that day. To the imago of Nikolos Daru Ede, he said, "For us to leave Tannahill, this might be possible, yes. We might flee to the stars. Across the Vild to Thiells. Is this what you would choose?"

"*Would* I choose to flee?" Ede wondered aloud. It seemed almost that he was talking to himself, computing risks and probabilities. "Where is the greater danger, to stay here in the palace or to chance the streets between here and the light-field?"

"I do not know. Truly, it is impossible to know."

"And if we *did* reach the light-field," Ede continued, "if we fled to the stars, we would have to leave my body behind."

Just then an explosion shook the windows of the palace, and Danlo slowly nodded his head. He hadn't forgotten Ede's purpose in helping him seek Tannahill or his promise to help Ede recover his frozen body.

"Yes," Danlo said. "But someday we might return. Someday, if Harrah defeats Bertram and the Iviomils are constrained."

"But as well we might never return," the Ede said. "The Lord of your Order might forbid you to return here, or an exploding star might catch your lightship in its blast, or—"

"Yes, this is true," Danlo said. Then he sighed because he hated interrupting anyone, even the programed imago of a man who had once been a god. "Who can see his own fate?"

"If we might never return, then I choose to remain."

"But the choice is not yours to make," Danlo said, smiling.

"Of course not—I have no power to move your lightship, do I, Pilot?"

"The choice is not mine, either," Danlo said. "The battle for the light-field is not yet won."

Two days later, however, Harrah Ivi en li Ede knocked at Danlo's door to tell him of a great victory. For the Holy Ivi to pay him a visit with the whole world fairly falling apart around them surprised Danlo; it was the first time he had spoken with her face to face since the day before his Walk with the Dead.

"Please come in," Danlo said as he held the door open.

For a moment, Harrah stood in the hallway, sighing as she looked down at a sleeping man who had recently been wounded in the battle for the light-field. The entire hallway was filled with the wounded lying in makeshift beds of foam cushions and plastic sheets. The air stank with the usual hydroxyls and sulfates and aldehydes—and with the terrible new smells of blood and pus and burned flesh. Women and children, their white kimonos stained with red, hurried among the groaning Architects; they brought them food, water, and for the fortunate few, cups of alaqua tea to take away a little of their pain. Although Harrah had recently changed into a fresh kimono for her visit with Danlo, streaks of blood smeared the silk where a man with a bandaged face had reached out to touch her. For the Holy Ivi—or for any-one—to walk through the hallways of the palace was no easy feat.

"Please sit with me a while, if you'd like," Danlo said. "Please sit, Blessed Ivi—you must be very tired."

Again Harrah sighed and rubbed the loose skin around her eyes. She looked deathly tired, with her soft brown eyes sunken in sadness and her whole face haggard and pale. For the first time in her life, she seemed almost as old as her years—all 128 of them, as Danlo recalled.

"Thank you," Harrah said. Her once-clear voice sounded hoarse and weak as if she'd been talking continually for many days. "We would love to sit with you."

Danlo invited her into his altar room, where he helped her down onto the white cushions on the floor. In her trembling hands she carried a devotionary similar to Danlo's; not even the Holy Ivi of the Cybernetic Universal Church liked to leave her rooms without her familiar computer. With a smile, Danlo took it from her and set it beside his devotionary on the altar. Then he sat cross-legged facing her.

"I have no tea to offer you, Blessed Ivi. I am sorry."

"Please don't be," Harrah said. "We've drunk too much tea today already."

Danlo smiled sadly as he looked into her eyes. Although Harrah was usually as honest as she was kind, he did not think that she was telling the truth. With tea being reserved mostly for the wounded, Danlo thought it unlikely that she had drunk more than one thin cup of mint tea since the morning facing ceremony. He himself had had nothing except water.

"You look tired, Pilot," Harrah said as she looked at Danlo.

"We are all tired, aren't we?"

"We've heard that you haven't slept since the third battle for the light-field began. Three days, Pilot."

"It . . . is hard to sleep with the people crying out for water to drink."

As if in response to the pain burning in Danlo's eyes, a soft moan came through the open doors to Danlo's adjoining sleeping chamber. There, amid the flowers and luxurious furnishings pushed to the edge of the room, four men lay dying on the floor. One of them was the palace keeper Thomas Ivieehl. Danlo had spent most of the day preparing tea for him (and the others), as well as changing bandages and emptying bowls of blood or bile—or any of the other fluids that leaked from a man's body when it has been burned and broken.

"How can you go three days without sleeping?" Harrah asked.

Danlo smiled, then rubbed his eyes. "And in that time, Blessed Harrah, how much sleep have *you* taken?"

"But we are the Holy Ivi of our people," she said. "Despite Bertram Jaspari's claim to the contrary."

"I will sleep when I must," Danlo said. "When I can."

Harrah sighed at Danlo's stubbornness, which was nearly as great as her own. She said, "We're sorry that we haven't been able to congratulate you since your tests. To see you, face to face. But we've been preoccupied."

"I understand."

"Congratulations, indeed, Danlo wi Soli Ringess. You *are* the Lightbringer, aren't you?"

Despite his exhaustion, this question amused Danlo. In truth, with each new horror he beheld and with each hour of sleep lost, he found himself often taking refuge in humor—sometimes the black humor of those forced to deal every day with death, but more often in his keen sense of irony and in the universe's essential strangeness. And so as he often did, he smiled and answered her question with a question: "I do not know—*am* I the Lightbringer?"

"We believe that you are," Harrah said. She, too, was smiling, though not in amusement but rather in all the brilliance of her faith. And in awe. Although she knew that Danlo was just a man, even as he had always said, she could see his luminous self

as clearly as if Ede the God had set a star to shine at the center of
his forehead. "Everyone believes this, Pilot. Even Bertram and
all the Iviomils fear that you are—although they won't permit
themselves to see what they really believe."

"So many people . . . have died over these beliefs." Danlo
listened to one of the men, Timur Hastivi, coughing in his sleeping chamber. "So many beliefs, so much death."

"Indeed," Harrah said. "But we've won a great battle. The
light-field is ours. At least, Ornice Olorun's light-field—the Iviomils still hold those of Amaris, Elimat, and Karkut, and a hundred other smaller cities. We've come to tell you this."

"I had already heard."

"We've come to tell you that your ship is unharmed. The
Iviomils tried to open it, but they were killed before they could
find their way in."

Danlo shut his eyes for a moment. He envisioned a cadre of
red-kimonoed Iviomils swarming over his lightship with lasers
and drills. He saw them cursing at the hardness of black diamond, cursing and dying as circles of the Worthy in their white
kimonos closed in around them and killed them with plasma
flames and heat tlolts.

"Yes," he said, "it is almost impossible for anyone other than
a pilot to open a lightship."

"You're free to leave, Pilot. We hold all the streets, all the
lifts between the palace and the light-field."

"Free to leave." Danlo said these few words as if their
sounds made no sense.

"Your mission to our Church has been accomplished," Harrah told him.

"Truly?"

"This morning we interfaced Ede's Eternal Computer. And
we received a New Program to replace the Programs of Increase
and Totality. We'll install the New Program tomorrow morning."

"I see."

"Never again, we pray, will it be part of the Program of the
Church to destroy the stars."

Danlo said nothing but only bowed his head in giving thanks
to this kindly woman.

"You may bring the news of your accomplishment to the
Lords of your Order."

Again, Danlo bowed his head.

"And to the Narain heretics—as their emissary, you may tell
them that there will be peace between us."

"If you'd like, Blessed Harrah."

"We had supposed that you'd be overjoyed to leave Tannahill."

Danlo looked at the altar where his devotionary sat next to hers. He looked at her imago of Nikolos Daru Ede beaming joy into the room, and then at his Ede, who kept an identical expression on his glowing face should Harrah chance to look that way.

"But I cannot leave yet," Danlo said. "I . . . have promises to keep."

"Promises to whom?"

"To your people. As you say, they believe that I am the Lightbringer."

"Indeed they do."

"I am a symbol, yes? If I were to flee to the stars now, many of your people would not understand."

"Indeed they wouldn't."

"Such an act, at this time, might even weaken your cause."

"We might still lose the war, we're afraid."

"I will stay until the war is decided, then." Here he smiled at himself and said, "What good is a Lightbringer if he leaves only darkness in his passing?"

"We were hoping you'd stay," Harrah admitted. "Just as we hope that when you leave, some day you'll return."

Danlo wanted to tell her that, yes, someday he would return, and soon, but just then a soft cry from his sleeping chamber caught his attention. He heard plastic sheets crinkling, then panting and moaning. Suddenly, he said, "Please excuse me for a moment, Blessed Harrah."

With astonishing energy for one who had denied himself sleep, he sprang to his feet and went into the other room. Sometime later—in truth, after a long time—he returned and sat back down.

"It is Thomas Ivieehl," he said. "He has much pain."

"We'd heard that he'd been burned in the battle for the lightfield."

"Yes," Danlo said. Now he was as far from amusement or humor as a man could be. He looked down at his hands as if he could almost feel his ivory skin burning and blackening into char.

"We'd heard that he was dying."

"Yes," Danlo said softly. "He is dying."

"We'd heard that the Lightbringer was caring for the dying,"

Harrah said. "And we allowed this only because you are who you are."

"I am sorry, Blessed Harrah. But there are so many who will die. Who could have dreamed that there would be so many?"

"But the living require our care, too."

"I . . . know."

"We'd heard that you saved a man," Harrah said. "Alesar Iviunn—wasn't that his name?"

Danlo smiled sadly as he nodded his head. He remembered how he had stayed awake pouring water into Alesar's mouth and playing his flute for him.

"You're the Lightbringer," Harrah said. "A man without fear who will heal the living and walk with the dead. Many people are saying that you can heal the dying, too."

"No," Danlo said. "The dying, the people . . . only they can heal themselves."

"It's said that you bear light in your hands, and your touch is like that of the sun upon a flower."

Danlo closed his eyes in remembrance of what he had seen inside himself during the light offering. He said, "We are all just light, yes? This splendid light. It is inside all things. It *is* all things, truly. It . . . knows itself. It moves itself, makes itself move. And it makes *itself,* from itself, onstreaming, on and on, the new patterns, the power, the purpose, I . . . I know that it is possible for anyone to heal himself. I can almost see it, this blessed way. I can feel it, in my hands, in my blood, and deeper—it burns in each atom of my being like fire. All of us are alive with this flame, Blessed Harrah. It burns to remake itself. And we burn to remake ourselves, and we all know how, truly we do. But we do not know . . . that we know."

For a long time after Danlo had stopped speaking, Harrah looked at him as she might a child born with his eyes fully open and laughing in delight at all the beauties of the world. Or weeping at its pain. She seemed to be listening to the sounds around them: Thomas Ivieehl's moans spilling out of Danlo's sleeping chamber like blood; bombs exploding in other levels of the city; the deep *whoosh* of their individual breaths. Near the altar, the parrotock began squawking in its steel cage. Because the red-and-blue bird made so much noise, Danlo had moved it from his sleeping chamber lest it disturb the dying of the men who lay there.

"You came to Tannahill with many purposes," Harrah finally said. Her voice was very soft, almost a whisper. "As an emissary of the Narain and a pilot of your Order. And, perhaps, as a man who sought his father.''

''Yes,'' Danlo said, listening to the deep sound inside his chest.

''And perhaps the greatest of your purposes—or at least the one nearest your heart—was to find a cure for the Plague virus.''

''The slow evil,'' Danlo said, remembering.

''A disease for which no cure is known.''

But I know the cure, Danlo thought. *Here, now, on this lost world, I have found it. The Entity was right—I have always known. And someday I will find the way to use this knowledge.*

''But there *is* a cure,'' he told her. ''Someday, I must bring it to my people. They are dying, Blessed Harrah. Dying slowly, but still dying.''

''When we first told you that there was no cure, we were sad beyond the power of words to express.'' As Harrah spoke, her eyes fell moist with tears. For a moment, it was hard for Danlo to know which cure she meant: that of the doomed Architects or the great Plague or the pain of the universe itself. ''But now, Pilot, from what you've said here today, it seems there really might be a possibility of a cure.''

''Yes . . . a possibility,'' Danlo said. What was truly possible? *Infinite possibilities.* He looked down at his hands while he thought of Tamara Ten Ashtoreth—the real Tamara whose soul had been mutilated beneath a cleansing heaume in Neverness not long before. For the ten thousandth time, he wondered if there might be a way to help her regain her lost memories.

Harrah took a deep breath and looked at Danlo with all the love a flower might have for the sun. She said, ''We're glad that you'll remain with us for a while. But we must tell you that the palace really isn't safe.''

''Is any place truly safe, Blessed Harrah?''

''We believe that Bertram will attempt one last attack on the palace. We wouldn't wish for any harm to come to you.''

Now Harrah gazed at him as only a grandmother fearing for the life of one of her children. Danlo felt the sudden wetness of water in his own eyes. Although he had seen Harrah only a few times, he realized that he had come to love her.

''And I would not wish any harm for you,'' he said.

Danlo covered his eyes, wiping them with the palm of his hand. An image of red-robed Iviomils ripping through the rooms of the palace burned in his brain. For the first time, he felt the inadequacy of ahimsa in the face of war. He had sworn never to

harm another, even in defense of his own life, and this was as it
should be. But if some battle-mad Iviomil were to burst into
Danlo's room at that very moment wielding a laser or a nerve
knife, he didn't know how he would protect this lovely old
woman.

"We've lived a very long time," Harrah said. "But you're
still young."

Danlo leaned over to pick up his flute from where it rested on
a table near the altar. He held it in his hands and looked at it for a
long time. What power would a couple feet of bamboo have, he
wondered, against an eye tlolt or laser cannon or the fire of a
hydrogen bomb?

"You're young," Harrah repeated, "and you've done nothing
to preserve that youth against the taking of your life."

"I will not let the programers make a pallaton of myself
again. I am sorry."

"No, *we* are sorry." She reached out to him with open hands
as if warming herself in the sun. "We would not wish to see this
treasure that sits before us lost to death."

Danlo remembered the terrible beauty that he had seen as he
had sat beneath the cube of lights in Hall of Heaven; even now he
could almost see the shimmering consciousness of every atom
inside himself. "But, Blessed Harrah," he said, smiling, "there
is no true death."

Although this might be true, there was certainly dying. At that
moment, in Danlo's sleeping chamber, Thomas Ivieehl chose to
let out a particularly anguished moan. He began calling for water,
calling for his son lost in the first battle for the light field, and
then, after a while, calling for God.

"I must go to him," Danlo said. He stood and bowed to
Harrah. "He has been my friend."

"We understand," Harrah said. She smiled at him, even
though as Holy Ivi of the Eternal Church, she was unused to
anyone leaving her presence without asking her permission.

Danlo gripped his flute in his hand and sighed. "I must be
with all of them for a while. No one should be left to die alone."

"We understand," Harrah said again. She looked down at his
flute. "Will you play a song for them?"

"Yes, a song," Danlo said. "It is almost all that I can give
them."

"We, too, believe that there is no true death," Harrah said.
"We Architects—this is the teaching of the Church."

Danlo bowed his head in honor of the power of her faith, if not the doctrines of the Cybernetic Universal Church.

"We also believe that these men will not die in vain," Harrah continued. She pointed into Danlo's sleeping chamber. "We will win the war, Pilot. The dying will end. And a new age for our Church will begin."

"I hope you win your war . . . soon."

"Will you allow us to pray for Thomas Ivieehl?" she asked him. "And for the other men? Sometimes there's a great power in prayer."

Danlo smiled and nodded his head. "Yes, if you'd like—we will pray together."

So saying, he took Harrah's arm in his, and they walked into the other room.

In Harrah's hopes for a favorable outcome to the war, she would be both right and wrong. As she had foretold, the armies and bands of Architects who followed her did indeed triumph over Bertram Jaspari's Iviomils. Bertram, gambling on winning an empire of many worlds and the souls of countless Architects, staked everything on the shock of terror and quick attack. But his armies had failed to capture most of his critical objectives, and even the campaign of assassination and terror that Malaclypse of Qallar unleashed upon the Architects did not move them from their purpose.

The Architects are a tough and tenacious people, much used to hunger, suffering, and self-sacrifice. It was Bertram's great mistake that where he counted on these traits in his Iviomils, he had supposed that the Architects of the Juriddik and Danladi sects, and especially the peace-loving Elidis, had grown soft in their souls and weak in faith. But he did not truly know his own people. He had supposed that when he clothed his Iviomils in the ancient red kimonos told of in the *Commentaries* and led them in a glorious facifah to purify the Church, many Architects would wish to join them in glory. And those who did not, he planned to terrorize into accepting his rule. But terror is the wrong weapon with which to touch people's hearts. Bertram should have known this. And Malaclypse Redring *did* know this, and it must be recorded here that after the first shocks of violence had failed to kill Harrah or to cow her, Malaclypse advised Bertram against the senseless slaughters that marked that last days of the war, not because he wished to avoid more killing, but only because the terror was alienating the great mass of Architects and driving them into the ranks of Harrah's armies. It was simply bad strategy.

But Bertram did not listen to him. Day by day, in a thousand cities across Tannahill as Harrah's Worthy began to recapture the light-fields and food factories, Bertram grew desperate. Since the Worthy so badly outnumbered his Iviomils, he reasoned that if he could strike without mercy at Harrah's strength in such cities as Tlon and Yevivi, where almost the entire populace had remained loyal to her, he might reduce the odds against him. This he soon did. One of his armies seized Tlon's air factories and cut off the oxygen to nine levels of that city. A million people died blue-faced and gasping for breath. But this massive murder only rallied millions of previously peaceful Architects against Bertram.

Everywhere, on every level of every city in Tannahill, the Worthy fell against Bertram's armies with outrage and wrath. By the war's twenty-ninth day, a quarter of the Iviomils had been killed or captured, and Bertram began to lose light-fields and tube nexi almost by the hour. And so inevitably he came to *his* critical hour as the false Ivi, or rather his moment of choice. And he chose badly. It must have been obvious to him that he had lost the war. He might have surrendered to Harrah, abased himself, and admitted that he had fallen into the worst of negative programs. He might have begged her forgiveness. Harrah, who was always too kind to her enemies, might have forgiven him, for was it not written in *Man's Journey* that even the most vile hakra could cleanse himself of his negative programs and turn his face toward God? But Bertram's was the face of vanity and cruelty, and he wished for revenge. And so this zealous man so lacking in true grace once again chose murder and death.

On the thirty-third day of the war, a cadre of Iviomils managed to smuggle a bomb into an apartment block in the heart of Montellivi. This was the city of Harrah's birth, and the number of her sisters, cousins, grandnieces, and other relatives who still lived there could be numbered in hundreds of thousands. Montellivi had always been a stronghold of the Juriddik sect, and the few Iviomil cadres that banded together there had been broken and swept from its streets like so many shards of glass. And so, wishing for revenge, at Bertram's command, one of the surviving cadres exploded a bomb. But this was no ordinary plastic bomb that might have melted out a few levels of the city and killed a few tens of thousands of people. It was a hydrogen bomb. One of the many factories that the Iviomils had captured in Amaris began to make such bombs out of lasers and the heavier isotopes of hydrogen. The bomb's explosion vaporized ten million Architects in a flash of a moment. Millions more died during the next few days of seared lungs and burns blackening much of their bodies. Many men and women were blinded in the initial blast. Many Iviomils—those who hadn't received the alarm to flee the city—were wounded or died as well.

The shock of this tragedy was felt almost immediately in the Hall of the Koivuniemin half a world away. When even the bloody-minded Jedrek Iviongeon pointed out that the bomb must have killed innocent Iviomil children whose pallatons had never been preserved onto diamond discs, Bertram's response stunned the assembled Elders.

"It's true that Iviomils have died today. We know that some of these must have been children who never should have been touched by horrors of battle. We had no time to make pallatons of their young minds; this is unfortunate, but only one of the many necessary tragedies of war. The Elder Iviongeon has observed that it will be impossible for these children to be vastened in Ede in the usual way. So it must be. We can't tell you how this distresses us. But in war, people die, even children. We must remember that they were Iviomils. And we must remember that we Iviomils fight our facifah to the greater glory of God's Ininite Program for the Universe. Because God will not forget his children. And we Iviomils must never forget the power of God. At the end of time, at the omega point, there will be a Second Creation. Is this not written in the *Last Things*? Some may doubt this promise, but we Iviomils are those chosen few who must believe the truth: God will absorb all things and all information into His infinite body. Our children who died in Montellivi *will* be vastened in Ede someday. We must not worry over the fate of those who died there. Our task was only to destroy this city of naraids and heretics; let God be judge and preserve those Iviomils who never turned their faces from Him."

And then, when Bertram and his Koivuniemin began to debate similar attacks against other cities and Jedrek Iviongeon voiced a similar objection, Bertram was more blunt. Concerning the fate of the Architects in Raizel, Bertram was heard to say, "Kill them all! Let God sort the souls of those who have remained faithful to him!"

This remark signaled the end of Bertram's false architetcy on Tannahill. Jedrek Iviongeon, along with ten other Elders, immediately stood up, smoothed out the folds of their red kimonos and left the Hall of the Koivuniemin. Within three days, Iviomils everywhere began to desert Bertram and surrender to Harrah's keepers and Readers. Bertram lost all but his most fanatical followers—which, considering his next move, was perhaps just what he wanted. For he had decided to flee the planet. His Iviomils (those remaining loyal to him) still held many of Tannahill's light-fields. And so he called his faithful to gather at the greatest of these, in the cities of Amaris, Elimat, and Karkut. On these three fields he had assembled a great fleet of shuttles that would ferry his armies to the deep ships and seedships waiting in near space above Tannahill. Bertram Jaspari was a shallow man but he was not stupid; he had prepared well for retreat. The captains of the ships were Iviomils sworn to bring missionaries to the far stars of the Vild. Now they would bring Bertram's armies—and his facifah—to whatever star in the galaxy he commanded them to fall.

For these captains would not be left alone to pilot almost blindly through the manifold's strange, dark spaces, as the Architects had been doomed to do for so long. Sivan wi Mawi Sarkissian, the renegade pilot of Neverness, in his *Red Dragon,* would lead the Iviomils on their Great Pilgrimage, as they called it. Malaclypse Redring of Qallar would accompany Bertram in his seedship named the *Glory of God* and help him found a new Church (which Bertram called the True Church) somewhere among the stars as far from Tannahill as they could find.

And so it happened. So ended the War of Terror, if not the War—and certainly not war itself. Because Bertram had only fifty-three ships filled with foodstuffs and the factories needed to build new cities on alien worlds, he had to leave many Iviomils behind. Most of these devout men and women—there were millions of them—despaired upon seeing Bertram's fleet vanish into the night. Rather than surrender to the deep cleansings that awaited them should they rejoin the Old Church, they chose to fight to the death.

It took Harrah's Worthy many days to track them into their apartments, or into bombed-out temples, or into the dark, wet tunnels below the deepest levels of Ornice Olorun and other cities. The Worthy slayed them one by one, and they took their red-swathed bodies away to be burned in the great plasma ovens. During this time of hunger and chaos, there was much burning of bodies, for the dead lay everywhere, on the light-fields and the streets, or rotting in the hospices, hotels, or even on the estates of the Elder Architects. Quickly, however, Harrah reestablished her authority, even in the far cities of Iviennet and Bavoll and other former Iviomil strongholds. The dead were cared for as the Algorithm prescribed, and their pallatons were brought to Ornice Olorun and loaded into the many computers in the House of Eternity. Altogether, perhaps some thirty-four million Architects died in the war. Given the incredible fertility of the Architects, however, the surviving populations might expect to make up these losses in much less than a year.

But no longer would the Church require women to bear five—or fifty—children. As Harrah had promised, she had redefined the Programs of Increase and Totality. She had received a New Program for the Church, and she had installed it during the worst days of the war. Now, with peace ordering the life of this vast planetary city called Tannahill, the Architects accepted the New Program with gratitude and relief. Few spoke against Harrah. Fewer still opposed her openly, for only those of rare faith (or foolishness) wished to be counted as Iviomils.

When Danlo had played his last song for the last of the wounded Architects brought into his rooms (Thomas Ivieehl had died on the evening of Harrah's visit), he prepared to leave Tannahill. It took him only moments to place his few possessions in the plain wooden chest that he brought with him wherever he went. He had few people to say good-bye to. One promise that he had made, he resolved to keep: he would ask Harrah about the ultimate fate of Ede's body. And so one day he arranged to have tea with her in her rooms.

As witness to his sincerity (or effrontery), he brought his devotionary computer to this meeting and smiled all along his walk down the now-empty hallways because he couldn't imagine how he might ask the Holy Ivi of the Cybernetic Universal Church for the body of the man who had become a god. But he never quite had to put this question to her. After cups of cool peppermint tea had been poured into little plastic cups, with the Ede imago glowing out of the devotionary and watching him, just as he broached the matter that he had come to discuss, Harrah was called away to attend the dying of one of her sisters in another part of the palace. And Danlo returned to his rooms bearing a little jeweled computer in his hands rather than Harrah's promise that the Lightbringer might take possession of the frozen body of Nikolos Daru Ede. But Harrah had not disregarded Danlo, nor did she like to dismiss him even for the most dire of needs. The next day, after the evening meal, she invited Danlo to meet her across Ornice Olorun at Ede's tomb.

Later that night Danlo arrived at this great, white monument to the father of the Church. Although Ede's Tomb and the glittering Temple nearby had been spared destruction, he saw signs of the war everywhere. Where once the people of Tannahill had been able to enter the Tomb freely and with ease, now a light fence surrounded it north, west, east, and south. And many keepers in stained white kimonos stood watchfully with lasers ready in front of the fence. Behind it, trees had been uprooted or burned to char; ragged holes still pocked the lawns and walkways—the work of bombs planted into the soil, perhaps, or of heat tlolts misfired and rocketing into the ground. As four of Harrah's keepers escorted Danlo up the steps of Ede's Tomb, he smelled burned plastic. In many places along the building, blackened grooves scored its smooth white walls. One of the false pillars marking the entranceway apparently had been struck by a missile, for a great section the size of a man's torso had been blasted out of its center. But the worst work of the war awaited Danlo inside. He made his way into the vast open spaces surrounding the central dais of the Tomb. Usually swarms of Architects gathered there day and night to view Ede's body in its clary crypt. But that evening, few people were present to honor Ede. Danlo stopped and stared at the dais reflecting the lights high above. The clary crypt was gone. Someone had stolen Ede's body. Despite the irony of the moment, he did not smile as he looked down at the devotionary computer that he carried in his hands. Ede's imago, he saw, was staring at the place where his ancient, frozen body so recently had lain. His face, made of nothing but light, was frozen into a familiar program of despair.

"Thank you for coming, Pilot."

The voice of Harrah Ivi en li Ede echoed in the spaces of the near-empty tomb. Danlo turned to see her slowly approaching him. She wore a white dobra on her head and a long, flowing kimono embroidered with gold. The Architects who waited near the dais must have thought her resplendent and holy, for their faces beamed awe as if they looked upon Ede himself and not just His High Holy Ivi. But Danlo thought she looked very small against the blue and white tiled floor of the Tomb, almost as if she had shrunk during these past days, as if the sufferings of the war had caused her to pull back inside her drooping skin and step very carefully. As she came closer, she smiled at Danlo, and he could see that her eyes were bright as ever. Sadder, perhaps, and yet strangely deeper. She still fairly blazed with her intense love·

of life, but she was tired, very tired. He knew immediately that she was getting ready to die.

"Blessed Harrah, thank you for inviting me," Danlo said, and he bowed.

Harrah returned his bow, painfully. She nodded at the four keepers following her. "We will speak with the Lightbringer now," she told them. So saying, she moved over to Danlo and took his arm. Together they slowly walked across the room. At the Tomb's southernmost part, in a little porch beneath the great windows, Harrah eased herself down upon one of the plain plastic benches where pilgrims or other Architects might sit and look upon the fleshly remains of Nikolos Daru Ede.

"He is gone," Harrah said, pointing across the long room to the upraised dais. There, upon the bare plastic slab, a group of five men and women worked to install some lacy black machinery that looked almost like a sulki grid. "We can't believe He is gone, but He is."

"Yes," Danlo said. He sat on the bench beside Harrah, and he looked at the dais and then back at her. "I see."

"Bertram Jaspari has desecrated the Tomb. He has stolen His body."

"I see." Danlo set his devotionary computer upon a nearby bench. The hologram of Ede filled the air with all the heaviness of a stone sculpture.

"We wanted you to know the truth of this, Pilot. We wanted you to see this sacrilege with your own eyes."

"Thank you. But ... . why?"

"Because we believe that you have a mysterious interest in Ede's body."

Danlo glanced at the imago of Ede, but he said nothing. He wondered if Ede, now that his body was lost, would want to cark himself into an eternal computer like any other Architect; or perhaps he would wish for a more profound vastening in hoping to retrace his path toward godhood.

"And," Harrah continued, "because you might help us get it back."

Here the Ede glowing out of the devotionary flashed Danlo a quick hand sign that meant, "Yes, yes!"

"You would wish me to return Ede's body to you?" Danlo asked her.

Harrah slowly shook her head. "No, only to help us to locate it so that we may ask for its return. When you leave us, as you soon will, you'll make long journeys from star to star. It may be that somewhere in the universe, someday, you'll chance to discover where the Iviomils have taken our Ede.''

"That is possible," Danlo said, smiling. He didn't tell her that in the galaxy's vast light-distances and billions of stars, it was unlikely that he—or anyone else—would find Bertram by chance alone.

For a while Harrah watched her programers working at the center of the room, and then she turned to Danlo and asked, "You've decided to leave us, haven't you?"

"Yes," Danlo said. "I must. I shall leave tonight."

"Because of Bertram?"

Danlo smiled grimly and nodded his head. "I must journey to Thiells and speak with the Lords of my Order. They must be told what has happened here."

"We're sorry that we allowed Bertram to escape," Harrah said.

"I am sorry, too. But some things cannot be helped."

Harrah motioned for Danlo to lean closer to her, and he let his forehead fall down almost touching her lips. And then, in a low voice, she said, "There's something that we must tell you. On one of the deep ships that Bertram stole, he installed a morrashar.''

"I am afraid that I do not know this word," Danlo said.

"A morrashar is a huge, black engine that fills an entire deep ship. It generates streams of graviphotons and fires them into a sun."

Danlo suddenly backed away from Harrah as if she had breathed fire at him instead of gentle words. He said, "A star killer."

"A star killer, Pilot."

"How did Bertram acquire this shaida thing?"

"His engineers made it for him. We Architects were the first people to discover this technology."

"I see."

"We hope that we are the only people."

"Do you still consider the Iviomils as your people, then?"

"Indeed we do."

"But there is to be no more killing of stars. You have announced your New Program—will the Iviomils ever accept it?"

Harrah sighed as if she were expelling a painful breath that she had been holding inside for too many years. "We believe that as long as Bertram leads them, they will never return to the Church."

"No, I think not," Danlo told her. And then, reading the look of worry in Harrah's eyes, he said, "As long as Bertram wields a star killer, you would not want him to return to Tannahill, would you?"

"After Bertram destroyed Montellivi," Harrah confessed, "there was a time when we couldn't imagine a worse crime. And then he fled into space, and we feared that he would destroy our sun."

"There . . . are other suns," Danlo said, remembering.

He closed his eyes, and he saw a vast array of lights that went shimmering on and on through the infinite depths of the universe. One of these beautiful lights was the Star of Neverness. Another was the Narain's star, all red and round like a drop of blood.

"We would like to believe," Harrah said, "that Bertram will come to cleanse himself of his negative programs."

"So many stars." Danlo continued as if he hadn't really been listening to her. "In our galaxy alone, three hundred billion stars—who would have dreamed that God would make so many?"

"We *have* to believe this, Pilot. For Bertram to have exploded a hydrogen bomb in Montellivi—this is a terrible hakr that will haunt him forever."

The stars are the children of God alone in the night, he remembered.

And then he said, "Bertram Jaspari, all the Iviomils—they could create another Vild."

"No, Pilot, no." Harrah said these words with all the anguish of hope, but there was no certainty in her voice, no strength.

"He has a star killer," Danlo said. "And he will enforce the rule of the old Program of Increase."

"We're sorry, Pilot."

"No," Danlo said. Gently, he took her cold, trembling hands in his own. "*I* am sorry. I have been lost in my own fears and therefore ungenerous. You have risked everything in helping me. And lost so much. This war . . . would not have been fought if I hadn't come to Tannahill. Truly. My mission—the mission of my Order. To heal the Vild. This is accomplished, yes? You will send out your Readers to the stars. And they will find the lost Architects of the Long Pilgrimage, and they will kill no more stars forever. I must thank you for this. For your great courage in receiving and installing the New Program."

A sudden fear fell across Harrah's face just then. Danlo understood that her interfacing of Ede's eternal computer had been fraught with danger and difficulty. He remembered, then, something that the Solid State Entity had told him: that the Silicon God was using the Cybernetic Universal Church to create the Vild. He wondered about the origin of the Program of Totality. Was it possible that somehow the Silicon God might be the source of this star killing program? Had the Silicon God, centuries ago, found a way to infect Ede's eternal computer with a plan to destroy the universe, much as he had carked the killing surreality into Ede the God? He did not know. He might never know, for if such a program ran within the eternal computer, it would be too subtle for any Holy Ivi to detect, much less discuss. The instructions of the Silicon God would whisper in the mind almost like the sweet, soft voice of one's own consciousness. It would take an extraordinary mind to distinguish between the false voice and the true.

"Interfacing Ede's eternal computer is the hardest thing we've ever done," Harrah told him. "If Bertram knew how hard, he never would have sought to be the Holy Ivi."

That was all she ever said concerning her experience with this holiest of artifacts. She turned to look toward the center of the Tomb, where her programers had finished their work. One of them, a portly old woman whose child-bearing days were long past, caught Harrah's attention and waved to her. Harrah then bowed her head as if according to some prearranged plan. The programers all stepped back from the dais. Harrah's keepers and the other Architects who had business in the Tomb that night stared at the bare slab where Ede had once lain. Now, in His place, the fine, black lace-work of a sulki grid shone darkly beneath the Tomb lights. Everyone, even Harrah, seemed to be waiting for something. What this event would be, Danlo could only guess.

"Now, please," Harrah said, again bowing her head.

Danlo was also was staring at the dais, and he fairly jumped to see the sulki grid disappear. One moment it was there, and in the next moment gone. And in its place, like a lightship suddenly falling out of the manifold into realspace, was the clary crypt of Nikolos Daru Ede. Or rather an illusion of this sacred object. The powerful sulki grid generated an imago of infinitely greater realism than the holograms of the devotionary computers. It would be almost impossible for the human eye to distinguish this imago from the true crypt—the one that Bertram had stolen. It was long and cut with clear angles across its seemingly clary surfaces, and it glittered with colors. Soon swarms of Architects would form their queues outside Ede's tomb and pass slowly by to view the cast-off body of their God. And all of them would attest that they had looked through half an inch of clary within the crypt to see the bald head and soft, smiling face of Nikolos Daru Ede.

"We ask you to keep this a secret," Harrah said to Danlo. "We don't wish our people to know that His body is gone."

"If you'd like, I will tell no one," Danlo said.

"You see, they've already lost so much, suffered so much."

"As have you, Blessed Harrah."

At this, Harrah looked down at her hands and said, "Our sisters and our granddaughters—so many of our family."

"Yes."

"All the Architects who died, even the Iviomils—you see, Pilot, they were all our family."

"I . . . know."

Harrah buried her face in her hands, then, and she began to weep. Danlo, not caring what her keepers might think, sat beside her on the bench and held her in his arms. But he was the Lightbringer, after all, and they looked away in trust that he would not harm her.

"Blessed Harrah," Danlo said as he felt the silent sobs tearing through her frail chest. "Blessed Harrah."

After a while, Harrah composed herself and sat straight upon her bench. She reminded Danlo that it was unseemly for anyone, even the Lightbringer, to touch the person of the Holy Ivi. And so Danlo moved away from her slightly. He might have smiled at her fierce will to accomplish all her duties toward life, but something in her eyes troubled him. For there was no light there, no joy, no hope, only resignation in the face of life's bitterness and pain.

"Blessed Harrah," he said again.

When Harrah finally looked at him, her eyes were almost as full of water as dark oceans floating in the infinite deeps of space. Her face was dark with grief, and her soul had fallen cold in contemplation of death. Danlo looked at her for a long time, watching and waiting—waiting until he felt the hot rush of tears burning in his own eyes. Through this window to the suffering that they shared, he passed into a clearer vision of her. He saw her pride, as hard as diamond, as well as her kindness, her nobility and grace. In some ways she was the loveliest woman he had ever known. But she wept in the silent sadness of herself, and she ached with a terrible loneliness as if she were the last star left alive in all the black void of the night.

His love for her, he realized, was without bound, like life itself. He marveled at the immense strangeness of life, its power, its mystery, its infinite possibilities. There was always a light inside light, memory of the past, dreams of the future, a flower unfolding from inside itself in colors of blue and white and gold like an infinite lotus opening out into the universe. As he looked deeper and deeper, he saw Harrah not only as an old woman wounded in her soul, but as a child full of prayers and hopes, as mother and lover, as a newborn baby trying to drink in the wonder of the world. He saw her as a devoted Reader who had great plans for her Church and as a grandmother who took her greatest delight in sending presents to her children's children. He saw her as she still might some day be. For her life was not yet done. She might live perhaps another thirty years—or thirty million. She would return to her faith if only she could return to herself, and she would be a great light leading the Church into a new age. *Each man and woman is a star,* he remembered. But no one, not even the High Holy Ivi of the Cybernetic Universal Church, could ever be doomed to shine alone.

"Harrah, Harrah."

Although Danlo's lips remained closed and his voice unmoving, he called to her with another, deeper part of himself. "Harrah, Harrah," he asked with his eyes, "Who am I? What am I?"

And in the same silent way, Harrah answered him, "You are the Lightbringer."

"No, no—I am only a mirror, nothing more. Look at me and you will see only yourself."

There was a moment, then. There was a moment of memory and miracle when Danlo returned to the onstreaming light inside himself. He was a mirror for Harrah's soul, truly, but he was also something much more. His eyes shone like deep, blue, liquid jewels and his heart was a blazing diamond full of fire and love. His whole being fell numinous and clear, not really like silvered glass at all, but rather like some impossible crystalline substance perfectly transparent to the light of his deepest consciousness. This light beyond light poured out of him with all the splendor of a star. It passed from his eyes to hers. It touched her deepest self and fired her will to live. Inside Harrah, as in everyone, dwelled all the wild possibilities of life. In the intense illumination of the moment, she finally saw this. She sat there smiling at Danlo and dancing with him soul to soul in the terrible quick beauty of their eyelight. And all this passed between them wordlessly and whisperlessly, in utter silence. None of the programmers or keepers (or even the little glowing Ede imago) would ever know how Harrah Ivi en li Ede at last came into her own secret light.

"Thank you, Pilot," she said after she wiped her eyes and found her voice. "Thank you, Danlo of the Stars. We shall miss you."

"Thank you, Blessed Harrah. I shall miss you, too."

Danlo suddenly stood up then. He himself felt as wild as any star, though not only with animajii—this limitless joy of life— but also with a terrible new energy. His eyes were like dark blue windows open upon all the glories of space and time. Or all the terrors of the manifold. An immense strangeness as cold and clear as a deep winter night fell over him; from far away, it seemed, he could see the future approaching with all the fury of ice clouds driven by the wind. He bowed to Harrah, slowly, deeply, with infinite grace. Then he slowly walked to the side door of the Tomb where it gave out onto a wide balcony. There, as Danlo stood beside a white, plastic railing, he had a clear sight of the great dome above the city of Ornice Olorun and of the sky beyond. As with most nights on Tannahill, few stars were burning through the haze of pollution swaddling the planet. But Danlo hadn't come here to look at the stars. Or rather, not *these* stars shining down upon the city with their weak, old light. While Harrah followed him out onto the balcony and leaned on the railing beside him, he gazed at the sky.

As he often did while waiting for the future to unfold, he began to count his heartbeats. He watched and he waited, and with each surge of blood inside his chest, somewhere on Tannahill a child was born and an old man or woman died. And somewhere in the universe a star died, too, in fiery clouds of hydrogen exploding outward into a sphere of light. Danlo listened to the rhythms of his heart, and he could almost hear the supernovas being born, one after another, ringing like bells, roaring like a fiery wind, throbbing and booming, in the Sculptor Group of galaxies and in the Canes Venatici, and closer to home, within the nearer stars of the Vild. He could almost see their killing light. For that was the terrible beauty of a different kind of light, the light of pure consciousness that shined everywhere at once upon all things.

Each man and woman is a star.

While Harrah breathed slowly by his side and his heart counted out each anguished moment of time one by one, he looked toward the east. There, some sixty-eight degrees above the horizon where the sky boiled like black ink, he looked far out into space in the direction from which his lightship had come to Tannahill. He looked for the star of Alumit Bridge, so close and yet invisible to his naked eye. He began to count backward from a hundred as he thought of Isas Lel and Lieswyr Ivioss and the other Narain men and women whom he had known.

One hundred . . . ninety-nine . . . ninety-eight . . . ninety-seven . . .

He remembered the great city of Iviunir in its thirty levels where the Narain people lived and the glittering Field where they carked out their icons in their millions and hoped to find their way toward the divine.

Sixty-six . . . sixty-five . . . sixty-four . . . sixty-three . . .

Somewhere, in a part of the Field that the Narain called Heaven, dwelled the Transcended Ones, Maralah and Tyr and Manannan, and that great composite being whom Danlo knew as Shahar. He remembered Shahar well. As he stared at the heavens connecting Tannahill to the star of Alumit Bridge, he remembered being absorbed into Shahar and letting wave upon wave of intense love wash through him like an ocean of light.

Twenty-two . . . twenty-one . . . twenty . . . nineteen . . .

Love, he remembered, was the true secret of the universe. It connected man to woman, and man to man—and everyone, man, woman, and child, to each other. All peoples, even those who sought to transcend their physical selves and evolve into pure, luminous beings, lived for that perfect love beyond love.

Four . . . three . . . two . . . one . . .

Infinite possibilities, he thought. *Infinite pain.*

He waited almost forever for the light to fall upon him, and then he finally saw it. The star of the Narain people appeared as a single, silver point piercing the blackness of the universe. And then it exploded outward into infinity in all directions. He looked up into Tannahill's dark sky, and when the brilliant light blinded him, he grabbed his head and fell down to one knee gasping for breath. It almost surprised him that Harrah did not scream at the burning pain of it and throw her hands across her face. In truth, she only stared into the east where he had stared as if awaiting nothing more than the rising of the sun. She seemed mystified at Danlo's sudden anguish, as if she couldn't understand that Bertram Jaspari had just killed a star with a man-made machine called a morrashar. She seemed not to grasp the terrible meaning of a moment when an exploding star killed many millions of people and Danlo clutched his chest as if his own heart had suddenly burst.

But then he remembered something. Harrah could not possibly see this new supernova, at least not with her eyes. In a single moment of time so recently past, the sun of Alumit Bridge had died into light, but it would be some forty years before this light crossed the spaces of the Vild and lit up Tannahill's sky. In truth, with Alumit Bridge orbiting the Narain's star at a distance of a hundred million miles, it would be many moments yet before the light fell upon Iviunir and her sister cities and incinerated every living thing on the planet.

"Pilot, are you well? Do you need to sit down?"

Harrah's soft, gentle words floated like pearls out into the night. Slowly Danlo stood up with his hand pressing his left eye. He wondered if he should tell her of this new supernova and the death of a people who had once been of the Eternal Church. He decided that it would be best if he did not. Even a great soul such as Harrah could only bear so much pain at one time. And what did he truly know? He might only be dreaming or scrying, beholding colors and contours of a reality that might never come to be. Soon he would take his lightship out into the Vild to confirm or belie this terrible vision that took his breath away. But then, in letting the star's almost infinite illumination touch his consciousness and burn through every atom of his being, he knew the truth of what he saw beyond any hope or doubt.

They helped me find Tannahill so that they might have peace. But I have brought them only war. And worse, total annihilation. Oh, Ahira, Ahira—what have I done?

"Pilot?"

Someday, Danlo knew, he or other pilots of his Order would have to hunt down Bertram Jaspari and restrain him—perhaps even destroy him. Someday soon there would be battles fought among the stars and war in the heavens, and he would come at last to his journey's end.

"Pilot, Pilot—what do you see?"

"I see light," Danlo answered truthfully. He turned to look at Harrah. "Only light. It . . . is everywhere, yes?"

Perhaps Harrah thought that he was speaking of hope, for she touched her hand to his face and smiled. And in a strange way, perhaps there truly *was* hope, not for the Narain who would finally get their wish of vanishing into a ball of light, but for all people who still lived in their very human bodies breathing the cool night air and listening to the music of the voices of family and friends. Perhaps the Architects were right to worship the death of the stars, for out of the dying, new elements of life were always being born. Perhaps there was even hope for him. Strangely, during his moment of greatest despair, he had found his father inside himself, and inside too, the possibility of curing a disease that had no cure. Although he had brought war to two worlds and perhaps out into the stars, he had brought peace as well, for his mission to Tannahill had accomplished the greatest of his purposes, which was to heal the Vild of its sickness. And he had brought something else. Harrah Ivi en li Ede named him as the Lightbringer but what was this mysterious light that he had brought? He looked at Harrah's deeply lined face, now bright in the flawlessness of her rare and splendid spirit. He looked once again at the furious radiance of the supernova beyond the sky and within the darkness of his own soul. There were, he decided, many ways of bringing light. Which was the most powerful? Someday he might know. Someday he might plunge once again into the shimmering ocean of consciousness inside himself and remain there until all the light of creation was his to behold. Then he would at last be a true human being—a true Lightbringer who might look upon the wounds of the world with smiling eyes and bear the greatest force in the universe in his hands.

But now he was only a man. He was only a pilot who longed to return home. And so he looked strangely at Harrah and offered her his arm. Together they would walk back through Ede's Tomb and perhaps linger a moment to appreciate the tragedy of a man who had tried to become as God. He would gather up his devotionary computer, his bamboo flute, and his wooden chest containing all the wordly things that mattered to him. He would say farewell to Harrah Ivi en li Ede, this blessed woman whom he loved like the mother he had never known. And then he would take his lightship out into the galaxy where the stars were always bright and beautiful and the light of the universe went on and on forever into the wild.

ABOUT THE AUTHOR

David Zindell's short story "Shanidar" was a prizewinning entry in the Writers of the Future Contest. In 1986 he was nominated for the John W. Campbell Award for best new writer. Both his novels, *Neverness* and *The Broken God,* were nominated for the Arthur C. Clarke Award. He lives in Boulder, Colorado, with his wife and children, where he is at work on the final volume in his *Requiem for Homo Sapiens.*

STEPHEN R. DONALDSON

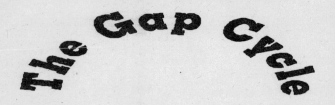
The Gap Cycle

Angus Thermopyle and Nick Succorso: two ore pirates with legendary reputations. Morn Hyland: a United Mining Company police officer, beautiful, dedicated, and deadly. Together they are drawn into an adventure of dark passions, perilous alliances, and dubious heroism in a future where technology has blossomed with fabulous possibilities, where a shadowy presence lurks just beyond our vision and people cross the Gap at faster-than-light speeds. . . .